ACROSS REALTIME

'Now Allison began to feel the bedrock fear that was gnawing at Angus Quiller. For many people, the completely inexplicable is worse than death. Allison was such a person. The crash – even Fred's death – she could cope with. The amnesia explanation had been so convenient. But now, almost half an hour had passed. There was no sign of aircraft, much less of rescue. Allison found herself whispering, reciting all the crazy alternatives. "You think we're in some kind of parallel world, or on the planet of another star – or in the future?" *A future where alien invaders set their silver castle-mountains down on the California shore?*

Quiller shrugged, started to speak, seemed to think better of it – then finally burst out with, "Allison, you know that . . . cross near the edge of the crater?"

She nodded.

"It was old, the stuff carved on it was badly weathered, but I could see . . . It had your name on it and . . . today's date."

Just the one cross, and just the one name. For a long while they were both silent.'

Also in Millennium

A FIRE UPON THE DEEP

Vernor Vinge is also the author of the highly acclaimed *A Fire Upon the Deep* and *True Names*. He has published short fiction in *Analog* and other SF magazines. A professor of mathematics and a computer scientist at San Diego State University, he writes fiction based on the theories of today that may well become the facts of tomorrow.

ACROSS REALTIME

VERNOR VINGE

MILLENNIUM

This collected edition first published in
Great Britain in 1993 by Millennium
The Orion Publishing Group
5 Upper St Martin's Lane
London WC2H 9EA

Millennium Paperback
Number Twenty

ISBN: 1 85798 147 2

THE PEACE WAR

To *my parents,*
Clarence L. Vinge and Ada Grace Vinge,
with love

I am grateful to:

Chuck Glines and Bil Townsend of the US Forest Service for talking to me about Los Padres National Forest;

Jim Concannon and Concannon Winery of Livermore, California, for their hospitality and a very interesting tour of the Concannon Winery;

Lea Braff, Jim Frenkel, Mike Cannis, Sharon Jarvis, and Joan D. Vinge for all their help and ideas.

FLASHBACK

One hundred kilometers below and nearly two hundred away, the shore of the Beaufort Sea didn't look much like the common image of the arctic: Summer was far advanced in the Northern Hemisphere, and a pale green spread across the land, shading here and there to the darker tones of grass. Life had a tenacious hold, leaving only an occasional peninsula or mountain range gray and bone.

Captain Allison Parker, USAF, shifted as far as the restraint harness would permit, trying to get the best view she could over the pilot's shoulder. During the greater part of a mission, she had a much better view than any of the "truck-drivers," but she never tired of looking out, and when the view was the hardest to obtain, it became the most desirable. Angus Quiller, the pilot, leaned forward, all his attention on the retrofire readout. Angus was a nice guy, but he didn't waste time looking out. Like many pilots—and some mission specialists—he had accepted his environment without much continuing wonder.

But Allison had always been the type to look out windows. When she was very young, her father had taken her flying. She could never decide what would be the most fun: to look out the windows at the ground—or to learn to fly. Until she was old enough to get her own license, she had settled for looking at the ground. Later, she discovered that without combat aircraft experience she would never pilot the machines that went as high as she wanted to go. So again she had settled for a job that would let her look out the windows. Sometimes she thought the electronics, the geography, the espionage angles of her job were all unimportant compared to the pleasure that came from simply looking down at the world as it really is.

"My compliments to your autopilot, Fred. That burn puts us right down the slot." Angus never gave Fred Torres, the command pilot, any credit. It was always the autopilot or ground control that was responsible for anything good that happened when Fred was in charge. Torres grunted something similarly insulting, then said to Allison, "Hope you're enjoying this. It's not often we fly this thing around the block just for a pretty girl."

Allison grinned but didn't reply. What Fred said was true. Ordinarily a mission was planned several weeks in advance and carried multiple tasks that kept it up for three or four days. But this one had dragged the two-man crew off a weekend leave and stuck them on the end of a flight that was an unscheduled quick look, just fifteen orbits and back to Vandenberg. This was clearly a deep-range, global reconnaissance—though Fred and Angus probably knew little more. Except that the newspapers had been pretty grim the last few weeks.

The Beaufort Sea slid out of sight to the north. The sortie craft was in an inverted, nose-down attitude that gave some specialists a sick stomach but that just made Allison feel she was looking at the world pass by overhead. She hoped that when the Air Force got its permanent recon platform, she would be stationed there.

Fred Torres—or his autopilot, depending on your point of view—slowly pitched the orbiter through 180 degrees to bring it into entry attitude. For an instant the craft was pointing straight down. Glacial scouring could never be an abstraction to someone who had looked down from this height: the land was clearly scraped and grooved, like ground before a dozer blade. Tiny puddles had been left behind: hundreds of Canadian lakes, so many that Allison could follow the sun in specular glints that shifted from one to another.

They pitched still further. The southern horizon, blue and misty, fell into and then out of view. The ground wouldn't be visible again until they were much lower, at altitudes some normal aircraft could attain. Allison sat back and pulled the restraint more tightly over her shoulders. She patted the optical disk pack tied down beside her. It contained her reason for being here. There were going to be a lot of relieved generals—and some even more relieved politicians—when she got back. The "detonations" the Livermore crew had detected must have been glitches. The Soviets were as innocent as those bastards ever were. She had scanned them with all her "normal" equipment, as well as with deep penetration gear known only to certain military intelligence agencies, and had detected no new offensive preparations. Only . . .

. . . Only the deep probes she had made on her own over Livermore were unsettling. She had been looking forward to her date with Paul Hoehler, if only to enjoy the expression on his face when she told him that the results of her test were secret. He had been so sure his bosses were up to something sinister at Livermore. She now saw that Paul may have been right; there was something going on at Livermore. It might have gone undetected without her deep-probe equipment; there had been an obvious effort at concealment. But one thing Allison Parker knew was her high-intensity reactor profiles, and there was a new one down there that didn't show up on the AFIA listings. And she had detected other things—probe-opaque spheres below ground in the vicinity of the reactor.

That was also as Paul Hoehler had predicted.

NMV specialists like Allison Parker had a lot of freedom to make ad lib additions to their snoop schedules; that had saved more than one mission. She would be in no trouble for the unscheduled probe of a US lab, as long as a thorough report was made. But if Paul was right, then this would cause a major scandal. And if Paul was wrong, then *he* would be in major trouble, perhaps on the road to jail.

Allison felt her body settle gently into the acceleration couch as creaking sounds came through the orbiter's frame. Beyond the forward ports, the black of space was beginning to flicker in pale shades of orange and red. The colors grew stronger and the sensation of weight increased. She knew it was still less than half a gee, though after a day in orbit it felt like more. Quiller said something about transferring to laser comm. Allison tried to imagine the land eighty kilometers below, Taiga forest giving way to farm land and then the Canadian Rockies— but it was not as much fun as actually being able to see it.

Still about four hundred seconds till final pitch-over. Her mind drifted idly, wondering what ultimately would happen between Paul and herself. She had gone out with better-looking men, but no one smarter. In fact, that was probably part of the problem. Hoehler was

7

clearly in love with her, but she wasn't allowed to talk technical with him, and what nonclassified work he did made no sense to her. Furthermore, he was obviously something of a troublemaker on the job—a paradox considering his almost clumsy diffidence. A physical attraction can only last for a limited time, and Allison wondered how long it would take him to tire of her—or vice versa. This latest thing about Livermore wasn't going to help.

The fire colors faded from the sky, which now had a faint tinge of blue in it. Fred—who claimed he intended to retire to the airlines— spoke up. "Welcome, lady and gentleman, to the beautiful skies of California . . . or maybe it's still Oregon."

The nose pitched down from reentry attitude. The view was much like that from a commercial flyer, if you could ignore the slight curvature of the horizon and the darkness of the sky. California's Great Valley was a green corridor across their path. To the right, faded in the haze, was San Francisco Bay. They would pass about ninety kilometers east of Livermore. The place seemed to be the center of everything on this flight: It had been incorrect reports from their detector array which convinced the military and the politicians that Sov treachery was in the offing. And that detector was part of the same project Hoehler was so suspicious of—for reasons he would not fully reveal.

Allison Parker's world ended with that thought.

1

The Old California Shopping Center was the Santa Ynez Police Company's biggest account—and one of Miguel Rosas' most enjoyable beats. On this beautiful Sunday afternoon, the Center had hundreds of customers, people who had traveled many kilometers along Old 101 to be there. This Sunday was especially busy: All during the week, produce and quality reports had shown that the stores would have best buys. And it wouldn't rain till late. Mike wandered up and down the malls, stopping every now and then to talk or go into a shop and have a closer look at the merchandise. Most people knew how effective the shoplift-detection gear was, and so far he hadn't had any business whatsoever.

Which was okay with Mike. Rosas had been officially employed by the Santa Ynez Police Company for three years. And before that, all the way back to when he and his sisters had arrived in California, he had been associated with the company. Sheriff Wentz had more or less adopted him, and so he had grown up with police work, and was doing the job of a paid undersheriff by the time he was thirteen. Wentz had encouraged him to look at technical jobs, but somehow police work was always the most attractive. The SYP Company was a popular outfit that did business with most of the families around Vandenberg. The pay was good, the area was peaceful, and Mike had the feeling that he was really doing something to help people.

Mike left the shopping area and climbed the grassy hill that management kept nicely shorn and cleaned. From the top he could look across the Center to see all the shops and the brilliantly dyed fabrics that shaded the arcades.

He tweaked up his caller in case they wanted him to come down for some traffic control. Horses and wagons were not permitted beyond the outer parking area. Normally this was a convenience, but there were so many customers this afternoon that the owners might want to relax the rules.

Near the top of the hill, basking in the double sunlight, Paul Naismith sat in front of his chessboard. Every few months, Paul came down to the coast, sometimes to Santa Ynez, sometimes to towns further north. Naismith and Bill Morales would come in early enough to get a good parking spot, Paul would set up his chessboard, and Bill would go off to shop for him. Come evening, the Tinkers would trot out their specialties and he might do some trading. For now the old man slouched behind his chessboard and munched his lunch.

Mike approached the other diffidently. Naismith was not personally forbidding. He was easy to talk to, in fact. But Mike knew him better than most—and knew the old man's cordiality was a mask for things as strange and deep as his public reputation implied.

"Game, Mike?" Naismith asked.

"Sorry, Mr. Naismith, I'm on duty." *Besides, I know you never lose except on purpose.*

The older man waved impatiently. He glanced over Mike's shoulder at something among the shops, then lurched to his feet. "Ah. I'm not going to snare anyone this afternoon. Might as well go down and window-shop."

Mike recognized the idiom, though there were no "windows" in the shopping center, unless you counted the glass covers on the jewelry and electronics displays. Naismith's generation was still a majority, so even the most archaic slang remained in use. Mike picked up some litter but couldn't find the miscreants responsible. He stowed the trash and caught up with Naismith on the way down to the shops.

The food vendors were doing well, as predicted. Their tables were overflowing with bananas and cacao and other local produce, as well as things from farther away, such as apples. On the right, the game area was still the province of the kids. That would change when evening came. The curtains and canopies were bright and billowing in the light breeze, but it wasn't till dark that the internal illumination of the displays would glow and dance their magic. For now, all was muted, many of the games powered down. Even chess and the other symbiotic games were doing a slow business. It was almost a matter of custom to wait till the evening for the buying and selling of such frivolous equipment.

The only crowd, five or six youngsters, stood around Gerry Tellman's Celest game. What was going on here? A little black kid was playing— had been playing for fifteen minutes, Mike realized. Tellman had Celest running at a high level of realism, and he was not a generous man. Hmmm.

Ahead of him, Naismith creaked toward the game. Apparently his curiosity was pricked, too.

Inside the shop it was shady and cool. Tellman perched on a scuffed wood table and glared at his small customer. The boy looked to be ten or eleven and was clearly an outlander: His hair was bushy, his clothes filthy. His arms were so thin that he must be a victim of disease or poor diet. He was chewing on something that Mike suspected was tobacco —definitely not the sort of behavior you'd see in a local boy.

The kid clutched a wad of Bank of Santa Ynez gAu notes. From the look on Tellman's face, Rosas could guess where they came from.

"Otra vez," the boy said, returning Tellman's glare. The proprietor hesitated, looked around the circle of faces, and noticed the adults.

"Aw right," agreed Tellman, "but this'll have to be the last time . . . *Esta es el final, entiende?"* he repeated in pidgin Spanish. "I, uh, I gotta go to lunch." This remark was probably for the benefit of Naismith and Rosas.

The kid shrugged. "Okay."

Tellman initialized the Celest board—to level nine, Rosas noticed. The kid studied the setup with a calculating look. Tellman's display was a flat one, showing a hypothetical solar system as seen from above the plane of rotation. The three planets were small disks of light moving around the primary. Their size gave a clue to mass; the precise values appeared near the bottom of the display. Departure and arrival planets moved in visibly eccentric orbits, the departure planet at one rev every five seconds—fast enough so precession was clearly occurring. Between it and the destination planet moved a third world, also in an eccentric orbit. Rosas grimaced. No doubt the only reason Tellman left the prob-

11

lem coplanar was that he didn't have a holo display for his Celest. Mike had never seen anyone without a symbiotic processor play the departure/destination version of Celest at level nine. The timer on the display showed that the player—the kid—had ten seconds to launch his rocket and try to make it to the destination. From the fuel display, Rosas was certain that there was not enough energy available to make the flight in a direct orbit. A cushion shot on top of everything else!

The kid laid all his bank notes on the table and squinted at the screen. Six seconds left. He grasped the control handles and twitched them. The tiny golden spark that represented his spacecraft fell away from the green disk of the departure world, *inward* toward the yellow sun about which all revolved. He had used more than nine-tenths of his fuel and had boosted in the wrong direction. The children around him murmured their displeasure, and a smirk came over Tellman's face. The smirk froze.

As the spacecraft came near the sun, the kid gave the controls another twitch, a boost which—together with the gravity of the primary —sent the glowing dot far out into the mock solar system. It edged across the two-meter screen, slowing at the greater remove, heading not for the destination planet but for the intermediary. Rosas gave a low, involuntary whistle. He had played Celest, both alone and with a processor. The game was nearly a century old and almost as popular as chess; it made you remember what the human race had almost attained. Yet he had never seen such a two-cushion shot by an unaided player.

Tellman's smile remained but his face was turning a bit gray. The vehicle drew close to the middle planet, catching up to it as it swung slowly about the primary. The kid made barely perceptible adjustments in the trajectory during the closing period. Fuel status on the display showed 0.001 full. The representation of the planet and the spacecraft merged for an instant, but did not record as a collision, for the tiny dot moved quickly away, going for the far reaches of the screen.

Around them, the other children jostled and hooted. They smelled a winner, and old Tellman was going to lose a little of the money he had been winning off them earlier in the day. Rosas and Naismith and Tellman just watched and held their breaths. With virtually no fuel left, it would be a matter of luck whether contact finally occurred.

The reddish disk of the destination planet swam placidly along while the mock spacecraft arced higher and higher, slower and slower, their paths becoming almost tangent. The craft was accelerating now, falling into the gravity well of the destination, giving the tantalizing impression of success that always comes with a close shot. Closer and closer. And the two lights became one on the board.

"Intercept" the display announced, and the stats streamed across the lower part of the screen. Rosas and Naismith looked at each other. The kid had done it.

Tellman was very pale now. He looked at the bills the boy had wagered. "Sorry, kid, but I don't have that much here right now." He started to repeat the excuse in Spanish, but the kid erupted with an unintelligible flood of Spañolnegro abuse. Rosas looked meaningfully at Tellman. He was hired to protect customers as well as proprietors. If Tellman didn't pay off, he could kiss his lease good-bye. The Shopping Center already got enough flak from parents whose children had lost money here. And if the kid were clever enough to press charges . . . ?

The proprietor finally spoke over youthful screaming. "Okay, so I'll pay. *Pago, pago* . . . you little son of a bitch." He pulled a handful of gAu notes out of his cash box and shoved them at the boy. "Now *get out.*"

The black kid was out the door before anyone else. Rosas eyed his departure thoughtfully. Tellman went on, plaintively, talking as much to himself as anyone else. "I don't know. I just don't know. The little bastard has been in here all morning. I swear he had never seen a game board before. But he watched and watched. Diego Martinez had to explain it to him. He started playing. Had barely enough money. And he just got better and better. I never seen anything like it. . . . In fact—" he brightened and looked at Mike, "in fact, I think I been set up. I betcha the kid is carrying a processor and just pretending to be young and dumb. Hey, Rosas, how about that? I should be protected. There's some sorta con here, especially on that last game. He—"

"—really did have a snowball's chance, eh, Telly?" Rosas finished where the proprietor had broken off. "Yeah, I know. You had a sure win. The odds should have been a thousand to one—not the even money you gave him. But I know symbiotic processing, and there's no way he could do it without some really expensive equipment." Out of the corner of his eye, he saw Naismith nod agreement. "Still"—he rubbed his jaw and looked out into the brightness beyond the entrance —"I'd like to know more about him."

Naismith followed him out of the tent, while behind them Tellman sputtered. Most of the children were still visible, standing in clumps along the Tinkers' mall.

The mysterious winner was nowhere to be seen. And yet he should have been. The game area opened onto the central lawn which gave a clear view down all the malls. Mike spun around a couple times, puzzled. Naismith caught up with him. "I think the boy has been about two jumps ahead of us since we started watching him, Mike. Notice how he didn't argue when Tellman gave him the boot. Your uniform must have spooked him."

"Yeah. Bet he ran like hell the second he got outside."

"I don't know. I think he's more subtle than that." Naismith put a finger to his lips and motioned Rosas to follow him around the banners that lined the side of the game shop. There was not much need for stealth. The shoppers were noisy, and the loading of furniture onto several carts behind the refurbishers' pavilion was accompanied by shouting and laughter.

The early afternoon breeze off Vandenberg set the colored fabric billowing. Double sunlight left nothing to shadow. Still, they almost tripped over the boy, curled up under the edge of a tarp. The boy exploded like a bent spring, directly into Mike's arms. If Rosas had been of the older generation, there would have been no contest: Ingrained respect for children and an unwillingness to damage them would have let the kid slip from his grasp. But the undersheriff was willing to play fairly rough, and for a moment there was a wild mass of swinging arms and legs. Mike saw something gleam in the boy's hand, and then pain ripped through his arm.

Rosas fell to his knees as the boy, still clutching the knife, pulled loose and sprinted away. He was vaguely conscious of red spreading through the tan fabric of his left sleeve. He narrowed his eyes against the pain and drew his service stunner.

"No!" Naismith's shout was a reflex born of having grown up with slug guns and later having lived through the first era in history when life was truly sacred.

The kid went down and lay twitching in the grass. Mike holstered his pistol and struggled to his feet, his right hand clutching at the wound. It looked superficial, but it hurt like hell. "Call Seymour," Mike grated at the old man. "We're going to have to carry that little bastard to the station."

2

The Santa Ynez Police Company was the largest protection service south of San Jose. After all, Santa Ynez was the first town north of Santa Barbara and the Aztlán border. Sheriff Seymour Wentz had three full-time deputies and contracts with eighty percent of the locals. That amounted to almost four thousand customers.

Wentz's office was perched on a good-sized hill overlooking Old 101. From it one could follow the movements of Peace Authority freighters for several kilometers north and south. Right now, no one but Paul Naismith was admiring the view. Miguel Rosas watched gloomily as Seymour spent half an hour on the phone to Santa Barbara, and then even managed to patch through to the ghetto in Pasadena. As Mike expected, no one south of the border could help. The rulers of Aztlán spent their gold trying to prevent "illegal labor emigration" from Los Angeles but never wasted time tracking the people who made it. The *sabio* in Pasadena seemed initially excited by the description, then froze up and denied any interest in the boy. The only other lead was with a contract labor gang that had passed through Santa Ynez earlier in the week, heading for the cacao farms near Santa Maria. Sy had some success with that. One Larry Faulk, labor contract agent, was persuaded to talk to them. The nattily dressed agent was not happy to see them.

"Certainly, Sheriff, I recognize the runt. Name is Wili Wáchendon." He spelled it out. The "w"s sounded like a hybrid of "w" with "v" and "b." Such was the evolution of Spañolnegro. "He missed my crew's departure yesterday, and I can't say that I or anyone else up here is sorry."

"Look, Mr. Faulk. This child has clearly been mistreated by your people." He waved over his shoulder at where the kid—Wili—lay in his cell. Unconscious, he looked even more starved and pathetic than he had in motion.

"Ha!" came Faulk's reply over the fiber. "I notice you have the punk locked up; and I also see your deputy has his arm bandaged." He pointed at Rosas, who stared back almost sullenly. "I'll bet little Wili has been practicing his people-carving hobby. Sheriff, Wili Wáchendon may have had a hard time someplace; I think he's on the run from the Ndelante Ali. But I never roughed him up. You know how labor contractors work. Maybe it was different in the good old days, but now we are agents, we get ten percent, and our crews can dump on us any time they please. At the wages they get, they're always shifting around, bidding for new contracts, squeezing for money. I have to be damn popular and effective or they would get someone else.

"This kid has been worthless from the beginning. He's always looked half-starved; I think he's a sicker. How he got from LA to the border is . . ." His next words were drowned out by a freighter whizzing along the highway beneath the station. Mike glanced out the window at the behemoth diesel as it moved off southward carrying liquified natural gas to the Peace Authority Enclave in Los Angeles. ". . . took him because he claimed he could run my books. Now, the little bas—the kid may know something about accounting. But he's a lazy thief, too. And I can prove it. If your company hassles me about this when I come back through Santa Ynez, I'll sue you into oblivion."

There were a couple more verbal go-arounds, and then Sheriff Wentz rang off. He turned in his chair. "You know, Mike, I think he's telling the truth. We don't see it so much in the new generation, but children like your Sally and Arta—"

Mike nodded glumly and hoped Sy wouldn't pursue it. His Sally and Arta, his little sisters. Dead years ago. They had been twins, five years younger than he, born when his parents had lived in Phoenix. They had made it to California with him, but they had always been sick. They both died before they were twenty and never looked to be older than

17

ten. Mike knew who had caused that bit of hell. It was something he never spoke of.

"The generation before that had it worse. But back then it was just another sort of plague and people didn't notice especially." The diseases, the sterility, had brought a kind of world never dreamed of by the bomb makers of the previous century. "If this Wili is like your sisters, I'd estimate he's about fifteen. No wonder he's brighter than he looks."

"It's more than that, Boss. The kid is really smart. You should have seen what he did to Tellman's Celest."

Wentz shrugged. "Whatever. Now we've got to decide what to do with him. I wonder whether Fred Bartlett would take him in." This was gentle racism; the Bartletts were black.

"Boss, he'd eat 'em alive." Rosas patted his bandaged arm.

"Well, hell, you think of something better, Mike. We've got four thousand customers. There must be someone who can help. . . . A lost child with no one to take care of him—it's unheard of!"

Some child! But Mike couldn't forget Sally and Arta. "Yeah."

Through this conversation, Naismith had been silent, almost ignoring the two peace officers. He seemed more interested in the view of Old 101 than what they were talking about. Now he twisted in the wooden chair to face the sheriff and his deputy. "I'll take the kid on, Sy."

Rosas and Wentz looked at him in stupefied silence. Paul Naismith was considered old in a land where two-thirds of the population was past fifty. Wentz licked his lips, apparently unsure how to refuse him. "See here, Paul, you heard what Mike said. The kid practically killed him this afternoon. I know how people your, uh, age feel about children, but . . ."

The old man shook his head, caught Mike with a quick glance that was neither abstracted nor feeble. "You know they've been after me to take on an apprentice for years, Sy. Well, I've decided. Besides trying to kill Mike, he played Celest like a master. The gravity-well maneuver is one I've never seen discovered unaided."

"Mike told me. It's slick, but I see a lot of players do it. We almost all use it. Is it really that clever?"

"Depending on your background, it's more than clever. Isaac New-

18

ton didn't do a lot more when he deduced elliptical orbits from the inverse square law."

"Look, Paul . . . I'm truly sorry, but even with Bill and Irma, it's just too dangerous."

Mike thought about the pain in his arm. And then about the twin sisters he had once had. "Uh, Boss, could you and I have a little talk?"

Wentz raised an eyebrow. "So . . . ? Okay. 'Scuse us a minute, Paul."

There was a moment of embarrassed silence as the two left the room. Naismith rubbed his cheek with a faintly palsied hand and gazed across Highway 101 at the pale lights just coming on in the Shopping Center. So very much had changed and all the years in between were blurred now. Shopping Center? All of Santa Ynez would have been lost in the crowd at a good high-school basketball game in the 1990s. These days a county with seven thousand people was considered a thriving concern.

It was just past sunset now, and the office was growing steadily darker. The room's displays were vaguely glowing ghosts hovering in the near distance. Cameras from down in the shopping areas drove most of those displays. Paul could see that business was picking up there. The Tinkers and mechanics and 'furbishers had trotted out their wares, and crowds were hanging about the aerial displays. Across the room, other screens showed pale red and green, relaying infrared images from cameras purchased by Wentz's clients.

In the next room the two officers' talk was a faint murmur. Naismith leaned back and pushed up his hearing aid. For a moment the sound of his lung and heart action was overpoweringly loud in his ears. Then the filters recognized the periodic noises and they were diminished, and he could hear Wentz and Rosas more clearly than any unaided human. Not many people could boast such equipment, but Naismith demanded high pay and Tinkers from Norcross to Beijing were more than happy to supply him with better-than-average prosthetics.

Rosas' voice came clearly: ". . . think Paul Naismith can take care of himself, Boss. He's lived in the mountains for years. And the Moraleses are tough and not more than fifty-five. In the old days there were some nasty bandits and ex-military up there—"

"Still are," Wentz put in.

19

"Nothing like when there were still a lot of weapons floating around. Naismith was old even when they were going strong, and he survived. I've heard about his place. He has gadgets we won't see for years. He isn't called the Tinker wizard for nothing. I—"

The rest was blotted out by a loud creaking that rose to near painful intensity in Naismith's ear, then faded as the filters damped out the amplification. Naismith looked wildly around, then sheepishly realized it was a microquake. They happened all the time this near Vandenberg. Most were barely noticeable—unless one used special amplification, as Paul was now. The roar had been a slight creaking of wall timbers. It passed . . . and he could hear the two peace officers once more.

". . . what he said about needing an apprentice is true, Boss. It hasn't been just us in Middle California who've been after him. I know people in Medford and Norcross who are scared witless he'll die without leaving a successor. He's hands-down the best algorithms man in North America—I'd say in the world except I want to be conservative. You know that comm gear you have back in the control room? I know it's close to your heart, your precious toy and mine. Well, the bandwidth compression that makes possible all those nice color pictures coming over the fiber and the microwave would be plain impossible without the tricks he's sold the Tinkers. And that's not all—"

"All right!" Wentz laughed. "I can tell you took it serious when I told you to specialize on our high tech clients. I know Middle California would be a backwater without him, but—"

"And it will be again, once he's gone, unless he can find an apprentice. They've been trying for years to get him to take on some students, or even to teach classes like before the Crash, but he's refused. And I think he's right. Unless you are terribly creative to begin with, there's no way you can make new algorithms. I think he's been waiting—not taking anyone on—and watching. I think today he found his apprentice. The kid's mean . . . he'd kill. And I don't know what he really wants besides money. But he has one thing that all the good intentions and motivation in the world can't get us, and that's brains. You should have seen him on the Celest, Boss. . . ."

The argument—or lecture—went on for several more minutes, but the outcome was predictable. The wizard of the Tinkers had at long last got himself an apprentice.

3

Night and triple moonlight. Wili lay in the back of the buckboard, heavily bundled in blankets. The soft springs absorbed most of the bumps and lurches as the wagon passed over the tilting, broken concrete. The only sounds Wili heard were the cool wind through the trees, the steady *clapclapclap* of the horse's rubberized shoes, its occasional snort in the darkness. They had not yet reached the great black forest that stretched north to south; it seemed like all Middle California was spread out around him. The sea fog which so often made the nights here dark was absent, and the moonlight gave the air an almost luminous blue tone. Directly west—the direction Wili faced—Santa Ynez lay frozen in the still light. Few lights were visible, but the pattern of the streets was clear, and there was a hint of orange and violet from the open square of the bazaar.

Wili wriggled deeper in the blankets, the tingling paralysis in his limbs mostly gone now; the warmth in his arms and legs, the cold air on his face, and the vision spread below him was as good as any drug high he'd ever stolen in Pasadena. The land was beautiful, but it had not turned out to be the easy pickings he had hoped for when he had defected from the Ndelante and headed north. There were unpeopled ruins, that was true: He could see what must have been the pre-Crash location of Santa Ynez, rectangular tracings all overgrown and no lights at all.

The ruins were bigger than the modern version of the town, but

21

nothing like the promise of the LA Basin, where kilometer after kilometer of ruins—much of it unlooted—stretched as far as a man could walk in a week. And if one wanted some more exciting, more profitable way of getting rich, there were the Jonque mansions in the hills above the Basin. From those high vantage points, Los Angeles had its own fairyland aspect: Horizon to horizon had sparkled with little fires that marked towns in the ruins. Here and there glowed the incandescent lights of Jonque outposts. And at the center, a luminous, crystal growth, stood the towers of the Peace Authority Enclave. Wili sighed. That had all been before his world in the Ndelante Ali had fallen apart, before he discovered Old Ebenezer's con. . . . If ever he returned, it would be a contest between the Ndelante and the Jonques over who'd skin him first.

Wili couldn't go back.

But he had seen one thing on this journey north that made it worth being chased here. That one thing made this landscape forever more spectacular than LA's. He looked over Santa Ynez at the object of his wonder.

The silver dome rose out of the sea, into the moonlight. Even at this remove and altitude, it still seemed to tower. People called it many things, and even in Pasadena he had heard of it, though he'd never believed the stories. Larry Faulk called it Mount Vandenberg. The old man Naismith—the one who even now was whistling aimlessly as his servant drove their wagon into the hills—he had called it the Vandenberg Bobble. But whatever they called it, it transcended the name.

In its size and perfection it seemed to transcend nature itself. From Santa Barbara he had seen it. It was a hemisphere at least twenty kilometers across. Where it fell into the Pacific, Wili could see multiple lines of moon-lit surf breaking soundlessly against its curving arc. On its inland side, the lake they called Lompoc was still and dark.

Perfect, perfect. The shape was an abstraction beyond reality. Its mirror-perfect surface caught the moon and held it in a second image, just as clear as the first. And so the night had two moons, one very high in the sky, the other shining from the dome. Out in the sea, the more normal reflection was a faint silver bar lying straight to the ocean's horizon. Three moons' worth of light in all! During the day, the vast mirror captured the sun in a similar way. Larry Faulk claimed the farmers planted their lands to take advantage of the double sunlight.

Who had made Vandenberg Dome? The One True God? Some Jonque or Anglo god? And if made by man, how? What could be inside? Wili dozed, imagining the burglary of all burglaries—to get inside and steal what treasures would be hidden by a treasure so great as that Dome. . . .

When he woke, they were in the forest, rolling upward still, the trees deep and dark around them. The taller pines moved and spoke unsettlingly in the wind. This was more of a forest than he had ever seen. The real moon was low now; an occasional splash of silver shouldered past the branches and lay upon further trees, glistening on their needles. Over his head, a band of night, brighter than the trees, was visible. The stars were there.

The Anglo's servant had slowed the horse. The ancient concrete road was gone; the path was scarcely wide enough for the cart. Wili tried to face forward, but the blankets and remaining effects of the cop's stunner prevented this. Now the old man spoke quietly into the darkness. *Password!* Wili doubled forward to see if the cops had discovered his other knife. No. It was still there, strapped to the inside of his calf. Old men running labor camps were something he knew a lot about from LA. He was one slave this old man was not going to own.

After a moment, a *woman's* voice came back, cheerfully telling them to come ahead. The horse took up its former pace. Wili saw no sign of the speaker.

The cart turned through the next switchback, its tires nearly soundless in the carpet of pine needles that layered the road. Another hundred meters, another turn, and—

It was a palace! Trees and vines closed in on all sides of the structure, but it was clearly a palace, though more open than the fortresses of the Jonque *jefes* in Los Angeles. Those lords usually rebuilt pre-Crash mansions, installed electrified fences and machine-gun nests for security. This place was old, too, but in other ways strange. There was no outward sign of defenses—which could only mean that the owner must control the land for kilometers all around. But Wili had seen no guardian forts on their trip up here. These northerners could not be as stupid and defenseless as they seemed.

The cart drove the length of the mansion. The trail broadened into a clearing before the entrance, and Wili had the best view yet. It was smaller than the palaces of LA. If the inner court was a reasonable size, then it couldn't house all the servants and family of a great *jefe*. But the building was massive, the wood and stone expertly joined. What moonlight was left glinted off metal tracery and shone streaming images of the moon's face in the polish of the wood. The roof was darker, barely reflecting. There were gables and a strange turret: dark spheres, in diameters varying from five centimeters to almost two meters, impaled on a glinting needle.

"Wake up. We are here." Hands undid the blankets, and the old man gently shook his shoulder. It took an effort to keep from lashing out. He grunted faintly, pretended he was slowly waking. *"Estamos llegado, chico,"* the servant, Morales, said. Wili let himself be helped from the cart. In truth he was still a little unsteady on his feet, but the less they knew of his capabilities the better. Let them think he was weak, and ignorant of English.

A servant came running out of the main entrance (or could the servants' entrance be so grand?). No one else appeared, but Wili resolved to be docile until he knew more. The woman—like Morales, middle-aged—greeted the two men warmly, then guided Wili across the stone flagging to the entrance. The boy kept his eyes down, pretending to be dopey. Out of the corner of his eye, though, he saw something more—a silver net like some giant spider web stretched between a tree and the side of the mansion.

Past the huge cavern doors, a light glowed dimly, and Wili saw that the place was the equal of anything in Pasadena, though there were no obvious art treasures or golden statuary lying about. They led him up (not down! What sort of *jefe* put his lowest servants on an upper floor?) a wide staircase, and into a room under the eaves. The only light was the moon's, coming through a window more than large enough to escape by.

"¿Tienes hambre?" the woman asked him.

Wili shook his head dumbly, surprised at himself. He really wasn't hungry; it must be some residual effect of the stunner. She showed him a toilet in an adjoining room and told him to get some sleep.

And then he was left alone!

Wili lay on the bed and looked out over the forest. He thought he could see a glint from the Vandenberg Dome. His luck was almost past marveling at. He thanked the One God he had not bolted at the

24

entrance to the mansion. Whoever was the master here knew nothing of security and employed fools. A week here and he would know every small thing worth stealing. In a week he would be gone with enough treasure to live for a long, long time!

FLASHFORWARD

Captain Allison Parker's new world began with the sound of tearing metal.

For several seconds she just perceived and reacted, not trying to explain anything to herself: The hull was breached. Quiller was trying to crawl back toward her. There was blood on his face. Through rents in the hull she could see trees and pale sky. *Trees?*

Her mind locked out the wonder, and she struggled from her harness. She snapped the disk pack to her side and pulled down the light helmet with its ten-minute air supply. Without thinking, she was following the hull-breach procedures that had been drilled into all of them so many times. If she had thought about it she might have left off the helmet—there were sounds of birds and wind-rustled trees—and she would have died.

Allison pulled Quiller away from the panel and saw why the harness had not protected him: The front of the shuttle was caved in toward the pilot. Another few centimeters and he would have been crushed. A harsh, crackling sound came clearly through the thin shell of her helmet. She slipped Quiller's in place and turned the oxygen feed. She recognized the smell that still hung in her helmet: The tracer stench that tagged their landing fuel.

Angus Quiller straightened out of her grasp. He looked around dazedly. "Fred?" he shouted.

Outside, the improbable trees were beginning to flare. God only

26

knew how long the forward hull would keep the fire in the nose tanks from breaking into the crew area.

Allison and Quiller pulled themselves forward . . . and saw what had happened to Fred Torres. The terrible sound that had begun this nightmare had been the left front of the vehicle coming down into the flight deck. The back of Fred's acceleration couch was intact, but Allison could see that the man was beyond help. Quiller had been very lucky.

They looked through the rent that was almost directly over their heads. It was ragged and long, perhaps wide enough to escape through. Allison glanced across the cabin at the main hatch. It was subtly bowed in; they would never get out that way. Even through their pressure suits, they could now feel the heat. The sky beyond the rent was no longer blue. They were looking up a flue of smoke and flame that climbed the nearby pines.

Quiller made a stirrup with his hands and boosted the NMV specialist though the ragged tear in the hull. Allison's head popped through. Under anything less than these circumstances she would have screamed at what she saw sitting in the flames: an immense dark octopus shape, its limbs afire, cracked and swaying. Allison wriggled her shoulders free of the hole and pulled herself up. Then she reached down for the pilot. At the same time, some part of her mind realized that what she had seen was not an octopus but the mass of roots of a rather large tree which somehow had fallen downward on the nose of the sortie craft. This was what had killed Fred Torres.

Quiller leaped up to grab her hand. For a moment his broader form stuck in the opening, but after a single coordinated push and tug he came through—leaving part of his equipment harness on the jagged metal of the broken hull.

They were at the bottom of a long crater, now filled with heat and reddish smoke. Without their oxygen, they would have had no chance. Even so, the fire was intense. The forward area was well involved, sending rivulets of fire toward the rear, where most of the landing fuel was tanked. She looked wildly around, absorbing what she saw without further surprise, simply trying to find a way out.

Quiller pointed at the right wing section. If they could run along it, a short jump would take them to the cascade of brush and small trees that had fallen into the crater. It wasn't till much later that she wondered how all that brush had come to lie *above* the orbiter when it crashed.

Seconds later they were climbing hand-over-hand up the wall of brush and vines. The fire edged steadily through the soggy mass below them and sent flaming streamers ahead along the pine needles imbedded in the vines. At the top they turned for a moment and looked down. As they watched, the cargo bay broke in half and the sortie craft slumped into the strange emptiness below it. Thus died all Allison's millions of dollars of optical and deep-probe equipment. Her hand tightened on the disk pack that still hung by her side.

The main tank blew, and simultaneously Allison's right leg buckled beneath her. She dropped to the ground, Quiller a second behind her. "Damn stupidity," she heard him say as debris showered down on them, "us standing here gawking at a bomb. Let's move out."

Allison tried to stand, saw the red oozing from the side of her leg. The pilot stooped and carried her through the damp brush, twenty or thirty meters upwind from the crater. He set her down and bent to look at the wound. He pulled a knife from his crash kit and sawed the tough suit fabric from around her wound.

"You're lucky. Whatever it was passed right through the side of your leg. I'd call this a nick, except it goes so deep." He sprayed the area with first-aid glue, and the pain subsided to a throbbing pressure that kept time with her pulse.

The heavy red smoke was drifting steadily away from them. The orbiter itself was hidden by the crater's edge. The explosions were continuing irregularly but without great force. They should be safe here. He helped her out of her pressure suit, then struggled out of his own.

Quiller walked several paces back toward the wreck. He bent and picked up a strange, carven shape. "Looks like it got thrown here by the blast." It was a Christian cross, its base still covered with dirt.

"We crashed in a damn cemetery." Allison tried to laugh, but it made her dizzy. Quiller didn't reply. He studied the cross for some seconds. Finally he set it down and came back to look at Allison's leg. "That stopped the bleeding. I don't see any other punctures. How do you feel?"

Allison glanced down at the red on her gray flight fatigues. Pretty colors, except when it's your own red. "Give me some time to sit here. I bet I'll be able to walk to the rescue choppers when they come."

"Hmm. Okay, I'm going to take a look around. . . . There may be a road nearby." He unclipped the crash kit and set it beside her. "Be back in fifteen minutes."

4

They started on Wili the next morning. It was the woman, Irma, who brought him down, fed him breakfast in the tiny alcove off the main dining room. She was a pleasant woman, but young enough to be strong, and she spoke very good Spanish. Wili did not trust her. But no one threatened him, and the food seemed endless; he ate so much that his eternal gnawing hunger was almost satisfied. All this time Irma talked—but without saying a great deal, as though she knew he was concentrating on his enormous breakfast. No other servants were visible. In fact, Wili was beginning to think the mansion was untenanted, that these three must be housekeeping staff holding the mansion for their absent lord. That *jefe* was very powerful or very stupid, because even in the light of day, Wili could see no evidence of defenses. If he could be gone before the *jefe* returned . . .

"—and do you know why you are here, Wili?" Irma said as she collected the plates from the mosaicked surface of the breakfast table.

Wili nodded, pretending shyness. Sure he knew. Everyone needed workers, and the old and middle-aged often needed whole gangs to keep them living in style. But he said, "To help you?"

"Not me, Wili. Paul. You will be his apprentice. He has looked a long time, and he has chosen you."

That figured. The old gardener—or whatever he was—looked to be eighty if he was a day. Right now Wili was being treated royally. But he suspected that was simply because the old man and his two flunkies

30

were making illegitimate use of their master's house. No doubt there would be hell to pay when the *jefe* returned. "And . . . and what am I to do for My Lady?" Wili spoke with his best diffidence.

"Whatever Paul asks."

She led him around to the back of the mansion where a large pool, almost a lake, spread away under the pines. The water looked clear, though here and there floated small clots of pine needles. Toward the center, out from under the trees, it reflected the brilliant blue of the sky. Downslope, through an opening in the trees, Wili could see thunderheads gathering about Vandenberg.

"Now off with your clothes and we'll see about giving you a bath." She moved to undo the buttons on his shirt, an adult helping a child.

Wili recoiled. "No!" To be naked here with the woman!

Irma laughed and pinned his arm, continued to unbutton the shirt. For an instant, Wili forgot his pose—that he was a child, and an obedient one. Of course this treatment would be unthinkable within the Ndelante. And even in Jonque territory, the body was respected. No woman forced baths and nakedness on males.

But Irma was strong. As she pulled the shirt over his head, he lunged for the knife strapped to his leg, and brought it up toward her face. Irma screamed. Even as she did, Wili was cursing himself.

"No, no! I am going to tell Paul." She backed away, her hands held between them, as if to protect herself. Wili knew he could run away now (and he couldn't imagine these three catching him)—or he could do what was necessary to stay. For now he wanted to stay.

He dropped the knife and groveled. "Please, Lady, I acted without thought." Which was true. "Please forgive me. I will do anything to make it up." Even, even . . .

The woman stopped, came back, and picked up the knife. She obviously had no experience as a foreman, to trust anything he said. The whole situation was alien and unpredictable. Wili would almost have preferred the lash, the predictability. Irma shook her head, and when she spoke there was still a little fear in her voice. Wili was sure she now knew that he was a good deal older than he looked; she made no move to touch him. "Very well. This is between us, Wili. I will not tell Paul." She smiled, and Wili had the feeling there was something she was not telling him. She reached her arm out full length and handed him the

31

brush and soap. Wili stripped, waded into the chill water, and scrubbed.

"Dress in these," she said after he was out and had dried himself. The new clothes were soft and clean, a minor piece of loot all by themselves. Irma was almost her old self as they walked back to the mansion, and Wili felt safe in asking the question that had been on his mind all that morning: "My Lady, I notice we are all alone here, the four of us—or at least so it appears. When will the protection of the manor lord be returned to us?"

Irma stopped and after a second, laughed. "What manor lord? Your Spanish is so strange. You seem to think this is a castle that should have serfs and troops all around." She continued, almost to herself, "Though perhaps that is your reality. I have never lived in the South.

"You have already met the lord of the manor, Wili." She saw his uncomprehending stare. "It's Paul Naismith, the man who brought you here from Santa Ynez."

"And . . ." Wili could scarcely trust himself to ask the question, ". . . you all, the three of you, are alone here?"

"Certainly. But don't worry. You are much safer here than you ever were in the South, I am sure."

I am sure, too, My Lady. Safe as a coyote among chickens. If ever he'd made a right decision, it had been his escape to Middle California. To think that Paul Naismith and the others had the manor to themselves—it was a wonder the Jonques had not overrun this land long ago. The thought almost kindled his suspicions. But then the prospects of what he could do here overwhelmed all. There was no reason he should have to leave with his loot. Wili Wáchendon, weak as he was, could probably be ruler here—if he was clever enough during the next few weeks. At the very least he would be rich forever. If Naismith were the *jefe*, and if Wili were to be his apprentice, then in essence he was being adopted by the manor lord. That happened occasionally in Los Angeles. Even the richest families were cursed with sterility. Such families often sought an appropriate heir. The adopted one was usually highborn, an orphan of another family, perhaps the survivor of a vendetta. But there were not many children to go around, especially in the old days. Wili knew of at least one case where the oldsters adopted from the Basin—not a black child, of course, but still, a boy from a peasant family. Such was the stuff of dreams; Wili could scarcely believe that it was being offered to him. If he played his cards right, he would eventually own all of this—and without having to steal a single thing, or risk torture and execution! It was . . . unnatural. But if these people were crazy, he would certainly do what he could to profit by it.

Wili hurried after Irma as she returned to the house.

A week passed, then two. Naismith was nowhere to be seen, and Bill and Irma Morales would only say that he was traveling on "business." Wili began to wonder if "apprenticeship" really meant what he had thought. He was treated well, but not with the fawning courtesy that should be shown the heir-apparent of a manor. Perhaps he was on some sort of probation: Irma woke him at dawn, and after breakfast he spent most of the day—assuming it wasn't raining—in the manor's small fields, weeding, planting, hoeing. It wasn't hard work—in fact, it reminded him of what Larry Faulk's labor company did—but it was deadly boring.

On rainy days, when the weather around Vandenberg blew inland, he stayed indoors and helped Irma with cleaning. He had scarcely more enthusiasm for this, but it did give him a chance to snoop: The mansion had no interior court, but in some ways it was more elaborate than he had first imagined. He and Irma cleaned some large rooms hidden below ground level. Irma would say nothing about them, though they appeared to be for meetings or banquets. The building's floor space, if not the available food supply, implied a large household. Perhaps that was how these innocents protected themselves: They simply hid until their enemies got tired of searching for them. But it didn't really make sense. If he were a bandit, he'd burn the place down or else occupy it. He wouldn't simply go away because he could find no one to kill. And yet there was no evidence of past violence in the polished hardwood walls or the deep, soft carpeting.

In the evenings, the two treated him more as they should the adopted son of a lord. He was allowed to sit in the main living room and play Celest or chess. The Celest was every bit as fascinating as the one in Santa Ynez. But he never could attain quite the accuracy he'd had that first time. He began to suspect that part of his win had been luck. It was the precision of his eye and hand that betrayed him, not his physical intuition. Delays of a thousandth of a second in a cushion shot could cause a miss at the destination. Bill said there were mechanical aids to overcome this difficulty, but Wili had little trust for such. He spent many hours hunched before the glowing volume of the Celest, while on the other side of the room Bill and Irma watched the holo. (After the first couple of days, the shows seemed uniformly dull—either local gossip, or flat television game shows from the last century.)

Playing chess with Bill was almost as boring as the holo. After a few games, he could easily beat the caretaker. The programmed version was much more fun than playing Bill.

As the days passed, and Naismith did not return, Wili's boredom intensified. He reconsidered his options. After all this time, no one had offered him the master's rooms, no one had shown him the appropriate deference. (And no tobacco was available, though that by itself was something he could live with.) Perhaps it was all some benign labor contract operation, like Larry Faulk's. If this were the Anglo idea of adoption, he wanted none of it, and his situation became simply a grand opportunity for burglary.

Wili began with small things: jeweled ashtrays from the subterranean rooms, a pocket Celest he found in an empty bedroom. He picked a tree out of sight behind the pond and hid his loot in a waterproof bag there. The burglaries, small as they were, gave him a sense of worth and made life a lot less boring. Even the pain in his gut lessened and the food seemed to taste better.

Wili might have been content to balance indefinitely between the prospect of inheriting the estate and stealing it, but for one thing: The mansion was haunted. It was not the air of mystery or the hidden rooms. There was something alive in the house. Sometimes he heard a woman's voice—not Irma's, but the one he had heard talk to Naismith on the trail. Wili saw the creature once. It was well past midnight. He was sneaking back to the mansion after stashing his latest acquisitions. Wili oozed along the edge of the veranda, moving silently from shadow to shadow. And suddenly there was someone behind him, standing full in the moonlight. It was a woman, tall and Anglo. Her hair, silver in the light, was cut in an alien style. The clothes were like something out of the Moraleses' old-time television: She turned to look straight at him. There was a faint smile on her face. He bolted—and the creature twisted, vanished.

Wili was a fast shadow through the veranda doors, up the stairs, and into his room. He jammed a chair under the doorknob and lay for many minutes, heart pounding. *What had he seen?* How he would like to believe it was a trick of the moonlight: The creature had vanished as if by the flick of a mirror, and large parts of the walls surrounding the veranda were of slick black glass. But tricks of the eye do not have such detail, do not smile faint smiles. What then? Television? Wili had seen plenty of flat video, and since coming to Middle California had used holo tanks. Tonight went beyond all that. Besides, the vision had turned to look *right at him.*

So that left . . . a haunting. It made sense. No one—certainly no woman—had dressed like that since before the plagues. Old Naismith would have been young then. Could this be the ghost of a dead love? Such tales were common in the ruins of LA, but until now Wili had been skeptical.

Any thought of inheriting the estate was gone. The question was, Could he get out of this alive?—and with how much loot? Wili watched the doorknob with horrified fascination. If he lived through this night, then it was probably safe to stay a few more days. The vision might be just the warning of a jealous spirit. Such a ghost would not begrudge him a few more trinkets, as long as he departed when Naismith returned.

Wili got very little sleep that night.

5

The horsemen—four of them, with a row of five pack mules—arrived the afternoon of a slow, rainy day. It had been thundering and windy earlier, but now the rains off Vandenberg came down in a steady drizzle from a sky so overcast that it already seemed evening.

When Wili saw the four, and saw that none of them was Naismith, he faded around the mansion, toward the pond and his cache. Then he stopped for a foolish moment, wondering if he should run back and warn Irma and Bill.

But the two stupid caretakers were already running down the front steps to greet the intruders: an enormous fat fellow and three rifle-carrying men-at-arms. As he skulked in the bushes, Bill turned and seemed to look directly at his hiding place. "Wili, come help our guests."

Mustering what dignity he could, the boy emerged and walked toward the group. The old fat one dismounted. He looked like a Jonque, but his English was strangely accented. "Ah, so this is his apprentice, *hein?* I have wondered if the master would ever find a successor and what sort of person he might be." He patted the bristling Wili on the head, making the usual error about the boy's age.

The gesture was patronizing, but Wili thought there was a hint of respect, almost awe, in his voice. Perhaps this slob was not a Jonque and had never seen a black before. The fellow stared silently at Wili for a moment and then seemed to notice the rain. He gave an exaggerated shiver and most of the group moved up the steps. Bill and Wili were left to take the animals around to the outbuilding.

Four guests. That was not the end. By twos and threes and fours, all through the afternoon and evening, others drifted in. The horses and mules quickly overflowed the small outbuilding, and Bill showed Wili hidden stables. There were no servants. The guests themselves, or at least the more junior of them, carried the baggage indoors and helped with the animals. Much of the luggage was not taken to their rooms, but disappeared into the halls below ground. The rest turned out to be food and drink—which made sense, since the manor produced only enough to feed three or four people.

Night and more rain. The last of the visitors arrived—and one of these was Naismith. The old man took his apprentice aside. "Ah, Wili, you have remained." His Spanish was as stilted as ever, and he paused frequently as if waiting for some unseen speaker to supply him with a missing word. "After the meetings, when our guests have gone, you and I must talk on your course of study. You are too old to delay. For now, though, help Irma and Bill and do not . . . bother . . . our guests." He looked at Wili as though suspecting the boy might do what Wili had indeed been considering. There was many a fat purse to be seen among these naive travelers.

"A new apprentice has nothing to tell his elders, and there is little he can learn from them in this short time." With that the old man departed for the halls beneath his small castle, and Wili was left to work with Irma and two of the visitors in the dimly lit kitchen.

Their mysterious guests stayed all that night and through the next day. Most kept to their rooms and the meeting halls. Several helped Bill with repairs on the outbuilding. Even here they behaved strangely: For instance, the roof of the stable badly needed work. But when the sun came out, the men wouldn't touch it. They seemed only willing to work on things where there was shade. And they never worked outside in groups of more than two or three. Bill claimed this was all Naismith's wish.

The next evening, there was a banquet in one of the halls. Wili, Bill, and Irma brought the food in, but that was all they got to see. The heavy doors were locked and the three of them went back up to the living room. After the Moraleses had settled down with the holo, Wili drifted away as if to go to his room.

He cut through the kitchen to the side stairs. The thick carpet made speedy, soundless progress possible, and a moment later he was peeking round at the entrance to the meeting hall. There were no guards, but the oak doors remained closed. A wood tripod carried a sign of gold on black. Wili silently crossed the hall and touched the sign. The velvet was deep but the gold was just painted on. It was cracked here and there and seemed very old. The letters said:

NCC

And below this, hand-lettered on vellum, was:

2047

Wili stepped back, more puzzled than ever. Why? Who was there to read the sign, when the doors were shut and locked? Did these people believe in spirit spells? Wili crept to the door and set his ear against the dark wood. He heard . . .

Nothing. Nothing but the rush of blood in his ear. These doors were thick, but he should at least hear the murmur of voices. He could hear the sound of a century-old game show from all the way up in the living room, but the other side of this door might as well be the inside of a mountain.

Wili fled upstairs, and was a model of propriety until their guests departed the next day.

There was no single leave-taking; they left as they had come. Strange customs indeed, the Anglos had.

But one thing was as in the South. They left gifts. And the gifts were conveniently piled on the wide table in the mansion's entrance way. Wili tried to pretend disinterest, but he felt his eyes must be visibly bugging out of his head whenever he walked by. Till now he had not seen much that was like the portable wealth of Los Angeles, but here were rubies, emeralds, diamonds, gold. There were gadgets, too, in artfully carved boxes of wood and silver. He couldn't tell if they were games or holos or what. There was so much here that a fortune could be taken and not be missed.

The last were gone by midnight. Wili crouched at the window of his attic room and watched them depart. They quickly disappeared down the trail, and the beat of hooves ceased soon after that. Wili suspected that, like the others, these three had left the main trail and were departing along some special path of their own.

Wili did not go back to his bed. The moon's waning crescent slowly rose and the hours passed. Wili tried to see familiar spots along the coast, but the fog had rolled in, and only the Vandenberg Dome rose into sight. He waited till just before morning twilight. There were no sounds from below. Even the horses were quiet. Only the faint buzzing of insects edged the silence. If he was going to have part of that treasure, he would have to act now, moonlight or not.

Wili slipped down the stairs, his hand lightly touching the haft of his knife. (It was not the same one he had flashed at Irma. That he had made a great show of giving up. This was a short carving knife from the kitchen set.) There had been no more ghostly apparitions since that night on the veranda. Wili had almost convinced himself that it had been an illusion, or some holographic scare show. Nevertheless, he had no desire to stay.

There, glinting in the moonlight, was his treasure. It looked even more beautiful than by lamplight. Far away, he heard Bill turn over, begin to snore. Wili silently filled his sack with the smallest, most clearly valuable items on the table. It was hard not to be greedy, but he stopped when the bag was only half-full. Five kilos would have to do! More wealth than Old Ebenezer passed to the lower Ndelante in a year! And now out the back, around the pond, and to his cache.

Wili crept out onto the veranda, his heart suddenly pounding. This would be the spirit's last chance to get him.

¡Dio! There *was* someone out there. Wili stood absolutely still, not breathing. It was Naismith. The old man sat on a lounge chair, his body bundled against the chill. He seemed to be gazing into the sky— but not at the moon, since he was in the shadows. Naismith was looking away from Wili; this could not be an ambush. Nevertheless, the boy's hand tightened on his knife. After a moment, he moved again, away from the old man and toward the pond.

"Come here to sit," said Naismith, without turning his head. Wili almost bolted, then realized that if the old man could be out here stargazing, there was no reason why the excuse should not also serve him. He set his sack of treasure down in the shadows and moved closer to Naismith.

"That's close enough. Sit. Why are you here so late, young one?"

"The same as you, I think, My Lord. . . . To view the sky." What else could the old man be out here for?

"That's a good reason." The tone was neutral, and Wili could not tell if there was a smile or a scowl on his face; he could barely make out the other's profile. Wili's hand tightened nervously on the haft of his knife. He had never actually killed anyone before, but he knew the penalties for burglary.

"But I don't admire the sky as a whole," Naismith continued, "though it is beautiful. I like the morning and the late evening especially, because then it is possible to see the—" there was one of his characteristic pauses as he seemed to listen for the right word, "satellites. See? There are two visible right now." He pointed first near the zenith and then waved at something close to the horizon. Wili followed his first gesture, and saw a tiny point of light moving slowly, effortlessly across the sky. Too slow to be an aircraft, much too slow to be a meteor: It was a moving star, of course. For a moment, he had thought the old man was going to show him something really magical. Wili shrugged and somehow Naismith seemed to catch the gesture.

"Not impressed, eh? There were men there once, Wili. But no more."

It was hard for Wili to conceal his scorn. How could that be? With aircraft you could see the vehicle. These little lights were like the stars and as meaningless. But he said nothing and a long silence overcame them. "You don't believe me, do you, Wili? But it is true. There were men and women there, so high up you can't see the form of their craft."

Wili relaxed, squatted before the other's chair. He tried to sound humble. "But then, Lord, what keeps them up? Even aircraft must come down for fuel."

Naismith chuckled. "That from the expert Celest player! Think, Wili. The universe is a great game of Celest. Those moving lights are swinging about the Earth, just like planets on a game display.

¡Del Nico Dio! Wili sat on the flags with an audible thump. A wave

of dizziness passed over him. The sky would never be the same. Wili's cosmology had—until that moment—been an unexamined flatland image. Now, suddenly, he found the interior cosmos of Celest surrounding him forever and ever, with no up or down, but only the vast central force field that was the Earth, with the moon and all those moving stars circling about. And he couldn't disguise from himself the distances involved; he was far too familiar with Celest to do that. He felt like an infinitesimal shrinking toward some unknowable zero.

His mind tumbled over and over in the dark, caught between the relationships flashing through his mind and the night sky that swung overhead. So all those objects had their own gravity, and all moved—at least in some small way—at the behest of all the others. An image of the solar system not too different from the reality slowly formed in his mind. When at last he spoke, his voice was very small, and his humility was not pretended, "But then the game, it represents trips that men have actually made? To the moon, to the stars that move? You . . . we . . . can do *that?*"

"We *could* do that, Wili. We could do that and more. But no longer."

"But why *not?*" It was as though the universe had suddenly been taken back from his grasp. His voice was almost a wail.

"In the beginning, it was the War. Fifty years ago there were men alive up there. They starved or they came back to Earth. After the War there were the plagues. Now . . . Now we could do it again. It would be different from before, but we could do it . . . if it weren't for the Peace Authority." The last two words were in English. He paused and then said, *"Mundopaz."*

Wili looked into the sky. The Peace Authority. They had always seemed a part of the universe as far away and indifferent as the stars themselves. He saw their jets and occasionally their helicopters. The major highways passed two or three of their freighters every hour. They had their enclave in Los Angeles. The Ndelante Ali had never considered hitting it; better to burgle the feudal manors of Aztlán. And Wili remembered that even the lords of Aztlán, for all their arrogance, never spoke of the Peace Authority except in neutral tones. It was fitting in a way that something so nearly supernatural should have stolen the stars from mankind. Fitting, yet, now he knew, intolerable.

"They brought us peace, Wili, but the price was very high." A meteor flashed across the sky, and Wili wondered if that had been a piece of man's work, too. Naismith's voice suddenly became business-like. "I said we must talk, and this is the perfect time for it. I want you for my apprentice. But this is no good unless you want it also. Some-how, I don't think our goals are the same. I think you want wealth: I know what's in the bag yonder. I know what's in the tree behind the pond."

Naismith's voice was dry, cool. Wili's eyes hung on the point where the meteor had swept to nothingness. This was like a dream. In Los Angeles, he would be on his way to the headsman now, an adopted son caught in treachery. "But what will wealth get you, Wili? Minimal security, until someone takes it from you. Even if you could rule here, you would still be nothing more than a petty lord, insecure.

"Beyond wealth, Wili, there is power, and I think you have seen enough so that you can appreciate it, even if you never thought to have any."

Power. Yes. To control others the way he had been controlled. To make others fear as he had feared. Now he saw the power in Naismith. What else could really explain this man's castle? And Wili had thought the spirit a jealous lover. Hah! Spirit or projection, it was this man's servant. An hour ago, this insight alone would have made him stay and return all he had stolen. Somehow, he still couldn't take his eyes off the sky.

"And beyond power, Wili, there is knowledge—which some say is power." He had slipped into his native English, and Wili didn't bother to pretend ignorance. "Whether it is power or not depends on the will and the wisdom of its user. As my apprentice, Wili, I can offer you knowledge, for a surety; power, perhaps; wealth, only what you have already seen."

The crescent moon had cleared the pines now. It was one more thing that would never be the same for Wili.

Naismith looked at the boy and held out his hand. Wili offered his knife hilt-first. The other accepted it with no show of surprise. They stood and walked back to the house.

6

Many things were the same after that night. They were the outward things: Wili worked in the gardens almost as much as before. Even with the gifts of food the visitors had brought, they still needed to work to feed themselves. (Wili's appetite was greater than the others'. It didn't seem to help; he remained as undernourished and stunted as ever.) But in the afternoons and evenings he worked with Naismith's machines.

It turned out the ghost was one of those machines. Jill, the old man called her, was actually an interface program run on a special processor system. She was good, almost like a person. With the projection equipment Naismith had built into the walls of the veranda, she could even appear in open space. Jill was the perfect tutor, infinitely patient but with enough "humanity" to make Wili want to please her. Hour after hour, she flashed language questions at him. It was like some verbal Celest. In a matter of weeks, Wili progressed from being barely literate to having a fair command of technical written English.

At the same time, Naismith began teaching him math. At first Wili was contemptuous of these problems. He could do arithmetic as fast as Naismith. But he discovered that there was more to math than the four basic arithmetic operations. There were roots and transcendental functions; there were the relationships that drove both Celest and the planets.

Naismith's machines showed him functions as graphs and related

43

function operations to those pictures. As the days passed, the functions became very specialized and interesting. One night, Naismith sat at the controls and caused a string of rectangles of varying width to appear on the screen. They looked like irregular crenellations on some battlement. Below the first plot, the old man produced a second and then a third, each somewhat like the first but with more and narrower rectangles. The heights bounced back and forth between 1 and −1.

"Well," he said, turning from the display, "what is the pattern? Can you show me the next three plots in this series?" It was a game they had been playing for several days now. Of course, it was all a matter of opinion what really constituted a pattern, and sometimes there was more than one answer that would satisfy a person's taste, but it was amazing how often Wili felt a certain rightness in some answers and an unesthetic blankness in others. He looked at the screen for several seconds. This was harder than Celest, where he merely cranked on deterministic relationships. Hmmm. The squares got smaller, the heights stayed the same, the minimum rectangle width decreased by a factor of two on every new line. He reached out and slid his finger across the screen, sketching the three graphs of his answer.

"Good," said Naismith. "And I think you see how you could make more plots, until the rectangles became so narrow that you couldn't finger-sketch or even display them properly.

"Now look at this." He drew another row of crenellations, one clearly not in the sequence: The heights were not restricted to 1 and −1. "Write me that as the sum and differences of the functions we've already plotted. Decompose it into the other functions." Wili scowled at the display; worse than "guess the pattern," this was. Then he saw it: three of the first graph minus four copies of the third graph plus . . .

His answer was right, but Wili's pride was short-lived, since the old man followed this problem with similar decomposition questions that took Wili many minutes to solve . . . until Naismith showed him a little trick—something called orthogonal decomposition—that used a peculiar and wonderful property of these graphs, these "walsh waves" he called them. The insight brought a feeling of awe just a little like learning about the moving stars, to know that hidden away in the patterns were realities that might take him days to discover by himself.

Wili spent a week dreaming up other orthogonal families and was disappointed to discover that most of them were already famous—haar waves, trig waves—and that others were special cases of general families known for more than two hundred years. He was ready for Naismith's books now. He dived into them, rushed past the preliminary chapters, pushed himself toward the frontier where any new insights would be beyond the farthest reach of previous explorers.

In the outside world, in the fields and the forest that now were such a small part of his consciousness, summer moved into fall. They worked longer hours, to get what crops remained into storage before the frosts. Even Naismith did his best to help, though the others tried to prevent this. The old man was not weak, but there was an air of physical fragility about him.

From the high end of the bean patch, Wili could see over the pines. The leafy forests had changed color and were a band of orange-red beyond the evergreen. The land along the coast was clouded over, but Wili suspected that the jungle there was still wet and green. Vandenberg Dome seemed to hang in the clouds, as awesome as ever. Wili knew more about it now, and someday he would discover all its secrets. It was simply a matter of asking the right questions—of himself and of Paul Naismith.

Indoors, in his greater universe, Wili had completed his first pass through functional analysis and now undertook a three-pronged expedition that Naismith had set for him: into finite Galois theory, stochastics, and electromagnetics. There was a goal in sight, though (Wili was pleased to see) there was no ultimate end to what could be learned. Naismith had a project, and it would be Wili's if he was clever enough.

Wili saw why Naismith was valued and saw the peculiar service he provided to people all over the continent. Naismith solved problems. Almost every day the old man was on the phone, sometimes talking to people locally—like Miguel Rosas down in Santa Ynez—but just as often to people in Fremont, or in places so far away that it was night on the screen while still day here in Middle California. He talked to people in English and in Spanish, and in languages that Wili had never heard. He talked to people who were neither Jonques nor Anglos nor blacks.

Wili had learned enough now to see that these were not nearly as simple as making local calls. Communication between towns along the coast was trivial over the fiber, where almost any bandwidth could be accommodated. For longer distances, such as from Naismith's palace to the coast, it was still relatively easy to have video communication: The coherent radiators on the roof could put out microwave and infrared beams in any direction. On a clear day, when the IR radiator could be used, it was almost as good as a fiber (even with all the tricks Naismith used to disguise their location). But for talking around the curve of the Earth, across forests and rivers where no fiber had been strung and no line of sight existed, it was a different story: Naismith used what he called "short-waves" (which were really in the one- to ten-meter range). These were quite unsuitable for high-fidelity communication. To transmit video—even the wavery black-and-white flat pictures Naismith used in his transcontinental calls—took incredibly clever coding schemes and some real-time adaptation to changing conditions in the upper atmosphere.

The people at the other end brought Naismith problems, and he came back with answers. Not immediately, of course; it often took him weeks, but he eventually thought of something. At least the people at the other end seemed happy. Though it was still unclear to Wili how gratitude on the other side of the continent could help Naismith, he was beginning to understand what had paid for the palace and how Naismith could afford full-scale holo projectors. It was one of these problems that Naismith turned over to his apprentice. If he succeeded, they might actually be able to steal pictures off the Authority's snooper satellites.

It wasn't only people that appeared on the screens.

One evening shortly after the first snowfall of the season, Wili came in from the stable to find Naismith watching what appeared to be an empty patch of snow-covered ground. The picture jerked every few seconds, as if the camera were held by a drunkard. Wili sat down beside the old man. His stomach was more upset than usual and the swinging of the picture did nothing to help the situation—but his curiosity gave him no rest. The camera suddenly swung up to eye level and looked through the pine trees at a house, barely visible in the evening gloom. Wili gasped—it was the building they were sitting in.

Naismith turned from the screen and smiled. "It's a deer, I think. South of the house. I've been following her for the last couple of nights." It took Wili a second to realize he was referring to what was holding the camera. Wili tried to imagine how anyone could catch a deer and strap a camera on it. Naismith must have noticed his puzzlement. "Just a second." He rummaged through a nearby drawer and handed Wili a tiny brown ball. "That's a camera like the one on the critter. It's wide enough so I have resolution about as good as the human eye. And I can shift the decoding parameters so it will 'look' in different directions without the deer's having to move.

"Jill, move the look axis, will you?"

"Right, Paul." The view slid upward till they were looking into overhanging branches and then down the other side. Wili and Naismith saw a scrawny back and part of a furry ear.

Wili looked at the object Paul had placed in his hand. The "camera" was only three or four millimeters across. It felt warm and almost sticky in Wili's hand. It was a far cry from the lensed contraptions he had seen in Jonque villas. "So you just stick them to the fur, true?" said Wili.

Naismith shook his head. "Even easier than that. I can get these in hundred lots from the Greens in Norcross. I scatter them through the forest, on branches and such. All sorts of animals pick them up. It provides just a little extra security. The hills are safer than they were years ago, but there are still a few bandits."

"Umm." If Naismith had weapons to match his senses, the manor was better protected than any castle in Los Angeles. "This would be greater protection if you could have people watching all the views all the time."

Naismith smiled, and Wili thought of Jill. He knew enough now to see that the program could be made to do just that.

Wili watched for more than an hour as Naismith showed him scenes from a number of cameras, including one from a bird. That gave the same sweeping view he imagined could be seen from Peace Authority aircraft.

When at last he went to his room, Wili sat for a long while looking out the garret window at the snow-covered trees, looking at what he had just seen with godlike clarity from dozens of other eyes. Finally he stood up, trying to ignore the cramp in his gut that had become so persistent these last few weeks. He removed his clothes from the closet and laid them on the bed, then inspected every square centimeter with his eyes and fingers. His favorite jacket and his usual work pants both had tiny brown balls stuck to cuffs or seams. Wili removed them; they looked so innocuous in the room's pale lamplight.

47

He put them in a dresser drawer and returned his clothes to the closet.

He lay awake for many minutes, thinking about a place and time he had resolved never to dwell on again. What could a hovel in Glendora have in common with a palace in the mountains? Nothing. Everything. There had been safety there. There had been Uncle Sylvester. He had learned there, too—arithmetic and a little reading. Before the Jonques, before the Ndelante—it had been a child's paradise, a time lost forever.

Wili quietly got up and slipped the cameras back into his clothing. Maybe not lost forever.

7

January passed, an almost uninterrupted snowstorm. The winds coming off Vandenberg brought ever-higher drifts that eventually reached the mansion's second story and would have totally blocked the entrances if not for the heroic efforts of Bill and Irma. The pain in Wili's middle became constant, intense. Winters had always been bad for him, but this one was worse than ever before, and the others eventually became aware of it. He could not suppress the occasional grimace, the faint groan. He was always hungry, always eating—and yet losing weight.

But there was great good, too. He was beyond the frontiers of Naismith's books! Paul claimed that no previous human had insight on the coding problem that he had attacked! Wili didn't need Naismith's machines now; the images in his mind were so much more complete. He sat in the living room for hours—through most of his waking time—almost unaware of the outside world, almost unaware of his pain, dreaming of the problem and his schemes for its defeat. All existence was groups and graphs and endless combinatorical refinements on the decryption scheme he hoped would break the problem.

But when he ate and even when he slept, the pain levered itself back into his soul.

It was Irma, not Wili, who noticed that the paler skin on his palms had a yellow cast beneath the brown. She sat beside him at the dining table, holding his small hands in her large, calloused ones. Wili bristled at her touch. He was here to eat, not to be inspected. But Paul stood behind her.

"And the nails look discolored, too." She reached across to one of Wili's yellowed fingernails and gave it a gentle tug. Without sound or pain, the nail came away at its root. Wili stared stupidly for a second, then jerked his hand back with a shriek. Pain was one thing; this was the nightmare of a body slowly dismembering itself. For an instant terror blotted out his gut pain the way mathematics had done before.

They moved him to a basement room, where he could be warm all the time. Wili found himself in bed most of each day. His only view of the outside, of the cloudswept purity of Vandenberg, was via the holo. The mountain snows were too deep to pass travelers; there would be no doctors. But Naismith moved cameras and high-bandwidth equipment into the room, and once when Wili was not lost in dreaming, he saw that someone from far away was looking on, was being interrogated by Naismith. The old man seemed very angry.

Wili reached out to touch his sleeve. "It will be all right, Uncle Syl —Paul. This problem I have always had and worst in the winters. I will be okay in the spring."

Naismith smiled and nodded, then turned away.

But Wili was not delirious in any normal sense. During the long hours an average patient would have lain staring at the ceiling or watching the holo and trying to ignore his pain, Wili dreamed on and on about the communications problem that had resisted his manifold efforts all these weeks. When the others were absent, there was still Jill, taking notes, ready to call for help; she was more real than any of them. It was hard to imagine that her voice and pretty face had ever seemed threatening.

In a sense, he had already solved the problem, but his scheme was too slow; he needed $n*\log(n)$ time for this application. He was far beyond the tools provided by his brief, intense education. Something new, something clever was needed, and by the One True God he would find it!

And when the solution did come it was like a sun rising on a clear morning, which was appropriate since this was the first clear day in almost a month. Bill brought him up to ground level to sit in the sunlight before the newly cleared windows. The sky was not just clear, but an intense blue. The snow was piled deep, a blinding white. Icicles grew down from every edge and corner, dripping tiny diamonds in the warm light.

Wili had been dictating to Jill for nearly an hour when the old man came down for breakfast. He took one look over Wili's shoulder and then grabbed his reader, saying not a word to Wili or anyone else. Naismith paused many times, his eyes half-closed in concentration. He was about a third of the way through when Wili finished. He looked up when Wili stopped talking. "You got it?"

Wili nodded, grinning. "Sure, and in n*log(n) time, too." He glanced at Naismith's reader. "You're still looking at the filter setting up. The real trick isn't for a hundred more lines." He scanned forward. Naismith looked at it for a long time, finally nodded. "I, I think I see. I'll have to study it, but I think . . . My little Ramanujan. How do you feel?"

"Great," he said, filled with elation, "but tired. The pain has been less these last days, I think. Who is Ramanujan?"

"Twentieth-century mathematician. An Indian. There are a lot of similarities: You both started out without much formal education. You are both very, very good."

Wili smiled, the warmth of the sun barely matching what he felt. These were the first words of real praise he had heard from Naismith. He resolved to look up everything on file about this Ramanujan. . . . His mind drifted, freed from the fixation of the last weeks. Through the pines, he could see the sun on Vandenberg. There were so many mysteries left to master. . . .

8

Naismith made some phone calls the next day. The first was to Miguel Rosas at the SYP Company. Rosas was undersheriff to Sy Wentz, but the Tinkers around Vandenberg hired him for almost all their police operations.

The cop's dark face seemed a touch pale after he watched Naismith's video replay. "Okay," he finally said, "who *was* Ramanujan?"

Naismith felt the tears coming back to his eyes. "That was a bad slip; now the boy is sure to look him up. Ramanujan was everything I told Wili: a really brilliant fellow, without much college education." This wouldn't impress Mike, Naismith knew. There were no colleges now, just apprenticeships. "He was invited to England to work with some of the best number theorists of the time. He got TB, died young."

". . . Oh. I get the connection, Paul. But I hope you don't think that bringing Wili into the mountains did anything to hurt him."

"His problem is worse during winters, and our winters are fierce compared to LA's. This has pushed him over the edge."

"Bull! It may have aggravated his problem, but he got better food here and more of it. Face it, Paul. This sort of wasting just gets worse and worse. You've seen it before."

"More than you!" That and the more acute diseases of the plague years had come close to destroying mankind. Then Naismith brought himself up short, remembering Miguel's two little sisters. Three orphans from Arizona they had been, but only one survived. Every winter, the girls had sickened again. When they died, their bodies were near-skeletons. The young cop had seen more of it than most in his generation.

"Listen, Mike, we've got to do something. Two or three years is the most he has. But hell, even before the War a good pharmaceutical lab could have cured this sort of thing. We were on the verge of cracking DNA coding and—"

"Even then, Paul? Where do you think the plagues came from? That's not just Peace Authority jive. We know the Peace is almost as scared of bioresearch as they are that someone might find the secret of their bobbles. They bobbled Yakima a few years ago just because one of their agents found a recombination analyzer in the city hospital. That's ten thousand people asphyxiated because of a silly antique. Face it: The bastards who started the plagues are forty years dead—and good riddance."

Naismith sighed. His conscience was going to hurt him on this—a little matter of protecting your customers. "You're wrong, Mike. I have business with lots of people. I have a good idea what most of them do."

Rosas' head snapped up. "Bioscience labs, even in our time?"

"Yes. At least three, perhaps ten. I can't be sure, since of course they don't admit to it. And there's only one whose location is certain."

"Jesus, Paul, how can you deal with such vermin?"

Naismith shrugged. "The Peace Authority is the real enemy. In spite of what you say, it's only their word that the bioscience people caused the plagues, trying to win back for their governments what all the armies could not. I *know* the Peace." He stopped for a moment, remembering treachery that had been a personal, secret thing for fifty years.

"I've tried to convince you tech people: The Authority can't tolerate you. You follow their laws: You don't make high-density power sources, don't make vehicles or experiment with nucleonics or biology. But if the Authority knew what was going on *within* the rules . . . You must have heard about the NCC: I showed conclusively that the Peace is beginning to catch on to us. They are beginning to understand how far we have gone without big power sources and universities and old-style capital industry. They are beginning to realize how far our electronics is ahead of their best. When they see us clearly, they'll step on us the way they have on all opposition, and we're going to have to *fight.*"

"You've been saying that for as long as I can remember, Paul, but—"

"But secretly you Tinkers aren't that unhappy with the status quo. You've read about the wars before the War, and you're afraid of what could happen if suddenly the Authority lost power. Even though you deceive the Peace, you're secretly glad they're there. Well, let me tell you something, Mike." The words came in an uncontrollable rush. "I knew the mob you call the Peace Authority when they were just a bunch of R and D administrators and petty crooks. They were at the right place and the right time to pull the biggest con and rip-off of all history. They have zero interest in humanity or progress. That's the reason they've never invented anything of their own."

He stopped, shocked by his outburst. But he saw from Rosas' face that his revelation had not been understood. The old man sat back, tried to relax. "Sorry, I wandered off. What's important right now is this: A lot of people—from Beijing to Norcross—owe me. If we had a patent system and royalties it would be a lot more gAu than has ever trickled in. I want to call those IOUs due. I want my friends to get Wili to the bioscience underground.

"And if the past isn't enough, think about this: I'm seventy-eight. If it's not Wili, it's no one. I've never been modest: I know I'm the best mathman the Tinkers have. Wili's not merely a replacement for me. He is actually better, or will be with a few years' experience. You know the problem he just cracked? It's the thing the Middle California Tinkers have been bugging me about for three years: eavesdropping on the Authority's recon satellites."

Rosas' eyes widened slightly.

"Yes. That problem. You know what's involved. Wili's come up with a scheme I think will satisfy your friends, one that runs a very small chance of detection. Wili did it in six weeks, with just the technical background he picked up from me last fall. His technique is radical, and I think it will provide leverage on several other problems. You're going to need someone like him over the next ten years."

"Um." Rosas fiddled with his gold-and-blue sheriff's brassard. "Where is this lab?"

"Just north of San Diego."

"That close? Wow." He looked away. "So the problem is getting him down there. The Aztlán nobility is damned unpleasant about blacks coming in from the north, at least under normal circumstances."

" 'Normal circumstances'?"

"Yes. The North American Chess Federation championships are in La Jolla this April. That means that some of the best high tech people around are going to be down there—legitimately. The Authority has even offered transportation to entrants from the East Coast, and they hardly ever sully their aircraft with us ordinary humans. If I were as paranoid as you, I would be suspicious. But the Peace seems to be playing it just for the propaganda value. Chess is even more popular in Europe than here; I think the Authority is building up to sponsorship of the world championships in Berne next year.

"In any case, it provides a cover and perfect protection from the Aztlán: black or Anglo, they've never touched anyone under Peace Authority protection."

Naismith found himself grinning. Some good luck after all the bad. There were tears in his eyes once more, but now for a different reason. "Thanks, Mike. I needed this more than anything I've ever asked for."

Rosas smiled briefly in return.

FLASHFORWARD

Allison didn't know much about plant identification (from less than one hundred kilometers anyway), but there was something very odd about this forest. In places it was overgrown right down to the ground; in other places, it was nearly clear. Everywhere a dense canopy of leaves and vines prevented anything more than fragmented views of the sky. It reminded her of the scraggly second growth forests of Northern California, except there was such a jumble of types: conifers, eucalyptus, even something that looked like a sickly manzanita. The air was very warm, and muggy. She rolled back the sleeves of her flight fatigues.

The fire was barely audible now. This forest was so wet that it could not spread. Except for the pain in her leg, Allison could almost believe she were in a park on some picnic. In fact, they might be rescued by *real* picnickers before the Air Force arrived.

She heard Quiller's progress back toward her long before she could see him. When he finally came into view, the pilot's expression was glum. He asked again about her injury.

"I—I think I'm fine. I pinched it shut and resprayed." She paused and returned his somber look. "Only . . ."

"Only what?"

"Only . . . to be honest, Angus, the crash did something to my memory. I don't remember a thing from right after entry till we were on the ground. What went wrong anyway? Where did we end up?"

Angus Quiller's face seemed frozen. Finally he said, "Allison, I think your memory is fine—as good as mine, anyway. You see, I don't have any memory from someplace over Northern California till the hull started busting up on the ground. In fact, I don't think there *was* anything to remember."

"What?"

"I think we were something like forty klicks up and then we were down on a planetary surface—just like that." He snapped his fingers. "I think we've fallen into some damn fantasy." Allison just stared at him, realizing that he was probably the more distressed of the two of them. Quiller must have interpreted the look correctly. "Really, Allison, unless you believe that we could have exactly the same amount of amnesia, then the only explanation is . . . I mean one minute we're on a perfectly ordinary reconnaissance operation, and the next we're . . . we're here, just like in a lot of movies I saw when I was a kid."

"Parallel amnesia is still more believable than that, Angus." *If only I could figure out where we are.*

The pilot nodded. "Yes, but you didn't climb a tree and take a look around, Allison. Plant life aside, this area looks vaguely like the California coast. We're boxed in by hills, but in one direction I could see that the forests go down almost to the sea. And . . ."

"And?"

"There's something out there on the coast, Allison. It's a mountain, a silver mountain sticking kilometers into the sky. There's never been anything on Earth like that."

Now Allison began to feel the bedrock fear that was gnawing at Angus Quiller. For many people, the completely inexplicable is worse than death. Allison was such a person. The crash—even Fred's death—she could cope with. The amnesia explanation had been so convenient. But now, almost half an hour had passed. There was no sign of aircraft, much less of rescue. Allison found herself whispering, reciting all the crazy alternatives. "You think we're in some kind of parallel world, or on the planet of another star—or in the future?" *A future where alien invaders set their silvery castle-mountains down on the California shore?*

Quiller shrugged, started to speak, seemed to think better of it— then finally burst out with, "Allison, you know that . . . cross near the edge of the crater?"

She nodded.

"It was old, the stuff carved on it was badly weathered, but I could see . . . It had your name on it and . . . and today's date."

Just the one cross, and just the one name. For a long while they were both silent.

9

It was April. The three travelers moved through the forest under a clear, clean sky. The wind made the eucs and vines sway above them, sending down misty sprays of water. But at the level of the mud road, the air was warm and still.

Wili slogged along, reveling in the strength he felt returning to his limbs. He been fine these last few weeks. In the past, he always felt good for a couple months after being really sick, but this last winter had been so bad he'd wondered if he would get better. They had left Santa Ynez three hours earlier, right after the morning rain stopped. Yet he was barely tired and cheerfully refused the others' suggestions that he get back into the cart.

Every so often the road climbed above the surrounding trees and they could see a ways. There was still snow in the mountains to the east. In the west there was no snow, only the rolling rain forests, Lake Lompoc spread sky-blue at the base of the Dome—and the whole landscape appearing again in that vast, towering mirror.

It was strange to leave the home in the mountains. If Paul were not with them, it would have been more unpleasant than Wili could admit.

Wili had known for a week that Naismith intended to take him to the coast, and then travel south to La Jolla—and a possible cure. It was knowledge that made him more anxious than ever to get back in shape. But it wasn't until Jeremy Kaladze met them at Santa Ynez that Wili realized how unusual this first part of the journey might be. Wili eyed the other boy surreptitiously. As usual, Jeremy was talking about everything in sight, now running ahead of them to point out a peculiar rockfall or side path, now falling behind Naismith's cart to study something he had almost missed. After nearly a day's acquaintance, Wili still couldn't decide how old the boy was. Only very small children in the Ndelante Ali displayed his brand of open enthusiasm. On the other hand, Jeremy was nearly two meters tall and played a good game of chess.

"Yes sir, Dr. Naismith," said Jeremy—he was the only person Wili had ever heard call Paul a doctor—"Colonel Kaladze came down along this road. It was a night drop, and they lost a third of the Red Arrow Battalion, but I guess the Russian government thought it must be important. If we went a kilometer down those ravines, we'd see the biggest pile of armored vehicles you can imagine. Their parachutes didn't open right." Wili looked in the direction indicated, saw nothing but green undergrowth and the suggestion of a trail. In LA the oldsters were always talking about the glorious past, but somehow it was strange that in the middle of this utter peace a war was buried, and that this boy talked about ancient history as if it were a living yesterday. His grandfather, Lt. Col. Nikolai Sergeivich Kaladze, had commanded one of the Russian air drops, made before it became clear that the Peace Authority (then a nameless organization of bureaucrats and scientists) had made warfare obsolete.

Red Arrow's mission was to discover the secret of the mysterious force-field weapon the Americans had apparently invented. Of course, they discovered the Americans were just as mystified as everyone else by the strange silvery bubbles, baubles—bobbles?—that were springing up so mysteriously, sometimes preventing bombs from exploding, more often removing critical installations.

In that chaos, when everyone was losing a war that no one had started, the Russian airborne forces and what was left of the American army fought their own war with weapon systems that now had no depot maintenance. The conflict continued for several months, declining in violence until both sides were slugging it out with small arms. Then the Authority had miraculously appeared, announcing itself as the guardian of peace and the maker of the bobbles.

The remnant of the Russian forces retreated into the mountains, hiding as the nation they invaded began to recover. Then the war viruses came, released (the Peace Authority claimed) by the Americans in a last attempt to retain national autonomy. The Russian guerrillas sat on the fringes of the world and watched for some chance to move. None came. Billions died and fertility dropped to near zero in the years following the War. The species called Homo sapiens came very close to extinction. The Russians in the hills became old men, leading ragged tribes.

But Colonel Kaladze had been captured early (through no fault of his own), before the viruses, when the hospitals still functioned. There had been a nurse, and eventually a marriage. Fifty years later, the Kaladze farm covered hundreds of hectares along the south edge of the Vandenberg Dome. That land was one of the few places north of Central America where bananas and cacao could be farmed. Like so much of what had happened to Colonel Kaladze in the last half century, it would have been impossible without the bobbles, in particular the Vandenberg one: The doubled sunlight was as intense as could be found at any latitude, and the high obstacle the Dome created in the atmosphere caused more than 250 centimeters of rain a year in a land that was otherwise quite dry. Nikolai Sergeivich Kaladze had ended up a regular Kentucky colonel—even if he was originally from Georgia.

Most of this Wili learned in the first ninety minutes of Jeremy's unceasing chatter.

In late afternoon they stopped to eat. Belying his gentle exterior, Jeremy was a hunting enthusiast, though apparently not a very expert one. The boy needed several shots to bring down just one bird. Wili would have preferred the food they had brought along, but it seemed only polite to try what Jeremy shot. Six months before, politeness would have been the last consideration to enter his mind.

They trudged on, no longer quite so enthusiastic. This was the shortest route to Red Arrow Farm but it was still a solid ten-hour hike from Santa Ynez. Given their late start, they would probably have to spend the night on this side of the Lompoc ferry crossing. Jeremy's chatter slowed as the sun slanted toward the Pacific and spread double shadows behind them. In the middle of a long discussion (monologue) on his various girl friends, Jeremy turned to look up at Naismith. Speaking very quietly, he said, "You know, sir, I think we are being followed."

The old man seemed to be half-dozing in his seat, letting Berta, his horse, pull him along without guidance. "I know," he said. "Almost two kilometers back. If I had more gear, I could know precisely, but it looks like five to ten men on foot, moving a little faster than we are. They'll catch up by nightfall."

Wili felt a chill that was not in the afternoon air. Jeremy's stories of Russian bandits were a bit pale compared to what he had seen with the Ndelante Ali, but they were bad enough. "Can you call ahead, Paul?"

Naismith shrugged. "I don't want to broadcast; they might jump on us immediately. Jeremy's people are the nearest folks who could help, and even on a fast horse that's a couple hours. We're going to have to handle most of this ourselves."

Wili glared at Jeremy, whose distant relatives—the ones he had been bragging about all day—were apparently out to ambush them. The boy's wide face was pale. "But I was mostly farking you. No one has actually seen one of the outlaw bands down this far in . . . well, in ages."

"I know," Naismith muttered agreement. "Still, it's a fact we're being crowded from behind." He looked at Berta, as if wondering if there was any way the three of them might outrun ten men on foot. "How good is that cannon you carry, Jeremy?"

The boy raised the weapon. Except for its elaborate telescopic sight and chopped barrel, it looked pretty ordinary to Wili: a typical New Mexico autorifle, heavy and simple. The clip probably carried ten 8-mm rounds. With the barrel cut down, it wouldn't be much more accurate than a pistol. Wili had successfully dodged such fire from a distance of one hundred meters. Jeremy patted the rifle, apparently ignorant of all this, "Really hot stuff, sir. It's smart."

"And the ammunition?"

"That too. One clip anyway."

Naismith smiled a jagged smile. " 'Kolya really coddles you youngsters—but I'm glad of it. Okay." He seemed to reach a decision. "It's going to depend on you, Jeremy. I didn't bring anything that heavy. . . . An hour walk from here is a trail that goes south. We should be able to reach it by twilight. A half hour along that path is a bobble. I know there's a clear line of sight from there to your farm. And the bobble should confuse our 'friends,' assuming they aren't familiar with the land this close to the coast."

New surprise showed on Jeremy's face. "Sure. We know about that bobble, but how did you? It's real small."

"Never you mind. I go for hikes, too. Let's just hope they let us get there."

They proceeded down the road, even Jeremy's tongue momentarily stilled. The sun was straight ahead. It would set behind Vandenberg. Its reflection in the Dome edged higher and higher, as if to touch the true sun at the moment of sunset. The air was warmer and the green of the trees more intense than in any normal sunset. Wili could hear no evidence of the men his friends said were pursuing.

Finally the two suns kissed. The true disk slipped behind the Dome into eclipse. For several minutes, Wili thought he saw a ghostly light hanging over the Dome above the point of the sun's setting.

"I've noticed that, too," Naismith replied to Wili's unspoken question. "I think it's the corona, the glow around the sun that's ordinarily invisible. That's the only explanation I can think of, anyway."

The pale light slowly disappeared, leaving a sky that went from orange to green to deepest blue. Naismith urged Berta to a slightly faster walk and the two boys swung onto the back of the cart. Jeremy slipped a new clip into his rifle and settled down to cover the road.

Finally they reached the cutoff. The path was as small as any Jeremy had pointed to during the day, too narrow for the cart. Naismith carefully climbed down and unhitched Berta, then distributed various pieces of equipment to the boys.

"Come on. I've left enough on the cart to satisfy them . . . I hope." They set off southward with Berta. The trail narrowed till Wili wondered if Paul was lost. Far behind them, he heard an occasional branch snap, and now even the sound of voices. He and Jeremy looked at each other. "They're loud enough," the boy muttered. Naismith didn't say anything, just switched Berta to move a bit faster. If the bandits weren't satisfied with the wagon, the three of them would have to make a stand, and evidently he wanted that to be further on.

The sounds of their pursuers were louder now, surely past the wagon. Paul guided Berta to the side. For a moment the horse looked back at them stupidly. Then Naismith seemed to say something in its ear and the animal moved off quickly into the shadows. It was still not really dark. Wili thought he could see green in the treetops, and the sky held only a few bright stars.

They headed into a deep and narrow ravine, an apparent cul-de-sac.

Wili looked ahead and saw—*three figures coming toward them out of a brightly lit tunnel!* He bolted up the side of the ravine, but Jeremy grabbed his jacket and pointed silently toward the strange figures: Now one of *them* was holding another and pointing. *Reflections.* That's what he was seeing. Down there at the back of the ravine, a giant curved mirror showed Jeremy and Naismith and himself silhouetted against the evening sky.

Very quietly, they slid down through the underbrush to the base of the mirror, then began climbing around its sides. Wili couldn't resist: Here at last was a bobble. It was much smaller than Vandenberg, but a bobble nevertheless. He paused and reached out to touch the silvery surface—then snatched his hand back in shock. Even in the cool evening air, the mirror was warm as blood. He peered closer, saw the dark image of his head swell before him. There was not a nick, not a scratch in that surface. Up close, it was as perfect as Vandenberg appeared from a distance, as transcendentally perfect as mathematics itself. Then Jeremy's hand closed again on his jacket and he was dragged upward around the sphere.

The forest floor was level with the top. A large tree grew at the edge of the soil, its roots almost like tentacles around the top of the sphere. Wili hunkered down between the roots and looked back along the ravine. Naismith watched a dim display while Jeremy slid forward and panned the approaches through his rifle sight. From their vantage Wili could see that the ravine was an elongated crater, with the bobble—which was about thirty meters across—forming the south end. The history seemed obvious: Somehow, this bobble had fallen out of the sky, carving a groove in the hills before finally coming to rest. The trees above it had grown in the decades since the War. Given another century, the sphere might be completely buried.

For a moment they sat breathless. A cicada started buzzing, the noise so loud he wondered if they would even hear their pursuers. "They may not fall for this." Naismith spoke almost to himself. "Jeremy, I want you to scatter these around behind us as far as you can in five minutes." He handed the boy something, probably tiny cameras like those around the manor. Jeremy hesitated, and Naismith said, "Don't worry, we won't be needing your rifle for at least that long. If they try to come up behind us, I want to know about it."

The vague shadow that was Jeremy Kaladze nodded and crawled off into the darkness. Naismith turned to Wili and pressed a coherent transmitter into his hands. "Try to get this as far up as you can." He gestured at the conifer among whose roots they crouched.

Wili moved out more quietly than the other boy. This had been Wili's specialty, though in the Los Angeles Basin there were more ruins than forests. The muck of the forest floor quickly soaked his legs and sleeves, but he kept close to the ground. As he oozed up to the base of the tree, he struck his knee against something hard and artificial. He stopped and felt out the obstacle: an ancient stone cross, a Christian cemetery cross really. Something limp and fragrant lay in the needle mulch beside it—flowers?

Then he was climbing swiftly up the tree. The branches were so regularly spaced they might as well have been stair steps. He was soon out of breath. He was just out of condition; at least he hoped that was the explanation.

The tree trunk narrowed and began to sway in response to his movement. He was above the nearby trees, pointed, dark forms all around him. He was really not very high up; almost all the trees in the rain forest were young.

Jupiter and Venus blazed like lanterns, and the stars were out. Only a faint yellow glow showed over Vandenberg and the western horizon. He could see all the way to the base of the Dome; this was high enough. Wili fastened the emitter so it would have a clear line of sight to the west. Then he paused a moment, letting the evening breeze turn his pants and sleeves cold on his skin. There were no lights anywhere. Help was very far away.

They would have to depend on Naismith's gadgets and Jeremy's inexperienced trigger finger.

He almost slid down the tree and was back at Naismith's side soon after that. The old man scarcely seemed to notice his arrival, so intent was he on the little display. "Jeremy?" Wili whispered.

"He's okay. Still laying out the cameras." Paul was looking through first one and then another of the little devices. The pictures were terribly faint, but recognizable. Wili wondered how long his batteries would last. "Fact is, our friends are coming in along the path we left for them." In the display, evidently from some camera Paul had dropped along the way, Wili could see an occasional booted foot.

"How long?"

"Five or ten minutes. Jeremy'll be back in plenty of time." Naismith took something out of his pack—the master for the transmitter Wili had set in the tree. He fiddled with the phase aimer and spoke softly, trying to raise the Strela farm. After long seconds, an insectlike voice answered from the device, and the old man was explaining their situation.

"Got to sign off. Low on juice," he finished. Behind them, Jeremy slid into place and unlimbered his rifle. "Your grandpa's people are coming, Jeremy, but it'll be hours. Everyone's at the house."

They waited. Jeremy looked over Naismith's shoulder for a moment. Finally he said. "Are they sons of the originals? They don't walk like old men."

"I know," said Naismith.

Jeremy crawled to the edge of the crater. He settled into a prone position and rested his rifle on a large root. He scanned back and forth through the sight.

The minutes passed, and Wili's curiosity slowly increased. What was the old man planning? What was there about this bobble that could be a threat to anyone? Not that he wasn't impressed. If they lived through to morning, he would see it by daylight and that would be one of the first joys of survival. There was something almost alive about the warmth he had felt in its surface, though now he realized it was probably just the reflected heat of his own body. He remembered what Naismith once had told him. Bobbles reflected everything; nothing could pass through, in either direction. What was within might as well be in a separate, tiny universe. Somewhere beneath their feet lay the wreckage of an aircraft or missile, embobbled by the Peace Authority when they put down the national armies of the world. Even if the crew of that aircraft could have survived the crash, they would have suffocated in short order. There were worse ways to die: Wili had always sought the ultimate hiding place, the ultimate safety. To his inner heart, the bobbles seemed to be such.

Voices. They were not loud, but there was no attempt at secrecy. There were footsteps, the sounds of branches snapping. In Naismith's fast-dimming display, Wili could see at least five pairs of feet. They walked past a bent and twisted tree he remembered just two hundred meters back. Wili strained his ears to make sense of their words, but it was neither English nor Spanish. Jeremy muttered, "Russian, after all!"

Finally, the enemy came over the ridge that marked the far end of the ravine. Unsurprisingly, they were not in a single file now. Wili counted ten figures strung out against the starry sky. Almost as a man, the group froze, then dove for cover with their guns firing full automatic. The three on the bobble hugged the dirt as rounds whizzed by, thunking into the trees. Ricochets off the bobble sounded like heavy hail on a roof. Wili kept his face stuck firmly in the moist bed of forest needles and wondered how long the three of them could last.

10

"**G**entlemen of the Peace Authority, Greater Tucson has been destroyed." The New Mexico Air Force general slapped his riding crop against the topographical map by way of emphasis. A neat red disk had been laid over the downtown district, and paler pink showed the fallout footprint. It all looked very precise, though Hamilton Avery suspected it was more show than fact. The government in Albuquerque had communication equipment nearly on a par with the Peace but it would take aircraft or satellite recon to get a detailed report on one of their western cities this quickly: The detonation had happened less than ten hours earlier.

The general—Avery couldn't see his name tag, and it probably didn't matter anyway—continued. "That's three thousand men, women, and children immediately dead, and God knows how many hundreds to die of radiation poisoning in the months to come." He glared across the conference table at Avery and the assistants he'd brought to give his delegation the properly important image.

For a moment it seemed as though the officer had finished speaking, but in fact he was just catching his breath. Hamilton Avery settled back and let the blast roll over him. "You of the Peace Authority deny us aircraft, tanks. You have weakened what is left of the nation that spawned you until we must use force simply to protect our borders from states that were once friendly. But what have you given us in return?" The man's face was getting red. The implication had been there, but the fool insisted on spelling it out: If the Peace Authority couldn't protect the Republic from nuclear weapons, then it could scarcely be the organization it advertised itself to be. And the general claimed the Tucson blast was incontrovertible proof that some nation possessed nukes and was using them, despite the Authority and all its satellites and aircraft and bobble generators.

On the Republic's side of the table, a few heads nodded agreement, but those individuals were far too cautious to say aloud what their scapegoat was shouting to the four walls. Hamilton pretended to listen; best to let this fellow hang himself. Avery's subordinates followed his lead, though for some it was an effort. After three generations of undisputed rule, many Authority people took their power to be God-given. *Hamilton knew better.*

He studied those seated around the general. Several were Army generals, one just back from the Colorado. The others were civilians. Hamilton knew this group. In the early years, he had thought the Republic of New Mexico was the greatest threat to the Peace in North America, and he had watched them accordingly. This was the Strategic Studies Committee. It ranked higher in the New Mexico government than the Group of Forty or the National Security Council—and, of course, higher than the cabinet. Every generation, governments seemed to breed a new inner circle out of the older, which was then used as a sop to satisfy larger numbers of less influential people. These men, together with the President, were the real power in the Republic. Their "strategic studies" extended from the Colorado to the Mississippi. New Mexico was a powerful nation. They could invent the bobble and nuclear weapons all over again if they were allowed.

They were easy to frighten nonetheless. This Air Force general couldn't be a full-fledged member of the group. The NMAF manned a few hot-air balloons and dreamed of the good old days. The closest they ever got to modern aircraft was a courtesy flight on an Authority plane. He was here to say things their government wanted said but did not have the courage to spit out directly.

The old officer finally ran down, and sat down. Hamilton gathered his papers and moved to the podium. He looked mildly across at the New Mexico officials and let the silence lengthen to significance.

It was probably a mistake to come here in person. Talking to national governments was normally done by officers two levels below him in the Peace Authority. Appearing in person could easily give these people an idea of the true importance of the incident. Nevertheless, he had wanted to see these men close up. There was an outside chance they were involved in the menace to the Peace he had discovered the last few months.

Finally he began. "Thank you, General, uh, Halberstamm. We understand your anxiety, but wish to emphasize the Peace Authority's long-standing promise. No nuclear weapon has exploded in nearly fifty years and none exploded yesterday in Greater Tucson."

The general spluttered. "Sir! The radiation! The blast! How can you say—"

Avery raised his hand and smiled for silence. There was a sense of noblesse oblige and faint menace in the action. "In a moment, General. Bear with me. It is true: There was an explosion and some radiation. But I assure you no one besides the Authority has nuclear weapons. If there were, we would deal with them by methods you all know.

"In fact, if you consult your records, you will find that the center of the blast area coincides with the site of a ten-meter confinement sphere generated"—he pretended to consult his notes—"5 July 1997."

He saw various degrees of shock, but no questions broke the silence. He wondered how surprised they really were. From the beginning, he'd known there was no point in trying to cover up the source of the blast. Old Alex Schelling, the President's science adviser, would have put two and two together correctly.

"I know that several of you have studied the open literature on confinement," *and you, Schelling, have spent a good many thousand cautious man-hours out in the Sandia ruins, trying to duplicate the effect,* "but a review is in order.

"Confinement spheres—bobbles—are not so much force fields as they are partitions, separating the in- and outside of their surfaces into distinct universes. Gravity alone can penetrate. The Tucson bobble was originally generated around an ICBM over the arctic. It fell to earth near its target, the missile fields at Tucson. The hell bomb inside exploded harmlessly, in the universe on the far side of the bobble's surface.

"As you know, it takes the enormous energy output of the Authority's generator in Livermore to create even the smallest confinement sphere. In fact, that is why the Peace Authority has banned all energy-intensive usages, to safeguard this secret of keeping the Peace. But once established you know that a bobble is stable and requires no further inputs to maintain itself."

"Lasting forever," put in old Schelling. It was not quite a question.

"That's what we all thought, sir. But nothing lasts forever. Even black holes undergo quantum decay. Even normal matter must eventually do so, though on a time-scale beyond imagination. A decay analysis has not been done for confinement spheres until quite recently." He nodded to an assistant who passed three heavy manuscripts across the table to the NM officials. Schelling scarcely concealed his eagerness as he flipped past the Peace Authority Secret seal—the highest classification a government official ever saw—and began reading.

"So, gentlemen, it appears that—like all things—bobbles do decay. The time constant depends on the sphere's radius and the mass enclosed. The Tucson blast was a tragic, fluke accident."

"And you're telling us that every time one of the damn things goes, it's going to make a bang as bad as the bombs you're supposed to be protecting us from?"

Avery permitted himself to glare at the general. "No, I am not. I thought my description of the Tucson incident was clear: There was an exploded nuclear weapon inside that confinement."

"Fifty years ago, Mr. Avery, *fifty* years ago."

Hamilton stepped back from the podium. "Mr. Halberstamm, can you imagine what it's like inside a ten-meter bobble? Nothing comes in or goes out. If you explode a nuke in such a place, there is nowhere to cool off. In a matter of milliseconds, thermodynamic equilibrium is reached, but at a temperature of several million degrees. The innocent-seeming bobble, buried in Tucson all these decades, contained the heart of a fireball. When the bobble decayed, the explosion was finally released."

There was an uneasy stirring among the Strategic Studies Committee as those worthies considered the thousands of bobbles that littered North America. Geraldo Alvarez, a presidential confidant of such power that he had no formal position whatsoever, raised his hand and asked diffidently, "How frequently does the Authority expect this to happen?"

"Dr. Schelling can describe the statistics in detail, but in principle the decay is exactly like that of other quantum processes: We can only

71

speak of what will happen to large numbers of objects. We could go for a century or two and not have a single incident. On the other hand, it is conceivable that three or four might decay in a single year. But even for the smallest bobbles, we estimate a time constant of decay greater than ten million years."

"So they go off like atoms with a given half-life, rather than chicken eggs hatching all at once?"

"Exactly, sir. A good analogy. And in one regard, I can be more specific and encouraging: Most bobbles do not contain nuclear explosions. And large bobbles—even if they contain 'fossil' explosions—will be harmless. For instance, we estimate the equilibrium temperature produced by a nuke inside the Vandenberg or Langley bobbles to be less than one hundred degrees. There would be some property damage around the perimeter, but nothing like in Tucson.

"And now, gentlemen, I'm going to give our side of the meeting over to Liaison Officers Rankin and Nakamura." He nodded at his third-level people. "In particular, you must decide with them how much public attention to give this incident." *And it better not be much!* "I must fly to Los Angeles. Aztlán detected the explosion, and they deserve an explanation, too."

He gestured his top Albuquerque man, the usual Peace rep to the highest levels of the Republic, to leave with him. They walked out, ignoring the tightened lips and red faces across the table. It was necessary to keep these people in their place, and one of the best ways of doing that was to emphasize that New Mexico was just one fish among many.

Minutes later they were out of the nondescript building and on the street. Fortunately, there were no reporters. The NM press was under fair control; besides, the existence of the Strategic Studies Committee was itself a secret.

He and Brent, the chief liaison officer here, climbed into the limo, and the horses pulled them into the afternoon traffic. Since Avery's visit was unofficial, he used local vehicles, and there was no escort; he had an excellent view. The layout was similar to that of the capitol of the old United States, if you could ignore the bare mountains that jaggedly edged the sky. He could see at least a dozen other vehicles on the wide boulevard. Albuquerque was almost as busy and cosmopolitan as an Authority Enclave. But that made sense: The Republic of New Mexico was one of the most powerful and populous nations on Earth.

He glanced at Brent. "Are we clean?"

The younger man looked briefly puzzled, then said, "Yessir. We went over the limo with those new procedures."

"Okay. I want to take the detail reports with me, but summarize. Are Schelling and Alvarez and company as innocently surprised as they claim?"

"I'd stake the Peace on it, sir." From the look on Brent's face, the fellow understood that was exactly what he was doing. "They don't have anything like the equipment you warned us of. You've always supported a strong counter-intel department here. We haven't let you down; we'd know if they were anywhere near being a threat."

"Hmm." The assessment agreed with Avery's every intuition. The Republic government would do whatever they could get away with. But that was why he'd kept watch on them all these years: He knew they didn't have the tech power to be behind what he was seeing.

He sat back in the padded leather seat. So Schelling was "innocent." Well then, would he buy the story Avery was peddling? Was it really a story at all? Every word Hamilton spoke in that meeting was the absolute truth, reviewed and rereviewed by the science teams at Livermore. . . . But the whole truth it was not. The NM officials did not know about the ten-meter bobble burst in Central Asia. The theory could explain that incident, too, but who could believe that two decays would happen within a year after fifty years of stability?

Like chicken eggs hatching all at once. That was the image Alvarez had used. The science team was certain it was simple, half-life decay, but they hadn't seen the big picture, the evidence that had been trickling in for better than a year. *Like eggs hatching* . . . When it comes to survival, the rules of evidence become an art, and Avery felt with dread certainty that someone, somewhere, had figured how to cancel bobbles.

11

The bandits' rifle fire lit the trees. There came another volley and another. Wili heard Jeremy move, as if getting ready to jump up and return fire. He realized the Russians must be shooting at themselves. The reflection that had fooled him had taken them in, too. What would happen when they realized it was only a bobble that faced them? A bobble and one rifle in the hands of an incompetent marksman?

The gunfire came to a ragged stop. "Now, Jeremy!" Naismith said. The larger boy jumped into the open and swung his weapon wildly across the ravine. He fired the whole clip. The rifle stuttered in an irregular way, as though on the verge of jamming. Its muzzle flash lit the ravine. The enemy was invisible, except for one fellow vaguely seen against the light-colored rock at the side of the cleft. That one had bad luck: he was almost lifted off his feet by the impact of bullet on chest, and slammed back against the rock.

Cries of pain rose from all along the ravine. How had Jeremy done it? Even one hit was fantastic luck. And Jeremy Kaladze was the fellow who in daylight could miss the broad side of a barn.

Jeremy slammed down beside him. "Did I g-get them all?" There was an edge of horror in his voice. But he slipped another clip into his sawed-off weapon.

There was no return fire. But wait. The bandit lying by the outcrop —he was up and running! The hit should have left him dead or crawl-

ing. Through the bushes below, he could hear the others picking themselves up and running for the far end of the ravine. One by one, they
appeared in silhouette, still running.

Jeremy rose to his knees, but Naismith pulled him down.

"You're right, son. There's something strange with them. Let's not
press our luck."

They lay for a long time in the ringing silence, till at last the animal
sounds resumed and the starlight seemed bright. There was no sign of
humans inside of five hundred meters.

Projections? Jeremy wondered aloud. *Zombies?* Wili thought silently
to himself. But they could be neither. They had been hit; they had
gone down. Then they had gotten up and run in a panic—and that was
unlike the zombies of Ndelante legend. Naismith had no speculations
he was willing to share.

It was raining again by the time their rescuers arrived.

Only nine o'clock on an April morning and already the air was a hot,
humid thirty degrees. Thunderheads hung high on the arch of the
Dome. It would rain in the afternoon. Wili Wáchendon and Jeremy
Sergeivich Kaladze walked down the wide, graveled road that led from
the main farmhouse toward outbuildings by the Dome. They made a
strange sight: One boy near two meters tall, white and lanky; the other
short, thin, and black, apparently subadolescent. But Wili was beginning to realize that there were similarities, too. It turned out they were
the same age—fifteen. And the other boy was sharp, though not in the
same class as Wili. He had never tried to intimidate with his size. If
anything, he seemed slightly in awe of Wili (if that were possible in
one as rambunctious and outspoken as Jeremy Sergeivich).

"The Colonel says"—Jeremy and the others never called Old
Kaladze "grandfather," though there seemed to be no fear in their
attitude, and a lot of affection—"the Colonel says the farm is being
watched, has been since the three of us got here."

"Oh? The bandits?"

"Don't know. We can't afford the equipment Dr. Naismith can buy
—those micro-cameras and such. But we have a telescope and twenty-
four-hour camera on top of the barn. The processor attached to it
detected several flashes from the trees"—he swept his hand toward the

ridgeline where the rain forest came down almost to the farm's banana plants—"that are probably reflections from old-style optics."

Wili shivered in the warm sunlight. There were lots of people here compared to Naismith's mansion in the wilderness, but it was not a properly fortified site: There were no walls, watchtowers, observation balloons. There were many very young children, and most of the adults were over fifty. That was a typical age distribution, but one unsuitable for defense. Wili wondered what secret resources the Kaladzes might have.

"So what are you going to do?"

"Nothing much. There can't be too many of 'em; they're awful shy. We'd go out after them if *we* had more people. As it is, we've got four smart rifles and men who can use them. And Sheriff Wentz knows about the situation. . . . C'mon, don't worry." He didn't notice Wili bristle. The smaller boy hid it well. He was beginning to realize that there was scarcely a mean bone in Jeremy's body. "I want to show you the stuff we have here."

He turned off the gravel road and walked toward a large, one-story building. It could scarcely be a barn; the entire roof was covered with solar batteries. "If it weren't for the Vandenberg Bobble, I think Middle California would be most famous for Red Arrow Products—that's our trade name. We're not as sophisticated as the Greens in Norcross, or as big as the Qens in Beijing, but the things we do are the best."

Wili pretended indifference. "This place is just a big farm, it looks like to me."

"Sure, and Dr. Naismith is just a hermit. It is big and it's terrific farmland. But where do you think my family got the money to buy it? We've been real lucky: Grandmother and the Colonel had four children after the War, and each of them had at least two. We're practically a clan, and we've adopted other folk, people who can figure out things we can't. The Colonel believes in diversification; between the farm and our software, we're unsinkable."

Jeremy pounded on the heavy white door. There was no answer, but it swung slowly inward and the boys entered. Down each side of the long building, windows let in morning light and enough breeze to make it relatively comfortable. He had an impression of elegant chaos. Ornamental plants surrounded scattered desks. There was more than one aquarium. Most of the desks were unoccupied: Some sort of conference was going on at the far end of the room. The men waved to Jeremy but continued with what sounded perilously close to being an argument.

"Lots more people here than usual. Most guys like to work from home. Look." He pointed to one of the few seated workers. The man seemed unaware of them. In the holo above his desk floated colored shapes, shapes that shifted and turned. The man watched intently. He nodded to himself, and suddenly the pattern was tripled and sheared. Somehow he was in control of the display. Wili recognized the composition of linear and nonlinear transformations: Inside his head, Wili had played with those through most of the winter.

"What's he doing?"

Jeremy's normal loudness was muted. "Who do you think implements those algorithms you and Dr. Naismith invent?" He swept his hand across the room. "We've done some of the most complicated implementations in the world."

Wili just stared at him. "Look, Wili. I know you have all sorts of wonderful machines up in the mountains. Where do you think they come from?"

Wili pondered. He had never really thought about it! His education had moved very fast along the paths Naismith laid out. One price for this progress was that in most respects Wili's opinions about what made things work were a combination of mathematical abstraction and Ndelante myth. "I guess I thought Paul made most of them."

"Dr. Naismith is an amazing man, but it takes hundreds of people all over the world to make all the things he needs. Mike Rosas says it's like a pyramid: At the top there are just a few men—say Naismith in algorithms or Masaryk in surface physics—guys who can invent really new things. With the Peace Authority Bans on big organizations, these people got to work alone, and there probably aren't more than five or ten of them in the whole world. Next down in the pyramid are software houses like ours. We take algorithms and implement them so that machines can run them."

Wili watched the programmatic phantoms shift and turn above the desk. Those shapes were at once familiar and alien. It was as if his own ideas had been transformed into some strange form of Celest. "But these people don't *make* anything. Where do the machines come from?"

"You're right; without hardware to run our programs, we're just daydreamers. That's the next level of the pyramid. Standard processors are cheap. Before the plagues, several families from Sunnyvale settled in Santa Maria. They brought a truckload of gamma-ray etching gear. It's been improved a lot since. We import purified base materials from Oregon. And special-purpose stuff comes from even further: For instance, the Greens make the best synthetic optics."

Jeremy started for the door. "I'd show you more here except they seem awfully busy today. That's probably your fault. The Colonel seems real excited about whatever you and Dr. Naismith invented this winter." He stopped and looked at Wili, as though hoping for some inside information. And Wili wondered to himself, *How can I explain?* He could hardly describe the algorithm in a few words. It was a delicate matter of coding schemes, of packing and unpacking certain objects very cleverly and very quickly. Then he realized that the other was interested in its *effects*, in the ability it could give the Tinkers to listen to the Authority satellites.

His uncertainty was misinterpreted, for the taller boy laughed. "Never mind, I won't push you. Fact is, I probably shouldn't know. C'mon, there's one thing more I want to show you—though maybe it should be a secret, too. The Colonel thinks the Peace Authority might issue a Ban if they knew about it."

They continued down the farm's main road, which ran directly into the side of the Vandenberg Dome some thousand meters further on. It made Wili dizzy just to look in that direction. This close, there was no feeling of the overall shape of the Dome. In a sense, it was invisible, a vast vertical mirror. In it he saw the rolling hills of the farm, the landscape that spread away behind them: There were a couple of small sailboats making for the north shore of Lake Lompoc, and he could see the ferry docked on the near side of the Salsipuedes fiord.

As they walked closer to the bobble, he saw that the ground right at the edge was torn, twisted. Rain off the Dome had gouged a deep river around the base, runoff to Lake Lompoc. The ground shook faintly but constantly with tiny earthquakes. Wili tried to imagine the other half of the bobble, extending kilometers into the earth. No wonder the world trembled around this obstruction. He looked up and swayed.

"Gets you, doesn't it?" Jeremy grabbed his arm and steadied him. "I grew up close to it, and I still fall flat on my behind when I stand here and imagine trying to climb the thing." They scrambled up the embanked mud and looked down at the river. Even though it hadn't rained for hours, the waters moved fast and muddy, gouging at the land. Across the river, a phantom Jeremy and Wili stared back. "It's dangerous to get much closer. The water channel extends a ways underground. We've had some pretty big landslides.

"That's not why I brought you here, anyway." He led Wili down the embankment toward a small building. "There's another level in Mike's pyramid: the folks who make things like carts and houses and plows. The refurbishers still do a lot of that, but they're running out of ruins, at least around here. The new stuff is made just like it was hundreds of years ago. It's expensive and takes a lot of work—the type of thing the Republic of New Mexico or Aztlán is good at. Well, we can program processors to control moving-parts machines. I don't see why we can't make a moving-parts machine to *make* all those other things. That's my own special project."

"Yes, but that's Banned. Are you telling me—"

"Moving-parts machines aren't Banned. Not directly. It's high-energy, high-speed stuff the Authority is death on. They don't want anyone making bombs or bobbles and starting another War." The building looked like the one they had left up the road, but with fewer windows.

An ancient metal pylon stuck out of the ground near the entrance. Wili looked at it curiously, and Jeremy said, "It doesn't have anything to do with my project. When I was little, you could still see numbers painted on it. It's off the wing of a pre-Authority airplane. The Colonel thinks it must have been taking off from Vandenberg Air Force Base at the instant they were bobbled: Half of it fell out here, and the rest crashed inside the Dome."

He followed Jeremy into the building. It was much dimmer than inside the software house. Something moved; something made high-pitched humming noises. It took Wili a second to realize that he and Jeremy were the only living things present. Jeremy led him down an aisle toward the sounds. A small conveyer belt stretched into the darkness. Five tiny arms that ended in mechanical hands were making a . . . what? It was barely two meters long and one high. It had wheels, though smaller than those on a cart. There was no room for passengers or cargo. Beyond this machine aborning, Wili saw at least four completed copies.

"This is my fabricator." Jeremy touched one of the mechanical arms.

The machine immediately stopped its precise movements, as though in respect to a master. "It can't do the whole job, only the motor windings and the wiring. But I'm going to improve it."

Wili was more interested in what was being fabricated. "What . . . are they?" He pointed to the vehicles.

"Farm tractors, of course! They're not big. They can't carry passengers; you have to walk behind them. But they can draw a plow, and do planting. They can be charged off the roof batteries. It's a dangerous first project, I know. But I wanted to make something nice. The tractors aren't really vehicles; I don't think the Authority will even notice. If they do, we'll just make something else. My fabricators are flexible."

They'll Ban your fabricators, too. Not surprisingly, Wili had absorbed Paul's opinion of the Peace Authority. They had Banned the research that could cure his own problems. They were like all the other tyrannies, only more powerful.

But Wili said none of this aloud. He walked to the nearest completed "tractor" and put his hand on the motor shell, half expecting to feel some electric power. This was, after all, a machine that could move under its own power. How many times had he dreamed of driving an automobile. He knew it was the fondest wish of some minor Jonque aristocrats that one of their sons might be accepted as an Authority truck driver.

"You know, Jeremy, this thing *can* carry a passenger. I bet I could sit here on its back and still reach the controls."

A grin slowly spread across Jeremy's face. "By golly, I see what you mean. If only I weren't so big, I could, too. Why, you could be an automobilist! C'mon, let's move this one outside. There's smooth ground behind the building where we can—"

A faint *beep* came from the phone at Jeremy's waist. He frowned and raised the device to his ear. "Okay. Sorry.

"Wili, the Colonel and Dr. Naismith want to see us—and they mean right now. I guess we were expected to hang around the main house and wait on their pleasure." It was closest Wili ever heard Jeremy come to disrespect for his elders. They started toward the door. "We'll come back before the afternoon rain and try to ride."

But there was sadness in his voice, and Wili looked back into the shadowed room. Somehow he doubted he would return any time soon.

12

It might have been a council of war. Colonel Kaladze certainly looked the part. In some ways Kaladze reminded Wili of the bosses in the Ndelante Ali: He was almost eighty, yet ramrod straight. His hair was cut as theirs, about five millimeters long everywhere, even on the face. The silvery stubble was stark against his tan. His gray-green work clothes were unremarkable except for their starched and shiny neatness. His blue eyes were capable of great good humor—Wili remembered from the welcoming dinner—but this morning they were set and hard. Next to him Miguel Rosas—even armed and wearing his sheriff's brassard—looked like a loose civilian.

Paul looked the same as always, but he avoided Wili's eyes. And that was the most ominous sign of all.

"Be seated, gentlemen," the old Russian spoke to the boys. All his sons—except Jeremy's father, who was on a sales expedition to Corvallis—were present. "Wili, Jeremy, you'll be leaving for San Diego earlier than we had planned. The Authority desires to sponsor the North American Chess Tourney, much as they've sponsored the Olympics these last few years: They are providing special transportation, and have moved up the semifinals correspondingly."

This was like a burglar who finds his victim passing out engraved invitations, thought Wili.

Even Jeremy seemed a little worried by it: "What will this do to

Wili's plan to, uh, get some help down there? Can he do this right under their noses?"

"I think so. Mike thinks so." He glanced at Miguel Rosas, who gave a brief nod. "At worst, the Authority is suspicious of us Tinkers as a group. They don't have any special reason to be watching Wili. In any case, if we are to participate, our group must be ready for their truck convoy. It will pass the farm in less than fifteen hours."

Truck convoy. The boys stared at each other. For an instant, any danger seemed small. The Authority was going to let them ride like kings down the coast of California all the way to La Jolla! "All who go must leave the farm in two or three hours to reach Highway One-oh-one before the convoy passes through." He grinned at Ivan, his eldest son. "Even if the Authority is watching, even if Wili didn't need help, Kaladzes would still be going. You boys can't fool me. I know you've been looking forward to this for a long time. I know all the time you've wasted on programs you think are unbeatable."

Ivan Nikolayevich seemed startled, then smiled back. "Besides, there are people there we've known for years and never met in person. It would be even more suspicious if we pulled out now."

Wili looked across the table at Naismith. "Is it okay, Paul?"

Suddenly Naismith seemed much older even than the Colonel. He lowered his head and spoke softly. "Yes, Wili. It's our best chance to get you some help. . . . But we've hired Mike to go instead of me. I can't come along. You see—"

Paul's voice continued, but Wili heard no more. *Paul will not come. This one chance to find a cure and Paul will not come.* For a moment that lasted long inside his head, the room whirled down to a tiny point and was replaced by Wili's earliest memories:

Claremont Street, seen through an unglazed window, seen from a small bed. The first five years of his life, he had spent most of every day in that bed, staring out into the empty street. Even in that he had been lucky. At that time Glendora had been an outland, beyond the reach of the Jonque lords and the milder tyranny of the Ndelante Ali. Wili, those first few years, was so weak he could scarcely eat even when food was right at hand. Survival had depended on his Uncle Sly. If he still lived, Sylvester would be older than Naismith himself. When Wili's parents wanted to give their sickly newborn to the coyotes and the hawks, it had been Uncle Sly who argued and pleaded and finally persuaded them to abandon Wili's worthless body to him instead. Wili would never forget the old man's face—so black and gnarled, fringed with silver hair. Outside he was so different from Naismith, inside so like him.

For Sylvester Washington (he insisted on the Anglo pronunciation of his last name) had been over thirty when the War came. He had been a schoolteacher, and he would not give up his last child easily. He made a bed for Wili, and made sure it faced on to the street so that the invalid boy could see and hear as much as possible. Sylvester Washington talked to him hours every day. Where similar children wasted and starved, Wili slowly grew. His earliest memories, after the view of Claremont Street through the window hole, were of Uncle Sly playing number games with him, forcing him to work with his mind when he could do nothing with his body.

Later the old man helped the boy exercise his body, too. But that was after dark, in the dusty yard behind the ruin he called their "ranch house." Night after night, Wili crawled across the warm earth, till finally his legs were strong enough to stand on. Sly would not let him stop till he could walk.

But he never took him out during the day, saying that it was too dangerous. The boy didn't see why. The street beyond his window was always quiet and empty.

Wili was almost six years old when he found the answer to that mystery, and his world ended. Sylvester had already left for work at the secret pond his friends had built above the Ndelante irrigation project. He had promised to come home early with something special, a reward for all the walking.

Wili was tired of the terrible daytime heat within the hovel. He peered through the crooked doorway and then walked slowly out onto the street, reveling in his freedom. He walked down the empty street and suddenly realized that a few more steps would take him to the intersection of Claremont and Catalina—and beyond the furthest reach of his previous explorations. He wandered down Catalina for fifteen or twenty minutes. What a wonderland: vacant ruins desiccating in the sun. They were all sizes, and of subtly different colors depending on the original paint. Rusted metal hulks sat like giant insects along one side of the street.

More than one house in twenty was occupied. The area had been looted and relooted. But—as Wili learned in later adventures—parts of the Basin were still untouched. Even fifty years after the War there were treasure hoards in the farthest suburbs. Aztlán did not claim a recovery tax for nothing.

Wili was not yet six, but he did not lose his way; he avoided houses that might be occupied and kept to the shadows. After a time he tired and started back. He stopped now and then to watch some lizard scurry from one hole to another. Gaining confidence, he cut across a grocery store parking lot, walked under a sign proclaiming bargains fifty years dead, and turned back onto Claremont. Then everything seemed to happen at once.

There was Uncle Sly, home early from the pond, struggling to carry a bag slung over his back. He saw Wili and his jaw fell. He dropped the bag and started running toward the boy. At the same time the sound of hooves came from a side alley. Five young Jonques burst into the sunlight—labor raiders. One swept the boy up while the rest held off old Sly with their whips. Lying on his belly across the saddle, Wili twisted about and got one last look. There was Sylvester Washington, already far down the street. He was wringing his hands, making no sound, making no effort to save him from the strange men who were taking Wili away.

Wili survived. Five years later he was sold to the Ndelante Ali. Two more years and he had some reputation for his burgling. Eventually, Wili returned to that intersection on Claremont Street. The house was still there; things don't change suddenly in the Basin. But the house was empty. Uncle Sly was gone.

And now he would lose Paul Naismith, too.

The boy's walleyed stare must have been taken for attentiveness. Naismith was talking, still not looking directly at Wili. "You are really to be thanked for the discovery, Wili. What we've seen is . . . well, it's strange and wonderful and maybe ominous. I *have* to stay. Do you understand?"

Wili didn't really mean the words, but they came anyway. "I understand you won't come along. I understand some silly piece of math is more important."

Worse, the words didn't anger Paul. His head bowed slightly. "Yes. There are some things more important to me than any person. Let me tell you what we saw—"

"Paul, if Mike and Jeremy and Wili are to be in the mouth of the lion, there is no sense in their knowing more right now."

"As you say, 'Kolya." Naismith rose and walked slowly to the door. "Please excuse me."

There was a short silence, broken by the Colonel. "We'll have to work fast to get you three on the way in time. Ivan, show me just what your chess fans want to send with Jeremy. If the Authority is providing transport, maybe Mike and the boys can take a more elaborate processor." He departed with his sons and Jeremy.

That left Wili and Mike. The boy stood and turned to the door.

"Just a minute, you." Mike's voice had the hard edge Wili remembered from their first encounter months before. The undersheriff came around the table and pushed Wili back into his chair. "You think Paul has deserted you. Maybe he has, but from what I can tell, they've discovered something more important than the lot of us. I don't know exactly what it is, or I couldn't go with you and Jeremy either. Get it? We can't afford to let Naismith fall into Authority hands.

"Consider yourself damn lucky we're going through with Paul's harebrained scheme to get you cured. He's the only man on Earth who could've convinced Kaladze to deal even indirectly with the bioscience swine." He glared down at Wili, as if expecting some counterattack. The boy was silent and avoided his eyes.

"Okay. I'll be waiting for you in the dining house." Rosas stalked out of the room.

Wili was motionless for a long time. There were no tears; there had been none since that afternoon very long ago on Claremont Street. He didn't blame Sylvester Washington and he didn't blame Paul Naismith. They had done as much as one man can do for another. But ultimately there is only one person who can't run away from your problems.

13

Still five meters up, the twin-rotor chopper sent a shower of grit across the Tradetower helipad. From her place in the main cabin, Della Lu watched the bystanders grab their hats and squint into the wash. Old Hamilton Avery was the only fellow who kept his aplomb.

As the chopper touched down, one of her crew slid open the front hatch and waved at the standing VIPs. Through her silvered window, she saw Director Avery nod and turn to shake hands with Smythe, the LA franchise owner. Then Avery walked alone toward the crewman, who had not stepped down from the doorway.

Smythe was probably the most powerful Peacer in Southern California. She wondered what he thought when his boss submitted to such a cavalier pickup. She smiled lopsidedly. Hell, she was in charge of the operation, and she.didn't know what was coming off either.

The rotors spun up even as she heard the hatch slam. Her crew had their orders: The helipad dropped away as the chopper rose like some magic elevator from the top of the Tradetower. They slid out from the roof and she looked down eighty stories at the street.

As the helicopter turned toward LAX and Santa Monica, Della came to her feet. An instant later Avery entered her cabin. He looked completely relaxed yet completely formal, his dress both casual and expensive. In theory, the Board of Directors of the Peace Authority was a committee of equals. In fact, Hamilton Avery had been the driving force behind it for as long as Della Lu had been following inner politics. Though not a famous man, he was the most powerful one in the world.

"My dear! So good to see you." Avery walked quickly to her, shook her hand as if she were an equal and not an officer three levels below him. She let the silver-haired Director take her elbow and lead her to a seat. One might think she was his guest.

They sat down, and the director looked quickly about the cabin. It was a solid, mobile command room. There was no bar, no carpets. With her priority, she could have had such, but Della had not gotten to her present job by sucking up to her bosses.

The aircraft hummed steadily westward, the chop of the blades muted by the office's heavy insulation. Below, Della could see Peace Authority housing. The Enclave was really a corridor that extended from Santa Monica and LAX on the coast, inland to what had once been the center of Los Angeles. It was the largest Enclave in the world. More than fifty thousand people lived down there, mostly near the News Service studios. And they lived well. She saw swimming pools and tennis courts on the three-acre suburban lots that passed below.

In the north glowered the castles and fortified roads of the Aztlán aristocrats. They had governmental responsibility for the region, but without Banned technology their "palaces" were medieval dumps. Like the Republic of New Mexico, Aztlán watched the Authority with impotent jealousy and dreamed of the good old days.

Avery looked up from the view. "I noticed you had the Beijing insignia painted over."

"Yes, sir. It was clear from your message that you didn't want people to guess you were using people from off North America." That was one of the few things that was crystal clear. Three days before she had been at the Beijing Enclave, just returned from her final survey of the Central Asian situation. Then a megabyte of detailed instructions came over the satellite from Livermore—and not to the Beijing franchise owner, but to one Della Lu, third-level counter-guerrilla cop and general hatchetman. She was assigned a cargo jet—its freight being this chopper—and told to fly across the Pacific to LAX. No one was to emerge at any intermediate stop. At LAX, the freighter crew was to disgorge the chopper with her people, and return immediately.

Avery nodded approvingly. "Good. I need someone who doesn't need everything spelled out. Have you had a chance to read the New Mexico report?"

"Yes, sir." She had spent the flight studying the report and boning up on North American politics. She had been gone three years; there'd have been a lot of catching up to do—even without the Tucson crisis.

"Do you think the Republic bought our story?"

She thought back on the meeting tape and the dossiers. "Yes. Ironically, the most suspicious of them were also the most ignorant. Schelling bought it hook, line, and sinker. He knows enough theory to see that it's reasonable."

Avery nodded.

"But they'll continue to believe only if no more bobbles burst. And I understand it's happened at least twice more during the last few weeks. I don't believe the quantum decay explanation. The old USA missile fields are littered with thousands of bobbles. If decays continue to happen, they won't be missed."

Avery nodded again, didn't seem especially upset by her analysis.

The chopper did a gentle bank over Santa Monica, giving her a close-up view of the largest mansions in the Enclave. She had a glimpse of the Authority beach and the ruined Aztlán shoreline further south, and then they were over the ocean. They flew south several kilometers before turning inland. They would fly in vast circles until the meeting was over. Even the Tucson event could not explain this mission. Della almost frowned.

Avery raised a well-manicured hand. "What you say is correct, but may be irrelevant. It depends on what the true explanation turns out to be. Have you considered the possibility that someone has discovered how to destroy bobbles, that we are seeing their experiments?"

"The choice of 'experiment sites' is very strange, sir: the Ross Iceshelf, Tucson, Ulan Ude. And I don't see how such an organization could escape direct detection."

Fifty-five years ago, before the War, what had become the Peace Authority had been a contract laboratory, a corporation run under federal grants to do certain esoteric—and militarily productive—research. That research had produced the bobbles, force fields whose generation took a minimum of thirty minutes of power from the largest nuclear plant in the lab. The old US government had not been told of the discovery; Avery's father had seen to that. Instead, the lab directors played their own version of geopolitics. Even at the rarefied bureaucratic heights Della inhabited, there was no solid evidence that the Avery lab had started the War, but she had her suspicions.

In the years following the great collapse, the Authority had stripped the rest of the world of high-energy technology. The most dangerous governments—such as that of the United States—were destroyed, and their territories left in a state that ranged from the village anarchy of Middle California, to the medievalism of Aztlán, to the fascism of New Mexico. Where governments did exist, they were just strong enough to collect the Authority Impost. These little countries were in some ways sovereign. They even fought their little wars—but without the capital industry and high-energy weapons that made war a threat to the race.

Della doubted that, outside the Enclaves, there existed the technical expertise to reproduce the old inventions, much less improve on them. And if someone did discover the secret of the bobble, Authority satellites would detect the construction of the power plants and factories needed to implement the invention.

"I know, I may sound paranoid. But one thing you youngsters don't understand is how technologically stultified the Authority is." He glanced at her, as though expecting debate. "We have all the universities and all the big labs. We control most degreed persons on Earth. Nevertheless, we do very little research. I should know, since I can remember my father's lab right before the War—and even more, because I've made sure no really imaginative projects got funded since.

"Our factories can produce most any product that existed before the War." He slapped his hand against the bulkhead. "This is a good, reliable craft, probably built in the last five years. But the design is almost sixty years old."

He paused and his tone became less casual. "During the last six months, I've concluded we've made a serious mistake in this. There are people operating under our very noses who have technology substantially in advance of pre-War levels."

"I hope you're not thinking of the Mongolian nationalists, sir. I tried to make it clear in my reports that their nuclear weapons were from old Soviet stockpiles. Most weren't usable. And without those bombs they were just pony sol—"

89

"No, my dear Della, that's not what I am thinking of." He slid a plastic box across the table. "Look inside."

Five small objects sat in the velvet lining. Lu held one in the sunlight. "A bullet?" It looked like an 8-mm. She couldn't tell if it had been fired; there was some damage, but no rifling marks. Something dark and glossy stained the nose.

"That's right. But a bullet with a brain. Let me tell you how we came across that little gem.

"Since I became suspicious of these backyard scientists, these Tinkers, I've been trying to infiltrate. It hasn't been easy. In most of North America, we have tolerated no governments. Even though it's cost us on the Impost, the risk of nationalism seemed too high. Now I see that was a mistake. Somehow they've gone further than any of the governed areas—and we have no easy way to watch them, except from orbit.

"Anyway, I sent teams into the ungoverned lands, using whatever cover was appropriate. In Middle California, for instance, it was easiest to pretend they were descendents of the old Soviet invasion force. Their instructions were to hang around in the mountains and ambush likely-looking travelers. I figured we would gradually accumulate information without any official raids. Last week, one crew ambushed three locals in the forests east of Vandenberg. The quarry had only one gun, a New Mexico eight-millimeter. It was nearly dark, but from a distance of forty meters the enemy hit every one of the ten-man crew—with one burst from the eight-millimeter."

"The New Mexico eight-millimeter only has a ten-round clip. That's—"

"A perfect target score, my dear. And my men swear the weapon was fired on full automatic. If they hadn't been wearing body armor, or if the rounds had had normal velocity, not one of them would have lived to tell the story. Ten armed men killed by one man and a handmade gun. Magic. And you're holding a piece of that magic. Others have been through every test and dissection that Livermore labs could come up with. You've heard of smart bombs? Sure, your air units in Mongolia used them. Well, Miss Lu, these are smart bullets.

"The round has a video eye up front, connected to a processor as powerful as anything we can pack in a suitcase—and our suitcase version would cost a hundred thousand monets. Evidently the gun barrel isn't rifled; the round can change attitude in flight to close with its target."

Della rolled the metal marble in her palm. "So it's under the control of the gunman?"

"Only indirectly, and only at 'launch' time. There must be a processor on the gun that queues the targets, and chooses the firing instant. The processor on the bullet is more than powerful enough to latch the assigned target. Rather interesting, eh?"

Della nodded. She remembered how delicate the attack gear on the A511's had been—and how expensive. They'd needed a steady supply of replacement boards from Beijing. If these things could be made cheaply enough to throw away . . . ?

Hamilton Avery gave a small smile, apparently satisfied with her reaction. "That's not all. Take a look at the other things in the box."

Della dropped the bullet onto the velvet padding and picked up a brownish ball. It was slightly sticky on her fingers. There were no markings, no variations in its surface. She raised her eyebrows.

"That is a bug, Della. Not one of your ordinary, audio bugs, but full video—we expect in all directions, at that. Something to do with Fourier optics, my experts tell me. It can record, or transmit a very short distance. We've guessed all this from x-ray micrographs of the interior. We don't even have equipment that can interface with it!"

"You're sure it's not recording right now?"

"Oh yes. They fried its guts before I took it. The microscopists claim there's not a working junction in there.

"Now I think you see the reason for all the precautions."

Della nodded slowly. The bobble bursts were not the reason; he expected their true enemies already knew all about those. Yes, Avery was being clever—and he was as frightened as his cool personality would ever allow.

They sat silently for about thirty seconds. The chopper made another turn, and the sunlight swept across Della's face. They were flying east over Long Beach toward Anaheim—those were the names in the history books anyway. The street pattern stretched off into gray-orange haze. It gave a false sense of order. The reality was kilometer on kilometer of abandoned, burned-out wilderness. It was hard to believe that this threat could grow in North America. But, after the fact, it made sense. If you deny big industry and big research to people, they will look for other ways of getting what they need.

. . . And if they could make these things, maybe they were clever enough to go beyond all the beautiful quantum-mechanical theories and figure a way to burst bobbles.

"You think they've infiltrated the Authority?"

"I'm sure of it. We swept our labs and conference rooms. We found seventeen bugs on the West Coast, two in China, and a few more in Europe. There were no repeaters near the overseas finds, so we think they were unintentional exports. The plague appears to spread from California."

"So they know we're on to them."

"Yes, but little more. They've made some big mistakes and we've had a bit of good luck: We have an informer in the California group. He came to us less than two weeks ago, out of the blue. I think he's legitimate. What he's told us matches our discoveries but goes a good deal further. We're going to run these people to ground. And do it officially. We haven't made an example of anyone in a long time, not since the Yakima incident.

"Your role in this will be crucial, Della. You are a woman, and outside the Authority the frailer sex is disregarded nowadays."

Not only outside the Authority, thought Della.

"You'll be invisible to the enemy, until it's too late."

"You mean a *field* job?"

"Why, yes, my dear. You've certainly had rougher assignments."

"Yes, but—" *but I was a field director in Mongolia.*

Avery put his hand on Della's. "This is no demotion. You'll be responsible only to me. As communications permit, you'll control the California operation. But we need our very best out there on the ground, someone who knows the land and can be given a credible cover." Della had been born and raised in San Francisco. For three generations, her family had been 'furbishers—and Authority plants.

"And there is a very special thing I want done. This may be more important than all the rest of the operation." Avery laid a color picture on the table. The photo was grainy, blown up to near the resolution limit. She saw a group of men standing in front of a barn: northern farmers—except for the black child talking to a tall boy who carried an NM 8-mm. She could guess who these were.

"See the guy in the middle—by the one with the soldier frizz."

His face was scarcely more than a blotch, but he looked perfectly ordinary, seventy or eighty years old. Della could walk through a crowd in any North American enclave and see a dozen such.

"We think that's Paul Hoehler." He glanced at his agent. "The name doesn't mean anything to you, does it? Well, you won't find it in the history books, but I remember him. Back in Livermore, right before the War. I was just a kid. He was in my father's lab and . . . he's the man who invented the bobble."

Della's attention snapped back to the photo. She knew she had just been let in on one of those secrets which was kept from everyone, which would otherwise die with the last of the old Directors. She tried to see something remarkable in the fuzzy features.

"Oh, Schmidt, Kashihara, Bhadra, they got the thing into projectable form. But it was one of Hoehler's bright ideas. The hell of it is, the man wasn't—isn't—even a physicist.

"Anyway, he disappeared right after the War started. Very clever. He didn't wait to do any moral posturing, to give us a chance to put him away. Next to eliminating the national armies, catching him was one of our highest priorities. We never got him. After ten or fifteen years, when we had control of all the remaining labs and reactors, the search for Dr. Hoehler died. But now, after all these years, when we see bobbles being burst, we have rediscovered him. . . . You can see why I'm convinced the 'bobble decay' is not natural."

Avery tapped the picture. "This is the man, Della. In the next weeks, we'll take Peace action against hundreds of people. But it will all be for nothing if you can't nail this one man."

FLASHFORWARD

Allison's wound showed no sign of reopening, and she didn't think there was much internal bleeding. It hurt, but she could walk. She and Quiller set up camp—more a hiding place than a camp, really—about twenty minutes from the crash site.

The fire had put a long plume of reddish smoke into the sky. If there was a sane explanation for all this, that plume would attract Air Force rescue. And if it attracted unfriendlies first, then they were far enough away from the crash to escape. She hoped.

The day passed, warm and beautiful—and untouched by any sign of other human life. Allison found herself impatient and talkative. She had theories: A cabin leak on their last revolution could almost explain things. Hypoxia can sneak up on you before you know it—hadn't something like that killed three Sov pilots in the early days of space? Hell, it could probably account for all sorts of jumbled memories. Somehow their reentry sequence had been delayed. They'd ended up in the Australian jungles. . . . No that wasn't right, not if the problem had really happened on the last rev. Perhaps Madagascar was a possibility. That People's Republic would not exactly welcome them. They would have to stay undercover till Air Force tracking and reconnaissance spotted the crash site. . . . A strike-rescue could come any time now, say with the Air Force covering a VTOL Marine landing.

Angus didn't buy it. "There's the dome, Allison. No country on Earth could build something like that without us knowing about it. I swear it's kilometers high." He waved at the second sun that stood in the west. The two suns were difficult to see through the forest cover. But during their hike from the crash site they'd had better views. When Allison looked directly at the false sun with narrowed eyes, she could see that the disk was a distorted oval—clearly a reflection off some vast curved surface. "I know it's huge, Angus. But it doesn't have to be a physical structure. Maybe it's some sort of inversion layer effect."

"You're only seeing the part that's way off the ground, where there's nothing to reflect except sky. If you climb one of the taller trees, you'd see the coastline reflected in the dome's base."

"Hmm." She didn't have to climb any trees to believe him. What she couldn't believe was his explanation.

"Face it, Allison. We're nowhere in the world we knew. Yet the tombstone shows we're still on Earth."

The tombstone. So much smaller than the dome, yet so much harder to explain. "You still think it's the future?"

Angus nodded. "Nothing else fits. I don't know how fast something like stone carving wears: I suppose we can't be more than a thousand years ahead." He grinned. "An ordinary, Buck Rogers-like interval."

She smiled back. "Better Buck Rogers than *The Last Remake* or *Planet of the Apes.*"

"Yeah. I never like it where they kill off all the 'extra' time-travelers."

Allison gazed through the forest canopy at the second sun. There had to be some other explanation.

They argued it back and forth for hours, in the end agreeing to give the "rescued from Madagascar" theory twenty-four hours to show success. After that they would hike down to the coast, and then along it till they found some form of humanity.

It was late afternoon when they heard it: a whistling scream that grew abruptly to a roar.

"*Aircraft!*" Allison struggled to her feet.

Angus shook himself, and looked into the sky. Then he was standing, too, all but dancing from one foot to the other.

Something dark and arrow-shaped swept over them. "An A-five-eleven, by God," exulted Angus. "Somehow you were right, Allison!" He hugged her.

There were at least three jets. The air was filled with their sound. And it was a joint operation. They glimpsed the third coming to a hover just three hundred meters away. It was one of the new Sikorsky troop carriers. Only the Marines flew those.

They started down the narrow path toward the nearest of the ships, Allison's gait a limping jog. Suddenly Angus' hand closed on her arm. She spun around, off balance. The pilot was pointing through a large gap in the branches, at the hovering Sikorsky. *"Paisley?"* was all he said.

"What?" Then she saw it. The outer third of the wings was covered with an extravagant paisley pattern. In the middle was set a green phi or theta symbol. It was utterly unlike any military insignia she had ever seen.

14

The atmosphere of an open chess tournament hadn't changed much in the last hundred years. A visitor from 1948 might wonder at the plush, handmade clothing and the strange haircuts. But the important things—the informality mixed with intense concentration, the wide range of ages, the silence on the floor, the long tables and rows of players—all would be instantly recognizable.

Only one important thing had changed, and that might take the hypothetical time-traveler a while to notice: The contestants did not play alone. Teams were not allowed, but virtually all serious players had assistance, usually in the form of a gray box sitting by the board or on the floor near their feet. The more conservative players used small keyboards to communicate with their programs. Others seemed unconnected to any aid but every so often would look off into the distance, lost in concentration. A few of these were players in the old sense, disdaining all programmatic magic.

Wili was the most successful of these atavists. His eyes flickered down the row of boards, trying to decide who were the truly human players and who were the fakes. Beyond the end of the table, the Pacific Ocean was a blue band shining through the open windows of the pavilion.

Wili pulled his attention back to his own game, trying to ignore the crowd of spectators and trying even less successfully to ignore his opponent. Though barely out of a Ruy Lopez opening—that's what Jeremy

97

had called it the other night, anyway—Wili had a good feeling about the game. A strong kingside attack should now be possible, unless his opponent had a complete surprise up her sleeve. This would be his fifth straight win. That accounted for the crowd. He was the only purely human player still undefeated. Wili smiled to himself. This was a totally unexpected by-product of the expedition, but a very pleasant one. He had never been admired for anything (unless his reputation within the Ndelante counted as admirable). It would be a pleasure to show these people how useless their machines really were. For the moment he forgot that every added attention would make it harder for him to fade away when the time came.

Wili considered the board a second longer, then pushed his bishop pawn, starting a sequence of events that ought to be unstoppable. He punched his clock, and finally raised his eyes to look at his opponent.

Dark brown eyes looked back at him. The girl—woman; she must be in her twenties—smiled at Wili as she acknowledged his move. She leaned forward, and raised an input/output band to her temple. Soft black hair spilled across that hand.

Almost ten minutes passed. Some of the spectators began drifting off. Wili just sat and tried to pretend he was not looking at the girl. She was just over one meter fifty, scarcely taller than he. And she was the most beautiful creature he had ever seen. He could sit this close to her and not have to say anything, not have to make conversation. . . . Wili rather wished the game might last forever.

When she finally moved, it was another pawn push. Very strange, very risky. She was definitely a soft player: In the last three days, Wili had played more chess than in the last three months. Almost all of it had been against assisted players. Some were mere servants to their machines. You could trust them never to make a simple mistake, and to take advantage of any you made. Playing them was like fighting a bull, impossible if you attack head on, easy once you identify the weak points. Other players, like Jeremy, were soft, more fallible, but full of intricate surprises. Jeremy said his program interacted with his own creativity. He claimed it made him better than either machine or human alone. Wili would only agree that it was better than being the slave of a processor.

This Della Lu, her play was as soft as her skin. Her last move was full of risk and—he saw now—full of potential. A machine alone could never have proposed it.

Rosas and Jeremy drifted into view behind her. Rosas was not entered in the tournament. Jeremy and his Red Arrow special were doing well, but he had a bye on this round. Jeremy caught his eye; they wanted him outside. Wili felt a flash of irritation.

Finally he decided on the best attack. His knight came out from the third rank, brazen ahead of the pawns. He pushed the clock; several minutes passed. The girl reached for her king . . . and turned it over! She stood, extended her hand across the table to Wili. "A nice game. Thank you very much." She spoke in English, with a faint Bay Area twang.

Wili tried to cover his surprise. She had lost, he was sure of that. But for her to see it this early. . . . She must be almost as clever as he. Wili held her cool hand a moment, then remembered to shake it. He stood and gargled something unintelligible, but it was too late. The spectators closed in with their congratulations. Wili found himself shaking hands all around, and some of those hands were jeweled, belonged to Jonque aristocrats. This was, he was told, the first time in five years an unaided player had made it to the final rounds. Some thought he had a chance of winning it all, and how long had it been since a plain human had been North American champion?

By the time he was out of his circle of admirers, Della Lu had retired in graceful defeat. Anyway, Miguel Rosas and Jeremy Sergeivich were waiting to grab him. "A good win," Mike said, setting his arm across the boy's shoulder. "I'll bet you'd like to get some fresh air after all that concentration."

Wili agreed ungraciously and allowed himself to be guided out. At least they managed to avoid the two Peace reporters who were covering the event.

The Fonda la Jolla pavilions were built over one of the most beautiful beaches in Aztlán. Across the bay, two thousand meters away, gray-green vineyards topped the tan-and-orange cliffs. Wili could follow those cliffs and the surf north and north till they vanished in the haze somewhere near Los Angeles.

They started up the lawn toward the resort's restaurant. Beyond it were the ruins of old La Jolla: There was more stonework than in Pasadena. It was dry and pale, without the hidden life of the Basin. No wonder the Jonque lords had chosen La Jolla for their resort. The place was far from both slums and estates. The lords could meet here in truce, their rivalries ignored. Wili wondered what the Authority had done to persuade them to allow the tournament here, though it was possible that the popularity of the game alone explained it.

"I found Paul's friends, Wili," said Rosas.

"Huh?" He came back to their real problems with an unpleasant lurch. "When do we go?"

"This evening. After your next game. You've got to lose it."

"*What?* Why?"

"Look," Mike spoke intensely, "we're risking a lot for you. Give us an excuse to drop this project and *we will.*"

Wili bit his lip. Jeremy followed in silence, and Wili realized that Rosas was right for once. Both of them had put their freedom, maybe even their lives, on the line for him—or was it really for Paul? No matter. Next to bobble research, bioscience was the blackest crime in the Authority's book. And they were mixing in it to get him cured.

Rosas took Wili's silence for the acquiescence it was. "Okay. I said you'll have to lose the next one. Make a big scene about it, something that will give us the excuse to get you outside and away from everyone else." He gave the boy a sidelong glance. "You won't find it too hard to do that, will you?"

"Where is . . . it . . . anyway?" asked Jeremy.

But Rosas just shook his head, and once inside the restaurant there was no chance for further conversation.

Roberto Richardson, the tournament roster said. That was his next opponent, the one he must lose to. *This is going to be even harder than I thought.* Wili watched his fat opponent walk across the pavilion toward the game table. Richardson was the most obnoxious of Jonque types, the Anglo. And worse, the pattern of his jacket showed he was from the estates above Pasadena. There were very few Anglos in the nobility of Aztlán. Richardson was as pale as Jeremy Sergeivich, and Wili shuddered to think of the compensating nastiness the man must contain. He probably had the worst-treated labor gangs in Pasadena. His type always took it out on the serfs, trying to convince his peers that he was just as much a lord as they.

Most Jonques kept only a single bodyguard in the pavilion. Richardson was surrounded by four.

The big man smiled down at Wili as he put his equipment on the table and attached a scalp connector. He extended a fat white hand, and Wili shook it. "I am told you are a former countryman of mine, from Pasadena, no less." He used the formal "you."

Wili nodded. There was nothing but good fellowship on the other's face, as though their social differences were some historical oddity. "But now I live in Middle California."

"Ah, yes. Well, you could scarcely have developed your talents in Los Angeles, could you, son?" He sat down, and the clock was started. Appropriately, Richardson had white.

The game went fast at first, but Wili felt badgered by the other's chatter. The Jonque was all quite friendly, asking him if he liked Middle California, saying how nice it must be to get away from his "disadvantaged condition" in the Basin. Under other circumstances, Wili would have told the Jonque off—there was probably no danger doing so in the truce area. But Rosas had told him to let the game go at least an hour before making an argument.

It was ten moves into the game before Wili realized how far astray his anger was taking him. He looked at Richardson's queen side opening and saw that the advantage of position was firmly in his fat opponent's hands. The conversation had not distracted Richardson in the least. Wili looked over his opponent's shoulder at the pale ocean. On the horizon, undisturbed and far away, an Authority tanker moved slowly north. Nearer, two Aztlán sail freighters headed the other way. He concentrated on their silent, peaceful motion till Richardson's comments were reduced to unintelligible mumbling. Then he looked down at the board and put all his concentration into recovery.

Richardson's talk continued for several moments, then faded away completely. The pale aristocrat eyed Wili with a faintly nonplussed expression, but did not become angry. Wili did not notice. For him, the only evidence of his opponent was in the moves of the game. Even when Mike and Jeremy came in, even when his previous opponent, Della Lu, stopped by the table, Wili did not notice.

For Wili was in trouble. This was his weakest opening of the tournament, and—psychological warfare aside—this was his strongest opponent. Richardson's play was both hard and soft: He didn't make mistakes and there was imagination in everything he did. Jeremy had said something about Richardson's being a strong opponent, one who had a fast machine, superb interactive programs, and the intelligence to use them. That had been several days ago, and Wili had forgotten. He was finding out firsthand now.

The attack matured over the next five moves, a tightening noose about Wili's playing space. The enemy—Wili no longer thought of him by name, or even as a person—could see many moves into the future, could pursue broad strategy even beyond that. Wili had almost met his match.

Each move took longer and longer as the players lapsed into catatonic evaluation of their fate. Finally, with the endgame in sight, Wili pulled the sharpest finesse of his short career. His enemy was left with two rooks—against Wili's knight, bishop, and three well-placed pawns. To win he needed some combinatoric jewel, something as clever as his invention of the previous winter. Only now he had twenty minutes, not twenty weeks.

With every move, the pressure in his head increased. He felt like a runner racing an automobile, or like the John Henry of Naismith's story disks. His naked intelligence was fighting an artificial monster, a machine that analyzed a million combinations in the time he could look at one.

The pain shifted from his temples to his nose and eyes. It was a stinging sensation that brought him out of the depths, into the real world.

Smoke! Richardson had lit an enormous cigar. The tarry smoke drifted across the table into Wili's face.

"Put that out." Wili's voice was flat, the rage barely controlled.

Richardson's eyes widened in innocent surprise. He stubbed out his expensive light. "I'm sorry. I knew Northerners might not be comfortable with this, but you blacks get enough smoke in your eyes." He smiled. Wili half rose, his hands making fists. Someone pushed him back into his chair. Richardson eyed him with tolerant contempt, as if to say "race will out."

Wili tried to ignore the look and the crowd around the table. He had to win now!

He stared and stared at the board. Done right, he was sure those pawns could march through the enemy's fire. But his time was running out and he couldn't recapture his previous mental state.

His enemy was making no mistakes; *his* play was as infernally deep as ever.

Three more moves. Wili's pawns were going to die. All of them. The spectators might not see it yet, but Wili did, and so did Richardson.

Wili swallowed, fighting nausea. He reached for his king, to turn it on its side and so resign. Unwillingly, his eyes slid across the board and met Richardson's. "You played a good game, son. The best I've ever seen from an unaided player."

There was no overt mockery in the other's voice, but by now Wili knew better. He lunged across the table, grabbing for Richardson's throat. The guards were fast. Wili found himself suspended above the table, held by a half-dozen not-too-gentle hands. He screamed at Richardson, the Spañolnegro curses expert and obscene.

The Jonque stepped back from the table and motioned his guards to lower Wili to the floor. He caught Rosas' eye and said mildly, "Why don't you take your little Alekhine outside to cool off?"

Rosas nodded. He and Jeremy frog-marched the still-struggling loser toward the door. Behind them, Wili heard Richardson trying to convince the tournament directors—with all apparent sincerity—to let Wili continue in the tournament.

15

Moments later, they were outside and shed of gawkers. Wili's feet settled back on the turf and he walked more or less willingly between Rosas and Jeremy.

For the first time in years, for the first time since he lost Uncle Sly, Wili found himself crying. He covered his face with his hands, trying to separate himself from the outside world. There could be no keener humiliation than this.

"Let's take him down past the buses, Jeremy. A little walk will do him good."

"It really was a good game, Wili," said Jeremy. "I told you Richardson's rated Expert. You came close to beating him."

Wili barely heard. "I had that Jonque bastard. *I had him!* When he lit that cigar, I lost my concentration. I tell you, if he did not cheat, I would have killed him."

They walked thirty meters, and Wili gradually quieted. Then he realized there had been no encouraging reply. He dropped his hands and glared at Jeremy. "Well, don't you think so?"

Jeremy was stricken, honesty fighting with friendship. "Richardson is a Mouth, you're right. He goes after everyone like that; he seems to think it's part of the game. You notice how it hardly affected his concentration? He just checkpoints his program when he gets talking, so he can dump back into his original mental set any time. He never loses a beat."

"And so I should have won." Wili was not going to let the other wriggle out of the question.

"Well, uh, Wili, look. You're the best unaided player I've ever seen. You lasted more rounds than any other purely-human. But be honest: Didn't you feel something different when you played him? I mean apart from his lip? Wasn't he a little more tricky than the earlier players . . . a little more deadly?"

Wili thought back to the image of John Henry and the steam drill. And he suddenly remembered that Expert was the low end of champion class. He began to see Jeremy's point. "So you really think the machines and the scalp connects make a difference?"

Jeremy nodded. It was no more than bookkeeping and memory enhancement, but if it could turn Roberto Richardson into a genius, what would it do for . . . ? Wili remembered Paul's faint smile at Wili's disdain of mechanical aids. He remembered the hours Paul himself spent in processor connect. "Can you show me how to use such things, Jeremy? Not just for chess?"

"Sure. It will take a while. We have to tailor the program to the user, and it takes time to learn to interpret a scalp connect. But come next year, you'll beat anything—animal, vegetable, or mineral." He laughed.

"Okay," Rosas said suddenly. "We can talk now."

Wili looked up. They had walked far past the parking lots. They were moving down a dusty road that went north around the bay, to the vineyards. The hotel was lost to sight. It was like waking from a dream suddenly to realize that the game and argument were mere camouflage.

"You did a real good job, Wili. That was exactly the incident we needed, and it happened at just the right time." The sun was about twenty minutes above the horizon, its light already misted. Orange twilight was growing. A puffy fog gathered along the beach like some silent army, preparing for its assault inland.

Wili wiped his face with the back of his arm. "No act."

"Nevertheless, it couldn't have worked out better. I don't think anybody will be surprised if you don't show till morning."

"Great."

The road descended. The only vegetation was aromatic brush bearing tiny purple flowers; it grew, scraggly, around the foundations and the ruined walls.

The fog moved over the coast, scruffy clots of haze, quite different from an inland fog; these were more like real clouds brought close to earth. The sun shone through the mists. The cliffsides were still visible, turning steadily more gold—a dry color that contrasted with the damp of the air.

As they reached beach level, the sun went behind the dense cloud deck at the horizon and spread into an orange band. The colors faded and the fog became more substantial. Only a single star, almost overhead, could penetrate the murk.

The road narrowed. The ocean side was lined with eucalyptus, their branches rattling in the breeze. They passed a large sign that proclaimed that the State's Highway—this dirt road—was now passing through Viñas Scripps. Beyond the trees, Wili could see regular rows of vertical stakes. The vines were dim gargoyles on the stakes. They walked steadily higher, but the invading fog kept pace, became even thicker. The surf was loud, even sixty meters above the beach.

"I think we're all alone up here," Jeremy said in a low voice.

"Of course, without this fog, we'd be clear as Vandenberg to anyone at the hotel."

"That's one reason for doing it tonight."

They passed an occasional wagon, no doubt used to carry grapes up the grade to the winery. The way widened to the left and split into a separate road. They followed the turnoff and saw an orange glow floating in the darkness. It was an oil lamp hung at the entrance to a wide adobe building. A sign—probably grand and colorful in the day—announced in Spanish and English that this was the central winery of Viñas Scripps and that tours for gentlemen and their ladies could be scheduled for the daylight hours. Only empty winery carts were parked in the lot fronting the building.

The three walked almost shyly to the entrance. Rosas tapped on the door. It was opened by a thirtyish Anglo woman. They stepped inside, but she said immediately, "Tours during daylight hours only, gentlemen." The last word had a downward inflection; it was clear they were not even minor aristocrats. Wili wondered that she opened the door at all.

Mike replied that they had left the tournament at Fonda la Jolla while it was still day and hadn't realized the walk was so long. "We've come all the way from Santa Ynez, in part to see your famous winery and its equipment. . . ."

"From Santa Ynez," the woman repeated and appeared to commiserate. She seemed younger in the light, but not nearly as pretty as Della Lu. Wili's attention wandered to the posters that covered the foyer walls. They illustrated the various stages of the grape-growing and wine-making processes. "Let me check with my supervisor. He may still be up; in which case, perhaps." She shrugged.

She left them alone. Rosas nodded to Jeremy and Wili. So this was the secret laboratory Paul had discovered. Wili had suspected from the moment the buses pulled into La Jolla. This part of the country was so empty that there hadn't been many possibilities.

Finally a man (the supervisor?) appeared at the door. "Mr. Rosas?" he said in English. "Please come this way." Jeremy and Wili looked at each other. Mr. *Rosas.* Apparently they had passed inspection.

Beyond the door was a wide stairway. By the light of their guide's electric flash, Wili saw that the walls were of natural rock. This was the cave system the winery signs boasted of. They reached the floor and walked across a room filled with enormous wooden casks. An overpowering but not unpleasant yeasty smell filled the cavern. Three young workers nodded to them but did not speak. The supervisor walked behind one of the casks. The back of the wooden cylinder came silently open, revealing a spiral stair. There was barely enough room on it for Jeremy to stand sideways.

"Sorry about the tight fit," the supervisor said. "We can actually pull the stairs downward, out of the cask, so even a thorough search won't find the entrance." He pushed a button on the wall, and a green glow spread down the shaft. Jeremy gave a start of surprise. "Tailored biolight," the man explained. "The stuff uses the carbon dioxide we exhale. Can you imagine what it would do to indoor lighting if we were allowed to market it?" He continued in this vein as they descended, talking about the harmless bioscience inventions that could make so much difference to today's world if only they weren't Banned.

At the bottom, there was another cavern. This one's ceiling was covered with glowing green. It was bright enough to read by, at least where it clumped up, over tables and instrument boards. Everyone looked five weeks dead in the fungal glow. It was very quiet; not even surfsound penetrated the rock. There was no one else in the room.

He led them to a table covered with worn linen sheeting. He patted the table and glanced at Wili. "You're the fellow we've been, uh, hired to help?"

"That's right," said Rosas when Wili gave only a shrug.

"Well, sit up here and I'll take a look at you."

Wili did so, cautiously. There was no antiseptic smell, no needles. He expected the man to tell him to strip, but no such command was given. The supervisor had neither the arrogant indifference of a slave gang vet, nor the solicitous manner of the doctor Paul had called during the winter.

"First off, I want to know if there are any structural problems. . . . Let me see, I've got my scope around here somewhere." He rummaged in an ancient metal cabinet.

Rosas scowled. "You don't have any assistants?"

"Oh, dear me, no." The other did not look up from his search. "There are only five of us here at a time. Before the War, there were dozens of bioscientists in La Jolla. But when we went underground, things changed. For a while, we planned to start a pharmaceutical house as a cover. The Authority hasn't Banned those, you know. But it was just too risky. They would naturally suspect anyone in the drug business.

"So we set up Scripps Vineyards. It's nearly ideal. We can openly ship and receive biologically active materials. And some of our development activities can take place right in our own fields. The location is good, too. We're only five kilometers from Old Five. The beach caves were used for smuggling even before the War, even before the United States . . . Aha, here it is." He pulled a plastic cylinder into the light. He walked to another cabinet and returned with a metal hoop nearly 150 centimeters across. There was a click as he slid it into the base of the cylinder. It looked a little foolish, like a butterfly hoop without a net.

"Anyway," he continued as he approached Wili, "the disadvantage is that we can only support a very few 'vineyard technicians' at a time. It's a shame. There's so much to learn. There's so much good we could do for the world." He passed the loop around the table and Wili's body. At the same time he watched the display at the foot of the table.

Rosas said, "I'm sure. Just like the good you did with the plag—" He broke off as the screen came to life. The colors were vivid, glowing with their own light. They seemed more alive than anything else in the green-tinted lab. For a moment it looked like the sort of abstract design that's so easy to generate. Then Wili noticed movement and asymmetries. As the supervisor slid the hoop back over Wili's chest, the elliptical shape shrank dramatically, then grew again as the hoop moved by his head. Wili rose to his elbows in surprise, and the image broadened.

"Lie back down. You don't have to be motionless, but let me choose the view angle."

Wili lay back and felt almost violated. They were seeing a cross section of his own guts, taken in the plane of the hoop! The supervisor brought it back to Wili's chest. They watched his heart squeezing, *thuddub thuddub.* The bioscientist made an adjustment, and the view swelled until the heart filled the display. They could see the blood surge in and out of each chamber. A second display blinked on beside the first, this new one filled with numbers of unknown meaning.

The supervisor continued for ten or fifteen minutes, examining all of Wili's torso. Finally, he removed the hoop and studied the summary data on the displays. "So much for the floor show.

"I won't even have to do a genopsy on you, my boy. It's clear that your problem is one we've cured before." He looked at Rosas, finally responding to the other's hostility. "You object to our price, Mr. Rosas?"

The undersheriff started to answer, but the supervisor waved him quiet. "The price is high. We always need the latest electronic equipment. During the last fifty years, the Authority has allowed you Tinkers to flourish. I daresay, you're far ahead of the Authority's own technology. On the other hand, we few poor people in bioresearch have lived in fear, have had to hide in caves to continue our work. And since the Authority has convinced you that we're monsters, most of you won't even sell to us.

"Nevertheless, we've worked miracles these fifty years, Mr. Rosas. If we'd had your freedom, we'd have worked more than miracles. Earth would be Eden now."

"Or a charnel house," Rosas muttered.

The supervisor nodded, seemed only slightly angered. "You say that even when you need us. The plagues warped both you and the Authority. If it hadn't been for those strange accidents, how different things would be. In fact, given a free hand, we could have saved people like this boy from ever having been diseased."

"How?" asked Wili.

"Why, with another plague," the other replied lightly, reminding Wili of the "mad scientists" in the old TV shows Irma and Bill watched. To suggest a plague after all the plagues had done. "Yes, another. You see, your problem was caused by genetic damage to your parents. The most elegant countermeasure would be to tailor a virus that moves through the population, correcting just those genotypes that cause the problem."

Fascination with experiment was clear in his voice. Wili didn't know what to think of his savior, this man of goodwill who might be more dangerous than the Peace Authority and all the Jonque aristocrats put together.

The supervisor sighed and turned off the display. "And yes, I suppose we are crazier than before, maybe even less responsible. After all, we've pinned our whole lives on our beliefs, while the rest of you could drift in the open light without fearing the Authority. . . .

"In any case, there are other ways of curing your disease, and we've known them for decades." He glanced at Rosas. "Safer ways." He walked part way down the corridor to a locker and glanced at a display by the door. "Looks like we have enough on hand." He filled an ordinary looking glass bottle from the locker and returned. "Don't worry, no plague stuff. This is simply a parasite—I should say a symbiont." He laughed shortly. "In fact, it's a type of yeast. If you take five tablets every day till the bottle's empty, you'll establish a stable culture in your gut. You should notice some improvement within ten days."

He put the jar in Wili's hand. The boy stared. Just "—here, take this and all your problems will be gone by morning—" or in ten days, or whatever. Where was the sacrifice, the pain? Salvation came this fast in dreams alone.

Rosas did not seem impressed. "Very well. Red Arrow and the others will pay as promised: programs and hardware to your specifications for three years." The words were spoken with some effort, and Wili realized just how reluctant a guide Miguel Rosas had been—and how important Paul Naismith's wishes were to the Tinkers.

The supervisor nodded, for the first time cowed by Rosas' hostility, for the first time realizing that the trade would produce no general gratitude or friendship.

Wili jumped down from the table and they started back to the stairs.

They had not gone ten steps when Jeremy said, "Sir, you said Eden?" His voice sounded diffident, almost frightened. But still curious. After all, Jeremy was the one who dared the Authority with his self-powered vehicles. Jeremy was the one who always talked of science remaking the world. "You said Eden. What could you do besides cure a few diseases?"

The supervisor seemed to realize there was no mockery in the question. He stopped under a bright patch of ceiling and gestured Jeremy Sergeivich closer. "There are many things, son. But here is one. . . . How old do you think I am? How old do you think the others at the winery are?"

Discounting the greenish light that made everyone look dead, Wili tried to guess. The skin was smooth and firm, with just a hint of wrinkles around the eyes. The hair looked natural and full. He had thought forty before. Now he would say even younger.

And the others they had seen? About the same. Yet in any normal group of adults, more than half were past fifty. And then Wili remembered that when the supervisor spoke of the War, he talked like an oldster, of time in personal memory. "We" decided this, and "we" did that.

He had been adult at the time of the War. He was as old as Naismith or Kaladze.

Jeremy's jaw sagged, and after a moment he nodded shyly. His question had been answered. The supervisor smiled at the boy. "So you see, Mr. Rosas talks of risks—and they may be as great as he claims. But what's to gain is very great, too." He turned and walked the short distance to the stairs door—

—which opened in his face. It was one of the workers from the cask room. "Juan," the man began, talking fast, "the place is being deep-probed. There are helicopters circling the fields. Lights everywhere."

16

The supervisor stepped back, and the man came off the spiral stair. "What! Why didn't you call down? Never mind, I know. Have you powered down all Banned equipment?" The man nodded. "Where is the boss?"

"She's sticking at the front desk. So are the others. She's going to try to brazen it out."

"Hmm." The supervisor hesitated only a second. "It's really the only thing to do. Our shielding should hold up. They can inspect the cask room all they want." He looked at the three Northerners. "We two are going up and say hello to the forces of worldwide law and order. If they ask, we'll tell them you've already departed along the beach route."

Wili's cure might still be safe.

The supervisor made some quick adjustment at a wall panel. The fungus gradually dimmed, leaving a single streak that wobbled off into the dark. "Follow the glow and you'll eventually reach the beach. Mr. Rosas, I hope you understand the risk we take in letting you go. If we survive, I expect you to make good on our bargain."

Rosas nodded, then awkwardly accepted the other's flashlight. He turned and hustled Jeremy and Wili off into the dark. Behind them, Wili heard the two bioscientists climbing the stairs to their own fate.

The dim band turned twice, and the corridor became barely shoulder wide. The stone was moist and irregular under Wili's hand. The tunnel went downhill now and was deathly dark. Mike flicked on his light and urged them to a near run. "Do you know what the Authority would do to a lab?"

Jeremy was hot on Wili's heels, occasionally bumping into the smaller boy, though never quite hard enough to make them lose their balance. What would the Authority do? Wili's answer was half a pant. "Bobble it?"

Of course. Why risk a conventional raid? If they even had strong suspicions, the safest action would be to embobble the whole place, killing the scientists and isolating whatever death seed might be stored here. Even without the Authority's reputation of harsh punishment for Banned research, it made complete sense. Any second now, they might find themselves inside a vast silver sphere. Inside.

Dio, perhaps it had happened already. Wili half stumbled at the thought, nearly losing his grip on the glass jar that was the reason for the whole adventure. They would not know till they ran headlong into the wall. They would live for hours, maybe days, but when the air gave out they would die as all the thousands before them must have died, at Vandenberg and Point Loma and Huachuca and . . .

The ceiling came lower, till it was barely centimeters above Wili's head. Jeremy and Mike pounded clumsily along, bent over yet trying to run at full speed. Light and shadow danced jaggedly about them.

Wili watched ahead for three figures running toward them: The first sign of embobblement would be their own reflections ahead of them. And there *was* something moving up there. Close.

"Wait! Wait!" he screamed. The three came to an untidy stop before—a door, an almost ordinary door. Its surface was metallic, and that accounted for the reflection. He pushed the opener. The door swung outward, and they could hear the surf. Mike doused the light.

They started down a stairway, but too fast. Wili heard someone trip and an instant later he was hit from behind. The three tumbled down the steps. Stone bit savagely into his arms and back. Wili's fingers spasmed open and the jar flew into space, its landing marked by the sound of breaking glass.

Life's blood spattering down unseen steps.

He felt Jeremy scramble past him. "Your flashlight, Mike, quick."

After a second, light filled the stairs. If any Peace cops were on the beach looking inland . . . ?

113

It was a risk they took for him.

Wili and Jeremy scrabbled back and forth across the stairs, unmindful of the glass shards. In seconds they had recovered the tablets—along with considerable dirt and glass. They dumped it in Jeremy's waterproof hiking bag. The boy dropped a piece of paper into the bag. "Directions, I bet." He zipped it shut and handed it to Wili.

Rosas kept the light on a second longer, and the three memorized the path they must follow. The steps were scarcely more than water-worn corrugations. The cave was free of any other human touch.

Darkness again, and the three started carefully downward, still moving faster than was really comfortable. If only they had a night scope. Such equipment wasn't Banned, but the Tinkers didn't flaunt it. The only high tech equipment they'd brought to La Jolla was the Red Arrow chess processor.

Wili thought he saw light ahead. Over the surf drone he heard a *thupthupthup* that grew first louder and then faded. A helicopter.

They made a final turn and saw the outside world through the vertical crack that was the entrance to the cave. The evening mist curled in, not as thick as earlier. A horizontal band of pale gray hung at eye level. After a moment, he realized the glow was thirty or forty meters away—the surf line. Every few seconds, something bright reflected off the surf and waters beyond.

Behind him Rosas whispered, "Light splash from their search beams on top of the bluff. We may be in luck." He pushed past Jeremy and led them to the opening. They hid there a few seconds and looked as far as they could up and down the beach. No one was visible, though there were a number of aircraft circling the area. Below the entrance spread a rubble of large boulders, big enough to hide their progress.

It happened just as they stepped away from the entrance: A deep, bell-like tone was followed by the cracking and crashing of rock now free of its parent strata. The avalanche proceeded all around them, thousands of tons of rock adding itself to the natural debris of the coastline. They cowered beneath the noise, waiting to be crushed.

But nothing fell close by, and when Wili finally looked up, he saw why. Silhouetted against the mist and occasional stars was the perfect curve of a sphere. The bobble had to be two or three hundred meters across, extending from the lowest of the winery's caves to well over the top of the bluff and from the inland vineyards to just beyond the edge of the cliffs.

"They did it. They really did it," Rosas muttered to himself.

Wili almost shouted with relief. A few centimeters the other way and they would have been entombed.

Jeremy!

Wili ran to the edge of the sphere. The other boy had been standing right behind them, surely close enough to be safe. Then where was he? Wili beat his fists against the blood warm surface. Rosas' hand closed over his mouth and he felt himself lifted off the ground. Wili struggled for a moment in enforced silence, then went limp. Rosas set him down.

"I know." Mike's voice was a strangled whisper. "He must be on the other side. But let's make sure." He flicked on his light—almost as brightly as he had risked in the cave—and they walked several meters back and forth along the line where the bobble passed into the rocks. They did not find Jeremy, but—

Rosas' flash stopped for a moment, freezing one tiny patch of ground in its light. Then the light winked out, but not before Wili saw two tiny spots of red, two . . . fingertips . . . lying in the dirt.

Just centimeters away, Jeremy must lie writhing in pain, staring into the darkness, feeling the blood on his hands. The wound could not be fatal. Instead, the boy would have hours still to die. Perhaps he would return to the labs, and sit with the others—waiting for the air to run out. The ultimate excommunication.

"You have the bag?" Rosas' voice quavered.

The question caught Wili as he was reaching for the mangled fingers. He stopped, straightened. "Yes."

"Well then, let's go." The words were curt. The tone was clamped-down hysteria.

The undersheriff grabbed Wili's shoulder and urged him down the jumble of half-seen rocks. The air was filled with dust and the cold moistness of the fog. The fresh broken rock was already wet and slippery. They clung close to the largest boulders, fearing both landslides and detection from the air. The bobble and bluffs cut a black edge into the hazy aura of the lights that swept the ground above. They could hear both trucks and aircraft up there.

But no one was down on the beach. As they crawled and climbed across the rocks, Wili wondered at this. Could it be the Authority did not know about the caves?

They didn't speak for a long time. Rosas was leading them slowly back toward the hotel. It might work. They could finish the tournament, get on the buses, and return to Middle California as though nothing had happened. As though Jeremy had never existed.

It took nearly two hours to reach the beach below the hotel. The fog was much thinner now. The tide had advanced; phosphorescent surf pounded close by, pushing surging tendrils of foam near their feet.

The hotel was brightly lit, more than he remembered on previous evenings. There were lots of lights in the parking areas, too. They hunkered down between two large rocks and inspected the scene. There were far too many lights. The parking lots were swarming with vehicles and men in Peacer green. To one side stood a ragged formation of civilians—prisoners? They stood in the glare of the trucks' lights, with their hands clasped on top of their heads. A steady procession of soldiers brought boxes and displays—the chess-assist equipment—from the hotel. It was much too far away to see faces, but Wili thought he recognized Roberto Richardson's fat form and flashy jacket there among the prisoners. He felt a quick thrill to see the Jonque standing like some recaptured slave.

"They raided everybody. . . . Just like Paul said, they finally decided to clean us all out." Anger was back in Mike's voice.

Where was the girl, Della Lu? He looked back and forth over the forlorn group of prisoners. She was so short. Either she was standing in back, or she was not there. Some of the buses were leaving. Maybe she had already been taken.

They had had amazing luck avoiding the bobble, avoiding detection, and avoiding the hotel raid. That luck must end now: They had lost Jeremy. They had lost the equipment at the hotel. Aztlán territory extended northward three hundred kilometers. They would have to walk more than a hundred klicks through wilderness just to reach the Basin. Even if the Authority was not looking for them, they could not avoid the Jonque barons, who would take Wili for a runaway slave—and Rosas for a peasant till they heard him talk, and then for a spy.

And if by some miracle they could reach Middle California, what then? This last was the most depressing thought of all. Paul Naismith had often talked of what would happen when the Authority finally saw the Tinkers as enemies. Apparently that time had come. All across the continent (all across the world? Wili remembered that some of the best chip engraving was done in France and China) the Authority would be cracking down. The Kaladze farm might even now be a smoking ruin, its people lined up with hands on heads, waiting to be shipped off to oblivion. And Paul would be one of them—if he wasn't already dead.

They sat in the cleft of the boulders for a long time, moving only to stay ahead of the tide. The sounds of soldiers and vehicles diminished. One by one the searchlights went out. One by one the buses rolled away—what had seemed marvelous carriages of speed and comfort just a few days before, now cattle cars.

If the idiots didn't search the beach, he and Rosas might have to walk north after all.

It must have been about three in the morning. The surf was just past its highest advance. There were still troopers on the hill near the hotel, but they didn't seem especially vigilant. Rosas was beginning to talk about starting north while it was still dark.

They heard a regular, scritching sound on the rocks just a few meters away. The two fugitives peeked out of their hiding place. Someone was pushing a small boat into the water, trying to get it past the surf.

"I think that girl could use some help," Mike remarked.

Wili looked closer. It was a girl, wet and bedraggled, but familiar: Della Lu had not been captured after all!

17

aul Naismith was grateful that even in these normally placid times there were still a few paranoids around—in addition to himself, that is. In some ways, 'Kolya Kaladze was an even worse case than he. The old Russian had devoted a significant fraction of his "farm's" budget to constructing a marvelous system of secret passages, hidden paths, small arms caches, and redoubts. Naismith had been able to travel more than ten kilometers from the farm, all the way around the Salsipuedes, without ever being exposed to the sky—or to the unwelcome visitors that lurked about the farm.

Now well into the hills, he felt relatively safe. There was little doubt that the Authority had observed the same event he had. Sooner or later they would divert resources from their various emergencies and come investigate the peculiar red smoke plume. Paul hoped to be long gone before that happened. In the meantime, he would take advantage of this incredible good luck. Revenge had waited, impotent, these fifty years, but its time might now come.

Naismith geed the horse. The cart and horse were not what he had come to the farm with. 'Kolya had supplied everything—including a silly, old-lady disguise which he suspected was more embarrassing than effective.

Nikolai had not stinted, but neither had he been happy about the departure. Naismith slouched back on the padded seat and thought ruefully of that last argument. They had been sitting on the porch of the main house. The blinds were drawn, and a tiny singing vibration in the air told Naismith that the window panes were incapable of responding to a laser-driven audio probe. The Peace Authority "bandits" —what an appropriate cover—had made no move. Except for what was coming over the radio, and what Paul had seen, there was no sign that the world was turning upside down.

Kaladze understood the situation—or thought he did—and wanted no part of Naismith's project. "I tell you honestly, Paul, I do not understand you. We are relatively safe here. No matter what the Peacers say, they can't act against us all at once; that's why they grabbed our friends at the tournament. For hostages." He paused, probably thinking of a certain three hostages. Just now, they had no way of knowing if Jeremy and Wili and Mike were dead or alive, captive or free. Taking hostages might turn out to be an effective strategy indeed. "If we keep our heads down, there's no special reason to believe they'll invade Red Arrow Farm. You'll be as safe here as anywhere. *But,*" Nikolai rushed on as if to forestall an immediate response, "if you leave now, you'll be alone and in the open. You want to head for one of the few spots in North America where the Peacers are guaranteed to swarm. For which risk, you get *nothing.*"

"You are three times wrong, old friend," Paul answered quietly, barely able to suppress his frantic impatience to be gone. He ticked off the points. "First, your second claim: If I leave right now, I can probably get there before the Authority. They have much else to worry about. Since we got Wili's invention working. I and my programs have spent every second monitoring the Peacer recon satellites for evidence of bobble decay. I'll bet the Authority itself doesn't have the monitor capability I do. It's possible they don't yet realize that a bobble burst up there in the hills this morning.

"As to your third claim: The risk *is* worth the candle. I stand to win the greatest prize of all, the means to destroy the Authority. Something or someone is causing bobbles to burst. So there is some defense against the bobbles. If I can discover that secret—"

Kaladze shrugged. "So? You'd still need a nuclear power generator to do anything with the knowledge."

"Maybe . . . Finally, my response to your first claim: You—we— are not at all safe lying low on the farm. For years, I tried to convince you the Authority is deadly once it sees you as a danger. You're right, they can't attack everywhere at once. But they'll use the La Jolla hostages to identify you, and to draw you out. Even if they don't have Mike and the boys, Red Arrow Farm will be high on their hit-list. And if they suspect I'm here, they'll raid you just as soon as they have enough force in the area. They have some reason to fear me."

"They want *you?*" Kaladze's jaw sagged. "Then why haven't they simply bobbled us?"

Paul grinned. "Most likely, their 'bandit' reconnaissance didn't recognize me—or maybe they want to be sure I'm inside their cage when they lock it." *Avery missed me once before. He can't stand uncertainty.*

"Bottom line, 'Kolya: The Peace Authority is out to get us. We must give them the best fight we can. Finding out what's bursting the bobbles might give us the whole game." No need to tell 'Kolya that he would be doing it even if the Peacers hadn't raided the tournament. Like most Tinkers, Nikolai Kaladze had never been in direct conflict with the Authority. Though he was as old as Naismith, he had not seen firsthand the betrayal that had brought the Authority to power. Even the denial of bioproducts to children like Wili was not seen by today's people as real tyranny. But now at last there was the technical and—if the Authority was foolish enough to keep up its pressure on the likes of Kaladze—the political opportunity to overturn the Peacers.

The argument continued for thirty minutes, with Naismith slowly prevailing. The real problem in getting 'Kolya's help was to convince him that Paul had a chance of discovering anything from a simple inspection of this latest bobble burst. In the end, Naismith was successful, though he had to reveal a few secrets out of his past that might later cause him considerable trouble.

The path Naismith followed leveled briefly as it passed over a ridgeline. If it weren't for the forest, he could see the crater from here. He had to stop daydreaming and decide just how to make his approach. There was still no sign of Peacers, but if he were picked up near the site, the old-lady disguise would be no protection.

He guided his horse off the path some thousand meters inland of the crater. Fifty meters into the brush, he got down from the cart. Under ordinary circumstances there was more than enough cover to hide horse and vehicle. Today, and here, he couldn't be so confident.

It was a chance he must take. For fifty years, bobbles—and the one up ahead, in particular—had haunted him. For fifty years he had tried to convince himself that all this was not his fault. For fifty years he had hoped for some way to undo what his old bosses had made of his invention.

He took his pack off the cart and awkwardly slipped it on. The rest of the way would be on foot. Naismith trudged grimly back up the forested hillside, wondering how long it would be before the pack harness began to cut, wondering if he would run out of breath first. What was a casual walk for a sixty-year-old might be life-threatening for someone his age. He tried to ignore the creaking of his trick knee and the rasping of his breath.

Aircraft. The sound passed over but did not fade into the distance. Another and another. Damn it.

Naismith took out some gear and began monitoring the remotes that Jeremy had scattered the night of the ambush. He was still three thousand meters from the crater, but some of the pellets might be in enough sun to be charged up and transmitting.

He searched methodically through the entire packet space his probes could transmit on. The ones nearest the crater were gone or so deeply embedded in the forest floor that all he could see was the sky above them. There had been a fire, maybe even a small explosion, when this bobble burst. But no ordinary fire could have burned within the bobble for fifty years. If a nuclear explosion had been trapped inside, there would have been something much more spectacular than a fire when it burst. (And Naismith knew this one: There had been no nuke in it.) That was the unique thing about this bobble burst; it might explain the whole mystery.

He had fragmentary views of uniforms. Peacer troops. They had left their aircraft and were spreading around the crater. Naismith piped the audio to his hearing aid. He was so close. But it would be crazy to go any nearer now. Maybe if they didn't leave too many troops, he could sneak in tomorrow morning. He had arrived too late to scoop them and too early to avoid them. Naismith swore softly to himself and unwrapped the lightweight camping bag Kaladze had given him. All the time he watched the tiny screen he had propped against a nearby tree trunk. The controlling program shifted the scene between the five best views he had discovered in his initial survey. It would also alert him if anyone started moving in his direction.

Naismith settled back and tried to relax. He could hear lots of activity, but it must be right down in the crater, since he could see none of it.

The sun slowly drifted west. Another time, Naismith would have admired the beautiful day: temperatures in the high twenties, birds singing. The strange forests around Vandenberg might be unique: Dry climate vegetation suddenly plunged into something resembling the rainy tropics. God only knew what the climax forms would be like.

Today, all he could think of was getting at that crater just a few thousand meters to the north.

Even so, he was almost dozing when a distant rifle shot brought him to full alertness. He diddled the display a moment and had some good luck: He saw a man in gray and silver, running almost directly away from the camera. Naismith strained close to the screen, his jaw sagging. More shots. He zoomed on the figure. Gray and silver. He hadn't seen an outfit like that since before the War. For a moment his mind offered no interpretation, just cranked on as a stunned observer. Three troopers rushed past the camera. They must have been shooting over the fellow's head, but he wasn't stopping and now the trio fired again. The man in gray spun and dropped. For a moment, the three soldiers seemed as stricken as their target. Then they ran forward, shouting recriminations at each other.

The screen was alive with uniforms. There was a sudden silence at the arrival of a tweedy civilian. The man in charge. From his high-pitched expostulations, Naismith guessed he was unhappy with events. A stretcher was brought up and the still form was carted off. Naismith changed the phase of his camera and followed the victim down the path that led northward from the crater.

Minutes later the shriek of turbines splashed off the hills, and a needle-nosed form rose into the sky north of Naismith. The craft vectored into horizontal flight and sprinted southward, passing low over Naismith's hiding place.

The birds and insects were deathly silent the next several minutes, almost as silent and awestruck as Paul's own imagination. *He knew now.* The bursting bobbles were not caused by quantum decay. The bursting bobbles were not the work of some anti-Peacer underground. He fought down hysterical laughter. He had invented the damn things, provided his bosses with fifty years of empire, but he and they had never realized that—though his invention worked superbly—his theory was a crock of sewage from beginning to end.

He knew that now. The Peacers would know it in a matter of hours, if they had not already guessed. They would fly in a whole division with their science teams. He would likely die with his secret if he didn't slip out now and head eastward for his mountain home.

. . . But when Naismith finally moved, it was not back to his horse. He went north. Carefully, quietly, he moved toward the crater: For there was a corollary to his discovery, and it was more important than his life, perhaps even more important than his hatred of the Peace Authority.

18

Naismith stopped often, both to rest and to consult the screen that he had strapped to his forearm. The scattered cameras showed fewer than thirty troopers. If he had guessed their locations correctly, he might be able to crawl in quite close. He made a two-hundred-meter detour just to avoid one of them; the fellow was well concealed and was quietly listening and watching. Naismith suffered the rocks and brambles with equal silence. He carefully inspected the ground just ahead of him for branches and other noise-makers. Every move must be a considered one. This was something he had very little practice at, but he had to do it right the first time.

He was very close to his goal now: Naismith looked up from the display and peered into a small ravine. This was the place! Her suddenly still form was huddled deep within the brush. If he hadn't known from the scanners exactly where to look, he would not have noticed the flecks of silver beyond the leaves and branches. During the last half hour he had watched her move slowly south, trying to edge away from the troopers at the crater rim. Another fifteen minutes, and she would blunder into the soldier Naismith had noticed.

He slid down the cleft, through clouds of midges that swirled in the musty dampness. He was sure she could see him now. But he was obviously no soldier, and he was crawling along just as cautiously as she. Paul lost sight of her the last three or four meters of his approach. He didn't look for her, instead eased into the depths of shadow that drowned her hiding place.

Suddenly a hand slammed over his mouth and he found himself spun onto his back and forced to the ground. He looked up into a pair of startlingly blue eyes.

The young woman waited to see if Naismith would struggle, then released his shoulder and placed her finger to her lips. Naismith nodded, and after a second she removed her hand from his mouth. She lowered her head to his ear and whispered, "Who are you? Do you know how to get away from them?"

Naismith realized with wry bleakness that she had not seen through his disguise: She thought she'd landed some dazed crone. Perhaps that was best. He had no idea what she imagined was going on, but it could hardly be any approximation to reality. There was no truthful answer she would understand, much less believe. Naismith licked his lips in apparent nervousness and whispered back, "They're after me, too. If they catch us they'll kill us, just like your friend." *Oops.* "We've got to turn from the way you're going. I saw one of 'em hiding just ahead."

The young woman frowned, her suspicion clear. Naismith's omniscience was showing. "So you know a way out?"

He nodded. "My horse and wagon are southeast of all this ruckus. I know ways we can sneak past these folks. I have a little farm up in—"

His words were lost in a steadily increasing roar that passed almost overhead. They looked up and had a quick impression of something large and winged, fire glowing from ports at wings and tail. Another troop carrier. He could hear others following. This was the beginning of the real invasion. The only place they could land would be on the main road north of the crater. But given another half hour, there would be wall-to-wall troopers here and not even a mouse could escape.

Naismith rolled to his knees and pulled at her hand. She had no choice now. They stood and walked quickly back the way he had come. The sound of the jets was a continuous rumble; they could have shouted and still not been heard. They had perhaps fifteen minutes to move as fast as they were able.

Greenish twilight had fallen on the forest floor. In his mottled brown dress, Naismith would be hard to spot, but the girl's flight fatigues made her a perfect target. He held her hand, urging her to paths he thought safe. He glanced at his wrist again and again, trying to see where the invaders were posted. The girl was busy looking in all directions and didn't notice his display.

The sounds fell behind them. The jets were still loud, but the soldiers' voices were fading in the distance. A dove lilted nearby.

They were trotting now, where the undergrowth thinned. Naismith's lungs burned and a steady pain pushed in his chest. The woman had a limp, but her breath came effortlessly. No doubt she was slowing her pace to his.

Finally he was forced to a stumbling walk. She put her arm around his shoulder to keep him steady. Naismith grimaced but did not complain. He should be grateful that he could even walk, he supposed. But somehow it seemed a great injustice that a short run could be nearly fatal to someone who still felt young inside. He croaked directions, telling the girl where the horse and cart were hidden.

Ten minutes more, and he heard a faint nickering. There was no sign of an ambush. From here, he knew dozens of trails into the mountains, trails that guerrillas of bygone years had worked hard to conceal. With even a small amount of further luck, they could escape. Paul sagged against the side of the cart. The forest rippled and darkened before him. Not now, Lord, *not now!*

His vision cleared, but he didn't have the strength to hoist himself onto the cart. The young woman's arm slipped to his waist, while her other went under his legs. Paul was a little taller than she, but he didn't weigh much anymore, and she was strong. She lifted him easily into the back, then almost dropped him in surprise. "You're not a—"

Naismith gave her a weak grin. "A woman? You're right. In fact, there's scarcely a thing you've seen today that is what it seems." Her eyes widened even further.

Paul was almost beyond speech now. He pointed her at one of the hidden paths. It should get them safely away, if she could follow it.

And then the world darkened and fell away from him.

19

The ocean was placid today, but the fishing boat was small. Della Lu stood at the railing and looked down into the sun-sparkled water with a sick fascination. In all the Peace, she had as much counter-subversive experience as anyone. In a sense her experience had begun as soon as she was old enough to understand her parents' true job. And as an adult, she had planned and participated in airborne assaults, had directed the embobbling of three Mongolian strongholds, had been as tough as her vision of the Peace demanded . . . but until now she had never been in a watercraft bigger than a canoe.

Was it possible she could be seasick? Every three seconds, the swell rose to within a couple meters of her face, then sank back to reveal scum-covered timbers below the waterline. It had been vaguely pleasant at first, but one thing she'd learned during the last thirty-six hours was that *it never ended*. She had no doubt she would feel fine just knowing the motion could be stopped at her whim. But short of calling off this charade, there was no way to get away from it.

Della ordered her guts to sleep and her nose to ignore the stench of sardines. She looked up from the waterline to the horizon. She really had a lot to be proud of. In North America—and in Middle California, especially—the Authority's espionage service was an abomination. There had been no threats from this region in many, many years. The Peace kept most of the continent in a state of anarchy. Satellite reconnaissance could spot the smallest agglomeration of power there. Only

127

in the nation states, like Aztlán and New Mexico, did the Directors see any need for spies. Things were very different in the great land-ocean that was Central Asia.

But Della was managing. In a matter of days, she had improvised from her Asian experience to come up with something that might work against the threat Avery saw here. She had not simply copied her Mongolian procedures. In North America, the subversives had penetrated—at least in an electronic sense—some of the Authority secrets. Communications, for instance: Della's eyes caught on the Authority freighter near the horizon. She could not report directly from her little fishing boat without risking her cover. So she had a laser installed near the waterline, and with it talked to the freighter—which surcrypted the messages and sent them through normal Authority channels to Hamilton Avery and the operations Della was directing for him.

Laughter. One of the fisherman said something in Spanish, something about "persons much inclined to sleep." Miguel Rosas had climbed out of the boat's tiny cabin. He smiled wanly at their jokes as he picked his way past the nets. (Those fishermen were a weak point in her cover. They were real, hired for the job. Given time, they would likely figure out whom they were working for. The Authority should have a whole cadre of professionals for jobs like this. Hell, that had been the original purpose in planting her grandparents in San Francisco: The Authority had been worried about the large port so close to the most important enclave. They reasoned that 'furbishers would be the most likely to notice any buildup of military materiel. If only they had chosen to plant them among Tinkers instead. As it was, the years passed and no threat developed, and the Authority never expanded their counter-underground.)

Della smiled at him, but didn't speak till the Californian was standing beside her. "How is the boy?"

Rosas frowned. "Still sleeping. I hope he's okay. He's not in good health, you know."

Della was not worried. She had doctored the black kid's bread, what the fishermen fed him last night. It wouldn't do the boy any harm, but he should sleep for several more hours. It was important that she and Rosas have a private conversation, and this might be the last natural opportunity for it.

She looked up at him, keeping her expression innocent and friendly.

*He doesn't look weak. He doesn't look like a man who would betray his
people.* . . . And yet he had. So his motives were very important if
they were to manipulate him further. Finally she said, "We want to
thank you for uncovering the lab in La Jolla."

The undersheriff's face became rigid, and he straightened.

Lu cocked her head quizzically. "You mean you didn't guess who I
am?"

Rosas slumped back against the railing, looked dully over the side. "I
suspected. It was all too pat: our escape, these fellows picking us up. I
didn't think you'd be a woman, though. That's so old-fashioned." His
dark hands clenched the wood till the knuckles shone pale. "Damn it,
lady, you and your men killed Jere—killed one of the two I was here to
protect. And then you grabbed all those innocent people at the tournament. *Why?* Have you gone crazy?"

The man hadn't guessed that the tournament raid was the heart of
Avery's operation: the biolab had been secondary, important mainly
because it had brought Miguel Rosas to them. They needed hostages,
information.

"I'm sorry our attack on the lab killed one of your people, Mr. Rosas.
That wasn't our intent." This was true, though it might give her a
welcome leverage of guilt. "You could have simply told us its location,
not insisted on a 'Judas kiss' identification. You must realize, we
couldn't take any chance that what was in the lab might get out. . . ."

Rosas was nodding, almost to himself. *That must be it,* Lu thought.
The man had a pathological hatred of bioscience, far beyond the average person's simple fear. That was what had driven him to betrayal.
"As for the raid on the tournament, we had very good reasons for that,
reasons which you will someday understand and support. For now you
must trust us, just as the whole world has trusted us these last fifty
years, and follow our direction."

"Direction? The hell you say. I did what I had to do, but that's the
end to my cooperation. You can lock me up like the rest."

"I think not. Your safe return to Middle California is a high priority
with us. You and I and Wili will put ashore at Santa Barbara. From
there we should be able to get to Red Arrow Farm. We'll be heroes, the
only survivors of the infamous La Jolla raid." She saw the defiance on
his face. "You really have no choice, Miguel Rosas. You have betrayed
your friends, your employers, and all the people we arrested at the

tournament. If you don't go along, we will let it be known you were behind the raids, that you have been our agent for years."

"That's a damn lie!" His outburst was clipped short as he realized its irrelevance.

"On the other hand, if you do help us . . . well, then you will be serving a great good"—Rosas did not sneer, but clearly he did not believe it either—"and when all this is over you will be very rich, if necessary protected by the Peace for the rest of your life." It was a strategy that had worked on many, and not just during the history of the Peace: Take a weak person, encourage him to betrayal (for whatever reason), and then use the stick of exposure and the carrot of wealth to force him to do far more than he'd ever have had the courage or motive for in the beginning. Hamilton Avery was confident it would work here and had refused her the time for anything more subtle. Miguel Rosas might get them a line on the Hoehler fellow.

Della watched him carefully, trying to pierce his tense expression and see whether he was strong enough to sacrifice himself.

The undersheriff stared at the gulls that circled the boat and called raucously to their brethren as the first catch was drawn aboard. For a moment he seemed lost in the swirl of wings, and his jaw muscles slowly relaxed.

Finally he looked back at her. "You must be very good at chess. I can't believe the Authority has chess programs that could play the way you did Wili."

Della almost laughed at the irrelevance of the statement, but she answered honestly. "You're right; they don't. But I scarcely know the moves. What you all thought was my computer was actually a phone link to Livermore. We had our hottest players up there going over my game, figuring out the best moves and then sending them down to me."

Now Rosas did laugh. His hand came down on her shoulder. She almost struck before she realized this was a pat and not a blow. "I had wondered. I had really wondered.

"Lady, I hate your guts, and after today I hate everything you stand for. But you have my soul now." The laughter was gone from his voice. "What are you going to make me do?"

No, Miguel, I don't have your soul, and I see that I never will. Della was suddenly afraid—for no reason that could ever convince Hamilton

Avery—that Miguel Rosas was not their tool. Certainly, he was naive; outside the Aztlán and New Mexico, most North Americans were. But whatever weakness caused him to betray the Scripps lab ended there. And somehow she knew that whatever decision he had just made could not be changed by gradually forcing him to more and more treacherous acts. There was something very strong in Rosas. Even after his act of betrayal, those who counted him friend might still be lucky to know him.

"To do? Not a great deal. Sometime tonight we reach Santa Barbara. I want you to take me along when we put ashore. When we reach Middle California, you'll back up my story. I want to see the Tinkers firsthand." She paused. "There is one thing. Of all the subversives, there is one most dangerous to world peace. A man named Paul Hoehler." Rosas did not react. "We've seen him at Red Arrow Farm. We want to know what he's doing. We want to know where he is."

That had become the whole point of the operation for Hamilton Avery. The Director had an abiding paranoia about Hoehler. He was convinced that the bursting bobbles were not a natural phenomenon, that someone in Middle California was responsible. Up till yesterday, she had considered it all dangerous fantasy, distorting their strategy, obscuring the long-term threat of Tinker science. Now she was not so sure. Last night, Avery called to tell her about the spacecraft the Peace had discovered in the hills east of Vandenberg. The crash was only hours old and reports were still fragmentary, but it was clear that the enemy had a manned space operation. If they could do that in secret, then almost anything was possible. This was a time for greater ruthlessness than ever she had needed in Mongolia.

Above and around, the gulls swooped through the chill blue glare, circling closer and closer as the fish piled up at the rear of the boat. Rosas' gaze was lost among the scavengers. Della, for all her skill, could not tell whether she had a forced ally or a double traitor. For both their sakes she hoped he was the former.

131

20

Parties and fairs were common among the West Coast Tinkers. Sometimes it was difficult to tell one from the other, so large were the parties and so informal the fairs. When he was a child, the high points of Rosas' existence had been such events: tables laden with food, kids and oldsters come from kilometers around to enjoy each other's company in the bright outdoors of sunny days or crowded into warm and happy dining rooms while rain swept by outside.

The La Jolla crackdown had changed much of that. Rosas strained to appear attentive as he listened to a Kaladze niece marvel at their escape and long trek back to Middle California. His mind roamed grim and nervous across the scene of their welcome-home party. Only Kaladze's family attended. There was no one from other farms or from Santa Ynez; even Seymour Wentz had not come. The Peacers were not to suspect that anything special was happening at Red Arrow Farm.

But Sy was not totally missing. He and some of the neighbors had shown up on line of sight from their homes inland. Sometime this evening they would have a council of war.

I wonder if can face Sy and not give away what really happened in La Jolla?

Wilma Wentz—Kaladze's niece and Sy's sister-in-law, a woman in her late forties—was struggling to be heard over music that came from a speaker hidden in a nearby tree. "But I still don't understand how you managed once you reached Santa Barbara. You and a black boy and

132

an Asian woman traveling together. We know the Authority had asked
Aztlán to stop you. How did you get past the border?"

Rosas wished his face were in shadows, not lit by the pale glow-bulbs
that were strung between the trees. Wilma was only a woman, but she
was clever and more than once had caught him out when he was a
child. He must be as careful with her as anyone. He laughed. "It was
simple, Wilma—once Della suggested it: We stuck our heads right
back into the lion's mouth. We found a Peacer fuel station and climbed
into the undercarriage of one of the tankers. No Aztlán cop stops one
of those. We had a nonstop ride from there to the station south of
Santa Ynez." Even so, it had not been fun. There had been kilometer
after kilometer of noise and diesel fumes. More than once during the
two-hour trip they had nearly fainted, fallen past the spinning axles
onto the concrete of Old 101. But Lu had been adamant: Their return
must be realistically difficult. No one, including Wili, must suspect.

Wilma's eyes grew slightly round. "Oh, that Della Lu. She is so
wonderful. Don't you think?"

Rosas looked over Wilma's head to where Della was making herself
popular with the womenfolk. "Yes, she is wonderful." She had them all
agog with her tales of life in San Francisco. No matter how much (and
how suicidally) he might wish it, she never slipped up. She was a
supernaturally good liar. How he hated that small Asian face, those
clean good looks. He had never known anyone—man, woman or animal—who was so attractive and yet so evil. He forced his eyes away
from her, trying to forget the slim shoulders, the ready smile, the power
to destroy him and all the good he had ever done. . . .

"It's marvelous to have you back, Mikey." Wilma's voice was suddenly very soft. "But I'm sorry for those poor people down at La Jolla
and in that secret lab."

And Jeremy. Jeremy who was left behind forever. She was too kind to
say it, too kind to remind him that he had not brought back one of
those he had been hired to protect. The kindness rubbed unknowingly
on deeper guilt. Rosas could not conceal the harshness in his voice.
"Don't you worry about the biosci people, Wilma. They were an evil
we had to use to cure Wili. As for the others—I promise you we'll get
them back." He reached out to squeeze her hand. *All but Jeremy.*

"*Da,*" said a voice behind him. "We will get all the rest back indeed." It was Nikolai Kaladze, who had snuck up on them with his

usual lack of warning. "But now that is what we are ready to discuss, Wilma, my dear."

"Oh." She accepted the implied dismissal, a thoroughly modern woman. She turned to gather up the women and younger men, to leave the important matters to the seniors.

Della looked momentarily surprised at this turn of events. She smiled and waved to Mike just as she left. He would like to think he'd seen anger in her face, but she was too good an actress for that. He could only imagine her rage at being kicked out of the meeting. He hoped she'd been counting on attending it.

In minutes, the party was over, the women and children gone. The music from the trees softened, and insect sounds grew louder. Seymour Wentz's holo remained. His image could almost be mistaken for that of someone sitting at the far end of the picnic table. Thirty seconds passed, and several more electronic visitors appeared. One was on a flat, black-and-white display—someone from very far indeed. Rosas wondered how well his transmission was shielded. Then he recognized the sender, one of the Greens from Norcross. With them, it was probably safe.

Wili drifted in, nodded silently to Mike. The boy had been very quiet since that night in La Jolla.

"All present?" Colonel Kaladze sat down at the head of the table. Images far outnumbered the flesh-and-blood now. Only Mike, Wili, and Kaladze and his sons were truly here. The rest were images in holo tanks. The still night air, the pale glow of bulbs, the aged faces, and Wili—dark, small, yet somehow powerful. The scene struck Rosas like something out of a fantasy: a dark elfin prince, holding his council of war at midnight in faerie-lit forest.

The participants looked at each other for a moment, perhaps feeling the strangeness themselves. Finally, Ivan Nikolayevich said to his father, "Colonel, with all due respect, is it proper that someone so young and unknown as Mr. Wáchendon should sit at this meeting?"

Before the eldest could speak, Rosas interrupted, a further breach of decorum. "I asked that he stay. He shared our trip south, and he knows more about some of the technical problems we face than any of us." Mike nodded apologetically to Kaladze.

Sy Wentz grinned crookedly at him. "As long as we're ignoring all the rules of propriety, I want to ask about our communications secu-rity."

Kaladze sounded only faintly irritated by the usurpations. "Rest as-sured, Sheriff. This part of the woods is in a little valley, blocked from the inland. And I think we have more confusion gear in these trees than there are leaves." He glanced at a display. "No leaks from this end. If you line-of-sighters take even minimum precautions, we're safe." He glanced at the man from Norcross.

"Don't worry about me. I'm using knife-edges, convergent corridors —all sorts of good stuff. The Peacers could monitor forever and not even realize they were hearing a transmission. Gentlemen, you may not realize how primitive the enemy is. Since the La Jolla kidnappings, we've planted some of our bugs in their labs. The great Peace Authori-ty's electronic expert expertise is fifty years obsolete. We found re-searchers ecstatic at achieving component densities of ten million per square millimeter." There were surprised chuckles from around the table. The Green smiled, baring bad teeth. "In field operations, they are much worse."

"So all they have are the bombs, the jets, the tanks, the armies, and the bobbles."

"Correct. We are very much like Stone Age hunters fighting a mam-moth: We have the numbers and the brains, and the other side has the physical power. I predict our fate will be similar to the hunters'. We'll suffer casualties, but the enemy will eventually be defeated."

"What an encouraging point of view," Sy put in dryly.

"One thing I would like to know," said a hardware man from San Louis Obispo. "Who put this bee in their drawers? The last ten years we've been careful not to flaunt our best products; we agreed not to bug the Peacers. That's history now, but I get the feeling that *some-body* deliberately scared them. The bugs we've just planted report they were all upset about high tech stuff they found in their labs earlier this year. . . . Anybody want to fess up?"

He looked around the table; no one replied. But Mike felt a sudden certainty. There was at least one man who might wish to rub the Authority's nose in the Tinkers' superiority, one man who always wanted a scrap. Two weeks ago, he would have felt betrayed by the action. Mike smiled sadly to himself; he was not the only person who could risk his friends' lives for a Cause.

The Green shrugged. "If that's all there were to it, they'd do something more subtle than take hostages. The Peacers think we've discovered something that's an immediate threat. Their internal communications are full of demands that someone named Paul Hoehler be found. They think he's in Middle California. That's why there are so many Peacer units in your area, 'Kolya."

"Yes, you're quite right," said Kaladze. "In fact that's the real reason I asked for this meeting. Paul wanted it. Paul Hoehler, Paul Naismith —whatever we call him—has been the center of their fears for a long time. Only now, he may be as deadly as they believe. He may have something that can kill the 'mammoth' you speak of, Zeke. You see, Paul thinks he can generate bobbles without a nuclear power plant. He wants us to prepare—"

Wili's voice broke through the ripple of consternation that spread around the table. "No! Don't say more. You mean Paul will not be here tonight, even as a picture?" He sounded panicked.

Kaladze's eyebrows rose. "No. He intends to stay thoroughly . . . submerged . . . until he can broadcast his technique. You're the only person he—"

Wili was on his feet now, almost shaking. "But he has to see. He has to listen. He is maybe the only one who will believe me!"

The old soldier sat back. "Believe you about what?"

Rosas felt a chill crawl up his back. Wili was glaring down the table at him.

"Believe me when I tell you that Miguel Rosas is a traitor!" He looked from one visitor to the next but found no response. "It's true, I tell you. He knew about La Jolla from the beginning. He told the Peacers about the lab. He got J-J-Jeremy killed in that hole in the cliffs! And now he sits here while you say everything, while you tell him Paul's plan."

Wili's voice rose steadily to become childish and hysterical. Ivan and Sergei, big men in their late forties, started toward him. The Colonel motioned them back, and when Wili had finished, he responded mildly, "What's your evidence, son?"

"On the boat. You know, the 'lucky rescue' Mike is so happy to tell you of?" Wili spat. "Some rescue. It was a Peacer fake."

"Your proof, young man!" It was Sy Wentz, sticking up for his undersheriff of ten years.

136

"They thought they had me drugged, dead asleep. But I was some awake. I crawled up the cabin stairs. I saw him talking to that *puta de la Paz*, that monster Lu. She *thanked* him for betraying us! They know about Paul; you are right. And these two are up here sniffing around for him. They killed Jeremy. They—"

Wili stopped short, seemed to realize that the rush of words was carrying his cause backward.

Kaladze asked, "Could you really hear all they were saying?"

"N-no. There was the wind, and I was very dizzy. But—"

"That's enough, boy." Sy Wentz's voice boomed across the clearing. "We've known Mike since he was younger than you. Me and the Kaladzes shared his upbringing. He grew up *here*"—not in some Basin ghetto—"and we know where his loyalties are. He's risked his life more than once for customers. Hell, he even saved Paul's neck a couple of years ago."

"I'm sorry, Wili." Kaladze's voice was mild, quite unlike Sy's. "We do know Mike. And after this morning, I'm sure Miss Lu is what she appears. I called some friends in San Francisco: Her folks have been heavy-wagon 'furbishers for years up there. They recognized her picture. She and her brother went to La Jolla, just as she says."

Has she no limits? thought Rosas.

"*Caray.* I knew you'd not believe. If Paul was here—" The boy glared at Kaladze's sons. "Don't worry. I'll remain a gentleman." He turned and walked stiffly out of the clearing.

Rosas struggled to keep his expression one of simple surprise. If the boy had been a bit cooler, or Della a bit less superhuman, it would have been the end of Miguel Rosas. At that moment, he came terribly close to confessing what all the boy's accusations could not prove. But he said nothing. Mike wanted his revenge to precede his own destruction.

21

Nikolai Sergeivich and Sergei Nikolayevich were pale mauve sitting on the driver's bench ahead of Wili. The late night rain was a steady hushing all around them. For the last four kilometers, the old Russian's "secret tunnel" had been aboveground: When the cart got too near the walls, Wili could feel wet leaves and coarse netting brush against him. Through his night glasses, the wood glowed faintly warmer than the leaves or the netting, which must be some sort of camouflage. The walls were thickly woven, probably looked like heavy forest from the outside. Now that the roof of the passage was soaked, a retarded drizzle fell upon the four of them. Wili shifted his slicker against the trickle that was most persistent.

Without the night glasses the world was absolutely black. But his other senses had things to tell him about this camouflaged path that was taking them inland, past the watchers the Authority had strung around the farm. His nose told him they were far beyond the groves of banana trees that marked the eastern edge of the farm. On top of the smell of wet wood and roping, he thought he smelled lilacs, and that meant they must be about halfway to Highway 101. He wondered if Kaladze intended to accompany him that far.

Over the creaking of the cart's wheels, he could hear Miguel Rosas up ahead, leading the horses.

Wili's lips twisted, a voiceless snarl. No one had believed him. Here he was, a virtual prisoner of the people who should be his allies, and the whole lot of them were being led through the dark by the Jonque traitor! Wili slipped the heavy glasses back on and glared at the mauve blob that was the back of Rosas' head. Funny how Jonque skin was the same color as his own in the never-never world of the night glasses.

Where would their little trip end? He knew that Kaladze and son thought they were simply going to the end of the tunnel, to let Wili return to Naismith in the mountains. And the fools thought that Rosas would let them get away with it. For twenty minutes he had been almost twitchy, expecting a flash of real light ahead of them, sharp commands backed up by men in Authority green with rifles and stunners, the La Jolla betrayal all over again. But the minutes stretched on and on with nothing but the rain and the creaking of the cart's high wheels. The tunnel bent around the hills, occasionally descending underground, occasionally passing across timbers built over washouts. Considering how much it rained around Vandenberg, it must have taken a tremendous effort to keep this pathway functioning yet concealed. Too bad the old man was throwing it all away, thought Wili.

"Looks like we're near the end, sir." Rosas' whisper came back softly —ominously?—over the quiet drone of the rain. Wili rose to his knees to look over the Kaladzes' shoulders: The Jonque was pushing against a door, a door of webbed branches and leaves which nevertheless swung smoothly and silently. Brilliant light glowed through the opening. Wili almost bolted off the cart before his glasses adjusted and he realized that they were still undiscovered.

Wili slipped his glasses off for a second and saw that the night was still as dark as the back of his hand. He almost smiled; to the glasses, there were shades of absolute black. In the tunnel, the glasses had only their body heat to see by. Outside, even under a thick cloud deck, even in the middle of a rainy night, there must be enough ordinary light for them. This gear was far better than the night scope on Jeremy's rifle.

Rosas led the extra horse into the light. "Come ahead." Sergei Nikolayevich slapped the reins, and the cart squeezed slowly through the opening.

Rosas stood in a strange, shadowless landscape, but now the colors in his slicker and face didn't glow, and Wili could see his features clearly. The bulky glasses made his face unreadable. Wili shinnied down and walked to the center of the open space. All around them the trees hung close. Clouds glowed through occasional openings in the branches. Beyond Rosas, he could see an ordinary-looking path. He turned and looked at the doorway. Living shrubs grew from the cover.

The cart pulled forward until the elder Kaladze was even with the boy. Rosas came back to help the old man down, but the Russian shook his head. "We'll only be here a few minutes," he whispered.

His son looked up from some instrument in his lap. "We're the only man-sized animals nearby, Colonel."

"Good. Nevertheless, we still have much to do tonight back at home." For a moment, he sounded tired. "Wili, do you know why we three came the way out here with you?"

"No, sir." The "sir" came naturally when he talked to the Colonel. Next to Naismith himself, Wili had found more to respect in this man than anyone else. Jonque leaders—and the bosses of the Ndelante Ali —all demanded a respectful manner from their stooges, but old Kaladze actually gave his people something in return.

"Well, son, I wanted to convince you that you are important, and that what you must do is even more important. We didn't mean insult at the meeting last night; we just know that you are wrong about Mike." He lifted his hand a couple of centimeters, and Wili stifled the fresh pleading that rose to his lips. "I'm not going to try to convince you that you're wrong. I know you believe all you say. But even with such disagreement, we still need you desperately. You know that Paul Naismith is the key to all of this. He may be able to crack the secret of the bobbles. He may be able to get us out from under the Authority."

Wili nodded.

"Paul has told us that he needs you, that without your help his success will be delayed. They're looking for him, Wili. If they get him before he can help us—well, I don't think we'll have a chance. They'll treat us all like the Tinkers in La Jolla. So. We brought Elmir with us." He gestured at the mare Rosas had been leading. "Mike says you learned how to ride in LA."

Wili nodded again. That was an exaggeration; he knew how not to fall off. With the Ndelante Ali, getaways had occasionally been on horseback.

"We want you to return to Paul. We think you can make it from here. The path ahead crosses under Old One-oh-one. You shouldn't see anyone else unless you stray too far south. There's a trucker camp down that way."

For the first time Rosas spoke. "He must really need your help, Wili. The only thing that protects him is his hiding place. If you were captured and forced to talk—"

"*I* won't talk," Wili said and tried not to think of things he had seen happen to uncooperative prisoners in Pasadena.

"With the Authority there would be no choice."

"So? Is that what happened to you, Jonque Señor? Somehow, I don't think you planned from the beginning to betray us. What was it? I know you have fallen for the Chinese bitch. Is that what it was?" Wili heard his voice steadily rising. "Your price is so low?"

"Enough!" Kaladze's voice was not loud but its sharpness cut Wili short. The Colonel struggled off the driving bench to the ground, then bent till his face—eyes still obscured by the night glasses—was even with Wili's. Somehow, Wili could feel those eyes glaring through the dark plastic lenses.

"If anyone is to be bitter, it should be Sergei Nikolayevich and I, should it not? It is *I*, not you, who lost a grandson to the Authority bobble. If anyone is to be suspicious it should be *I*, not you. Mike Rosas saved your life. And I don't mean simply that he got you back here alive. He got you in and out of those secret labs; seconds either way and it would be all of you left trapped inside. And what you got in there was life itself. I saw you when you left for La Jolla: if you were so sick now, you would be too *weak* to afford the luxury of this anger."

That stopped Wili. Kaladze was right, though not about Rosas' innocence. These last eight days had been so busy, so full of fury and frustration, that he hadn't fully noticed: In previous summers his condition had always improved. But since he started eating that *stuff*, the pain had begun leaching away—faster than ever before. Since getting back to the farm, he had been eating with more pleasure than he had at any time in the last five years.

"Okay. I will help. On a condition."

Nikolai Sergeivich straightened but said nothing. Wili continued, "The game is lost if the Authority finds Naismith. Mike Rosas and the Lu woman maybe know where he is. If you promise—*on your honor*— to keep them for ten days away from all outside communication, then it will be worth it to me to do as you say."

Kaladze didn't answer immediately. It would be such an easy promise to give, to humor him in his "fantasies," but Wili knew that if the

Russian agreed to this, it would be a promise kept. Finally, "What you ask is very difficult, very inconvenient. It would almost mean locking them up." He glanced at Rosas.

"Sure. I'm willing." The traitor spoke quickly, almost eagerly, and Wili wondered what angle he was missing.

"Very well, sir, you have my word." Kaladze extended a thin, strong hand to shake Wili's. "Now let us be gone, before twilight herself joins our cozy discussions."

Sergei and Rosas turned the horse and cart around and carefully erased the marks of their presence. The traitor avoided Wili's look even as he swung the camouflaged door shut.

And Wili was alone with one small mare in darkest night. All around him the rain splattered just audibly. Despite the slicker, a small ribbon of wet was starting down his back.

Wili hadn't realized how difficult it was to lead a horse in such absolute dark; Rosas had made it look easy. Of course, Rosas didn't have to contend with odd branches which—if not bent carefully out of the way—would swipe the animal across the face. He almost lost control of poor Elmir the first time that happened. The path wound around the hills, disappeared entirely at places where the constant rains had enlarged last season's gullies. Only his visualization of Kaladze's maps saved him then.

It was at least fifteen kilometers to Old 101, a long, wet walk. Still, he was not really tired, and the pain in his muscles was the healthy feeling of exercise. Even at his best, he had never felt quite so bouncy. He patted the thin satchel nestled against his skin and said a short prayer to the One True God for continued good fortune.

There was plenty of time to think. Again and again, Wili came back to Rosas' apparent eagerness to accept house arrest for himself and the Lu woman. They must have something planned. Lu was so clever . . . so beautiful. He didn't know what had turned Rosas rotten, but he could almost believe that he did it simply for her. Were all *chicas chinas* like her? He had never seen a lady, black, Anglo, or Jonque, like Della Lu. Wili's mind wandered, imagining several final, victorious confrontations, until—night glasses and all—he almost walked over the edge of a washout half-full of racing water. It took him and Elmir fifteen minutes to get down and back up the mud-slicked sides of the gully, and he almost lost the glasses in the process.

It brought him back to reality. Lu was beautiful like oleander—or better—like a Glendora cat. She and Rosas had thought of something, and if he could not guess what it was, it could kill him.

Hours later he still hadn't figured it out. Twilight couldn't be far off now, and the rain had ceased. Wili stopped where a break in the forest gave him a view eastward. Parts of the sky were clear. They burned with tiny spots of flame. The trees cast multiple shadows (each a slightly different color). A long section of 101 was visible between the shoulders of the hills. There was no traffic, though to the south he saw shifting swaths of light that must be Authority road freighters. There was also a steady glow that might be the truckers' camp Kaladze had mentioned.

Directly below his viewpoint, a forested marsh extended right up to Old 101. The highway had been washed out and rebuilt many times, till it was little more than a timber bridge over the marshlands. He would have his choice of any of a hundred places to cross under.

It was farther away than it looked. By the time they were halfway there, the eastern sky was brightly lit, and Elmir seemed to have more faith in what he was doing.

He chose a lightly traveled path through the wet and started under the highway. Still he wondered what Lu and Rosas had planned. If they couldn't get a message out, then who could? Who knew where to look for Naismith and was also outside of Red Arrow Farm? Sudden understanding froze him in his tracks; Elmir's soft nose knocked him to his knees, but he scarcely noticed. *Of course!* Poor stupid little Wili, always ready to give his enemies a helping hand.

Wili got to his feet and walked back along Elmir, looking carefully for unwanted baggage. He ran his hand along the underside of her belly, and on the cinch found what he was looking for: The transmitter was large, almost two centimeters across. No doubt it had some sort of timer so it hadn't begun radiating back where the Kaladzes would have been sure to notice. He weighed the device with his hand. It was awfully big, probably an Authority bug. *But Rosas could have supplied something more subtle.* He went back to the horse and inspected her and her gear again, much more carefully. Then he took off his own clothes and did the same for them. The early morning air was chill, and muck oozed up between his toes. It felt great.

He looked very carefully, but found nothing more, which left him with nagging doubts. If it had just been Lu, he could understand. . . .

And there was still the question of what to do with the bug he had found. He got dressed and started to lead Elmir out from under the roadway. In the distance a rumbling grew louder and louder. The timbers began shaking, showering them with little globs of mud. Finally the land freighter passed directly overhead, and Wili wondered how the wooden trestle structure could take it.

It gave him an idea, though. There was that truckers' camp to the south, maybe just a couple of kilometers away. If he tied Elmir up here, he could probably make it in less than an hour. Not just Authority freighters used the stop. Ordinary truckers, with their big wagons and horse teams, would be there, too. It should be easy to sneak up early in the twilight and give one of those wagons a fifty-gram hitchhiker.

Wili chuckled out loud. So much for Missy Lu and Rosas. With a little luck, he'd have the Authority thinking Naismith was hiding in Seattle!

22

S he was trapped in some sort of gothic novel. And that was the least of her problems.

Allison Parker sat on an outcropping and looked off to the north. This far from the Dome the weather was as before, with maybe a bit more rain. If she looked neither right nor left, she could imagine that she was simply on a camping trip, taking her ease in the late morning coolness. Here she could imagine that Angus Quiller and Fred Torres were still alive, and that when she got back to Vandenberg, Paul Hoehler might be down from Livermore for a date.

But a glance to the left and she would see her rescuer's mansion, buried dark and deep in the trees. Even by day, there seemed something gloomy and alien about the building. Perhaps it was the owner. The old man, Naismith, seemed so furtive, so apparently gentle, yet still hiding some terrible secret or desire. And as in any gothic, his servants—themselves in their fifties—were equally furtive and close-mouthed.

Of course, a lot of mysteries had been solved these last days, the greatest the first night. When she had brought the old man in, the servants had been very surprised. All they would say was that the "master will explain all that needs explaining." "The master" was nearly unconscious at the time, so that was little help. Otherwise they had treated her well, feeding her and giving her clean, though ill-fitting clothes. Her bedroom was almost a dormer, its windows half in and half

145

out of the roof. The furniture was simple but elegant; the oiled burl dresser alone would have been worth thousands back . . . where she came from. She had sat on the bright patchwork quilt and thought darkly that there better be some explanations coming in the morning, or she was going to leg it back to the coast, unfriendly armies or no.

The huge house had been still and dead as the twilight deepened. Faint but clear against the silence, Allison could hear the sounds of applause and an audience laughing. It took her a second to realize that someone had turned on a television—though she hadn't seen a set during the day. *Ha!* Fifteen minutes of programming would tell her as much about this new universe as a month of talking to "Bill" and "Irma." She slid open her bedroom door and listened to the tiny, bright sounds.

The program was weirdly familiar, conjuring up memories of a time when she was barely tall enough to reach the on switch of her mother's TV. "Saturday Night"? It was either that or something very similar. She listened a few moments more, heard references to actors, politicians who had died before she ever entered college. She walked down the stairs, and sat with the Moraleses through an evening of old TV shows.

They hadn't objected, and as the days passed they'd opened up about some things. This was the future, about a half-century forward of her present. They told her of the war and the plagues that ended her world, and the force fields, the "bobbles," that birthed the new one.

But while some things were explained, others became mysteries in themselves. The old man didn't socialize, though the Moraleses said that he was recovered. The house was big and there were many rooms whose doors stayed closed. He—and whoever else was in the house besides the servants—was avoiding her. Eerie. She wasn't welcome here. The Morales were not unfriendly and had let her take a good share of the chores, but behind them she sensed the old man wishing she would go away. At the same time, they couldn't afford to have her go. They feared the occupying armies, the "Peace Authority," as much as she did; if she were captured, their hiding place would be found. So they continued to be her uneasy hosts.

She had seen the old man scarcely a handful of times since the first afternoon, and never to talk to. He was in the mansion though. She heard his voice behind closed doors, sometimes talking with a woman —not Irma Morales. That female voice was strangely familiar.

God, what I wouldn't give for a friendly face right now. Someone to talk to. Angus, Fred, Paul Hoehler.

Allison slid down from her rocky vantage point and paced angrily into the sunlight. On the coast, morning clouds still hung over the lowlands. The silver arch of the force field that enclosed Vandenberg and Lompoc seemed to float halfway up the sky. No structure could possibly be so big. Even mountains had the decency to introduce themselves with foothills and highlands. The Vandenberg Bobble simply rose, sheer and insubstantial as a dream. So that glistening hemisphere contained much of her old world, her old friends. They were trapped in timelessness in there, just as she and Angus and Fred had been trapped in the bobble projected around the sortie craft. And one day the Vandenberg Bobble would burst. . . .

Somewhere in the trees beyond her vision there was a cawing; a crow ascended above the pines, circled down at another point. Over the whine of insects, Allison heard padded clopping. A horse was coming up the narrow trail that went past her rock pile. Allison moved back into the shadows and watched.

Three minutes passed and a lone horseman came into view: It was a black male, so spindly it was hard to guess his age, except to say that he was young. He was dressed in dark greens, almost a camouflage outfit, and his hair was short and unbraided. He looked tired, but his eyes swept attentively back and forth across the trail ahead of him. The brown eyes flickered across her.

"Jill! How did you get so far from the veranda?" The words were spoken with a heavy Spanish accent; at this point it was an incongruity beneath Allison's notice. A broad grin split the boy's face as he slid off the horse and scrambled across the rocks toward her. "Naismith says that—" The words came to an abrupt halt along with the boy himself. He stood an arm's-length away, his jaw sagging in disbelief. "Jill? Is that really you?" He swung his hand in a flat arc toward Allison's midsection. The gesture was too slow to be a blow, but she wasn't taking any chances. She grabbed his wrist.

The boy actually squeaked—but with surprise, not pain. It was as if he could not believe she had actually touched him. She marched him back to the trail, and they started toward the house. She had his arm behind his back now. The boy did not struggle, though he didn't seem intimidated either. There was more shock and surprise in his eyes than fear.

Now that it was the other guy who was at a disadvantage, maybe she could get some answers. "You, Naismith, none of you have ever seen me before, yet you all seem to know me. I want to know why." She bent his arm a bit more, though not enough to hurt. The violence was in her voice.

"But, but I *have* seen you." He paused an instant, then rushed on. "In pictures, I mean."

It might not be the whole truth, but . . . Perhaps it was like those fantasies Angus used to read. Perhaps she was somehow important, and the world had been waiting for them to come out of stasis. In that case their pictures might be widely distributed.

They walked a dozen steps along the soft, needle-covered path. No, there was something more. These people acted as if they had known her as a person. Was that possible? Not for the boy, but Bill and Irma and certainly Naismith were old enough that she might have known them . . . before. She tried to imagine those faces fifty years younger. The servants couldn't have been more than children. The old man, he would have been around her own age.

She let the boy lead the way. She was more holding his hand than twisting his arm now; her mind was far away, thinking of the single tombstone with her name, thinking how much someone must have cared. They walked past the front of the house, descended the grade that led to a below-ground-level entrance. The door there was open, perhaps to let in the cool smells of morning. Naismith sat with his back to them, his attention all focused on the equipment he was playing with. Still holding his horse's reins, the boy leaned past the doorway and said, "Paul?"

Allison looked past the old man's shoulder at the screen he was watching: A horse and a boy and a woman stood looking through a doorway at an old man watching a screen that . . . Allison echoed the boy, but in a tone softer, sadder, more questioning. "Paul?"

The old man, who just last month had been young, turned at last to meet her.

23

There were few places on Earth that were busier or more populous than they had been before the War. Livermore was such a place. At its pre-War zenith, there had been the city and the clusters of commercial and federal labs scattered through the rolling hills. Those had been boom times, with the old Livermore Energy Laboratories managing dozens of major enterprises and a dozen-dozen contract operations from their square-mile reservation just outside of town. And one of those operations, unknown to the rest, had been the key to the future. Its manager, Hamilton Avery's father, had been clever enough to see what could be done with a certain staff scientist's invention, and had changed the course of history.

And so when the old world had disappeared behind silver bobbles, and burned beneath nuclear fireballs, and later withered in the war-plagues—Livermore had grown. First from all over the continent and then from all over the planet, the new rulers had brought their best and brightest here. Except for a brief lapse during the worst of the plague years, that growth had been near-exponential. And Peace had ruled the new world.

The heart of Authority power covered a thousand square kilometers, along a band that stretched westward toward the tiny Bay towns of Berkeley and Oakland. Even the Beijing and the Paris Enclaves had nothing to compare with Livermore. Hamilton Avery had wanted an

Eden here. He had had forty years and the wealth and genius of the planet to make one.

But still at the heart of the heart there was the Square Mile, the original federal labs, their century-old University of California architecture preserved amidst the sweep of one-thousand-meter bobbles, obsidian towers, and forested parks.

If the three of us are to meet, thought Avery, *what more appropriate place than here?* He had left his usual retinue on the greensward which edged the Square Mile. He and a single aide walked down the aged concrete sidewalk toward the gray building with the high narrow windows that had once held central offices.

Away from the carefully irrigated lawns and ornamental forests, the air was hot, more like the natural summer weather of the Livermore Valley. Already Avery's plain white shirt was sticking to his back.

Inside, the air-conditioning was loud and old-fashioned, but effective enough. He walked down ancient linoleum flooring, his footsteps echoing in the past. His aide opened the conference room's door before him and Hamilton Avery stepped forward to meet—or confront—his peers.

"Gentlemen." He reached across the conference table to shake first Kim Tioulang's hand, then Christian Gerrault's. The two were not happy; Avery had kept them waiting. *And the hell of it is, I didn't mean to.* Crisis had piled on top of crisis these last few hours, to the point that even a lifetime of political and diplomatic savvy was doing him no good.

Christian Gerrault, on the other hand, never had had much time for diplomacy. His piggish eyes were even more recessed in his fat face than they had seemed on the video. Or perhaps it was simply that he was angry: "You have a very great deal of explaining to do, monsieur. We are not your servants, to be summoned from halfway around the world."

Then why are you here, you fat fool? But out loud he said, "Christian —Monsieur le Directeur—it is precisely because we are the men who count that we must meet here today."

Gerrault threw up a meaty arm. "Pah! The television was always good enough before."

"The 'television,' monsieur, no longer works." The Central African looked disbelieving, but Avery knew Gerrault's people in Paris were clever enough to verify that the Atlantic comsat had been out of action for more than twenty-four hours. It had not been a gradual or partial failure, but an abrupt, total cessation of relayed communication.

But Gerrault simply shrugged, and his three bodyguards moved uneasily behind him. Avery shifted his gaze to Tioulang. The elderly Cambodian, Director for Asia, was not nearly so upset. K.T. was one of the originals: He had been a graduate student at Livermore before the War. He and Hamilton and some hundred others picked by Avery's father had been the founders of the new world. There were very few of them left now. Every year they must select a few more successors. Gerrault was the first director from outside the original group. *Is this the future?* He saw the same question in Tioulang's eyes. Christian was much more capable than he acted, but every year his jewels, his harems, his . . . excesses, became harder to ignore. After the old ones were gone, would he proclaim himself an emperor—or simply a god?

"K.T., Christian, you've been getting my reports. You know we have what amounts to an insurrection here. Even so, I haven't told you everything. Things have happened that you simply won't believe."

"*That* is entirely possible," said Gerrault.

Avery ignored the interruption. "Gentlemen, our enemy has spaceflight."

For a long moment there was only the sighing of the air-conditioning. Gerrault's sarcasm had evaporated, and it was Tioulang who raised protest. "But, Hamilton, the industrial base that requires! The Peace itself has only a small, unmanned program. We saw to it that all the big launch complexes were lost during the War." He realized he was rattling on with the obvious and waited for Avery to continue.

Avery motioned his aide to lay the pictures on the table. "I know, K.T. This should be impossible. But look: A fully functional sortie craft —the type the old USAF was flying just before the War—has crashed near the California-Aztlán border. This isn't a model or a mockup. It was totally destroyed in a fire subsequent to its landing, but my people assure me that it had just returned from orbit."

The two directors leaned forward to look at the holos. Tioulang said, "I take your word for this, Hamilton, but it could still be a hoax. I thought all those vehicles were accounted for, but perhaps there has been one in storage all these years. Granted, it is intimidating even as a hoax, but . . ."

"As you say. But there is no evidence of the vehicle's being dragged into the area—and that's heavy forest around the crash site. We are bringing as much of the wreck as we can back here for a close look. We should be able to discover if it was made since the War or if it is a refurbished model from before. We are also putting pressure on Albuquerque to search the old archives for evidence of a secret US launch site."

Gerrault tipped his massive form back to look at his bodyguards. Avery could imagine his suspicion. Finally the African seemed to reach a decision. He leaned forward and said quietly, "Survivors. Did you find anyone to question?"

Avery shook his head. "There were at least two aboard. One was killed on impact. The other was killed by . . . one of our investigating teams. An accident." The other's face twisted, and Avery imagined the slow death Christian would have given those responsible for any such accident. Avery had dealt quickly and harshly with the incompetents involved, but he had gotten no pleasure from it. "There was no identification on the crewman, beyond an embroidered name tag. His flight-suit was old US Air Force issue."

Tioulang steepled his fingers. "Granting the impossible, what were they up to?"

"It looks like a reconnaissance mission. We've brought the wreck back to the labs, but there is still equipment we can't identify."

Tioulang studied one of the aerial photos. "It probably came in from the north, maybe even overflew Livermore." He gave a wan smile. "History repeats. Remember that Air Force orbiter we bobbled? If they had reported what we were up to right at that critical moment . . . what a different world it would be today."

Days later Avery would wonder why Tioulang's comment didn't make him guess the truth. Perhaps it was Gerrault's interruption; the younger man was not interested in reminiscence. "This then explains why our communication satellites have failed!"

"We think so. We're trying to bring up the old radar watch we maintained through the twenties. It would help if both of you would do this, too.

"However you cut it, it seems we have our first effective opposition in nearly thirty years. Personally, I think they have been with us a long, long time. We've always ignored these 'Tinkers,' assuming that without big energy sources their technology could be no threat to us. 'Cottage industry,' we called it. When I showed you how far their electronics was ahead of ours, you seemed to think they were at most a threat to my West Coast holdings.

"Now it's clear that they have a worldwide operation in some ways equal to our own. I know there are Tinkers in Europe and China. They exist most places where there was a big electronics industry before the War. You should regard them as much a threat as I do mine."

"Yes, and we must flush out the important ones and . . ." Gerrault was in his element now. Visions of torture danced in his eyes.

"And," said Tioulang, "at the same time convince the rest of the world that the Tinkers are a direct threat to their safety. Remember that we all need goodwill. I have direct military control over most of China, but I could never keep India, Indonesia, and Japan in line if the people at the bottom didn't trust me more than their governments. There are more than twenty million people in those holdings."

"Ah, that is your problem. You are like the grasshopper, lounging in the summer of public approval. I am the industrious ant"—Gerrault looked down at his enormous torso and chuckled at the metaphor— "who has diligently worked to maintain garrisons from Oslo to Capetown. If this is 'winter' coming, I'll need no public approval." His eyes narrowed. "But I do need to know more about this new enemy of ours."

He glanced at Avery. "And I think Avery has cleverly provided us with a lever against them. I wondered why you supported their silly chess tournament in Aztlán, why you used your aircraft to transport their teams from all over the continent. Now I know: When you raided that tournament, you arrested some of the best Tinkers in the world. Oh, no doubt, just a few of them have knowledge of the conspiracy against us, but at the same time they must have many loved ones—and some of those will know more. If, one at a time, we try the prisoners for treason against Peace . . . why, I think we'll find someone who is willing to talk."

Avery nodded. He would get none of the pleasure out of the operation that Christian might. He would do only what was necessary to preserve the Peace. "And don't worry, K.T., we can do it without antagonizing the rest of our people.

"You see, the Tinkers use a lot of x- and gamma-ray lithography; they need it for microcircuit fabrication. Now, my public affairs people have put together a story that we've discovered the Tinkers are secretly upgrading these etching lasers for use as weapons lasers like the governments had before the War."

Tioulang smiled. "Ah. That's the sort of direct threat that should get us a lot of support. It's almost as effective as claiming they're involved in bioscience research."

"There." Gerrault raised his hands beneficently to his fellow directors. "We are all happy then. Your people are pacified, and we can go after the enemy with all vigor. You were right to call us, Avery; this is a matter that deserves our immediate and personal attention."

Avery felt grim pleasure in replying, "There is another matter, Christian, at least as important. Paul Hoehler is alive."

"The old-time mathematician you have such a fixation on? Yes, I know. You reported that in hushed and terrified tones several weeks ago."

"One of my best agents has infiltrated the Middle California Tinkers. She reports that Hoehler has succeeded—or is near to succeeding —in building a bobble generator."

It was the second bombshell he had laid on them, and in a way the greater. Spaceflight was one thing; several ordinary governments had had it before the War. But the bobble: For an enemy to have that was as unwelcome and incredible as hell opening a chapel. Gerrault was emphatic: "Absurd. How could one old man fall on a secret we have kept so carefully all these years?"

"You forget, Christian, that *one old man* invented the bobble in the first place! For ten years after the War, he moved from laboratory to laboratory always just ahead of us, always working on ways to bring us down. Then he disappeared so thoroughly that only I of all the originals believed he was out there somewhere plotting against us. And I was right; he has an incredible ability to survive."

"I'm sorry, Hamilton, but I have trouble believing, too. There is no hard evidence here, apparently just the word of a woman. I think you always have been overly distressed by Hoehler. He may have had some of the original ideas, but it was the rest of your father's team that really made the invention possible. Besides, it takes a fusion plant and some huge capacitors to power a generator. The Tinkers could never . . ."

Tioulang's voice trailed off as he realized that if you could hide space-launch facilities, you could certainly do the same for a fusion reactor.

"You see?" said Avery. Tioulang hadn't been in Father's research group, couldn't realize Hoehler's polymath talent. There had been others in the project, but it had been Hoehler on all the really theoretical fronts. Of course, history was not written that way. But stark after all the years, Avery remembered the rage on Hoehler's face when he realized that in addition to inventing "the monster" (as he called it), the development could never have been kept secret if he had not done the work of a lab full of specialists. It had been obvious the fellow was going to report them to LEL, and Father had trusted only Hamilton Avery to silence the mathematician. Avery had not succeeded in that assignment. It had been his first—and last—failure of resolve in all these years, but it was a failure that refused to be buried.

"He's out there, K.T., he really is. And my agent is Della Lu, who did the job in Mongolia that none of your people could. What she says you can believe. . . . Don't you see where we are if we fail to act? If they have spaceflight and the bobble, too, then they are our *superiors*. They can sweep us aside as easily as we did the old-time governments."

24

The *sabios* of the Ndelante Ali claimed the One True God knows all and sees all.

Those powers seemed Wili's, now that he had learned to use the scalp connect. He blushed to think of all the months he had dismissed symbiotic programs as crutches for weak minds. If only Jeremy —who had finally convinced him to try—could be here to see. If only Roberto Jonque Richardson were here to be crushed.

Jeremy had thought it would take months to learn. But for Wili, it was like suddenly remembering a skill he'd always had. Even Paul was surprised. It had taken a couple of days to calibrate the connector. At first, the sensations coming over the line had been subtle things, unrelated to their real significance. The mapping problem—the relating of sensation to meaning—was what took most people months. Jill had been a big help with that. Wili could talk to her at the same time he experimented with the signal parameters, telling her what he was seeing. Jill would then alter the output to match what Wili most expected. In a week he could communicate through the interface without opening his mouth or touching the keyboard. Another couple of days and he was transferring visual information over the channel.

The feeling of power was born. It was like being able to add extra rooms to his imagination. When a line of reasoning became too complex, he could simply expand into the machine's space. The low point of every day was when he had to disconnect. He was so stupid then.

Typing and vocal communication with Jill made him feel like a deaf-mute spelling out letters.

And every day he learned more tricks. Most he discovered himself, though some things—like concentration enhancement and Jill-programming—Paul showed him. Jill could proceed with projects during the time when Wili was disconnected and store results in a form that read like personal memories when Wili was able to reconnect. Using the interface that way was almost as good as being connected all the time. At least, once he reconnected, it seemed he'd been "awake" all the time.

Paul had already asked Jill to monitor the spy cameras that laced the hills around the mansion. When Wili was connected, he could watch them all himself. One hundred extra eyes.

And Wili/Jill monitored local Tinker transmissions and the Authority's recon satellites the same way. That was where the feeling of omni-science came strongest.

Both Tinkers and Peacers were waiting—and preparing in their own ways—for the secret of generating bobbles that Paul had promised. From Julian in the South to Seattle in the North and Norcross in the East, the Tinkers were withdrawing from view, trying to get their gear undercover and ready for whatever construction Paul might tell them was necessary. In the high tech areas of Europe and China, something similar was going on—though the Peace cops were so thick in Europe it was difficult to get away with anything there. Four of that continent's self-producing design machines had already been captured or destroyed.

It was harder to tell what was happening in the world's great outback. There were few Tinkers there—in all Australia, for instance, there were less than ten thousand humans—but the Authority was spread correspondingly thin. The people in those regions had radios and knew of the world situation, knew that with enough trouble elsewhere they might overthrow the local garrisons.

Except for Europe, the Authority was taking little direct action. They seemed to realize their enemy was too numerous to root out with a frontal assault. Instead the Peacers were engaged in an all-out search to find one Paul Naismith before Paul Naismith could make good on his promises to the rest of the world.

Jill?

Yes, Wili? Nothing was spoken aloud and no keys were tapped. Input/output was like imagination itself. And when Jill responded, he had a fleeting impression of the face and the smile that he would have seen in the holo if he'd been talking to her the old way. Wili could have bypassed Jill; most symbiotic programs didn't have an intermediate surrogate. But Jill was a friend. And though she occupied lots of program space, she reduced the confusion Wili still felt in dealing with the flood of input. So Wili frequently had Jill work in parallel with him, and called her when he wanted updates on the processes she supervised.

Show me the status of the search for Paul.

Wili's viewpoint was suddenly suspended over California. Silvery traces marked the flight paths of hundreds of aircraft. He sensed the altitude and speed of every craft. The picture was a summary of all Jill had learned monitoring the Authority's recon satellites and Tinker reports over the last twenty-four hours. The rectangular crisscross pattern was still centered over Northern California, though it was more diffuse and indecisive than on earlier days.

Wili smiled. Sending Della Lu's bug north had worked better than he'd hoped. The Peacers had been chasing their tails up there for more than a week. The satellites weren't doing them any good. One of the first fruits of Wili's new power was discovering how to disable the comm and recon satellites. At least, they appeared disabled to the Authority. Actually, the recon satellites were still broadcasting but according to an encryption scheme that must seem pure noise to the enemy. It had seemed an easy trick to Wili; once he conceived the possibility, he and Jill had implemented it in less than a day. But looking back—after having disconnected—Wili realized that it was deeper and trickier than his original method of tapping the satellites. What had taken him a winter of mind-busting effort was an afternoon's triviality now.

Of course, none of these tricks would have helped if Paul had not been very cautious all these years; he and Bill Morales had traveled great distances to shop at towns farther up the coast. Many Tinkers thought his hideout was in Northern California or even Oregon. As long as the Peacers didn't pick up any of the few people who had actually visited here—say at the NCC meeting—they might be safe.

Wili frowned. There was still the greatest threat. Miguel Rosas probably did not know the location, though he must suspect it was in Middle California. But Wili was sure Colonel Kaladze knew. It could only be a matter of time before Mike and the Lu woman ferreted out the secret. If subtlety were unsuccessful, then Lu would no doubt call in the Peace goons and try to beat it out of him. *Are they still on the farm?*

Yes. And there have been no outgoing calls from them. However, the Colonel's ten-day promise lapses tomorrow. Then Kaladze would no doubt let Lu call her "family" in San Francisco. But if she hadn't called in the Army already, she must not have anything critical to report to her bosses.

Wili had not told Paul what he knew of Mike and Lu. Perhaps he should. But after trying to tell Kaladze . . . Instead he'd been trying to identify Della Lu with independent evidence. More than ten percent of Jill's time was spent in the effort. So far she had nothing definite. The story about relatives in the Bay Area appeared to be true. If he had some way of tapping Peacer communication or records, things would be different. He saw now he should have disabled their recon satellites alone. If their comsats were usable, it would give them some advantage—but perhaps he could eventually break into their high crypto channels. As it was, he knew very little about what went on inside the Authority.

. . . and sometimes, he really wondered if Colonel Kaladze might be right. Wili had been half-delirious that morning on the boat; Mike and Della had been several meters away. Was it possible he'd misinterpreted what he heard? Was it possible they were innocent after all? *No!* By the One True God, he had heard what he had heard. Kaladze hadn't been there.

25

Sunlight still lay on the hills, but the lowlands and Lake Lompoc were shrouded in blue shadows. Paul sat on his veranda and listened to the news that Wili's electronic spies brought in from all over the world.

There was a small cough and Naismith looked up. For an instant he thought it was Allison standing there. Then he noticed how carefully she stood between him and the holo surface built into the wall. If he moved more than a few centimeters, parts of the image would be cut off. This was only Jill.

"Hi." He motioned for her to come and sit. She stepped forward, careful to generate those little moving sounds that made her projection seem more real, and sat in the image of a chair. Paul watched her face as she approached. There really were differences, he realized. Allison was very pretty, but he had made Jill's face beautiful. And of course the personalities were subtly different, too. It could not have been otherwise considering that he had done his design from memories forty-five years stale (or embellished), and considering that the design had grown by itself in response to his reactions. The real Allison was more outgoing, more impatient. And Allison's mere presence seemed to be changing Jill. The interface program had been much quieter these last days.

He smiled at her. "You've got the new bobble theory all worked out?"

She grinned back and was more like Allison than ever. "Your theory. I do nothing but crunch away—"

"I set up the theory. It would take a hundred lifetimes for me to do the symbolic math and see the theory's significance." It was a game they—he—had played many times before. The back-and-forth had always made Jill seem so real. "What have you got?"

"Everything seems consistent. There are a lot of things that were barred under your old theory, that are still impossible: It's still impossible to burst a bobble before its time. It's impossible to generate a bobble around an existing one. On the other hand—in theory at least —it should be possible to balk an enemy bobbler."

"Hmm . . ." Simply carrying a small bobble was a kind of defense against bobble attack—a very risky defense, once noticed: It would force the attacker to project smaller bobbles, or off-center ones, trying to find a volume that wasn't "banned." A device that could prevent bobbles from being formed nearby would be a tremendous improvement, and Naismith had guessed the new theory might allow such, but . . .

"Betcha that last will be an *engineering* impossibility for a long time. We should concentrate on making a low-power bobbler. That looks hard enough."

"Yes. Wili's right on schedule with that."

Jill's image suddenly froze, then flicked out of existence. Naismith heard the veranda door slide open. "Hi, Paul," came Allison's voice. She walked up the steps. "You out here by yourself?"

". . . Yes. Just thinking."

She walked to the edge of the veranda and looked westward. These last weeks, every day had brought more change in Paul's life and in the world beyond the mountains than a normal year. Yet for Allison, it was different. Her world had turned inside out in the space of an hour. He knew the present rate of change was agonizingly slow for her. She paced the stone flags, stopping occasionally to glare off into the sunset at the Vandenberg Bobble.

Allison. Allison. Few old men had dreams come quite so stunningly true. She was so young; her energy seemed to flash about her in every stride, in every quick movement of her arms. In some ways the memories of Allison lost were less hurtful than the present reality. Still, he was glad he had not succeeded in disguising what became of Paul Hoehler.

Allison suddenly looked back at him, and smiled. "Sorry about the pacing."

"No problem. I . . ."

She waved toward the west. The air was so clear that—except for the lake and the coastline reflected in its base—the Dome was almost invisible. "When will it burst, Paul? There were three thousand of us there the day I left. They had guns, aircraft. When will they come out?"

A month ago he would not have thought of the question. Two weeks ago he couldn't have answered. In those weeks a theory had been trashed and his new theory born. It was totally untested, but soon, soon that would change. "Uh. My answer's still guessing, Allison: The Authority technique, the only way I could think of then, is a brute force method. With it, the lifetime is about fifty years. So now I can represent radius or mass as a perturbation series about a fifty-year decay time. The smallest bobbles the Authority made were about ten meters across. They burst first. Your sortie craft was trapped in a thirty-meter bobble; it decayed a little later." Paul realized he was wandering and tried to force his answer into the mold she must want. He thought a moment. "Vandenberg ought to last fifty-five years."

"Five more years. Damn it." She walked back across the veranda. "I guess you'll have to win without them. I was wondering why you hadn't told your friends about me—you haven't even told them that time stops inside the bobbles. I thought maybe you expected to surprise the Peacers with their long-dead victims suddenly alive."

"You're close. You, me, Wili, and the Morales are the only ones who know. The Authority hasn't guessed—Wili says they've carted your orbiter up to Livermore as if it were full of clues. No doubt the fools think they've stumbled on some new conspiracy. . . . But then, I guess it's not so stupid. I'll bet you didn't have any paper records aboard the orbiter."

"Right. Even our notepads were display flats. We could trash everything in seconds if we fell among unfriendlies. The fire would leave them with nothing but slagged optical memory. And if they don't have the old fingerprint archives, they're not going to identify Fred or Angus."

"Anyway, I've told the Tinkers to be ready, that I'm going to tell them how to make bobble generators. Even then, I may not say anything about the stasis effect. That's something that could give us a real edge, but only if we use the knowledge at the right time. I don't want some leak to blow it."

Allison turned as if to pace back to the edge of the veranda, then noticed the display that Paul had been studying. Her hand rested lightly on his shoulder as she leaned over to look at the displays. "Looks like a recon pattern," she said.

"Yes. Wili and Jill synthesized it from the satellites we're tapping. This shows where Authority aircraft have been searching."

"For you."

"Probably." He touched the keyboard at the margin of the flat, and the last few days' activity were displayed.

"Those bums." There was no lightness in her voice. "They destroyed our country and then stole our own procedures. Those search patterns look SOP 1997 for medium-level air recon. I bet your damn Peacers never had an original thought in their lives. . . . Hmm. Run that by again." She knelt to look closely at the daily summaries. "I think today's sorties were the last for that area, Paul. Don't be surprised if they move the search several hundred klicks in the next day or two." In some ways, Allison's knowledge was fifty years dead and useless—in other ways, it could be just what they needed.

Paul gave a silent prayer of thanks to Hamilton Avery for having kept the heat on all these years, for having forced Paul Hoehler to disguise his identity and his location through decades when there would have otherwise been no reason to. "If they shift further north, fine. If they come all the way south. Hmm. We're well hidden, but we wouldn't last more than a couple days under that sort of scrutiny. Then . . ." He drew a finger across his throat and made a croaking noise.

"No way you could put this show on the road, huh?"

"Eventually we could. Have to start planning for it. I have an enclosed wagon. It may be big enough for the essential equipment. But right now, Allison . . . Look, we don't yet have anything but a lot of theories. I'm translating the physics into problems Wili can handle. With Jill, he's putting them into software as fast as he can."

"He seems to spend his time daydreaming, Paul."

Naismith shook his head. "Wili's the best." The boy had picked up symbiotic programming faster than Paul had ever seen, faster than he'd thought possible. The technique improved almost any programmer, but in Wili's case, it had turned a first-rank genius into something Naismith could no longer completely understand. Even when he was linked with Wili and Jill, the details of their algorithms were beyond him. It was curious, because off the symbiosis Wili was not that much brighter than the old man. Paul wondered if he could have been that good, too, if he had started young. "I think we're nearly there, Allison. Based on what we understand now, it ought to be possible to make bobbles with virtually no energy input. The actual hardware should be something Jill can prototype here."

Allison didn't come off her knees. Her face was just centimeters from his. "That Jill program is something. Just the motion holo for the face would have swamped our best array processors. . . . But why make it look like me, Paul? After all those years, did I really mean so much?"

Naismith tried to think of something flippant and diversionary, but no words came. She looked at him a second longer, and he wondered if she could see the young man trapped within.

"Oh, *Paul.*" Then her arms were around him, her cheek next to his. She held him as one would hold something very fragile, very old.

Two days later, Wili was ready.

They waited till after dark to make the test. In spite of Paul's claims, Wili wasn't sure how big the bobble would be, and even if it did not turn out to be a monster, its mirrorlike surface would be visible for hundreds of kilometers to anyone looking in the right direction in the daytime.

The three of them walked to the pond north of the house. Wili carried the bulky transmitter for his symb link. Near the pond's edge he set his equipment down and slipped on the scalp connector. Then he lit a candle and placed it on a large tree stump. It was a tiny spot of yellow, bright only because all else was so dark. A gray thread of smoke rose from the glow.

"We think the bobble, it will be small, but we don't want to take chances. Jill is going to make its lower edge to snip the top of this candle. Then if we're wrong, and it is huge—"

"Then as the night cools, the bobble will rise and be just another floater. By morning it could be many kilometers from here." Paul nodded. "Clever . . ."

He and Allison backed further away, Wili following. From thirty meters, the candle was a flickering yellow star on the stump. Wili motioned them to sit; even if the bobble was super-large, its lower surface would still clear them.

"You don't need any power source at all?" said Allison. "The Peace Authority uses fusion generators and you can do it for free?"

"In principle, it isn't difficult—once you have the right insight, once you know what really goes on inside the bobbles. And the new process is not quite free. We're using about a thousand joules here—compared to the gigajoules of the Authority generators. The trade-off is in complexity. If you have a fusion generator backing you up, you can bobble practically anything you can locate. But if you're like us, with solar cells and small capacitors, then you must finesse it.

"The projection needs to be supervised, and it's no ordinary process control problem. This test is about the easiest case: The target is motionless, close by, and we only want a one-meter field. Even so, it will involve—how much crunching do we need, Wili?"

"She needs thirty seconds initial at about ten billion flops, and then maybe one microsecond for 'assembly'—at something like a trillion."

Paul whistled. A *trillion* floating-point operations per second! Wili had said he could implement the discovery, but Paul hadn't realized just how expensive it might be. The gear would not be very portable. And long distance or very large bobbles might not be feasible.

Wili seemed to sense his disappointment. "We think we can do it with a slower processor. It maybe takes many minutes for the setup, but you could still bobble things that don't move or are real close."

"Yeah, we'll optimize later. Let's make a bobble, Wili."

The boy nodded.

Seconds passed. Something—an owl—thuttered over the clearing, and the candle went out. Nuts. He had hoped it would stay lit. It would have been a nice demonstration of the stasis effect to have the candle still burning later on when the bobble burst.

"Well?" Wili said. "What do you think?"

"You did it!" said Paul. The words were somewhere between a question and an exclamation.

"Jill did, anyway. I better grab it before it floats away."

Wili slipped off the scalp connector and sprinted across the clearing. He was already coming back before Naismith had walked halfway to the tree stump. The boy was holding something in front of him, something light on top and dark underneath. Paul and Allison moved close. It was about the size of a large beach ball, and in its upper hemisphere he could see reflected stars, even the Milky Way, all the way down to the dark of the tree line surrounding the pond. Three silhouettes marked the reflections of their own heads. Naismith extended his hand, felt it slide silkily off the bobble, felt the characteristic bloodwarm heat —the reflection of his hand's thermal radiation.

Wili had his arms extended around its girth and his chin pushed down on the top. He looked like a comedian doing a mock weight lift. "It feels like it will shoot from my hands if I don't hold it every way."

"Probably could. There's no friction."

Allison slipped her hand across the surface. "So that's a bobble. Will this one last fifty years, like the one . . . Angus and I were in?"

Paul shook his head. "No. That's for big ones done the old way. Eventually, I expect to have very flexible control, with duration only loosely related to size. How long does Jill estimate this one will last, Wili?"

Before the boy could reply, Jill's voice interrupted from the interface box. "There's a PANS bulletin coming over the high-speed channels. It puffs out to a thirty-minute program. I'm summarizing:

"Big story about threat to the Peace. Biggest since Huachuca plague-time. Says the Tinkers are the villains. Their leaders were captured in La Jolla raids last month. . . . The broadcast has video of Tinker 'weapons labs,' pictures of sinister-looking prisoners. . . .

"Prisoners to be tried for Treason against the Peace, starting immediately, in Los Angeles.

". . . all government and corporate stations must rebroadcast this at normal speed every six hours for the next two days."

There was a long silence after she finished. Wili held up the bobble. "They picked the wrong time to put the squeeze on *us!*"

Naismith shook his head. "It's the worst possible time for us. We're being forced to use this"—he patted the bobble—"when we've barely got a proof of principle. It puts us right where that punk Avery wants us."

26

The rain was heavy and very, very warm. High in the clouds, lightning chased itself around and around the Vandenberg Dome, never coming to earth. Thunder followed the arching, cloud-smeared glows.

Della Lu had seen more rain the last two weeks than would fall in a normal year in Beijing. It was a fitting backdrop for the dull routine of life here. If Avery hadn't finally gone for the spy trials, she would be seriously planning to escape Red Arrow hospitality—blown cover or not.

"Hey, you tired already? Or just daydreaming?" Mike had stopped and was looking back at her. He stood, arms akimbo, apparently disgusted. The transparent rain jacket made his tan shirt and pants glint metallic even in the gray light.

Della walked a little faster to catch up. They continued in silence for a hundred meters. No doubt they made an amusing pair: Two figures shrouded in rain gear, one tall, one so short. Since Wili's ten-day "probation period" had lapsed, the two of them had taken a walk every day. It was something she had insisted on, and—for a change—Rosas hadn't resisted. So far she had snooped as far north as Lake Lompoc and east to the ferry crossing.

Without Mike, her walks would've had to have been with the womenfolk. That would have been tricky. The women were *protected*, and had little freedom or responsibility. She spent most of every day with them, doing the light manual labor that was considered appropriate to her sex. She had been careful to be popular, and she had learned a lot, but all local intelligence. Just as with families in San Francisco, the women were not privy to what went on in the wider world. They were valued, but second-class, citizens. Even so, they were clever; it would be difficult to look in the places that really interested her without raising their suspicions.

Today was her longest walk, up to the highlands that overlooked Red Arrow's tiny sea landing. Despite Mike's passive deceptions, she had put together a pretty good picture of Old Kaladze's escape system. At least she knew its magnitude and technique. It was a small payoff for the boredom and the feeling that she was being held offstage from events she should be directing.

All that could change with the spy trials. If she could just light a fire under the right people . . .

The timbered path went back and forth across the hill they climbed. There were many repairs, and several looked quite recent, yet there were also washouts. It was like most things among the Tinkers. Their electronic gadgets were superlative (though it was clear now that the surveillance devices Avery had discovered were rare and expensive items amongst the Tinkers; they didn't normally spy on each other). But they were labor poor, and without power equipment, things like road maintenance and laundry were distinctly nineteenth century. And Della had the calluses to prove it.

Finally they reached the overlook point. A steady breeze swept across the hill, blowing the rain into their faces. There was only one tree at the top, though it was a fine, large conifer growing from the highest point. There was some kind of platform about halfway up.

Rosas put his arm across her shoulder, urging her toward the tree. "They had a tree house up here when I was a kid. There ought to be a good view."

Wood steps were built into the tree trunk. She noticed a heavy metallic cable that followed the steps upward. Electronics even here? Then she realized that it was a lightning guide. The Tinkers were very careful with their children.

Seconds later they were on the platform. The cabin was clean and dry with soft padding on the floor. There was a view south and west, somehow contrived to keep out the wind and rain. They shrugged out of their rain jackets and sat for a moment enjoying the sound of wet that surrounded this pocket of dry comfort. Mike crawled to the south-facing window. "A lot of good it will do you, but there it is."

The forested hills dropped away from the overlook. The coast was about four kilometers away, but the rain was so heavy that she had only a vague impression of sand dunes and marching surf. It looked like there was a small breakwater, but no boats at anchor. The landing was not actually on Red Arrow property, but they used it more than anyone else. Mike claimed that more people came to the farm from the ocean than overland. Della doubted that. It sounded like another little deception.

The undersheriff backed away from the opening and leaned against the wall beside her. "Has it really been worth it, Della?" There was a faint edge in his voice. It was clear by now that he had no intention of denouncing her—and implicating himself at the same time. But he was not hers. She had dealt with traitors before, men whose self-interest made them simple, reliable tools. Rosas was not such. He was waiting for the moment when the damage he could do her would be greatest. Till then he played the role of reluctant ally.

Indeed, had it been worth the trouble? He smiled, almost triumphantly. "You've been stuck here for more than two weeks. You've learned a little bit about one small corner of the ungoverned lands, and one group of Tinkers. I think you're more important to the Peacers than that. You're like a high-value piece voluntarily taken out of the game."

Della smiled back. He was saying aloud her own angry thoughts. The only thing that had kept her going was the thought that just a little more snooping might ferret out the location of Paul Hoehler/Naismith. It had seemed such an easy thing. But she gradually realized that Mike—and almost everyone else—didn't know where the old man lived. Maybe Kaladze did, but she'd need an interrogation lab to pry it out of him. Her only progress along that line had been right at the beginning, when she tagged the black boy's horse with a tracer.

Hallelujah, all that had changed. There was a chance now that she was in the best of strategic positions.

Mike's eyes narrowed, and Della realized he sensed some of her triumph. *Damn.* They had spent too much time together, had too many conversations that were not superficial. His hand closed on her upper arm and she was pulled close to his face. "Okay. What is it? What are you going to spring on us?" Her arm suddenly felt as though trapped in a vice.

Della suppressed reflexes that would have left him gargling on a crushed windpipe. Best that he think he had the age-old macho edge. She pretended shocked speechlessness. How much to say? When they were alone, Mike often spoke of her real purpose at Red Arrow. She knew he wasn't trying to compromise her to hidden listeners—he could do that directly whenever he chose. And he knew Red Arrow so well, it was unlikely they would be bugged without his knowledge. So the only danger was in telling him too much, in giving him the motive to blow the whole game. But maybe she should tell him a little; if it all came as a surprise, he might be harder to control. She tried to shrug. "I've got a couple maybes going for me. Your friend Hoehler—Naismith—says he has a prototype bobble generator. Maybe he does. In any case, it will be a while before the rest of you can build such. In the meantime, if the Peace can throw you off balance, can get you and Naismith to overextend yourselves . . ."

"The trials."

"Right." She wondered what Mike's reaction would be if he knew that she had recommended immediate treason trials for the La Jolla hostages. He'd made sure there were Kaladzes in earshot when she was allowed to call her family in San Francisco. She had sounded completely innocent, just telling her parents that she was safe among the Middle California Tinkers, though she mustn't say just where. No doubt Rosas guessed that some sort of prearranged signal scheme was being used, but he could never have known how elaborate it was. Tone codes were something that went right by native speakers of English. "The trials. If they could be used to panic Kaladze and his friends, we might get a look at Naismith's best stuff before it can do the Peace any real harm."

Mike laughed, his grip relaxing slightly. "*Panic* Nikolai Sergeivich? You might as well think to panic a charging bear."

Della did not fully plan what she did next, and that was very unusual for her. Her free hand moved up behind his neck, caressing the short cut hair. She raised herself to kiss him. Rosas jerked back for an instant, then responded. After a moment, she felt his weight on her and they slid to the soft padding that covered the floor of the tree house. Her arms roamed across his neck and wide shoulders and the kiss continued.

She had never before used her body to ensure loyalty. It had never been necessary. It certainly had never before been an attractive prospect. And it was doubtful it could do any good here. Mike had fallen to them out of honor; he could not rationalize the deaths he had caused. In his way, he was as unchangeable as she.

One of his arms wrapped around her back while his free hand pulled at her blouse. His hand slid under the fabric, across her smooth skin, to her breasts. The caresses were eager, rough. There was rage . . . and something else. Della stretched out against him, forcing one of her legs between his. For a long while the world went away and they let their passion speak for them.

. . . Lightning played its ring dance along the Dome that towered so high above them. When the thunder paused in its following march, they could hear the *shish* of warm rain continue all around.

Rosas held her gently now, his fingers slowly tracing the curve of her hip and waist. "What do you get out of being a Peace cop, Della? If you were one of the button-pushers, sitting safe and cozy up in Livermore, I could understand. But you've risked your life stooging for a tyranny, and turning me into something I never thought I'd be. Why?"

Della watched the lightning glow in the rain. She sighed. "Mike, I am for the Peace. Wait. I don't mean that as rote Authority mumbo jumbo. We *do* have something like peace all over the world now. The price is a tyranny, though milder than any in history. The price is twentieth-century types like me, who would sell their own grandmothers for an ideal. Last century produced nukes and bobbles and warplagues. You have been brushed by the plagues—that alone is what turned you into 'something you never thought you'd be.' But the others are just as bad. By the end of the century, those weapons were becoming cheaper and cheaper. Small nations were getting them. If the War hadn't come, I'll bet subnational groups and criminals would have had them. The human race could not survive mass-death technology so widely spread. The Peace has meant the end of sovereign nations and their control of technologies that could kill us all. Our only mistake was in not going far enough. We didn't regulate high tech electronics—and we're paying for that now."

The other was silent, but the anger was gone from his face. Della came to her knees and looked around. She almost laughed. It looked as if a small bomb had gone off in the tree house; their clothes were thrown all across the floor pads. She began dressing. After a moment, so did Mike. He didn't speak until they had on their rain slickers and had raised the trapdoor.

He grinned lopsidedly and stuck his hand out to Della. "Enemies?" he said.

"For sure." She grinned back, and they shook on it.

And even as they climbed out of the tree, she was wondering what it would take to move old Kaladze. Not panic; Mike was right about that. What about shame? Or anger?

Della's chance came the next day. The Kaladze clan had gathered for lunch, the big meal of the day. As was expected of a woman, Lu had helped with the cooking and laying out of the dinnerware, and the serving of the meal. Even after she was seated at the long, heavily laden table, there were constant interruptions to go out and get more food or replace this or that item.

The Authority channels were full of the "Treason against Peace" trials that Avery was staging in LA. Already there had been some death sentences. She knew Tinkers all across the continent were in frantic communication, and there was an increasing sense of dread. Even the women felt it. Naismith had announced his prototype bobble generator. A design had also been transmitted. Unfortunately, the only working model depended on processor networks and programs that would take the rest of the world weeks to grow. And even then, there were problems with the design that would cost still more time to overcome.

The menfolk took these two pieces of news and turned lunch into a debate. It was the first time she had seen them talk policy at a meal; it showed how critical the situation was. In principle the Tinkers now had the same ultimate weapon as the Authority. But the weapon was no good to them yet. In fact, if the Authority learned about it before the Tinkers had generators in production, it might precipitate the military attack they all feared. So what should be done about the prisoners in Los Angeles?

Lu sat quietly through fifteen minutes of this, until it became clear that caution was winning and the Kaladzes were going to keep a low profile until they could safely take advantage of Naismith/Hoehler's invention. Then she stood up with a shrill, inarticulate shout. The dining hall was instantly silent. The Kaladzes looked at her with shocked surprise. The woman sitting next to her made fluttering motions for her to sit down. Instead, Della shouted down the long table, "You cowardly *fools!* You would sit here and dither while they execute our people one by one in Los Angeles. You have a weapon now, this bobble generator. And even if you are not willing to risk your own necks, there are plenty of noble houses in Aztlán that are; at least a dozen of their senior sons were taken in La Jolla."

At the far end of the table, Nikolai Sergeivich came slowly to his feet. Even at that distance, he seemed to tower over her diminutive 155 centimeters. "Miss Lu. It is not we who have the bobble generator, but Paul Naismith. You know that he has only one, and that it is not completely practical. He won't give us—"

Della slammed the flat of her hand on the table, the pistol-shot noise cutting the other off and dragging everyone's attention back to her. "Then *make him!* He can't exist without you. He must be made to understand that our own flesh and blood are at stake here—" She stepped back from the table and looked them all up and down, then put surprise and scorn on her face. "But that's not true of you, is it? *My own brother is one of the hostages.* But to you, they are merely fellow Tinkers."

Under his stubbly beard, Kaladze's face became very pale. Della was taking a chance. Publicly disrespectful women were rare here, and when they surfaced—even as guests—they could expect immediate expulsion. But Della had gone a calculated distance *beyond* disrespect. She had attacked their courage, their manhood. She had spoken aloud of the guilt which—she hoped—was lying just below their caution.

Kaladze found his voice and said, "You are wrong, madam. They are not *merely* fellow Tinkers, but our brothers, too." And Della knew she had won. The Authority would get a crack at that bobble generator while it was still easy pickings.

She sat meekly down, her eyes cast shyly at the table. Two large tears started down her cheeks. But she said nothing more. Inside, a Cheshire cat smile spread from ear to ear: for the victory, and for the chance to get back at them for all the days of dumb servility. From the corner of her eye, she saw the stricken look on Mike's face. She had guessed right there, too. He would say nothing. He knew she lied, but those lies *were* a valid appeal to honor. He was caught, even knowing, in the trap with the others.

27

ztlán encompassed most of what had been Southern and Baja
California. It also claimed much of Arizona, though this was
sharply disputed by the Republic of New Mexico. In fact, Aztlán
was a loose confederation of local rulers, each with an immense estate.

Perhaps it was the challenge of the Authority Enclave in old Downtown, but nowhere in Aztlán were the castles grander than in North
Los Angeles. And of those castles, that of the Alcalde del Norte was a
giant among giants.

The carriage and its honor guard moved quickly up the well-main-
tained old-world road that led to El Norte's main entrance. In the
darkened interior, a single passenger—one Wili Wáchendon—sat on
velvet cushions and listened to the *clopclop* of the carriage team and
outriders. He was being treated like a lord. Well, not quite. He couldn't
get over the look of stunned surprise on the faces of the Aztlán troops
when they saw the travel-grimed black kid they were to escort from
Ojai to LA. He looked through tinted bulletproof glass at things he had
never expected to see—not by daylight anyway. On the right, the hill
rose sheer, pocked every fifty meters by machine-gun nests; on the left,
he saw a pike fence half-hidden in the palms. He remembered such
pikes, and what happened to unlucky burglars.

Beyond the palms, Wili could see much of the Basin. It was as big as
some countries, and—not even counting the Authority personnel in the
Enclave—there were more than eighty thousand people out there,

making it one of the largest cities on Earth. By now, midafternoon, the wood and petroleum cooking stoves of that population had raised a pall of darkish smoke that hung just under the temperature inversion and made it impossible to see the far hills.

They reached the southern ramparts and crossed the flagstone perimeter that surrounded the Alcalde's mansion. They rolled by a long building fronted with incredible sweeps of perfectly matched plate glass. There was not a bullet hole or shatter star to be seen. No enemy had reached this level in many years. The Alcalde had firm control of the land for kilometers on every side.

The carriage turned inward, and retainers rushed to slide open the glass walls. Wagon, horses, and guard continued inward, past more solid walls; this meeting would take place beyond sight of spying eyes. Wili gathered his equipment. He slipped on the scalp connector, but it was scant comfort. His processor was programmed for one task, and the interface gave him none of the omniscience he felt when working with Jill.

Wili felt like a chicken at a coyote convention. But there was a difference, he kept telling himself. He smiled at the collected coyotes and set his dusty gear on the glistening floor: *This* chicken laid bobbles.

He stood in the middle of the Alcalde's hall of audience, alone there except for the two stewards who had brought him the last hundred meters from the carriage. Four Jonques sat on a dais five meters away. They were not the most titled nobles in Aztlán—though one of them was the Alcalde—but he recognized the embroidery on their jackets. These were men the Ndelante Ali had never dared to burgle.

To the side, subordinate but not cringing, stood three very old blacks. Wili recognized Ebenezer, Pasadena Sabio of the Ndelante, a man so old and set in his ways that he had never even learned Spanish. He needed interpreters to convey his wishes to his own people. Of course, this increased his appearance of wisdom. As near as could be over such a large area, these seven men ruled the Basin and the lands to the east—ruled all but the Downtown and the Authority Enclave.

Wili's impudence was not lost on the coyotes. The youngest of the Jonque lords leaned forward to look down upon him. "*This* is Naismith's emissary? With *this* we are to bobble the Downtown, and rescue our brothers? It's a joke."

The youngest of the blacks—a man in his seventies—whispered in Ebenezer's ear, probably translating the Jonque's comments into English. The Old One's glance was cold and penetrating, and Wili wondered if Ebenezer remembered all the trouble a certain scrawny burglar had caused the Ndelante.

Wili bowed low to the seated noblemen. When he spoke it was in standard Spanish with what he hoped was a Middle California accent. It would be best to convince these people that he was not a native of Aztlán. "My Lords and Wise Ones, it is true that I am a mere messenger, a mere technician. But I have Naismith's invention here with me, I know how to operate it, and I know how it can be used to free the Authority's prisoners."

The Alcalde, a pleasant-looking man in his fifties, raised an eyebrow and said mildly, "You mean your companions are carrying it—disassembled perhaps?"

Companions? Wili reached down and opened his pack. "No, My Lord," he said, withdrawing the generator and processor, "this is the bobbler. Given the plans that Paul Naismith has broadcast, the Tinkers should be able to make these by the hundreds within six weeks. For now this is the only working model." He showed the ordinary-looking processor box around. Few things could look less like a weapon, and Wili could see the disbelief growing on their faces. A demonstration was in order. He concentrated briefly to let the interface know the parameters.

Five seconds passed and a perfect silver sphere just . . . appeared in the air before Wili's face. The bobble wasn't more than ten centimeters across, but it might have been ten kilometers for the reaction of his audience. He gave it the lightest of pushes, and the sphere—weighing exactly as much as an equivalent volume of air—drifted across the hall toward the nobles. Before it had traveled a meter, air currents had deflected it. The youngest of the Jonques, the loudmouthed one, shed his dignity and jumped off the dais to grab at the bobble.

"By God, it's real!" he said as he felt its surface.

Wili just smiled and imaged another command sequence. A second and a third sphere floated across the room. For bobbles this size, where the target was close by and homogeneous, the computations were so simple he could generate an almost continuous stream. For a few moments his audience lost some of its dignity.

Finally old Ebenezer raised a hand and said to Wili in English, "So, boy, you have all the Authority has. You can bobble all Downtown, and we go in and pick up the pieces. All their armies won't stand up to this."

Jonque heads jerked around, and Wili knew they understood the question. Most of them understood English and Spañolnegro—though they often pretended otherwise. He could see the processors humming away in their scheming minds: With this weapon, they could do a good deal more than rescue the hostages and boot the Authority out of Aztlán. If the Peacers were to be replaced, why shouldn't it be by them? And—as Wili had admitted—they had a six weeks' head start on the rest of the world.

Wili shook his head. "No, Wise One. You'd need more power—though still nothing like the fusion power the Authority uses. But even more important, this little generator isn't fast enough. The biggest it can make is about four hundred meters across, and to do that takes special conditions and several minutes setup time."

"Bah. So it's a toy. You could decapitate a few Authority troopers with it maybe, but when they bring out their machine guns and their aircraft you are dead." Señor Loudmouth was back in form. He reminded Wili of Roberto Richardson. Too bad this was going to help the likes of them.

"It's no toy, My Lord. If you follow the plan Paul Naismith has devised, it can rescue all the hostages." Actually it was a plan that Wili had thought of after the first test, when he had felt Jill's test bobble sliding around in his arms. But it would not do to say the scheme came from anyone less than Paul. "There are things about bobbles that you don't know yet, that no one, not even the Authority, knows yet."

"And what are those things, sir?" There was courtesy without sarcasm in the Alcalde's voice.

Across the hall, a couple entered the room. For an instant all Wili could see was their silhouettes against the piped sky light. But that was enough. "You two!" Mike looked almost as shocked as Wili felt, but Lu just smiled.

"Kaladze's representatives," the Alcalde supplied.

"By the One God, no! These are the Authority's representatives!"

"See here." It was Loudmouth. "These two have been vouched for by Kaladze, and he's the fellow who got this all organized."

178

"I'm not saying anything with them around."

Dead silence greeted this refusal, and Wili felt sudden, physical fear. The Jonque lords had very interesting rooms beneath their castles, places with . . . effective . . . equipment for persuading people to talk. This was going to be like the confrontation with the Kaladzes, only bloodier.

The Alcalde said, "I don't believe you. We've checked the Kaladzes carefully. We've even dismissed our own court so that this meeting would involve just those with the need to know. "But"—he sighed, and Wili saw that in some ways he was more flexible (or less trusting, anyway) than Nikolai Sergeivich—"perhaps it would be safer if you only spoke of what must be done, rather than the secrets behind it all. Then we will judge the risks, and decide if we must have more information just now."

Wili looked at Rosas and Lu. Was it possible to do this without giving away the secret—at least until it was too late for the Authority to counter it? Perhaps. "Are the hostages still being held on the top floor of the Tradetower?"

"The top two floors. Even with aircraft, an assault would be suicide."

"Yes, My Lord. But there is another way. I will need forty Julian-thirty-three storage cells"—other brands would do, but he was sure the Aztlán make was available—"and access to your weather service. Here is what you have to do. . . ." It wasn't until several hours later that Wili looked back and realized that the cripple from Glendora had been giving orders to the rulers of Aztlán and the wise men of the Ndelante Ali. If only Uncle Sly could have seen it.

Early afternoon the next day:

Wili crouched in the tenement ruins just east of the Downtown and studied the display. It was driven by a telescope the Ndelante had planted on the roof. The day was so clear that the view might have been that of a hawk hovering on the outskirts of the Enclave. Looking into the canyons between those buildings, Wili could see dozens of automobiles whisking Authority employees through the streets. Hundreds of bicycles—property of lower-ranking people—moved more slowly along the margins of the streets. And the pedestrians: There were actually crushes of people on the sidewalks by the larger buildings. An occasional helicopter buzzed through the spaces above. It was like some vision off an old video disk, but this was *real* and happening right now, one of the few places on Earth where the bustling past still lived.

Wili shut down the display and looked up at the faces—both Jonque and black—that surrounded him. "That's not too much help for this job. Winning is going to depend on how good your spies are."

"They're good enough." It was Ebenezer's sour-faced aide. The Ndelante Ali was a big organization, but Wili had a dark suspicion that the fellow recognized him from before. Getting home to Paul would depend on keeping his "friends" here intimidated by Naismith's reputation and gadgets. "The Peacers like to be served by people as well as machines. The Faithful have been in the Tradetower as late as this morning. The hostages are all on the top two floors. The next two floors are empty and alarm-ridden, and below that is at least one floor full of Peace Troopers. The utility core is also occupied, and you notice there is a helicopter and fixed-wing patrol. You'd almost think they're expecting a twentieth century armored assault, and not . . ."

And not one scrawny teenager and his miniature bobble blower. Wili silently completed the other's dour implication. He glanced at his hands: skinny maybe, but if he kept gaining weight as he had been these last weeks, he would soon be far from scrawny. And he felt like he could take on the Authority and the Jonques and the Ndelante Ali all at once. Wili grinned at the *sabio.* "What I've got is more effective than tanks and bombs. If you're sure exactly where they are, I'll have them out by nightfall." He turned to the Alcalde's man, a mild-looking old fellow who rarely spoke but got unnervingly crisp obedience from his men. "Were you able to get my equipment upstairs?"

"Yes, sir." *Sir!*

"Let's go, then." They walked back into the main part of the ruin, carefully staying in the shadows and out of sight of the aircraft that droned overhead. The tenement had once been thirty meters high, with row on row of external balconies looking west. Most of the facing had long ago collapsed, and the stairwells were exposed to the sky. The Alcalde's man was devious, though. Two of the younger Jonques had climbed an interior elevator shaft and rigged a sling to hoist the gear and their elders to the fourth-story vantage point that Wili required.

One by one, Ndelante and Jonques ascended. Wili knew such cooperation between the blood enemies would have been a total shock to most of the Faithful. These groups fought and killed under other circumstances—and used each other to justify all sorts of sacrifices from their own peoples. Those struggles were real and deadly, but the secret cooperation was real, too. Two years earlier, Wili had chanced on that secret; it was what finally turned him against the Ndelante.

The fourth-floor hallway creaked ominously under their feet. Outside it had been hot; in here it was like a dark oven. Through holes in the ancient linoleum, Wili could see into the wrecks of rooms and hallways below. Similar holes in the ceiling provided the hallway's only light. One of the Jonques opened a side door and stood carefully apart as Wili and the Ndelante people entered.

More than a half-tonne of Julian-thirty-three storage cells were racked against an interior wall. The balcony side of the room sagged precariously. Wili unpacked the processor and the bobble generator and set about connecting them to the Julians. The others squatted by the wall or in the hallway beyond. Rosas and Lu were there; Kaladze's representatives could not be denied, though Wili had managed to persuade the Alcalde's man to keep them—especially Della—away from the equipment, and away from the window.

Della looked up at him and smiled a strange, friendly smile; strange because no one else was looking to be taken in by the lie. *When will she make her move?* Would she try to signal to her bosses, or somehow steal the equipment herself? Last night, Wili had thought long and hard about how to defeat her. He had the self-bobbling parameters all ready. Bobbling himself and the equipment would be a last resort, since the current model didn't have much flexibility—he would be taken out of the game for about a year. More likely, one of them was going to end up very dead this day, and no wistful smile could change that.

He dragged the generator and its power cables and camouflage bag close to the ragged edge of the balcony. Under him the decaying concrete swayed like a tiny boat. It felt as if there was only a single support spar left. *Great.* He centered his equipment over the imagined spar and calibrated the mass- and ranging-sensors. The next minutes would be critical. In order that the computation be feasibly simple, the generator had to be clear of obstacles. But this made their operation relatively exposed. If the Authority had had anything like Paul's surveillance equipment, the plan would not have stood a chance.

Wili wet his finger and held it into the air. Even here, almost out of

doors, the day was stifling. The westerly breeze barely cooled his finger.
"How hot is it?" he asked unnecessarily; it was obviously hot enough.

"Outside air temperature is almost thirty-seven. That's about as hot
as it ever gets in LA, and it's the high for today."

Wili nodded. *Perfect.* He rechecked the center and radius coordinates, started the generator's processor, and then crawled back to the
others by the inner wall. "It takes about five minutes. Generating a
large bobble from two thousand meters is almost too much for this
processor."

"So"—Ebenezer's man gave him a sour smile—"you are going to
bobble something. Are you ready to share the secret of just what? Or
are we simply to watch and learn?"

On the far side of the room, the Alcalde's man was silent, but Wili
sensed his attention. Neither they nor their bosses could imagine the
bobble's being used as anything but an offensive weapon. They were
lacking one critical fact, a fact that would become known to all—
including the Authority—very soon.

Wili glanced at his watch: two minutes to go. There was no way he
could imagine Della preventing the rescue now. And he had some
quick explaining to do, or else—when his allies saw what he had done
—he might have deadly problems. "Okay," he said finally. "In ninety
seconds, my gadget is going to throw a bobble around the top floors of
the Tradetower."

"What?" The question came from four mouths, in two languages.
The Alcalde's man, so mild and respectful, was suddenly at his throat.
He held up his hand briefly as his men started toward the equipment
on the balcony. His other hand pressed against Wili's windpipe, just
short of pain, and Wili realized that he had seconds to convince him
not to topple the generator into the street. "The bobble will . . . pop
. . . later. . . . Time . . . stops inside," choked Wili. The pressure
on his throat eased; the goons edged back from the balcony. Wili saw
Jonque and *sabio* trade glances. There would have to be a lot more
explanations later, but for now they would cooperate.

A sudden, loud *click* marked the discharge of the Julians. All eyes
looked westward through the opening that once held a sliding glass
door. Faint "ah"s escaped from several pairs of lips.

The top of the Tradetower was in shadow, surmounted and dwarfed
by a four-hundred-meter sphere.

"The building, it must collapse," someone said. But it didn't. The bobble was only as massive as what it enclosed, and that was mostly empty air. There was a long moment of complete silence, broken only by the far, tiny wailing of sirens. Wili had known what to expect, but even so it took an effort to tear his attention from the sky and surreptitiously survey the others.

Lu was staring wide-eyed as any; even her schemes were momentarily submerged. But Rosas: The undersheriff looked back into Wili's gaze, a different kind of wonder on his face, the wonder of a man who suddenly discovers that some of his guilt is just a bad dream. Wili nodded faintly at him. *Yes, Jeremy is still alive, or at least will someday live again. You did not murder him, Mike.*

In the sky around the Tradetower, the helicopters swept in close to the silver curve of the bobble. From further up they could hear the whine of the fixed-wing patrol spreading in greater and greater circles around the Enclave. They had stepped on a hornets' nest and now those hornets were doing their best to decide what had happened and to deal with the enemy. Finally, the Jonque chief turned to the Ndelante *sabio.* "Can your people get us out from under all this?"

The black cocked his head, listening to his earphone, then replied, "Not till dark. We've got a tunnel head about two hundred meters from here, but the way they're patrolling, we probably couldn't make it. Right after sunset, before things cool off enough for their heat eyes to work good, that'll be the best time to sneak back. Till then we should stay away from windows and keep quiet. The last few months they've improved. Their snooper gear is almost as good as ours now."

The lot of them—blacks, Jonques, and Lu—moved carefully back into the hallway. Wili left his equipment sitting near the edge of the balcony; it was too risky to retrieve it just now. Fortunately, its camouflage bag resembled the nondescript rubble that surrounded it.

Wili sat with his back against the door. No one was going to get to the generator without his knowing it.

From in here, the sounds of the Enclave were fainter, but soon he heard something ominous and new: the rattle and growl of tracked vehicles.

After they were settled and lookouts were posted at the nearest peepholes, the *sabio* sat beside Wili and smiled. "And now, young friend, we have hours to sit, time for you to tell us just what you meant when you said that the bobble will burst, and that time stops inside." He spoke quietly, and—considering the present situation—it was a reasonable question. But Wili recognized the tone. On the other side of the hallway, the Alcalde's man leaned forward to listen. There was just enough light in the musty hallway for Wili to see the faint smile on Lu's face.

He must mix truth and lies just right. It would be a long afternoon.

28

The hallway was brighter now. As the sun set, its light came nearly horizontally through the rips near the ceiling and splashed bloody light down upon them. The air patrols had spread over a vast area, and the nearest tanks were several thousand meters away; Ebenezer's man had coordinated a series of clever decoy operations—the sort of thing Wili had seen done several times against the Jonques.

"¡Del Nico Dio!" It was almost a shriek. The lookout at the end of the hall jumped down from his perch. "It's happening. Just as he said. It's *flying!*"

Ebenezer's *sabio* made angry shushing motions, but the group moved quickly to the opening, the *sabio* and chief Jonque forcing their way to the front. Wili crawled between them and looked through one of the smaller chinks in the plaster and concrete: The evening haze was red. The sun sat half-dissolved in the deeper red beyond the Enclave towers.

And hanging just above the skyline was a vast new moon, a dark sphere edged by a crescent of red: The bobble had risen off the top of the Tradetower and was slowly drifting with the evening breeze toward the west.

"Mother of God," the Alcalde's man whispered to himself. Even with understanding, this was hard to grasp. The bobble, with its cargo of afternoon air, was lighter than the evening air around it, the largest hot-air balloon in history. And sailing into the sunset with it went the

Tinker hostages. The noise of aircraft came louder, as the hornets returned to their nest and buzzed around this latest development. One of the insects strayed too close to the vast smooth arc. Its rotor shattered; the helicopter fell away, turning and turning.

The *sabio* glanced down at Wili. "You're sure it will come inland?"

"Yes. Uh, Naismith studied the wind patterns very carefully. It's just a matter of time—weeks at most—before it grounds in the mountains. The Authority will know soon enough—along with the rest of the world—the secret of the bobbles, but they won't know just when this one will burst. If the bobble ends up far enough away, the other problems we are going to cause them will be so big they won't post a permanent force around it. Then, when it finally bursts . . ."

"I know, I know. When it finally bursts we're there to rescue them. But ten years is long to sleep."

It would actually be one year. That had been one of Wili's little lies. If Lu and the Peacers didn't know the potential for short-lived bobbles, then—

It suddenly occurred to him that Della Lu was no longer in his sight. He turned quickly from the wall and looked down the hallway. But she and Rosas were still there, sitting next to a couple of Jonque goons who had not joined the crush at the peephole. "Look, I think we should try to make it back to the tunnel now. The Peacers have plenty of new problems, and it's pretty dark down in the street."

Ebenezer's man smiled. "Now, what would you know about evading armed men in the Basin?" More than ever Wili was sure the *sabio* recognized him, but for now the other was not going to make anything of it. He turned to the Jonque chief. "The boy's probably right."

Wili retrieved the generator, and one by one they descended via the rope sling to the ruined garages below the apartment house. The last man slipped the rope from its mooring. The blacks spent several minutes removing all ground-level signs of their presence. The Ndelante were careful and skilled. There were ways of covering tracks in the ruins, even of restoring the patina of dust in ancient rooms. For forty years the depths of the LA Basin had been the ultimate fortress of the Ndelante; they knew their own turf.

Outside, the evening cool had begun. Two of the *sabio*'s men moved out ahead, and another two or three brought up the rear. Several carried night scopes. It was still light enough to read by; the sky above the street was soft red with occasional patches of pastel blue. But it was darkening quickly, and the others were barely more than shadows. Wili could sense the Jonques' uneasiness. Being caught at nightfall deep in the ruins would normally be the death of them. The high-level conniving between the Ndelante and the bosses of Aztlán did not ordinarily extend down to these streets.

Their point men led them through piles of fallen concrete; they never actually stepped out into the open street. Wili hitched up his pack and fell back slightly, keeping Rosas and Lu ahead of him. Behind him, he could hear the Jonque chief and—much quieter—Ebenezer's *sabio*.

Out of the buzzing of aircraft, the sound of a single helicopter came louder and louder. Wili and the others froze, then crouched down in silence. The craft was closer, closer. The *thwupthwupthwup* of its rotors was loud enough so that they could almost feel the overpressures. It was going to pass directly over them. This sort of thing had happened every twenty minutes or so during the afternoon, and should be nothing to worry about. Wili doubted if even observers on the rooftops could have spotted them here below. But this time:

As the copter passed over the roofline a flash of brilliant white appeared ahead of Wili. *Lu!* He had been worried she was smuggling some sophisticated homer, and here she was betraying them with a simple handflash!

The helicopter passed quickly across the street. But even before its rotor tones changed and it began to circle back, Wili and most of the Ndelante were already heading for deeper hidey-holes. Seconds later, when the aircraft passed back over the street, it really was empty. Wili couldn't see any of the others, but it sounded as if the Jonques were still rushing madly about, trying to find some way out of the jagged concrete jungle. A monstrously bright light swept back and forth along the street, throwing everything into stark blacks and whites.

As Wili had hoped, the searchlight was followed seconds later by rocket fire. The ground rose and fell under him. Faint behind the explosions, Wili could hear shards of metal and stone snicking back and forth between concrete piles. There were screams.

Heavy dust rose from the ruins. This was his best chance: Wili scuttled back a nearby alley, ignoring the haze and the falling rocks. Another half minute and the enemy would be able to see clearly again, but by then Wili (and probably the rest of the Ndelante) would be a hundred meters away, and moving under much greater cover than he had right here.

An observer might think he ran in mindless panic, but in fact Wili was very careful, was watching for any sign of a Ndelante trail. For more than forty years the Ndelante had been the de facto rulers of these ruins. They used little of it for living space, but they mined most of the vast Basin, and everywhere they went they left subtle improvements—escape hatches, tunnels, food caches—that weren't apparent unless one knew their marking codes. After less than twenty meters, Wili had found a marked path, and now ran at top speed through terrain that would have seemed impassable to anyone standing more than a few meters away. Some of the others were escaping along the same path: Wili could hear at least two pairs of feet some distance behind him, one heavy Jonque feet, the others barely audible. He did not slow down; better that they catch up.

The chopper pilot had lifted out of the space between the buildings and fired no more. No doubt the initial attack had not been to kill, but to jar his prey into the open. It was a decent strategy against any but the Ndelante.

The pilot flew back and forth now, lobbing stun bombs. They were so far away that Wili could barely feel them. In the distance, he heard the approach of more aircraft. Some of them sounded big. Troop carriers. Wili kept running. Till the enemy actually landed, it was better to run than to search for a good hiding place. He might even be able to get out of the drop area.

Five minutes later, Wili was nearly a kilometer away. He moved through a burned-out retail area, from cellar to cellar, each connected to the next by subtle breaks in the walls. His equipment pack had come loose and the whole thing banged painfully against him when he tried to move really fast. He stopped briefly to tighten the harness, but that only made the straps cut into his shoulders.

In one sense he was lost: He had no idea where he was, or how to get to the pickup point the Ndelante and the Jonques had established. On the other hand, he knew which direction he should run *from*, and—if he saw them—he could recognize the clues that would lead to some really safe hole that the Ndelante would look into after all the fuss died down.

Two kilometers run. Wili stopped to adjust the straps again. Maybe he should wait for the others to catch up. If there was a safety hole around here, they might know where it was. And then he noticed it, almost in front of him: an innocent pattern of scratches and breaks in the cornerstone of a bank building. Somewhere in the basement of that bank—in the old vault no doubt—were provisions and water and probably a hand comm. No wonder the Ndelante behind him had stayed so close to his trail. Wili left the dark of the alley and moved across the street in a broken run, flitting from one hiding place to the next. It was just like the old days—after Uncle Sly but before Paul and math and Jeremy—except that in those old days, he had more often than not been carried by his fellow burglars, since he was too weak for sustained running. Now he was as tough as any.

He started down the darkened stairs, his hands fishing outward in almost ritual motions to disarm the boobytraps the Ndelante were fond of leaving. Outside sounds came very faint down here, but he thought he heard the others, the surviving Jonque and however many Ndelante were with him. Just a few more steps and he would be in the—

After so much dark, the light from behind him was blinding. For an instant, Wili stared stupidly at his own shadow. Then he dropped and whirled, but there was no place to go, and the handflash followed him easily. He stared into the darkness around the point of light. He did not have to guess who was holding it.

"Keep your hands in view, Wili." Her voice was soft and reasonable. "I really do have a gun."

"You're doing your own dirty work now?"

"I figured if I called in the helicopters before catching up, you might bobble yourself." The direction of her voice changed. "Go outside and signal the choppers down."

"Okay." Rosas' voice had just the mixture of resentment and cowardice that Wili remembered from the fishing boat. His footsteps retreated up the stairs.

"Now take off the pack—slowly—and set it on the stairs."

Wili slipped off the straps and advanced up the stairs a pace or two. He stopped when she made a warning sound and set the generator down amidst fallen plaster and rat droppings. Then Wili sat, pretending to take the weight off his legs. If she were just a couple of meters closer. . . . "How could you follow me? No Jonque ever could; they

189

don't know the signs." His curiosity was only half pretense. If he hadn't been so scared and angry, he would have been humiliated: It had taken him years to learn the Ndelante signs, and here a woman—not even an Ndelante—had come for the first time into the Basin, and equaled him.

Lu advanced, waving him back from the stairs. She set her flash on the steps and began to undo the ties on his pack with her right hand. She did have a gun, an *Hacha* 15-mm, probably taken off one of the Jonques. The muzzle never wavered.

"Signs?" There was honest puzzlement in her voice. "No, Wili, I simply have excellent hearing and good legs. It was too dark for serious tracking." She glanced into the pack, then slipped the straps over one shoulder, retrieved her handflash, and stood up. She had everything now. *Through me, she even has Paul*, he suddenly realized. Wili thought of the holes the *Hacha* could make, and he knew what he must do.

Rosas came back down. "I swung my flash all around, but there's so much light and noise over there already, I don't think anyone noticed."

Lu made an irritated noise. "Those featherbrains. What they know about surveillance could be—"

And several things happened at once: Wili rushed her. Her light swerved and shadows leaped like monsters. There was a ripping, cracking sound. An instant later, Lu crashed into the wall and slid down the steps. Rosas stood over her crumpled form, a metal bar clutched in his hand. Something glistened dark and wet along the side of that bar. Wili took one hesitant step up the stairs, then another. Lu lay facedown. She was so small, scarcely taller than he. And so still now.

"Did . . . did you kill her?" He was vaguely surprised at the note of horror, almost accusation, in his voice.

Rosas' eyes were wide, staring. "I don't know; I t-tried to. S-sooner or later I had to do this. I'm *not* a traitor, Wili. But at Scripps—" He stopped, seemed to realize that this was not the time for long confessions. "Hell, let's get this thing off her." He picked up the gun that lay just beyond Lu's now limp hand. That action probably saved them.

As he rolled her on her side, Lu exploded, her legs striking at Rosas' midsection, knocking him backward onto Wili. The larger man was almost dead weight on the boy. By the time Wili pushed him aside, Della Lu was racing up the stairs. She ran with a slight stagger, and one arm hung at an awkward angle. She still had her handflash. "The gun, Mike, quick!"

But Rosas was doubled in a paroxysm of pain and near paralysis, faint *"unh, unh"* sounds escaping from his lips. Wili snatched the metal bar, and flew up the steps, diving low and to one side as he came onto the street.

The precaution was unnecessary: She had not waited in ambush. Amidst the wailing of faraway sirens, Wili could hear her departing footsteps. Wili looked vainly down the street in the direction of the sounds. She was out of sight, but he could track her down; this was country he knew.

There was a scrabbling noise from the entrance to the bank. "Wait." It was Rosas, half bent over, clutching his middle. "She won, Wili. She won." The words were choked, almost voiceless.

The interruption was enough to make Wili pause and realize that Lu had indeed won. She was hurt and unarmed, that was true. And with any luck, he could track her down in minutes. But by then she would have signaled gun and troop copters; they were much nearer than Mike had claimed.

She had won the Authority their own portable bobble generator.

And if Wili couldn't get far away in the next few minutes, the Authority would win much more. For a long second, he stared at the Jonque. The undersheriff was standing a bit straighter now, breathing at last, in great tormented gasps. He really should leave Rosas here. It would divert the troopers for valuable minutes, might even insure Wili's escape.

Mike looked back and seemed to realize what was going on in his head. Finally Wili stepped toward him. "C'mon. We'll get away from them yet."

In ten seconds the street was as empty as it had been all the years before.

29

The Jonque nobles believed him when Wili vouched for Mike. That was the second big risk he took to get them home. The first had been in evading the Ndelante Ali; they had walked out of the Basin on their own, had contacted the Alcalde's men directly. Not many Jonques had made it out of the operation, and their reports were confused. But the rescue was obviously a great success, so it wasn't hard to convince them that there had been no betrayal. Such explanations might not have washed with the Ndelante; they already distrusted Wili. And it was likely there were black survivors who had seen what really happened.

In any case, Naismith wanted Wili back immediately, and the Jonques knew where their hopes for continued survival lay. The two were on their way northward in a matter of hours. It was not nearly so luxurious a trip as coming down. They traveled back roads in camouflaged wagons, and balanced speed with caution. The Aztlán convoy knew it was prey to a vigilant enemy.

It was night when they were deposited on a barely marked trail north of Ojai. Wili listened to the sounds of the wagon and outriders fade into the lesser noises of the night. They stood unspeaking for a minute after, the same silence that had been between them through most of the last hours. Finally Wili shrugged and started up the dusty trail. It would get them to the cabin of a Tinker sympathizer on the other side of the border. At least one horse should be ready for them there.

He heard Mike close behind, but there was no talk. This was the first time they had really been alone since the walk out of the Basin—and then it had been necessary to keep very quiet. Yet even now, Rosas had nothing to say. "I'm not angry anymore, Mike." Wili spoke in Spanish; he wanted to say exactly what he meant. "You didn't kill Jeremy; I don't think you ever meant to hurt him. And you saved my life and probably Paul's when you jumped Lu."

The other made a noncommittal grunt. Otherwise there was just the sound of his steps in the dirt and the keening of insects in the dry underbrush. They went on another ten meters before Wili abruptly stopped and turned on the other. "Damnation! Why won't you talk? There is no one to hear but the hills and me. You have all the time in the world."

"Okay, Wili, I'll talk." There was little expression in the voice, and Mike's face was scarcely more than a shadow against the sky. "I don't know that it matters, but I'll talk." They continued the winding path upward. "I did everything you thought, though it wasn't for the Peacers and it wasn't for Della Lu. . . . Have you heard of the Huachuca plaguetime, Wili?"

He didn't wait for an answer but rambled on with a loose mixture of history—his own and the world's. The Huachuca had been the last of the warplagues. It hadn't killed that many in absolute numbers, perhaps a hundred million worldwide. But in 2015, that had been one human being in five. "I was born at Fort Huachuca, Wili. I don't remember it. We left when I was little. But before he died, my father told me a lot. He *knew* who caused the plagues, and that's why he left." The Rosas family had not left Huachuca because of the plague that bore its name. Death lapped all around the town, but that and the earlier plagues seemed scarcely to affect it.

Mike's sisters were born *after* they left; they had sickened and slowly died. The family had moved slowly north and west, from one dying town to the next. As in all the plagues, there was great material wealth for the survivors—but in the desert, when a town died, so did services that made further life possible. "My father left because he discovered the secret of Huachuca, Wili. They were like the La Jolla group, only more arrogant. Father was an orderly in their research hospital. He didn't have real technical training. Hell, he was just a kid when the War and the early plagues hit." By that time, government warfare—

and the governments themselves—were nearly dead. The old military machinery was too expensive to maintain. Any further state assaults on the Peace had to be with cheaper technologies. This was the story the Peacer histories told, but Mike's father had seen its truth. He had seen shipments going to the places that were first to report the plague, shipments that were postdated and later listed as medical supplies for the victims.

He even overheard a conversation, orders explicitly given. It was then he decided to leave. "He was a good man, Wili, but maybe a coward, too. He should have tried to expose the operation. He should have tried to convince the Peacers to kill those monsters. And they *were* monsters, Wili. By the teens, everyone knew the governments were finished. What Huachuca did was pure vengeance. . . . I remember when the Authority finally figured out where that plague came from. Father was still alive then, very sick though. I was only six, but he had told me the story over and over. I couldn't understand why he cried when I told him Huachuca had been bobbled; then I saw he was laughing, too. People really do cry for joy, Wili. They really do."

To their left, the ground fell almost vertically. Wili could not see if the drop was two meters or fifty. The Jonques had given him a night scope, but they'd told him its batteries would run down in less than an hour. He was saving it for later. In any case, the path was wide enough so that there was no real danger of falling. It followed the side of the hills, winding back and forth, reaching higher and higher. From his memory of the maps, he guessed they should soon reach the crest. Soon after that, they would be able to see the cabin.

Mike was silent for a long time, and Wili did not immediately reply. Six years old. Wili remembered when he was six. If coincidence and foolhardy determination had not thrust him into the truth, he would have gone through life convinced that Jonques had kidnapped him from Uncle Sly, and that—with Sly gone—the Ndelante were his only friends and defenders. Two years ago, he had learned better. The raid —yes, it had been Jonque—but done at the secret request of the Ndelante. Ebenezer had been angered by the unFaithful like Uncle Sly who used the water upstream from the Ndelante reservoir. Besides, the Faithful were ready to move into Glendora, and they needed an outside enemy to make their takeover easier. It worked the other way, too:

Jonque commoners without lords protector lived in constant fear of Ndelante raids.

Wili shrugged. It was not something he would say to Mike. Huachuca was probably everything he thought. Still, Wili had infinite cynicism when it came to the alleged motives of organizations.

Wili had seen treacheries big and small, organizational and personal. He knew Mike believed all he said, that he'd done in La Jolla what he thought right, that he'd done it and still tried to do the job of protecting Wili and Jeremy that he had been hired for.

The trail dipped, moved steadily downward. They were past the crest. Several hundred meters further on, the scrub forest opened up a little, and they could look into small valley. Wili motioned Mike down. He pulled the Jonque night scope from his pack and looked across the valley. It was heavier than the glasses Red Arrow had loaned him, but it had a magnifier, and it was easy to pick out the house and the trails that led in and out of the valley.

There were no lights in farmhouse. It might have been abandoned except that he could see two horses in the corral. "These people aren't Tinkers, but they are friends, Mike. I think it's safe. With those horses, we can get back to Paul in just a few days."

"What do you mean 'we,' Wili? Haven't you been listening? I did betray you. I'm the last person you should trust to know where Paul is."

"I listened. I know what you did, and why. That's more than I know about most people. And there's nothing there about betraying Paul or the Tinkers. True?"

"Yes. The Peacers aren't the monsters the plaguemakers were, but they are an enemy. I'll do most anything to stop them . . . only, I guess I couldn't kill Della. I almost came apart when I thought she was dead back in the ruins; I couldn't try again."

Wili was silent a moment. "Okay. Maybe I couldn't either."

"It's still a crazy risk for you to take. I should be going to Santa Ynez."

"They'll likely know, Mike. We got out of LA just ahead of the news that you ran with Della. Your sheriff might still accept you, but none of the others, I'll bet. Paul though, he needs another pair of strong hands; he may have to move fast. Bringing you in is safer than calling the Tinkers and telling them where to send help."

More silence. Wili raised the scope and took one more look up and down the valley. He felt Mike's hand on his shoulder. "Okay. But we tell Paul straight out about me, so he can decide what to do with me."

The boy nodded. "And, Wili . . . thanks."

They stood and started into the valley. Wili suddenly found himself grinning. He felt so proud. Not smug, just proud. For the first time in his life, he had been the strong shoulder for someone else.

30

What Wili had missed most, even more than Paul and the Moraleses, was the processor hookup. Now that he was back, he spent several hours every day in deep connect. Most of the rest of the time he wore the connector. In discussions with Paul and Allison, it was comforting to have those extra resources available, to feel the background programs proceeding.

Even more, it brought him a feeling of safety.

And safety was something that had drained away, day by day. Six months ago, he had thought the mansion perfectly hidden, so far away in the mountains, so artfully concealed in the trees. That was before the Peacers started looking for them, and before Allison Parker talked to him about aerial reconnaissance. For precious weeks the search had centered in Northern California and Oregon, but now it had been expanded and spread both south and east. Before, the only aircraft they ever saw was the LA/Livermore shuttle—and that was so far to the east, you had to know exactly where and when to look to see a faint glint of silver.

Now they saw aircraft several times a week. The patterns sketched across the sky formed a vast net—and they were the fish.

"All the camouflage in the world won't help, if they decide you're hiding in Middle California." Mike's voice was tight with urgency. He walked across the veranda and tugged at the green-and-brown shroud he and Bill Morales had hung over all the exposed stonework and hard

197

corners of the mansion. Gone were the days when they could sit out by the pond and admire the far view.

Paul protested. "It's no ordinary camouflage, it—"

"I know it was a lot of work. You've told me Allison and the Moraleses spent two weeks putting it together. I know she and Wili added a few electronic twists that make it even better than it looks. But, Paul"—he sat down and glared at Paul, as if to persuade by the force of his own conviction—"they have other ways. They can interrogate del Norte—or at least his subordinates. That will get them to Ojai. They've raided Red Arrow and Santa Ynez and the market towns further north. Apparently the few people—like Kaladze—who really know your location have escaped. But no matter how many red herrings you've dropped over the years, they're eventually going to narrow things down to this part of the country."

"And there's Della Lu," said Allison.

Mike's eyes widened, and Wili could see that the comment had almost unhorsed him. Then he seemed to realize that it was not a jibe. "Yes, there's Lu. I've always thought this place must be closer to Santa Ynez than the other trading towns: I laid my share of red herrings on Della. But she's very clever. She may figure it out. The point is this: In the near future, they'll put the whole hunt on this part of California. It won't be just a plane every other day. If they can spare the people, they might actually do ground sweeps."

"What are you suggesting, Mike?" Allison again.

"That we move. Take the big wagon, stuff it with all the equipment we need, and move. If we study the search patterns and time it right, I think we could get out of Middle California, maybe to someplace in Nevada. We have to pick a place we can reach without running into people on the way, and it has to be some ways from here; once they find the mansion, they'll try to trace us. . . . I know, it'll be risky, but it's our only chance if we want to last more than another month."

Now it was Paul's turn to be upset. "Damn it, we can't move. Not now. Even if we could bring all the important equipment—which we can't—it would still be impossible. I can't afford the time, Mike. The Tinkers need the improvements I'm sending out; they need those bobble generators if they're going to fight back. If we take a month's vacation now, the revolution will be lost. We'll be safe in some hole in Nevada—safe to watch everything we've worked for go down the tubes." He thought a moment and came up with another objection. "Hell, I bet we couldn't even keep in touch with the Tinkers afterwards. I've spent years putting together untraceable communication links from here. A lot of it depends on precise knowledge of local terrain and climate. Our comm would make us sitting ducks if we moved."

Throughout the discussion, Wili sat quietly at the edge of the veranda, where the sunlight came through the camouflage mesh most strongly. In the back of his mind, Jill was providing constant updates on the Authority broadcasts she monitored. From the recon satellites, he knew the location of all aircraft within a thousand kilometers. They might be captured, but they could never be surprised.

This omniscience was little use in the present debate. At one extreme, he "knew" millions of little facts that together formed their situation; at the other, he knew mathematical theories that governed those facts. In between, in matters of judgment, he sensed his incompetence. He looked at Allison. "What do you think? Who is right?"

She hesitated just a moment. "It's the reconnaissance angle I know." It was eerie watching Allison. She was Jill granted real-world existence. "If the Peacers are competent, then I don't see how Mike could be wrong." She looked at Naismith. "Paul, you say the Tinkers' revolt will be completely suppressed if we take time out to move. I don't know; that seems a much iffier contention. Of course, if you're *both* right, then we've had the course. . . ." She gazed up at the dappled sunlight coming through the green-brown mesh. "You know, Paul, I almost wish you and Wili hadn't trashed the Authority's satellite system."

"What?" Wili said abruptly. That sabotage was his big contribution. Besides, he hadn't "trashed" the system, only made it inaccessible to the Authority. "They would have found us long ago with their satellites, if I had not done that."

Allison held up her hand. "I believe it. From what I've seen, they don't have the resources or the admin structure for wide-air recon. I just meant that given time we could have sabotaged their old comm and recon system—in such a way that the Peacers would think it was still working." She smiled at the astonishment on their faces. "These last weeks, I've been studying what you know about their old system. It's really the automated USAF comm and recon scheme. We had it fully in place right before . . . everything blew up. In theory it could handle all our command and control functions. All you needed was the satellite system, the ground receivers and computers, and maybe a hundred specialists. In theory, it meant we didn't need air recon or land lines. In theory. OMBP was always twisting our arm to junk our other systems and rely on the automated one instead. They could cut our budget in half that way."

She grinned. "Of course we never went along. We needed the other systems. Besides, we knew how fragile the automated system was. It was slick, it was thorough, but one or two rotten apples on the maintenance staff could pervert it, generate false interpretations, fake communications. We demanded the budget for the other systems that would keep it honest.

"Now it's obvious that the Peacers just took it over. They either didn't know or didn't care about the dangers; in any case, I bet they didn't have the resources to run the other systems the Air Force could. If we could have infiltrated a couple people into their technical staff, we could be making them see whatever we wanted. They'd never find us out here." She shrugged. "But you're right; at this point it's just wishful thinking. It might have taken months or years to do something like that. You had to get results right away."

"Damn," said Paul. "All those years of clever planning, and I never . . ."

"Oh, Paul," she said softly. "You are a genius. But you couldn't know everything about everything. You couldn't be a one-man revolution."

"Yeah," said Mike. "And he couldn't convince the rest of us that there was anything worth revolting against."

Wili just stared, his eyes wide, his jaw slack. It would be harder than anything he had done before but . . . "Maybe you do not need spies, Allison. Maybe we can. . . . I've got to think about this. We've still got days. True, Mike?"

"Unless we have real bad luck. With good luck we might have weeks."

"Good. Let me think. I must think. . . ." He stood up and walked slowly indoors. Already the veranda, the sunlight, the others were forgotten.

* * *

It was not easy. In the months before he learned to use the mind connect, it would have been impossible; even a lifetime of effort would not have brought the necessary insights. Now creativity was in harness with his processors. He knew what he wanted to do. In a matter of hours he could test his ideas, separate false starts from true.

The recon problem was the most important—and probably the easiest. Now he didn't want to block Peacer reception. He wanted them to receive . . . lies. A lot of preprocessing was done aboard the satellites; just a few bytes altered here and there might be enough to create false perceptions on the ground. Somehow he had to break into those programs, but not in the heavy-handed way he had before. Afterward, the truth would be received by them alone. The enemy would see what Paul wanted them to see. Why, they could protect not just themselves, but many of the Tinkers as well!

Days passed. The answers came miraculously fast, and perilously slow. At the edge of his consciousness, Wili knew Paul was helping with the physics, and Allison was entering what she knew about the old USAF comm/recon system. It all helped, but the hard inner problem —how to subvert a system without seeming to and without any physical contact—remained his alone.

They finally tested it. Wili took his normal video off a satellite over Middle California, analyzed it quickly, and sent back subtle sabotage. On the next orbit, he simulated Peacer reception: A small puff of synthetic cloud appeared in the picture, just where he had asked. The satellite processors could keep up the illusion until they received coded instructions to do otherwise. It was a simple change. Once operational, they could make more complicated alterations: Certain vehicles might not be reported on the roads, certain houses might become invisible.

But the hard part had been done.

"Now all we have to do is let the Peacers know their recon birds are 'working' again," said Allison when he showed them his tests. She was grinning from ear to ear. At first Wili had wondered why she was so committed to the Tinker cause; everything she was loyal to had been dead fifty years. The Tinkers didn't even exist when her orbiter was bobbled. But it hadn't taken him long to understand: She was like Paul. She blamed the Peacers for taking away the old world. And in her case, that was a world fresh in memory. She might not know anything about the Tinkers, but her hate for the Authority was as deep as Paul's.

"Yeah," said Paul. "Wili could just return the comm protocols to their original state. All of a sudden the Peacers would have a live system again. But even as stupid as they are, they'd suspect something. We have to do this so they think that somehow *they* have solved the problem. Hmm. I'll bet Avery still has people working on this even now."

"Okay," said Wili. "I fix things so the satellites will not start sending to them until they do a complete recompile of their ground programs."

Paul nodded. "That sounds perfect. We might have to wait a few more days, but—"

Allison laughed. "—But I know programmers. They'll be happy to believe their latest changes have fixed the problem."

Wili smiled back. He was already imagining how similar things could be done to the Peacer communication system.

31

War had returned to the planet. Hamilton Avery read the Peace Authority News Service article and nodded to himself. The headline and the following story hit just the right note: For decades, the world had been at peace, thanks to the Authority and the cooperation of peace-loving individuals around the world. But now—as in the early days, when the bioscience clique had attempted its takeover—the power lust of an evil minority had thrown the lives of humankind into jeopardy. One could only pray that the ultimate losses would not be as great as those of the War and the plagues.

The news service story didn't say all this explicitly. It was targeted for high tech regions in the Americas and China and concentrated on "objective" reporting of Tinker atrocities and the evidence that the Tinkers were building energy weapons—and bobble generators. The Peace hadn't tried to cover up that last development: A four-hundred-meter bobble floating through the skies of LA is a bit difficult to explain, much less cover up.

Of course, these stories wouldn't convince the Tinkers themselves, but they were a minority in the population. The important thing was to keep other citizens—and the national militias—from joining the enemy.

The comm chimed softly. "Yes?"

"Sir, Director Gerrault is on the line again. He sounds very . . . upset."

Avery stifled a smile. The comm was voice-only, but even when alone, Avery tried to disguise his true feelings. "Director" Gerrault indeed! There might still be a place for that pupal Bonaparte in the organization, but hardly as a Director. Best to let him hang a few hours more. "Please report to Monsieur Gerrault—again—that the emergency situation here prevents my immediate response. I'll get to him as soon as humanly possible."

"Uh, yes sir. . . . Agent Lu is down here. She also wishes to see you."

"That's different. Send her right up."

Avery leaned back in his chair and steepled his fingers. Beyond the clear glass of the window wall, the lands around Livermore spread away in peace and silence. In the near distance—yet a hundred meters beneath his tower—were the black-and-ivory buildings of the modern centrum, each one separated from the others by green parkland. Farther away, near the horizon, the golden grasses of summer were broken here and there by clusters of oaks. It was hard to imagine such peace disrupted by the pitiful guerrilla efforts of the world's Tinkers.

Poor Gerrault. Avery remembered his boast of being the industrious ant who built armies and secret police while the American and Chinese Directors depended on the people's good will and trust. Gerrault had spread garrisons from Oslo to Capetown, from Dublin to Szczecin. He had enough troopers to convince the common folk that he was just another tyrant. When the Tinkers finally got Paul Hoehler's toy working, the people and the governments had not hesitated to throw in with them. And then . . . and then Gerrault had discovered that his garrisons were not nearly enough. Most were now overrun, not so much by the enemy's puny bobble generators, as by all the ordinary people who no longer believed in the Authority. At the same time, the Tinkers had moved against the heart of Gerrault's operation in Paris. Where the European Director's headquarters once stood, there was now a simple monument: a three-hundred-meter silver sphere. Gerrault had gotten out just before the debacle, and was now skulking about in the East European deserts, trying to avoid the Teuton militia, trying to arrange transportation to California or China. It was a fitting end to his tyranny, but it was going to be one hell of a problem retaking Europe after the rest of the Tinkers were put down.

There was a muted knock at the door, and Avery pressed "open," then stood with studied courtesy as Della Lu stepped into the room. He gestured to a comfortable chair near the end of his desk, and they both sat.

Week by week his show of courtesy toward this woman was less an act. He had come to realize that there was no one he trusted more than her. She was as competent as any man in his top departments, and there was a loyalty about her—not a loyalty to Avery personally, he realized, but to the whole concept of the Peace. Outside of the old-time Directors, he had never seen this sort of dedication. Nowadays, Authority middle-management was cynical, seemed to think that idealism was the affliction of fools and low-level flunkies. And if Della Lu was faking her dedication, even in that she was a world champion; Avery had forty years of demonstrated success in estimating others' characters.

"How is your arm?"

Lu clicked the light plastic cast with a fingernail. "Getting well slowly. But I can't complain. It was a compound fracture. I was lucky I didn't bleed to death. . . . You wanted my estimate of enemy potential in the Americas?"

Always business. "Yes. What can we expect?"

"I don't know this area the way I did Mongolia, but I've talked with your section chiefs and the franchise owners."

Avery grinned to himself. Between staff optimism and franchise-owner gloom she thought to find the truth. Clever.

"The Authority has plenty of good will in Old Mexico and America-central. Those people never had it so good, they don't trust what's left of their governments, and they have no large Tinker communities. Chile and Argentina we are probably going to lose: They have plenty of people capable of building generators from the plans that Hoehler broadcast. Without our satellite net we can't give our people down there the comm and recon support they need to win. If the locals want to kick us out badly enough, they'll be able—"

Avery held up a hand. "Our satellite problems have been cleared up."

"What? Since when?"

"Three days. I've kept it a secret within our technical branch, until we were sure it was not just a temporary fix."

"Hmm. I don't trust machines that choose their own time and place to work."

"Yes. We know now the Tinkers must have infiltrated some of our software departments and slipped tailor-made bugs into our controller codes. Over the last few weeks, the techs ran a bunch of tests, and they've finally spotted the changes. We've also increased physical security in the programming areas; it was criminally lax before. I don't think we'll lose satellite communications again."

She nodded. "This should make our counter-work a lot easier. I don't know whether it will be enough to prevent the temporary loss of the Far South, but it should be a big help in North America."

She leaned forward. "Sir, I have several recommendations about our local operations. First, I think we should stop wasting our time hunting for Hoehler. If we pick him up along with the other ringleaders, fine. But he's done about all the harm he—"

"No!" The word broke sharply from his lips. Avery looked over Lu's head at the portrait of Jackson Avery on the wall. The painting had been done from photos, several years after his father's death. The man's dress and haircut were archaic and severe. The gaze from those eyes was the uncompromising, unforgiving one he had seen so many times. Hamilton Avery had forbidden the cult of personality, and nowhere else in Livermore were there portraits of leaders. Yet he, a leader, was the follower of such a cult. For three decades he had lived beneath that picture. And every time he looked at it, he remembered his failure —so many years ago. "No," he said again, this time in a softer voice. "Second only to protecting Livermore itself, destroying Paul Hoehler must remain your highest priority.

"Don't you see, Miss Lu? People have said before, 'That Paul Hoehler, he has caused us a lot of harm, but there is nothing more he can do.' And yet Hoehler has always done more harm. He is a genius, Miss Lu, a mad genius who has hated us for fifty years. Personally, I think he's always known that bobbles don't last forever, and that time stops inside. I think he has chosen now to cause the Tinker revolt because he knew when the old bobbles would burst. Even if we are quick to rebobble the big places like Vandenberg and Langley, there are still thousands of smaller installations that will fall back into normal time during the next few years. Somehow he intends to use the old armies against us." Avery guessed that Lu's blank expression was hiding

skepticism. Like the other Directors, she just could not *believe* in Paul
Hoehler. He tried a different tack.

"There is objective evidence." He described the orbiter crash that
had so panicked the Directors ten weeks earlier. After the attack on the
LA Enclave, it was obvious that the orbiter was not from outer space,
but from the past. In fact, it must have been the Air Force snooper
Jackson Avery bobbled in those critical hours just before he won the
world for Peace. Livermore technical teams had been over the wreck
again and again, and one thing was certain: There had been a third
crewman. One had died as the bobble burst, one had been shot by
incompetent troopers, and one had . . . disappeared. That missing
crewman, suddenly waking in an unimagined future, could not have
escaped on his own. The Tinkers must have known that this bobble
was about to burst, must have known what was inside it.

Lu was no toady; clearly she was unconvinced. "But what use would
they have for such a crewman? Anything he could tell them would be
fifty years out of date."

What could he say? It all had the stench of Hoehler's work: devious,
incomprehensible, yet leading inexorably to some terrible conclusion
that would not be fully recognized until it was too late. But there was
no way he could convince even Lu. All he could do was give orders.
Pray God that was enough. Avery sat back and tried to reassume the air
of dignity he normally projected. "Forgive the lecture, Miss Lu. This is
really a policy issue. Suffice it to say that Paul Hoehler must remain one
of our prime targets. Please continue with your recommendations."

"Yes, sir." She was all respect again. "I'm sure you know that the
technical people have stripped down the Hoehler generator. The projector itself is well understood now. At least the scientists have come up
with theories that can explain what they previously thought impossible." Was there a faintly sarcastic edge to that comment? "The part we
can't reproduce is the computer support. If you want the power supply
to be portable, you need very complex, high-speed processing to get the
bobble on target. It's a trade-off we can't manage.

"But the techs have figured how to calibrate our generators. We can
now project bobbles lasting anywhere from ten to two hundred years.
They see theoretical limits on doing much better."

Avery nodded; he had been following those developments closely.

"Sir, this has political significance."

"How so?"

"We can turn what the Tinkers did to us in LA around. They bobbled their friends off the Tradetower to protect them. They know precisely how long it will last, and we don't. It's very clever: we'd look foolish putting a garrison at Big Bear to wait for our prisoners to 'return.' But it works the other way: Everyone knows now that bobbling is not permanent, is not fatal. This makes it the perfect way to take suspected enemies out of circulation. Some high Aztlán nobles were involved with this rescue. In the past we couldn't afford vengeance against such persons. If we went around shooting everyone we suspect of treason, we'd end up like the European Directorate. But now . . .

"I recommend we raid those we suspect of serious Tinkering, stage brief 'hearings'—don't even call them 'trials'—and then embobble everyone who might be a threat. Our news service can make this very reasonable and nonthreatening: We have already established that the Tinkers are involved with high-energy weapons research, and quite possibly with bioscience. Most people fear the second far more than the first, by the way. I infiltrated the Tinkers by taking advantage of that fear.

"These facts should be enough to keep the rest of the population from questioning the economic impact of taking out the Tinkers. At the same time, they will not fear us enough to band together. Even if we occasionally bobble popular or powerful persons, the public will know that this is being done without harm to the prisoners, and for a limited period of time—which we can announce in advance. The idea is that we are handling a temporary emergency with humanity, greater humanity than they could expect from mere governments."

Avery nodded, concealing his admiration. After reading of her performance in Mongolia, he had half expected Lu to be a female version of Christian Gerrault. But her ideas were sensible, subtle. When necessary she did not shrink from force, yet she also realized that the Authority was not all-powerful, that a balancing act was sometimes necessary to maintain the Peace. There really were people in this new generation who could carry on. If only this one were not a woman.

"I agree. Miss Lu, I want you to continue to report directly to me. I will inform the North American section that you have temporary authority for all operations in California and Aztlán—if things go well, I will push for more. In the meantime, let me know if any of the 'old hands' are not cooperating with you. This is not the time for jealousy."

Avery hesitated, unsure whether to end the meeting or bring Lu into the innermost circle. Finally he keyed a command to his display flat and handed it to Lu. Besides himself—and perhaps Tioulang—she was the only person really qualified to handle Operation Renaissance. "This is a summary. I'll want you to learn the details later; I could use your advice on how to split the operation into uncoupled subprojects that we can run at lower classifications."

Lu picked up the flat and saw the Special Material classification glowing at the top of the display. Not more than ten people now living had seen Special Materials; only top agents knew of the classification—and then only as a theoretical possibility. Special Materials were never committed to paper or transmitted; communication of such information was by courier with encrypted, booby-trapped ROMs that self-destructed after being read.

Lu's eyes flickered down the Renaissance summary. She nodded agreement as she read the description of Redoubt 001 and the bobble generator to be installed there. She pushed the page key and her eyes suddenly widened; she had reached the discussion that gave Renaissance its name. Her face paled as she read the page.

She finished and silently handed him the flat. "It's a terrifying possibility, is it not, Miss Lu?"

"Yes sir."

And even more than before, Avery knew he had made the right decision; Renaissance was a responsibility that *should* frighten. "Winning with Renaissance would in many ways be as bad as the destruction of the Peace. It is there as the ultimate contingency, and, *by God, we must win without it.*"

Avery was silent for a moment and then abruptly smiled. "But don't worry; think of it as caution to the point of paranoia. If we do a competent job, there's not a chance that we'll lose." He stood and came around his desk to show her to the door.

Lu stood, but did not move toward the door. Instead, she stepped toward the wide glass wall and looked at the golden hills along the horizon.

"Quite a view, isn't it?" Avery said, a bit nonplussed. She had been so purposeful, so militarily precise—yet now she tarried over a bit of landscape. "I can never decide whether I like it more when the hills are summer gold or spring green."

She nodded, but didn't seem to be listening to the chitchat. "There's one other thing, sir. One other thing I wanted to bring up. We have the power to crush the Tinkers in North America; the situation is not like Europe. But craft has won against power before. If I were on the other side . . ."

"Yes?"

"If I were making their strategy, I would attack Livermore and try to bobble our generator."

"Without high-energy sources they can't attack us from a distance."

She shrugged. "That's our scientists' solemn word. And six months ago they would have argued volumes that bobbles can't be generated without nuclear power. . . . But let's assume that they're right. Even then I would try to come up with some attack plan, some way of getting in close enough to bobble the Authority generator."

Avery looked out his window, seeing the beautiful land with Lu's vision: as a possible battlefield, to be analyzed for fields of fire and interdiction zones. At first glance it was impossible to imagine any group getting in undetected, but from camping trips long ago he remembered all the ravines out there. Thank God the recon satellites were back in operation.

That would protect against only part of the danger. There was still the possibility that the enemy might use traitors to smuggle a Tinker bobble generator into the area. Avery's attention turned inward, calculating. He smiled to himself. Either way it wouldn't do them any good. It was common knowledge that one of the Authority's bobble generators was at Livermore (the other being at Beijing). And there were thousands of Authority personnel who routinely entered the Livermore Enclave. But that was a big area, almost fifty kilometers in its longest dimension. Somewhere in there was the generator and its power supply, but out of all the millions on Earth, only five knew exactly where that generator was housed, and scarcely fifty had access. The bobbler had been built under the cover of projects Jackson Avery contracted for the old LEL. Those projects had been the usual combination of military and energy research. The LEL and the US military had been only too happy to have them proceed in secret and had made it possible for the elder Avery to build his gadgets underground and well away from his official headquarters. Avery had seen to it that not even the military liaison had really known where everything was. After the War, that secrecy had been maintained: In the early days, the remnants of the US government still had had enough power to destroy the bobbler if they had known its location.

And now that secrecy was paying off. The only way Hoehler could accomplish what Lu predicted was if he found some way of making Vandenberg-sized bobbles. . . . The old fear welled up: That was just the sort of thing the monster was capable of.

He looked at Lu with a feeling that surpassed respect and bordered on awe: She was not merely competent—she could actually think like Hoehler. He took her by the arm and led her to the door. "You've helped more than you can know, Miss Lu."

32

Allison had been in the new world more than ten weeks.

Sometimes it was the small things that were the hardest to get used to. You could forget for hours at a time that nearly everyone you ever knew was dead, and that those deaths had been mostly murder. But when night came, and indoors became nearly as dark as outside—that was strangeness she could not ignore. Paul had plenty of electronic equipment, most of it more sophisticated than anything in the twentieth century, yet his power supply was measured in watts, not kilowatts. So they sat in darkness illuminated by the flatscreen displays and tiny holos that were their eyes on the outer world. Here they were, conspirators plotting the overthrow of a world dictatorship—a dictatorship which possessed missiles and nukes—and they sat timidly in the dark.

Their quixotic conspiracy wasn't winning, but, by God, the enemy knew it was in a fight. Take the TV: The first couple of weeks it seemed that there were hardly any stations, and those were mostly run by families. The Moraleses spent most of their viewing time with old recordings. Then, after the LA rescue, the Authority had begun around-the-clock saturation broadcasting similar to twentieth-century Soviet feeds, and as little watched: It was all news, all stories about the heinous Tinkers and the courageous measures being taken by "your Peace Authority" to make the world safe from the Tinker threat.

Paul called those "measures" the Silvery Pogrom. Every day there were more pictures of convicted Tinkers and fellow-travelers disappearing into the bobble farm the Authority had established at Chico. Ten years, the announcers said, and those bobbles would burst and the felons would have their cases reviewed. Meantime, their property would also be held in stasis. Never in history, the audience was assured, had criminals and monsters been treated with more firmness or more fairness. Allison knew bullshit when she heard it; if she hadn't been bobbled herself, she would have assumed that it was a cover for extermination.

It was a strange feeling to have been present at the founding of the present order, and to be alive now, fifty years later. This great Authority, ruling the entire world—except now Europe and Africa—had grown from nothing more than that third-rate company Paul worked for in Livermore. What would have happened if she and Angus and Fred had made their flight a couple of days earlier, in time to return safely with the evidence?

Allison looked out the mansion's wide windows, into the twilight. Tears didn't come to her eyes anymore when she thought about it, but the pain was still there. If they had gotten back in time, her CO might have listened to Hoehler. They just might have been able to raid the Livermore labs before the brazen takeover that was called the "War" nowadays. And apparently the "War" had been just the beginning of decades of war and plague, now blamed on the losers. Just a couple of days' difference, and the world would not be a near-lifeless tomb, the United States a fading memory. To think that some lousy contractors could have brought down the greatest nation in history!

She turned back into the room, trying to see the three other conspirators in the dimness. An old man, a skinny kid, and Miguel Rosas. This was the heart of the conspiracy? Tonight, at least, Rosas sounded as pessimistic as she felt.

"Sure, Paul, your invention will bring them down eventually, but I'm telling you the Tinkers are all going to be dead or bobbled before that happens. The Peacers are moving *fast.*"

The old man shrugged. "Mike, I think you just need something to panic over. A few weeks back it was the Peacers' recon operation. Wili fixed that—more than fixed it—so now you have to worry about something else." Allison agreed with Mike, but there was truth in Paul's complaint. Mike seemed both haunted and trapped: haunted by what he had done in the past, trapped by his inability to do something to make up for that past. "The Tinkers have simply got to hide out long enough to make more bobblers and improve on 'em. Then we can fight back." Paul's voice was almost petulant, as though he thought that he had done all the hard work and now the Tinkers were incompetent to carry through with what remained. Sometimes Paul seemed exactly as she remembered him. But other times—like tonight—he just seemed old, and faintly befuddled.

"I'm sorry, Paul, but I think that Mike he is right." The black kid spoke up, his Spanish accent incongruous yet pleasant. The boy had a sharp tongue and a temper to go with it, but when he spoke to Paul—even in contradiction—he sounded respectful and diffident. "The Authority will not give us the time to succeed. They have bobbled the Alcalde del Norte himself. Red Arrow Farm is gone; if Colonel Kaladze was hiding there, then he is gone, too." On a clear day, dozens of tiny bobbles could be seen about the skirts of the Vandenberg Dome.

"But our control of Peacer recon. We should be able to protect large numbers of—" He noticed Wili shaking his head. "What? You don't have the processing power? I thought you—"

"That's not the big problem, Paul. Jill and I have tried to cover for many of the Tinkers that survived the first bobblings. But see: The first time the Peacers fall on to one of these groups, they will have a contradiction. They will see the satellites telling them something different than what is on the ground. Then our trick is worthless. Already we must remove protection from a couple of the groups we agreed on— They were going to be captured very soon no matter what, Paul." He spoke the last words quickly as he saw the old man straighten in his chair.

Allison put in, "I agree with Wili. We three may be able to hold out forever, but the Tinkers in California will be all gone in another couple of weeks. Controlling the enemy's comm and recon is an enormous advantage, but it's something they will learn about sooner or later. It's worthless except for short-term goals."

Paul was silent for a long moment. When he spoke again, it sounded like the Paul she had known so long ago, the fellow who never let a problem defeat him. "Okay. Then victory must be our *short-term* goal. . . . We'll attack Livermore, and bobble *their* generator."

"Paul, you can do that? You can cast a bobble hundreds of kilometers away, just like the Peacers?" From the corner of her eye, Allison saw Wili shake his head.

"No, but I can do better than in LA. If we could get Wili and enough equipment to within four thousand meters of the target, he could bobble it."

"Four thousand meters?" Rosas walked to the open windows. He looked out over the forest, seeming to enjoy the cool air that was beginning to sweep into the room. "Paul, Paul. I know you specialize in the impossible, but . . . In Los Angeles we needed a gang of porters just to carry the storage cells. A few weeks ago you wouldn't hear of taking a wagon off into the eastern wilderness. Now you want to haul a wagonful of equipment through some of the most open and well-populated country on Earth.

"And then, if you do get there, *all* you have to do is get those several tonnes of equipment within four thousand meters of the Peacer generator. Paul, I've been up to the Livermore Enclave. Three years ago. It was police service liaison with the Peacers. They've got enough firepower there to defeat an old-time army, enough aircraft that they don't need satellite pickups. You couldn't get within forty kilometers without an engraved invitation. Four thousand meters range is probably right inside their central compound."

"There is another problem, Paul." Wili spoke shyly. "I had thought about their generator, too. Someday, I know we must destroy it—and the one in Beijing. But Paul, I can't find it. I mean, the Authority publicity, it gives nice pictures of the generator building at Livermore, but they are fake. I know. Since I take over their communication system, I know everything they say to each other over the satellites. The generator in Beijing is very close to its official place, but the Livermore one is hidden. They never say its place, even in the most secret transmissions."

Paul slumped in his chair, defeat very obvious. "You're right, of course. The bastards built it in secret. They certainly kept the location secret while the governments were still powerful."

Allison stared from one to the other and felt crazy laughter creeping up her throat. They really didn't know. After all these years they didn't know. And just minutes before, she had been hurting herself with might-have-beens. The laughter burbled out, and she didn't try to stop it. The others looked at her with growing surprise. Her last mission, perhaps the last recon sortie the USAF ever flew, might yet serve its purpose.

Finally, she choked down the laughter and told them the cause for joy. ". . . so if you have a reader, I think we can find it."

There followed frantic calls for Irma, then even more frantic searches through attic storage for the old disk reader. An hour later, the reader sat on the living room table. It was bulky, gray, the Motorola insignia almost scratched away. Irma plugged it in and coaxed it to life. "It worked fine years ago. We used it to copy all our old disks onto solid storage. It uses a lot of power though; that's one reason we gave it up."

The reader's screen came to life, a brilliant glow that lit the whole room. This was the honest light Allison remembered. She had brought her disk pack down, and undone the combination lock. The disk was milspec, but it was commercial format; it should run on the Motorola. She slipped it into the reader. Her fingers danced across the keyboard, customizing off routines on the disk. Everything was so familiar; it was like suddenly being transported back to the before.

The screen turned white. Three mottled gray disks sat near the middle of the field. She pressed a key and the picture was overlaid with grids and legends.

Allison looked at the picture and almost started laughing again. She was about to reveal what was probably the most highly classified surveillance technique in the American arsenal. Twelve weeks "before," such an act would have been unthinkable. Now, it was a wonderful opportunity, an opportunity for the murdered past to win some small revenge. "Doesn't look like much, does it?" she said into the silence. "We're looking down at—I should say 'through'—Livermore." The date on the legend was 01JUL97.

She looked at Paul. "This is what you asked me to look for, Paul. Remember? I don't think you ever guessed just how good our gear really was."

"You mean, those gray things are old Avery's test projections?"

She nodded. "Of course, I didn't know what to make of them at the time. They're about five hundred meters down. Your employers were very cautious."

Wili looked from Allison to Paul and back, bewilderment growing. "But what is it that we are seeing?"

"We are seeing straight through the Earth. There's a type of light that shines from some parts of the sky. It can pass through almost anything."

"Like x-rays?" Mike said doubtfully.

"Something like x-rays." There was no point in talking about massy neutrinos and sticky detectors. They were just words to her, anyway. She could use the gear, and she understood the front-end engineering, but that was all. "The white background is a 'bright' region of the sky —seen straight through the Earth. Those three gray things are the *silhouettes* of bobbles far underground."

"So they're the only things that are opaque to this magic light," Mike said. "It looks like a good bobble hunter, Allison, but what good was it for anything else?" If you could see through literally everything, then you could see nothing.

"Oh, there is a very small amount of attenuation. This picture is from a single 'exposure,' without any preprocessing. I was astounded to see anything on it. Normally, we'd take a continuous stream of exposures, through varying chords of the Earth's crust, then · compute a picture of the target area. The math is pretty much like medical tomography." She keyed another command string. "Here's a sixty-meter map I built from all our observations."

Now the display showed intricate detail: A pink surface map of 1997 Livermore lay over the green, blue, and red representation of subsurface densities. Tunnels and other underground installations were obvious lines and rectangles in the picture.

Wili made an involuntary *ah*ing sound.

"So if we can figure out which of those things is the secret generator . . ." said Mike.

"I think I can narrow it down quite a bit." Paul stared intently at the display, already trying to identify function in the shapes.

"No need," said Allison. "We did a lot of analysis right on the sortie craft. I've got a database on the disk; I can subtract out everything the Air Force knew about." She typed the commands.

"And now the moment we've all been waiting for." There was an edge of triumph in the flippancy. The rectangles dimmed—all abut one on the southwest side of the Livermore Valley.

"You did it, Allison!" Paul stood back from the display and grabbed her hands. For an instant she thought he would dance her around the room. But after an awkward moment, he just squeezed her hands.

As he turned back to the display, she asked, "But can we be sure it's still there? If the Peacers know about this scanning technique—"

"They don't. I'm sure of it," said Wili.

Paul laughed. "We can do it, Mike! We can do it. Lord, I'm glad you all had the sense to push. I'd have sat here and let the whole thing die."

Suddenly the other three were all talking at once.

"Look. I see answers to your objections, and I have a feeling that once we start to take it seriously we can find even better answers. First off, it's not impossible to get ourselves and some equipment up there. One horse-drawn wagon is probably enough. Using back roads, and our 'invisibility,' we should be able to get at least to Fremont."

"And then?" said Allison.

"There are surviving Tinkers in the Bay Area. We all attack, throw in everything we have. If we do it right, they won't guess we control their comm and recon until we have our bobbler right on top of them."

Mike was grinning now, talking across the conversation at Wili. Allison raised her voice over the others'. "Paul, this has more holes than—"

"Sure, sure. But it's a start." The old man waved his hand airily, as if only trivial details remained. It was a typical Paulish gesture, something she remembered from the first day she met him. The "details" were usually nontrivial, but it was surprising how often his harebrained schemes worked anyway.

33

"**E**at Vandenberg Bananas. They Can't Be Beat." The banner was painted in yellow on a purple background. The letters were shaped as though built out of little bananas. Allison said it was the most asinine thing she had ever seen. Below the slogan, smaller letters spelled, "Andrews Farms, Santa Maria."

The signs were draped along the sides of their wagons. A light plastic shell was mounted above the green cargo. At every stop Allison and Paul carefully refilled the evap coolers that hung between the shell and the bananas. The two banana wagons were among the largest horse-drawn vehicles on the highway.

Mike and the Santa Maria Tinkers had rigged a hidden chamber in the middle of each wagon. The front wagon carried the bobbler and the storage cells; the other contained Wili, Mike, and most of the electronics.

Wili sat at the front of the cramped chamber and tried to see through the gap in the false cargo. No air was ducted from the coolers while they were stopped. Without it, the heat of the ripening bananas and the summer days could be a killer. Behind him, he felt Mike stir restlessly. They both spent the hottest part of the afternoons trying to nap. They weren't very successful; it was just too hot. Wili suspected they must stink so bad by now that the Peacers would *smell* them inside.

Paul's stooped figure passed through Wili's narrow field of view. His

219

disguise was pretty good; he didn't look anything like the blurred pictures the Peacers were circulating. A second later he saw Allison—in farmer's-daughter costume—walk by. There was a slight shifting of the load and the monotonous *clopclopclop* of the team resumed. They pulled out of the rest stop, past a weigh station moldering toward total ruin.

Wili pressed his face against the opening, both for the air and the view. They were hundreds of kilometers from Los Angeles; he had expected something more exciting. After all, the area around Vandenberg was almost a jungle. But no. Except for a misty stretch just after Salinas, everything stayed dry and hot. Through the hole in the bananas, he could see the ground rising gently ahead of them, sometimes golden grass, sometimes covered with chaparral. It looked just like the Basin, except that the ruins were sparse and only occasional. Mike said there were other differences, but he had a better eye for plants.

Just then a Peace Authority freighter zipped by in the fast lane. Its roar was surmounted by an arrogant horn blast. The banana wagon rocked in the wash and Wili got a faceful of dust. He sighed and lay back. Five days they had been on the road now. The worst of it was that, inside the wagon, he was out of touch; they couldn't disguise the antennas well enough to permit a link to the satellite net. And they didn't have enough power for Jill to run all the time. The only processors he could use were very primitive.

Every afternoon was like this: hotter and hotter till they couldn't even pretend to sleep, till they started grumping at each other. He almost wished they would have some problems.

This afternoon he might get that almost-wish. This afternoon they would reach Mission Pass and Livermore Valley.

The nights were very different. At twilight Paul and Allison would turn the wagons off Old 101 and drive the tired teams at least five kilometers into the hills. Wili and Mike came out of their hole, and Wili established communication with the satellite net. It was like suddenly coming awake to be back in connection with Jill and the net. They never had trouble finding the local Tinkers' cache. There were always food and fodder and freshly charged storage cells hidden near a spring or well. He and Paul used those power cells to survey the world through satellite eyes, to coordinate with the Tinkers in the Bay Area and China. They must all be ready at the same time.

The previous night the four of them had held their last council of war.

Some things that Allison and Mike had worried about turned out to be no problems at all. For instance, the Peacers could have set checkpoints hundreds of kilometers out along all highways leading to Livermore. They hadn't done so. The Authority obviously suspected an attack on their main base, but they were concentrating their firepower closer in. And their reserve force was chasing Wili's phantoms in the Great Valley. Now that the Authority had wiped away all public Tinkering, there was nothing obvious for them to look for. They couldn't harass every produce wagon or labor convoy on the coast.

But there were other problems that wouldn't go away. The previous night had been their last chance to look at those from a distance. "Anything after tonight, we're going to have to play by ear," Mike had said, stretching luxuriously in the open freedom of the evening.

Paul grunted at this. The old man sat facing them, his back to the valley. His wide farmer hat drooped down at the sides. "Easy for you to say, Mike. You're an action type. I've never been able to ad lib. I get everything worked out in advance. If something really unexpected happens I'm just no good at real-time flexibility." It made Wili sad to hear him say this. Paul was becoming indecisive again. Every night, he seemed a little more tired.

Allison Parker returned from settling the horses and sat down at the fourth corner of their little circle. She took off her bonnet. Her pale hair glinted in the light of their tiny campfire. "Well then, what are the problems we have to solve? You have the Bay Area Tinkers, what's left of them, all prepared to stage a diversion. You know exactly where the Peacer bobble generator is hidden. You have control of the enemy's communication and intelligence net—that alone is a greater advantage than most generals ever have."

Her voice was firm, matter-of-fact. It gave support by making concrete points rather than comforting noises, Wili thought.

There was a long silence. A few meters away they could hear the horses munching. Something fluttered through the darkness over their heads. Finally Allison continued. "Or is there doubt that you do control their communications? Do they really trust their satellite system?"

"Oh, they do. The Authority is spread very thin. About the only innovative thing they've ever done was to establish the old Chinese launch site at Shuangcheng. They have close and far reconnaissance from their satellites, as well as communications—both voice and computer." Wili nodded in agreement. He followed the discussion with only a fraction of his mind. The rest was off managing and updating the hundreds of ruses that must fit together to maintain their great deception. In particular, the faked Tinker movements in the Great Valley had to be wound down, but carefully so that the enemy would not realize they had put thousands of men there for no reason.

"And Wili says they don't seem to trust anything that comes over ground links," Paul continued. "Somehow they have the idea that if a machine is thousands of kilometers off in space, then it should be immune to meddling." He laughed shortly. "In their own way, those old bastards are as inflexible as I. Oh, they'll follow the ring in their nose, until the contradictions get too thick. *By then we must have won.*

". . . But there are so many, many things we have to get straight before that can happen." The sound of helplessness was back in his voice.

Mike sat up. "Okay. Let's take the hardest: how to get from their front door to the bobble generator."

"Front door? Oh, you mean the garrison on Mission Pass. Yes, that's the hardest question. They've strengthened that garrison enormously during the last week."

"Ha. If they're like most organizations, that'll just make them more confused—at least for a while. Look, Paul. By the time we arrive there, the Bay Area Tinkers should be attacking. You told me that some of them have maneuvered north and east of Livermore. They have bobble generators. In that sort of confusion there ought to be lots of ways to get our heavy-duty bobbler in close."

Wili smiled in the dark. Just a few days ago, it had been Rosas who'd been down on the plan. Now that they were close, though . . .

"Then name a few."

"Hell, we could go in just like we are—as banana vendors. We know they import the things."

Paul snorted. "Not in the middle of a war."

"Maybe. But *we* can control the moment the real fighting begins. Going in as we are would be a long shot, I admit, but if you don't want to improvise completely, you should be thinking about various ways things could happen. For instance, we might bobble the Pass and have our people grab the armor that's left and come down into the Livermore Valley on it with Wili covering for us. I know you've thought about that—all day I have to sit on those adapter cables you brought.

"Paul," he continued more quietly, "you've been the inspiration of several thousand people these last two weeks. These guys have their necks stuck way out. We're all willing to risk everything. But we need you more than ever now."

"Or put less diplomatically—I got us all into this pickle, so I can't give up on it now."

"Something like that."

". . . Okay." Paul was silent for a moment. "Maybe we could arrange it so that . . ." He was quiet again and Wili realized that the old Paul had reasserted himself—was trying to, anyway. "Mike, do you have any idea where this Lu person is now?"

"No." The undersheriff's voice was suddenly tight. "But she's important to them, Paul. I know that much. I wouldn't be surprised if she were at Livermore."

"Maybe you could talk to her. You know, pretend you're interested in betraying the Tinker forces we've lined up here."

"No! What I did had nothing to do with hurting . . ." His voice scaled down, and he continued more calmly. "I mean, I don't see what good it would do. She's too smart to believe anything like that."

Wili looked up through the branches of the dry oak that spread over their campsite. The stars should have been beautiful through those branches. Somehow they were more like tiny gleams in a dark-socketed skull. Even if he were never denounced, could poor Mike ever silence his internal inquisitor?

"Still, as you said about the other, it's something to think about." Paul shook his head sharply and rubbed his temples. "I am so tired. Look. I've got to talk to Jill about this. I'll think things out. I promise. But let's continue in the morning. Okay?"

Allison reached across as though to touch his shoulder, but Paul was already coming to his feet. He walked slowly away from the campfire. Allison started to get up, then sat down and looked at the other two. "There's something wrong. . . . There's something so wrong about Paul making a person out of a thing," she said softly. Wili didn't know what to say, and after a moment the three of them spread out their sleeping bags and crawled in.

Wili's lay between the cache of storage cells and the wagon with the processors. There should be enough juice for several hours' operation. He adjusted the scalp connect and wriggled into a comfortable position. He stared up at the half-sinister arches of the oaks and let his mind mesh with the system. He was going into deep connect now, something he avoided when he was with the others. It made his physical self dopey and uncoordinated.

Wili sensed Paul talking to Jill but did not try to participate.

His attention drifted to the tiny cameras they had scattered beyond the edges of the camp, then snapped onto a high-resolution picture from above. From there, their oaks were just one of many tiny clumps of darkness on a rolling map of paler grassland. The only light for kilometers around came from the embers that still glowed at the center of their camp. Wili smiled in his mind; that was the true view. The tiny light flicked out, and he looked down on the scene that was being reported to the Peace Authority. Nobody here but us coyotes.

This was the easiest part of the "high watch." He did it only for amusement; it was the sort of thing Jill and the satellite processors could manage without his conscious attention.

Wili drifted out from the individual viewpoints, his attention expanding to the whole West Coast and beyond, to the Tinkers near Beijing. There was much to do; a good deal more than Mike or Allison —or even Paul—might suspect. He talked to dozens of conspirators. These men had come to expect Paul's voice coming off Peacer satellites in the middle of the West Coast night. Wili must protect them as he did the banana wagons. They were a weak link. If any of them were captured, or turned traitor, the enemy would immediately know of Wili's electronic fraud. From them, "Paul's" instructions and recommendations were spread to hundreds.

In this state, Wili found it hard to imagine failure. All the details were there before him. As long as he was on hand to watch and supervise, there was nothing that could take him by surprise. It was a false optimism perhaps. He knew that Paul didn't feel it when he was linked up and helping. But Wili had gradually realized that Paul used the system without becoming part of it. To Paul it was like another programming tool, not like a part of his own mind. It was sad that someone so smart should miss this.

This real dream of power continued for several hours. As the cells slowly drained, operations were necessarily curtailed. The slow retreat from omniscience matched his own increasing drowsiness. Last thing before losing consciousness and power, he ferreted through Peacer archives and discovered the secret of Della Lu's family. Now that their cover was blown, they had moved to the Livermore Enclave, but Wili found two other spy families among the 'furbishers and warned the conspirators to avoid them.

Heat, sweat, dust on his face. Something was clanking and screaming in the distance. Wili lurched out of his daydreaming recollection of the previous evening. Beside him Rosas leaned close to the peephole. A splotch of light danced across his face as he tried to follow what was outside in spite of the swaying progress of the banana wagon.

"God. Look at all those Peacers," he said quietly. "We must be right at the Pass, Wili."

"Lemme see," the boy said groggily. Wili suppressed his own surprised exclamation. The wagons were still ascending the same gentle grade they'd been on for the last hour. Ahead he could see the wagon that contained Jill. What was new was the cause of all the clanking. Peacer armor. The vehicles were still on the horizon, coming off an interchange ahead. They were turning north toward the garrison at Mission Pass. "Must be the reinforcements from Medford." Wili had never seen so many vehicles with his own eyes. The line stretched from the interchange for as far as they could see. They were painted in dark green colors—quite an uncamouflage in this landscape. Many of them looked like tanks he had seen in old movies. Others were more like bricks on treads.

As they approached the interchange the clanking got louder and combined with the overtones of turbines. Soon the banana wagons caught up with the military. Civilian traffic was forced over to the rightmost lane. Powered freighters and horse-drawn wagons alike were slowed to the same crawl.

It was late afternoon. There was something big and loud behind them that cast a long shadow forward across the two banana wagons, and brought a small amount of coolness. But the tanks to the right raised a dust storm that more than made up for the lowered temperatures.

They drove like this for more than an hour. Where were the checkpoints? The road ahead still rose. They passed dozens of parked tanks, their crews working at mysterious tasks. Someone was fueling up. The smell of diesel oil came into the cramped hole along with the dust and the noise.

All was in shadow now. But finally Wili thought he could see part of the garrison. At least there was a building on the crest they were approaching. He remembered what things looked like from above. Most of the garrison's buildings were on the far side of the crest. Only a few positions—for observation and direct fire—were on this side.

Wili wondered what sort of armor they had back there now, considering what he was seeing on this side.

Wili and Mike traded time at the peephole as the spot on the horizon grew larger. The outpost sat like a huge boulder mostly submerged in the earth. There were slots cut in the armor, and he could see guns or lasers within. Wili was reminded of some of the twentieth-century fantasies Bill Morales liked to watch. These last few days—and hopefully the next few as well—were like Lucas' *Lord of the Rings*. Mike had even called Mission Pass the "front door" last night. Beyond these mountains (actually low hills) lay the "Great Enemy" 's ultimate redoubt. The mountains hid enemy underlings that watched for the hobbits or elves (or Tinkers) who must sneak through to the plains beyond, who must go right into the heart of evil and perform some simple act that would bring victory.

The similarity went further. This enemy had a supreme weapon (the big bobbler hidden in the Valley), but instead depended on earthly servants (the tanks and the troops) to do the dirty work. The Peacers hadn't bobbled anything for the last three days. That was a mystery, though Wili and Paul suspected the Authority was building up power reserves for the battle they saw coming.

Ahead of them, civilian traffic stopped at a checkpoint. Wili couldn't see exactly what was happening, but one by one—some slowly, some quickly—the wagons and freighters passed through. Finally their turn came. He heard Paul climb down from the driver's seat. A couple of Peacers approached. Both were armed, but they didn't seem especially tense. Twilight was deep now, and he could barely make out the color in their uniforms. The sky came down to the near horizon that was the crest of the Pass. The Earth's shadow, projected into the sky, made a dark wall beyond them. One carried a long metal pole. Some kind of weapon?

Paul hurried up from the back wagon. For a moment all three stood in his field of view. The troopers glanced at Paul and then up at where Allison was sitting. They obviously realized the two wagons were together. "Watcha got here, uncle?" asked the older of them.

"Bananas," Naismith replied unnecessarily. "You want some? My granddaughter and I've got to get them to Livermore before they spoil."

"I have bad news for you, then. Nothing's getting through here for a while." The three walked out of sight, back along the wagon.

"What?" Paul's voice rose, cracked. He was a better actor than Wili would have guessed. "B-but what's going on here? I'll lose business."

The younger soldier sounded sincerely apologetic. "We can't help it, sir. If you had followed the news, you'd know the enemies of Peace are on the move again. We're expecting an attack almost any time. Those damn Tinkers are going to bring back the bad old days."

"Oh no!" The anguish in the old man's voice seemed a compound of his personal problems and this new forecast of doom.

There was the sound of side curtains being dragged off the wagon. "Hey, Sarge, these things aren't even ripe."

"That's right," said Naismith. "I have to time things so when I arrive they'll be just ready to sell. . . . Here. Take a couple, officer."

"Um, thanks." Wili could imagine the Peacer holding a clump of bananas, trying to figure what to do with them. "Okay, Hanson, do your stuff." There was a rasping and a probing. So *that's* what the metal pole was. Both Wili and Miguel Rosas held their breath. Their hiding space was small, and it was covered with webbed padding. It could probably deceive a sonic probe. What about this more primitive search?

"It's clean."

"Okay. Let's look at your other wagon."

They walked to the forward wagon, the one that contained the bobbler and most of the storage cells. Their conversation faded into the general din of the checkpoint. Allison climbed down from her driver's seat and stood where Wili could see her.

Minutes passed. The band of shadow across the eastern sky climbed, became diffuse. Twilight moved toward night.

Electric lamps flashed on. Wili gasped. He had seen miraculous electronics these last months, but the sudden sheer power of those floodlights was as impressive as any of it. Every second they must eat as much electricity as Naismith's house did in a week.

Then he heard Paul's voice again. The old man had taken on a whining tone, and the trooper was a bit more curt than before. "Look, mister, *I* didn't decide to bring war here. You should count yourself lucky that you have any sort of protection from these monsters. Maybe things will blow over in time for you to save the load. For now, you're stuck. There's a parking area up ahead, near the crest. We have some latrines fixed there. You and your granddaughter can stay overnight, then decide if you want to stick it out or turn back. . . . Maybe you could sell part of the load in Fremont."

Paul sounded defeated, almost dazed. "Yes sir. Thanks for your help. Do as he says, Allison dear."

The wagons creaked forward, blue-white light splashing all around them like magic rain. From across the tiny hiding place, Wili heard the whisper of chuckle.

"Paul is really *good.* Now I wonder if all his whining last night was some sort of reverse whammy to get *our* spirits up."

Horse-drawn wagons and Authority freighters alike had parked in the big lot near the crest of the Pass. There were some electric lamps, but compared to the checkpoint it was almost dark. A good many people were stuck here overnight. Most of them milled around by cooking fires at the middle of the lot. The far end was dominated by the squat dome they had seen from far down the highway. Several armored vehicles were parked in front of it; they faced into the civilians.

The armored traffic on the highway had virtually ceased. For the first time in hours there was an absence of clank and turbines.

Paul came back around the side of the wagon. He and Allison adjusted the side curtains. Paul complained loudly to Allison about the disaster that had befallen them, and she was dutifully quiet. A trio of freighter drivers walked by. As they passed out of earshot, Naismith said quietly. "Wili, we're going to have to risk a hookup. I've connected you with the gear in the front wagon. Allison has pulled the narrow-beam antenna out of the bananas. I want contact with our . . . friends. We're going to need help to get any closer."

Wili grinned in the dark. It was a risk—but one he'd been aching to take. Sitting in this hole without processors was like being deaf, dumb, and blind. He attached the scalp connector and powered up.

There was a moment of disorientation as Jill and he meshed with the satellite net. Then he was looking out a dozen new eyes, listening on hundreds of Peacer comm channels. It would take him a little longer to contact the Tinkers. After all, they were humans.

A bit of his awareness still hung in their dark hiding place. With his true ears, Wili heard a car roar off the highway and park at the Peacer dome. The armor at the far end of the lot came to life. Something important was happening right here. Wili found a camera aboard the armor that could transmit to the satellite net. He looked out: The car's driver had jumped out and come to attention. Far across the lot, he could see civilians—somewhere among them Paul and Allison—turn to watch. He felt Mike crawl across him to look out the peephole. Wili juggled the viewpoints, at the same time continuing his efforts to reach the Tinkers, at the same time searching Authority RAM for the cause of the current commotion.

A door opened at the base of the Peacer station. White light spread from it across the asphalt. A Peacer was outlined in the doorway. A second followed him. And between them . . . a child? Someone small and slender, anyway. The figure stepped out of the larger shadows and looked across the parking lot. Light glinted off the black helmet of short hair. He heard Mike suck in a breath.

It was Della Lu.

34

Staff seemed satisfied with the preparations; even Avery accepted the plans.

Della Lu was not so happy. She looked speculatively at the stars on the shoulder of the perimeter commander. The officer looked back with barely concealed truculence. He thought he was tough. He thought she was more nonprofessional interference.

But she knew he was soft. All these troops were. They hadn't ever been in a real fight.

Lu considered the map he had displayed for her. As she, through Avery, had required, the armored units were being dispersed into the hills. Except for a few necessary and transient concentrations, the Tinkers would have to take them out a vehicle at a time. And satellite intelligence assured them that the enemy attack was many hours away, that the infiltrators weren't anywhere near the net of armor.

She pointed to the Mission Pass command post. "I see you stopped all incoming traffic. Why have them park so close to your command point here? A few of those people must be Tinker agents."

The general shrugged. "We inspected the vehicles four thousand meters down the road. That's beyond the range the intelligence people give for the enemy's homemade bobbler. Where we have them now, we can keep them under close watch and interrogate them more conveniently."

Della didn't like it. If even a single generator slipped through, this command post would be lost. Still, with the main attack at least twenty-four hours away, it might be safe to sit here a bit longer. There was time perhaps to go Tinker hunting in that parking area. Anybody they caught would probably be important to the enemy cause. She stepped back from the map display. "Very well, General, let's take a look at these civilians. Get your intelligence teams together. It's going to be a long night for them.

"In the meantime, I want you to move your command and control elements over the ridgeline. When things start happening, they'll be much safer in mobiles."

The officer looked at her for a moment, probably wondering just who she was sleeping with to give such orders. Finally he turned and spoke to a subordinate.

He glanced back at Della. "You want to be present at the interrogations?"

She nodded. "The first few, anyway. I'll pick them for you."

The parking-lot detention area was several hundred meters on a side. It looked almost like a fairground. Diesel freighters loomed over small horse-drawn carts and wagons. The truckers had already started fires. Some of their voices were almost cheerful. The delay by itself didn't worry them; their businesses were internal to the Authority and they stood to be reimbursed.

Lu walked past the staff car the general had ordered for them. The officer and his aides tagged along, uncertain what she would do next. She wasn't sure yet either, but once she got the feel of the crowd. . . .

If she were Miguel Rosas, she'd figure out some way to hijack one of the Peace Authority freighters. There was enough volume in a freighter to hide almost anything the Tinkers might make. Hmm. But the drivers generally knew each other and could probably recognize each other's rigs. The Tinkers would have to park their freighter away from the others, and avoid socializing. She and her entourage drifted through the shadows beyond the fires.

The freighters were clumped together; none was parked apart. That left the non-Peacer civilians. She turned away from the freighters and walked down a row of wagons. The people were ordinary enough: more than half in their fifties and sixties, the rest young apprentices. They did look uneasy—they stood to lose a lot of money if they had stay here

231

long—but there was little fear. They still believed the Authority's propaganda. And most of them were food shippers. None of their own people had been bobbled in the purges she had supervised the last few weeks. From somewhere over the hill she heard choppers. The intelligence crews would be here shortly.

Then she saw the banana wagons. They could only be from the Vandenberg area. No matter what intelligence was saying nowadays, she still thought Middle California was the center of the infestation. An old man and a woman about Lu's own age stood near the wagons. She felt tiny alarm bells going off.

Behind Della, the helicopters were landing. Dust blew cool and glowing around her. The choppers' lights cast her group's shadow toward the pair by the banana wagons. The old man raised his hand to shade his eyes; the woman just looked at them. There was something strange about her, a straightness in her posture, almost a soldier's bearing. For all that the other was tall and Caucasian, Della felt she was seeing someone very like herself.

Della clapped the general's arm, and when he turned to her she shouted over the sounds of blades and turbines, "There are your prime suspects—"

"The bitch! Is she some kind of mind reader?" Mike watched Lu's progress across the wide field. She still wasn't coming directly toward them, but edged slowly closer, like some cautious huntress. Mike cursed quietly. They seemed doomed at every step to face her and be bested by her.

The field grew bright; shadows shifted and lengthened. Choppers. Three of them. Each craft carried twin lamps hung below the cockpit. Lu's wolves, eyes glowing, settled down behind their mistress.

"Mike. Listen." Wili's voice was tense, but the words were slurred, the cadence irregular. He must be in deep connect. He sounded like one talking from a dream. "I'm running at full power; we'll be out of power in seconds—but that is all we have."

Mike looked out at the helicopters; Wili was right about that. "But what can we *do?*" he said.

"Our friends . . . going to distract her . . . no time to explain everything. Just do what I say."

Mike stared into the darkness. He could imagine the dazed look in

Wili's eyes, the slack features. He had seen it often enough the last few evenings. The boy was managing their own problems and coordinating the rest of the revolution, all at the same time. Rosas had played symbiotic games, but this was beyond his imagination. There was only one thing he could say. "Sure."

"You're going to take those two armored equipment carriers at . . . far side of the field. Do you see them?"

Mike had, earlier. They were two hundred meters off. There were guards posted next to them.

"When?"

"A minute. Kick loose the side of the wagon . . . now. When I say go . . . you jump, grab Allison, and run for them. Ignore everything else you see and hear. Everything."

Mike hesitated. He could guess what Wili intended, but—

"Move. Move. *Move!*" Wili's voice was abruptly urgent, angry—the dreamer frustrated. It was as unnerving as a scream. Mike turned and crashed his heels into the specially weakened wall. It had been intended as an emergency escape route. As the tacked nails gave way, Mike reflected that this was certainly an emergency—but they would be getting out in full view of Peacer guns.

Lu's general heard her order and turned to shout to his men. He was below his usual element here, directing operations firsthand. Della had to remind him, "Don't point. Have your people pick up others at the same time. We don't want to spook those two."

He nodded.

The rotors were winding down. Something like quiet should return to the field now, she thought . . .

. . . and was wrong. "Sir!" It was a driver in the field car. "We're losing armor to enemy action."

Lu whipped around the brass before they could do more than swear. She hopped into the car and looked at the display that glowed in front of the soldier. Her fingers danced over the command board as she brought up views and interpretation. The man stared at her for a horrified instant, then realized that she must be somebody very special.

Satellite photos showed eight silvery balls embedded in the hills north of them, eight silvery balls gleaming in starlight. Now there were nine. Patrols in the hills reported the same thing. One transmission ended in midsentence. Ten bobbles. The infiltration was twenty-four hours ahead of the schedule Avery's precious satellites and intelligence computers had predicted. The Tinkers must have dozens of manpack generators out there. If they were like the one Wili Wáchendon had carried, they were very short range. The enemy must be sneaking right up on their targets.

Della looked across the detention area at the banana wagons. Remarkably timed, this attack.

She slipped out of the car and walked back to the general and his staff. *Cool. Cool. They may hold off as long as we don't move on the wagons.*

"Looks bad, General. They're way ahead of our estimates. Some of them are already operating north of us." That much was true.

"My God. I've got to get back to command, lady. These interrogations will have to wait."

Lu smiled crookedly. The other still didn't get the point. "You do that. Might as well leave these people alone anyway." But the other was already walking away from her. He waved acknowledgment and got into the field car.

To the north she heard tac air, scrambled up from the Livermore Valley. Something flashed white, and far hills stood in momentary silhouette. That was one bobbler that wouldn't get them this night.

Della looked over the civilian encampment as though pondering what to do next. She was careful to give no special attention to the banana wagons. Apparently, they thought their diversion successful—at least she remained unbobbled.

She walked back to her personal chopper, which had come in with the interrogation teams. Lu's aircraft was smaller, only big enough for pilot, commander, and gunner. It bristled with sensor equipment and rocket pods. The tail boom might be painted with LA paisley, but these were her own people on this machine, veterans of the Mongolian campaign. She pulled herself onto the command seat and gave the pilot an emphatic up-and-away sign. They were off the ground immediately.

Della ignored this efficiency; she was already trying to get her priority call through to Avery. The little monochrome display in front of her pulsed red as her call stayed in the queue. She could imagine the madhouse Livermore Central had become the last few minutes. *But, damn you, Avery, this is not the time to forget I come first!*

Red. Red. Red. The call pattern disappeared, and the display was filled with a pale blob that might have been someone's face. "Make it quick." It was Hamilton Avery's voice. Other voices, some almost shouting, came from behind him.

She was ready. "No proof, but I know they've infiltrated right up to the Mission Pass Gate. I want you to lay a thousand-meter bobble just south of the CP—"

"No! We're still charging. If we start using it now, there won't be juice for rapid fire when we really need it, when they get over the ridgeline."

"Don't you see? The rest is diversion. Whatever I've found here must be *important.*"

But the link was broken; the screen glowed a faint, uniform red. Damn Avery and his caution! He was so afraid of Paul Hoehler, so certain the other would figure out a way to get into Livermore Valley, that he was actually making it possible for the enemy to do so.

She looked past the instrument displays. They were about four hundred meters up. Splashes of blue-white light from the pole lamps lit the detention area; the camp looked like some perfect model. There was little apparent motion, though the pilot's thermal scanner showed that some of the armor was alive, awaiting orders. The civilian camp was still and bluish white, little tents sitting by scarcely larger wagons. The darker clumps around the fires were crowds of people.

Della swallowed. If Avery wouldn't bobble the camp . . .

She knew, without looking, what her ship carried. She had stun bombs, but if those wagons were what she thought, they would be shielded. She touched her throat mike and spoke to her gunner. "Fire mission. Rockets on the civilian wagons. No napalm." The people around the campfires would survive. Most of them.

The gunner's "Roger" sounded in her ear. The air around the chopper glowed as if a small sun had suddenly risen behind them, and a roar blotted out the rotor thupping. Looking almost into the exhaust of the rocket stream dimmed all other lights to nothing.

Or almost nothing. For an instant, she glimpsed rockets coming *up* from below. . . .

Then their barrage exploded. In the air. Not halfway to the target. The fireballs seemed to *splash* across some unseen surface. The chopper staggered as shrapnel ripped through it. Someone screamed.

The aircraft tipped into an increasing bank that would soon turn them upside down. Della didn't think, didn't really notice the pilot slumped against his controls. She grabbed her copy of the stick, pulled, and jabbed at the throttle. *Ahead she saw another copter, on a collision path with theirs.* Then the pilot fell back, the stick came free, and her aircraft shot upward, escaping both ground and the mysterious other.

The gunner crawled up between them and looked at the pilot. "He's dead, ma'am."

Della listened, and also listened to the rotors. There was something ragged in their rhythm. She had heard worse. "Okay. Tie him down." Then she ignored them and flew the helicopter slowly around what had been the Mission Pass Gate.

The phantom missiles from below, the mysterious helicopter—all were explained now. Near the instant her gunner fired his rockets, someone had bobbled the Pass. She circled that great dark sphere, a perfect reflection of her lights following her. The bobble was a thousand meters across. But this hadn't been Avery relenting: Along with the civilian and freighter encampment, the bobble also contained the Gate's command post. Far below, Authority armor moved around the base, like ants suddenly cut off from the nest.

So. Perfect timing, once again. They had known she was going to attack, and known precisely when. Tinker communication and intelligence must be the equal of the Peace's. And whoever was down there had been important. The generator they carried must have been one of the most powerful the Tinkers had. When they had seen the alternative was death, they had opted out of the whole war.

She looked across at her chopper's reflection, seemingly a hundred meters off. The fact that they had bobbled themselves instead of her aircraft was evidence that the Hoehler technique—at least with small power sources—was not very good for moving targets. Something to remember.

At least now, instead of a hundred new deaths on her soul, the enemy had burdened her with just one, her pilot. And when this bobble burst—the minimum ten years from now or fifty—the war would be history. A flick of the eye to them, and there would be no more killing. She suddenly envied these losers very much.

She banked away and headed for Livermore Central.

35

"**N**ow!" Wili's command came abruptly, just seconds after Rosas had loosened the false wall. Mike crashed his heels one last time into the wood. It gave way, bananas and timber falling with it.

And suddenly there was light all around them. Not the blue-point lights the Authority had strung around the campground, but an all-enveloping white glare, brighter than any of the electrics.

"Run now. Run!" Wili's voice was faint from within the compartment. The undersheriff grabbed Allison and urged her across the field. Paul started to follow them, then turned back at Wili's call.

An Authority tank swiveled on its treads, its turret turning even faster. Behind him an unfamiliar voice shouted for him to stop. Mike and Allison only ran faster. And the tank disappeared in a ten-meter-wide silver sphere.

They ran past civilians cowering in the nebulous glare, past troopers and Authority equipment that one after another were bobbled before they could come into action.

Two hundred meters is a long way to sprint. It is more than long enough to think, and understand.

The glare all around them was only bright by comparison with night. This was simply morning light, masked and diffused by fog. Wili had bobbled the campground through to the next morning, or the morning after that—to some later time when the mass of the Authority's forces would have moved away from the Gate they now thought blocked. Now he was mopping up the Peacers that had been in the bobble. If they moved fast, they could be gone before the Peace discovered what had happened.

When Mike and Allison reached the armored carriers, they were unguarded—except for a pair of three-meter bobbles that gleamed on either side of them. Wili must have chosen these just because their crews were standing outside.

Mike clambered up over the treads and paused, panting. He turned and pulled Allison onto the vehicle. "Wili wants us to drive these to the wagons." He threw the open hatch and shrugged helplessly. "Can you do it?"

"Sure." She caught the edge of the hatch and swung down into the darkness. "C'mon."

Mike followed awkwardly, feeling a little stupid at his question. Allison was from the age of such machines, when everyone knew how to drive.

The smell of lubricants and diesel oil was faint perfume in the air. There was seating for three. Allison was already in the forward position, her hands moving tentatively over the controls. There were no windows and no displays—unless the pale-painted walls were screens. Wait. The third crew position faced to the rear, into formidable racks of electronic equipment. There were displays there.

"See here," said Allison. He turned and looked over her shoulder. She turned a handle, firing up the crawler's turbine. The whine ascended the scale, till Mike felt it through the metal walls and floor as much as through his ears.

Allison pointed. There *was* a display system on the panel in front of her. The letters and digits were bar-formed, but legible. "That's fuel. It's not full. Should be able to go at least fifty kilometers, though. These others, engine temperature, engine speed—as long as you have auto-driver set you'd best ignore them.

"Hold tight." She grabbed the driving sticks and demonstrated how to control the tracks. The vehicle slewed back and forth and around.

"How can you see out?"

Allison laughed. "A nineteenth-century solution. Bend down a little further." She tapped the hull above her head. Now he saw the shallow depression that ringed the driver's head, just above the level of her temples. "Three hundred and sixty degrees of periscopes. The position can be adjusted to suit." She demonstrated.

"Okay. You say Wili wants both the crawlers over to the banana wagons? I'll bring the other one." She slipped out of the driver's seat and disappeared through the hatch.

Mike stared at the controls. She had not turned off the engine. All he had to do was sit down and *drive*. He slid into the seat and stuck his head through the ring of periscope viewers. It was almost as if he had stood up through the hatch; he really could see all around.

Straight ahead, Naismith stood by the wagons. The old man was tearing at the side panels, sending his "precious bananas" cascading across the ground. To the left a puff of vapor came from the other armored carrier, and Mike heard Allison start its engine.

He looked past the lower edge of the periscope ring at the drive sticks. He touched the left tread control, and the carrier jerked incrementally till it was lined up on the wagons. Then he pressed both sticks, and he was moving forward! Mike accelerated to what must have been six or seven meters per second, as fast as a man could run. It was just like in the games. The trip was over in seconds. He cautiously slowed the carrier to a crawl the last few meters, and turned in the direction Paul motioned. Then he was stopped. The turbine's keening went on.

Allison had already opened the rear of the other vehicle and was sliding the bulky electronics gear out onto the dirt. Mike wondered at the mass of equipment the Peacers seemed to need in these vehicles. All of Sy Wentz's police electronics would fit in one of the carriers with room to spare. "Leave the comm and sense equipment aboard, Allison. Wili may be able to interface it." While Allison concentrated on the equipment she knew, Mike and Paul worked to move Wili's processor and the Tinker communications gear out of the banana wagons.

The boy came out of the gutted wagon. He was off the system now, but still seemed dazed, his efforts to help ineffectual. "I have used almost all, Paul. I can't even talk to the net anymore. If we can't use the generators on these"—he waved at the carriers—"we are dead."

That was the big question. Without foreplanning there wasn't a chance, but Paul had brought power interfaces and connector cables. They were based on Allison's specs. If, as with many things, the Peacers had not changed the old standards, then they had a chance.

They could almost fool themselves that the morning was quiet and still. Even the insects were silent. The air around them got steadily brighter, yet the morning fog was still so thick that the sun's disk was not visible. Far away, much farther than the ridgeline, they heard aircraft. Once or twice a minute there was a muffled explosion. Wili had started the Tinker forces on their invasion of the Livermore Valley, but from the north edge, where he had told them to mass through the night. Hopefully the diversion would be some help.

From the corner of his eyes, Mike had the constant impression of motion half-seen, of figures all across the campground working at projects similar to their own. He glanced across the field and saw the reason for the illusion: Wili had cast dozens of bobbles of varying sizes, all in a few seconds' time after the big, overnight bobble had burst. Some must hold just one or two men. Others, like the ones he had put around the main civilian campsite and the Peacer outpost, were more than fifty meters across. And in every one of them he could see the reflections of the four of them, working frantically to finish the transfer before the Peacers down in the Valley realized that the one big bobble had already burst.

It seemed longer, but the work took only minutes. Leaving most of the power cells behind, they didn't have more than fifty kilos of hardware. The processor and the larger bobble generator went into one carrier, while their own satellite comm equipment and a smaller bobbler went into the other. It was an incongruous sight, the Tinker gear sitting small and innocent in the green-painted equipment racks. Allison stood up in the now-spacious carrier and looked at Paul. "Are you satisfied?"

He nodded.

"Then it's smoke-test time." There was no humor in her voice. She turned a switch. Nothing smoked; displays flickered to life. Wili gave a whoop. The rest of the interfacing was software. It would take unaided programmers weeks. Hopefully, Paul and Wili could do it while they were on the move.

Allison, Paul, and Wili took one carrier. Mike—under protest—took the other. There was plenty of room for everyone and all the equipment in just one of the vehicles. "They expect to see rovers in pairs, Mike. I know it."

"Yes," said Allison. "Just follow my lead, Mike; I won't do anything fancy."

The two vehicles moved slowly out of the parking area, cautiously negotiating the field of mirrored tombstones. The whine of their engines drowned the sound of aircraft and occasional explosions that came from far beyond the ridgeline. As they neared the crest, the fog thinned and morning blue was visible. They were far enough from the parking area that—even without their electronics working—they might be mistaken for Peacers.

Then they were starting downward, past the last of the outer defenses. Soon they would know about the inner ones, and know if Allison's news, now fifty years old, was still the key to the destruction of the Peace.

36

Della Lu caught up on the situation reports as she ate breakfast. She wore a fresh jumpsuit, and her straight hair gleamed clean and black in the bright fluorescent lights of the command center. One might think she had just returned from a two-week vacation—not from a night spent running all over the hills, trying to pin down guerrilla positions.

The effect was calculated. The morning watch had just come on. They were for the most part rested, and had none of the harried impatience of the team that had been down here all night. If she were going to exercise command—or even influence—upon them, she must appear cool, analytical. And inside, Della almost was. She had taken time to clean up, time even for a short nap. Physically, things had been much worse in Mongolia. Mentally? Mentally, she was beginning, for the first time in her life, to feel outclassed.

Della looked across the ranked consoles. This was the heart of the Livermore command, which itself was the heart of operations worldwide. Before this morning she had never been in this room. In fact, she and most of the occupants didn't know quite where it was. One thing was sure: It was far underground, proof against nukes and gas and such old-fashioned things. Almost equally sure: It was within a few dozen meters of the Livermore bobble generator and its fusion power source. On some of the displays she could see command language for directing and triggering that generator. There was no point in having such control any more or less secure than the generator itself. They would both be in the deepest, most secret hole available.

A situation board covered most of the front wall. Right now it showed a composite interpretation of the land around Livermore, based on satellite reconnaissance. Apparently, the driving programs were not designed for other inputs. Reports from the men on the ground were entered on the display by computer clerks working at terminals connected to the command database. So far this morning, the board did not show any conflicts between the two sources of information. Enemy contact had been about zip for the last hour.

The situation was different elsewhere in the world: There had been no Authority presence in Europe or Africa for days. In Asia, events much like those in North America had taken place. Old Kim Tioulang was nearly as clever as Hamilton Avery, and he had some of the same blind spots. His bobble generator was just north of Beijing. The smaller displays showed the status of the conflict around it. The Chinese Tinkers hadn't built as many bobblers as their American cousins, and they hadn't penetrated as close to the heart of the Beijing complex. But it was late night there, and an attack was under way. The enemy had surprised K.T. just as it had the Livermore forces. The two bobble generators that were the backbone of Peacer power were both under attack, a simultaneous attack that seemed purposefully coordinated. The Tinkers had communications at least as good as the Authority's. At least.

According to the main display, sunrise was due in fifteen minutes, and a heavy fog covered most of the Valley. There were several possible enemy locations, but for now the Peace was holding off. The Tinker bobblers were extremely effective at close range; during the night, the Authority had lost more than twenty percent of its tank force. Better to wait till they had more information on the enemy. Better to wait till Avery let them use the big bobbler. Then they could take them on by the dozens, and at any range.

Lu finished breakfast, sat sipping coffee. Her eyes wandered about the room, half-consciously memorizing faces, displays, exits. The people in this brightly lit, quiet, air-conditioned bunker were living in a fantasy world. And none of them knew it. This was the end receptacle for megabytes of intelligence streaming in to the Peace from all over the world. Before that data arrived, it was already interpreted and winnowed by remote processors. Here it was finally integrated and put on the displays for the highest commanders to pass upon. These people thought their cute displays gave them some ultimate grip on reality. Lu knew that had never been true—and after last night she was sure the system was riddled with lies.

A door hissed open, and Hamilton Avery entered the command bunker. Behind him came Peace General Bertram Maitland, the chief military seat-warmer in the American Directorate. A typical button-pusher. Somehow she had to get past him and convince Avery to junk remote sensing and fight this one with people.

Maitland and Avery strode to an upper rank of terminals. Avery glanced down at Lu and motioned her to join them.

When she arrived, the general was already busy at a terminal, a large-screen model in a flashy red cabinet. He didn't look up. "Intelligence predicts they'll resume the attack shortly after sunrise. You can see indications of thermal activity on the situation board already. It's barely detectable, since they don't have powered vehicles. This time, though, we'll be ready for them." He punched a final command into the terminal, and a faint buzzing penetrated the walls of the bunker. Maitland gestured to the situation board. "There. We just put every one of the suspected enemy concentrations into stasis."

Avery smiled his controlled smile. Every day he seemed a little paler, a little more drawn. He dressed as nattily as always and spoke as coolly as always, but she could see that he was coming near the end of his strength. "That's good. Excellent. I knew if we waited for a full charge we could make up our losses. How many can we do?"

General Maitland considered. "It depends on the size you want. But we can make several thousand at least, with generation rates as high as one per second. I have it under program control now: Satellite recon and even our field commanders can report an enemy location and automatically get an embobblement." The almost subsonic buzz punctuated his words.

"No!" The two old men looked up at her, more surprised than angry. "No." Della repeated more quietly. "It's bad enough to trust these remote sensors for information If they actually control our bobbling, we could very well use all our reserves and get nothing." *Or worse, bobble our own people.* That thought had not occurred to her before.

Maitland's expression clouded. His antagonist was young, female, and had been promoted with unseemly speed past his favorites. If it weren't for Hamilton Avery, she would be out there on some battalion staff—and that only as reward for her apparent success in Asia. Lu turned her attention to Avery. "Please, Director. I know it's fantastic to suspect enemy interference in our satellite communications. But you yourself have said that nothing is beyond this Hoehler, and that whatever is the most fantastic is what he is most likely to do."

She had pushed the right button. Avery flinched, and his eyes turned to the situation board. Apparently the enemy attack predicted by Maitland had begun. Tiny red dots representing Tinker guerrillas were moving into the Valley. Already the Authority bobbler had acted several more times under automatic control. *And what if this is fraudulent, or even partly so?* There might be Tinkers in the Valley, moving through the deep ravines that netted the landscape, moving closer and closer. Now that the possibility was tied to Paul Hoehler, she could see that it had become almost a certainty in his mind.

"And you were the person who predicted he would attack us here," Avery said almost to himself and then turned to the officer. "General Maitland, abort the programmed response. I want a team of your people monitoring our ground forces—*no satellite relays*. They will determine when and what to embobble."

Maitland slapped the table. "Sir! That will slow response time to the point where some of them may get onto the inner grounds."

For an instant, Avery's face went slack, as if the conflicting threats had finally driven him over the edge. But when he responded, his voice was even, determined. "So? They still have no idea where our generator is. And we have enough conventional force to destroy such infiltrators ten times over. My order stands."

The officer glared at him for a moment. But Maitland had always been a person who followed orders. Avery would have replaced him decades before if that were not the case. He turned back to the terminal, canceled the program, and then talked through it to his analysts at the front of the room, relaying Avery's directive. The intermittent buzzing from beyond the walls ceased.

The Director motioned Lu to follow him. "Anything else?" he asked quietly, when they were out of Maitland's earshot.

Della didn't hesitate. "Yes. Ignore all automated remote intelligence. In the Livermore area, use line-of-sight communications—no relays.

We have plenty of people on the ground, and plenty of aircraft. We'll lose some equipment doing it, but we can set up a physical reconnaissance that will catch almost anyone moving around out there. For places further away, Asia especially, we're stuck with the satellites, but at least we should use them for voice and video communication only— no processed data." She barely stopped for breath.

"Okay, I'll do as you recommend. I want you to stay up here, but don't give orders to Maitland."

It took nearly twenty minutes, but in the end Maitland and his analysts had a jury-rigged system of aircraft sweeps that produced something like complete coverage of the Valley every thirty minutes. Unfortunately, most of the aircraft were not equipped with sophisticated sensors. In some cases, the reports were off eyeballs only. Without infrared and side-looking radar, almost anything could remain hidden in the deeper ravines. It made Maitland and his people very unhappy. During the twenties, they had let the old ground based system slide into oblivion. Instead, enormous resources had been put into the satellite system, one they thought gave them even finer protection, and worldwide. Now that system was being ignored; they might as well be refighting World War II.

Maitland pointed to the status board, which his men were painfully updating with the field reports that were coming in. "See? The people on the ground have missed almost all the concentrations we identified from orbit. The enemy is well-camouflaged. Without good sensors, we're just not going to see him."

"They have spotted several small teams, though."

Maitland shrugged. "Yes, sir. I take it we have permission to bobble them?"

There was a glint in Avery's eyes as he responded to the question. However Lu's theories turned out, Maitland's days with this job were numbered. "Immediately."

A small voice sounded from the general's terminal. "Sir, I'm having some trouble with the update of the Mission Pass area. Uh, two A-five-elevens have overflown the Pass. . . . They both say the bobble there is gone."

Their eyes snapped up to the situation board. The map was constructed with photographic precision. The Mission Pass bobble, the Tinker bobble that had nearly killed her the night before, glinted silver and serene on that board. The satellite system still saw it—or reported seeing it.

Gone. Avery went even paler. Maitland sucked his breath back between his teeth. Here was direct, incontrovertible evidence. They had been taken, fooled. And now they had only the vaguest idea where the enemy might really be and what he might do. "My God. She was right! She was right all along."

Della was not listening. There was no triumph in her. She had been fooled, too. She had believed the techs' smug assurance that ten years was the theoretical minimum for the duration of a bobble. How could she have missed this? *Last night I had them, I'll bet. I had Hoehler and Wili and Mike and everyone who counts. . . . And I let them escape through time to today.* Her mind racing frantically through the implications. If twenty-four-hour bobbles could be cast, then what about sixty-second bobbles—or one-second ones? What advantage could the other side gain from such? *Why, they could—*

"Ma'am?" Someone touched her elbow. Her attention returned to the brightly lit command room. It was Maitland's aide. The general had spoken to her. Della's eyes focused on the two old men.

"I'm sorry. What did you say?"

The general's voice was flat but not hostile. Even surprise was leached from him now. Everything he depended on had failed him. "We just got a call on the satellite network. Max priority and max encryption." That could only be a Director—and the only other surviving director was K.T. in China. "Caller demands to talk to you. Says his name is Miguel Rosas."

37

Mike drove. Fifty meters ahead, almost swallowed up in the fog, he could see the other crawler. Inside it were Paul and Wili and Allison, with Allison driving. It was easy to keep up until Allison trucked off the broad roadway into the hills. He came down a hillside a little fast, and nearly lost control.

"You okay?" Paul's voice sounded anxiously in his ear. He'd established the laser link just seconds before.

Mike twitched the controls tentatively. "Yeah. But why come straight down that hill?"

"Sorry, Mike." It was Jill—no, Allison. "Sideways would have been worse; might have slipped treads."

Then they were moving through open country. The ring of periscopes was not as good as a wraparound holo, but it did give the sensation that his head was in the open. The keening of the engine covered any natural morning sounds. Except for their crawlers, and a crow flickering past in the mist, nothing moved. The grass was sere and golden, the dirt beneath white and gravelly. An occasional dwarf oak loomed out of the fog and forced Allison and then Mike to detour. He should be able to smell morning dew on the grass, but the only smells were of diesel fuel and paint.

And now the morning fog began to part. Blue filtered through from above. Then the blue became sky. Mike felt like a swimmer come to the surface of a misty sea, looking across the waters at far hills.

There was the war, and it was more fantastic than any old-time movie:

Silver balls floated by the dozens through the sky. Far away, Peacer jets were dark bugs trailing grimy vapor. They swooped and climbed. Their dives ended in flares of color as they strafed Tinker infiltrators on the far side of the Valley. Bombs and napalm burned orange and black through the sea of fog. He saw one diving aircraft replaced by a silvery sphere—which continued the plane's trajectory into the earth. The pilot might wake decades from now—as Allison Parker had done—and wonder what had become of his world. That was a lucky shot. Mike knew the Tinker bobblers were small, not even as powerful as the one Wili brought to LA. Their range with accuracy was only a hundred meters, and the largest bobble they could cast was five or ten meters across. On the other hand, they could be used defensively. The last Mike had heard, the Bay Area Tinkers had got the minimum duration down to fifteen seconds; just a little better and "flicker" tactics would be possible.

Here and there, peeping out of the mist, were bobbles set in the ground: Peacer armor bobbled during the night fighting or Tinkers caught by the monster in the valley. The only difference was size.

The nose of the crawler dipped steeply, and Mike grunted in surprise, his attention back on his driving. He took the little valley much more slowly than the last one. The forward crawler was almost up the other side when he reached the bottom. His carrier moved quickly through a small stream, and then he was almost laid on his back as it climbed the far side. He pushed the throttle far forward. Power screamed through the treads. The crawler came over the lip of the embankment fast, nose high and fell with a crash.

"The trees ahead. We'll stop there for a couple of minutes." It was Wili's voice. Mike followed the other crawler into an open stand of twisted oaks. Far across the Livermore Valley, two dark gnats peeled off from the general swarm that hovered above the Tinker insurgents and flew toward them. That must be the reason Wili wanted to get under cover. Mike looked up through the scrawny branches and wondered what sort of protection the trees really gave. Even the most primitive thermal sensor should be able to see them sitting here with hot engines.

The jets roared by a couple thousand meters to the west. Their thunder dwindled to nothing. Mike looked again across Livermore Valley.

Where the fighting was heaviest, new bobbles shone almost once a second. With the engines idling, Mike thought he could hear the thunder and thump of more conventional weapons. Two jets dived upon a hidden target and the mists were crisscrossed with their laser fire. The target tried something new: A haze of bobbles—too small to distinguish at this distance—appeared between aircraft and ground. There was a flash of sudden red stars within that haze as the energy beams reflected again and again from the multiple mirrors. It was hard to tell if it made an effective shield. Then he noticed the jets staggering out of their drive. One exploded. The other trailed smoke and flame in a long arc toward the ground. Mike suddenly wondered what would happen to a jet engine if it sucked in a dozen two-centimeter bobbles.

Wili's voice came again. "Mike. The Peacers are going to discover that we have been faking their satellite reception."

"When?" asked Mike.

"Any second. They are changing to aircraft reconnaissance."

Mike looked around him, wishing suddenly that he were on foot. It would be so much easier to hide a human-sized target than a crawler. "So we can't depend on being 'invisible' anymore."

"No. *We* can. I am also speaking with Peacer control on the direct line-of-sight." These last words were spoken by a deep, male voice. Mike started, then realized he was not talking directly to Wili. The fake had a perfect Oregon accent, though the syntax was still Wili's; hopefully that would go unnoticed in the rush of battle. He tried to imagine the manifold images Wili must be projecting to allies and enemies. "They think we're Peacer recon. They have fourteen other crawlers moving around their inner area. As long as we follow their directions, we won't be attacked. . . . And they want us to move closer in."

Closer in. If Wili could get just another five thousand meters closer, he could bobble the Peacer generator.

"Okay. Just tell us which way to go."

"I will, Mike. But there's something else I want you to do first."

"Sure."

"I'm going to give you a satellite connection to Authority High

Command. Call them. Insist to speak with Della Lu. Tell her everything you know about our tricks—"

Mike's hands tightened on the drive sticks. "No!"

"—except that we control these two crawlers."

"But *why?*"

"Do it, Mike. If you call now, you'll be able to give away our satellite trick before they have proof. Maybe they will think you're still loyal. It will distract them, anyway. Give away anything you want. I'll listen too. I'll learn more what's passing at their center. Please, Mike."

Mike gritted his teeth. "Okay, Wili. Put 'em on."

Allison Parker grinned savagely to herself. She hadn't driven a crawler in almost three years—fifty-three if you counted years like the rest of the universe. At the time, she'd thought it a silly waste of taxpayer's money to have recon specialists take a tour with a base security outfit. The idea had been that anyone who collected intelligence should be familiar with the groundside problems of security and deception. Becoming a tank driver had been fun, but she never expected to see the inside of one of these things again.

Yet here she was. Allison gunned the engines, and the little armored carrier almost flew out of the thicket of scrub oak where they'd been hiding. She recognized these hills, even with the hovering spheres and napalm bursting in the distance. Time didn't change some things. Their path ran parallel to a series of cairnlike concrete structures, the ruins of the power lines that had stretched across the Valley. Why, she and . . . Paul . . . had hiked along precisely this way . . . so long ago.

She tried to shake free of the painful double images. The sun was fast burning off the morning fog. Soon the concealment the Tinkers were using to such advantage would be gone. If they couldn't win by then, they never would.

In her earphone, she heard a strange voice reporting their position to the Peacer command center. It was eerie: She knew the message came ultimately from Wili. But he was sitting right behind her and had not spoken a word. The last time she looked, he seemed asleep.

The deception was working. They were doing what Peacer control said, but they were also coming closer and closer to the edge of the inner security area.

251

"Paul. What I saw from orbit is only about six thousand meters north of here. We'll be closest in another couple of minutes. Is that close enough?"

Paul touched his scalp connector, seemed to think. "No. We'd have to be motionless for almost an hour to bobble from that range. The best trade-off is still four thousand meters. I—Wili—has a spot in mind; he and Jill are doing prelim computations on the assumption we can reach it. Even so, he'll need about thirty seconds once we get there."

After a moment Paul added, "In a couple minutes, we'll break our cover. Wili will stop transmitting and you'll drive like hell straight for their bobbler."

Allison looked through the periscoped hull. The crawler was so close to the security perimeter, the towers and domes of the Enclave blocked her view to the north. The Enclave was a city, and their final dash would take them well inside its boundaries. "We'll be sitting ducks." Her sentence was punctuated by the swelling roar of a stub-winged jet that swept almost directly over them. She hadn't seen or heard it till that instant. But the aircraft wasn't strafing. It was loafing along at less than one hundred meters per second, a low-level recon.

"We have a good chance." Wili's voice came suddenly in her earphone. "We won't make our run until the patrol planes are in good position. We should be in their blind spot for almost five minutes."

"And they'll have other things to worry about," said Paul. "I've been talking to the Tinkers coming in on foot. They all know the site of the Peacer generator now. Some of them have gotten pretty close, closer than we. They don't have our equipment—but the Authority can't know that for sure. When Wili gives the signal, they'll come out of hiding and make their own dash inwards."

The war went far beyond their crawlers, beyond even the Livermore Valley. Paul said a similar battle was being played out in China.

Even so, victory or defeat seemed to depend on what happened to this one crawler in the next few minutes.

38

Della slipped on the earpiece and adjusted the microphone to her throat. She had the undivided attention of Avery, Maitland, and everyone else in earshot. None of them except Hamilton Avery had heard of one Miguel Rosas, but they all knew he had no business on a maximum security channel. "Mike?"

A familiar voice came from the earpiece and the speaker on the terminal. "Hello, Della. I've got some news for you."

"Just calling on this line is news enough. So your people have cracked our comm and recon system."

"Right the first time."

"Where are you calling from?"

"The ridgeline southwest of you. I don't want to say more—I still don't trust your friends. . . . It's just that I trust mine even less." This last was spoken low, almost muttered. "Look. There are other things you don't know. The Tinkers know exactly where your bobbler is hidden."

"What?" Avery turned abruptly to the situation board and motioned for Maitland to check it out.

"How can they know? You have spies? Carry-in bugs?"

Mike's forced chuckle echoed from the speaker. "It's a long story, Della. You would be amused. The old US Air Force had it spotted—just too late to save the world from you. The Tinkers stumbled on the secret only a few weeks ago."

Della glanced questioningly at the Director, but Avery was looking over Maitland's shoulder, at the terminal. The general's people were frantically typing queries, posting results. The general looked up at the Director. "It's possible, sir. Most of the infiltrators are north and west of the Enclave. But the ones closest to the inner zone boundary are also the closest to the generator; they seem to have a preference for that sector."

"It could be an artifact of our increased surveillance in that area."

"Yes, sir." But now Maitland did not sound complacent. Avery nodded to himself. He hadn't believed his own explanation. "Very well. Concentrate tactical air there. I see you have two armored vehicles already tracking along the boundary. Keep them there. Bring in more. I want what infantry we have moved there, too."

"Right. Once we locate them, they're no threat. We have all the firepower."

Della spoke again to Mike. "Where is Paul Hoehler—the man you call Naismith?" Avery stiffened at the question, and his attention returned to her, an almost physical force.

"Look, I really don't know. They have me working a pointer relay; some of our people don't have their own satellite receivers."

Della cut the connection and said to Avery, "I think he's lying, Director. Our only lever on Mike Rosas is his hatred for certain Tinker potentials, in particular bioscience. He'll resist hurting his personal friends."

"He *knows* Hoehler?" Avery seemed astounded to find someone so close to the ultimate antagonist. "If he knows where Hoehler is . . ." The Director's eyes unfocused. "You've got to squeeze that out of him, Della. Take this conversation off the speaker and talk to him. Promise him anything, tell him anything, but find Hoehler." With a visible effort he turned back to Maitland. "Get me Tioulang in Beijing. I know, I know. Nothing is secure." He smiled, an almost skeletal grimace. "But I don't care if they know what I tell him."

Della resumed the link with Mike. Now that the speaker was off, his voice would sound in her ear only. And with the throat mike, her side of the conversation would be inaudible to those around her. "This is just you and me now, Mike. The brass thinks they got everything they can out of you."

"Oh yeah? And what do you think?"

"I think some large but unknown percentage of what you are telling me is bullshit."

"I guessed that. But you're still talking."

"I think we're both betting we can learn more than the other from talking. Besides—" Her eyes fixed on the Renaissance trigger box sitting on the table before Hamilton Avery. With a small part of her attention she followed what Avery was saying to his counterpart in Beijing. "Besides, I don't think you know what you're up against."

"Enlighten me."

"The Tinker goal is to bobble the Livermore generator. Similarly for the attack on Beijing. You don't realize that if we consider the Peace truly endangered, we will embobble *ourselves*, and continue the struggle decades in the future."

"Hmm. Like the trick we played on you at Mission Pass."

"But on a much larger scale."

"Well, it won't help you. Some of us will wait—and we'll know where to wait. Besides, the Authority's power isn't just in Livermore and Beijing. You need your heavy industry, too."

Della smiled to herself. Mike's phrasing was tacit admission he was still a Tinker. There were deceptions here—deceptions she could penetrate given a little time—but neither of them was pretending loyalties they did not have. Time to give away a little information, information that would do them no good now: "There are a few things you don't know. The Peace has more than two bobble generators."

There was a moment of silence in her ear. "I don't believe you— How many?"

Della laughed quietly. Maitland glanced up at her, then turned back to his terminal. "That is a secret. We've been working on them ever since we suspected Tinker infiltration—spies, we thought. Only a few people know, and we never spoke of it on our comm net. More important than the number is the location; you won't know about them till they come out at you."

There was a longer silence. She had made a point.

"And what other things make 'Peace' unbeatable?" There was sarcasm and something else in his words. In the middle of the sentence, his voice seem to catch—as if he had just lifted something. As was usual with a high-crypto channel, there were no background sounds. But the data massaging left enough in the voice to recognize tones and sublinguistical things like this sudden exhalation. The sound, almost a grunt, had not been repeated. If she could just get him to talk a little more.

There was a secret that might do it. Renaissance. Besides, it was something she owed him, perhaps owed all the enemy. "You should know that if you force this on us, we'll not let you grow strong during our absence. The Authority"—for once calling it "the Peace" stuck in her throat—"has planted nukes in the Valley. And we have such bombs on rockets. If we bobble up . . . if we bobble up, your pretty Tinker culture gets bombed back to the Stone Age, and we'll build anew when we come out."

Still a longer silence. *Is he talking to someone else? Has he broken the connection?* "Mike?"

"Della, why are you on their side?"

He'd asked her that once before. She bit her lip. "I—I didn't dream up Renaissance, Mike. I think we can win without it. The world has had decades now more peaceful than any in human history. When we took over, the race was at the edge of the precipice. You know that. The nation states were bad enough; they would have destroyed civilization if left to themselves. But even worse, their weapons had become so cheap that small groups—some reasonable, some monstrous—would have had them. If the world could barely tolerate a dozen killer nations, how could it survive thousands of psychotics with rad bombs and war plagues?

"I know you understand what I'm saying. You felt that way about bioscience. *There are other things as bad, Mike.*" She stopped abruptly, wondering who was manipulating whom. And suddenly she realized that Mike, the enemy, was one of the few people she could ever talk to, one of the few people who could understand the . . . things . . . she had done. And perhaps he was the only person—outside of herself—whose disapproval could move her.

"I understand," came Mike's voice. "Maybe history will say the Authority gave the human race time to save itself, to come up with new institutions. You've had fifty years; it hasn't been all bad. . . . But no matter what either of us wants, it's ending now. And this 'Renaissance' will destroy whatever good you've done." His voice caught again.

"Don't worry. We'll win fair and square and there'll be no Renaissance." She was watching the main display. One of the crawlers had turned almost directly inward, toward the heart of the Enclave. Della cut audio and got the attention of Maitland's aide. She nodded questioningly at the crawler symbol on the display.

The colonel leaned across from his chair and said quietly, "They saw Tinkers within the perimeter. They're chasing."

The symbol moved in little jerks, updated by the nearly manual control they had been reduced to. Suddenly the crawler symbol disappeared from the board. Avery sucked in his breath. An analyst looked at his displays and said almost immediately, "We lost laser comm. They may have been bobbled . . . or may be out of sight."

Possible. The ground was rough, even inside the Enclave boundary. Riding a crawler over that would be an exciting thing. . . . And then Della understood the mystery in Mike's speech. *"Mr. Director."* Her shout cut across all other voices. "That crawler isn't looking for the enemy. It *is* the enemy!"

39

While they drove parallel to the perimeter fence, the ground was not too rough. When they turned inward, it would be a different story. There was a system of ditches running along the fence.

Beyond that was the interior of the Enclave. Allison risked a glance every now and then. It was like the future she had always imagined: spires, tall buildings, wide swaths of green. Paul said Authority ground troops were moving into the area, but right now all was peaceful, abandoned.

Wait. Three men came running out of the ditches. They paused at the fence and then were somehow through. Two of them carried heavy backpacks. These were their Tinker allies. One waved to their crawler, and then they disappeared among the buildings.

"Turn here. Follow them inward," said Paul. "Wili's told the Peacer command we're in hot pursuit."

Allison pushed/pulled on the control sticks. The armored vehicle spun on its treads, one reversed, the other still pulling forward. Through the side periscope she saw Mike's crawler, moving off to the north. No doubt Wili had told him not to turn.

They shot forward at top speed, the engines an eerie screaming all around them. Beside Allison, Paul was gasping. Thirty kph across open terrain was rough as any air maneuver. Then they were falling, and the view ahead was filled with concrete. They flew over the edge of the ditch and crashed downward onto the floor. The restraint webbing couldn't entirely absorb the shock. For a moment Allison was in a daze, her hands freezing the controls into fast forward. The crawler ran up the steep far wall and teetered there an instant, as if unsure whether to proceed upward or fall on its back.

Then they slammed down on the other side, collapsing the fence. Whatever automatic defenses lived here must be temporarily disabled.

She ground clear of the concrete-and-steel rubble, then risked a glance at Paul. "Oh, my God." He was slumped forward, a wash of red spread down his face. Red was smeared on the wall in front of him. Somehow he had not tied down properly.

Allison slowed the crawler. She twisted in her seat, saw that the boy remained comatose. "Wili! Paul's hurt!"

A woman's voice shrieked in her ear, *"You dumb bitch!"*

Wili twisted, his face agonized, like someone trying to waken from a dream.

But if he woke, if his dream died, then all their dreams would die. "Drive, Allison. Please drive." Wili's synthetic voice came cool from her earpiece. "Paul . . . Paul wants this more than anything." Behind her, the boy's real voice was softly moaning. And Paul moved not at all.

Allison closed out everything but her job: They were on a surfaced street. She rammed the throttle forward, took the crawler up to seventy kph. She had only vague impressions of the buildings on either side of them. It looked like residential housing, though more opulent than in her time. All was deserted. Coming up on a T-intersection. Over the roofs of the multistory residences, the towers at the center of the Enclave seemed no nearer.

Wili's voice continued. "Right at the intersection. Then left and left. Foot soldiers are coming from east. So far they think we're one of them, but I'm breaking laser contact . . . *now*"—Allison whipped into the turn—"and they should guess what we are very soon."

They continued so for several minutes. It was like dealing with an ordinary voice program: Turn right. Turn left. Slow down. Keep to the edge of the street.

"Five hundred meters. Take the service alley here. They're onto us. Gunships coming. They can't locate us precisely enough to bobble. Whoever sees us is to shoot." He was silent again as Allison negotiated the alley. Still no sign of life from Paul.

"He still lives, Allison. I can still . . . hear . . . him a little."

Through the front periscope she had a glimpse of something dark and fast cross the narrow band of sky between the houses.

"Pull under that overhang. Stop. Throttle up to charge the cells. Thirty seconds for local conditions and I'll be ready to fire."

The moment they were stopped, Allison was out of her harness and bending over Paul. "Now leave me. I need to think. Take Paul. Save Paul."

She looked at the boy. He still hadn't opened his eyes. He was further off than she had ever seen him.

"But, Wili—"

His body twitched, and the synthetic voice was suddenly angry in her ear. "I need time to think, and I don't have it. Their planes are on the way. Get out. *Get out!*"

Allison unbuckled Paul and removed the scalp connector. He was breathing, but his face remained slack. She cranked at the rear doors, praying that nothing had been warped by their fall into the ditch. The doors popped open and cool morning air drifted in, along with the increased keening of the engines.

She ripped off her headset and struggled to get the old man's body over her shoulder. As she staggered past Wili, she noticed his lips were moving. She bent down awkwardly to listen. The boy was mumbling, "Run, run, run, run . . ."

Allison did her best.

40

No one understood the conflict as Wili did. Even when he was linked with Jill, Paul had only a secondhand view. And after Paul, there was no one who saw more than fragments of the picture. It was Wili who ran the Tinker side of the show—and to some extent the Peacer side, too. Without his directions in Paul's voice, the thousands of separate operations going on all over the Earth would be so scattered in time and effect that the Authority would have little trouble keeping its own control system going.

But Wili knew his time would end very, very soon.

From the crawler's recon camera, he watched Paul and Allison moving away into the managerial residences. Their footsteps came fainter in his exterior microphones. Would he ever know if Paul survived?

Through the narrow gap between the sides of the alley a Peacer satellite floated beyond the blue sky. One reason he had chosen this parking spot was to have that line of sight. In ninety seconds, the radio star would slide behind carven wooden eaves. He would lose it, and thus its relay to synchronous altitude, and thus his control of things worldwide. He would be deaf, dumb, and blind. But ninety seconds from now, it wouldn't matter; he and all the other Tinkers would win or lose in sixty.

The whole system had spasmed when Paul was knocked out. Jill had stopped responding. For several minutes, Wili had struggled with all the high-level computations. Now Jill was coming back on line; she was almost finished with the local state computations. The capacitors would be fully charged seconds after that. Wili surveyed the world one last time.

From orbit he saw golden morning spread across Northern California. Livermore Valley sparkled with a false dew that was really dozens —hundreds—of bobbles. Unaided humans would need many versions of this picture to understand what Wili saw at once.

There were ground troops a couple of thousand meters east of him. They had fanned out, obviously didn't know where he was. The tricky course he had given Allison would keep him safe from them for at least five minutes.

Jets had been diverted from the north side of the Valley. He watched them crawl across the landscape at nearly four hundred meters per second. They were the real threat. They could see him before the capacitors were charged. There was no way to divert them or to trick them. The pilots had been instructed to use their own eyes, to find the crawler, and to destroy it. Even if they failed in the last, they would report an accurate position—and the Livermore bobbler would get him.

He burst-transmitted a last message to the Tinker teams in the Valley: Paul's voice announced the imminent bobbling and assigned new missions. Because of Wili's deceptions, their casualties had been light; that might change now. He told them what he had learned about Renaissance and redirected them against the missile sites he had detected. He wondered fleetingly how many would feel betrayed to learn of Renaissance, would wish that he—Paul—would stop the assault. But if Paul were really here, if Paul could think as fast as Wili, he'd've done the same.

He must end the Peace so quickly that Renaissance died, too.

Wili passed from one satellite to another, till he was looking down on Beijing at midnight. Without Wili's close supervision, the fighting had been bloodier: There were bobbles scattered through the ruins of the old city, but there were bodies, too, bodies that would not live again. The Chinese Tinkers had to get in very close; they did not have a powerful bobbler or the Wili/Jill processor. Even so, they might win. Wili had guided three teams to less than one thousand meters of the Beijing bobbler. He sent his last advice, showing them a transient gap in the defense.

Messages sent or automatically sending. Now there was only his own mission. The mission all else depended on.

From high above, Wili saw an aircraft sweep south over the alley. (Its boom crashed around the carrier, but Wili's own senses were locked out and he barely felt it.) The pilot *must* have seen him. How long till the follow-up bomb run?

The Authority's great bobbler was four thousand meters north of him. He and Jill had made a deadly minimax decision in deciding on that range. He "looked at" the capacitors. They were still ten seconds from the overcharge he needed. Ten seconds? The charge rate was declining as charge approached the necessary level. Their haywired interface to the crawler's electrical generator was failing. Extrapolation along the failure curve: thirty seconds to charge.

The other aircraft had been alerted. Wili saw courses change. More extrapolation: It would be very, very close. He could save himself by self-bobbling, the simplest of all generations. He could save himself and lose the war.

Wili watched in an omniscient daze, watched from above as death crept down on the tiny crawler.

Something itched. Something demanded attention. He relaxed his hold, let resources be diverted . . . and Jill's image floated up.

Wili! Go! You can still go! Jill flooded him with a last burst of data, showing that all processes would proceed automatically to completion. Then she cut him off.

And Wili was alone in the crawler. He looked around, vision blurred, suddenly aware of sweat and diesel fuel and turbine noise. He groped for his harness release, then rolled off onto the floor. He barely felt the scalp connector tear free. He came to his feet and blundered out the rear doors into the sunlight.

He didn't hear the jets' approach.

Paul moaned. Allison couldn't tell if he was trying to say something or was simply responding to the rough handling. She got under his weight and stagger-ran across the alley toward a stone-walled patio. The gate was open; there was no lock. Allison kicked aside a child's tricycle and laid Paul down behind the waist-high wall. Should be safe from shrapnel here, except—she glanced over her shoulder at the glass wall that stretched across the interior side of the patio. Beyond was carpeting, elegant furniture. That glass could come showering down if the building got hit. She started to pull Paul behind the marble table that dominated the patio.

"No! Wili. Did he make it?" He struggled weakly against her hands.

The sky to the north showed patches of smoke, smudged exhaust trails, a vagrant floating bobble where someone had missed a target—but that was all. Wili had not acted; the crawler sat motionless, its engines screaming. Somewhere else she heard treads.

The boom was like a wall of sound smashing over them. Windows on both sides of the street flew inward. Allison had a flickering impression of the aircraft as it swept over the street. Her attention jerked back to the sky, scanned. A dark gnat hung there, surrounded by the dirty aureole of its exhaust. There was no sound from this follow-up craft; it was coming straight in. The length of the street—and the crawler—would be visible to it. She watched it a moment, then dived to the tiled patio deck next to Paul.

Scarcely time to swear, and the ground smashed up into them.

Allison didn't lose consciousness, but for a long moment she didn't really know where she was. A girl in a gingham dress leaned over an old man, seeing red spread across a beautiful tile floor.

A million garbage cans dropped and rattled around her.

Allison touched her face, felt dust and untorn skin. The blood wasn't hers.

How bad was he hurt?

The old man looked up at her. He brushed her hands away with some last manic strength. "Allison. Did we win . . . please? After all these years, to get that bastard Avery." His speech slurred into mumbling.

Allison came to her knees and looked over the wall. The street was in ruins, riddled with flying debris. The crawler had been hit, its front end destroyed. Fire spread crackling from what was left of its fuel. Under the treads something else burned green and violent. And the sky to the north . . .

. . . was as empty as before. No bobble stood where she knew the Peace generator was hidden. The battle might yet go on for hours, but Allison knew that they had lost. She looked down at the old man and tried to smile. "It's there, Paul. You won."

41

"**W**e got one of them, sir. Ground troops have brought in three survivors. They're—"

"From the nearer one? Where is that second crawler?" Hamilton Avery leaned over the console, his hands pale against the base of the keyboard.

"We don't know, sir. We have three thousand men on foot in that area. We'll have it in a matter of minutes, even if tac air doesn't get it first. About the three we picked—"

Avery angrily cut the connection. He sat down abruptly, chewed at his lip. "He's getting closer, I know it. Everything we do seems a victory, but is really a defeat." He clenched his fists, and Della could imagine him screaming to himself: *What can we do?* She had seen administrators go over the edge in Mongolia, frozen into inaction or suicidal overreaction. The difference was that *she* had been the boss in Mongolia. Here . . .

Avery opened his fists with visible effort. "Very well. What is the status of Beijing? Is the enemy any closer than before?"

General Maitland spoke to his terminal. He looked at the response in silence. Then, "Director, we have lost comm with them. The recon birds show the Beijing generator has been bobbled. . . ." He paused as though waiting for some explosion from his boss. But Avery was composed again. Only the faint glassiness of his stare admitted his terror.

"—and of course that could be faked, too," Avery said quietly. "Try

for direct radio confirmation . . . from someone known to us."
Maitland nodded, started to turn away. "And, General. Begin the computations to bobble us up." He absently caressed the Renaissance trigger that sat on the table before him. "I can tell you the coordinates."

Maitland relayed the order to try for shortwave communication with Beijing. But he personally entered the coordinates as Avery spoke them. As Maitland set up the rest of the program, Della eased into a chair behind the Director. "Sir, there is no need for this."

Hamilton Avery smiled his old, genteel smile, but he wasn't listening to her. "Perhaps not, my dear. That is why we are checking for confirmation from Beijing." He flipped open the Renaissance box, revealing a key pad. A red light began blinking on the top. Avery fiddled with a second cover, which protected some kind of button. "Strange. When I was a child, people talked about 'pushing the button' as though there was a magic red button that could bring nuclear war. I doubt if ever power was just so concentrated . . . But here I have almost exactly that, Della. One big red button. We've worked hard these last few months to make it effective. You know, we really didn't have that many nukes before. We never saw how they might be necessary to preserve the Peace. But if Beijing is really gone, this will be the only way."

He looked into Della's eyes. "It won't be so bad, my dear. We've been very selective. We know the areas where our enemy is concentrated; making them uninhabitable won't have any lasting effect on the race."

To her left, Maitland had completed his preparations. The display showed the standard menu she had seen in his earlier operations. Even by Authority standards, it looked old-fashioned. Quite likely the control software was unchanged from the first years of the Authority.

Maitland had overridden all the fail-safes. At the bottom of the display, outsized capitals blinked:

WARNING!
THE ABOVE TARGETS ARE FRIENDLY.
CONTINUE?

A simple "yes< CR >" would bobble the industrial core of the Authority into the next century.

"We have shortwave communication with Peace forces at Beijing,

Director." The voice came unseen, but it was recognizably Maitland's chief aide. "These are troops originally from the Vancouver franchise. Several of them are known to people here. At least we can verify these are really our men."

"And?" Avery asked quietly.

"The center of the Beijing Enclave is bobbled, sir. They can see it from their positions. The fighting has pretty much ended. Apparently the enemy is lying low, waiting for our reaction. Your instructions are requested."

"In a minute," Avery smiled. "General, you may proceed as planned." That minute would be more than fifty years in the future.

"yes<CR>," the general typed. The familiar buzzing hum sounded irregularly, and one after another the locations on the list were marked as bobbled: Los Angeles Enclave, Brasilia Enclave, Redoubt 001 . . . It was quickly done, what no enemy could ever do. All other activity in the room ceased; they all knew. The Authority was now committed. In fact, most of the Authority was gone from the world by that act. All that remained was this one generator, this one command center—and the hundreds of nuclear bombs that Avery's little red button would rain upon the Earth.

Maitland set up the last target, and the console showed:

FINAL WARNING!
PROJECTION WILL SELF-ENCLOSE.
CONTINUE?

Now Hamilton Avery was punching an elaborate pass-code into his red trigger box. In seconds, he would issue the command that would poison sections of continents. Then Maitland could bobble them into a future made safe for the "Peace."

The shock in Della's face must finally have registered on him. "I am not a monster, Miss Lu. I have never used more than the absolute minimum force necessary to preserve the Peace. After I launch Renaissance, we will bobble up, and then we will be in a future where the Peace can be reestablished. And though it will be an instant to us, I assure you I will always feel the guilt for the price that had to be paid." He gestured at his trigger box. "It is a responsibility I take solely upon myself."

That's damned magnanimous of you. She wondered fleetingly if hard-boiled types like Della Lu and Hamilton Avery always ended up like this—rationalizing the destruction of all they claimed to protect.

Maybe not. Her decision had been building for weeks, ever since she had learned of Renaissance. It had dominated everything after her talk with Mike. Della glanced around the room, wished she had her sidearm: She would need it during the next few minutes. She touched her throat and said clearly, "See you later, Mike."

There was quick understanding on Avery's face, but he didn't have a chance. With her right hand she flicked the red box down the table, out of Avery's reach. Almost simultaneously, she smashed Maitland's throat with the edge of her left. Turning, she leaned over the general's collapsing form—and typed:

"yes<CR>"

42

Wili moped across the lawn, his hands stuck deep in his pockets, his face turned downward. He kicked up little puffs of dust where the grass was brownest. The new tenants were lazy about watering, or else maybe the irrigation pipes were busted.

This part of Livermore had been untouched by the fighting; the losers had departed peaceably enough, once they saw bobbles sprout over their most important resources. Except for the dying grass, it was beautiful here, the buildings as luxurious as Wili could imagine. When they turned on full electric power, it made the Jonque palaces in LA look like hovels. And most anything here—the aircraft, the automobiles, the mansions—could be his.

Just my luck. I get everything I ever wanted, and then I lose the people that are more important. Paul had decided to drop out. It made sense and Wili was not angry about it, but it hurt anyway. Wili thought back to their meeting, just half an hour before. He had guessed the moment he'd seen Paul's face. Wili had tried to ignore it, had rushed into the subject he'd thought they were to talk about: "I just talked to those doctors we flew in from France, Paul. They say my insides are as normal as anything. They measured me every way"—he had undergone dozens of painful tests, massive indignities compared to what had been done to him at Scripps, and yet much less powerful. The French doctors were not bioscientists, but simply the best medical staff the European director would tolerate—"and they say I'm using my food, that

269

I'm growing fast." He grinned. "Bet I will be more than one meter seventy."

Paul leaned back in his chair and returned the smile. The old man was looking good himself. He'd had a bad concussion during the battle, and for a while the doctors weren't sure he would survive. "I'll bet too. It's exactly what I'd been hoping. You're going to be around for a long time, and the world's going to be a better place for it. And . . ." His voice trailed off, and he didn't meet the boy's look. Wili held his breath, praying *Dio* his guess wouldn't be correct. They sat in silence for an awkward moment. Wili looked around, trying to pretend that nothing of import was to be said. Naismith had appropriated the office of some Peacer bigwig. It had a beautiful view of the hills to the south, yet it was plainer than most, almost as if it had been designed for the old man all along. The walls were unadorned, though there was a darker rectangle of paint on the wall facing Paul's desk. A picture had hung there once. Wili wondered about that.

Finally Naismith spoke. "Strange. I think I've done penance for blindly giving them the bobble in the first place. I have accomplished everything I dreamed of all these years since the Authority destroyed the world. . . . And yet—Wili, I'm going to drop out, fifty years at least."

"Paul! Why?" It was said now, and Wili couldn't keep the pain from his voice.

"Many reasons. Many good reasons." Naismith leaned forward intently. "I'm very old, Wili. I think you'll see many from my generation go. We know the bioscience people in stasis at Scripps have ways of helping us."

"But there are others. They can't be the only ones with the secret."

"Maybe. The bioscience types are surfacing very slowly. They can't be sure if humanity will accept them, even though the plagues are decades past."

"Well, *stay.* Wait and see." Wili cast wildly about, came up with a reason that might be strong enough. "Paul, if you go, you may never see Allison again. I thought—"

"You thought I loved Allison, that I hated the Authority on her account as much as any." His voice went low. "You are right, Wili, *and don't you ever tell her that!* The fact that she lives, that she is just as I always remembered her, is a miracle that goes beyond all my dreams.

But she is another reason I must leave, and soon. It hurts every day to see her; she likes me, but almost as a stranger. The man she knew has died, and I see pity in her more than anything else. I must escape from that."

He stopped. "There's something else too. . . . Wili, I wonder about Jill. Did I lose the only one I ever really had? I have the craziest dreams from when I was knocked out. She was trying like hell to bring me back. She seemed as real as anyone . . . and more caring. But there's no way that program could have been sentient; we're nowhere near systems that powerful. No *person* sacrificed her life for us." The look in his eyes made the sentence a question.

It was a question that had hovered in Wili's mind ever since Jill had driven him out of the crawler. He thought back. He had known Jill . . . used the Jill program . . . for almost nine months. Her projection had been there when he was sick; she had helped him learn symbiotic programming. Something inside him had always thought her one of his best friends. He tried not to guess how much stronger Paul's feelings must be. Wili remembered Jill's hysterical reaction when Paul had been hurt; she had disappeared from the net for minutes, only coming back at the last second to try to save Wili. And Jill was complex, complex enough that any attempt at duplication would fail; part of her "identity" came from the exact pattern of processor interconnection that had developed during her first years with Paul.

Yet Wili had been inside the program; he had seen the limitations, the inflexibilities. He shook his head. "Yes, Paul. The Jill program was not a person. Maybe someday we'll have systems big enough, but . . . Jill was j-just a s-simulation." And Wili believed what he was saying. So why were they sitting here with tears in their eyes?

The silence stretched into a minute as two people remembered a love and a sacrifice that couldn't really exist. Finally, Wili forced the weirdness away and looked at the old man. If Paul had been alone before, what now?

"I could go with you, Paul," and Wili didn't know if he was begging or offering.

Naismith shook himself and seemed to come back to the present. "I can't stop you, but I hope you don't." He smiled. "Don't worry about me. I didn't last this long by being a sentimental fool *all* the time.

"Your time is now, Wili. There is a lot for you to do."

"Yes. I guess. There's still Mike. He needs . . ." Wili stopped, seeing the look on Paul's face. *"No!* Not Mike too?"

"Yes. But not for several months. Mike is not very popular just now. Oh, he came through in the end; I don't think we'd've won without him. But the Tinkers know what he did in La Jolla. And he knows; he's having trouble living with it."

"So he's going to run away." *Too.*

"No. At least that's not the whole story. Mike has some things to do. The first is Jeremy. From the logs here at Livermore, I can figure to within a few days when the boy will come out of stasis. It's about fifty years from now. Mike is going to come out a year or so before that. Remember, Jeremy is standing near the sea entrance. He could very likely be killed by falling rock when the bobble finally bursts. Mike is going to make sure that doesn't happen.

"A couple years after that, the bobble around the Peacer generator here in Livermore will burst. Mike will be here for that. Among other things, he's going to try to save Della Lu. You know, we would have lost without her. The Peacers had *won,* yet they were going ahead with that crazy world-wrecker scheme. Both Mike and I agree she must have bobbled their projector. Things are going to be mighty dangerous for her the first few minutes after they come out of stasis."

Wili nodded without looking up. He still didn't understand Della Lu. She was tougher and meaner, in some ways, than anyone he had known in LA. But in others—well, he knew why Mike cared for her, even after everything she had done. He hoped Mike could save her.

"And that's about the time I'm coming back, Wili. A lot of people don't realize it, but the war isn't over. The enemy has lost a major battle, but has escaped forward through time. We've identified most of their bobbled refuges, but Mike thinks there are some secret ones underground. Maybe they'll come out the same time as the Livermore generator, maybe a lot later. This is a danger that goes into the foreseeable future. Someone has to be around to fight those battles, just in case the locals don't believe in the threat."

"And that will be you?"

"I'll be there. At least through Round Two."

So that was that. Paul was right, Wili knew. But it still felt like the losses of the past: Uncle Sly, the trek to La Jolla without Paul. "Wili, you can do it. You don't *need* me. When I am forgotten, you will still be remembered—for what you will do as much as for what you already did." Naismith looked intently at the boy.

Wili forced a smile and stood. "You will be proud to hear of me when you return." He turned. He must leave with those words.

Paul stopped him, smiled. "It's not just yet, Wili. I'll be here for another two or three weeks, at least."

And Wili turned again, ran around the desk, and hugged Paul Naismith as hard as he dared.

Screeching tires and, "*Hey!* You wanna get killed?"

Wili looked up in startled shock as the half-tonne truck swerved around him and accelerated down the street. It wasn't the first time in the last ten days he'd nearly daydreamed himself into a collision. These automobiles were so fast, they were on top of you before you knew it. Wili trotted back to the curb and looked around. He had wandered a thousand meters from Paul's office. He recognized the area. This part of the Enclave contained the Authority's archives and automatic logging devices. The Tinkers were taking the place apart. Somehow, it had been missed in the last frantic bobbling, and Allison was determined to learn every Peacer secret that existed outside of Stasis. Wili sheepishly realized where his feet had been leading him: to visit all his friends, to find out if *any*one thought the present was worth staying in.

"Are you okay, Mr. Wáchendon?" Two workers came running up, attracted by the sounds of near calamity. Wili had gotten over being recognized everywhere (after all, he did have an unusual appearance for hereabouts), but the obvious respect he received was harder to accept. "Damn Peacer drivers," one of them said. "I wonder if some of 'em don't know they lost the war."

"*Sí.* Fine," answered Wili, wishing he hadn't made such a fool of himself. "Is Allison Parker here?"

They led him into a nearby building. The air-conditioning was running full blast. It was downright chilly by Wili's standards. But Allison was there, dressed in vaguely military-looking shirt and pants, directing some sort of packing operation. Her men were filling large cartons with plastic disks—old-world memory devices, Wili suspected. Allison was concentrating on the job, smiling and intent. For an instant Wili had that old double vision, was seeing his other friend with this body . . . the one who never really existed. The mortal had outlived the ghost.

Then the worker beside him said diffidently, "Captain Parker?" and the spell was broken.

Allison looked up and grinned broadly. "Hey, Wili!" She walked over and draped an arm across his shoulders. "I've been so busy this last week, I haven't seen any of my old friends. What's happening?" She led him toward an interior doorway, paused there and said over her shoulder, "Finish Series E. I'll be back in a few minutes." Wili smiled to himself. From the day of victory, Allison had made it clear she wouldn't tolerate second-class citizenship. Considering the fact that she was their only expert on twentieth-century military intelligence, the Tinkers had little choice but to accept her attitude.

As they walked down a narrow hall, neither spoke. Allison's office was a bit warmer than the outer room, and free of fan noises. Her desk was covered with printouts. A Peacer display device sat at its center. She waved him to a seat and patted the display. "I know, everything they have here is childish by Tinker standards. But it works and at least I understand it."

"Allison, a-are you going to drop out, too?" Wili blurted out.

The question brought her up short. "Drop out? You mean bobble up? Not on your life, kiddo. I just came back, remember? I have a lot to do." Then she saw how seriously he meant the question. "Oh, Wili. I'm sorry. You know about Mike and Paul, don't you?" She stopped, frowned at some sadness of her own. "I think it makes sense for them to go, Wili. Really.

"But *not* for me." The enthusiasm was back in her voice. "Paul talks about this battle being just Round One of some 'war through time.' Well, he's wrong about one thing. The first round was fifty years ago. I don't know if those Peacer bastards are responsible for the plagues, but I do know they destroyed the world we had. They did destroy the United States of America." Her lips settled into a thin line.

"I'm going back over their records. I'm going to identify every single bobble they cast during the takeover. I'll bet there are more than a hundred thousand of my people out there in stasis. They're all coming back into normal time during the next few years. Paul has a program that uses the Peacer logs to compute exactly when. Apparently, all the projections were for fifty/sixty years, with the smallest bursting first. There's still Vandenberg and Langley and dozens more. That's a pitiful fraction of the millions we once were, but I'm going to be there and I'm going to save all I can."

"Save?"

She shrugged. "The environment around the bobbles can be dangerous the first few seconds. I was nearly killed coming out. They'll be disoriented as hell. They have nukes in there; I don't want those fired off in a panic. And I don't know if your plagues are really dead. Was I just lucky? I'm going to have to dig up some bioscience people."

"Yes," said Wili, and told her about the wreckage Jeremy had shown him back on the Kaladze farm. Somewhere, high in the air within the Vandenberg stasis, was *part* of a jet aircraft. The pilot might still be alive, but how could he survive the first instants of normal time?

Allison nodded as he spoke, and made some notes. "Yes. That's the sort of thing I mean. We'll have a hard time saving that fellow, but we'll try."

She leaned back in her chair. "That's only half of what I must do. Wili, the Tinkers are so bright in many ways, but in others . . . well, 'naive' is the only word that springs to mind. It's not their fault, I know. For generations they've had no say in what happens outside their own villages. The Authority didn't tolerate governments—at least as they were known in the twentieth century. A few places were permitted small republics; most were lucky to get feudalism, like in Aztlán.

"With the Authority gone, most of America—outside of the Southwest—has no government at all. It's fallen back into anarchy. Power is in the hands of private police forces like Mike worked for. It's peaceful just now, because the people in these protection rackets don't realize the vacuum the Authority's departure has created. But when they do, there'll be bloody chaos."

She smiled. "I see I'm not getting through. I can't blame you; you don't have anything to refer to. The Tinker society has been a very peaceful one. But that's the problem. They're like sheep—and they're going to get massacred if they don't change. Just look at what's happened here:

"For a few weeks we had something like an army. But now the sheep have broken down into their little interest groups, their families, their businesses. They've divided up the territory, and God help me if some of them aren't selling it, selling the weapons, selling the vehicles—and to whoever has the gold! It's suicide!"

And Wili saw that she might be right. Earlier that week he had run into Roberto Richardson, the Jonque bastard who'd beaten him at La Jolla. Richardson had been one of the hostages, but he had escaped before the LA rescue. The fat slob was the type who could always land on his feet, and running. He was up here at Livermore, dripping gAu. And he was buying everything that moved: autos, tanks, crawlers, aircraft.

The man was a strange one. He'd made a big show of being friendly, and Wili was cool enough now to take advantage. Wili asked the Jonque what he was going to do with his loot. Richardson had been vague, but said he wasn't returning to Aztlán. "I like the freedom here, Wáchendon. No rules. Think I may move north. It could be very profitable." And he'd had some advice for Wili, advice that just now seemed without ulterior motive: "Don't go back to LA, Wáchendon. The Alcade loves you—at least for the moment. But the Ndelante has figured out who you are, and old Ebenezer doesn't care how big a hero you are up here at Livermore."

Wili looked back at Allison. "What can you do to stop it?"

"The things I've already said for a start. A hundred thousand new people, most with my attitudes, should help the education process. And when the dust has settled, I'm hoping we'll have something like a decent government. It won't be in Aztlán. Those guys are straight out of the sixteenth century; wouldn't be surprised if they're the biggest of the new land grabbers. And it won't be the ungoverned lands that most of the US has become. In all of North America, there seems to be only one representative democracy left—the Republic of New Mexico. It's pretty pitiful geographically, doesn't control much more than old New Mexico. But they seem to have the ideals we need. I think a lot of my old friends will think the same.

"And that's just the beginning, Wili. That's just housekeeping. The last fifty years have been a dark age in some ways. But technology has progressed. Your electronics is as far advanced as I imagined it would be.

"Wili, the human race was on the edge of something great. Given another few years, we would have colonized the inner solar system. That dream is still close to people's consciousness—I've seen how popular Celest is. We can have that dream for real now, and easier than we twentieth-century types could have done it. I'll bet that, hiding away in the theory of bobbles, there are ideas that will make it trivial."

They talked for a long while, probably longer than the busy Allison had imagined they would. When he left, Wili was as much in a daze as when he arrived—only now his mind was in the clouds. He was going to learn some physics. Math was the heart of everything, but you had to have something to apply it to. With his own mind and the tools he had learned to use, he would make those things Allison dreamed of. And if Allison's fears about the next few years turned out to be true, he would be around to help out on that, too.

MAROONED
IN REALTIME

I am grateful to:

Mike Gannis for many super ideas related to this story; Sara Baase, John L. Carroll, Howard Davidson, Jim Frenkel, Dipak Gupta, Jay Hill, Sharon Jarvis, and Joan D. Vinge for all their help and suggestions.

Other people have created zoologies and/or geographies of the future. Though they are different from what is described in this story, they are wonderfully interesting:

Dougal Dixon, *After Man*, St. Martin's Press, New York, 1981. Christopher Scotese and Alfred Ziegler, as described in "The Shape of Tomorrow," by Dennis Overbye, *Discover*, November, 1982, pp. 20–25.

To all those Marooned without hope of rescue

1

On the day of the big rescue, Wil Brierson took a walk on the beach. Surely this was one afternoon when it would be totally empty.

The sky was clear, but the usual sea mist kept visibility to a few kilometers. The beach, the low dunes, the sea—all were closed in by faint haze that seemed centered on his viewpoint. Wil moped along just beyond the waves, where the water soaked the sand flat and cool. His ninety-kilo tread left perfect barefoot images trailing behind. Wil ignored the sea birds that skirled about. He walked head down, watching the water ooze up around his toes at every step. A humid breeze carried the smell of seaweed, sharp and pleasant. Every half minute the waves peaked and clear sea water flooded around his ankles. Except during storms, this was all the "surf" one ever saw on the Inland Sea. Walking like this, he could almost imagine that he was back by Lake Michigan, so long ago. Every summer, he and Virginia had camped on the lakeshore. Almost, he could imagine that he was returning from a noontime stroll on some very muggy Michigan day, and that if he walked far enough he would find Virginia and Anne and Billy waiting impatiently around the campfire, teasing him for going off alone.

Almost . . .

Wil looked up. Thirty meters further on was the cause of all the seabird clamor. A tribe of fishermonkeys was playing at water's edge. The monkeys must have noticed him by now. In past weeks, they would have disappeared into the sea at the first sight of human or machine. Now they stayed ashore. As he approached, the younger ones waddled toward him. Wil went to one knee and they crowded round, their webbed fingers searching curiously at his pockets. One removed a data card. Wil grinned, tugged the card from the monkey's grasp. "Aha! A pickpocket. You're under arrest!"

"Forever the policeman, eh, Inspector?" The voice was feminine, the tone light. It came from somewhere over his head. Wil leaned back. A remote-controlled flier hung just a few meters above him.

He grinned. "Just keeping in practice. Is that you, Marta? I thought you were preparing for this evening's 'festivities.' "

"I am. And part of the preparation is to get foolish people off the beach. The fireworks won't wait till night."

"What?"

"That Steve Fraley—he's making a big scene, trying to argue Yelén into postponing the rescue. She's decided to do it a little early, just to let Steve know who's boss." Marta laughed. Wil couldn't tell if her amusement was directed at Yelén Korolev's irritation or at Fraley. "So please to move your tail, sir. I have some other people to harass yet. I expect you back in town before this flier."

"Yes, ma'am!" Wil gave a mock salute and turned to jog back the way he had come. He had gone about thirty meters when a banshee shriek erupted behind him. He glanced over his shoulder and saw the flier diving in the other direction, lights flashing, sirens blaring. Against that assault, the new-found sophistication of the fishermonkeys dissolved. They panicked, and with the screaming flier between them and the sea their only choice was to grab the kids and scramble up into the dunes. Marta's flier followed, dropping noise bombs on either side of them. Flier and monkeys disappeared over the top of the sand into the jungle, and the noise faded. Wil wondered briefly how far Marta would have to chase them to get them into a safe area. He knew she was equal parts softheartedness and practicality. She'd never scare the animals away from the beach unless there was some chance they could make it to safe haven. Wil smiled to himself. He wouldn't be surprised if Marta had chosen the season and the day of the blow-off to minimize deaths to wildlife.

Three minutes later, Brierson was near the top of the rickety stairs that led to the monorail. He looked down and saw that he hadn't been the only person on the beach. Someone was strolling toward the base of the stairway. Over half a million centuries, the Korolevs had rescued or recruited quite a collection of weirds, but at least they all *looked* fairly normal. This . . . person . . . was different. The stranger carried a variable parasol, and was naked except for a loincloth and shoulder purse. His skin was pale, pasty. As he started up the stairs, the parasol tilted back to reveal a hairless, egglike head. And Wil saw that the stranger might just as well be a she (or an it). The creature was short and slender, its movements delicate. There were faint swellings around its nipples.

Brierson waved hesitantly; it was good policy to meet all the new neighbors, especially the advanced travelers. But then it looked up at Brierson, and even across twenty meters those dark eyes penetrated with cold indifference. The small mouth twitched, but no words came. Wil swallowed and turned to continue up the plastic stairs. There might be some neighbors it was better to learn of secondhand.

Korolev. That was the official name of the town (as officially named by Yelén Korolev). There were almost as many rival names as there were inhabitants. Wil's Indian friends wanted to call it Newest Delhi. The government (in irrevocable exile) of New Mexico wanted to call it New Albuquerque. Optimists liked Second Chance, pessimists Last Chance. For megalomaniacs it was the Great Urb.

Whatever its name, the town nestled in the foothills of the Indonesian Alps, high enough so that equatorial heat and humidity was moderated to an almost uniform pleasantness. Here the Korolevs and their friends had finally assembled the rescued from all the ages. Almost everyone's architectural taste had been catered to. The New Mexican statists had a main street lined with large (mostly empty) buildings that Wil thought epitomized their bureaucracy. Most others from the twenty-first century—Wil included—lived in small groups of homes very like those they'd known before. The advanced travelers lived higher in the mountains.

Town Korolev was built on a scale to accommodate thousands. At the moment the population was less than two hundred, every living human being. They needed more; Yelén Korolev knew where to get one hundred more. She was determined to rescue them.

Steven Fraley, President of the Republic of New Mexico, was determined that those hundred remain unrescued. He was still arguing the case when Brierson arrived. ". . . and you don't appreciate the history of our era, madam. The Peacers came near to exterminating the human race. Sure, saving this group will get you a few more warm bodies, but you risk the survival of our whole colony, of the entire human race, in doing so."

Yelén Korolev looked calm, but Wil knew her well enough to recognize the signs of an impending explosion: there were rosy patches on her cheeks, yet her features were otherwise even paler than usual. She ran a hand through her blond hair. "Mr. Fraley, I really do know the history of your era. Remember that almost all of us—no matter what our present age and experience—have our childhoods within a couple hundred years of one another. The Peace Authority"—her lips twitched in a quick smile at the name—"may have started the general war of 1997. They may even be responsible for the terrible plagues of the early twenty-first century. But as governments go, they were relatively benign. This group in Kampuchea"—she waved toward the north—"went into stasis in 2048, when the Peacers were overthrown. That was before decent health care was available. It's entirely possible that none of the original criminals are present."

Fraley opened and closed his mouth, but no words came. Finally: "Haven't you heard of their 'Renaissance' scheme? In '48 they were ready to kill by the millions again. Those guys under Kampuchea probably got more hell-bombs than a dog has fleas. That base was their secret ace in the hole. If they hadn't screwed up their stasis, they'd've come out in 2100 and blown us away. And you probably wouldn't even have been born—"

Yelén cut into the torrent. "Hell-bombs? Popguns. Even you know that. Mr. Fraley, getting another hundred people into our colony will make our settlement just big enough to survive. Marta and I haven't spent our lives setting this up just to see it die like the undermanned attempts of the past. The only reason we postponed the founding of Korolev till megayear fifty was so we could rescue those Peacers when their bobble bursts."

She turned to her partner. "Is everybody accounted for?"

Marta Korolev had sat through the argument in silence, her dark features relaxed, her eyes closed. Her headband put her in communication with the estate's autonomous devices. No doubt she had managed a half dozen fliers during the last half hour, scouring the countryside for any truant colonists the Korolev satellites had spotted. Now she opened her eyes. "Everybody's accounted for and safe. In fact"—she caught sight of Wil standing at the back of the amphitheater and grinned— "almost everyone is here on the castle grounds. I think we can provide you people with quite a show this afternoon." She either hadn't followed or—more likely—had chosen to ignore the dispute between Yelén and Fraley.

"Okay, let's get started." A rustle of anticipation passed through the audience. Many were from the twenty-first century, like Wil. But they'd seen enough of the advanced travelers to know that such a statement was more than enough signal for spectacular events to happen.

From his place at the top of the amphitheater, Wil had a good view to the north. The forests of the higher elevations fell away to a gray-green blur that was the equatorial jungle. Beyond that, haze obscured even the existence of the Inland Sea. Even on the rare, clear day when the sea mists lifted, the Kampuchean Alps were hidden beyond the horizon. Nevertheless, the rescue should be visible; he was a bit surprised that the bluish white of the northern horizon was undisturbed.

"Things will get more exciting, I promise." Yelén's voice brought his eyes back to the stage. Two large displays floated behind her. They made an incongruous contrast with the moss- and gold-encrusted temple that covered the land beyond the stage. Castle Korolev was typical of the flamboyance of the advanced residences. The underlying stonework and statuary—modeled vaguely on Angkor Wat—had been built half a thousand years earlier, then left for mountain rains to wear at, for moss to cover, for trees to penetrate. Afterwards, construction robots hid all the subtle machinery of late twenty-second-century technology within the "ruins." Wil respected that technology. Here was a place where no sparrow could fall unremarked. The owners were as safe from a quiet knife in the back as from a ballistic missile attack.

"As Mr. Fraley says, the Peacer bobble was supposed to be a secret. It was originally underground. It is much further underground now— somebody blundered. What was to be a fifty-year jump became something . . . longer. As near as we can figure, their bobble should burst sometime in the next few thousand years; they've been in stasis fifty million years. During that time, continents drifted and new rifts formed. Parts of Kampuchea slid deep beneath new mountains." The display behind her lit with a multicolored transect of the Kampuchean Alps. The surface crust appeared as blue, shading into yellow and orange at the greater depths. Right at the margin of orange and magma red was a tiny black disk—the Peacer bobble, afloat against the ceiling of hell.

Inside the bobble, time was stopped. Those within were as they'd been at that instant of a near-forgotten war when the losers decided to escape to the future. No force could affect a bobble's contents; no force could affect its duration—not the heart of a star, not the heart of a lover.

But when the bobble burst, when the stasis ended . . . The Peacers were about forty kilometers down. There would be a moment of noise and heat and pain as the magma swallowed them. One hundred men and women would die, and a certain endangered species would move one more step toward final extinction.

The Korolevs proposed to raise the bobble to the surface, where it would be safe for the few remaining millennia of its duration. Yelén waved at the display. "This was taken just before we started the operation. Here's the ongoing view."

The picture flickered. The red magma boundary had risen thousands of meters above the bobble. Pinheads of white light flashed in the orange and yellow that represented the solid crust. In the place of each of those lights, red blossomed and spread, almost—Wil winced at the thought—like blood from a stab wound. "Each of those sparkles is a hundred-megaton bomb. In the last few seconds, we've released more energy than all mankind's wars put together."

The red spread as the wounds coalesced into a vast hemorrhage in the bosom of Kampuchea. The magma was still twenty kilometers below ground level. The bombs were timed so there was a constant sparkling just above the highest level of red, bringing the melt closer and closer to the surface. At the bottom of the display, the Peacer bobble floated, serene and untouched. On this scale, its motion towards the surface was imperceptible.

Wil pulled his attention from the display and looked beyond the amphitheater. There was no change: the northern horizon was still haze and pale blue. The rescue site was fifteen hundred kilometers away, but even so, he'd expected something spectacular. The minutes

288

passed. A cool breeze swept slow around the theater, rustling the almost-jacarandas that bounded the stage, sending the perfume of their large flowers across the audience. A family of spiders in one tree had built a for-show web in its upper branches. The web silk gleamed in rainbow colors against the sky.

The elapsed-time clock on the display showed almost four minutes. The Korolev pattern of bomb bursts was still thousands of meters short of the surface.

President Fraley rose from his seat. "Madame Korolev, please. There is still time to stop this. I know you've rescued all types, cranks, joyriders, criminals, victims. But these are *monsters.*" For once, Wil thought he heard sincerity—perhaps even fear—in the New Mexican's voice. *And he might be right.* If the rumors were true, if the Peacers had created the plagues of the early twenty-first century, then they were responsible for the deaths of billions. If they had succeeded with their Renaissance Project, they would have killed most of the survivors.

Yelén Korolev glanced down at Fraley but didn't reply. The New Mexican stiffened, then waved abruptly to his people. One hundred men and women—most in NM fatigues—came quickly to their feet. It was a dramatic gesture, if nothing else: the amphitheater would be almost empty with them gone.

"Mr. President, I suggest you and the others sit back down." It was Marta Korolev. Her tone was as pleasant as ever, but the insult in the words brought a flush to Steve Fraley's face. He gestured angrily and turned to the stone steps that led from the theater.

Wil was more inclined to take her words literally: Yelén might use sarcasm and imperious authority, but Marta usually meant her advice only to help. He looked again to the north. Over the jungle slopes there was a wavering, a rippling. *Oops.* With sudden understanding, Wil slid onto a nearby bench.

The ground shock arrived an instant later. It was a soundless, rolling motion that took Fraley's feet right out from under him. Steve's lieutenants quickly helped him up, but the man was livid. He glared death at Marta, then stomped quickly—and carefully—up the steps. He didn't notice Wil till he was almost past him. The Republic of New Mexico kept a special place in its fecal pantheon for W. W. Brierson; having Wil witness this humiliation was the last straw. Then the generals hustled their President on. Those who followed glared briefly at Brierson, or avoided looking at him entirely.

Their departing footsteps came clearly from beyond the amphitheater. Seconds later they had fired up the engines on their armored personnel carriers and were rumbling off to their part of town. All through this, the earthquake continued. For someone who had grown up in Michigan, it was uncanny. The rolling, rocking motion was almost silent. But the birds were silent too, and the spiders on the forshow web motionless. From deep within the castle's stonework there was creaking.

On the transect, magma red had nearly reached the surface. The tiny lights that represented bombs flickered just below ground, and the last yellow of solid earth just . . . evaporated.

Still the nuking continued, carving a wide red sea.

And finally there was action on the northern horizon. Finally there was direct evidence of the cataclysm there. The pale blue was lit again and again by something very bright, something that punched through the haze like a sunrise trying to happen. Just above the flashes a band of white, almost like a second horizon, slowly rose. The top had been blown off the northern foothills of the Kampuchean Alps.

A sigh spread through the audience. Wil looked down, saw several people pointing upwards. Faintly purple, barely brighter than the sky, the wraith extended almost straight overhead from north to south. A daytime aurora?

Strange lightning flickered on the slopes below the castle. The air in the amphitheater was charged with static electricity, yet all was unholy silent. The sound of the rescue would come loud even from fifteen hundred kilometers around the earth, but that sound was still an hour away, chugging across the Kampuchean Alps towards the Inland Sea.

And the Peacer bobble, like flotsam loosed from ice by a summer sun, was free to float to the surface.

2

Everyone agreed with Marta that the show had been impressive. Many didn't realize that the "show" wouldn't end with one afternoon of fireworks. The curtain calls would go on for some time, much more dismal than impressive.

The rescue blasting had been about a hundred times as energetic as the nineteenth-century Krakatoa blow-off. Billions of tonnes of ash and rock were pumped into the stratosphere that afternoon. The sun was a rare sight in the days that followed, at best a dim reddish disk through the murk. In Korolev, there was a heavy frost on the ground every morning. The almost-jacarandas were wilted and dying. Their spider families were dead or moved to burrows. Even in the jungles along the coast, temperatures rarely got above fourteen degrees now.

It rained most of every day—but not water: the dust was settling out. When it came down dry, it was like gray-brown snow, piling obscene drifts on houses and trees and the bodies of small animals; the New Mexicans ruined the last of their jetcopters learning what rock dust does to turbines. Things were even worse when it came down wet, a black fluid that changed the drifts to mud. It was small consolation that the bombs were clean, and the dust a "natural product."

Korolev robots quickly rebuilt the monorails. Wil and the Dasgupta brothers took a trip down to the sea.

The dunes were gone, blasted inland by the rescue-day tsunamis. The trees south of the dunes were laid out flat, all pointing away from

291

the sea. There was no green; all was covered with ash. Even the sea had a layer of scum on it. Miraculously, some fishermonkeys lived. Wil saw small groups on the beach, grooming the ash from each other's pelts. They spent most of their time in the water, which was still warm.

The rescue itself was an undoubted success. The Peacer bobble now sat on the surface. The third day after the detonation, a Korolev flier visited the blast site. The pictures it sent back were striking. Gale-force winds, still laden with ash, drove across gray scabland. Glowing orange-red peeked through netted cracks in the scab. At the center of this slowly freezing lake of rock sat a perfect sphere, the bobble. It floated two-thirds out of the rock. Of course, no nicks or scour marred its surface. No trace of ash or rock adhered. In fact, it was all but invisible: its mirror surface reflected the scene around it, showing the net of glowing cracks stretching back into the haze.

A typical bobble, in an untypical place.

"All things shall pass." That was Rohan Dasgupta's favorite mis-quote. In a few months, the molten lake would freeze over, and an unprotected man could walk right to the side of the Peacer bobble. About the same time, the blackout and the mud rains would end. For a few years there would be brilliant sunsets and unusually cool weather. Wounded trees would recover, seedlings would replace those that had died. In a century or two, nature would have forgotten this affront, and the Peacer bobble would reflect forest green.

Yet it would be unknown thousands of years before the bobble burst, and the men and women within could join the colony.

As usual, the Korolevs had a plan. As usual, the low-techs had little choice but to tag along.

"Hey, we're having a party tonight. Want to come?"

Wil and the others looked up from their shoveling. After three hours mucking around in the ash, they all looked pretty much the same. Black, white, Chinese, Indian, Aztlán—all were covered with gray ash.

The vision that confronted them was dressed in sparkling white. Her flying platform hovered just above the long pile of ash that the low-techs had pushed into the street. She was one of the Robinson daughters. Tammy? In any case, she looked like some twentieth-century fashion plate: blond, tan, seventeen, friendly.

Dilip Dasgupta grinned back at her. "We'd sure like to. But tonight?

If we don't get this ash away from the houses before the Korolevs bobble up, we'll be stuck with it forever." Wil's back and arms were one big ache, but he had to agree. They had been doing this for two days, ever since the Korolevs announced tonight's departure. If they could get all the gray stuff pushed back from the houses before they bobbled up, it would be sluiced away by a thousand years of weather when they came back. Everyone on the street had pitched in, though with lots of grumbling—directed mostly at the Korolevs. The New Mexicans had even sent over some enlisted men with wheelbarrows and shovels. Wil wondered about that: he couldn't believe that someone like Fraley was really overcome by a spirit of cooperation. This was either honest helpfulness on the part of lower officers, or else a subtle effort to bring the other low-techs into the NM camp, future allies against the Korolevs and the Peacers.

The Robinson girl leaned on her platform, and it drifted closer to Dasgupta. She looked up and down the street, then spoke with an air of confidentiality. "My folks like Yelén and Marta a lot—*really*. But Daddy thinks they carry some things too far. You Early Birds are going to be at our level of tech in a few decades anyway. Why should you have to slave like this?"

She bit at a fingernail. "I really wish you could come to our party. . . . Hey! Why don't we do this: You keep working, say till about six. Maybe you can get it all cleaned by then, anyway. But if you can't, don't worry. My folks' robots can take care of what's left while you go get ready for the party." She smiled, then continued almost shyly. "Do you think that would be okay? Could you come then?"

Dilip looked at his brother Rohan, then replied, deadpan, "Why, uh, yes. With that backup, I think we could make it."

"Great! Now look. It's at our house starting around eight. So don't work past six, okay? And don't bother eating, either. We've got lots of food. The party'll go till the Witching Hour. That will leave you plenty of time to get home before the Korolevs bobble up."

Her flier drifted sideways and climbed beyond the trees that encircled the houses. "See you!" Twelve sweaty shovel pushers watched her departure in numbed silence.

A smile spread slowly across Dilip's wide face. He looked at his shovel, then rolled his eyes at the others. Finally he shouted, "Screw it!", threw the shovel to the ground, and jumped up and down on it.

This provoked a heartfelt cheer from the others, the NM corporals included. In moments, the newly liberated workers had departed for their homes.

Only Brierson remained on the street, still looking in the direction taken by the Robinson girl. He felt as much curiosity as gratitude. Wil had done his best to know the high-techs: for all their idiosyncrasies, they'd seemed united behind the Korolevs. But no matter how friendly the disagreement, he saw now that they had factions, too. *I wonder what the Robinsons are selling.*

The public area of the Robinsons' place was friendlier than the Korolevs'. Incandescent lamps hung from oaken beams. The teak dance floor opened onto a buffet room, an outdoor terrace, and a darkened theater where the hosts promised some extraordinary home movies later.

While guests were still arriving, the younger Robinson children ran noisily about the dance floor, dodging among the guests in a wild game of tag. They were tolerated, more than tolerated. They were the only children in the world.

In some sense, almost everyone present was an exile. Some had been shanghaied, some had jumped to escape punishment (deserved and otherwise), some (like the Dasguptas) thought that stepping out of time for a couple of centuries while their investments multiplied would make them rich. On the whole, their initial jumps had been short—into the twenty-fourth, twenty-fifth, twenty-sixth centuries.

But somewhere in the twenty-third, the rest of humanity disappeared. The travelers coming out just after the Extinction found ruins. Some—the most frivolous, and the most hurried of the criminals—had brought nothing with them. These starved, or lived a few pitiful years in the decaying mausoleum that was Earth. The better-equipped ones —the New Mexicans, for example—had the means to return to stasis. They bobbled forward through the third millennium, praying to find civilization revived. All they found was a world sinking back to nature, Man's works vanishing beneath jungle and forest and sea.

Even these travelers could survive only a few years in realtime. They had no medical support, no way to maintain their machines or produce food. Their equipment would soon fail, leaving them stranded in the wilderness.

But a few, a very few, had left at the close of the twenty-second century—when technology gave individuals greater wealth than whole twentieth-century nations. These few could maintain and reproduce all but the most advanced of their tools. Most departed civilization with a deliberate spirit of adventure. They had the resources to save the less fortunate scattered through the centuries, the millennia, and finally the megayears that passed.

Except for the Robinsons, no one had children. That was something reserved for the future, when humankind's ghosts made one last try at reclaiming the race's existence. So the kids who played raucous tag across the dance floor were a greater wonder than any high-tech magic. When the Robinson daughters gathered up their younger siblings for bed, there was a moment of strange, sad silence.

Wil drifted through the buffet room, stopping here and there to talk with his new acquaintances. He was determined to know everyone eventually. Quite a goal: if successful, he would know every living member of the human race. The largest group—and for Wil the most difficult to know—were the New Mexicans. Fraley himself was nowhere in sight, but most of his people were here. He spotted the corporals who had helped with the shoveling, and they introduced him to some others. Things were friendly till an NM officer joined the group.

Wil excused himself and moved slowly toward the dance floor. Most of the advanced travelers were at the party, and they were mingling. A crowd surrounded Juan Chanson. The archeologist was arguing his theory of the Extinction. "Invasion. Extermination. That's the beginning and the end of it." He spoke a clipped, rattling dialect of English that made his opinions seem even more impressive.

"But, Professor," someone—Rohan Dasgupta—objected, "my brother and I came out of stasis in 2465. That couldn't have been more than two centuries after the Extinction. Newer Delhi was in ruins. Many of the buildings had completely fallen in. But we saw no evidence of nuking or lasing."

"Sure. I agree. Not around Delhi. But you must realize, my boy, you saw a very small part of the picture, indeed. It's a great misfortune that most of those who returned right after the Extinction didn't have the means to study what they saw. I can show you pictures . . . LA a fifty-kilometer crater, Beijing a large lake. Even now, with the right equipment, you can find evidence of those blasts.

"I've spent centuries tracking down and interviewing the travelers who were alive in the late third millennium. Why, I even interviewed you." Chanson's eyes unfocused for a fraction of a second. Like most of the high-techs, he wore an interface band around his temples. A moment's thought could bring a flood of memory. "You and your brother. That was around 10000 AD, after the Korolevs rescued you—"

Dasgupta nodded eagerly. For him, it had been just weeks before. "Yes, they had moved us to Canada. I still don't know why—"

"Safety, my boy, safety. The Laurentian Shield is a stable place for long-term storage, almost as good as a cometary orbit." He waved his hand dismissingly. "The point is, *I* and a few other investigators have pieced together these separate bits of evidence. It is tricky; twenty-third-century civilization maintained vast databases, but the media had decayed to uselessness within a few decades of the Extinction. We have fewer contemporary records from the era than we do from the Mayans'. But there are enough . . . I can show you: my reconstruction of the Norcross invasion graffiti, the punched vanadium tape that W. W. Sánchez found on Charon. These are the death screams of the human race.

"Looking at the evidence, any reasonable person must agree the Extinction was the result of wholesale violence directed against populations that were somehow defenseless.

"Now, there are *some* who claim the human race simply killed itself, that we finally had the world-ending war people worried about in the twentieth century. . . ." He glanced at Monica Raines. The pinch-faced artist smiled back sourly but didn't rise to the bait. Monica belonged to the "People Are No Damned Good" school of philosophy. The Extinction held no mysteries for her. After a moment, Chanson continued. "But if you really *study* the evidence, you'll see the traces of outside interference, you'll see that our race was murdered by something . . . from outside."

The woman next to Rohan gave a little gasp. "But these . . . these aliens. What became of them? Why, if they return—we're sitting ducks here!"

Wil stepped back from the fringes of the group and continued toward the dance floor. Behind him, he heard Juan Chanson's triumphant "Exactly! That is the practical point of my investigations. We must mount guard on the solar frontiers—" His words were lost in the background chatter. Wil shrugged to himself. Juan was one of the most approachable of the high-techs, and Wil had heard his spiel before. There was no question the Extinction was the central mystery of their lives. But rehashing the issue in casual conversation was like arguing theology—and depressing, to boot.

A dozen couples danced. On the stage, Alice Robinson and daughter Amy were running the music. Amy played something that looked like a guitar. Alice's instrument was a more conventional console. They improvised on a base of automatic music generators. Having two real humans out front, whose voices and hands were making part of the music, made the band exciting and real.

They played everything from Strauss waltzes, to the Beatles, to W. W. Arai. A couple of the Arai pieces Wil had never heard: they must have been written after his . . . departure. Partners changed from dance to dance. The Arai tunes brought more than thirty people onto the floor. Wil stayed at the edge of the floor, for the moment content to observe. On the other side, he saw Marta Korolev; her partner was not in evidence.

Marta stood swaying, snapping her fingers to the music, a faint smile on her face. She looked a little like Virginia: her chocolate skin was almost the shade Wil remembered. No doubt Marta's father or mother came from America. But the other side of her family was clearly Chinese.

Appearance aside, there were other similarities. Marta had Virginia's outgoing good humor. She combined common sense with uncommon sympathy. Wil watched her for many minutes, trying not to seem to watch. Several of the bolder partiers—Dilip was first—asked her to dance. She accepted enthusiastically, and soon was on the floor for almost every tune. She was very good to watch. If only—

A hand touched his shoulder and a feminine voice sounded in his ear. "Hey, Mr. Brierson, is it true you're a policeman?"

Wil looked into blue eyes just centimeters from his. Tammy Robinson stood on tiptoe to shout into his ear. Now that she had his attention, she stood down, which still left her a respectable 180 centimeters tall. She was dressed in the same spotless white as before. Her interface band looked like a bit of jewelry, holding back her long hair. Her grin was bounded by dimples; even her eyes seemed to be smiling.

Brierson grinned back. "Yes. At least, I used to be a cop."

"Oh, wow." She took his arm in hers and edged them away from the loudness. "I never met a policeman before. But I guess that's not saying a lot."

"Oh?"

"Yeah. I was born about ten megayears after the Singularity—the Extinction, Juan calls it. I've read and watched all about cops and criminals and soldiers, but till now I've never actually met any."

Wil laughed. "Well, now you can meet all three."

Tammy was abashed. "I'm sorry. I'm really not that ignorant. I know that police are different from criminals and soldiers. But it's so strange: they're all careers that can't even exist unless lots of people decide to live together."

Lots of people. Like more than a single family. Brierson glimpsed the abyss that separated them.

"I think you'll like having other people around, Tammy."

She smiled and squeezed his arm. "Daddy always says that. Now I'm beginning to understand."

"Just think. Before you're a hundred, Korolev Town will be almost like a city. There could be a couple of thousand people for you to know, people more interesting and worthwhile than criminals."

"Ugh. We're not going to stay for that. I want to be with lots of people—hundreds at least. But how could you stand to be locked in one little corner of time?" She looked at him, seemed suddenly to realize that Brierson's whole life had been stuck in a single century. "Gee. How can I explain it? Look—where you come from, there was air and space travel, right?" Brierson nodded. "You could go anywhere you wanted. Now, suppose instead you had to spend your life in a house in a deep valley. Sometimes you hear stories about other places, but you can never climb out of the valley. Wouldn't that drive you crazy?

"That's how I'd feel about making a permanent stop at Korolev. We've been stopped for six weeks now. That's not long compared to some of our stops, but it's long enough for me to get the feeling: The animals aren't changing. I look out and the mountains just *sit* there." She made a little sound of frustration. "Oh, I can't explain it. But

298

you'll see some of what I mean tonight. Daddy's going to show the video we made. It's beautiful!"

Wil smiled. Bobbles didn't change the fact that time was a one-way trip.

She saw the denial in his eyes. "You must feel like I do. Just a little? I mean, why did you go into stasis in the first place?"

He shook his head. "Tammy, there are lots of people here who never asked to be bobbled. . . . I was shanghaied." A crummy embezzlement case it had been. When he thought back, it was so fresh in his mind, in many ways more real than the world of the last few weeks. The assignment had seemed as safe as houses. The need for an armed investigator had been a formality, required by his company's archaic regs: the amount stolen was just over the ten thousand gAu. But someone had been desperate or careless . . . or just plain vicious. Most jurisdictions of Wil's era counted offensive bobbling of more than a century as manslaughter: Wil's stasis had lasted one thousand centuries. Of course, Wil did not consider the crime to be the murder of one W. W. Brierson. The crime was much more terrible than that. The crime was the destruction of the world he had known, the family he loved.

Tammy's eyes grew wide as he told his story. She tried to understand, but Wil thought there was more wonder than sympathy in her look. He stopped short, embarrassed.

He was trying to think of a suitable change of subject when he noticed the pale figure on the far side of the dance floor. It was the person he'd seen at the beach. "Tammy, who's that?" He nodded in the direction of the stranger.

Tammy pulled her gaze away from his face and looked across the room. "Oh! She's weird, isn't she? She's a spacer. Can you imagine? In fifty million years, she could travel all over the Galaxy. We think she's more than nine thousand years old. And all that time alone." Tammy shivered.

Nine thousand years. That would make her the oldest human Wil had ever seen. She certainly looked more human tonight than on the beach. For one thing, she wore more clothes: a blouse and skirt that were definitely feminine. Now her skull was covered with short black stubble. Her face was smooth and pale. Wil guessed that when her hair

299

grew out, she might look like a normal young woman—Chinese, probably.

A half-meter of emptiness surrounded the spacer; elsewhere the crowd was packed close. Many clapped and sang; there was scarcely a person who could resist tapping a foot or nodding in time to the music. But the spacer stood quietly, almost motionless, her dark eyes staring impassively into the dancers. Occasionally her arm or leg would twitch, as if in some broken resonance with the tunes.

She seemed to sense Wil's gaze. She looked back at him, her eyes expressionless, analytical. This woman had seen more than the Robinsons, the Korolevs—more than all the high-techs put together. Was it his imagination that he suddenly felt like a bug on a slide? The woman's lips moved, the twitching motion he remembered from the beach. Then it had seemed a coldly alien, almost insectile gesture. Now Wil had a flash of insight: After nine thousand years alone, nine thousand years on God knows how many worlds, would a person still remember the simple things—like how to smile?

"C'mon, Mr. Brierson, let's dance." Tammy Robinson's hand was insistent on his elbow.

Wil danced more that night than since he'd been dating Virginia. The Robinson kid just wouldn't quit. She didn't really have more stamina than Brierson. He kept in condition and kept his bio-age around twenty; with his large frame and tendency to overweight he couldn't afford to be fashionably middle-aged. But Tammy had the *enthusiasm* of a seventeen-year-old. Paint her a different color and she reminded him of his daughter Anne: cuddly, bright, and just a bit predatory when it came to the males she wanted.

The music swept them round and round, taking Marta Korolev in and out of his view. Marta danced only a few times with any one partner and spent considerable time off the floor, talking. This evening would leave the Korolev reputation substantially mellowed. Later, when he saw her depart for the theater, he suppressed a sigh of relief. It had been a depressing little game, watching her and watching her, and all the time pretending not to.

The lights brightened and the music faded. "It's about an hour to midnight, folks," came Don Robinson's voice. "You're welcome to dance till the Witching Hour, but I've got some pictures and ideas I'd like to share with you. If you're interested, please step down the hall."

"That's the video I was telling you about. You've got to hear what Daddy has to say." Tammy led him off the floor, even though another song was starting. The music had lost some of its vibrancy. Amy and Alice Robinson had left the bandstand. The rest of the evening would be uninterpreted recordings.

Behind them, the crowd around the dance floor was breaking up. There had been hints through the evening that this last entertainment would be the most spectacular. Almost everyone would be in the Robinsons' theater.

As they walked down the hall, the lights above them went dim. The theater itself was awash with blue light. A four-meter globe of Earth hung above the seats. It was an effect Wil had seen before, though never on this scale. Given several satellite views it was possible to construct a holo of the entire planet and hang its blue-green perfection before the viewer. From the entrance to the theater, the world was in quarter phase, morning just touching the Himalayas. Moonlight glinted faintly off the Indian Ocean. The continental outlines were the familiar ones from the Age of Man.

Yet there was something strange about the image. It took Wil a second to realize just what: There were no clouds.

He was about to walk around the globe to the seating when he noticed two shadows beyond the dark side. It looked like Don Robinson and Marta Korolev. Wil paused, resisting Tammy's urging that they hurry to get the best seats. The room was rapidly filling with partygoers, but Wil guessed he was the only one who had noticed Robinson and Korolev. There was something strange here: Korolev's bearing was tense. Every few seconds she chopped at the air between them. The shadow that was Don Robinson stood motionless, even as Korolev became more excited. Wil had the impression of short, unsatisfactory replies being given to impassioned demands. Wil couldn't hear the words; either they were behind a sound screen, or they weren't talking out loud. Finally Robinson turned and walked out of sight behind the globe. Marta followed, still gesturing.

Even Tammy hadn't noticed. She led Brierson to the edge of the audience area and they sat. A minute passed. Wil saw Marta emerge from beyond the sunlit hemisphere and walk behind the audience to sit near the door.

Then there was music, just loud enough to still the audience. Tammy touched Wil's hand. "Oh. Here comes Daddy."

Don Robinson suddenly appeared by the sunside hemisphere. He cast no shadow on the globe, though both shone in the synthetic sunlight. "Good evening, everyone. I thought to end our party with this little light show—and a few ideas I'm hoping you'll think about." He held up his hand and grinned disarmingly. "I promise, mostly pictures!"

His image turned to pat the surface of the globe familiarly. "All but a lucky few of us began our journey down time unprepared. That first bobbling was an accident or was intended as a single jump to what we guessed would be a friendlier future civilization. Unfortunately—as we all discovered—there is no such civilization, and many of us were stranded." Robinson's voice was friendly, smooth, the tone traditionally associated with the selling of breakfast food or religion. It irritated Wil that Robinson said "we" and "us" even when he was speaking specifically of the low-tech travelers.

"Now, there were a few who were well equipped. Some of these have worked to rescue the stranded, to bring us all together where we can freely decide humanity's new course. My family, Juan Chanson, and others did what we could—but it was the Korolevs who had the resources to bring this off. Marta Korolev is here tonight." He waved generously in her direction. "I think Marta and Yelén deserve a big hand." There was polite applause.

He patted the globe again. "Don't worry. I'm getting to our friend here. . . . One problem with all this rescuing is that most of us have spent the last fifty million years in long-term stasis, waiting for all the 'principals' to be gathered for this final debate. Fifty million years is a long time to be gone; a lot has happened.

"That's what I want to share with you tonight. Alice and the kids and I were among the fortunate. We have advanced bobblers and plenty of autonomous devices. We've been out of stasis hundreds of times. We've been able to live and grow along with the Earth. The pictures I'm going to show you tonight are the 'home movies,' if you will, of our trip to the present.

"I'm going to start with the big picture—the Earth from space. The

302

image you see here is really a composite—I've averaged out the cloud cover. It was recorded early in the fourth millennium, just after the Age of Man. This is our starting point.

"Let's begin the journey." Robinson vanished and they had an unobstructed view of the globe. Now Wil noticed a gray haze that seemed to waver around the polar ice cap. "We're moving forward about half a megayear per minute. The camera satellites were programmed to take pictures at the same local time every year. At this rate, even climate cycles are visible only as a softening of picture definition." The gray haze—it must be the edge of the Antarctic ice pack! Wil looked more carefully at Asia. There was a blurring, a fantastically rapid mottling of greens and tans. Droughts and wetness. Forest and jungle battling savanna and desert. In the north, white flickered like lightning. Suddenly the glaring whiteness flashed southwards. It surged and retreated, again, again. In less than a quarter of a minute it was gone back to the northern horizon. Except for shimmering whiteness in the Himalayas, the greens and tans lived once more across Asia. "We had a pretty good ice age there," Robinson explained. "It lasted more than one hundred thousand years. . . . We're beyond the immediate neighborhood of Man now. I'm going to speed us up . . . to five megayears per minute."

Wil glanced at Marta Korolev. She was watching the show, but her face held an uncharacteristic look of displeasure. Her hands were clenched into fists.

Tammy Robinson leaned from her seat to whisper, "This is where it really gets good, Mr. Brierson!"

Wil turned back to the display, but his attention was split between the view and the mystery of Marta's anger.

Five million years every minute. Glacier and desert and forest and jungle blended. One color or another might fleetingly dominate the pastel haze, but the overall impression was stable and soothing. Only now . . . only now the continents themselves were moving! A murmur passed around the room as the audience realized what they were seeing. Australia had moved north, sliding into the eastern islands of the Indonesian archipelago. Mountains puckered along the collision. This part of the world was near the sunrise line. Low sunlight cast the new mountains in relief.

There was sound, too. From the surface of the globe, Wil heard something that reminded him of wood surfaces squeaking wetly across each other. A sound like crumpling paper accompanied the birth of the Indonesian Alps. "Those noises are real, friends," said Don Robinson. "We kept a system of seismophones on the surface. What you're hearing are long-term averages of seismic action. It took thousands of major earthquakes to make every second of those sounds."

As he spoke, Australia and Indonesia merged, the combination continuing its slide northwards, turning slightly as it came. Already the form of the Inland Sea could be discerned. "No one predicted what happened next," continued Robinson's travelogue. "There! Notice the rift spreading through Kampuchea, breaking the Asian plate." A string of narrow lakes appeared across Southeast Asia. "In a moment, we'll see the new platelet reverse direction and ram *back* into China—to build the Kampuchean Alps."

From the corner of his eye, Brierson saw Marta heading for the door. *What is going on here?* He started to get up, found that Tammy's arm was still around his.

"Wait. Why are you going, Mr. Brierson?" she whispered, starting to get up.

"I've got to check on something, Tammy."

"But—" She seemed to realize that extended discussion would detract from her father's show. She sat down, looking puzzled and a little hurt.

"Sorry, Tam," Wil whispered. He headed for the door. Behind him, continents crashed.

The Witching Hour. The time between midnight and the start of the next day. It was more like seventy-five minutes than an hour. Since the Age of Man, the Earth's rotation had slowed. Now, at fifty megayears, the day was a little over twenty-five hours long. Rather than change the definition of the second or the hour, the Korolevs had decreed (just another of their decrees) that the standard day should consist of twenty-four hours plus whatever time it took to complete one rotation. Yelén called the extra time the Fudge Factor. Everyone else called it the Witching Hour.

Wil walked through the Witching Hour, looking for some sign of Marta Korolev. He was still on the Robinson estate, that was obvious: as advanced travelers, the Robinsons had plenty of robots. Rescue-day ash had been meticulously cleaned from the stone seats, the fountains, the trees, even the ground. The scent of almost-jacarandas floated in the cool night breeze.

Even without the tiny lights that floated along the paths, Wil could have found his way without difficulty. For the first time since the blow-off, the night was clear—well, not really *clear*, but he could see the moon. Its wan light was only faintly reddened by stratospheric ash. The old girl looked pretty much as she had in Wil's time, though the stains of industrial pollution were gone. Rohan Dasgupta claimed the moon was a little farther out now, that there would never again be a total eclipse of the sun. The difference was not enough for Wil to see.

The reddish silver light fell bright across the Robinsons' gardens, but Marta was nowhere in sight. Wil stopped, let his breath out, and listened. There were footsteps. He jogged in their direction and caught up with Korolev still inside the estate.

"Marta, wait." She had already stopped and turned to face him. Something dark and massive floated a few meters above her. Wil glanced at it and slowed to a walk. These autonomous devices still made him uneasy. They hadn't existed in his time, and no matter how often he was told they were safe, it was still unnerving to think of the firepower they controlled—independent of the direct commands of their masters. With her protector floating nearby, Marta was almost as safe as back in Castle Korolev.

Now that he'd caught up with her, he didn't know quite what to say. "What's the matter, Marta? I mean, is anything wrong?"

At first, he thought she would not answer. She stood with balled fists. The moonlight showed tear streaks on her face. She slumped and brought her hands up to her temples. "That b-bastard Robinson. That slimy bastard!" The words were choked.

Wil stepped closer. The protection device moved forward, keeping him in clear view. "What happened?"

"You want to know? I'll tell you . . . but let's sit down. I-I don't think I can stand much longer. I'm s-so *mad.*" She walked to a nearby bench and sat. Wil lowered his bulk beside her, then started. To the hand, the bench felt like stone, but it yielded to main body weight like a cushion.

Marta put a hand on his arm, and for an instant he thought she might touch her head to his shoulder. The world was a very empty place now, and Marta reminded him so much of things lost. . . . But coming between the Korolevs was probably the single most boorish, the single most dangerous, thing he could do. Wil said abruptly, "This may not be the best place to talk." He waved at the fountain and the carefully tended trees. "I'll bet the Robinsons monitor the whole estate."

"Hah! We're screened." Marta moved her hand from his arm. "Besides, Don knows what I think of him.

"All these years, they've pretended to support our plan. We helped them, gave them factory designs that didn't exist when they left civilization. All the time, they were just waiting—taking their pretty pictures—while we did all the work, bringing what was left of the human race to one place and time.

"And now that we have everyone together, now that we need everyone's cooperation, *now* they start sweet-talking people away from us. Well, I'll tell you, Wil. Our settlement is humankind's last chance. I'll do anything, *anything,* to protect it." Marta had always seemed so cheerful, optimistic. That made her fury even more striking. But the one did not make hypocrisy of the other. Marta was like a mother cat, suddenly ferocious and deadly in protecting her kittens.

"So the Robinsons want to break up the town? Do they want their own colony?"

Marta nodded. "But not like you think. Those lunatics want to continue down time, sightseeing their way into eternity. Robinson figures if he can persuade most of us to come along, he'll have a stable system. He calls it a 'timelike urbanization.' For the next few billion years, his colony would spend about a month per megayear outside of stasis. As the sun goes off main sequence, they'll move into space and bobble through longer and longer jumps. He literally wants to follow the evolution of the whole goddamned universe!"

Brierson remembered Tammy Robinson's impatience with living at the same rate as the universe. She'd been campaigning for the scheme her father must now be selling to the audience back in the theater.

Wil shook his head and chuckled. "Sorry. I'm not laughing at you, Marta. It's just that compared to the things you should be worrying about, this is ludicrous.

"Look. Most of the low-techs are like me. It's been only weeks of objective time since I left civilization. Even the New Mexicans spent only a few years in realtime before you rescued them. We haven't lived centuries 'on the road' like you advanced types. We're still hurting. More than anything, we want to stop and rebuild."

"But Robinson is so slick."

"He's so slick you can scrape the grease off. You've been away from that kind for a long, long time. Back in civilization, we were exposed to sales pressure almost every day. . . . There's only one lever he has, and that's something you should be worrying about in any case."

Marta smiled wanly. "Yelén and I worry about so many things, Wil. You have something new for us?"

"Maybe." Wil was silent for a moment. The fountain across from their bench burbled loud. There were soft hooting sounds in trees. He hadn't expected this opportunity. Until now the Korolevs had been approachable enough, but they didn't seem to listen. "We're all grateful to you and Yelén. You saved us from death—or at least from life alone in an empty world. We have a chance to start the human race again. . . . But at the same time, a lot of low-techs resent you advanced travelers in your castles above town. They resent the fact that you make all the decisions, that you decide what you will share and what we will work at."

"I know. We haven't explained things very well. We seem omnipotent. But don't you see, Wil? We high-techs are a few people from around 2200 who brought our era's version of good-quality camping and survival gear. Sure, we can make most any consumer product of your time. But we *can't* reproduce the most advanced of our own devices. When those finally break, we'll be as helpless as you."

"I thought your autons were good for hundreds of years."

"Sure, if we use them for ourselves alone. Supporting an army of low-techs cuts us down to less than a century. We *need* each other, Wil. Apart, both groups face dead ends. Together, we have a chance. We can supply you with databases, equipment, and a good approximation to a twenty-first-century standard of living—for a few decades. As our support decays, you provide the human hands and minds and ingenuity to fill the gaps. If we can get a high birth rate, and build a twenty-first-century infrastructure, we may pull this out."

"Willing hands? Like the ash shoveling we've had to do?" He didn't mean the question to sound nasty, but it came out that way.

She touched his arm again. "No, Wil. That was dumb of us. Arrogant." She paused, her eyes searching his.

"Have you ever been ramjetting, Wil?"

"Huh? Uh, no." In general, Wil didn't go *looking* for trouble.

"But it was a big sport in your time, wasn't it? Sort of like hang gliding, but a lot more exciting—especially for the purists who didn't carry bobblers. Our situation reminds me of a typical ramjet catastrophe: You're twenty thousand meters up, ramming along. All of a sudden your jet flames out. It's an interesting problem. Those little rigs didn't mass more than a few hundred kilos; they didn't carry turbines. So all you can do is dive hell down. If you can get your airspeed above Mach one, you can usually relight the ram; if not, you make a nice crater.

"Well, we're sitting pretty right now. But the underlying civilization has flamed out. We have a *long* way to fall. Counting the Peacers, there will be almost three hundred low-techs. With your help we ought to be able to relight at some decent level of technology—say twentieth or twenty-first century. If we can, we'll quickly climb back. If we can't, if we fall to a premachine age when our autons fail . . . we'll be just too primitive and too few to survive. So. The ash shoveling was unnecessary. But I can't disguise the fact that there will be hard times, terribly hard work."

She looked down. "I know you've heard most of this before, Wil. It's a hard package to sell, isn't it? But I thought I would have more time. I thought I could convince most of you of our goodwill. . . . I never counted on Don Robinson and his slick promises and good-fellowship."

Marta looked so forlorn. He reached out to pat her shoulder. No doubt Robinson had plans similar to the Korolevs', plans that would remain secret until the low-techs were safely suckered into his family's journey. "I think that most of us low-techs will see through Robinson. If you make it clear where his promises must be lies. If you can come down from the castle. Concentrate on Fraley; if Robinson convinces him, you might lose the New Mexicans. Fraley isn't dumb, but he is rigid and he lets his anger run away with him. He really does hate the Peacers." *Almost as much as he hates me.*

Half a minute passed. Marta gave a short, bitter laugh. "So many enemies. The Korolevs hate the Robinsons, the NMs hate the Peacers, almost everybody hates the Korolevs."

"And Monica Raines hates all mankind."

This time her laugh was lighter. "Yes. Poor Monica." Marta leaned toward him and this time really did rest her head against his shoulder. Wil's arm slipped automatically across her back. She sighed. "We're two hundred people, just about all that's left. And I swear we have more jealousy and scheming than twentieth-century Asia."

They sat in silence, her head against him, his hand resting lightly against her back. He felt the tension slowly leave her body. For Wil it was different. *Oh, Virginia, what to do?* Marta felt so good. It would be so easy to caress that back, to slide his hand down to her waist. Most likely there'd be a moment of embarrassed backing away. But if she responded . . . If she responded, they'd be adding one more set of jealousies to the brew.

So Wil's hand did not move. In later times, he often wondered if things might have gone differently had he not chosen the path of sanity and caution.

He thought wildly for a moment, finally discovered a topic that was sure to break the mood. "You know I'm one of the shanghaied ones, Marta."

"Mm-hmm."

"The crime is a strange one, bobbling someone into the far future. It may be murder, but the court can't know for sure. In my time, most jurisdictions had a special punishment for it."

Silence.

"They'd bobble survival equipment and the trial record next to the victim. Then they'd take the bastard who created the problem and bobble him too—so he'd come out of stasis just *after* the victim. . . ."

The spell was broken. Marta pulled slowly back. She could tell what was coming. "Sometimes the courts couldn't know the duration."

Wil nodded. "In my case, I'll bet the duration was known. *And* I'll bet even more that there was a conviction. There were only three suspects; I was closing in on that damn embezzler. That's why he panicked."

He paused. "Did you rescue him, Marta? Did you rescue the . . . person . . . who did this to me?"

She shook her head. Her openness deserted her when she had to lie.

"You've got to tell me, Marta. I don't need revenge"—perhaps a small lie there—"but I do need to know."

She shook her head again but this time replied. "We can't, Wil. We need everyone. Can't you see that all such crimes are meaningless now?"

"For my own protection—"

She got up, and after a second Wil did, too.

"No. We've given him a new face and a new name. He has no motive for harming you now, and we've warned him what we'll do if he tries."

Brierson shrugged.

"Hey, Wil, have I made myself another enemy?"

"N-no. I could never be your enemy. And I want the settlement to succeed as much as you and Yelén."

"I know." She raised her hand in a half-wave. "G'night, Wil."

"Good night."

She walked into the darkness, her robot protector floating close above her shoulder.

3

Things had changed by "next" morning. At first, the changes were what Brierson had expected.

Gone was the drear ash and dirty sky. Dawn splashed sunlight across his bed; he could see a wedge of blue between green-leafed trees. Wil came slowly awake, something deep inside saying it was all a dream. He closed his eyes, opened them again, and stared into the brightness.

They did it. "By God, they really did it." He rolled out of bed and pulled on some clothes. He shouldn't really be surprised. The Korolevs had announced their plan. Sometime in the morning hours, after the Robinson party was over and when their surveillance showed everyone safe at home, they had bobbled every building in the settlement. Through unknown centuries they bobbled forward, coming out of stasis for a few seconds every year, just long enough to check if the Peacer bobble had burst.

Wil rushed down the stairs, past the kitchen. Breakfast could be skipped. Just to see the green and the blue and the clean sunlight made him feel like a kid at Christmas. Then he was outside, standing in the sunlight. The street was nearly gone. Almost-jacarandas had sprouted through its surface. Their lowest flowers floated a meter above his head. Spider families scampered through the leaves. The huge pile of ash that he and the Dasguptas and the others had pushed into the middle of the street was gone, washed away by a hundred—a thousand?—rainy seasons. The only sign of that long-ago pollution was around Wil's house. A circular arc marked where the stasis field had intersected the ground. Outside was green and growing; inside was covered with gray ash, the trees and plants dying.

As Wil wandered through the young forest that the street had become, the wrongness of the scene gradually percolated through: Everything was alive, but there was not another human, not a single robot. Had everyone wakened earlier, say at the moment the bobbles burst?

He walked down to the Dasguptas' place. Half hidden by the brush, he saw someone big and black heading his way—his own reflection. The Dasguptas were still in stasis. The trees grew right up to their bobble. Rainbow webs floated around it, but the surface was untouched. Neither vines nor spiders could find purchase on that mirrored smoothness.

Wil ran through the forest, panic rising in him. Now that he knew what to look for, they were easy to spot: the sun's image glinted off two, three, half a dozen bobbles. Only his had burst. He looked at the trees, the birds, and the spiders. The scene was scarcely pleasing now. How long could he live without civilization? The rest might come out of stasis in moments or a hundred years, or a thousand; he had no way of knowing. In the meantime Wil was alone, perhaps the only living man on Earth.

He left the street and scrambled up a rise into older trees. From the top, he should be able to see some of the estates of the advanced travelers. The fear tightened at his throat. Sun and sky sat in the green of the hills; there were bobbles where the palaces of Juan Chanson and Phil Genet should be. He looked south, towards Castle Korolev.

Spires, gold and green! No bobble there!

And in the air above the castle, he saw three close-set dots: fliers, moving fast and straight towards him, like some old-time fighters on a strafing run. The trio was over him in seconds. The middle flier descended and invited him into its passenger cabin.

The ground fell slantingly away. He had a moment's vision of the Inland Sea, blue through coastal haze. There were bobbles around the advanced estates, around the NM quarter of town. To the west were several large ones—around the autofactories? Everything was in stasis except the Korolev estate. He was above the castle now, coming down fast. The gardens and towers looked as before, but an enormous circle circumscribed the estate—a subtle yet abrupt change in the tone of the forest's green. Like himself, the Korolevs had been in stasis up to the recent past. For some reason they were leaving the rest bobbled. For some reason they wanted private words with W. W. Brierson.

The Korolev library had no bookcases weighted down with data cartridges or paper-and-ink books. Data could be accessed anywhere; the library was a place to sit and think (with appropriate support devices) or to hold a small conference. The walls were lined with holo windows showing the surrounding countryside. Yelén Korolev sat at the middle of a long marble table. She motioned Wil to sit across from her.

"Where's Marta?" Brierson asked automatically.

"Marta is . . . dead, Inspector Brierson." Yelén's voice was even flatter than usual. "Murdered."

Time seemed to stop. *Marta. Dead?* He had taken bullets with less physical sensation than those words brought. His mouth opened, but the questions wouldn't come. In any case, Yelén had questions of her own. "And I want to know what you had to do with it, Brierson."

Wil shook his head, in confusion more than denial.

She slapped the marble tabletop. "Wake up, mister! I'm talking to you. You're the last person who saw her alive. She rejected your advances. Did that make it worth killing her, Brierson? *Did it?*"

The insanity of the accusation brought Wil back to his senses. He stared at Yelén, realizing that she was in a much worse state than he. Like Marta, Yelén Korolev had been raised in late twenty-second-century Hainan. But Yelén had no trace of Chinese blood. She was descended from the Russians who had filtered out of Central Asia after the 1997 debacle. Her fair Slavic features were normally cool, occasionally showing ironic humor. Those features were as smooth as ever now, but the woman kept running her hand across her chin, her forefinger tracing again and again the edge of her lip. She was in a state of walleyed shock that Wil had seen only a couple of times before—and those times had been filled with sudden death. From the corner of his eye, he saw one of her protection robots float around the far side of the table—keeping her widely separated from its target.

"Yelén," he finally said, trying to keep his voice calm and reasonable, "till this moment I didn't know about Marta. I liked . . . respected . . . her more than anyone in the settlement. I could never harm her."

Korolev stared at him a long moment, then let out a shaky breath. The feeling of deadly tension lessened. "I know what you tried to do that night, Brierson. I know how you thought to repay our charity. I'll always hate your guts because of it. . . . But you're telling the truth about one thing: There's no way you—or any low-tech—could have killed Marta."

She looked through him, remembering her lost partner, or perhaps communicating through her headband. When she spoke again her voice was softer, almost lost. "You were a policeman, in a century where murder was still common. You're even famous. When I was a kid, I read all about you. . . . I'll do anything to get Marta's killer, Inspector."

Wil leaned forward. "What happened, Yelén?" he said quietly.

"She—she was marooned—left outside all our bobbles."

For a moment, Wil didn't understand. Then he remembered walking the deserted street and wondering if he was all alone, wondering how many years would pass before the other bobbles burst. Before, he had thought that being shanghaied into the future was the most terrible bobble crime. Now he saw that being marooned in an empty present could be just as awful.

"How long was she alone, Yelén?"

"Forty years. *Just forty goddamned years.* But she had no health care. She had no robots. She had just the clothes on her back. I'm p-proud of her. She lasted forty years. She survived the wilderness, the loneliness, her own aging. For forty years. And she almost won through. Another ten years—" Her voice broke and she covered her eyes. "Back up, Korolev," she said. "Just the facts.

"You know we have to move down time to when the Peacer bobble bursts. We planned to begin the move the night of the party. After everyone was indoors, we'd bobble forward in three-month steps. Every three months, the bobbles would burst and our sensors would take a few microseconds to check the fast-flicker autons, to see if the Peacers were still in stasis. If they were, we'd automatically bobble up for another three months. Even if we waited a hundred thousand years, all you'd have seen was a second or so of flickering and flashing.

"So. That was the plan. What happened was that the first jump was a century long—for everyone in near-Earth space. The other advanced travelers had agreed to follow our programming on this. They were in

314

stasis, too. The difference between three months and a century was not enough to alarm their controller programs. Marta was alone. Once she figured out that the flicker interval was more than three months, she hiked around the Inland Sea to the Peace Authority bobble."

That was a twenty-five-hundred-kilometer hike.

Yelén noticed the wonder on his face. "We're survivors, Inspector. We didn't last this long by letting difficulties stop us.

"Anyway, the area around the Peace bobble is still a vitrified plain. It took her decades, but she built a sign there." The window behind Yelén suddenly became a view from space. At that distance, the bobble was just a glint of sunlight with a spiky shadow. A jagged black line extended northwards from it. Apparently the picture was taken at local dawn, and the black strip was the shadow of Marta's monument. It must have been several meters high and dozens of kilometers long. The image lasted only seconds, the space of time Yelén imagined it.

"You may not know this, but we have lots of equipment at the Lagrange zones. Some of it is in kiloyear stasis. Some is flickering with a period of decades. None of it is carefully watching the ground . . . but that line structure was enough to trip even a high-threshold monitor. Eventually, the robots sent a lander to investigate. . . . They were just a few years too late."

Wil forced his mind past thinking on what the lander found. Thank God Yelén's imagination didn't flash that on the windows.

For now—method: "How could this be done? I thought an old-time army couldn't match the security of your household automation."

"That's true. No low-tech could break in. At first glance, even the advanced travelers couldn't manage this: it's possible to outfight a high-tech—but the battles are abrupt and obvious. What happened here was sabotage. And I think I have it figured out. Somebody used our external comm to talk to the scheduling programs. Those weren't as secure as they should be. Marta was cut out of the check roster, and a one-century total blackout was substituted for the original flicker scheme. The murderer was lucky: if he had tried for anything longer, it would have tripped all sorts of alarms."

"Could it happen again?"

"No. Whoever did it is good, Brierson. But basically they took advantage of a bug. That bug no longer exists. And I'm being much more careful about how my machines accept outside comm now."

Wil nodded. This was a century beyond him, even if his specialty had been forensic computing. He'd just have to take her word that there was no further danger—of this sort of assassination. Wil's strength was in the human side. For instance:

"Motive. Who would want Marta dead?"

Yelén's laugh was bitter. "My suspects." The windows of the library became a mosaic of the settlement's population. Some had only small pictures—all the New Mexicans fitted on a single panel. Others—Brierson, for instance—rated more space. "Almost everybody conceives some grudge against us. But you twenty-first-century types just don't have the background to pull this off. No matter how attractive the notion"—she looked at Wil—"you're off the list." The pictures of the low-techs vanished from the windows.

The rest stood like posters against the landscape beyond. These were all the advanced travelers (Yelén excepted): the Robinsons, Juan Chanson, Monica Raines, Philippe Genet, Tunç Blumenthal, Jason Mudge —and the woman Tammy said was a spacer.

"The motive, Inspector Brierson? I can't afford to consider that it was anything less than the destruction of our settlement. One of these people wants humanity permanently extinct, or—more likely—wants to run their own show with the people we've rescued; it would probably come to the same thing."

"But why Marta? Killing her has tipped their hand without—"

"Without stopping the Korolev Plan? You don't understand, Brierson." She ran a hand through her blond hair and stared down at the table. "I don't think any of you understand. You know I'm an engineer. You know I'm a hardheaded type who's made a lot of unpopular decisions. The plan would never have gotten this far without me.

"What you don't know is that Marta was the brains behind it all. Back in civilization, Marta was a project manager. One of the best. She had this figured out even before we left civilization. She could see that technology and people were headed into some sort of singularity in the twenty-third century. She really wanted to help the people who were stranded down time. . . . Now we have the settlement. To make it succeed is going to take the special genius she had. I know how to make the gadgets work, and I can outshoot most anyone in a clean fight. But it could all fall apart now, without Marta. We are so few here; there are so many internal jealousies.

"I think the killer knew this, too."

Wil nodded, a little surprised that Yelén realized her own failings so clearly.

"I'm going to have my hands full, Brierson. I intend to spend many decades of my life preparing for the time when the Peacers come out and I bring the settlement back. If Marta's dream is to succeed, I can't afford to use my own time hunting the killer. *But I want that killer, Brierson.* Sometimes . . . sometimes I feel a little crazy, I want him so bad. I'll give you any reasonable support in this. Will you take the case?"

Even at fifty megayears, there was still a job for Wil Brierson.

There was one obvious thing he should demand, something he would not hesitate to require if he were back in civilization. He glanced at Yelén's auton, still hovering at the end of the table. Here . . . it might be better to wait for witnesses. Powerful ones. Finally he said, "I'll need personal transportation. Physical protection. Some means of publicly communicating with the entire settlement—I'll want their cooperation on this problem."

"Done."

"I'll also need your databases, at least where they deal with people in the settlement. I want to know where and when everyone originated, and exactly how they got bobbled past the Extinction."

Korolev's eyes narrowed. "Is this for your personal vendetta, Brierson? The past is dead. I'll not have you stirring up trouble with people who were once your enemies. Besides, the low-techs aren't suspects; there's no need for you to be sniffing around them."

Wil shook his head. This was just like old times: the customers deciding what the professional should see. "You're a high-tech, Yelén. But you're using a low-tech person, namely me. What makes you think the enemy doesn't have *his* accomplices?" People like Steve Fraley were the puppets now. They yearned to be the puppeteers. Playing Korolev against her enemy was a game the New Mexican President would love.

"Mph. Okay. You'll get the databases—but with your shanghai case locked out."

"And I want the sort of high-speed interface you have."

"Do you know how to use it?" Her hand brushed absently at her headband.

"Uh, no."

"Then forget it. The modern versions are a lot easier to learn than the kind you had, but I grew up with one and I still can't properly visualize with it. If you don't start as a child, you may spend years and never get the hang of it."

"Look, Yelén. Time is the one thing we've got. It's God knows how many thousands of years till the Peacers come out and you restart the settlement. Even if it took me fifty years to learn, it wouldn't interfere."

"Time is something *you* don't have, mister. If you spend a century tooling up for this job, you'll lose the viewpoint that's your value to me."

She had a point. He remembered how Marta had misunderstood the effect of Robinson's sales pitch.

"Sure," she continued, "there are high-tech angles to the murder. Maybe they're the most important angles. But I've already got expert help in that department."

"Oh? Someone you can trust among the high-techs?" He waved at the mug shots on the walls.

Korolev smiled thinly. "Someone I can *dis*trust less than the others. Never forget, Brierson, my devices will be watching all of you." She thought for a moment. "I was hoping she'd be back in time for this meeting. She's the least likely to have a motive. In all the megayears, she's never been tangled in our little schemes. You two will work together. I think you'll find your skills complementary. She knows technology, but she's a little . . . strange." Yelén was silent again; Wil wondered if he would ever get used to this silent communion between human and machines.

There was movement at the corner of his vision. Wil turned and saw that a third person sat by the table. It was the spacer woman. He hadn't heard a door opening or footsteps. . . . Then he noticed that she sat back from the table, and her seat was angled slightly off true. The holo was better than any he'd seen before.

She nodded solemnly at Yelén. "Ms. Korolev. I'm still in high orbit, but we can talk if you wish."

"Good. I wanted to introduce you to your partner." She smiled at some private joke. "Ms. Lu, this is Wil Brierson. Inspector Brierson, Della Lu."

He'd heard that name before but couldn't remember just where. The short Asian looked much as she had at the party. He guessed she hadn't been out of stasis for more than a few days: her hair was the same dark fuzz as before.

Lu stared at Korolev for several seconds after she made the introduction, then turned to look at Brierson. If the delay were not a mannerism, she must be out beyond the moon. "I've read good things about you, Inspector," she said and made a smile that didn't involve her eyes. She spoke carefully, each word an isolated thing, but otherwise her English was much like Wil's North American dialect.

Before Brierson could reply, Korolev said, "What of our prime suspects, Ms. Lu?"

Another four-beat pause. "The Robinsons refused to stop." The library windows showed a view from space. In one direction, Wil could see a bright blue disk and a fainter, gray one—the Earth and the moon. Through the window behind Lu hung a bobble, sun and Earth and moon reflected in its surface. The sphere was surrounded by a spidery metal structure, swollen here and there into more solid structures. Dozens of tiny silver balls moved in slow orbit about the central one. Every few seconds the bobbles vanished, replaced by a much larger one that contained even the spidery superstructure. There was a flash of light, and then the scene returned to its first phase.

"By the time I caught up with them, they were off antigravity and using impulse boost. Their flicker rate was constant. It was easy to pace them."

Quack, quack. For a moment, Wil was totally lost. Then he realized he was seeing a nuke drive, *very* close up. The idea was so simple that it had been used even in his time: Just eject a bomb, then go into stasis for a few seconds while it detonates and gives you a big push. When you came out of stasis, drop off another bomb and repeat the process. Of course, it was deadly to bystanders. To get these pictures, Della Lu must have matched the Robinsons' bobble cycle exactly, and used her own bombs to keep up.

"Notice that when the drive bobble bursts, they immediately generate a smaller one just inside their defense frame. A battle would have taken several thousand years of outside time to resolve."

Objects in stasis had absolute protection against the outside world. But bobbles eventually burst: if the duration was short, your enemy would still be waiting, ready to shoot; if the duration was long, your enemy might drop your bobble into the sun—and absolute protection would end in absolute catastrophe. Apparently the advanced travelers used a hierarchy of autonomous fighters, flickering in and out of real-time. While in realtime, their processors decided on the duration of the next embobblement. The shortest-period devices stayed in sync with longer-period ones, relaying conclusions up a chain of command. At the top, the travelers' command bobble might have a relatively long period.

"So they got away?" Hidden by time and interstellar depths.

Pause, pause, pause, pause. "Not entirely. They claimed innocence, and left a spokesman to demonstrate their good faith." One of the windows brightened into a picture of Tammy Robinson. She looked even paler than usual. Wil felt a flash of anger at Don Robinson. Clever it might be, but what sort of person leaves his teenage kid to face a murder investigation? Lu continued. "I have her with me. We should be landing in sixty minutes."

"Good. Ms. Lu, I would like you and Brierson to interview her then." Beyond the windows, forests replaced the black and bright of space. "I want you to get her story before you and Brierson leave for the restart of Town Korolev."

Wil glanced at the spacer. She was strange, but apparently capable. And she was as powerful a witness as he could get. He ignored Yelén's auton and tried to put the proper note of peremptory confidence in his voice when he said, "One other thing, Yelén."

"Well?"

"We need a complete copy of the diary."

"How— What diary!"

"The one Marta kept all the years she was marooned."

Yelén's mouth clamped shut as she realized he must be bluffing— and that she had already lost the game. Wil kept his eyes on Yelén, but he noticed the auton rise: there was more than one bluff to play here.

"It's none of your business, Brierson. I've read it: Marta had no idea who marooned her."

"I want it, Yelén."

"Well, you can just stick it!" She half-rose from her seat, then sat. "You're the last person I want pawing through Marta's private—" She turned to Lu. "Maybe I could show parts of it to you."

Wil didn't let the spacer reply. "No. Where I come from, conceal-ment of evidence was usually a crime, Yelén. That's meaningless here, but if you don't give me the diary—all of it, and everything associated with it—I'll drop the case, and I'll ask Lu to drop the case."

Yelén's fists were clenched. She started to speak, stopped. A faint tremor shook her face. Finally: "Okay. You'll have it. *Now get out of my sight!*"

4

ammy Robinson was a very frightened young woman; Wil didn't
need police experience to see that. She paced back and forth
across the room, hysteria sparking from the high edge in her
voice. "How can you keep me in this cell? It's a dungeon!"

The walls were unadorned, off-white. But Wil could see doors opening onto a bedroom, a kitchen. There were stairs, perhaps to a study.
Her quarters covered about 150 square meters—a little cramped by
Wil's standards, but scarcely a punishing confinement. He stepped
away from Della Lu and put his hand on Tammy's shoulder. "These
are ship's quarters, Tam. Della Lu never expected to have passengers."
That was only a guess, but it felt right. Lu's holdings were compact,
built both vertically and horizontally. All the advanced travelers could
take their households into space—but Lu's was designed to stay there,
to be a home even in solar systems without planets. "You are in cus-
tody, but once we get to Town Korolev, you'll get better housing."

Della Lu tilted her head to one side. "Yes. Yelén Korolev is going to
take care of you then. She has much better—"

"No!" It was almost a scream. Tammy's eyes showed white all
around the irises. "I surrendered to you, Della Lu. And in good faith. I
won't tell you anything if you . . . Korolev will—" She put her hand
over her mouth and collapsed on a nearby sofa.

Wil sat down beside her as Della Lu pulled up a chair to sit facing
them. Lu's black pants and high-collared jacket looked military, but she

sat on the edge of her chair and watched Tammy's consternation with childlike curiosity. Wil cast a meaningful look in her direction (as if that would do any good) before continuing. "Tammy, there's no way we'll let Yelén get at you."

Tammy was upset, but no fool. She looked past Wil at the spacer. "Is that a promise, Della Lu?"

Lu gave an odd chuckle, but this time she didn't blow it. "Yes. And it's a promise I can keep."

They stared at each other a silent moment. Then the girl shuddered, her whole body relaxing. "Okay. I'll talk. Of course I'll talk. That's the whole reason I stayed behind: to clear my family's name."

"You know what's happened to Marta?"

"I've heard Yelén's accusations. When we came out of that strange, overlong bobblement, she was all over the comm links. She said poor Marta got marooned in the present . . . that she *died* there." Frank horror showed on Tammy's face.

"That's right. Someone sabotaged the Korolev jump program. It lasted a century instead of three months, and left Marta outside of stasis."

"And my dad's the chief suspect?" Incredulously.

Wil nodded. "I saw your father arguing with Marta, Tam. And later she told me how your family wants the people of Town Korolev to join you. . . . Your plans would benefit if the settlement failed."

"Sure. But we're not some gang of twentieth-century thugs, Wil. We *know* we have something more attractive than the Korolevs' rehash of civilization. It'll take the average person a while to see this, but given a fair chance they'll come with us. Instead, Yelén's forced us to run for our lives."

"You don't think Marta's been killed?" said Lu.

Tammy shrugged. "No. That would be hard to fake, especially if you"—she was looking at Della—"insist on studying the remains. I think Marta was murdered—and I think Yelén is the murderer. All the talk about outside sabotage is just short of ridiculous."

This was certainly Wil's biggest worry. In his time, domestic violence was a leading cause of death. Yelén seemed the most powerful of the high-techs. If she were the villain, life might be short for successful investigators. But aloud: "She's truly broken up over losing Marta. If she's faking, she's very good at it."

Tammy's response was quick. "I don't think she's faking it. I think she killed Marta for some crazy personal reason, and terribly regrets the necessity. But now that it's done, she's going to use it to destroy all opposition to the great Korolev plan."

"Um." He, W. W. Brierson, might be the cause of Marta's death. Suppose Yelén conceived that she was losing her love to another. For some disturbed souls, such a loss was logically equivalent to the death of the beloved. They could murder—and then honestly blame the loss on others. . . . Wil remembered the irrational hatred in Yelén's eyes when he walked into her library.

He looked at Tammy with new respect. She'd never seemed this bright before. In fact . . . he felt just a little bit manipulated. For all her terror, the girl was a very cool character. "Tammy," he said quietly, "just how old are you, really?"

"I—" The tear-streaked adolescent face froze for a second. Then: "I've lived ninety years, Wil."

Forty years longer than I. Some daughter figure.

"B-but that's not a secret." New tears filled her eyes. "I'd've told anyone who asked. A-and I'm not faking my personality. I try to keep a fresh, open mind. We're going to live a long time, and Daddy says it helps if we grow up slowly, if we don't freeze into adult mind-sets like they did in the old days."

The Lu creature gave one of her strange little laughs. "That depends on how long you plan to live," she said to no one in particular.

Brierson suddenly realized that it was wishful thinking to regard himself an expert on human nature. *Once* he had been; now that expertise might be as obsolete as the rest of his knowledge. When he left civilization, life-prolonging medicine had been just a few decades old. At that time, Tammy's deception would have been almost impossible. Yelén Korolev had had about two hundred years to teach herself to lie. Della Lu was so disconnected from humanity, it was hard to make sense of her at all. How could he judge what such people said?

Might as well continue the sympathetic role. He patted Tammy's hand. "Okay, Tam. I'm glad you told us."

She smiled halfheartedly. "Don't you see, Wil? My dad's a suspect because we disagreed with Marta. We left to protect the family; my staying behind shows we're not running from an investigation. . . . But Yelén is. On the way down, Della Lu told me how Yelén wants you back in stasis right away. She'll be left all alone at the scene of the crime. By the time you two come out, the evidence will be tens of thousands years stale—heck, what evidence there is will've been manufactured by her.

"Now, I brought the family records for the weeks before our party. You and Della Lu should study them. They may be dull, but at least they're the truth."

Wil nodded. It was obvious the Robinsons had their story together. He let the interview go on another fifteen minutes, until Tammy seemed calm and almost relaxed. Lu spoke occasionally, her interjections sometimes perceptive, more often obscure. It was evident that—in itself—clearing the family name was of little importance to the Robinsons. When they were headed, present opinion would be less than dust. But the family still wanted recruits. Tammy's parents were convinced that the people of Town Korolev would eventually realize that settling in the present was a dead end, and that time itself was the proper place for humanity. It might take a few decades, but if Tammy could survive the murder investigation, she would be free to wait and persuade. And eventually she would catch up with her family. Her parents had set a number of rendezvous in the megayears to come. Their exact locations were something she refused to reveal.

"You want to pace your lives, and live as long as the universe?" asked Lu.

"At least."

The spacer giggled. "And what will you do at the end?"

"That depends on how it ends." Tammy's eyes lit. "Daddy thinks that all the mysteries people have ever wondered on—even the Extinction—may be revealed there. It's the ultimate rendezvous for all thinking beings. If time is cyclic, we'll bobble through to the beginning and Man will be universal."

"And if the universe is open and dies forever?"

"Then perhaps we and the others can change that." Tammy shrugged. "But if we can't—well, we'll still be there. We will have seen it all. Daddy says we'll raise a glass and toast the memory of all of you that went before." She was still smiling.

And Brierson wondered if this might be the craziest of all his new acquaintances.

* * *

Afterwards, Wil tried to plan out the investigation with Della Lu. It was not easy.

"Was Ms. Robinson distressed at the beginning of the interview?" asked Lu.

Wil rolled his eyes heavenward. "Yes, I believe she was."

"Ah. I thought so, too."

"Look, uh, Della. What Tammy says about Yelén makes sense. It's absurd for the cops—us—to leave the murder scene like this. Back in Michigan, we would have dropped any customer who demanded such a thing. Now, Yelén is right that my hanging around to investigate the physical evidence would be amateurish. But your equipment is as good as hers—"

"Better."

"—and she should be willing to let you postpone bobbling long enough to gather evidence."

Lu was silent for a moment—talking through her headband? "Ms. Korolev wants to be alone for emotional reasons."

"Hmph. She has thousands of years to be alone before the Peacers come out. You should at least do an autopsy and record the physical evidence."

"Very well. Ms. Korolev is a suspect, then?"

Wil spread his hands. "At this stage, she and the Robinsons have to be at the top of our list. Once we start poking around, it may be easy to scratch her. Just now it would be totally unprofessional to have *her* do the field investigation."

"Is Ms. Korolev friendly towards you?"

"Huh? Not especially. What does that have to do with the investigation?"

"Nothing. I'm trying to find a . . ."—she seemed to search for the word—"a role model for talking to you."

Wil smiled faintly, thinking back to Yelén's hostility. "I'd appreciate it if you wouldn't model on her."

"Okay." Unsmiling.

If Lu were as smart with gadgets as she was dumb with people, they would make the best detective team in history. "There is something else, something very important, that I need. Yelén has promised me physical protection and access to her databases. I'd like to have your protection, too—at least till we can clear her."

"Certainly. If you wish, I'll manage your jump forward, too."

"And I'd like access to your databases." Cross-checking Korolev couldn't hurt.

The spacer hesitated. "Okay. But some of the information isn't very accessible."

Wil looked around Della's cabin—command bridge? It was even smaller than Tammy's quarters, and almost as stark. A small cluster of roses grew from Della's desk; their scent filled the air. A watercolor landscape hung on the wall facing the spacer. The life tones and shadows were subtly wrong, as if the artist were clumsy . . . or the scene not of this Earth.

And Brierson was putting his life in this person's hands. In this universe of strangers, he must trust some more than others, but . . . "How old are you, Della?"

"I've lived nine thousand years, Mr. Brierson. I have been away . . . a long time. I have seen much." Her dark eyes took on that cold, far look he remembered from their first encounters. For a moment, she looked past him, perhaps at the watercolor, perhaps beyond. Then the expressionless gaze returned to his face. "I think it's time I rejoined the human race."

5

Some fifty thousand years later, all that was left of the only world empire in history, the Peace Authority, returned to normal time. They were welcomed by Korolev autons, and discouraged from interfering with the bobbles on the south side of the Inland Sea. They had three months to consider their new circumstances before those bobbles burst.

What Marta and Yelén had worked so long for was ready to begin.

Thousands of tonnes of equipment were given to the low-techs, along with farms, factories, mines. The gifts were to individuals, supposedly based on their expertise back in civilization. The Dasgupta brothers received two vanloads of communication equipment. To Wil's amazement, they immediately traded the gear to an NM signal officer —for a thousand-hectare farm. And Korolev didn't object. She did point out which equipment was likely to fail first, and provide databases to those who wanted to plan for the future.

Many of the ungoverned low-techs loved it: survival with profit. Within weeks they had a thousand schemes for combining high-tech equipment with primitive production lines. Both would coexist for decades, with the failing high-tech restricted to a smaller and smaller role. In the end there would be a viable infrastructure.

The governments were not so pleased. Both Peacers and NMs were heavily armed, but as long as Korolev stood guard over the Inland Sea, all that twenty-first-century might was about as persuasive as the brass cannon on a courthouse lawn. Both had had time to understand the situation. They watched each other carefully, and united in their complaints against Korolev and the other high-techs. Their propaganda noted how carefully the high-techs coordinated the giveaway, how restricted it really was: no weapons were given, no bobbler technology, no aircraft, no autons, no medical equipment. "Korolev gives the illusion of freedom, not the reality."

The excitement of the founding came muted to Wil. He went to some of the parties. Sometimes he watched the Peacer or NM news. But he had little time to participate. He had a job, in some ways like his of long ago; he had a murderer to catch. Unless something seemed connected with that goal, it drifted by him, irrelevant.

Marta's murder was a major piece of news. Even with a civilization to build, people still found time to talk about it. Now that she was gone, everyone remembered her friendliness. Every unpopular Korolev policy was greeted with a sigh of "If only Marta were alive, this would be different." At first, Wil was at the center of the parties. But he had little to say. Besides, he was in a unique—and uncomfortable—position: Wil was a low-tech, but with the perks of a high. He could fly anywhere he wanted; the other low-techs were confined to Korolev-supplied "public" transportation. He had his own protection autons, supplied by Della and Yelén; other low-techs watched with ill-concealed nervousness when those floated into view. These advantages were nontransferable, and it wasn't long before Wil was more shunned than sought.

One of the Korolevs' fundamental principles had already been violated: the settlement was physically scattered now. The Peacers had refused to move across the Inland Sea to Town Korolev. With dazzling impudence, they demanded that Yelén set them up with their own town on the north shore. That put them more than nine hundred kilometers from the rest of humanity—a distance more psychological than real, since it was a fifteen-minute flight on Yelén's new trans-sea shuttle. Nevertheless, it was a surprise that she yielded.

The surviving Korolev was . . . changed. Wil had talked to her only twice since the colony's return to realtime. The first time had been something of a shock. She looked almost the same as before, but there was a moment of nonrecognition in her eyes. "Ah, Brierson," she said mildly. Her only comment about Lu's providing him protection was to say that she would continue to do so also. Her hostility was muted; she'd had a long time to bury her grief.

Yelén had spent a hundred years following Marta's travels around the sea. She and her devices had stored and cataloged and studied everything that might bear on the murder. Marta's was already the most thoroughly investigated murder in the history of the human race. *But only if this investigator is not herself the murderer,* said a little voice in the back of Wil's head.

Yelén had done another thing with the century she stayed behind: She had tried to reeducate herself. "There's only one of us left, Inspector. I've tried to live double. I've learned everything I can about Marta's specialty. I've dreamed through Marta's memories of every project she managed." A shadow of doubt crossed her face. "I hope it's enough." The Yelén he'd known before the murder would not have shown such weakness.

So, armed with Marta's knowledge and trying to imitate Marta's attitudes, Yelén had relented and let the Peacers establish North Shore. She'd set up the trans-sea flier service. She'd encouraged a couple of the high-techs—Genet and Blumenthal—to move their principal estates there.

And the murder investigation had truly been left to Lu and Brierson.

Though he had talked to Korolev only twice, he saw Della Lu almost every day. She had produced a list of suspects. She agreed with Korolev: the crime was completely beyond the low-techs. Of the high-techs, Yelén and the Robinsons were still the best suspects. (Fortunately Lu was cagey enough not to report *all* their suspicions to Yelén.)

At first, Wil thought the manner of the murder was a critical clue. He'd brought it up with Della early on. "If the murderer could bypass Marta's protection, why not kill her outright? This business of marooning her is nicely poetic, but it left a real possibility that she might be rescued."

Della shook her head. "You don't understand." Her face was framed with smooth black hair now. She'd stayed behind for nine months, the longest Yelén would allow. No breakthroughs resulted from the stay, but it had been long enough for her hair to grow out. She looked like a normal young woman now, and she could talk for minutes at a time without producing a jarring inanity, without getting that far, cold look. Lu was still the weirdest of the advanced travelers, but she was no longer in a class by herself. "The Korolev protection system is good. It's fast. It's smart. Whoever killed Marta did it with software. The killer found a chink in the Korolev defensive logic and very cleverly exploited it. Extending the stasis period to one century was not by itself life-threatening. Leaving Marta outside of stasis was not by itself life-threatening."

"Together they were deadly."

"True. And the defense system would have normally noticed that. I'm simplifying. What the killer did was more complicated. My point is, if he had tried anything more direct, there is no amount of clever programming that could have fooled the system. There was no surefire way he could murder Marta. Doing it this way gave the killer the best chance of success."

"Unless the killer is Yelén. I assume she could override all the system safeguards?"

"Yes."

But doing so would clearly show her guilt.

"Hmm. Marooning Marta left her defenseless. Why couldn't the murderer arrange an accident for her then? It doesn't make sense that she was allowed to live forty years."

Della thought a moment. "You're suggesting the killer could have bobbled everyone else for a century, and delayed bobbling himself?"

"Sure. A few minutes' delay would've been enough. Is that so hard?"

"By itself, it's trivial. But everyone was linked with the Korolev system for that jump. If anyone had delayed, it would show up in everyone's records. I'm an expert on autonomous systems, Wil. Yelén has shown me her system's design. It's a tight job, only a year older than mine. For anyone—except Yelén—to alter those jump records would be . . ."

"Impossible?" These systems people never changed. They could work miracles, but at the same time they claimed perfectly reasonable requests were impossible.

"No, maybe not impossible. If the killer had planned ahead, he might have an auton that didn't appear on his stasis roster. It could have been left outside of stasis without being noticed. But I don't see how the jump records themselves could be altered unless the killer had thoroughly infiltrated the Korolev system."

So they were dealing with a fairly impromptu act. And the queer circumstances of Marta's death were nothing more than a twenty-third-century version of a knife in the back.

6

Korolev had delivered Marta's diary soon after the colony returned to realtime. Wil's demand for it was one thing that could still bring a flare of anger to her face. In fact, Wil didn't really want to see the thing. But getting a copy, and getting Della to verify that it was undoctored, was essential. Until then, Yelén was logically the best suspect on his list. Now that he had the diary, it was easier to accept his intuition that Yelén was innocent. He set out to read Yelén's summaries and Della's cross-checking. If nothing showed up there, the diary would be a low-priority item.

Yelén had sent down an enormous amount of material. It included high-resolution holos of all Marta's writing. Yelén supplied a powerful overdoc; Wil could sort the pages by pH if he wanted. A note in the overdoc said the originals were in stasis, available at five days' notice.

The originals. Wil hadn't thought about it: How could you make a diary without even a data pad? Brief messages could be carved on the side of a tree or chiseled in rock, but for a diary you'd need something like paper and pen. Marta had been marooned for forty years, plenty of time to experiment. Her earliest writing was berry-juice ink on the soft insides of tree bark. She left the heavy pages in a rock cairn sealed with mud. When they were recovered fifty years later, the bark had rotted and the juice stains were invisible. Yelén and her autons had studied the fragile remains. Microanalysis showed where the berry stains had been; the first chapters were not lost. Apparently Marta had recognized the danger: the "paper" in the later cairns was made from reed strips. The dark green ink was scarcely faded.

The first entries were mainly narrative. At the other end of the diary, after she had been decades alone, the pages were filled with drawings, essays, and poems. Forty years is a long time if you have to live it alone, second by second. Not counting recopied material, Marta wrote more than two million words before she died. (Yelén had supplied him with a commercial database, GreenInc. Wil looked at some of the items in it; the diary was as long as twenty noninteractive novels.) Her medium was far bulkier than old-time paper, and she traveled thousands of kilometers in her time. Whenever she moved, she built a new cairn for her writing. The first few pages in each repeated especially important things—directions to the previous cairns, for instance. Later, Yelén found every one. Nothing had been lost, though one cairn had been flooded. Even there, the reconstructions were nearly complete.

Wil spent an afternoon going through Yelén's synopsis and Della's corresponding analysis. There were no surprises.

Afterwards, Wil couldn't resist looking for references to himself. There were four clusters, the most recent listed first. Wil punched it up:

Year 38.137 Cairn #4
Lat 14.36N Long 1.01E [K-meridian]
—ask for heuristic cross-reference—

was the header Yelén's overdoc printed across the top of the display. Below it was cursive green lettering. A blinking red arrow marked the reference:

< < . . . and if I don't make it, dearest Lelya, please don't spend your time trying to solve this mystery. Live for both of us; live for the project. If you must do anything with it, delegate the responsibility. There was that policeman. A low-tech. I can't remember his name. (Oh, the millionth time I pray for an interface band, or even a data set!) Give him the job, and then concentrate on what is important. . . . > >

Wil sat back and wished the context searcher weren't so damned smart. She didn't even remember his name! He tried to tell himself that she had lived almost forty years beyond their acquaintance when she wrote these words. Would he remember her name forty years from now? *(Yes!)* To think of all his soul-searching, to think how close they seemed that last night, and how noble he had been to back off—when all the time he was just another low-tech to her.

With a quick sweep of his hand, Wil cleared the other references from the display. *Let it lie, Wil. Let it lie.* He stood up, walked to the window of his study. He had important work to do. There was the interview with Monica Raines, and then with Juan Chanson. He should be researching for those.

So after a moment he returned to his desk . . . and jumped the display to the first entry in Marta's diary:

<<The Journal of Marta Qih-hui Qen Korolev
Dearest Lelya, >> it began. Every entry was addressed to "Lelya."

"GreenInc. Question," said Wil. "What is 'Lelya'?" He pointed to the word in the diary. A side display filled with the three most likely possibilities. The first was: "Diminutive of the name Yeléna." Wil nodded to himself; that had been his guess. He continued reading from the central display.

<<Dearest Lelya,

<<It's now 181 days since everyone left—and that's the only thing I'm sure of.

<<Starting this journal is something of an admission of defeat. Till now, I had kept careful track of time, and that seemed all that was necessary; you remember we had planned a flicker cycle of ninety days. Yesterday the second flicker should have happened—yet I saw nothing.

<<So I guess I have to take the longer view. (What a mild way to say it. Yesterday, all I could do was cry.) I've got to have someone to "talk" to.

<<And I've got a lot to say, Lelya. You know how I like to talk. The hardest thing is the act of writing. I don't know how civilization got started, if literacy involved the effort I've had to make. This bark is easy to find, but I'm afraid it won't age well. Have to think about that. The "ink" is easy, too. But the reed pen I've made leaks and blobs. And if I say something wrong, I can only paint out the errors. (I understand why calligraphy was such a high art.) It takes a long time to write even the simplest things. But I have an advantage now: I have lots and lots of time. All the time in the world. >>

The reconstruction of the original showed awkward block letters and numerous scratch-outs. Wil wondered how many years it had been before she developed the cursive style he'd seen at the end of her diary.

< < By the time you read this, you'll probably have all the explanations (hopefully from me direct!), but I want to tell you what I remember.

< < There was the party at the Robinsons. I left early, so mad at Don that I could spit. They've really done us dirt, you know that? Anyway, it was past the Witching Hour and I was walking the forest path to the house. Fred was about five meters up, in front of me; I remember the moonlight glinting off his hull. > >

Fred? The diary's overdoc said that was the auton with Marta that night. Wil hadn't realized they were personalized. You never heard them addressed by name. Come to think of it, that wasn't surprising; the high-techs generally talked to their mechanicals via headband.

< < From Fred I had a good view over three octaves. There was no one close by. There were no autons shadowing me. It's about an hour's walk up to the house. I had taken longer. I wanted to be cool when I talked to you about Don's little game. I was almost to the great steps when it happened. Fred had no hint. There was a cinnamon burst of static and then he crashed to the ground. It's the most startled I've ever been, Lelya. Our whole lives we've had autons giving us extra eyes. This is the first time I can remember not having *any* warning of a problem.

< < Ahead of me, the great steps were gone. There was my reflection staring back. Fred was lying at the edge of the bobble. He'd been cut in half by the stasis field.

< < We've had some rough times, Lelya, like when we fought the graverobbers. They were so strong, I thought the battle might carry us past fifty megayears and ruin everything. You remember how I was after that. Well, this was worse. I think I went a little crazy. I kept telling myself it was all a dream. (Even now, six months later, that sometimes seems the best explanation.) I ran along the bobble's edge. Things were as peaceful and silent as before, but now the ground was treacherous beneath my feet and branches clawed at me. I didn't have Fred to be my high eyes. The bobble was hundreds of meters across. It met the ground just beyond the great steps. It didn't cut through any large trees. It was obviously the bobblement we'd planned for the property.

‹‹ Well, if you're reading this, you already know the rest. The Robinsons' place was bobbled. Genet's was bobbled. It took me three days to hike across all of Korolev Town: everything was bobbled. It looked exactly like the jump we'd programmed except for two things: (1) (obviously) poor little Marta had been left outside, and (2) all automatic equipment was *in* stasis.

‹‹ Those first weeks, I could still hope that every ninety days the stasis would flicker off while the autons checked the Peacer bobble. I couldn't imagine how all this had happened (I still can't), yet it might turn out to be one of those stupid mistakes one can laugh about afterwards. All I had to do was stay alive for ninety days.

‹‹ There's damn little outside stasis, Lelya. There was no question of salvaging Fred. Looking at that compact pile of junk, I was surprised how little I could do with it—even if his power supply had been on my side of the bobble. Monica Raines is right about one thing: Without autons, we might as well be savages. They are our hands. And that's not the most horrible part: Without processor and db support, I'm a cripple, my mind stuck in molasses. When a question occurs to me, the only data is what's wedged in my own gray matter. The only eyes I see from are my own, fixed in space and time, seeing only a narrow band of the spectrum. To imagine that before our time people lived their whole lives in this lobotomized state! Maybe it helped that they didn't know anything better.

‹‹ But Monica is wrong about something else: I didn't just sit down and starve. All my time in survival sports paid off. The Robinsons had left a pile of trash just on our side of the property line. (That figures.) At a glance you might not think there was much worthwhile: a hundred kilos of botched gold fittings, an organic sludge pond that made me want to puke, and—get this—a dozen cutter blades. So what if they've lost their micrometer edge? They're still sharp enough to cut a hair lengthwise. They're about half a kilo each, single diamond crystals. I lashed them onto wood hafts. I also found some shovels on a pile of rock ash in town.

‹‹ I remembered the large carnivores we spotted coming in. If they're still around, they're lying low. After a couple of weeks, I was beginning to feel safe. My traps worked, though not as well as on a sport trip; the wildlife hasn't recovered from the Peacer rescue. Just as we'd planned, the south gallery of the house was left out of stasis.

(Remember how you thought it hadn't aged enough?) It's all naked stone, stairs and towers and halls, but it makes good shelter—and parts are easy to barricade.

< < I didn't remember how long the lookabout would last, so I decided to hit you over the head with my message. I lashed a frame between the trees at the bottom of the great stairs. I spread bark across the framework and used wet ash to spell HELP in letters three meters high. There's no way it could be missed by the monitor on top of the library. I had the sign done a good week ahead of time.

< < Day ninety was worse than waiting for the judge's call in arbitration. No day ever seemed so long. I sat right by my sign and watched my reflection in the bobble. Lelya, *nothing happened*. You aren't on a three-month flicker, or the monitor isn't watching. I never hated my own face as much as I did that day, watching it in the side of the bobble. > >

Of course, Marta had not given up. The next pages described how she had built similar signs near the bobbles of all the advanced travelers.

< < Day 180 just passed, and the bobbles still sit. I cried a lot. I miss you so. Survival games were fun, but not forever.

< < I've got to settle down for the long haul. I'm going to make those billboards sturdier. I want them to last at least a hundred years. How long can *I* last? Without health care, people used to live about a century. I've kept my bio-age at twenty-five years, so I should have seventy-five left. Without the databases I can't be sure, but I bet seventy-five is a lower bound. There should be some residual effect from my last medical treatment, and I'm full of panphages. On the other hand, old people were fragile, weren't they? If I have to protect myself and get my own food, that could be a factor.

< < Okay. Let's be pessimistic. Say I can only last seventy-five years. What's my best chance for getting rescued?

< < You can bet I've thought about that a lot, Lelya. So much depends on what caused this catastrophe—and all the clues are on your side of the bobble. I've got ideas, but without the databases I can't tell what's plausible. > > She went on to list the string of unrelated errors that would be necessary to leave *her* outside and all the autons inside, and to change the flicker period. Sabotage was the only possible explanation; she knew that someone had tried to kill her.

<< I'm not lying down to die. I can't think technical anymore, but I'll bet you still have a fairly short flicker period. Besides, we have gear lots of other places: at the Lagrange zones, the West End mines, the Peacer bobble. With luck, there will be lookabouts in the next seventy-five years. And didn't we leave autonomous devices in realtime in Canada? I think there's a land bridge to America in this era. If I can get there, maybe I could make my own rescue.

<< So most of the time, I'm optimistic.

<< But suppose I don't make it? Then I'm the murder victim, and some kind of witness, too. Even though you'll never get Fred's record of the Robinsons' recruiting party, you'll hear about it elsewhere. That's the only clue I have.

<< Don't let them break up our settlement, Lelya. >>

7

The morning of the Monica Raines interview did not begin well. Wil was still asleep when the house announced that Della Lu was waiting outside.

Wil groaned, slowly rising from the unpleasant dreams that haunted his mornings. Then he realized the time, and the day. "Sorry, sorry. I'll be right down." He rolled out of bed and staggered into the bathroom. Who had decided on this early start, anyway? Then he remembered it had been himself; something about time zones.

Even downstairs, he was still a bit foggy. He grabbed a box lunch from the kitchen. The bright colors on the package were advertising fifty million years old. When Korolev said she was providing twenty-first-century support, she meant it. The autofactories were running off the same programs as the original manufacturers. The effect was more weird than homey. He tucked the lunch into his shoulder bag along with his data set. Something in the back of his mind was saying he should take more; after all, he was going a third of the way around the world today. He shook his head. Sure, and he'd probably be back in five hours. Even the lunch was unnecessary. Wil gave final instructions to the house and stepped into the morning coolness.

It was the sort of morning that should change the ways of night owls. Green loomed high around the house, the trees glistening damply in the sun. Everything felt clean and bright, just created. Except for the birds, it was quiet. He walked across the mossy street toward Lu's

340

enclosed flier. Two protection devices—one from Yelén and one from Della—left their posts above his house and drifted along with him.

"Hey, Wil! Wait a minute." Dilip Dasgupta waved from his house, fifty meters down the road. "Where are you going?"

"Calafia," Brierson called back.

"Wow." Rohan and Dilip were both up and dressed. They jogged down the road to him.

"This part of the murder investigation?" said Dilip.

"You look awful, Wil," said Rohan.

Brierson ignored Rohan. "Yeah. We're flying out to see Monica Raines."

"Ah! A suspect."

"No. We're still fact-finding, Dilip. I want to talk to all the high-techs."

"Oh." He sounded like a football fan disappointed by his team's hard luck. A few days earlier, the disappointment would have been tinged with fear. Everyone had been edgy then, guessing that Marta's murder might be the prelude to a massive assault on the settlement.

"Wil, I mean it." Rohan was not to be sidetracked. "You really looked dragged out. And it's not just this morning, so early and all. Don't let this case shut you off from your friends. You gotta mingle, Wil. . . . Like, this morning we're going on a fishing expedition off North Shore. It's something the Peacers organized. That Genet fellow is coming along in case we run into anything too big to handle. You know, I don't see why governments got such a bad name. Both the Peacers and the New Mexicans aren't much different from social clubs or college fraternities. They've been real nice to everybody."

"Yes, and face it, Wil, we're starting new lives here. Most of the human race is tied up in those two groups now. There are lots of women there, lots of people you'd like to know."

Brierson grinned, embarrassed and a bit touched. "You're right. I should keep up with things."

Rohan reached up to slap him on the shoulder. "Hey, if you get back in the afternoon, you might have the Lu person drop you off at North Shore. I bet there'll still be something going."

"Okay!" Wil turned and walked toward Lu's aircraft. The Dasguptas were right about some things. How wrong they were about others: A smile came back to his lips as he imagined Steve Fraley's reaction to hearing the Republic of New Mexico likened to a social club.

"Good morning, Wil." Lu's face was impassive. She seemed not at all impatient at the delay. "Is 1.5 g's okay?"

"Sure, sure." Brierson settled into a chair, not quite sure what she was talking about. At least he didn't have to worry about *her* questioning his mood. Short of laughter or smiles or tears, she still seemed incapable of reading facial expressions.

He sank slowly into the seat cushions as the flier's acceleration added a physical lassitude to his mental one. He'd been using the GreenInc database for more than the investigation of Marta's murder. Last night he'd tracked his family to the end of the twenty-second century. He was proud of what his children had become: Anne the astronaut, Billy the cop and later the story-maker. As far as he could tell, Virginia had never remarried. The three of them had disappeared into the twenty-third century, along with his parents, his sister, and all the rest of humanity.

In 2140 and 2180 they had bobbled gifts to accompany him. GreenInc said it was the best survival equipment their money could buy. It had all been lost to the graverobbers, the scavenging travelers that existed in the first megayears after Man. Perhaps that was just as well. There would have been family video in those care packages. That would have been very hard to view.

. . . But all along he'd had the secret dream that Virginia might come after him herself, at least when the kids had their own families. It was strange: He would have pleaded with her not to come, yet now he felt . . . betrayed.

The faint whistling from beyond the windows had long faded, but the gut-tugging acceleration continued. Wil's attention returned to the flier. He looked straight out. Cloud-speckled ocean stood like a blue wall beside them. He looked up through the transparent dome—and saw the curve of the Earth, pale blue meeting the black of space. They were hundreds of klicks up, driving forward at a steady acceleration that was nothing like the ballistic trajectories he was used to.

"How long?" he managed to say.

"It is slow, isn't it?" Della said. "Now that the settlement is founded, Yelén doesn't want us to use nukes in near space. At this acceleration, it'll be another half hour to North America."

An island chain trundled rapidly across his field of view. Much nearer, he saw the autons that protected him at home; the two flew formation with Della's craft.

"I still don't understand why you want to go out of your way to interview Ms. Raines. How is she special?"

Wil shrugged. "I like to do the reluctant ones first. She's not interested in coming back in person, and I want these interviews to be face to face."

Della said, "That's wise. Most of us could do almost anything on a holo channel. . . . But she's one of the least powerful of the hightechs. I can't imagine her as the killer."

A few minutes later, Della turned the flier over. It was a skew turn that for a moment had them accelerating straight down into the Pacific. Wil was glad there had not been time for breakfast. When they entered the atmosphere off the west coast of Calafia, they were moving barely fast enough to put a glow in the flier's hull.

Calafia. It was one of the Korolevs' more appropriate namings. In Wil's time, one of the clichés of regional insult was the prediction that California would one day fall into the sea. It never happened. Instead, California had *put* to sea, sliding along the San Andreas Fault, earthquake by earthquake, millennium after millennium—till the southwest coast of North America became a fifteen-hundred-kilometer island. It was indeed Calafia, the vast, narrow island that Spanish mariners had (prematurely) identified fifty million years earlier.

Della covered the last few hundred kilometers in a low approach. The beach passed quickly beneath. North and south, for as far as he could see, breakers marched on perfect sand. Nowhere was there town or road. The world was in an interglacial period now, much as in the Age of Man. That coastline really *did* look like California's. It didn't raise the same nostalgia as Michigan might, but he felt his throat tighten nevertheless. He and Virginia had often visited southern California in the 2090s, after the disgovernance of Aztlán.

They scudded over hills mantled with evergreens. Afternoon sunlight cast everything in jagged relief. Beyond the hills, the vegetation was sere and grayish green. Beyond that was prairie and the Calafia straits.

* * *

"Okay. So what dumb questions do you want to ask?" Monica Raines did not look back as she led them down to her—blind, she called it. Wil and Della hurried after her. He was not put off by the artist's brusqueness. In the past, she'd made no secret of her dislike for the Korolevs and their plans.

The wood stairs descended through tree-shrouded dimness. The smell of mesquite hung in the air. At the bottom, invisible among vines and branches, was a small cabin. Its floor was deeply carpeted, with pillows scattered about. One side of the room had no wall, but overlooked the beginning of the plainsland. A battery of equipment—optics?—was mounted at the edge of this open side.

"I'd appreciate it if you'd keep your voices down," said Monica. "We're less than one hundred meters from the starter nest." She fiddled with the equipment; she was not wearing a headband. A display flat lit with the picture of two . . . vultures? They strutted around a small pile of stones and brush. The picture was wavery with heat shimmers. Wil sighted over the optics: Sure enough, he could just make out two birds in the valley below the blind.

"Why use a telescope?" Lu asked softly. "With tracer cameras, you could—"

"Yeah, I use them, too. Gimme remotes," she said to the thin air. Several other displays came to life. The pictures were dim even in the darkened room. "I don't like to scatter tracers all around; they mess up the environment. Besides, I don't have any good ones left." She jerked a thumb at the main display. "If you're lucky, these dragon birds are gonna give you a real show."

Dragon birds? Wil looked again at the misshapen bodies, the featherless heads and necks. They still looked like vultures to him. The duncolored creatures strutted round and round the pile, occasionally puffing out their chests. Off to one side, he saw a smaller one, sitting and watching. The strangest thing about them was the bladelike ridge that ran across the top of their beaks.

Monica sat cross-legged on the floor. Wil sat down more awkwardly and punched up some notes on his data set. Della Lu remained standing, drifting around the room, looking at the pictures on the wall. They were famous pictures: *Death on a Bicycle, Death Visits the Amusement Park*. . . . They'd been a fad in the 2050s, at the time of the longevity breakthrough, when people realized that but for accidents or violence, they could live forever. Death was suddenly a pleasant old man, freed from his longtime burden. He rolled awkwardly along on his first bicycle ride, his scythe sticking up like a flag. Children ran beside him, smiling and laughing. Wil remembered the pictures well; he'd been a kid himself then. But here, fifty million years after the extinction of the human race, they seemed more macabre than cute.

Wil pulled his attention back to Monica Raines. "You know that Yelén Korolev has commissioned Ms. Lu and me to investigate the murder. Basically, I'm to provide the old-fashioned nosing around—like in the detective stories—and Della Lu is doing the high-tech analysis. It may seem frivolous, but this is the way I've always operated: I want to talk to you face to face, get your thoughts about the crime." *And try to find out what you had to do with it,* he didn't say; Wil's approach was as nonthreatening and casual as possible. "This is all voluntary. We aren't claiming any contractual authority."

The corner of Raines' mouth turned down. "My 'thoughts about the crime,' Mr. Brierson, are that I had nothing to do with it. To put it in your detective jargon: I have no motive, as I have no interest in the Korolevs' pitiful attempt to resurrect mankind. I had no opportunity, as my protection equipment is much more limited than theirs."

"You are a high-tech, though."

"Only by the era of my origin. When I left civilization, I took the bare necessities for survival. I didn't bring software to build autofactories. I have air/space capability and some explosives, but they're the minimum needed to exit stasis safely." She gestured at Lu. "Your high-tech partner can verify all this."

Della dropped bonelessly to a cross-legged position and propped her chin on her hands. For an instant she looked like a young girl. "You'll give me access to your databases?"

"Yes."

The spacer nodded, and then her attention drifted away again. She was watching the picture off the telescope. The dragon birds had stopped their strutting. Now they were taking turns *throwing* small rocks into the nestlike structure between them. Wil had never seen anything like it. The birds would hunt about at the edge of the pile of stones and brush. They seemed very selective. What they grasped in their beaks glittered. Then, with a quick flip of the head, the pebble was cast into the pile. At the same time, the thrower flapped briefly into the air.

Raines followed Della's glance. The artist's face split with a smile less cynical than usual. "Notice how they face downwind when they do that."

"They're fire makers?" asked Lu.

Raines' head snapped up. "You're the spacer. You've seen things like this before?"

"Once. In the LMC. But they weren't . . . birds, exactly."

Raines was silent for a moment. Curiosity and wonder seemed to battle against her natural desire to remain one up on her visitors. The latter won, but she sounded friendlier as she continued. "Things have to be just right before they'll try. It's been a dry summer, and they've built their starter-pyre at the edge of an area that hasn't burned in decades. Notice that there's a good breeze blowing along the hillsides."

Lu was smiling now, too. "Yes. So that flapping reflex when they throw—that's to give the sparks a little help?"

"Right. It can be—oh, look, look!" There wasn't much to see. Wil had noticed a faint spark when the last pebble struck the rocks in the nest—the starter-pyre, Monica called it. Now a wisp of smoke rose from the straw that covered the leeward side of the pile. The vulture stayed close to the smoke, moved its wings in long sweeps. Its rattling call echoed up the ravine. "Nope. It didn't quite catch. . . . Sometimes the dragon's *too* successful, by the way. They burn like torches if their feathers catch fire. I think that's why the males work in pairs: one's a spare."

"But when the game works . . ." said Lu.

"When the game works, you get a nice brush fire sweeping away from the dragon birds."

"How do they benefit by starting fires?" asked Wil; he already had a bad feeling he knew the answer.

"It makes for good eating, Mr. Brierson. These scavengers don't wait for lunch to drop dead on its own. A fire like this can spread faster than some animals can run. After it's over, there's plenty of cooked meat. Those beak ridges are for scraping the char off their prey. The dragons get so fat afterwards, they can barely waddle. A good burn marks the start of a really successful breeding season."

Wil felt a little sick. He'd watched nature films all the way back to the flat-screen Disneys, but he never could accept the talk about the beauty and balance of nature—when illustrated by grotesque forms of sudden death.

Things got worse. Della asked, "So they get mainly small animals?"

Raines nodded. "But there are a few interesting exceptions." She brought another display to life. "These pictures are from a camera about four thousand meters east of here." The picture jogged and bounced. Wil glimpsed shaggy creatures rooting through dense brush. They were built low to the ground, yet seemed vaguely apelike.

"Marvelous what the primates can become, isn't it? The design is so multipurpose, so *centered*. Except for one disastrous dead end, they are by far the most interesting of the mammals. At one time or another, I've seen them adapt to almost every slot available for large land animals, and more: the fishermonkeys are almost in the penguin slot. I'm watching them very closely; someday they may become exclusively water animals." Enthusiasm was bright on her normally saturnine features.

"You think mankind *devolved* into the fishermonkeys and these . . . things?" Wil pointed at the display. He couldn't keep the revulsion from his voice.

Raines sniffed. "That's absurd. And presumptuous, really. Homo sapiens was about the most self-deadly variation in the theme of life. The species insulated itself from physical stress for so long that what few individuals survived the destruction of technology would have been totally unable to live on their own. No, the present-day primates are descended from those in wilderness estates at the time mankind did itself in."

She laughed softly at the look on Wil's face. "You have no business making value judgments on the dragons, Mr. Brierson. Theirs is a beautiful variation. It's survived half a million years—almost as long as Man's experiment with fire. The starter-pyres began as small piles of glitter, a kind of sexual display for the males. The first fires were accidental, but the adaptation has been refined over hundreds of thousands of years. It doesn't provide them with all their food, or even most of it. But it's an extra advantage. As a mating ritual, it even survives climatic wet spells. When summers are dry again, it is still ready to use.

"This is how fire was meant to be used, Mr. Brierson. The dragons have little impact on the average tonnage burned; they just redistribute the fires to their advantage. Their way is self-limiting, fitting the balance of nature. Man perverted fire, used it for unlimited destruction."

Every one crazier than the last, thought Wil. Monica Raines sat surrounded and served by the fruits of that "perversion," and all she could do was bitch. She sounded like something out of the twentieth century. "So you don't believe Juan Chanson's theory that man was exterminated by aliens?"

"There's no need for such an invention. Can't you see, Mr. Brierson? The trends were all there, undeniable. Mankind's systems grew more and more complicated, their demands more and more rapacious. Have you seen the mines the Korolevs built west of the Inland Sea? They stretch for dozens of kilometers—open pits, autons everywhere. By the late twenty-second century, *that's* the scale of resources demanded by a single individual. Science gave each human animal the presumption to act like a little god. The Earth just couldn't take it. Hell, I'll bet there wasn't even a war. I'll bet the whole structure collapsed under its own weight, leaving the rapists at the mercy of their victim—nature."

"There's the asteroid belt. Industry could be moved off-planet." In fact, Wil had seen the beginnings of that in his time.

"No. This was an exponential process. Moving into space just postponed the debacle a few decades." She rose to her knees and looked at the telescope display. The vultures had resumed their slow strutting about the rock pile. "Too bad. I don't think we'll get a fire today. They try hardest in the early afternoon."

"If you feel this way about humans, why are you out of stasis just now?" said Lu.

Wil added, "Did you think you could persuade the new settlement to behave more . . . respectfully toward nature?"

Raines made one of her turned-down smiles. "Certainly not. You haven't seen any propaganda from me, have you? I couldn't care less. This settlement is the biggest I've seen, but it will fail like all the others, and there will be peace on Earth once more. I, um . . . it's just a coincidence we're all out of stasis at the same time." She hesitated. "I—I am an artist, Ms. Lu. I use the scientist's tools, but with the heart of an artist. Back in civilization, I could see the Extinction coming: there would be no one left to rape nature, but neither would there be anyone to praise her handiwork.

"So I proceed down through time, averaging a year alive in each megayear, making my pictures, taking my notes. Sometimes I stay out for just a day, sometimes for a week or a month. The last few megayears, I've been very active. The social spiders are fascinating, and now—just in the last half million years—the dragon birds have appeared. It's not surprising that we all should be living at the same time."

There was something fishy about the explanation. A year of observing time spread through a million years left an awful lot of empty space. The settlement had only been active for a few months. The odds against meeting her seemed very high. Raines sat uneasily, almost fidgeting under his gaze. She was lying, but why? The obvious explanation was certainly an innocent one. For all her hostility, Monica Raines was still a human being. Even if she could not admit it to herself, she still needed others to share the things she did.

"But my staying is no coincidence, Mr. Brierson. I've got my pictures; I'm ready to go. Besides, I expect the next few centuries—the time it takes you people to die off—will be ugly ones. I'd be long gone except for Yelén. She demands I stay in this era. She says she'll drop me into the sun if I bobble up. The bitch." Apparently Raines didn't have as much firepower as the Robinsons. Wil wondered if any of the other high-techs were staying under duress. "So you can see why I'm willing to cooperate. Get her off my back."

Despite the sour words, she was eager to talk. She showed them her video of the early dragon birds, back when starting fires was almost an accident. In her fifty-year voyage she had created archives that would have shamed the national libraries of the twentieth century. And Don Robinson was not the only one who made home movies. Monica's automation could rearrange her data into terrifying homotopies, where creatures caught in the blowtorch of time flowed and melted from one form to another. She seemed determined to show them everything, and Della Lu, at least, seemed willing to watch.

When they left the blind, deep twilight lay across the grassland. Raines accompanied them to the top of her little canyon. A dry, warm wind rattled through the chaparral; the dragon birds should have no trouble starting their fire if the weather stayed like this. They stood for a moment at the top of the ridgeline. They could see for kilometers in all directions. Bands of orange and red crossed the western horizon. A hint of green lay above that, then violet and starry blackness. Nowhere was there a single artificial light. A smell like honey floated in the breeze.

"It's beautiful, isn't it?" Raines said softly.

Untouched forever and ever. Could she really want that? "Yes, but someday intelligence will evolve again. Even if you're right about humanity, the world won't stay peaceful forever."

She didn't answer immediately. "It could happen. There are a couple of species that seem to be at the brink of sentience—the spiders for one." She looked back at him, her face lit by the twilight band. Was she blushing? Somehow, his question had hit home. "If it happens . . . well, I'll be here, right from the beginning of their awareness. I'm not against intelligence by itself, just the abuse of it. Perhaps I can nudge them away from the arrogance of my race." Like an elder god, leading the new creatures in the way of the right. Monica Raines would find people who could properly appreciate her—even if she had to help in their creation.

Lu's flier drove steadily back over the Pacific. The sun rose swiftly from around the shoulder of the Earth. According to his data set it was barely noon in the Asian time zone. The bright sunlight and blue sky (which was really the Pacific below) made such an emotional difference. Just minutes ago all had been darkness and poor Monica's murky thoughts.

"Crazies," said Wil.

"What?"

"All these advanced travelers. I could go a year in police work and not meet anyone as strange: Yelén Korolev, who seems to be jealous of me just for liking her girlfriend, and who moped alone for a century after we jumped forward; cute little Tammy Robinson—who is old enough to be my mother—and whose object in life is to celebrate New Year's at the end of time; Monica Raines, who would make a twentieth-century ecofanatic look like a strip miner." *And then there's Della Lu, who has lived so long she has to study to seem human at all.*

He stopped short and looked guiltily at Della. She grinned knowingly at him, and the smile seemed to reach all the way to her eyes. Damn. There were times now she seemed totally aware. "What do you expect, Wil? We were all a little strange to begin with; we left civilization voluntarily. Since then, we have spent hundreds—sometimes thousands —of years getting here. That takes a power of will you would call monomania."

"Not all the high-techs started out crazy. I mean . . . your original motive was short-range exploration, right?"

"By your standards it wasn't short range. I had just lost someone I cared about very much; I wanted to be alone. The Gatewood's Star mission was a twelve-hundred-year round trip. By the time I got back, I had overshot the Singularity—what Monica and Juan call the Extinction. That's when I left on my really long missions. You've missed all the reasonable high-techs, Wil. They settled down in the first few megayears after Man and made the best of it. You're left with *la crud de la crud,* so to speak."

She had a point. The low-techs were a lot easier to talk to. Wil had thought that a matter of culture similarity, but now he saw that it went deeper. The low-techs were people who had been shanghaied, or had short-term goals (like the Dasguptas and their foolish investment schemes). Even the New Mexicans, who had an abundance of unpleasant notions, had not spent more than a few years in realtime since leaving civilization.

Okay, so all the suspects were nuts. The problem was to find the nut that was also rotten.

"What about Raines? For all her talk of indifference, she's clearly hostile to the Korolevs. Perhaps she killed Marta just to speed up the 'natural process' of the settlement's collapse."

"I don't think so, Wil. I snooped around while we were talking with her. She has good bobbling equipment, and enough automation to run her observation program, but she's virtually defenseless. She doesn't have the depth to fool the Korolev scheduling programs. . . . In fact, she's terribly underequipped. If she keeps living a year per megayear, she won't last more than a couple of hundred megayears before her autons begin to fail. Then she's going to find out about nature first-hand. . . . You should compliment me, Wil; I'm following your advice about the interviews. I didn't laugh when she started on peace and the balance of nature."

Brierson smiled. "Yes. You were a good cointerrogator. . . . But I don't think she plans on traveling forever. Her real goal is to play god to the next intelligent race that evolves on Earth."

"The *next* intelligent race? Then she doesn't realize how rare intelligence is. You may think those fire-making birds are freaks, but let me tell you something: Such developments are a thousand times more common than the evolution of intelligence. Chances are the sun will go red giant long before intelligence reappears on Earth."

"Hmm." He was scarcely in a position to argue. Della Lu was the only living human, perhaps the only person in history, who really knew about such things. "Okay, so she's unrealistic . . . or maybe she's hiding her true resources, at the Lagrange zones or in the wilderness. Can you be sure she's not playing dumb?"

"Not yet. But when she gives me access to her records, I'll run consistency checks. I have faith in my automation. Raines left civilization seven years before me. Whatever automation she took, mine is better. If she's hiding anything, I will know."

One less suspect, probably. That was a sort of progress.

They flew silently for several minutes, the blue of the Earth on one side, the sun sliding down the other. He could see one of the protection autons, a bright fleck floating against the clouds.

Perhaps he should take the afternoon off, go to the Peacer meeting at North Shore. Still, there was something about Monica Raines. "Della, how do you think Raines would feel if the settlement were a success? Would she be so indifferent to us if she thought we might do permanent damage?"

"I think she would be surprised, and very angry . . . and impotent."

"I wonder. Let's suppose she doesn't have the usual high-tech battle equipment. If she simply wanted to destroy the settlement, she might not need anything spectacular: perhaps a disease, something with a long incubation period."

Lu's eyes widened almost comically. He had noticed the same mannerism in Yelén Korolev. It had something to do with their direct data interface: When confronted with a surprising question demanding heavy analysis, they seemed first startled and then dazed. Several seconds passed. "That's just barely possible. She has a bioscience background, and a small autolab would be hard to spot. The Korolevs' medical automation is good, but it's not designed for warfare. . . ."

She smiled. "That's an interesting idea, Wil. A properly designed virus could evade the panphages and infect everyone before any symptoms appeared. Bobbling out of the area would be no defense."

"Interesting" was not the word Brierson would have used. The diseases spread after the 1997 war had killed most of the human race. Even in Wil's time, less than forty million people lived in North America. By then the terror was gone, and the world was a friendly place, but still—better bombs and bullets than bugs. He licked his lips. "I suppose we don't have to worry about it immediately. She must know how deadly the high-tech response would be. But if our settlement is *too* successful . . ."

"Yes. I've put this on my list. Now that we're aware of the possibility, it shouldn't be hard to guard against. I have exploration-duty medical equipment. It's smart and very paranoid."

"Yeah." *Nothing to worry about, Wil.* They had lost a murder suspect—and possibly gained a genocidal maniac.

8

Wil didn't make it to the party at North Shore.

At first, the Raines thing had him wound up, and then— well, someone had killed Marta. Most likely that someone wanted the settlement to fail. And he was no nearer cracking the case today than a week ago. Parties would have to wait.

He meshed his data set with the house archives. He could have used the house displays direct, but he felt more at ease with his portable. . . . Besides, it was one of the few things that had come with him through time. Its memory was an attic filled with a thousand private souvenirs; the date it displayed, 16 February 2100, was when he would be if his old life had continued.

Wil heated his lunch pack and munched absentmindedly at hot vegetables as he scanned his progress. He was behind in his reading; just another good reason to stay home this afternoon. People outside police work didn't realize how much of criminal investigation involved drawing conclusions from databases—usually public databases, at that. Wil's "reading" was the most likely source of real evidence. There was no shortage of things to look at. His house archive was far bigger than any other low-tech's. In addition to the 2201 edition of GreenInc, he had copies of parts of Korolev's and Lu's personal databases.

Wil had insisted on having his own copies. He didn't want networked stuff. He didn't want it changing mysteriously depending on the whim of the original owners. The price of such independence was a certain incoherence. His own processors had to accommodate idiosyncrasies in the structure of the imported data. With Yelén's databases, it wasn't too bad. They were designed both for headband use and for old-fashioned query languages. Her engineering jargon was sometimes incomprehensible, but he could get by.

Della's db's were a different story. Her copy of GreenInc was a year more recent than Yelén's, but a note announced that the later parts had been severely damaged during her travels. That was an understatement. Whole sections from the late twenty-second were jumbled or just plain missing. Her personal database appeared to be intact, but it used a customized headband design. His processors found it almost impossible to talk to the retrieval programs. Usually the output seemed to be allegorical hallucinations; occasionally he was blocked by the fragments of a personality simulator. Not for the first time in his life, Wil wished he could use interface headbands. They had existed in his time. If you had great native intelligence and a certain turn of imagination, they made computers a direct extension of your mind; otherwise, the bands were little more than electronic drug-tripping. Wil sighed. Yelén said the headbands from her era were easier to use; if only she had given him the time to learn how.

Della had nine thousand years of exploration packed away in her database. He'd had tantalizing glimpses—a world where plants floated in the sky, pictures of stars crowding close about something dark and *visibly* moving, a low-orbit shot of a planet green and cratered. On one planet, bathed in the glow of a giant red sun, he saw something that looked like ruins. Nowhere else had he seen any sign of intelligence. Was it so rare that all Della ever saw were ruins or fossils of ruins—of civilizations lasting a few millennia, and missed by millions of years? He hadn't yet asked her about what she'd seen. The murder was their immediate business, and until recently she'd been difficult to talk to. But now that he thought about it, she was awfully closemouthed about her travels.

His other researches were going better. He'd studied most of the high-techs. None of them—except Yelén and Marta—had any special relationship back in civilization. The conclusion couldn't be absolute, of course. The biography companies only had so many spies. If someone was hiding something, and was also out of the public eye, then that something could stay hidden.

Philippe Genet was one of the least documented. Wil couldn't find any reference to him before 2160, when he began advertising his services as a construction contractor. At that time, he was at least forty years old. You'd have to live like a hermit or have lots of money to go forty years and not get on a junk-mail list or have a published credit rating. There was another possibility: Perhaps Genet had been in stasis before 2160. Wil had not pursued that very far; it would open a whole new tree of investigation. Between 2160 and when Genet left civilization in 2201, the trail was sparse but visible. He had not been convicted of any crimes that involved public punishment. He hadn't been seen at public events, or written anything for public scrutiny. From his advertising—and the advertising that was focused back on him—it was clear that his construction business was successful, but not so successful as to attract the attention of the trade journals. Consumer ratings of his work were solid but not spectacular; he came out low in "customer relations." In the 2190s, he followed the herd and began specializing in space construction. Nowhere could Wil find anything that might be a motive. However, with his construction background, Genet was probably one of the best armed of the travelers.

Genet's conservative, quiet background hardly seemed to fit jumping into the future. He was a must for an early interview; at the least, it would be nice to meet a high-tech who was not a crazy.

In terms of documentation, Della Lu was at the other extreme. Brierson should have recognized her name the first time he heard it, even attached to its present owner. That name was important in the history books of Wil's childhood. If not for her, the 2048 revolt against the Peace Authority would have been a catastrophic failure. Della had been a double agent.

Wil had just reread the history of that war. To the Peacers, Lu was a secret-police cop who had infiltrated the rebels. In fact, it was the other way around: During the rebel assault on Livermore, Della Lu was stationed at the heart of the Peacer command. Right under her bosses' noses, she bobbled the Peace's command center and herself. End of battle; end of Peace Authority. The rest of their forces surrendered, or bobbled themselves. The Peacers now living on North Shore had been a secret Asian garrison designed to take the war into the future; unfortunately for them, they took it a little too *far* into the future.

What Della did took guts. She had been surrounded by the people she betrayed; when the bobble burst she could expect little better than a quick death.

All that had happened in 2048, two years before Wil was born. He could remember, as a kid, reading the histories and hoping that some way would be found to save the brave Della Lu when the Livermore bobble finally burst. Brierson hadn't lived to see that rescue. He was shanghaied in 2100, just before Della came out of stasis. His entire life in civilization had passed in what was no time at all to Della Lu.

Now he could view the rescue, and follow Lu through the twenty-second century. From the beginning, she was a celebrity. The biographers paid their *paparazzi*, and no part of her life was free of scrutiny. How much she had changed. Oh, the face was the same, and the twenty-second-century Della Lu often wore her hair short. But there was a precision and a force to her movements then. She reminded Wil of a cop, even a soldier. There were also humor and happiness in the recordings, things the present Lu seemed to be relearning. She'd married a Tinker, Miguel Rosas—and here Wil recognized the model for the personality simulator he'd found in Della's database. In the 2150s, they'd been famous all over again, this time for exploring the outer Solar System. Rosas died on their expedition to the Dark Companion. Della had left civilization for Gatewood's Star in 2202.

Wil finished lunch, letting the display roll through the bio summaries he'd constructed so far. It was an ironic thing, impossible before the invention of the bobble: Della Lu was an historical figure in his past, yet *he* was an historical figure in hers. She'd mentioned reading of him after her rescue, admiring someone who had "single-handedly stopped the New Mexican incursion." Brierson smiled sourly. He'd just been at the right place at the right time. If he hadn't been there, the invasion would have ended a little later, a little more bloodily; it was people like Kiki van Steen and Armadillo Schwartz who really stopped the invasion of Kansas. All through his police career, his company had hyped Wil. It was good for business, and usually bad for Wil. The customers seemed to expect miracles when W. W. Brierson was assigned to their case. His reputation almost got him killed during the Kansas thing. *Hell. Fifty million years later, that propaganda is still haunting me.* If he'd been just another policeman, Yelén Korolev might never have thought to give him this case. What she needed was a real investigator, not an enforcement type who had been promoted beyond all competence.

So what if he "knew" people? It scarcely seemed to help here. He had plenty of suspects, plenty of motives, and no hard facts. GreenInc was big and detailed; there were hundreds of possibilities he should look into. But what would get him closer to finding Marta's killer?

Wil put his head in his hands. Virginia had always said it was healthy for a person to wallow in self-pity every once in a while.

"You have a call from Yelén Korolev."

"Ugh." He sat back. "Okay, house. Put her on."

The conference holo showed Yelén sitting in her library. She looked tired, but then she always looked tired these days. Wil restrained the impulse to brush at his hair; no doubt he looked equally dragged out.

"Hello, Brierson. I just talked to Della about Monica Raines. You've eliminated her as a suspect."

"Uh, yes. But did Della tell you that Raines might be—"

"Yeah, the biowar thing. That's . . . good thinking. You know, I told Raines I'd kill her if she tried to bobble out of this era. Now I wonder. If she's not a suspect in the murder and yet is a threat to the settlement, perhaps I should 'persuade' her to take a jump—at least a megayear. What do you think?"

"Hmm. I'd wait till we've studied her personal database. Lu says she can protect us against biological attack. In any case, I don't think Raines would try something unless mankind looks like a successful re-run. It's even possible she'd be more of a threat to humanity a million years from now."

"Yeah. I can't be absolutely sure of our own dispersion in time. I hope we're successfully rooted here, but—" She nodded abruptly. "Okay. That scheme is on hold. How's the investigation going otherwise?"

Brierson suggested Lu survey the weapon systems of the advanced travelers, and then outlined his own efforts with GreenInc. Korolev listened quietly. Gone was the blazing anger of their original confrontation. In its place was a kind of dogged determination.

When he finished, she didn't look pleased, but her words were mild. "You've spent a lot of time searching the civilized eras for clues. That's okay; after all, we come from there. But you should realize that the advanced travelers—excepting Jason Mudge—have lived most of their lives *since* the Singularity.

"At one time or another, there were about fifty of us. Physically we were independent, living at our own rates. But there was communication; there were meetings. Once it became clear that the rest of humanity was gone, all of us had our plans. Marta said it was a loose society, maybe a society of ghosts. And it got smaller and smaller. The high-techs you see now are the hard cases, Inspector. The overt criminals, the graverobbers, were killed thirty million years ago. The easygoing travelers, like Bil Sánchez, dropped off early. People would stop for a few hundred years, and try to start a family or a town; you could have a whole world for the stopping. Most we never saw again, but then sometimes a group—or parts of it—would appear megayears down time. Our lives are threaded loosely around one another. You should be studying my personal databases about that, Brierson."

"Hmm. These early settlements—they all failed. Was there evidence of sabotage?" If Marta's murder was part of a pattern . . .

"That's what I want *you* to look for, Inspector." A little of the old scorn appeared. "Till now I never thought so. From the standpoint of the dropouts, they weren't all failures. Several couples simply wanted to live their lives stopped in one era. Modern health care can keep the body alive a very long time; we discovered other limits. Time passes, personalities change. Very few of us have lived more than a thousand years. Neither our minds nor our machines last forever. To reestablish civilization, you need the interactions of many people, you need a good-sized gene pool and stability over several generations of population growth. That's almost impossible with small groups—especially when everyone has bobblers and every quarrel has the potential for breaking up the settlement."

Yelén leaned forward abruptly. "Brierson, even if Marta's murder is not part of a conspiracy against the settlement—even then, I—I'm not sure if I can hold things together."

Yelén really had changed. He had never expected her to come crying on *his* shoulder. "The low-techs won't stay in this era?"

She shook her head. "They have no choice. You're familiar with the Wächendon suppressor field?"

"Sure. No new bobbles can be generated in a suppressor field." The invention had cost as many lives as it had saved, since the field made it impossible to escape the weapons that burn and maim.

Yelén nodded. "That's close enough. I've got most of Australasia under a Wáchendon field. The New Mexicans and the Peacers and the rest of the low-techs are stuck in this era until they discover how to counter the field. That should take at least ten years. We hoped they'd put down roots and be willing to stay by then." Yelén stared at the pink marble of her library table. "And the plan would work, Inspector," she said softly, taking her turn at self-pity. "Marta's plan would work if it weren't for those goddamned statist bastards."

"Steve Fraley?"

"Not just him. The top Peacers—Kim Tioulang and his gang—are as bad. They just won't cooperate with me. There are one hundred and one NMs and one hundred and fifteen Peacers. That's better than two-thirds of the settlement. Fraley and Tioulang think they *own* their groups. The hell of it is, the rank and file seem to agree! It's twentieth-century insanity, but it makes them powerful beyond all reason. They both want to run the whole show. Have you noticed their recruiting? They want the rest of the low-techs to become their 'citizens.' They won't be satisfied till one is supreme. They may reinvent high-tech just for the privilege of breaking up the settlement."

"Have you talked about this with the other high-techs?"

She rubbed nervously at her chin. *If only Marta were here;* the words all but spoke themselves. "A little, but most of 'em are more confused than I. Della was some help; she actually *was* a statist once. But she's hard to talk to. Have you noticed? She shifts personalities like clothes, as though she's trying to find something that fits.

"Inspector, you don't go back quite as far as Della, but there were still governments in your time. Hell, you caused the collapse of one of them. How can this sort of primitivism be successful now?"

Brierson winced. So now he had caused the disgovernance of New Mexico, had he? Wil sat back and—just like in the old days—tried to come up with something that would satisfy the inflated expectations of his customer. "Yelén, I agree that governments are a form of deception —though not necessarily for the rulers, who usually benefit from them. Most of the citizens, most of the time, must be convinced that the national interest is more important than their own. To you this must seem like an incredible piece of mass hypnotism, backed up by the public disciplining of dissenters."

Yelén nodded. "And the 'mass hypnotism' is the important thing. Any time they want, the NM rank and file could just give Fraley the finger and walk away; he couldn't kill 'em all. Instead they stay, his tools."

"Yes, but in a way this gives *them* power, too. If they walk, where's to go? There are no other groups. There is no ungoverned society like in my time."

"Sure there is. The Earth is empty, and almost a third of the low-techs are ungovs. There's nothing to keep people from settling down to their own interests."

Wil shook his head, surprised at his own insight, surprised at his voicing it to Yelén. Before, he wouldn't have thought to argue with her. But she seemed sincerely interested in his opinion. "Don't you see, Yelén? There are no ungoverned now. There are the Peacers, the NMs —but over all the low-techs there is the government of Yelén Korolev."

"What? I am *not* a government!" Red rose in her face. "I don't tax. I don't conscript. I only want to do what's right for people." Even if she was changed, at that moment Wil was glad for Lu's auton hovering above his house.

Wil chose his next words carefully. "That's all true. But you have two of the three essential attributes of government: First, the low-techs believe—correctly, I think—that you have the power of life and death over them. Second, you use that belief—however gently—to make them put your goals ahead of theirs."

It was pop social science from Wil's era, but it seemed to have a real effect on Korolev. She rubbed her chin. "So you figure that, at least subconsciously, the low-techs feel they have to choose sides?"

"Yes. And as the most powerful governing force, you could easily come out the most distrusted."

"What is your advice, then?"

"I, uh . . . ." Wil had painted himself into a corner. *Yes. Suppose I'm right. What then?* The little settlement at fifty megayears was totally different from the society of Wil's time. It was entirely possible that without Korolev force, the handful of seeds collected here would be blown away on the winds of time. And separately, those seeds would never bloom.

Back in civilization, Wil had never thought much on "great issues." Even in school, he hadn't liked nitpicking arguments about religion or natural rights. The world made sense and seemed to respond appropriately to his actions. Since he had lost Virginia, everything was so terribly on its head. Could there really be a situation so weird that he would advocate government? He felt like a Victorian pushing sodomy.

Yelén gave him a lopsided grin. "You know, Marta said some of the same things. You don't have her training, but you seem to have her sense. My gentle Machiavelli didn't shrink from the consequences, though. I've got to be popular, yet I've still got to have my way. . . ."

She looked at him, seemed to reach a decision. "Look, Inspector, I want you to mix more. Both the NMs and the Peacers have regular recruiting parties. Go to the next Peacer one. Listen to what they're saying. Maybe you can explain them to me. And maybe you can explain *me* to *them*. You were a popular person in your time. Tell people what you think—even what you don't like about me. If they have to choose sides, I think I'm their best bet."

Wil nodded. First the Dasguptas and now Korolev: Was there a conspiracy to get W. W. Brierson back in circulation? "What about the investigation?"

Yelén was silent for a moment. "I need you for both, Brierson. I mourned Marta for a hundred years. I traced her around the Inland Sea a meter at a time. I've got records or bobble samples of everything she did and everything she wrote. I—I think I'm over the rage. The most important thing in my life now is to see that Marta didn't die in vain. I will do *anything* to make the settlement succeed. That means finding the killer, but it also means selling my case to the low-techs."

9

That night he took another look at Marta's diary. It was a very low-priority item now, but he couldn't concentrate on anything more technical. Yelén had read the diary several times. In their literal-minded way, her autons had gone over the text in even more detail, and Lu's had cross-checked the analysis. Marta knew she had been murdered, but said again and again that she had no clues beyond her description of the evening of the party. According to the overdoc, she rarely repeated the details in later years, and when she did it was clear that her earlier memories were the more precise.

Now Wil browsed the earliest sections. Marta had stayed near Town Korolev for more than a year. Though she said otherwise, it was clear she hoped for rescue in some small multiple of ninety days. Even if that rescue didn't come, she had lots of preparing to do: She planned to walk to Canada, halfway around the world.

<< . . . but klick for klick it barely qualifies as an intermediate survival course, >>she wrote. << It will take years, and I may miss a lookabout back here at Town Korolev, but that's okay. Along the way, I'll put billboards at the West End mines and the Peacer bobble. Once I get your attention, give me a sign, Lelya: Nuke the sky for a week of nights. I'll find open ground, and wait for the autons. >>

Marta knew the territory near Korolev. Her shelter in the realtime wing of the castle was secure, close to water and adequate hunting. It was a good place to collect her energy for the trek ahead. She experimented with the weapons and tools she'd known from survival sport. In the end she settled on a diamond-bladed pike and knife and a short bow. She kept the other diamond blades in reserve; she wasn't going to waste them on arrowheads. She built a travois from a section of Fred's hull. It was enough to do some testing. She made several cautious trips covering a few kilometers.

< < Dearest Lelya— If I am ever to leave, I suppose it should be now. The plan is still to sail to our mines at West End and then head north to the Peacer bobble, and Canada far beyond that. Tomorrow I depart for the coast; tonight I finish packing. Would you believe, I have made so much equipment, I actually have *lists;* the age of data processing has arrived!

< < Hope I see you before I write more. —Love, Marta. > >

That was the last of the bark tablets she left at the castle. Two hundred kilometers along the southern coast of the sea, Yelén found the second of Marta's cairns, a three-meter-high pile of rock at the edge of the jacaranda forests. This was one of the best preserved of Marta's sites. She'd built a cabin there; it was still standing when Yelén studied it a century later.

Six months had passed since Marta left the castle in the mountains. She was still optimistic, though she had hoped to reach the mines before stopping. There had been problems, one of them painful and deadly. During her time at the cabin, Marta described her adventures since leaving the castle.

< < I followed our monorail to the coast. You know I said it was a waste to build that thing when we were going to leave it behind anyway. Well, now I'm glad you listened to Genet and not me. That right-of-way cuts straight through the forest. I avoided some tricky rock climbing just by sliding the travois along the rail's underframe. It was like a practice hike—which I needed more than I realized.

< < I've forgotten a lot, Lelya. I have just one poor brainful of memories now. If I'd known I was to be marooned, I would have loaded quite a different set. (But if I'd foreseen that, I probably could have avoided the whole adventure! Sigh. I should be glad I never offloaded our survival courses.) Anyway, my mind is full of our plans for the settlement, the stuff I was thinking about the night of the party. I have only a casual recollection of maps. I know we did lots of wildlife studies, and

were hooked into Monica's work, too. But that's all gone. Where the plants are like the ones back in civilization, I recognize them.

< < For the rest, I have fragments of memory that are sometimes worse than useless: take the spiders and their jacaranda forests. These are *nothing* like the scattered trees and isolated webs up at Town Korolev. Here the trees are huge, and the forests go on forever. That much was obvious from the ground, walking along the monorail. We had slashed through that forest, but it towered on either side. The brush that had grown along the path was already covered by matted spider webbing. Ah, if I had remembered then what I've learned since, I'd probably be at the mines by now!

< < Instead, I wandered along beneath the rail (where for some reason the webs didn't come) and admired the gray silk that spread down from the jacarandas. I didn't dare cut through the webs to look into the forest; at that time, I was still scared of the spiders. They're little things, like the ones in the mountains, but if you look close you can see thousands of them moving in the webs. I was afraid they might be like army ants, ready to swarm down on whoever jiggled their silk. Eventually, I found a break in the shroud where I could step through without touching the threads. . . . Lelya, it's a different world in there, quieter and more peaceful than the deepest redwood grove. Dim green light is everywhere—the really thick webs are at the fringes of the forests. (And of course I didn't find the explanation for that till later.) There's no underbrush, no animals—only a musty smell and a greenish haze in the air. (I'll bet you're laughing at me now, because *you* already know what made that smell.) Anyway, I was impressed. It's like a cathedral . . . or a tomb.

< < I only spent an hour in there the first time; I was still nervous about the spiders. Besides, the point of this trip was to reach the sea. I still planned to make a raft and sail direct to the West End. Failing that, short hops along the coast ought to bring me to the mines faster than any overland walk. So I thought.

< < It was storming the day I came in sight of the shore. I knew we had wrecked the coast with our tsunami, but I wasn't prepared for what I saw. The jungle was blasted flat for kilometers back from the sea. The tree trunks were piled three and four deep, all pointing away from the water. I remember thinking that at least I would have plenty of lumber for my raft.

< < I sheltered the travois and went a ways onto the coastal plain. The going was treacherous. Rotted vines swathed the trunks. Tree bark sloughed away under my weight. The topmost trunks were relatively clear, but slime slick. I crawled/walked from trunk to trunk. All the while, the storm was getting worse. The last time I'd been to the beach was to round up Wil Brierson . . . > >

A reader smiled. *She did remember my name!* Somewhere in the adventures of her next forty years she forgot, but for a while she had remembered.

< < . . . just before we raised the Peacers. It had been a warm, misty place. Today was different: lightning, thunder, wind-driven rain. No way was I going to get to water's edge this afternoon. I crawled along a tree trunk to its uptorn fan of roots, and peeked over. Fantasyland. There were three waterspouts out there. They slid back and forth, the further ones pale and translucent. The third had drifted inland, though it was still a couple of klicks away. Dirt and timber splashed up from its tip. I crawled out of the wind and listened to the roar. As long as it didn't get louder, I should be safe from heaven's dirty finger.

< < All this raised serious questions about my plan to take a shortcut across the sea. No doubt this was an exceptional storm, but what about ordinary squalls? How common were they? The Inland Sea is a lot like the old Mediterranean. I thought of a guy named Odysseus who spent half his life being blown from one side of that pond to the other. I wished we had taken maritime sports more seriously. Sailing to Catalina barely qualified us as novices; we didn't even make our own boat. The notion of hugging the coast didn't look good either. I remembered the pictures: our tsunami had smashed the whole southern coast. There were no beaches or harbors left on this side of the sea, just millions of tonnes of broken wood and mud. I would have to carry all my food even if I stayed close to the shore.

< < So there I was, kind of discouraged and awfully wet. My schedule was in shambles. And that was a laugh. I have all the time in the world; that's the problem.

< < There was a super-close lightning bolt. From the corner of my eye I saw *something* rushing me. As I turned, it dropped on my shoulder, grabbing for my neck. An instant later something else landed on my middle, and on my leg. I bet I screamed as loud as ever in my life; it was lost in the thunder.

< < . . . They were *fishermonkeys*, Lelya. Three of them. They clung tight as leeches; one had its face buried in my middle. But they weren't biting. I sat rigid for a moment, ready to start smashing in all directions. The one on my leg had its eyes screwed shut. All three were shivering, and holding me so tight it hurt. I gradually relaxed, and set my hand on the fellow who had grabbed my middle. Through the seallike fur, I could feel its shivering ease a little.

< < They were like little children, running to Momma when the lightning got too bad. We sat in the lee of that root fan through the worst of the storm. They scarcely moved the whole time, their warm bodies stuck to my leg, belly, and shoulder.

< < The storm gentled to an even rain, and the temperature climbed back into the thirties. The three didn't rush off. They sat, looking at me solemnly. Now, even *I* don't believe that nature is full of cuddly creatures just waiting to love a human. I began to have some unhappy suspicions. I got up, climbed over the side of the trunk. The three followed, then ran a little way to one side, stopped, and chittered at me. I walked to them, and they ran off again, and stopped again. Already I was thinking of them as Hewey, Dewey, and Lewey. (How did Disney spell those names?) Of course, fishermonkeys look nothing like ducks, either real or caricatured. But there was a cooperative madness about them that made the names inescapable.

< < Our lurching game of tag went on for fifty meters. Then we came to a pile that had recently slipped: I could see where the trunks had turned, exposing unweathered wood. The three didn't try to climb these. They led me around them . . . to where a larger monkey was pinned between two trunks. It wasn't hard to guess what had happened. A good-sized stream flowed beneath the pile. Probably the four had been fishing there. When the storm came up, they hid in the wooden cave formed by the tree trunks. No doubt the wind and the added water in the stream had upset the woodpile.

< < The three patted and pulled at their friend, but halfheartedly; the body wasn't warm. I could see that its chest was crushed. Perhaps this had been their mother. Or maybe it was the dominant male— Unca Donald even.

< < It made me sadder than it should, Lelya. I knew our rescuing the Peacers was going to blow a hole in the ecosystem; I'd already done my rationalizing, cried my tears. But . . . I wondered how many

fishermonkeys were left on the south shore. I bet they were scattered in small groups all through the dead jungle. And now this. The four of us sat for a time, consoling each other, I hope. > >

< < If sea travel was out, my options were a bit constrained. The jungle parallels the coast and extends inland to the two-thousand-meter level. It would take me a hundred years to get around the sea by hacking my way through that, with every stream at right angles to my line of travel. That left the jacaranda forests—back up where the air is cool, and the spiders spin their webs.

< < Oh. I took the fishermonkeys with me. In fact, they refused to be left behind. I was now mother, or dominant male, or whatever. These three had all the mobility of penguins. During the days, they spent most of the time on the travois. When I stopped to rest, they'd be off —racing each other around, trying to tease me into the chase. Then Dewey would come to sit by me. He was the odd man out. Literally. Hewey was a girl and Lewey the other male. (It took a while to figure this out. The fishers' sexual equipment is better hidden than in the monkeys of our time.) It was all very platonic, but sometimes Dewey needed another friend.

< < I can just see you, Lelya, shaking your head and muttering about sentimental weakness. But remember what I've said so many times: If we can survive and still be sentimental, life is a lot more fun. Besides, there were coldly calculated reasons for lugging my little friends back to the jac forest. The fishers are not entirely sea creatures. The fact that they can fish from streams shows that. These three ate berries and roots. Plants haven't changed as much as animals over these fifty megayears, but some of the changes can be inconvenient. For instance, Dewey *et al.* wouldn't touch the water I got from a traveler's palm; on the way down, that stuff had made me sick. > >

Here the diary had many pages of drawings, enhanced by Yelén's autons to show the dyes' original colors. These were not as skillfully drawn as those Wil had seen later in the diary—when Marta had had years of practice—but they were better than anything he could do. She had brief notes by each picture: < < Dewey wouldn't touch this when green, otherwise okay . . . > > or < < Looks like trillium; raises blisters like poison ivy. > >

Wil looked carefully at the first few pages, then skipped ahead to where Marta entered the jacaranda forest.

< < I was a bit frightened at first. The fishers picked up on it, edging moodily around on the travois and whimpering. Walking through the jac forest just seemed too *easy*. The air is wet and moist, yet not nearly so uncomfortable as in a rain forest. The mist I'd seen earlier is always present. The musky, choking smell is there, too, though you don't notice it after the first few minutes. The light coming through the canopy is shadowless and green. Floating down from the heights are occasional leaves and twigs. There are no animals; except at the edges of the forest, the spiders stick to the canopy. There are no trees but the jacs, and no vines. The ground cover is a moist carpet. In the top few centimeters you can see leaf fragments, perhaps little bits of spiders. Walking through it kicks up a murkier version of what hangs all through the air. A thousand meters into the forest, the only sounds you hear are those you make yourself. The place is beautiful, and heaven to hike through.

< < But you see why I was nervous, Lelya? Just a few hundred meters downslope was a *jungle*, a thickly grown, life-gone-to-crazy-excess jungle. There had to be something pretty fearsome keeping all competing plants and all animal pests out of the jac forest. I still had visions of spider armies sweeping down the trees and sucking the juice out of intruders.

< < I was very cautious the first few days. I walked close to the northern edge of the forest, close enough so I could hear the sounds of the jungle.

< < It didn't take long to see that the jungle/jac border is a war zone. As you walk toward the border, the forest floor is broken by the corpses of ordinary trees. The deadwood furthest in is scarcely recognizable lumps; closer to the border you can see whole trees, some still standing. What had been the leafy parts are drowned in ancient webs. Rank on rank of mushrooms cover the wood. Their colors are beautiful pastels . . . and the fishers wouldn't touch them.

< < Walk a bit further and you're out from under the jacs. Here the jungle is alive and fighting to stay that way. Here the spiderwebs are thickest, a tight dark layer across the treetops. Those webs are silver kudzu, Lelya. The critical battle in this war is the jungle top trying to grow past the shroud, and the spiders trying to lay still more silk on top.

You know how fast things grow in a rain forest; the plants themselves play the shade-out game, growing a dozen centimeters in twenty-four hours. The spiders have to hustle to keep ahead. Since those first days, I've climbed into the jungle canopy just outside the jac forest and watched. On a busy day, the top of the kudzu web almost seems to froth, the little buggers are pumping out so much new silk.

< < Where the jungle trees are still living, you do see animals. Webs fan from tree to tree, black with trapped insects. For larger animals, the silk is no barrier. Snakes, lizards, catlike predators—I've seen them all in the thirty-meter-wide band that the spiders' kudzu shades. But they don't have dens there. They are fleeing, or chasing, or very sick. There are no monsters to scare them back; they just don't like to stay. By now I had some theories, but it was almost a week before I knew for sure.

< < Once or twice a day, we walked to the jungle's edge. There I did some easy hunting and we ate the berries the fishers liked. At night, we slept several hundred meters into the jacs, farther than any other animals dared come. And as long as I stayed far enough inside the forest, we made very good time. Even old jac trunks molder quickly away and the ubiquitous mulch smooths out most ground irregularities. The only obstacles were the many streams that crossed our path. Down in the jungle, the brush along these streams would have been virtually impassable. Here, the mulch extended right to the water's edge. The water itself was clear, though where a stream broadened and the water slowed, there was greenish scum on the surface. There were fish.

< < Ordinarily, I don't mind drinking from a stream, even in the tropics. Any blood or gut parasites are just a tasty meal for my panphages. Here I was more careful. The first one we came to, I hung back and watched my committee of experts. They sniffed around, took a drink or two, and jumped in. A few seconds later they had their dinner. From then on, I didn't hesitate to ford the streams, floating the travois ahead of me.

< < But by the fifth day, Hewey was beginning to drag. She didn't come off the travois to play. Dewey and Lewey patted and groomed her, but she would not be jollied. By the next afternoon, they were equally droopy. There were sniffles and tiny coughs. It was about what I had expected. Now for the important questions:

< < I found a campsite on the jungle side of the border. It was hell compared to the comfort we'd enjoyed in the jacs, but it was defensible

and at the edge of a lake. By then the three were so weak I had to fish and forage for them.

< < I watched them for a week, trying to analyze the odds, trying to guess what once I could have remembered in an instant. It was the greenish mist, I was sure. The stuff floated down endlessly from the top of the jacarandas. Other stuff came down too, but most of it was identifiable—leaves, bits of spider, things that might have been caterpillar parts. I had a fair estimate of the spider biomass; the jac tops were actually bowed down in places. The green mist . . . it was spider shit. That by itself was no big deal. The thing is, if you lived in the forest, you breathed a lot of it. Almost anything that fine would eventually cause health problems. It was clear now the spiders had gone a step further. There was something downright poisonous in that haze. Mycotoxins? The word pops to mind, but damn it, I have nowhere to remember more. It had to be more than an irritant. Apparently nothing had evolved a defense. Yet it wasn't super fast-acting. The fishers had lasted several days. The big question was, how fast would it affect a larger animal (such as yours truly)? And was recovery a simple matter of leaving the forest?

< < I got the answer to the second question in a couple of days. All three came out of their funk. Eventually they were fishing and rowdying as enthusiastically as ever. So I had the old decision to make, this time with a bit more information: Should I hike through the jac forest as far and fast as I was able? Or should I hack my way crosswise through a thousand klicks of jungle? My guinea pigs looked as good as new; I decided to continue with the forest route, till I had symptoms.

< < It would mean leaving Dewey and Hewey and Lewey. I *hoped* I was leaving them better off than when I found them. That pond was alive with fish, as good as anything back in civilization. The fishermonkeys were quick to rush into the water at the first hint of land predators. The only threat from the water was something large and croc-like that didn't look very fast. It wasn't precisely like the jungle they had once known by the seashore, but I would stay long enough to build them a sanctuary.

< < I ignored the fact that my survival craft was from a different era. For once, being sentimental was deadly.

< < The morning of the seventh day, it was obvious that something big had died nearby. The moist air always carried the scents of life and

371

death, but a heavy overtone of putrefaction had been added. Hewey and Lewey ignored it, were busy chasing each other around the water's edge. Dewey was not in sight. Usually when the others squeezed him out he came to me; sometimes he just went off to sulk. I called to him. No answer. I'd seen him an hour earlier, so it couldn't be his demise the breeze announced.

< < I was just getting worried when Dewey raced out of the bushes, chittering gleefully. He held a huge black beetle between his hands. > >

A drawing covered the rest of the page. The creature looked like a stinkbug, but according to the overdoc it was more than ten centimeters long. Its enormous abdomen accounted for most of that size. The chitin was thick and black, laced by a network of deep grooves.

< < Dewey ran right up to Hewey, brushing Lewey aside. For once he had an offering that might give him precedence. And Hewey was impressed. She poked at the armored ball, jumped back in surprise when the bug gave a whistling *tweet*. In seconds they were rolling it back and forth between them, entranced by the teakettle noises and acrid bursts of steam that came from the thing.

< < I was as curious too. As I started toward them, Dewey grabbed the beetle to hold it up to me. Suddenly he screamed and tossed the bug toward me. It struck the top of my right foot—and exploded.

< < I didn't know such pain could exist, Lelya. Even worse, I couldn't turn it *off*. I don't think I lost consciousness, but for a while the world beyond that pain scarcely existed. Finally I came back far enough to feel the wetness that flowed from the wound. The small bones in my foot were shattered. Chitin fragments had cut deep into my foot and lower leg. Dewey was bleeding too—but his wound was a nick compared to mine.

< < I've named them grenade beetles. I know now they're a carrion eater—with a defense worthy of a twenty-first-century armadillo. When hassled, their metabolism becomes an acidulous pressure cooker. They don't want to die; they give plenty of warning. No creature from this region would deliberately give them any trouble. But if goaded to the bursting point, their death is an explosion that will kill any small attacker outright, and bring lingering death to most larger ones.

< < I don't remember much of the next few days, Lelya. I had to cause myself even greater pain trying to set the bones of my foot. It hurt almost as much to pick out the fragments of chitin. They smelled

of rot, of the corpse that beetle had been into. God only knows what infections my panphages saved me from.

< < The fishermonkeys tried to help. They brought berries and fish. I improved. I could crawl, even walk with a makeshift crutch—though it hurt like hell.

< < Other creatures knew I was hurt. Various things nosed about my shelter, but were chased off by the fishers. I woke one morning to loud fishermonkey screeching. Something big shuffled by, and the monkey's cry ended in a horrible squeak.

< < That afternoon, Hewey and Lewey were back, but I never saw Dewey again.

< < A jungle does not tolerate convalescents. Unless I could get back to the jac forest, I would be dead very soon. And if the remaining fishers were half as loyal as Dewey, they would be dead, too. That evening, I put the berries and freshest fish onto my travois. Meter by meter, I dragged it back to the jac forest. Hewey and Lewey followed me partway in. Even their foolish penguin walk was enough to keep up. But they feared the forest now, or maybe they weren't as crazy as Dewey, for eventually they fell behind. I still remember their calling after me. > >

This was Marta's closest brush with death for many years. If there had not been good fishing in the first stream she found or if the jac forest had been any less gentle than she imagined, she would not have survived.

The weeks passed, and then a month. Her shattered foot slowly healed. She spent nearly a year by that stream just inside the forest, returning to the jungle only occasionally—for fresh fruit, and to check on the fishers, and to hear some sounds beyond herself. It became her second major camp, the one with the cabin and the cairn. She had plenty of time to bring her diary up to date, and to scout the forest. It was not everywhere the same. There were patches of older, dying jacarandas. The spiders hung their display webs across those trees, turning the light blue and red. Most of her descriptions of the forest gave Wil the impression of unending catacombs, but this was a cathedral, the webs stained glass. Marta couldn't remember the purpose of the display webs. She stayed for days under one of them, trying to fathom the mystery. Something sexual, she guessed: but for the spiders . . . or the trees? For a weird instant, Wil felt impelled to look up the answer for her; she of all people deserved to know. Then he shook his head and deliberately paged his data set.

Marta figured out most of the spiders' life cycle. She'd seen the enormous quantities of insect life trapped on the perimeter barriers, and she guessed at the tonnage that must be captured on the canopy. She also noticed how often the fallen leaves were fragmented, and correctly guessed that the spiders maintained caterpillar farms much as ants keep aphids. She did as much as any naturalist without tools could.

< < But the forest never made me sick, Lelya. A mystery. In fifty million years, has Evolution's arms race drifted so far that I'm outside the range of the spider-shit toxin? I can't believe that, since the poison seems to work on everything that moves. More likely, there's something in my medical systems, the panphages or whatever, that's protecting me. > >

Wil looked up from the transcript. There was more, of course, almost two million words more.

He stood, walked to the window, and turned off the lights. Down the street, the Dasguptas' place was still dark. It was a clear night; the stars were a pale dust across the sky, outlining the treetops. This day seemed awfully long. Maybe it was the trip to Calafia and going through two sunsets in one day. More likely it was the diary. He knew he was going to keep reading it. He knew he was going to give it more time than the investigation justified. Damn.

10

For Wil Brierson, dreams had always waited at the end of sleep. In earlier times, they had waited to entertain and enlighten. Now, they lay in ambush.

Goodbye, goodbye, goodbye. Wil cried and cried, but no sounds came and scarcely any tears. He was holding hands with someone, someone who didn't speak. Everything was shades of pale blue. Her face was Virginia's, and also Marta's. She smiled sadly, a smile that could not deny the truth they both knew. . . . *Goodbye, goodbye, goodbye.* His lungs were empty, yet still he cried, forcing out the last of his breath. He could see through her now, to blue beyond. She was gone, and what he might have saved was lost forever.

Wil woke with an abrupt gasp for breath. He had exhaled so far it hurt. He looked up at the gray ceiling and remembered an advertisement from his childhood. They'd been pushing medical monitors; something about 6:00 AM being a good time to die, that lots of people suffered sleep apnea and heart attacks just before waking—and wouldn't everyone be safer if everyone bought automatic monitors.

It couldn't happen with modern medical treatment. Besides, the autons Yelén and Della had floating above the house were monitoring him. And a second besides—Wil smiled sourly to himself—the clock said 10:00 AM. He had slept nearly nine hours. He swung his bulk out of bed, feeling as if he had slept less than half that.

He lumbered into the bathroom, washed away the strange wetness he found around his eyes. All through his career, he'd done his best to project an appearance of calm strength. It hadn't been hard: He was built like a tank, and he was naturally a low-blood-pressure type. There were a few cases that had made him nervous, but that had been reasonable, since bullets were flying. In police work, he'd seen a fair number of people crack up. For all the publicity given cases like the Kansas Incursion, most of the violence in his era was simple domestic stuff, folks driven around the bend by job or family pressures.

He smiled wryly at the face in the mirror. He had never imagined it could happen to him. The end of sleep was a walk down night paths now. He had a feeling things were going to get worse. Yet there was a part of him that was as analytical as always, that was following his morning dreams and daytime tension with surprised interest, taking notes at his own dismemberment.

Downstairs, Wil threw open the windows, let the morning sounds and smells drift in. He was damned if he'd let this funk paralyze him. Later in the day, Lu was coming over. They would talk about the weapons survey, and decide who to interview next. In the meantime, there was lots of work to do. Yelén was right about studying the high-techs' lives since the Extinction. In particular, he wanted to learn about Sánchez's aborted settlement.

He was barely started on this project when Juan Chanson dropped by. In person. "Wil, my boy! I was hoping we might have a chat."

Brierson let him in, wondering why the high-tech hadn't called ahead. Chanson strode quickly around the living room. As usual, he was energetic to the point of twitchiness. " *'Blas Spañol,* Wil?" he said.

"Sí," Brierson replied without thinking; he could get by, anyway.

"Buen," the archeologist continued in Spañolnegro. "I really get tired of English, you know. Never can get just the right word. I'll wager some people think me a fool because of it."

Wil nodded at the rush of words. In Spañolnegro, Chanson talked even faster than in English. It was an impressive—and nearly unintelligible—achievement.

Chanson stopped his nervous tour of the living room. He jerked a thumb at the ceiling. "I suppose our high-tech friends are taking in every word?"

"Uh, no. They're monitoring body function, but I would have to call for help before our words would be interpreted." *And I asked Lu to make sure Yelén did no eavesdropping.*

Chanson smiled knowingly. "So they tell you, no doubt." He placed a gray oblong on the table; a red light blinked at one end. "Now the promises are true. Whatever we say goes unrecorded." He waved for Brierson to be seated.

"We've talked about the Extinction, have we not?"

"*Sí.*" Several times.

Chanson waved his hand. "Of course. I talk to everybody about it. Yet how many believe? Fifty million years ago, the human race was *murdered*, Wil. Isn't that important to you?"

Brierson sat back. This would shoot the morning. "Juan, the Extinction is very important to me." Was it really? Wil had been shanghaied more than a century before it. To his heart, that was when Virginia and Anne and W. W. Jr. had died—even if the biographies said they lived into the twenty-third century. He had been shanghaied across a hundred thousand years; that was many times longer than all recorded history. Now he lived at fifty megayears. Even without the capital-e Extinction, this was so deep in the future that no one could expect the human race to still exist. "But most high-techs don't think there was an alien invasion. Alice Robinson said the race died out over the whole twenty-third century, and that there weren't signs of violence until very late. Besides, if there were an invasion, you'd think we'd have all sorts of refugees from the twenty-third. Instead we have *nobody*—except the last of you high-techs from 2201 and 2202."

Chanson sniffed. "The Robinsons are fools. They fit the facts to their rosy preconceptions. I've spent thousands of years of my life piecing this together, Wil. I've mapped every square centimeter of Earth and Luna with every diagnostic known to man. Bil Sánchez did the same for the rest of the Solar System. I've interviewed the rescued lowtechs. Most of the high-techs think I'm a crank, I've so thoroughly abused their hospitality. There's a lot I don't understand about the aliens—but there's a lot that I do. There are no refugees from the twenty-third because the invaders could jam bobble generators; they had some superpowerful version of the Wáchendon suppressor. The extermination was not like twentieth-century nuclear war, over in a matter of weeks. I've dated the Norcross graffiti at 2230. Apparently, the aliens were using specifically antihuman weapons early in the war.

On the other hand, the vanadium tape Billy Sánchez found on Charon appears to be from late in the century. It ties in with the new craters there and in the asteroids. At the end, the aliens dug out the deep resistance with nukes."

"I don't know, Juan. It's so far in the past now—how can we prove or disprove anyone's theories? What's important is to make sure our settlement succeeds and humanity has another chance."

Chanson leaned across the table, even more intense than before. "Exactly. But don't you see? The aliens had bobblers, too. What destroyed civilization threatens to destroy us now."

"After fifty million years? What could be the motive?"

"I don't know. There are limits to physical investigation, no matter how patient. But I think it was a close thing back in the twenty-third. The aliens pulled out all the stops at the end, and it was barely enough. After the war, they were very weak—perhaps on the edge of extinction themselves. They were gone from the Solar System for millions of years. But make no mistake, Wil. They have not forgotten us."

"You expect another invasion."

"That's what I've always feared, but I'm beginning to feel otherwise. There are too few of them; their game is stealth now. They aim to divide and destroy. Marta's murder was only the beginning."

"*What?*"

Chanson flashed a quick, angry smile. "The game is not so academic now, is it, my boy? Think on it: With that murder, they crippled us. Marta was the brains behind the Korolev plan."

"You claim they're here *among* us? I should think you high-techs can monitor things coming into the system."

"Certainly, though the others don't bother. One of the safest places for long-term storage is on cometary orbits. Such bobbles return every hundred thousand years or so. Only *I* seem to realize that a few more return than go out. At least half my time has been spent building a surveillance net. Over the megayears I intercepted three coming in with substantial hyperbolic excess. Two came out of stasis in the inner Solar System, surrounded by my forces. *They came out shooting,* Wil."

"Did they use the super Wáchendon suppressor?"

"No. I think their surviving equipment is scarcely better than ours. With my superior position, I managed to destroy both of them."

Wil looked at the little man with new respect. Like all the high-

378

techs, he was a monomaniac; anyone who pursued one objective for centuries would be. His conclusions had been ridiculed by most of the others, yet he stuck by them and had done his best to protect the others from a threat only he could see. If Chanson was right . . . Wil's mouth was suddenly dry. He could see where this was leading. "What about the third one, Juan?" he said quietly.

Again that angry smile. "That one was much more recent, *much* more clever. It did a lookabout before I was in position. I was outmaneuvered. By the time I got back to Earth, it was already here, claiming to be human—claiming to be Della Lu, long-lost spacer. Your partner is a monster, my boy."

Wil tried not to think about the firepower that floated over their heads. "Is there any solid evidence? Della Lu was a real person."

Chanson laughed. "They're weak now. Subterfuge may be all that's left them—and surely they have copies of GreenInc. Did you see this 'Della Lu' right after she arrived? It would be a joke to call that thing human. The claim she's so old that normal human attributes have faded is nonsense. *I'm* more than two thousand years old, and *my* behavior is perfectly normal."

"But she was alone all that time." Wil's words defended her, but he was remembering the encounter on the beach, Lu's insectile manner, her cold stare. "Surely a medical exam would settle this."

"Maybe. Maybe not. I have reason to think the exterminators are of nearly human structure. If their life sciences are as good as ours, they could rearrange their innards to human standards. As for subtle chemical tests—our ignorance of them and their technology is simply too great to risk accepting negative evidence as proof."

"Who else have you told?"

"Yelén. Philippe. You can be sure I'm making no public accusations. The Lu creature knows *someone* attacked her coming in, but I don't think she knows who. She may even think it was an automatic action. Even if she's alone, she is terribly dangerous, Wil. We can't afford to move against her until all the high-techs are willing to act together. I pray this will happen before she destroys the settlement.

"I don't know if Philippe believes me, but I think he'd act if the rest could be won over. As for Yelén, well . . . I already said she was the lesser of the Korolevs. She's done some passive testing and can't believe the enemy could make such a good counterfeit. She's totally unimpressed by Lu's erratic behavior. Basically, Yelén has no imagination.

"You may be the key, Wil. You see Lu every day. Sooner or later she is going to slip, and you will *know* that what I say is true. It is vitally important you prepare yourself for that moment. With luck, it will be something small, something you can pretend to ignore. If you can cover your knowledge, she may let you live.

"And if she lets you live, then maybe we can convince Yelén."

And if she doesn't let me live, no doubt that will be evidence too. One way or another, Chanson had a use for him.

11

Della Lu arrived in early afternoon. Wil stepped outside to watch her land. The autons supplied by Yelén and Della were faithfully keeping station several hundred meters above the house. He wondered what a battle between those two machines would be like, and whether he could survive it. Before, he'd been grateful for Lu's protection against Yelén. Now it worked both ways. Brierson kept his face placid as the spacer walked toward him.

"Hi, Wil." Even with his recollection of the early Della, it was hard now to believe that Chanson could be right. Lu wore a pink blouse and belled pants. Her hair was cut in bangs that swayed girlishly as she walked. Her smile seemed natural and spontaneous.

"Hi, Della." He grinned back with a smile he hoped seemed just as natural and spontaneous. She entered the house ahead of him.

"Yelén and I have a disagreement we'd like you to . . ." She stopped talking and her body tensed. She sidled around the living-room table, her eyes flicking across its surface. Abruptly something round and silver gleamed there. She picked it up. "Did you know you were bugged?"

"No!" Wil walked to the table. A spherical notch about a centimeter across had been cut from it. The notch was where Chanson had set his bug stomper.

She held up the silver sphere—an exact match for the notch—and said, "Sorry to nick your table. I wanted to bobble it first thing. Some bugs bite when they are discovered."

Wil looked at his face reflected perfect and tiny in the ball. It could contain anything. "How did you spot it?"

She shrugged. "It was too small for my auton to see. I've got some built-in enhancements." She tapped her head. "I'm a little more capable than an ordinary human. I can see into the UV and IR, for instance. . . . Most of the high-techs don't bother with such improvements, but they can be useful sometimes."

Hmm. Wil had lived several years with medical electronics jammed inside his skull; he hadn't liked it one bit.

Della walked across the room and sat on the arm of one of his easy chairs. She swung her feet onto the seat and braced her chin on her hands. The childlike mannerisms were a strange contrast to her words. "My auton says Juan Chanson was your last visitor. Did he get near the table?"

"Yes. That's where we were sitting."

"Hmm. It was a dumb trick, ran a high risk of detection. What did he want, anyway?"

Wil was ready for the question. His response was prompt but casual. "He rambled, as usual. He's discovered I speak Spañolnegro. I'm afraid I'll be his favorite audience from now on."

"I think there's more to it than that. I haven't been able to get an appointment for us to interview him. He won't say no, but he has endless excuses. Philippe Genet is the only other person who seems to be avoiding us. We should put these people at the top of our interview list."

She was doing a better job of proving Juan's case than Juan himself. "Let me think about it. . . . What was it you and Yelén wanted to know?"

"Oh, that. Yelén wants to keep Tammy bobbled for a century or so, till the low-techs are 'firmly rooted.' "

"And you don't."

"No. I have several reasons. I promised the Robinsons Tammy would be safe. That's why I refuse to turn her over to Yelén. But I also promised them that Tammy would be given a chance to clear the family name. She claims that means she should be free to operate in the present."

"I'll bet Don Robinson couldn't care less about his good name. Things are too hot for the family, but he still wants recruits. If Tammy is bobbled she won't be doing any recruiting."

"Yes. Those are almost Yelén's words." Della moved off the chair arm and sat like an adult. She steepled her hands and stared at them a moment. "When I was very young—even younger than you—I was a Peacer cop. I don't know if you understand what that means. The Peace Authority was a government, no matter what its claims. As a government cop, my morality was very different from yours. The long-range goals of the Authority were the basis of that morality. My own interests and the interests of others were secondary—though I truly believed that survival depended on achieving the Authority's goals. The history books talk mostly about how I stopped Project Renaissance and brought down the Peacers, but I also did some . . . pretty rough things for the Authority; look up my management of the Mongolian Campaign.

"That youngest version of Della Lu would have no problem here: leaving Tammy free is a risk—a very small risk—to the goal of a successful colony. That Della Lu would not hesitate to bobble her, perhaps even execute her, to avoid that risk.

"But I grew out of that." Her steepled hands collapsed, and her expression softened. "For a hundred years I lived in a civilization where individuals set their own goals and guarded their own welfare. That Della Lu sees what Tammy is going through. That Della Lu believes in keeping promises made."

Wil forced himself to think on the question. "I believe in abiding by contracts, too, though I'm not quite sure what was agreed to here. I'm inclined to release Tammy. Let her proselytize, but without her headband. I doubt she remembers enough technology to make any difference."

"It's possible the Robinsons left an equipment cache someplace where Tammy and her recruits could get it."

"If they did, that would be pretty good evidence they knew about the murder beforehand. Why don't we release her, but bug her mercilessly. If she does more than talk, we'll bobble her. Tammy and her family are the best suspects. If we keep her locked up, it's possible we'll never solve the murder. . . . Do you think Yelén would go for that?"

"Yes. That's more or less the argument I made. She said okay if you agreed."

Wil's eyebrows rose. He was both surprised and flattered. "That's settled, then." He looked through the window, trying to think how the conversation might be turned to the topic that was really bothering him. "You know, Della, I had a family. From what I read in GreenInc, they lived right through to the Extinction. I hate to think that Monica is right—that humankind just committed suicide. And Juan's theories are just as obnoxious. How do you think it ended?" He hoped the camouflage hid his real interest. And it wasn't entirely camouflage: He'd be grateful to get a nonviolent explanation for the end of civilization.

Della smiled at the question. She seemed without suspicion. "It's always easier to seem wise if you're selling pessimism. That makes Juan and Monica seem smarter than they really are. The truth is . . . there was no Extinction."

"What?"

"*Something* happened, but we have only circumstantial evidence what it was."

"Yes, but that 'something' killed every human outside of stasis." He could not disguise his sarcasm.

She shrugged. "I don't think so. Let me give you my interpretation of the circumstantial evidence:

"During the last two thousand years of civilization, almost every measure of progress showed exponential growth. From the nineteenth century on, this was obvious. People began extrapolating the trends. The results were absurd: vehicles traveling faster than sound by the mid-twentieth century, men on the moon a bit later. All this was achieved, yet progress continued. Simple-minded extrapolations of energy production and computer power and vehicle speeds gave meaninglessly large answers for the late twenty-first century. The more sophisticated forecasters pointed out that real growth eventually saturates; the numbers coming out of the extrapolations were just too big to be believed."

"Hmph. Seems to me they were right. I really don't think 2100 was more different from 2000 than 2000 was from 1900. We had prolongevity and economical space travel, but those were in the range of conservative twentieth-century prediction."

"Yes, but don't forget the 1997 war. It just about eliminated the human race. It took more than fifty years to dig out of that. After 2100 we were back on the exponential track. By 2200, all but the blind could see that something fantastic lay in our immediate future. We had practical immortality. We had the beginnings of interstellar travel. We had networks that effectively increased human intelligence—with bigger increases coming."

She stopped, seemed to change the subject. "Wil, have you ever wondered what became of your namesake?"

"The original W.W.? . . . Say," he said, with sudden realization, "you actually *knew* him, didn't you?"

She smiled briefly. "I *met* Wili Wáchendon a couple of times. He was a sickly teenager, and we were on the opposite sides of a war. But what became of him after the fall of the Peacers?"

"Well, he invented too many things for me to remember. He spent most of his time in space. By the 2090s, you didn't hear much about him."

"Right. And if you follow him in GreenInc, you'll see the trend continued. Wili was a first-rate genius. Even then he could use an interface band better than I can now. I figure that, as time passed, he had less and less in common with people like us. His mind was somewhere else."

"And you think that's what happened to all mankind eventually?"

She nodded. "By 2200, we could increase human intelligence itself. And intelligence is the basis of all progress. My guess is that by midcentury, any goal—any goal you can state objectively, without internal contradictions—could be achieved. And what would things be like fifty years after *that?* There would still be goals and there would still be striving, but not what we could understand.

"To call that time 'the Extinction' is absurd. It was a Singularity, a place where extrapolation breaks down and new models must be applied. And those new models are beyond our intelligence."

Della's face was aglow. It was hard for Wil to believe that this was the fabrication of an "exterminator." In the beginning at least, these had been human ideas and human dreams.

"It's a funny thing, Wil. I left civilization in 2202. Miguel had died just a few years earlier. That meant more to me than any Big Picture. I wanted to be alone for a while, and the Gatewood's Star mission seemed ideal. I spent forty years there, and was bobbled out for almost twelve hundred. I fully expected that when I got back, civilization would be unintelligible." Her smile twisted. "I was very surprised to find Earth empty. But then, what could be less intelligible than a total absence of intelligence? From the nineteenth century on, futurists wondered about the destiny of science. And now, from the other side of the Singularity, the mystery is just as deep.

"There was no Extinction, Wil. Mankind simply graduated, and you and I and the rest missed graduation night."

"So three billion people just stepped into another plane. This begins to sound like religion, Della."

She shrugged. "Just talking about superhuman intelligence gets us into something like religion." She grinned. "If you really want the religious version . . . have you met Jason Mudge? He claims that the Second Coming of Christ was sometime in the twenty-third century. The Faithful were saved, the unfaithful destroyed—and the rest of us are truant."

Wil smiled back; he had heard of Mudge. His notion of the Second Coming could explain things too—in one respect better than Lu's theory. "I like your ideas better. But what's your explanation for the physical destruction? Chanson isn't the only person who thinks that nukes and bioweapons were used towards the end of the twenty-third."

Della hesitated. "That's the one thing that doesn't fit. When I returned to Earth in 3400, there was plenty of evidence of war. The craters were already overgrown, but from orbit I could see that metropolitan areas had been hit. Chanson and the Korolevs have better records; they were active all through the fourth millennium, trying to figure out what had happened, and trying to rescue short-term low-techs. It looks like a classic nuclear war, fought without bobbles. The evidence of biowarfare is much more tenuous.

"I don't know, Wil. There must be an explanation. The trends in the twenty-second century were *so* strong that I can't believe the race committed suicide. Maybe it was a fireworks celebration. Or maybe . . . do you know about survival sport?"

"That was after my time. I read about it in GreenInc."

"Physical fitness has always been a big thing in civilization. By the late twenty-second, medical care automatically maintained body fitness, so people worked on other things. Most middle-class folk had Earthside estates of several thousand hectares. There were shared estates bigger than some twentieth-century nations. Fitness came to mean the ability to survive without technology. The players were dropped naked into a wilderness—arctic, rain forest, you name it—that had been secretly picked by the judges. No technology was allowed, though medical autons kept close track of the contestants; it could get to be pretty rough. Even people who didn't compete would often spend several weeks a year living under conditions that would be deadly to twentieth-century city-dwellers. By 2200, individuals were probably tougher than ever before. All they lacked was the bloody-mindedness of earlier times."

Wil nodded. Marta had certainly demonstrated what Lu was saying. "How does this explain the nuke war?"

"It's a little farfetched, but . . . imagine things just before the race fell into the Singularity. Individuals might be only 'slightly' superhuman, and might still be interested in the primitive. For them, nuclear war might be a game of strength and fitness."

"You're right; that does sound farfetched."

She shrugged.

"Would you say Juan is in the minority, thinking mankind was exterminated?"

"I think so; I know Yelén agrees with me. But remember that—until very recently—I didn't have much chance to talk to anyone. I was back in the Solar System for a few years around 3400. During that time, no one was out of stasis. They'd left plenty of messages, though: The Korolevs were already talking about a rendezvous at fifty megayears. Juan Chanson had an auton at L4 blatting his theories to all who would listen. It was clear to me that with the evidence at hand, they could argue forever without proving things one way or the other.

"I wanted certainty. And I thought I could have it." She made that twisted smile again.

"So *that's* why you went back into space."

"Yes. What had happened to us must have happened—must *be happening*—over and over again throughout the universe. From the twentieth century on, astronomers watched for evidence of intelligence beyond the Solar System. They never saw any. We wonder about the great silence on Earth after 2300. They wondered about the silence among the stars. Their mystery is just the spacelike version of ours.

"There is a difference. In space, I can travel any direction I wish. I was sure that eventually I would find a race at the edge of the Singularity."

Listening to her, Wil felt a strange mix of fear and frustration. One way or another, this person must *know* where others could only speculate. Yet what she told him and the truth could be entirely different things. And the questions that might distinguish lie from truth might provoke a deadly response. "I've tried to use your databases, Della. They're very hard to understand."

"That's not surprising. Over the years, there was some nonrepairable damage; parts of my GreenInc are so messed up I don't even use them. And my personal db's . . . well, I've customized them quite a bit."

"Surely you want people to know what you've seen?" Yet Della had always been strangely closemouthed about her time Out There.

She hesitated. "Once I did. Now I'm not sure. There are people who don't want to know the truth. . . . Wil, someone fired on me when I entered the Solar System."

"What?" Brierson hoped his surprise sounded real. "Who was it?"

"I don't know. I was a thousand AUs out, and the guns were automatic. My guess is Juan Chanson. He seems to be the most paranoid about outsiders, and I was clearly hyperbolic."

Wil suddenly wondered about the "aliens" Juan said he had destroyed. How many of them had been returning spacers? Some of Juan's theories could be self-proving. "You were lucky," he said, probing gently, "to get past an ambush."

"Not lucky. I've been shot at before. Any time I'm less than a quarter light-year from a star, I'm ready to fight—usually ready to run, too."

"So there *are* other civilizations!"

For a long moment, Della didn't answer. Her personality shifted yet again. Expression drained from her face, and she seemed almost as cold as in their first meetings.

"Intelligent life is a rare development.

"I spent nine thousand years on this, spread across fifty million years of realtime. I averaged less than a twentieth light speed. But that was fast enough. I had time to visit the Large Magellanic Cloud and the Fornax System, besides our own galaxy. I had time to stop at tens of thousands of places, at astrophysical freaks and normal stars. I saw some strange things, mostly near deep gravity wells. Maybe it was engineering, but I couldn't prove it, even to myself.

"I found that most slow-spinning stars have planets. About ten percent of these have an Earth-type planet. And almost all such planets have life.

"If Monica Raines loves the purity of life without intelligence, she loves one of the most common things in the universe. . . . In all my nine thousand years, I found two intelligent races." Her eyes stared into Wil's. "Both times I was too late. The first was in Fornax. I missed them by several billion years; even their asteroid settlements were ground to dust. There were no bobbles, and it was impossible to tell if their ending had been abrupt.

"The other was a nearer thing, both in space and time: a G2 star about a third of the way around the Galaxy from here. The world was beautiful, larger than Earth, its atmosphere so dense that many plants were airborne. The race was centaurlike; I learned that much. I missed them by a couple of hundred megayears. Their databases had evaporated, but their space settlements were almost undamaged.

"They had vanished just as abruptly as humankind did from Earth. One century they were there, the next—nothing. But there were differences. For one thing, there was no sign of nuclear war. For another, the centaur-folk had started a couple of interstellar colonies. I visited them. I found evidence of growing population, of independent technological progress, and then . . . their own Singularities. I lived two thousand years in those systems, spread out over a half megayear. I studied them as carefully as Chanson and Sánchez did our solar system.

"There were bobbles in the centaur systems. Not as many as near Earth, but this was a lot longer after their Singularity. I knew if I hung around, I'd run into somebody."

"Did you?"

Della nodded. "But what sort of person would you expect two hundred megayears after civilization? . . . The centaur came out shooting. I nuked out; I ran fifty light-years, past where the centaur had any interest. Then, over the next million years, I sneaked back. Sure enough, he was back in stasis, depending on occasional lookabouts and his autons for protection. I left plenty of robot transmitters, some with autons. If he gave them half a chance, they would teach him my language and convince him I was peaceful. . . .

"His realtime forces attacked the minute they heard my transmissions. I lost half my auton defense holding them off. I almost lost my life; that's where my db's were damaged. A thousand years later, the centaur himself came out of stasis. Then *all* his forces attacked. Our machines fought another thousand years. The centaur stayed out of stasis the whole time. I learned a lot. He was willing to talk even if he had forgotten how to listen.

"He was alone, had been the last twenty thousand years of his life. Once upon a time, he'd been no nuttier than most of us, but those twenty thousand years had burned the soul from him." She was silent for a moment—thinking on what nine thousand years could do? "He was caught on behavior tracks he could never—could never want to—break. He thought of his solar system as a mausoleum, to be protected from desecration. One by one, he had destroyed the last centaurs as they came out of stasis. He had fought at least four travelers from outside his system. God knows who they were—centaur spacers, or 'Della Lus' of other races.

"But, like us, he couldn't replace his autons. He had lost most of them when I found him; I wouldn't have stood a chance a hundred megayears earlier. I suppose, if I had stayed long enough, I could have beaten him. The price would have been my living more thousands of years; the price would have been *my* soul. In the end, I decided to let him be." She was silent for a long while, the coldness slowly departing from her face, to be replaced by . . . tears? Were they for the last centaur—or for the millennia she had spent, never finding more than the mystery she began with?

"Nine thousand years . . . was not enough. Artifacts from beyond the Singularity are so vast that doubters can easily deny them. And the pattern of progress followed by vanishment can be twisted to any explanation—especially on Earth, where there are signs of war."

There was a difference between Della's propaganda and the others', Wil realized. She was the only one who seemed plagued by uncertainty, by any continuing need for proof. It was hard to believe that such an ambiguous, doubt-ridden story could be an alien cover. Hell, she seemed more human than Chanson.

Della smiled but did not brush the wetness from her lashes. "In the end, there is only one way to know for a fact what the Singularity is. You have to be there when it happens. . . . The Korolevs have

390

brought together everybody that's left. I think we have enough people. It may take a couple of centuries, but if we can restart civilization *we will make our own Singularity.*

"And *this* time, I won't miss graduation night."

12

il was at the North Shore party later that week.

Virtually everyone was there, even some high-techs. Della and Yelén were absent—and Tammy was more or less forbidden from attending these outings—but he saw Blumenthal and Genet. Today they looked almost like anyone else. Their autons hovered high, all but lost in the afternoon light. For the first time since taking the Korolev case, Wil didn't feel like an outsider. His own autons were indistinguishable from the others, and even when visible, the fliers seemed no more intimidating than party balloons.

There were two of these affairs each week, one at Town Korolev sponsored by New Mexico, the other run by the Peacers here at North Shore. Just as Rohan said, both groups were doing their best to gladhand the uncommitted. Wil wondered if ever in history governments had been forced to tread so softly.

Clusters of people sat on blankets all across the lawn. Other folks were lining up at the barbecue pits. Most were dressed in shorts and tops. There was no sure way of telling Peacers from NMs from ungovs, though most of the blue blankets belonged to the Republic. Steve Fraley himself was attending. His staff seemed a little stiff, sitting on lawn chairs, but they were not in uniform. The top Peacer, Kim Tioulang, walked over and shook Steve's hand. From this distance, their conversation looked entirely cordial. . . .

So Yelén figured he should mingle, observe, find out just how unpopular her plans were. Okay. Wil smiled faintly and leaned back on his elbows. It had been a matter of duty to come to this picnic, to do just what the Dasgupta brothers—and simple common sense—had already suggested. Now he was very glad he was here, and the feeling had nothing to do with duty.

In some ways, the North Shore scenery was the most spectacular he'd seen. It was strikingly different from the south side of the Inland Sea. Here, forty-meter cliffs fell straight to narrow beaches. The lawns that spread inland from the cliffs were as friendly as any park in civilization. A few hundred meters further north, the clifftop bench ended in steep hills shrouded by trees and flowers—climbing and climbing, till they stood faintly bluish against the sky. Three waterfalls streamed down from those heights. It was like something out of a fairy tale.

But the view was only the smallest part of Wil's pleasure. He'd seen so much beautiful country the last few weeks—all untouched and pristine as any city-hater could wish. Something in the back of his mind thought it the beauty of a tomb—and he a ghost come to cry for the dead. He brought his gaze back from the heights and looked across the crowds of picnickers. *Crowds*, by God! His smile returned, unthinking. Two hundred, three hundred people, all in one spot. Here he could see that they really did have a chance, that there could be children and a human future, and a use for beauty.

"Hey, lazybones, if you're not going to help with the food, at least give us room to sit down!" It was Rohan, a big grin on his face. He and Dilip were back from the food lines. Two women accompanied them. The four sat down, laughing briefly at Wil's embarrassment. Rohan's friend was a pretty Asian; she nodded pleasantly to him. The other woman was a stunning, dark-haired Anglo; Dilip really knew how to pick 'em. "Wil, this is Gail Parker. Gail's an EMC—"

"ECM," the girl corrected.

"Right, an ECM officer on Fraley's staff."

She wore thigh-length shorts, with a cotton top; he'd never have guessed she was an NM staffer. She stuck out her hand. "I've always wondered what you were like, Inspector. Ever since I was a little girl, they've been telling me about that big, black, badass northerner name of W. W. Brierson. . . ." She looked him up and down. "You don't look so dangerous." Wil took her hand uncertainly, then noticed the mischievous gleam in her eyes. He'd met a number of New Mexicans since the failed NM invasion of the ungoverned lands. A few didn't even recognize his name. Many were frankly grateful, thinking he had speeded the disgovernance of New Mexico. Others—the die-hard statists of Fraley's stripe—hated Wil out of all proportion to his significance.

Gail Parker's reaction was totally unexpected . . . and fun. He smiled, and tried to match her tone. "Well, ma'am, I'm big and black, but I'm really not such a badass."

Gail's reply was interrupted by an immensely loud voice echoing across the picnic grounds. "FRIENDS—" There was a pause. Then the amplified voice continued more quietly. "Oops, that was a bit much. . . . Friends, may I take a few moments of your time."

Rohan's friend said quietly, "So wonderful; a speech." Her English was heavily accented, but Wil thought he heard sarcasm. He had hoped that with Don Robinson's departure he would be spared any more "friends" speeches. He looked down the lawn at the speaker. It was the Peacer boss who had been talking to Fraley a few moments earlier. Dilip handed a carton of beer over Wil's shoulder. "I advise you to drink up, 'friend,'" he said. "It may be the only thing that saves you." Wil nodded solemnly and broke the seal on the carton.

The spindly Peacer continued. "This is the third week we of the Peace have hosted a party. If you have been to the others, you know we have a message to get across, but we haven't bothered you with speeches. Well, by now we hope we've 'sucked you in' enough so you'll give me a hearing." He laughed nervously, and there were responding chuckles from the audience, almost out of sympathy. Wil chugged some beer and watched the speaker narrowly. He'd bet anything the guy really was nervous and shy—not used to haranguing the masses. But Wil had read up on Tioulang. From 2010 till the fall of the Peace Authority in 2048, Kim Tioulang had been the Director for Asia. He had ruled a third of the planet. So maybe his diffidence reflected nothing more than the fact that if you're a big-enough dictator, you don't have to impress anyone with your manner.

"Incidentally, I warned President Fraley of my intention to propagandize this afternoon, and offered him the 'floor' in rebuttal. He graciously declined the offer."

Fraley stood up and made a megaphone of his hands. "I'll get you all at *our* party." There was laughter, and Wil felt the corners of his mouth turn down. He *knew* Fraley was a martinet; it was annoying to see the man behave with any grace.

Tioulang turned back to the mass of picnickers. "Okay. What am I trying to convince you of? To join the Peace. Failing that, to show solidarity with the interests of the low-techs—as represented by the Peace and the Republic of New Mexico. . . . Why do I ask this? The Peace Authority came and went before many of you were born—and the stories you've heard about it are the usual ones that history's winners lay on the losers. But I can tell you one thing: The Peace Authority has always stood for the survival of humanity, and the welfare of human beings everywhere."

The Peacer's voice went soft. "Ladies and gentlemen, one thing is beyond argument: What we do during the next few years will determine if the human race lives or dies. It depends on *us*. For the sake of humanity, we can't afford to follow blindly after Korolev or any high-tech—Don't mistake me: I admire Korolev and the others. I am deeply grateful to them. They gave the race a second chance. And the Korolev scheme seems very simple, very generous. By running her factories way over redline, Yelén has promised to keep us at a moderate standard of living for a few decades." Tioulang gestured at the beer freezers and the barbecue pits, acknowledging their provenance. "She tells us that this will wreck her equipment centuries before it would otherwise break down. As the years pass, first one and then another of her systems will fail. And we will be left dependent on whatever resources we have developed.

"So we have a few decades to make it . . . or fade into savagery. Korolev and the others have provided us with tools and the databases to create our own means of production. I think we all understand the challenge. I shook some hands this afternoon. I noticed calluses that weren't there earlier. I talked to people that have been working twelve-, fifteen-hour days. Before long, these little meetings will be our only break from the struggle."

Tioulang paused a moment, and the Asian girl laughed softly. "Here it comes, everybody."

"To this point, no sane person can have disagreement. But what the Peace Authority—and our friends of the Republic—do resist is Yelén Korolev's method. Hers is the age-old story of the absentee landlord, the queen in the castle and the serfs in the fields. By some scheme that is never revealed, she parcels out data and equipment to individuals—never to organizations. The only way individuals can make sense of such a hopeless jumble is by following Korolev directions . . . by developing the habit of serfdom."

Wil set the beer down. The Peacer had one hundred percent of his attention now. Certainly Yelén was listening to the spiel, but would she understand Tioulang's point? Probably not; it was something new to Wil, and he'd thought he appreciated all the reasons for resenting Korolev. Tioulang's interpretation was a subtle—perhaps even an unconscious—distortion of Marta's plan. Yelén gave tools and production equipment to individuals, according to what hobbies or occupations they had had back in civilization. If those individuals chose to turn the gear over to the Peace or the Republic, that was their business; certainly Yelén had not forbidden such transfers.

In fact, she hadn't given any orders about how to use the gifts. She had simply made her production databases and planning programs public. Anyone could use those data and programs to make deals and coordinate development. The ones who coordinated best would certainly come out ahead, but it was scarcely a "jumble" . . . except perhaps to statists. Wil looked across the picnickers. He couldn't imagine the ungoverned being taken in by Tioulang's argument. Marta's plan was about as close to "business as usual" as you could come under the present circumstances, but it was alien weirdness to the Peacers and most of the NMs. That difference in perception might be enough to bring everything down.

Kim Tioulang was also watching the audience, waiting to see if his point had sunk in. "I don't think any of us want to be serfs, but how can we prevent it, given Korolev's overwhelming technical superiority? . . . I have a secret for you. The high-techs need us more than we need them. Without any high-techs at all, the human race would still have a chance. We have—we *are*—the one thing that is really needed: people. Between the Peace, the Republic, and the, uh, unaffiliated, we low-techs are almost three hundred human beings. That's more than in any settlement since the Extinction. Our biologists tell us it is enough —just barely enough—genetic diversity to restart the human race. Without our numbers, the high-techs are doomed. And they know it.

"So the most important thing is that we hang together. We are in a position to reinvent democracy and the rule of the majority."

Behind Wil, Gail Parker said, "God, what a hypocrite. The Peace never had any interest in elections when *they* were in the saddle."

"If I've convinced you of the need for unity—and frankly, the need is so obvious that I don't need much persuasiveness there—there is still the question of why the Peace is a better bet for you than the Republic.

"Think about it. The human race has been at the brink before. In the early part of the twenty-first century, plagues destroyed billions. Then, as now, technology remained widely available. Then, as now, the problem was the depopulation of the Earth. In all humility, my friends, the Peace Authority has more experience in solving our present problem than any group in history. We brought the human race *back* from the brink. Whatever else may be said of the Peace, *we* are the acknowledged experts in these matters. . . ."

Tioulang shrugged diffidently. "That's really all I had to say. These are important things to think about. Whatever your decisions, I hope you'll think about them carefully. My people and I are happy to take any questions, but let's do it one on one." He cut the amplifier.

There was a buzz of conversation. A fair-sized crowd followed Tioulang back to his pavilion by the beer locker. Wil shook his head. The guy had made some points. But people didn't believe everything he said. Just behind Wil, Gail Parker was giving the Dasguptas a quick rehash of history. The Peace Authority was the great devil of the early twenty-first century, and Wil had lived near enough to that era to know that their reputation could not be entirely a smear. Tioulang's diffident, friendly manner might soften the harsh outlines of history, but few were going to buy his view of the Peace.

What some *did* buy—Wil realized unhappily as he listened to nearby ungovs—was Tioulang's overall viewpoint. They accepted his claim that Korolev's policies were designed to keep them down. They seemed to agree that "solidarity" was their great weapon against the "queen on the hill." And the Peacer's call for a reestablishment of democracy was especially popular. Wil could understand the NMs buying that; majority rule was the heart of their system. But what if the majority decided that everyone with dark skin should work for free? Or that Kansas should be invaded? He couldn't believe the ungoverned would accept such a notion. But some appeared to. This was a matter of survival, and the will of the majority was working in their favor. How quickly cracks the veneer of civilization.

Brierson rolled to his feet. "I'm getting some food. Need anything more?"

Dilip looked up from the discussion with Parker. "Er, no. We're stocked."

"Okay. Be back in a little while." Wil wandered down the lawn, treading carefully around blankets and people. There seemed the same discouraging set of responses: the Peacers enthusiastic, NMs distrustful but recognizing the "basic wisdom" of Tioulang's speech, the ungovs of mixed opinions.

He reached the food, began filling a couple of plates. One good thing about all this deep philosophical debate: He didn't have to wait in line.

The voice behind him was a sardonic bass. "That Tioulang is really a clown, isn't he?"

Wil turned. An ally!

The speaker was a brown-haired Anglo, dressed in a heavy—and none too clean—robe. At one meter seventy, he was short enough so Wil could see the shaved patch on the top of his skull. The fellow had a permanent grin pasted on his face.

"Hello, Jason." Brierson tried to keep the irritation out of his voice. Of all the people here, that the only one to echo his thoughts was Jason Mudge, the cheated chiliast and professional crank! It was too much. Wil continued down the food line, piling his plates precariously high. Jason followed, not taking anything to eat, but bombarding Wil with the Mudge analysis of Tioulang's lunacy: Tioulang totally misunderstood Man's crisis. Tioulang was taking humanity back from the Faith. The Peacers and the NMs and the Korolevs—in fact, everybody—had closed their eyes to the possibility of redemption and the perils of further dis-Belief.

Wil grunted occasionally at the other's words, but avoided any meaningful response. Reaching the end of the line, he realized there was no way to get all this food across the lawn without slopping; he'd have to scarf some of it right here. He set the plates down and attacked one of the hot dogs.

Mudge circled closer, thinking Brierson had stopped to listen. Once his spiel began, he was a nonstop talker. Right now, his voice was "powered down." Earlier, he'd stood on the high ground north of the lawn and harangued them for a quarter hour. His voice had boomed across the picnic grounds, as loud as Tioulang's had been with amplification. Even at that volume, he'd spoken as fast as now, every word standing in block capitals. His message was very simple, though repeated again and again with different words: Present-day humans were Truants from the Second Coming of the Lord. (That Second Coming was presumably the Extinction.) He, Jason Mudge, was the prophet of the Third and Final Coming. All must repent, take the robes of the Forgiven, and await the Salvation that was soon to come.

At first, the harangue had been amusing. Someone shouted that with all these Comings, Mudge must not only be a prophet, but the Lord's Sexual Athlete as well. Such taunts only increased Jason's zeal; he would talk till the Crack of Doom if there remained any unrepentant. Finally, the Dasgupta brothers walked up from the lawn and had a brief chat with the prophet. That had been the end of the speechifying. Afterwards, Wil had asked them about it. Rohan had smiled shyly and replied, "We told him we'd throw him over the cliffs if he continued shouting at us." Knowing Dilip and Rohan, the threat was completely incredible. However, it worked on Mudge; he was a prophet who could not afford to become a martyr.

So now Jason toured the picnic grounds, looking for stragglers and other targets of opportunity. And W. W. Brierson was the current victim. Wil munched a curried egg roll and eyed the other man. Perhaps this wasn't entirely wasted time. Della and Yelén had lost all interest in Mudge, but this was the first time Wil had seen him up close.

Strictly speaking, Jason Mudge was a high-tech. He had left civilization in 2200. The GreenInc database showed him as a (very) obscure religious nut, who proclaimed that the Second Coming of Christ would occur at the end of the next century. Apparently ridicule is a constant of history: Mudge couldn't take the pressure, and bobbled through to 2299, thinking to come out during the final throes of the world of sin. Alas, 2299 was after the Singularity; Mudge arrived on an empty planet. As he would willingly—and at great length—explain, he had erred in his biblical computations. The Second Coming had in fact occurred in 2250. Furthermore, his errors were fated, as punishment for his arrogance in trying to "skip ahead to the good part." But the Lord in His infinite compassion had given Jason one more chance. As the prophet who had missed the Second Coming, Jason Mudge was the perfect shepherd for the lost flock that would be saved at the Third.

So much for religion. GreenInc had shown another side of the man. Up until 2197, he had worked as a systems programmer. When Wil noticed that, Mudge's name had moved several notches up the suspect list. Here was a certified nut who could reasonably want to see the Korolev effort fail. And the nut's specialty involved the sort of skills needed to sabotage the bobble fail-safes and maroon Marta.

Yelén was not so suspicious of him. She had said that by the late twenty-second century, most occupations involved systems. And with prolongevity, many people had several specialties. Mudge's path had crossed the Korolevs' several times since the Age of Man. The encounters were always the same: Mudge needed help. Of all the high-techs who had left civilization voluntarily, he was the most poorly equipped: He had a flier but no space capability. He owned no autons. His databases consisted of a couple of religion cartridges.

Yet he was still on Wil's list. It was a bit implausible that anyone would go this far to disguise his abilities, but Mudge *might* have something cached away. He had asked Yelén to put Mudge under surveillance, to see if he was communicating with hidden autons.

Now Wil had a chance to apply the "legendary Brierson savvy" firsthand. Watching Mudge, Wil realized the little man required virtually no feedback. As long as Wil was standing here facing him, the harangue would continue. No doubt he rarely talked to anyone who gave more. Could he respond at all once he got rolling? *Let's see.* Wil raised his hand and injected a random comment. "But we don't *need* supernatural explanations, Jason. Why, Juan Chanson says invaders caused the Extinction."

The Mudge diatribe continued for almost a second before he noticed there had been some real interaction. His mouth hung open for an instant, and then—he laughed. "*That* backslider? I don't see why you people believe anything he says. He has fallen from the Way of Christ, into the toils of science." The last was a dirty word in Jason's mouth. He shook his head, and his smile came back broader than ever. "But your question shows something. Indeed we must consider that—" The last prophet moved closer and launched still another attempt to make him understand . . .

. . . and Wil really did. Jason Mudge needed people. But somewhere in his past, the little man had concluded that the only way to get others' attention was with the cosmically important. And the harder he tried to explain, the more hostile was his audience—until it was a triumph to have an audience at all. If there was anything to the Brierson intuition, Yelén was right: Jason Mudge should come off the suspect list.

It might seem a small thing, the twenty-five-hour day. But that extra hour and bit was one of the nicest things about the new world. Almost everyone felt it. For the first time in their lives, there seemed to be enough time in the day to get things done, enough time to reflect. Surely, everyone agreed, they would soon adjust, and the days would be just as crowded as always. Yet the weeks passed and the effect persisted.

The picnic stretched through the long afternoon, lost much of the intentness that followed Tioulang's speech. Attention shifted to the volleyball nets on the north side of the lawn. For many, it was a mindless, pleasurable time.

It should have been so for Wil Brierson; he had always enjoyed such things. Today, the longer he stayed, the more uncomfortable he became. The reason? If all the human race was here, then the person who had shanghaied him was, too. Somewhere within two hundred meters was the cause of all his pain. Beforehand, he'd thought he could ignore that fact; he'd been faintly amused at the Korolev fears he might launch a vendetta against the shanghaier.

How little he knew himself. Wil found himself watching the other players, trying to find a face from the past. He muffed easy shots; worse, he crashed into a smaller player. Considering Brierson's ninety kilos, that was a distinct breach of etiquette.

After that, he stood on the sidelines. Did he really know what he was looking for? The embezzlement case had been so simple; a blind man could have tagged the culprit. Three suspects there had been: the Kid, the Executive, and the Janitor—that was how he'd thought of them. And given a few more days, he'd have had an arrest. Brierson's great mistake was to underestimate the crook's panic. Only trivial amounts had been stolen; what kind of crazyman would bobble the investigating officer, and guarantee a terrible punishment?

The Kid, the Exec, the Janitor. Wil wasn't even sure of their names just now, but he remembered their faces so clearly. No doubt, the Korolevs had disguised the fellow, but Wil was sure that given time he could see through such.

This is insane. He'd all but promised Yelén—and Marta before her —that he wouldn't go after the shanghaier. And what could he do if he found the bastard? If anything, life would be more unpleasant than before. . . . Still, his eyes wandered, thirty years of police skill in harness to his pain. Wil left the games and began a circuit of the grounds. More than half the picnickers were not involved with the volleyball. He moved with apparent aimlessness but kept track of everything in his field of vision, watching for any sign of evasion. Nothing.

After walking around the field, Brierson moved from group to group. His approach was relaxed, cheerful. In the old days, this appearance had almost always been genuine, even when he was on the job. Now it was a double deception. Somewhere above him, Yelén was watching his every move. . . . She should be pleased. He appeared to be doing exactly what she wanted of him: in the course of two hours, he interviewed about half the ungovs—all without giving the appearance of official scrutiny. He learned a lot. For instance, there were many people who saw through the governments' line. Good news for Yelén.

At the same time, Wil's private project continued. After ten or fifteen minutes of chatting, Wil could be sure that yet one more was not his quarry. He kept track of the faces and the names. Something inside him took pleasure in so thoroughly fooling Yelén.

The shanghaier was almost certainly a loner. How would such a type hide himself? Wil didn't know. He did discover that almost no one was really alone now. Faced with an empty Earth, people were hanging together, trying to help those who hurt the most. And he could see terrible grief in many, often hidden behind cheerfulness. The basket cases were the folks who had been out of stasis only a month or two; for them, the loss was so painfully fresh. Surely there had been some outright psychiatric breakdowns; what was Yelén doing about those? Hmm. It was entirely possible the shanghaier *wasn't* here. No matter. When he got home, he would match the people he'd met with the settlement lists. The holes would stand out. After the next party or the next, he'd have a good idea who he was after.

The sun slowly fell, a straight-down path that seemed faintly unreal to someone raised in midlatitudes. Shadows deepened. The green of lawn and hillsides was subtly changed by the reddening light; more than ever, the land looked like a fantasist's painting. The sky turned to gold and then to red. As twilight passed quickly into night, light panels came on by two of the volleyball courts. There were several bonfires—cheerful yellow light compared to the blue around the courts.

Wil had talked with most of the ungovs and perhaps twenty Peacers. Not an enormous group, but then he'd had to move slowly—to fool Yelén and to assure that *he* wasn't fooled by any disguise.

Darkness released him from the terrible compulsion; there was no point to an interview unless he was confident of the results. He wandered back towards the courts, relief verging on elation. Even his feeling of shame at deceiving Yelén was gone. In spite of himself, he had done good work for her this day. He'd seen issues and attitudes that she had never mentioned.

For instance:

There were people sitting away from the lights. Their talk was low and intense. He was almost back to the courts when he came on a large group—almost thirty people, all women. By the light of the nearest bonfire, he recognized Gail Parker and a few others. There were both ungovs and NMs here, maybe a few Peacers. Wil paused, and Parker looked up. Her gaze had none of its earlier friendliness. He drifted away, aware of several pairs of eyes following his retreat.

He knew the shape of their discussions. People like Kim Tioulang could make grandiose talk about reestablishing the human race. But that reestablishment demanded tremendous birth rates, for at least a century. Without womb tanks and postnatal automation, the job would fall on the women. It meant creating a serf class, but not the one Tioulang was so eager to warn against. These serfs might be beloved and cherished—and might believe in the rightness of it all as much as anyone—but they would carry the heavy burden. It had happened before. The plagues of the early twenty-first century had killed most of the race, and left many of the survivors sterile. The women of that period had a very restricted role, very different from women before or after. Wil's parents had grown up in that time: The only serious fights he could remember between them involved his mother's efforts to start her own business.

A motherhood serfdom would be much harder to establish this time around. These people were not coming back from plagues and a terrible war. Except for the Peacers, they were from the late twenty-first and the twenty-second. The women were highly trained, most with more than one career. As often as not, they were the bosses. As often as not, they initiated romance. Many of those from the twenty-second were sixty or seventy years old, no matter how young and lush their bodies. They were not people you could push around.

. . . And yet, and yet Gail and the others could see final extinction waiting irrevocably in the very near future . . . unless they made some terrible sacrifices. He understood their intent discussion and Gail's unfriendly stare. Which sacrifices to make, which to decline. What to demand, what to accept. Wil was glad he wasn't welcome in their councils.

Something moon-bright rose into the air ahead of him, quickly fell back. Wil looked up and broke into a trot, forcing the problem from his mind. The light rose again, sweeping fast-moving shadows across the lawn. Someone had brought a glowball! A crowd had already gathered along three sides of the volleyball court, blocking his view. Brierson edged around till he could see the play.

Wil found himself grinning stupidly. Glowballs were something new, just a couple of months old . . . at the time he was shanghaied. It might be old hat to some, but it was a complete novelty to the Peacers and even to the NMs. The ball had the same size and feel as a regulation volleyball—but its surface was brightly aglow. The teams were playing by this light alone, and Wil knew the first few games would be comic relief. If you kept your eye on the ball, then little else was bright enough to see. The ball became the center of the universe, a sphere that seemed to swell and shrink while everything else swung around it. After a few moments, you couldn't find your teammates—or even the ground. The NM and Peacer players spent almost as much time on their butts as standing. Laughter swept the far side of the court as three *spectators* fell down. This ball was better than the others Wil had seen. Whenever it touched out-of-bounds, it chimed and the light changed to yellow. *That* was an impressive trick.

Not everyone had problems. No doubt Tunç Blumenthal had always played with glowballs. In any case, Wil knew that Tunç's biggest problem was playing down to everyone else's level. The high-tech massed as much as Wil, but stood over two meters tall. He had the speed and coordination of a professional. Yet, when he held back and let others dominate the play, he didn't seem condescending. Tunç was the only high-tech who really mixed with the lows.

After a time, all players learned the proper strategy: less and less did they watch the ball directly. They watched each other. Most important, they watched the *shadows*. With the glowball, those shadows were twisting, shifting fingers—showing where the ball was and where it was going.

The games went quickly, but there was only one ball and many wanted to play. Wil gave up any immediate plans to get on the court. He wandered around the edge of the crowd, watching the shadows flick back and forth, highlighting a face for an instant, then plunging it into darkness. It was fun to see adults as fascinated as kids.

One face stopped him short: Kim Tioulang stood at the outskirts of the crowd, less than five meters from Brierson. He was alone. He might be a boss, but apparently he didn't need a herd of "aides" like Steve Fraley. The man was short, his face in shadow except when a high shot washed him in a quick down-and-up of light. His concentration was intense, but his expressionless gaze contained no hint of pleasure.

The man was strikingly frail. He was something that did not exist in Wil's time—except by suicidal choice or metabolic accident. Kim Tioulang's body was *old*; it was in the final stages of the degeneration which, before the mid-twenty-first, had limited life spans to less than a century.

There were so many different ways to think of time now. Kim had lived less than eighty years. He was young by comparison with the "teenagers" from the twenty-second. He had nothing on Yelén's three hundred years of realtime experience or the mind-destroying stretch of Della's nine thousand. Yet, in some ways, Tioulang was a more extreme case than either Korolev or Lu.

Brierson had read the GreenInc summary on the man. Kim Tioulang was born in 1967. That was two years before Man began the conquest of space, thirty years before the war and the plagues, at least fifty years before Della Lu was born. In a perverse sense, he *was* the oldest living human.

Tioulang had been born in Kampuchea, in the middle of one of the regional wars that pocked the late twentieth. Though limited in space and time, some of those wars were as horrible as what followed the 1997 collapse. Tioulang's childhood was drenched in death—and unlike the twenty-first-century plagues, where the murderers were faceless ambiguities, death in Kampuchea came person to person via bullets and hackings and deliberate starvation. GreenInc said the rest of Tioulang's family disappeared in the maelstrom . . . and little Kim ended up in the USA. He was a bright kid; by 1997 he was finishing a doctorate in physics. And working for the organization that overthrew the governments and became the Peace Authority.

From there, GreenInc had little but Peacer news stories and historical inference to document Tioulang's life. No one knew if Tioulang had anything to do with starting the plagues. (For that matter, there was no absolute proof the Peace had started them.) By 2010, the man was Director for Asia. He'd kept his third of the planet in line. He had a better reputation than the other Directors; he was no Christian Gerrault, "Butcher of Eurafrica." Except during the Mongolian insurrection, he managed to avoid large-scale bloodshed. He remained in power right up to the fall of the Peace in 2048—and that fall was for Tioulang less than four months past.

And so, even though Kim Tioulang predated the rest of living humanity by scant decades, his background put him in a class by himself. He was the only one who had grown up in a world where humans routinely killed other humans. He was the only one who had ruled, and killed to stay in power. Next to him, Steve Fraley was a high-school class president.

An arcing shot lifted the glowball above the crowd, putting Tioulang's face back in the light—and Wil saw that the Peacer was staring at him. The other smiled faintly, then stepped back from the crowd to stand beside Brierson. Up close, Wil saw that his face was mottled, pocked. Could old age alone do that?

"You're Brierson, the one who works for Korolev?" His voice was just loud enough to be heard over the laughs and shouting. Light danced back and forth around them.

Wil bridled, then decided he wasn't being accused of betraying the low-techs. "I'm investigating Marta Korolev's murder."

"Hmm." Tioulang folded his arms and looked away from Wil. "I've done some interesting reading the last few weeks, Mr. Brierson." He chuckled. "For me, it's like future history to see where the next hundred and fifty years took the world. . . . You know, those years turned out as well as ever I could hope. I always thought that without the Peace, humankind would exterminate itself. . . . And maybe it did eventually, but you went for more than a century without our help. I think the immortality thing must have something to do with it. Does it really work? You look around twenty years old—"

Brierson nodded. "But I'm fifty."

Tioulang scuffed at the lawn with his heel. His voice was almost wistful. "Yes. And apparently I can have it now, too. The long view—I can already see how it softens things, and how that's probably for the best.

"I've also read your histories of the Peace. You people make us out as monsters. The hell of it is, you have some of it right." He looked up at Wil, and his voice sharpened. "I meant what I said this afternoon. The human race is in a bind here; we of the Peace would make the best leaders. But I also meant it when I said we're willing to go with democracy; I see now it could really work.

"You are very important to us, Brierson. We know you have Korolev's ear—don't interrupt, please! We can talk to her whenever we wish, but we think she respects your opinions. If you believe what I am telling you, there is some chance she may too."

"Okay," said Wil. "But what *is* the message? You oppose Yelén's policies, want to run things under some government system with majority rule. What if your people don't win out? The NMs have a lot more in common with the ungovs and the high-techs than you. If we fall back to a government situation, they are more likely to be the leaders than you. Would you accept that?" *Or grab for power like you did at the end of the twentieth?*

Tioulang looked around, almost as though checking for eavesdroppers. "I expect we'll win, Brierson. The problems we face here are problems the Peace is especially well equipped to handle. Even if we don't win, we'll still be needed. I've talked to Steven Fraley. He may seem rough and tough to you . . . but not to me. He's a little bit of a fool, and likes to boss people around, but left to ourselves, we could get along."

"Left to yourselves?"

"That's the other thing I want to talk to you about." He shot a furtive glance past Wil. "There are forces at work Korolev should know about. Not everyone wants a peaceful solution. If a high-tech backs one faction, we—" The swinging light splashed over them. Tioulang's expression suddenly froze into something that might might have been hatred . . . or fear. "I can't talk more now. I can't talk." He turned and walked stiffly away.

Wil glanced in the opposite direction. There was no one special in the crowd there. What had spooked the Peacer? Wil drifted around the court, watching the game and the crowd.

Several minutes passed. The game ended. There were the usual cheerful arguments about who should be on the new teams. He heard Tunç Blumenthal say something about "trying something new" with the glowball. The random chatter lessened as Tunç talked to the players and they pulled down the volleyball net. When the new game started, Wil saw that Blumenthal had indeed tried something new.

Tunç stood at the serving line and punched the glowball across the court, over the heads of the other team. As it passed across the far court out-of-bounds, there was a flash of green light and the ball *bounced* as if from some unseen surface. It sailed up and back—and bounced downwards off an invisible ceiling. As it hit the ground, the glow turned to out-of-play yellow. Tunç served again, this time to the side. The ball bounced as from a side wall, then against the invisible far-court wall, then off the other side. The green flashes were accompanied by the sounds of solid rebounds. The crowd was silent except for scattered gasps of surprise. Were the teams trapped in there? The idea occurred to several of the players simultaneously. They ran to the invisible walls, reached out to touch them. One fellow lost his balance and fell off the court. "There's nothing there!"

Blumenthal gave some simple rules and they volleyed. At first it was chaos, but after a few minutes they were really playing the new game. It was fast, a strange cross between volleyball and closed-court handball. Wil couldn't imagine how this trick was managed, but it was spectacular. Before, the ball had moved in clean parabolas, broken only by the players' strokes. Now it careened off unseen surfaces, the shadows reversing field instantly.

"Ah, Brierson! What are you doing out here, man? You should be playing. I watched you earlier today. You're good."

Wil turned to the voice. It was Philippe Genet and two Peacer women friends. The women wore open jackets and bikini bottoms. Genet wore only shorts. The high-tech walked between the women, his hands inside their jackets, at their waists.

Wil laughed. "I'd need lots of practice to be good with something that wild. I imagine you could do pretty well, though."

The other shrugged and drew the women closer. Genet was Brierson's height but perhaps fifteen kilos less massive, verging on gauntness. He was a black, though several shades paler than Wil. "Do you have any idea where that glowball came from, Brierson?"

"No. One of the high-techs."

"That's certain. I don't know if you realize what a clever gadget that is. Oh, I'll bet you twenty-first-century types had something like it: put a HI light and a navigation processor in a ball and you could play a simple game of night volley. But look at that thing, Brierson." He nodded at the glowball, caroming back and forth off invisible barriers. "It has its own agrav unit. Together with the navigation processor, it's simulating the existence of reflecting walls. I was in the game earlier. That ball's a Collegiate Mark 3, a whole athletic department. If one team is short a player, just tell the ball—and in addition to boundary walls, it'll simulate the extra player. You can even play solitaire with it, specify whatever skill level and strategy you want for the other players."

Interesting. Wil found his attention divided between the description and the high-tech himself. This was the first time he'd talked to Genet. From a distance, the man had seemed sullen and closemouthed, quite in keeping with the business profile GreenInc had on him. Now he was talkative, almost jovial . . . and even less likable. The man had the arrogance of someone who was both very foolish and very rich. As he talked, Genet's hands roamed across the women's torsos. In the shifting of light and shadow, it was like watching a stop-action striptease. The performance was both repellent and strange. In Brierson's time, many people were easygoing about sex, whether for pleasure or pay. This was different; Genet treated the two like . . . property. They were fine furniture, to be fondled while he talked to Brierson. And they made no objection. These two were a far cry from the group with Gail Parker.

Genet glanced sidelong at Wil and smiled slowly. "Yes, Brierson, the glowball is high-tech. Collegiate didn't market the M.3 till . . ." He paused, consulting some database. "Till 2195. So it's strange, don't you think, that the New Mexicans are the people who brought it to the party?"

"Obviously some high-tech gave it to them earlier." Wil spoke a bit sharply, distracted by the other's hands.

"Obviously. But consider the implications, Brierson. The NMs are one of the two largest groups here. They are absolutely necessary to the success of the Korolev plan. From history—my history, your personal experience—we know they're used to running things. The only thing that keeps them from bulldozing the rest of you low-techs is their technical incompetence. . . . Now, just suppose some high-tech wanted to take over from Korolev. The easiest way to destroy her plan might be to back the NMs and feed them some autons and agravs and advanced bobblers. Korolev and the rest of us high-techs could not afford to put the NMs down; we need them if we are to reestablish civilization. We might just have to capitulate to whoever was behind the scheme."

Tioulang was trying to tell me something similar. The evening cool was suddenly chill. Strange that a thing as innocent as the glowball should be the first evidence since Marta's murder that someone was trying to take over. What did this do to his suspect list? Tammy Robinson might use such a bribe to recruit. Or maybe Chanson was right, and the force that ended civilization in the twenty-third was still at work. Or maybe the enemy simply desired to *own*, and was willing to risk the destruction of them all to achieve that end. He looked at Genet. Earlier in the day, Brierson had been upset to think they might slide back to governments and majority rule. Now he remembered that more evil and primitive institutions were possible. Genet oozed confidence, megalomania. Wil was suddenly sure the other was capable of planting such a clue, pointing it out, and then enjoying Wil's consternation and suspicion.

Some of that suspicion must have shown on his face. Genet's smile broadened. His hand brushed aside one girl's jacket, flaunting his "property." Wil relaxed fractionally; over the years, he had dealt with some pretty unpleasant people. Maybe this high-tech was an enemy and maybe not, but he wasn't going to get under Wil's skin.

"You know I'm working for Yelén on Marta's murder, Mr. Genet. What you tell me, I'll pass on to her. What do you suggest we do?"

Genet chuckled. "You'll 'pass it on,' will you? My dear Brierson, I don't doubt that every word we say is going directly to her. . . . But you're right. It's easier to pretend. And you low-techs are a good deal more congenial. Less back talk, anyway.

"As for what we should do: nothing overt just yet. We can't tell whether the glowball was a slip, or a subtle announcement of victory. I suggest we put the NMs under intense surveillance. If this was a slip, then it will be easy to prevent a takeover. Personally, I don't think the NMs have received much help yet; we'd see other evidence if they had." He watched the game for a few moments, then turned back to Wil. "You especially should be pleased by this turn of events, Brierson."

"I suppose so." Wil resented admitting anything to Genet. "If this is connected to Marta's murder, it may break the case."

"That's not what I meant. You were shanghaied, right?"

Wil gave a brief nod.

"Ever wonder what became of the fellow who bushwhacked you?" He paused, but Brierson couldn't even nod to that. "I'm sure dear Yelén would like this kept from you, but I think you deserve to know. They caught him; I've got records of the trial. I don't know how the skunk ever thought he could evade conviction. The court handed down the usual sentence: He was bobbled, timed to come out about a month after you. Personally, I think he deserved whatever you might do to him. But Marta and Yelén didn't work that way. They rescued everyone they could. They figured every warm body increases the colony's chances.

"Marta and Yelén made him promise to stay out of your way. Then they gave him a shallow disguise and turned him over to the NMs. They figured he could fade into the crowd there." Genet laughed. "So you see why I say this is an enjoyable twist of fate for you, Brierson. Putting pressure on the NMs gives you a chance to step on the insect who put you here." He saw the blank expression on Wil's face. "You think I'm putting you on? You can check it out easily enough. The NM Director, President—whatever they call him—has taken a real shine to your friend. The twerp is on Fraley's staff now. I saw them a few minutes ago, on the other side of this game."

Genet's gaunt face parted in a final smile. He gathered his "property" close and walked into the darkness. "Check it out, Brierson. You'll get your jollies yet."

Wil stood quietly for several minutes after the other left. He was looking at the game, but his eyes did not track the glowball anymore. Finally, he turned and walked along the outskirts of the crowd. The way was lit whenever the ball rose above the fans. That light flickered white and green and yellow, depending on whether the ball was live, striking a "wall," or out of play. Wil didn't notice the colors anymore.

Steve Fraley and his friends were sitting on the far side of the court. Somehow they had persuaded the other spectators to stand clear of the sidelines, so they had a good view even sitting down. Wil stayed in the crowd. From here he could observe with little chance that Fraley would notice.

There were fifteen in the group. Most looked like staff people, though Wil recognized a few ungovs. Fraley sat near the middle, with a couple of his top aides. They spent more time talking to the ungovs than watching the game. For a government type, ol' Steve had plenty of experience with the soft sell. Twice back in the 2090s he'd been elected President of the Republic.

It was an impressive achievement—and an empty one: By the end of the twenty-first, the New Mexico government was like a beach house when the dunes shift. War and territorial expansion were not feasible—the failure of the Kansas Incursion had shown that. And the Republic couldn't compete economically with the ungoverned lands. The grass was truly greener on the other side of the fence, and with unrestricted emigration, the situation only got worse. As a matter of frank competition, the government repealed regulation after regulation. Unlike Aztlán, the Republic never formally disgoverned. But in 2097, the NM Congress amended the constitution—over Fraley's veto—to renounce all mandatory taxing authority. Steve Fraley objected that what was left was not a government. He was obviously correct, but it didn't do him much good. What *was* left was a viable business. The Republic's police and court system didn't last; it simply wasn't competitive with existing companies. But the NM Congress did. Tourists from all over the world visited Albuquerque to pay "taxes," to vote, to see a real government in action. The ghost of the Republic lived for many years, a source of pride and profit to its citizens.

It was not enough for Steve Fraley. He used what was left of presidential authority to assemble the remnants of the NM military machine. With a hundred fellow right-thinkers he bobbled forward five hundred years—to a future where, it was hoped, sanity had returned.

Wil grimaced to himself. So, like all the cranks and crooks and victims who overshot the Singularity, Fraley and his friends ended up on the shore of a lake that had once been open ocean—fifty million years after Man.

Wil's eyes slid from Fraley to the aides beside him. Like many self-important types, these two kept their apparent age in the middle forties. Sleek and gray, they were the NM ideal of leadership. Wil remembered both from twenty-first-century news stories. Neither could be the . . . creature . . . he sought. He pushed through the crowd, closer to the open space around the NMs.

Several of those listening to Fraley's sales pitch were strangers. Wil stared at them, applying all the tests he had invented during the day.

Scarcely conscious of the movement, Wil edged out of the crowd. Now he could see all the NMs in Fraley's group. A few were paying attention to the discussions around Fraley; the rest were watching the game. Wil studied each one, matching what he saw with the Kid, the Exec, and the Janitor. There were several vague resemblances, but nothing certain. . . . He stopped, eyes caught on a middle-aged Asian. The fellow didn't resemble any of the three, yet there was something strange about him. He was as old as Fraley's top advisers, yet the game had all his attention. And this guy didn't have the others' air of assurance. He was balding, faintly pudgy. Wil stared at him, trying to imagine the man with a head of hair, and without eyefolds or facial flab.

Make those changes, and take thirty years off his apparent age . . . and you'd have . . . the Kid. The nephew of the guy who was robbed. This was the *thing* that had taken Virginia from him, that had taken Billy and Anne. This was the thing that had destroyed Brierson's whole world . . . and done it just to avoid a couple of years of reparation surcharge.

And what can I do if I find the bastard? Something cold and awful took over then, and thought ceased.

Wil found himself in the open area between the volleyball court and the NMs. He must have shouted; everyone was looking at him. Fraley stared openmouthed. For an instant, he looked afraid. Then he saw where Wil was headed, and he laughed.

There was no humor in the Kid's response. His head snapped up, instant recognition on his face. He sprang to his feet, his hands held awkwardly before him—whether an inept defense or a plea for mercy was not clear. It didn't matter. Wil's deliberate walk had become a lumbering run. Someone with his own voice was screaming. The NMs in his way scattered. Wil was barely conscious of body-blocking one who was insufficiently agile; the fellow simply bounced off him.

The Kid's face held sheer terror. He backpedaled frantically, tripped; this was one bind he would not escape.

13

Something flashed in the air above Wil, and his legs went numb. He went down, just short of where the Kid had been standing. Even as the breath smashed out of him, he was trying to get back to his knees. It was no good. He snorted blood, and rational thought resumed. Someone had stungunned him.

Around him there was shouting and people were still backing away, unsure if his berserker charge might continue. The game had broken off; the glowball's light was steady and unmoving. Wil touched his nose; bloodied but unbroken.

When he twisted back onto his elbows, the babble quieted.

Steve Fraley walked toward him, a wide grin on his face. "My, my, Inspector. Getting a little carried away, aren't you? I thought you were cooler than that. You, of all people, should know that we can't support the old grudges." As he got closer, Wil had to strain to look up at his face. Wil gave up and lowered his head. Beyond the NM President, at the limit of the glowball's illumination, he saw the Kid puking on the grass.

Fraley stepped close to the fallen Brierson, his sport shoes filling most of the near view. Wil wondered what it would be like to get one of those shoes in the face—and somehow he was sure that Steve was wondering the same thing.

"President Fraley." Yelén's voice spoke from somewhere above. "I certainly agree with you about grudges."

"Um, yes." Fraley retreated a couple of steps. When he spoke, it sounded as if he were looking upwards. "Thanks for stunning him, Ms. Korolev. Perhaps it's for the best that this happened. I think it's time you realized who you can trust to behave responsibly—and who you cannot."

Yelén did not reply. Several seconds passed. There was quiet conversation around him. He heard footsteps approach, then Tunç Blumenthal's voice. "We just want to move him away from the crowd, Yelén, give him a chance to get his legs back. Okay?"

"Okay."

Blumenthal helped Wil roll onto his back, then picked him up under the shoulders. Looking around, Wil saw that Rohan Dasgupta had grabbed his legs. But all Wil could feel was Blumenthal's hands; his legs were still dead meat. The two lugged him away from the light and the crowd. It was a struggle for the slender Rohan. Every few steps, Wil's rear dragged on the ground, a noise without sensation.

Finally, it was dark all around. They set him down, his back against a large boulder. The courts and bonfires were pools of light clustered below them. Blumenthal sat on his heels beside Wil. "Soon as you feel a tingling in those legs, I suggest you try walking, Wil Brierson. You'll have less an ache that way."

Wil nodded. It was the usual advice to stungun victims, at least when the heart wasn't involved.

"My God, Wil, what happened?" Curiosity struggled with embarrassment in Rohan's voice.

Brierson took a deep breath; the embers of his rage still glowed. "You've never seen me blow my stack, is that it, Rohan?" The world was so empty. Everybody he'd cared about was gone . . . and in their place was an anger he had never known. Wil shook his head. He'd never realized what an uncomfortable thing continuing anger could be.

They sat in silence a minute more. Pins-and-needles prickling started up Wil's feet. He'd never known a stun to wear off so quickly; another high-tech improvement, no doubt. He rolled onto his knees. "Let's see if I can walk." He climbed to his feet, using Dasgupta and Blumenthal as crutches.

"There's a path over here," said Blumenthal. "Just keep walking and it'll get easier."

They tottered off. The path turned downwards, leaving the picnic grounds behind the crest of a hill. The shouts and laughter faded, and soon the loudest sounds were the insects. There was a sweetish smell—flowers?—that he'd never noticed around Town Korolev. The air was cool, downright cold on those parts of his legs that had regained sensation.

At first, Wil had to put all his weight on Blumenthal and Dasgupta. His legs seemed scarcely more than stumps, his knees now locking, now bending loose with no effective coordination. After fifty meters his feet could feel the pebbles in the path and he was doing at least part of the navigating.

The night was clear and moonless. Somehow the stars alone were enough to see by—or maybe it was the Milky Way? Wil looked into the sky ahead of them. The pale light was strangely bright. It climbed out of the east, a broad band that narrowed and faded halfway up the sky. *East?* Could the megayears change even that? Wil almost stumbled, felt the others' grasp tighten. He looked higher, saw the real Milky Way slicing down from another direction.

Blumenthal chuckled. "There wasn't much going on at the Lagrange zones in your time, was there?"

"There were habitats at L4 and L5. They were easy to see, like bright stars," nothing like this stardust haze.

"Put enough stuff in Luna's orbit and you'll see more than just a few new stars. In my time, millions lived there. All Earth's heavy industry was there. Things were getting crowded. There's only so much thermal and chemical pollution you can dump before your factories begin to poison themselves."

Now Wil remembered things Marta and Yelén had said. "But it's mainly bobbles there now."

"Yes. This light isn't caused by factories and civilization. Third-body perturbations have long since flushed the original artifacts. Now it's a handy place for short-term storage, or to park observing equipment."

Wil stared at the pale glow. He wondered how many thousands of bobbles it took to make such a light. He knew Yelén still had much of her equipment off Earth. How many millions of tonnes were in "short-term storage" out there? For that matter, how many travelers were still in stasis, ignoring all the messages the Korolevs had laid down across the megayears? The light was ghostly in more ways than one.

They went another couple of hundred meters eastwards. Gradually

Wil's coordination returned, till he was walking without help and only an occasional wobble. His eyes were fully dark-adapted now. Light-colored flowers floated in the bushes to the side of the path, and when they nodded close the sweetish smell came stronger. He wondered if the path was natural or a piece of Korolev landscaping. He risked his balance by looking straight up. Sure enough, there was something dark against the stars. Yelén's auton—and probably Della's, too—was still with them.

The path meandered southwards, to the naked rock that edged the cliffs. From below came a faint sighing, the occasional slap of water against rock. It could have been Lake Michigan on a quiet night. Now for some mosquitoes to make him feel truly at home.

Blumenthal broke the long silence. "You were one of my childhood heroes, Wil Brierson." There was a smile in his voice.

"What?"

"Yes. You and Sherlock Holmes. I read every novel your son wrote."

Billy wrote . . . about me? GreenInc had said Billy's second career was as a novelist, but Wil hadn't had time to look at his writing.

"The adventures were fiction, even though you were the hero. He wrote 'em under the assumption that Derek Lindemann hadn't bumped you off. There were almost thirty novels; you had adventures all through the twenty-second."

"Derek Lindemann?" Dasgupta said. "Who . . . Oh, I *see.*"

Wil nodded. "Yeah, Rohan." Wimpy Derek Lindemann . . . the Kid. "The guy I tried to kill just now." But for a moment his anger seemed irrelevant. Wil smiled sadly in the darkness. To think that Billy had created a synthetic life for the one that had been ended. By God, he was going to read those novels!

He glanced at the high-tech. "Glad you enjoyed my adventures, Tunç. I assume you grew out of it. From what I hear, you were in construction."

"True and true. But had I wished to be a policeman, it would've been hard. By the late twenty-second, most habitats had fewer than one cop per million population. It was even worse in rural areas. A deplorable scarcity of crime, it was." Wil smiled. Blumenthal's accent was strange—almost singsong, a cross between Scottish and Amerasian. None of the other high-techs talked like this. In Wil's time, English dialect differences had been damping out; communication and travel were so fast in the Earth-Luna volume. Blumenthal had grown up in space, several days' travel time from the heartland.

"Besides, I wanted more to build things than to protect folks. At the beginning of the twenty-third, the world was changing faster than you can imagine. I'll wager there was more technical change in the first decade of the twenty-third than in all the centuries to the twenty-second. Have you noticed the differences among the advanced travelers? Monica Raines left civilization in 2195; no matter what she claims now, she bought the best equipment available. Juan Chanson left in 2200—with a much smaller investment. Yet Juan's gear is superior in every way. His autons have spent several thousand years in realtime, and are good for at least as much more. Monica has survived sixty years and has only one surviving auton. The difference was five years' progress in sport and camping equipment. The Korolevs left a year after Chanson. They bought an immense amount of equipment, yet for about the same investment as Chanson; a single year had depreciated the 2200 models that far. Juan, Yelén, Genet—they're aware of this. But I don't think any of them understand what nine more years of progress could bring. . . . You know I'm the last one out?"

Wil had read that in Yelén's summaries. The difference hadn't seemed terribly important. "You bobbled out in 2210?"

"True. Della Lu was latest before me, in 2202. We've never found anyone who lived closer to the Singularity."

Rohan said softly, "You should be the most powerful of all."

"Should be, perhaps. But the fact is, I'm not one of the willing travelers. I was more than happy to live when I was. I never had the least inclination to hop into the future, to start a new religion or break the stock market. . . . I'm sorry, Rohan Dasgupta, I—"

"It's okay. My brother and I were a little too greedy. We thought, 'What can go wrong? Our investments seem safe; after a century or two, they should make us very rich. And if they don't, well, the standard of living will be so high, even being poor we'll live better than the rich do now.' " Rohan sighed. "We bet on the progress you speak of. We didn't count on coming back to jungles and ruins and a world without people." They walked several paces in silence. Finally Rohan's curiosity got the better of him. "You were shanghaied, then, like Wil?"

"I . . . don't think so; since no one lived after me, it's impossible to know for sure. I was in heavy construction, and accidents happen. . . . How's the legs, Wil Brierson?"

"What?" The sudden change of topic took Wil by surprise. "Fine now." There were still pins and needles, but he had no trouble with coordination.

"Then let's start back, okay?"

They walked away from the cliffs, past the sweet blossoms. The campfires were invisible behind several ridgelines; they had come almost a thousand meters. They walked most of the way back with scarcely a word. Even Rohan was silent.

Wil's rage had cooled, leaving only ashes, sadness. He wondered what would happen the next time he saw Derek Lindemann. He remembered the abject terror on Lindemann's face. The disguise had been a good one. If Phil Genet hadn't pointed Wil right at the Kid, it might have been weeks before he nailed him. Lindemann had been seventeen, a gawky Anglo; now he looked fifty, a somewhat pudgy Asian. Clearly there had been cosmetic surgery. As for his age . . . well, when Yelén and Marta decided to do something, they could be brutally direct. Somewhere in the millions of years that Wil and the others spent bobbled, Derek Lindemann had lived thirty years of realtime without medical support. Perhaps the Korolevs had been out of stasis then, perhaps not; the autons that attended their bobble farm on the Canadian Shield would have been competent to provide for him. Thirty years the Kid lived essentially alone. Thirty years inward turning. The Lindemann that Wil knew had been a wimp. No doubt his embezzling was petty revenge against his relatives in the company. No doubt he bobbled Brierson out of naive panic. And for thirty years the Kid had lived with the fear that one day W. W. Brierson would recognize him.

"Thanks for . . . talking to me. I-I'm not usually like this." That was true, and perhaps the most unnerving part of the whole day. In thirty years of police work, he'd never blown up. Perhaps that wasn't surprising; knocking customers around was a quick way to get fired. But in Wil's case, being cool had come easy. He was truly the low-pressure type he seemed. How often *he* had been the calm one who talked others down from the high ledges of panic and rage. He'd never been the kind who went from anger to anger. In the last weeks, all that had changed, yet . . . "You've both lost as much as I, haven't you?" He thought back to all the people he had talked to this afternoon, and shame replaced his embarrassment. Maybe ol' W. W. Brierson had always been unflappable because he never had any real problems. When the crunch came, he was the weakest of all.

"It's okay," Blumenthal said. "There have been fights before. Some people are hurting more than others. And for each of us, some days are worse than others."

"Besides, you're special, Wil," said Rohan.

"Huh?"

"The rest of us have our hands full rebuilding civilization. Korolev is giving us enormous amounts of equipment. It needs lots of supervision; there's not enough automatic stuff to go around. We're working as hard as anyone in the twentieth century. I think most of the high-techs are, too. I know Tunç is.

"But you, Wil, what is your job? You work just as hard as any of us—but doing what? Trying to figure out who killed Marta. I'll bet that's fun. You have to spend all your time, off by yourself, thinking about things that have been lost. Even the laziest low-tech isn't in that bind. If someone wanted to drive you crazy, they couldn't have invented a better job for you."

Wil found himself smiling. He remembered the times Rohan had tried to get him to these picnics. "Your prescription?" he asked lightly.

"Well . . ." Rohan was suddenly diffident. "You could get off the case. But I hope you won't. We all want to know what happened to Marta. I liked her the most of all the high-techs. And her murder might be part of something that could kill the rest of us. . . . I think the important thing is that you realize what the problem is. You're not falling apart. You're just under more pressure than most of us.

"Also, there's no point in working on it all the time, is there? I'll bet you spend hours staring into blind alleys. Spend more time with the rest of humanity. Ha! You might even find some clues here!"

Wil thought back over the last two hours. On Rohan's last point there was no possible disagreement.

14

From North Shore to Town Korolev was about a thousand kilometers, most of it over the Inland Sea. Yelén didn't stint with the shuttle service between the two points. The two halves of the settlement were physically separate, but she was determined to make them close in every other way. When Wil left the picnic, there were three fliers waiting for southbound passengers. He ended up in one that was empty except for the Dasgupta brothers.

The agrav rose with the familiar silent acceleration that never became intense—and never ceased. The trip would take about fifteen minutes. Below them, the picnic fires dwindled, seemed to tilt sideways. The loudest sound was a distant scream of wind. It grew, then dwindled to nothing. The interior lighting turned the night beyond the windows into undetailed darkness. Except for the constant acceleration, they might have been sitting in an ordinary office waiting room.

They were going home ahead of most people. Wil was surprised to see Dilip leaving early. He remembered what the guy had been up to that afternoon. "What became of Gail Parker, Dilip? I thought . . ." Wil's voice trailed off as he remembered the unhappy caucus he'd stumbled onto.

The older Dasgupta shrugged, his normally rakish air deflated. "She . . . she didn't want to play. She was polite enough, but you know how things are. Every week the girls are a bit harder to get along with. I guess we've all got some hard decisions to make."

422

Wil changed the subject. "Either of you know who brought the glowball?"

Rohan grinned. No doubt he was pleased by what he thought an innocuous topic. "Wasn't that something? I've seen glowballs before, but nothing like that. Didn't Tunç Blumenthal bring it?"

Dilip shook his head. "I was there from the beginning. It was Fraley's people. I saw them get off the shuttle with it. Tunç didn't come along till they had played a couple of games."

Just as Phil Genet claimed.

Still under acceleration, the shuttle did a slow turn, the only evidence being a faint queasiness in the passengers' guts. Now they were flying tailfirst into the darkness. They were halfway home.

Wil settled back in his seat, let his mind wander back over the day. Detective work had been easier in civilization. There, most things were what they seemed. You had your employers, their clients, collateral services. In most cases, these were people you had worked with for years; you knew who you could trust. Here, it was paranoid heaven. Except for Lindemann, he knew no one from before. Virtually all the high-techs were twisted creatures. Chanson, Korolev, Raines, Lu—they had all lived longer than he, some for thousands of years. They were all screwier than the types he was used to dealing with. And Genet. Genet was not so strange; Wil had known a few like him. There were lots of mysteries about Genet's life in civilization, but one thing was clear as crystal after tonight: Phil Genet was a people-owner, barely under control. Whether or not he had killed anyone, murder was in his moral range.

On the other hand, Blumenthal seemed to be a genuinely nice guy. He was an involuntary traveler like Wil, but without the Lindemann burden.

Brierson suppressed a smile. In the standard mystery plot, such all-around niceness would be a sure sign of guilt. In the real world, things rarely worked that way. . . . *Damn.* In *this* real world, almost anything could be true. Okay, what grounds could there be for suspecting Blumenthal? Motive? Certainly none was visible. In fact, very little was known about Blumenthal. The 2201 GreenInc listed him as ten years old, a child employee in a family-owned mining company. There was scarcely more information about the company. It was small, operating mainly in the comet cloud. Wil had less hard information on Blumenthal than on any other high-tech, Genet excepted. As the last human to leave civilization, there had been no one to write Tunç's biography. It was only Tunç's word that he'd been bobbled in 2210. It could have been later, perhaps from the heart of the Singularity. He claimed an industrial accident had blown him into the sun. Come to think of it, what corroboration could there be for that either? And if it wasn't an accident, then most likely he was the loser in a battle of nukes and bobbles, where the victors wanted the vanquished permanently dead.

Wil suddenly wondered where Tunç stood on Chanson's list of potential aliens.

Scattered streetlamps shone friendly through the trees, and then the flier was on the ground. Wil and the Dasguptas piled out, feeling light-headed in the sudden return to one gravity.

They had landed on the street that ran past their homes. Wil said good night to Rohan and Dilip and walked slowly up the street toward his place. He couldn't remember when so many things, both physical and mental, had been jammed into one afternoon. The residual effects of the stun added overwhelming fatigue to it all. He glanced upwards but saw only leaves, backlit by a streetlamp. No doubt the autons were still up there, hidden behind the trees.

Such an innocuous thing, the glowball. And the explanation might be innocuous, too: Maybe Yelén had simply given it to the NMs, or maybe they'd swiped it themselves. Surely it was a trivial item in a high-tech's inventory. The fact that she hadn't demanded a late-night session was a good sign. After he got a good sleep, he might be able to laugh at Genet.

Wil walked along the edge of his lot. He reached the gate . . . and stopped cold. Crude letters were spraygunned across the gate and surrounding wall. They spelled the words LO TECH DONT MEAN NO TECH. The message had scarcely registered on his mind when white light drenched the scene. Yelén's auton had dropped to man-height beside Wil. Its spotlight fanned across the gateway.

Brierson stepped close to the wall. The paint was still wet. It glittered in the light. He stared numbly at the lettering.

Polka-dot paint, green on purple. The bright green disks were perfectly formed, even where the paint had dribbled downwards. It was the sort of thing you see often enough on data sets—and never in the real world.

Yelén's voice came from the auton. "Take a good look, Brierson. Then come inside; we've got to talk."

15

The lights came on even before he reached the house. Wil walked into the living room and collapsed in his favorite chair. Two conference holos were lit: Yelén was on one, Della the other. Neither looked happy. Korolev spoke first. "I want Tammy Robinson out of our time, Inspector."

Wil started to shrug, *Why ask me?* He glanced at Della Lu, remembered that he was damn close to being arbiter in this dispute. "Why?"

"It should be obvious now. The deal was that we would let her stay in realtime as long as she didn't interfere. Well, it's sure as hell clear someone is backing the NMs—and she's the best suspect."

"But suspect only," said Lu. The spacer's face and costume were a strange contrast. She wore frilly pants and halter, the sort of outfit Wil would have expected at the picnic. Yet he hadn't seen her there. Had she simply *peeped,* too shy or aloof to show up? Whatever personality matched the outfit, it scarcely fit her expression now. It was cold, determined. "I gave her my word that—"

Yelén slapped the table in front of her. "Promises be damned! The survival of the settlement comes first, Lu. You of all people should know that. If you won't bobble Robinson, then stand aside and let—"

Della smiled, and suddenly she seemed a lot deadlier, a lot more determined than Korolev—with all her temper—ever had. "I will not stand aside, Yelén."

"Um." Yelén sat back, perhaps remembering that Della was one of the most heavily armed of the travelers, perhaps thinking of the centuries of combat experience Lu had had with her weapons. She glanced at Brierson. "Will you talk some sense to her? We've got a life-and-death situation here."

"Maybe. But Tammy is only one suspect—and the one who is most carefully watched. If she was up to something, surely you'd have direct evidence?"

"Not necessarily. I figure I'll need a medium recon capability for at least another century of realtime. I can't afford a 'no-sparrow-shall-fall' network; I'd run out of consumables in a few months. I have kept a close watch on Robinson, but if her family stashed autons before they left, it wouldn't take much for her to communicate with them. All she has to do is give away some trinkets, make these low-techs a bit more dissatisfied. I'll bet she has high-performance bobblers hidden near the Inland Sea. If she can lead her little friends there, we'll be looking at a lot of long-term bobbles—and an end to the plan."

If the Robinsons had prepared their departure that carefully, they were probably responsible for Marta's murder, too. "How 'bout a compromise? Take her out of circulation for a few months."

"I promised her, Wil."

"I know. But this would be voluntary. Explain the situation to her. If she's innocent, she'll be as upset by all this as we are. A three-month absence won't hurt her announced goals, and will very likely prove her innocent. If it does, then she could have a lot more freedom afterwards."

"What if she doesn't agree?"

"I really think she will, Della." *If not, then we'll see if my integrity can stand up to Yelén as well as yours does.*

Yelén said, "I would buy a three-month bobbling—though we may go through this same argument again at the end of it."

"Okay. I'll talk to Tammy." Della looked down at her frilly outfit, and a strange expression crossed her face. Embarrassment? "I'll get back to you." Her image vanished.

Wil looked at the remaining holo. Yelén was in her library. Sunlight streamed through its fake windows. Night and day must have little meaning to Yelén; that made Wil feel even more tired.

Korolev diddled with something on her desk, then looked back at

Wil. "Thanks for the compromise. I was on the verge of doing something . . . rash."

"You're welcome." He closed his eyes a moment, almost succumbing to stun-induced sleepiness.

"Yes. Now we know our worst fears are true, Inspector. Agrav glowballs. Polka-dot paint. These are completely trivial things compared to what we have already given away. *But they are not on the gift inventory.* It's just like Phil says. Marta's murderer is not done with us. Someone or some*thing* is out there, taking over the low-techs."

"You don't sound so sure the Robinsons are behind it."

". . . No, that was partly wishful thinking. They have the clearest motive. Tammy would be the easiest to handle. . . . No. It could be almost any of the high-techs."

Brierson was too tired to keep his mouth shut. "Do we even know who those are?"

"What do you mean?"

"What if the murderer is masquerading as a low-tech? Maybe there's a surviving graverobber."

"That's absurd." But her eyes went wide, and for nearly fifteen seconds she was silent. "Yes, that's absurd," she repeated, with a trace less certainty. "I've got good records on all the rescues; we made most of them. We never saw any unusual equipment. Now, a masquerader might have his high-tech gear in separate storage, but we'd know if he moved much of it. . . . I don't know if you can understand, Brierson: We've had total control of their stasis from the beginning. An advanced traveler couldn't tolerate such domination."

"Okay." But he wondered if Lu's reaction would be the same.

"Good. Now I want to get your impression of what you saw today. I watched it all myself, but—"

Wil held up a hand. "How about waiting till tomorrow, Yelén? I'll have things sorted out better."

"No." The queen on the mountain wasn't angry, but she was going to have things her way. "There are things I need to know right now. For instance, what do you think spooked Kim Tioulang?"

"I have no idea. Could you see who he was looking at when he panicked?"

"Into the crowd. I didn't have enough cameras to be more definite.

428

My guess is he had lookouts posted, and one of them signaled that Mr. Bad was in the area."

Mr. Bad. Phil Genet. The connection was instantaneous, needed no supporting logic. "Why make a mystery of it? Give Tioulang some protection and ask him what he has in mind."

"I did. Now he won't talk."

"Surely you have truth drugs. Why not just bring him in and—" Wil stopped, suddenly ashamed. He was talking like some government policeman: "The needs of the State come first." He could rationalize, of course. This was a world without police contracts and legal systems. Till they were established, simple survival might justify such tactics. The argument was slippery, and Wil wondered how far he would slide into savagery before he found solid footing.

Yelén smiled at his embarrassment—whether from sympathy or amusement he could not tell. "I decided not to. Not yet, anyway. The low-techs hate me enough already. And it's just possible Tioulang might suicide under questioning. Some of the twentieth-century governments put pretty good psych-blocks in their people. If the Peacers inherited that filthy habit . . . Besides, he may not know any more than we do: Someone is backing the NM faction."

Wil remembered Tioulang's sudden panic; the man feared someone in particular. "You have him protected?"

"Yes. Almost as well as you, though he doesn't know it. For the time being I won't risk snatching him."

"You want to know my favorite candidate for villain? Phil Genet."

Yelén leaned forward. "Why?"

"He showed up just a few minutes after Tioulang took off. The man reeks of evil."

" 'Reeks of evil'? That's a professional opinion, is it?"

Wil rubbed his eyes. "Hey, you wanted to get my 'impressions,' remember?" But she was right; he wouldn't have put it that way if he'd been thinking straight.

"Phil's a sadist. I've known that for years. And I think he's worse now that we've got all the low-techs out of stasis—you little guys are such easy victims. I saw how he worked you over about Lindemann. I'm sorry about stunning you, Wil, but I can't tolerate any of the old grudges."

Wil nodded, faintly surprised. There was something near sympathy in her voice. In fact, he was grateful she had stunned him down. "Genet is capable of murder, Yelén."

"Lots of people are. What would you have done to Lindemann if . . . ? Look, neither of us likes Phil. That by itself is no big deal: I don't especially like you, and yet we get along. It's a matter of common interest. He helped Marta and me a lot. I doubt if we could have rescued the Peacers without his construction equipment. He's more than proved he wants the settlement to succeed."

"Maybe. But now that everyone has been brought together, perhaps your 'common interest' is dead. Maybe he wants to run the whole show."

"Hmm. He knows none of us have a chance if we start shooting. You think he's really crazy?"

"I don't know, Yelén. Look at the recording again. I had the feeling he wasn't taunting just me. He knew you'd be listening. I think he was laughing at you, too. Like he was on the verge of some triumph, something the sadist in him couldn't resist hinting at."

"So you think he set up the glowball—and was laughing at us all the time he was 'clueing you in.'" She pursed her lips. "It doesn't make sense . . . but I guess I'm paying for your intuition as much as anything else. I'll break a few more autons out of stasis, try to keep better tabs on Phil."

She sat back, and for a moment Wil thought she might be done with him. "Okay. I want to go over your other conversations." She noticed his expression. "Look, Inspector. I didn't ask you to socialize for your health. You're my low-tech point of view. We've got a murder here, incipient civil war, and everybody's general dislike for me. Just about everything we saw today has a connection with these things. I want your reactions while they're fresh."

So they reviewed the picnic. Literally. Yelén insisted on playing much of the video. She really did need help. Whether it was the centuries of living apart or her high-tech viewpoint Wil didn't know, but there were many things about the picnic she didn't understand. She had no sympathy for the women's dilemma. The first time they viewed the women's meeting, she made an obscure comment about "people having to pay for other people's mistakes." Was she referring to the Korolev failure to bring womb tanks?

Wil had her play the scene again, and he tried to explain. Finally she became a little angry. "Sure they've got to make sacrifices. But don't they realize it's the survival of the human race that's at stake?" She waved her hand. "I can't believe their nature is that different from earlier centuries. When the crunch comes, they'll do what they must."

Would the queen on the mountain also do her female duty? Would she have six kids—or twelve? Brierson didn't voice the question. He could do without a Korolev explosion.

The sunlight streaming through Yelén's windows slowly shifted from morning to afternoon. The clock on Wil's data set showed it was way past the Witching Hour. If they kept going, he'd be seeing *real* sunlight, through his own windows. Finally the analysis wound back to Wil's conversation with Jason Mudge. Korolev stopped him. "You can take Mudge off your list of suspects, Inspector."

Wil had been about to say the same. He simulated curiosity. "Why?"

"The jerk fell off the cliffs last night, right on his pointy head."

Brierson lurched to wakefulness. "You mean, he's *dead?*"

"Dead beyond all possible resuscitation, Inspector. For all his God-mongering, he was no teetotaler. The autopsy showed blood alcohol at 0.22 percent. He left the party a little before you ran into Lindemann. Apparently he couldn't find anyone who'd even pretend to listen. The last I saw he was weaving along the westward bluffs. He got about fifteen hundred meters down the path, must have slipped where it comes near the cliff edge. One of my routine patrols found the body just after you got back here. He'd been in the water a couple of hours."

He rested his chin in his palms and slowly shook his head. *Yelén. Yelén. We've talked all through the night, and all that time your autons have been investigating and dissecting . . . and never a word that a man has died.* "I asked you to keep an eye on him."

"Well, *I* decided not to. He just wasn't that important." Korolev was silent a moment. Something of his attitude must have penetrated. "Look, Brierson, I'm not happy he died. Eventually he might have dropped that 'Third Coming' garbage and been of some use. But face it: The man was a parasite, and having him out of the way is one less suspect—however farfetched."

"Okay, Yelén. It's okay."

He should have guessed the effect of his assurance. Yelén leaned forward. "Are you really that paranoid, Brierson? Do you think Mudge was murdered, too?"

Maybe. What might Mudge know that could make it worth silencing him? He owned little high-tech equipment, yet he did know systems. Maybe he'd been the murderer's pet vandal, now deemed a liability. Wil tried to remember what they had talked about, but all that came was the little guy's intent expression. Of course, Yelén would be willing to play the conversation back. Again and again. It was the last thing he wanted now. "Let our paranoias go their separate ways, Yelén. If I think of anything, I'll let you know."

For whatever reason, Korolev didn't push him. Fifteen minutes later she was off the comm.

Wil straggled up to his bedroom, relieved and disappointed to be alone at last.

16

As usual there was a morning dream, but not the dream in blue this time, not the dream of parting, of gasping sobs that emptied his lungs. This was the dream of the many houses. He woke again and again, always to a house that should have been familiar, yet wasn't. There were yards and neighbors, never quite understood. Sometimes he was married. Mostly he was alone; Virginia had just left or was at some other house. Sometimes he saw them—Virginia, Anne, Billy— and that was worse. Their conversations were short, about packing, a trip to be made. And then they were gone, leaving Wil to try to understand the purpose of the hidden rooms, the doors that wouldn't open.

When Wil really woke, it was with a desperate start, not the sobbing breathlessness of the blue dream. He felt a resentful relief, seeing the sun streaming past the almost-jacarandas into his bedroom. This was a house that didn't change from day to day, a house he had almost accepted—even if it was the source for some of the dreams. He lay back for a second; sometimes he almost recognized the others, too; one was a mixture of this place and the winter home they bought in California just before . . . the Lindemann case. Wil smiled weakly at himself. These morning entertainments had greater intensity than any novel he'd ever played. Too bad he wasn't a fan of the tearjerkers.

* * *

He glanced at his mail. There was a short note from Lu: Tammy had agreed to a three-month bobblement, subject to a ten-hour flicker. Good. The other items were from Yelén: megabytes of analysis on the party. Ugh. She'd expect him to know all this the next time they talked. He sat down, browsed through the top nodes. There were a couple of things he was especially curious about. Mudge, for instance.

Wil formatted the autopsy report in Michigan State Police style. He scanned the lab results; the familiar forms brought back memories, strangely pleasant for all that they involved the uglier side of his job. Jason Mudge had been as drunk as Yelén said. There was no trace of any other drug. She had not been exaggerating about his fall, either. The little guy had struck the rocks headfirst. Wil ran some simulations: A headfirst landing was consistent with the cliff's height and Mudge's stature—assuming he tripped and fell with no effort at recovery. Every lesion, every trauma on poor Mudge's body was accounted for; even the scratches on his arms were matched to microgram specks of flesh left on bushes that grew close to the path.

It was all very reasonable: The man had been seen drinking, had been seen leaving the picnic in a drunken state. From his desperate eagerness of the afternoon, Wil could imagine his state of mind by evening. He had wandered down the path, self-pity and booze exaggerating every movement. . . . If it had been anyone else, he might have been stopped. But to approach Jason Mudge was to risk sermons unending.

And so he was dead, like any number of drug-related semisuicides Wil had seen. Still, it was interesting that the actual cause of death was so perfectly, instantly fatal. Even if Yelén's autons had discovered Mudge immediately after his fall, they could not have saved him. Except for multiple gunshot wounds and explosions, Wil had never seen such thorough destruction of a brain.

It might be worth going over the fellow's past once more, in particular Wil's last conversation with Mudge. He remembered now. There had been some strange comment about Juan Chanson. Wil replayed the video from Yelén's auton. Yes, he implied Juan had once been a chiliast, too.

Now, that was easy to check. Brierson asked Yelén's GreenInc about the archeologist. . . . Chanson was well covered, despite his obscure specialty. As a kid, he had been involved with religion; both his parents had been Faithful of the Ndelante Ali. But by the time he reached college, whatever belief remained was mild and ecumenical. He was awarded a doctorate in Mayan archeology from the Universidad Politécnica de Ceres. Wil smiled to himself. In his time, Port Ceres had been a mining camp—to think that a few decades later it could support a university granting degrees like Chanson's!

Nowhere was there evidence of religious fanaticism or of any connection with Jason Mudge. In fact, there was no hint of his later preoccupation with alien invasions. Chanson bobbled out in 2200, and his motive was no nuttier than most: He thought a century or two of progress might give him the tools for a definitive study of the Mayan culture.

  . . . *Instead he wound up with the greatest archeological mystery of all time.*

Wil sighed. So in addition to the late Mr. Mudge's other flaws, he had been spreading lies about his rivals.

17

The next few days fell into a pattern, mostly a pleasant one: The afternoons he spent with one or another group of low-techs.

He saw several mines. They were still heavily automated. Many were open-pit affairs; fifty million years had created whole new ore beds. (The only richer pickings were in the asteroid belt, and one of Yelén's retrenchments was to give up most space activities.) The settlement's factories were like nothing that had existed in history, a weird combination of high-tech custom construction and the primitive production lines which would eventually dominate. Thanks to Gail Parker he even saw an NM tractor factory; he was surprised by a generally friendly reception.

In some ways the North Shore picnic had been misleading. Wil discovered that, although most people agreed with Tioulang's complaints against Korolev, few ungovs seriously considered giving their sovereignty to either the Peace or New Mexico. In fact, there had already been some quiet defections from the statist camps.

People were as busy as Rohan claimed. Ten-, twelve-hour days were the rule. And much of the remaining time was filled with scheming to maximize long-term gain. Most of the high-tech giveaways had already been traded several times. When he visited the Dasguptas' farm he saw they were also making farm machinery. He told them about the NM factory. Rohan just smiled innocently. Dilip leaned back against one of his home-brew tractors and crossed his arms. "Yes, I've talked to Gail about that. Fraley wants to buy us out. If the price is right, maybe we'll let him. Heh, heh. Both NMs and Peacers are heavy in tool production. I can see what's going on in their tiny brains. Ten years down the road, they figure on a classic peasant/factory confrontation—with them on top. Poor Fraley; sometimes I feel sorry for him. Even if the NMs and the Peace merged, they still wouldn't have all the factories, or even half the mines. Yelén says her databases and planning software will be available for centuries. There are ungov technical types better than anyone Fraley has. Rohan and I know commodity trading. Hell, a lot of us do, and market planning, too." He smirked happily. "In the end, he'll lose his shirt."

Wil grinned back. Dilip Dasgupta had never lacked for self-confidence. In this case he might be right . . . as long as the NMs and the Peace couldn't use force.

Wil's evening debriefings with Yelén were not quite so much fun, though they were more congenial than the one after the North Shore picnic. Her auton followed him everywhere, so she usually heard and saw everything he did. Sometimes it seemed that she wanted to rehash every detail; finding Marta's murderer was a goal never far from her mind, especially now that it seemed part of a general sabotage scheme. But just as often she wanted his estimate of the low-techs' attitudes and intentions. Their conversations were a weird mix of social science, paranoia, and murder investigation.

Tammy had been bobbled within hours of the picnic. Since then, there had been no signs of high-tech interference. Either she was responsible for it (and had been terribly clumsy), or the glowball and paint were part of something still inscrutable.

Apparently the low-techs were oblivious to this latest twist. Over the last few weeks they had seen and used an enormous amount of equipment; most had no way of knowing the source or "sanctity" of what was provided. And Yelén had erased the polka-dot graffiti from Wil's gate. On the other hand, it was certain that some NMs knew of the bootlegging, enough that Tioulang's spies had gotten the news. Knowing the NM organization, Wil couldn't imagine any conspiracy independent of Steve Fraley.

Yelén dithered with the notion of seizing Fraley and his staff for interrogation, in the end decided against it. There was the same problem as with grabbing Tioulang. Besides, Marta's plan seemed to be *working*. The first phases—the giveaway, the establishment of agreements among the low-techs—were delicate steps that depended on everyone's confidence and goodwill. Even in the best of circumstances —and the last few days did seem about as good as things could get— the low-techs had all sorts of reasons for disliking the queen on the mountain.

And that was one of Korolev's main interests in pumping Brierson. She took every complaint that appeared on the recordings and asked for Wil's analysis. More, she wanted to know the problems he sensed but that went unsaid. It was one of the happier parts of Wil's new job, one he suspected that most of the low-techs understood, too. . . . Would his reception at the NM tractor plant have been quite so cordial otherwise?

Yelén was amused by Dilip Dasgupta's dealings with New Mexico: "Good for him; no one should be taking any crap from those atavists.

"You know what Tioulang and Fraley did when I started Marta's giveaway?" she continued. "They told me how they had their disagreements, but that the future of the race was of supreme importance; their experts had gotten together, come up with a 'Unity Plan.' It specified production goals, resource allocation, just what every damn person was going to do for the next ten years. They expected me to jam this piece of wisdom down everyone's throat. . . . Idiots. I have software that's spent decades crunching on these problems, and *I* can't plan at the level of detail these jerks pretend to. Marta would be proud of me, though; I didn't laugh out loud. I just smiled sweetly and said anyone who wanted to follow their plan was certainly welcome to, but that I couldn't dream of enforcing it. They were insulted even so; I guess they thought I was being sarcastic. It was after that that Tioulang started peddling his line about majority rule and unity against the queen on the mountain."

Other items were more serious, and did not amuse her at all. There were 140 low-tech females. Since the founding of the settlement, her medical service had diagnosed only four pregnancies. "Two of the women requested abortions! I will *not* do abortions, Brierson! And I want every woman off contraceptive status."

They had talked around this problem before; Wil didn't know quite what to say. "This could just drive them into the arms of the NMs and

Peacers." Come to think of it, this was one issue where Korolev and the governments probably saw eye to eye. Fraley and Tioulang might make a show of supporting reproductive freedom, but he couldn't imagine it as more than a short-term ploy.

The anger left Yelén's voice. She was almost pleading. "Don't they see, Wil? There have been settlements before. Most were just a family or two, but some—like Sánchez's—were around half our size. They all failed. I think ours may be big enough. Just barely. If the women can average ten children each over the next thirty years, and if their daughters can perform similarly, then we'll have enough people to fill the gaps left as automation fails. But if they can't, then the technology will fail, and we'll actually lose population. All my simulations show that what's left won't be a viable species. In the end, there'll be a few high-techs living a few more subjective centuries with what's left of their equipment."

Marta's vision of a flamed-out ramjet diving Earthwards passed through Wil's mind. "I think the low-tech women want humanity back as much as you, Yelén. But it takes a while to get hardened to this situation. Things were so different back in civilization. A man or a woman could decide where and when and whether—"

"Inspector, don't you think that I know that? I lived forty years in civilization, and I know that what we have here stinks. . . . But it's all we've got."

There was a moment's awkward silence, then: "One thing I don't understand, Yelén. Of all the travelers, you and Marta had the best intuition about the future. Why didn't . . ." The words slipped out before he could stop them; he really wasn't trying to provoke a fight. "Why didn't you think to bring along automatic wombs and a zygote bank?"

Korolev's face reddened, but she didn't blow up. After a second she said, "We did. As usual, it was Marta's idea. I made the purchase. But . . . I screwed up." She looked away from Brierson. It was the first time he'd seen shame in her manner. "I, I didn't test the shipment enough. The company was rated AAAA; it should have been safe as houses. And we were so busy those last few weeks . . . but I should have been more careful." She shook her head. "We had plenty of time later, on the future side of the Singularity. The equipment was junk,

Brierson. The wombs and postnatal automation were shells, with just enough processing power to fake the diagnostics."

"And the zygotes?"

Yelén gave a bitter laugh. "Yes. With bobbles it should be impossible to mess that up, right? Wrong. The zygotes were malformed, the sort of nonviable stuff even Christians won't touch.

"I've studied that company through GreenInc; there's nothing that could have tipped us off. But after their last rating, the owners must have gutted their company. The behavior was criminal; when they were caught, it would take them decades to make reparations. Or maybe we were a one-shot fraud; maybe they knew I was making a long jump." She paused. The zip returned to her voice. "I wish they were here now. I wouldn't have to sue them; I'd just drop 'em into the sun.

"Sometimes innocent people have to pay for the mistakes of others, Inspector. That's how it is here. These women must start producing. Now."

Wil spread his hands. "Give them, give us some time."

"It may be hard for you to believe, but time is something we don't have a whole lot of. We waited fifty million years to get everyone together. But once this exercise is begun, there are certain deadlines. You've noticed that I haven't given away any medical equipment."

Wil nodded. Peacer and NM propaganda noticed it loudly. Everyone was welcome to *use* the high-techs' medical services, but, like their bobblers and fighting gear, their medical equipment had not been part of the giveaway.

"We have almost three hundred people here now. The high-end medical equipment is delicate stuff. It consumes irreplaceable materials; it wears out. This is already happening, Brierson, faster than a linear scale-up would predict. The synthesizers must constantly recalibrate to handle each individual."

There was a tightness in Wil's throat. He wondered if this was how a twentieth-century type might feel on being told of inoperable cancer. "How long do we have?"

She shrugged. "If we gave full support, and if the population did *not* increase, maybe fifty years. But the population must increase, or we won't be able to maintain the rest of our technology. The children will need plenty of health care. . . . Now, I don't know how long it will be before the new civilization can make its own medical equipment. It could take anywhere from fifty to two hundred years, depending on whether we have to mark time waiting for a really large population or can get exponential tech growth with only a few thousand people.

"No one need die of old age; I'm willing to bobble the deathbed cases. But there *will* be old age. I'm not supplying age maintenance—and, with certain exceptions, I will not for at least a quarter century."

Wil was a biological twenty. Once, he'd let it slide to thirty—and discovered that he was not a type that aged gracefully. He remembered the flab, the belly that swelled over his pants.

Yelén smiled at him coldly. "Aren't you going to ask me about the exceptions?"

Damn you, thought Wil.

When he didn't reply, she continued. "The trivial exception: those so foolish or unfortunate as to be over bio-forty right now. I'll set their clocks back once.

"The important exception: any woman, for as long as she stays pregnant." Yelén sat back, a look of grim satisfaction on her face. "*That* should supply any backbone that is missing."

Wil stared at her wonderingly. Just a few minutes before, Yelén had been acting as a civilized person might, all amused by the Peacer/NM plans for central control. Now she was talking about running the low-techs' personal lives.

There was a long silence. Yelén understood the point. He could tell by the way she tried to stare him down. Finally her gaze broke. "Damn it, Brierson, it has to be done. And it's moral, too. We high-techs each *own* our medical equipment. We've agreed on this action. Just how we invest our charity is surely our business."

They had argued the theory before. Yelén's logic was a thin thing, going a bit beyond what shipwreck law Wil knew. After all, the advanced travelers had brought the low-techs here, and would not allow them to bobble out of the era. More clearly than ever, he understood Yelén's reaction to Tammy. It would take so little to destroy the settlement. And over the next few years, disaffection was bound to grow.

Like it or not, Wil was working for a government. *Sieg Heil.*

18

The mornings Wil devoted to research. He still had a lot of background to soak up. He wanted a basic understanding of the settlers, both low-tech and high. They all had pasts and skills; the more he knew, the less he might be surprised. At the same time, there were specific questions (suspicions) raised by his field trips and discussions with Yelén.

For instance: What corroboration was there for Tunç Blumenthal's story? Was he the victim of an accident—or a battle? Had it happened in 2210—or later, perhaps from within the Singularity itself?

It turned out there was physical evidence: Blumenthal's spacecraft. It was a small vehicle (Tunç called it a repair boat), massing just over three tonnes. The bow end was missing—not cut by the smooth curve of a bobble, but flash-evaporated. That hull had a million times the opacity of lead; some monstrous burst of gamma had vaporized a good hunk of it just as the boat bobbled out.

The boat's drive was "ordinary" antigravity—but in this case, it was a built-in characteristic of the hull material. The comm and life-support systems bore familiar trademarks; their mechanism was virtually unintelligible. The recycler was thirty centimeters across; there were no moving parts. It appeared to be as efficient as a planetary ecology.

Tunç could explain most of this in general terms. But the detailed explanations—the theory and the specs—had been in the boat's database. And that had been in Tunç's jacket, in the forward compartment.

The volatilized forward compartment. The processors that remained were compatible with the Korolevs', and Yelén had played with them quite a bit.

At one extreme was the lattice of monoprocessors and bobblers embedded in the hull. The monos were no smarter than a twentieth-century home computer, but each was less than one angstrom unit across. Each ran a simple program loop, 1E17 times a second. That program watched its processor's brothers for signs of catastrophe—and triggered an attached bobbler accordingly. Yelén's fighter fleet had nothing like it.

At the other extreme was the computer in Tunç's headband. It was massively parallel, and as powerful as a corporate mainframe of Yelén's time. Marta thought that, even without its database, Tunç's headband made him as important to the plan as any of the other high-techs. They had given him a good part of their advanced equipment in exchange for its use.

Brierson smiled as he read the report. There were occasional comments by Marta, but Yelén was the engineer and this was mainly her work. Where he could follow it at all, the tone was a mix of awe and frustration. It read as he imagined Benjamin Franklin's analysis of a jet aircraft might read. Yelén could study the equipment, but without Tunç's explanations its purpose would have been a mystery. And even knowing the purpose and the underlying principles of operation, she couldn't see how such devices could be built or why they worked so perfectly.

Wil's grin faded. Almost two centuries separated Ben Franklin from jet planes. Less than a decade stood between Yelén's expertise and this "repair boat." Wil knew about the acceleration of progress. It had been a fact of his life. But even in his time, there had been limits on how fast the marketplace could absorb new developments. Even if all these inventions could be made in just nine years—what about the installed base of older equipment? What about compatibility with devices not yet upgraded? How could the world of real products be turned inside out in such a short time?

Wil looked away from the display. So there was physical evidence, but it didn't prove much except that Tunç had been as far beyond the high-techs as they were beyond Wil. It really was surprising that Chanson had not accused Tunç—rescued from the sun with inexplicable equipment and a story no one could check—of being another alien. Perhaps Juan's paranoia was not as all-encompassing as it seemed.

He really should have another chat with Blumenthal.

Wil used a comm channel that Yelén said was private. Blumenthal was as calm and reasonable as before. "Sure, I can talk. The work I do for Yelén is mainly programming; very flexible hours."

"Thanks. I wanted to talk more about how you got bobbled. You said it was possible you were shanghaied. . . ."

Blumenthal shrugged. "It is possible. Yet most likely an accident it was. You've read about my company's project?"

"Just Yelén's summaries."

Tunç hesitated, swapped out. "Ah, yes. What she says is fair. We *were* running a matter/antimatter distillery. But look at the numbers. Yelén's stations can distill perhaps a kilo per day—enough to power a small business. We were in a different class entirely. My partners and I specialized in close solar work, less than five radii out. We had easements on most of the sun's southern hemisphere. When I . . . left, we were distilling one hundred thousand *tonnes* of matter and antimatter every *second*. That's enough to dim the sun, though we arranged things so the effect wasn't perceptible from the ecliptic. Even so, there were complaints. An absolute condition of our insurance was that we move it out promptly and without leakage. A few days' production would be enough to damage an unprotected solar system."

"Yelén's summary said you were shipping to the Dark Companion?" Like a lot of Yelén's commentary, the rest of that report had been technical, unintelligible without a headband.

"True!" Tunç's face came alight. "Such a fine idea it was. Our parent company liked big construction projects. Originally, they wanted to stellate Jupiter, but they couldn't buy the necessary options. Then we came along with a much bigger project. We were going to *implode* the Dark Companion, fashion of it a small Tipler cylinder." He noticed Wil's blank expression. "A naked black hole, Wil! A space warp! A gate for faster-than-light travel! Of course the Dark Companion is so small that the aperture would be only a few meters wide, and have tidal strains above 1E13 g's per meter—but with bobbles it might be usable. If not, there were plans to probe through it to the galactic core, and siphon back the power to widen it."

Tunç paused, some of his enthusiasm gone. "That was the plan, anyway. In fact, the distillery was almost too much for us. We were on site for days at a time. It gets on your nerves after a while, knowing that beyond all the shielding, the sun is stretched from horizon to horizon. But we had to stay; we couldn't tolerate transmission delays. It took all of us linked to our mainframe to keep the brew stable.

"We had stability, but we weren't shipping quite everything out. Something near a tonne per second began accumulating over the south pole. We needed a quick fix or we'd lose performance bonuses. I took the repair boat across to work on it. The problem was just ten thousand kilometers from our station—a thirty-millisecond time lag. Intellect nets run fine with that much lag, but this was process control; we were taking a chance. We'd accumulated a two-hundred-thousand-tonne backlog by then. It was all in flicker storage—a slowly exploding bomb. I had to repackage it and boost it out."

Tunç shrugged. "That's the last I remember. Somehow, we lost control; part of that backlog recombined. My boat bobbled up. Now, I was on the sun side of the brew. The blast rammed me straight into Sol. There was no way my partners could save me."

Bobbled into the sun. It was almost high-tech slang for certain death. "How could you ever escape?"

Blumenthal smiled. "You haven't read about that? There is no way in heaven *I* could have. On the sun, the only way you can survive is to stay in stasis. My initial bobbling was only for a few seconds. When it lapsed, the fail-safe did a quick lookabout, saw where we were heading, and rebobbled—sixty-four thousand years. That was 'effective infinity' to its pinhead program.

"I've done some simulations since. I hit the surface fast enough to penetrate thousands of kilometers. The bobble spent a few years following convection currents around inside. It wasn't as dense as the inner sunstuff. Eventually I percolated back to near the surface. Then, every time the bobble floated over a blow-off, it was boosted tens of thousands of kilometers up. . . . For thirty thousand years a damn volleyball I was, flying up to the corona, falling back through the photosphere, floating around awhile, then getting thrown up again.

"That's where I was through the Singularity and during the time the short-term travelers were being rescued. That's where I would have died if it hadn't been for Bil Sánchez." He paused. "You never knew

Bil. He dropped out, died about twenty million years ago. He was a nut about Juan Chanson's extermination theory. Most of Chanson's proof is on Earth; W. W. Sánchez traveled all over the Solar System looking for evidence. He dug up things Chanson never guessed at.

"One thing Bil did was scan for bobbles. He was convinced that sooner or later he'd find one containing somebody or somemachine that had escaped the 'Extinction.' When he spotted my bobble in the sun, he thought he'd hit the jackpot. Their latest records—from 2201 —didn't show any such bobbling. It was just the weird place you might expect to find a survivor; even the exterminators couldn't have reached someone down there.

"But Bil Sánchez was patient. He noticed that every few thousand years, a really big solar flare would blast me way up. He and the Korolevs diverted a comet, stored it off Mercury. The next time I was boosted off the surface, they were ready: They dropped the comet into a sun-grazing orbit. It picked me off at the top of my bounce. Fortunately, the snowball didn't break up and my bobble stuck on its surface; we swung around the sun, up into the cool. From there, the situation was much like their other rescues. Thirty thousand years later, I was back in realtime."

"Tunç, you lived closer to the Extinction than anyone else. What do *you* think caused it?"

The spacer sat back, crossed his arms. "That's what they all ask. . . . Ah, Wil Brierson, if I only knew! I tell them I don't know. And they go away, seeing each his own theory reflected in my story." He seemed to realize the answer was not going to satisfy. "Very well, my theories. Theory Alpha: Possible it is that mankind was exterminated. What Bil found in the Charon catacombs is hard to explain any other way. But it can't be like Juan Chanson says. Bil had it better: Anything that could bump off the intellect nets in Earth/Luna would needs be superhuman. If it's still around, no brave talk will save us. That's why Bil Sánchez and his little colony dropped out. Poor man, he was frightened of what might happen to anything bigger.

"And Theory Beta: This is what Yelén believes, and probably Della too—though she is still so shy, I can't tell for sure. Humankind and its machines became something better, something . . . unknowable. And I saw things that fit with that, too.

"Ever since the Peace War there have been more or less autonomous devices. For centuries, folks had been saying that machines as smart as people were just around the corner. Most didn't realize how unimportant such a thing would be. What was needed was *greater* than human intelligence. Between our processors and ourselves, my era was achieving that.

"My own company was small; there were only eight of us. We were backward, rural; the rest of humanity was hundreds of light-seconds away. The larger spacing firms were better off. Their computers were correspondingly bigger, and they had thousands of people linked. I had friends at Charon Corp and Stellation Inc. They thought we were crazy to stay so isolated. And when we visited their habitats, when the comm lag got to less than a second, I could see what they meant. There was power and knowledge and joy in those companies. . . . And they could plan circles around us. Our only advantage was mobility.

"Yet even these corporations were fragments, a few thousand people here and there. By the beginning of the twenty-third, there were three *billion* people in the Earth/Luna volume. Three billion people and corresponding processing power—all less than three light-seconds apart.

"I . . . it was strange, talking to them. We attended a marketing conference at Luna in 2209. Even linked, we never did understand what was going on." He was quiet for a long moment. "So you see, either theory fits."

Wil was not going to let him off that easily. "But your project—you say it would have meant faster-than-light travel. Is there any evidence what became of that?"

Tunç nodded. "Bil Sánchez visited the Dark Companion a couple times. It's the same dead thing it always was. There's no sign it was ever modified. I think that scared him even more than what he found at Charon. I know it scares me. I doubt my accident was enough to scuttle the plan: our project would have given humanity a gate to the entire Galaxy . . . but it was also mankind's first piece of cosmic engineering. If it worked, we wanted to do the same to a number of stars. In the end, we might have built a small Arp object in this arm of the Galaxy. Bil thought we'd been 'uppity cockroaches'—and the real owners finally stepped on us. . . .

"But don't you be buying Theory Alpha just yet. I said the Singularity was a mirrored thing. Theory Beta explains it just as well. In 2207, we were the hottest project at Stellation Inc. They put everything they had into renting those easements around the sun. But after 2209, the edge was gone from their excitement. At the marketing conference at Luna, it almost seemed Stellation's backers were trying to sell our project as a *frivolity.*"

Tunç stopped, smiled. "So you have my thumbnail sketch of Great Events. You can get it all, clearer said with more detail, from Yelén's databases." He cocked his head to one side. "Do you like listening to others so much, Wil Brierson, that you visit me first?"

Wil grinned back. "I wanted to hear you firsthand." *And I still don't understand you.* "I'm one of the earlier low-techs, Tunç. I've never experienced direct connect—much less the mind links you talk about. But I know how much it hurts a high-tech to go without a headband." All through Marta's diary, that loss was a source of pain. "If I understand what you say about your time, you've lost much more. How can you be so *cool?*"

The faintest shadow crossed Tunç's face. "It's not a mystery, really. I was nineteen when I left civilization. I've lived fifty years since. I don't remember much of the time right after my rescue. Yelén says I was in a coma for months. They couldn't find anything wrong with my body; just no one was home.

"I told you my little company was backward, rural. That's only by comparison with our betters. There were eight of us, four women, four men. Maybe I should call it a group marriage, because it was that, too. But it was more. We spent every spare gAu on our processor system and the interfaces. When we were linked up, we were something . . . wonderful. But now all that's memories of memories—no more meaningful to me than to you." His voice was soft. "You know, we had a mascot: a poor, sweet girl, close to anencephalic. Even with prosthesis she was scarcely brighter than you or I. Most of the time she was happy." The expression on his face was wistful, puzzled. "And most of the time, I am happy, too."

19

Then there was Marta's diary. He had started reading it as a casual cross-check on Yelén and Della. It had become a dark addiction, the place he spent the hours after his late-night arguments with Yelén, the hours after returning from his field trips.

What might have happened if Wil had been less a gentleman the night of the Robinson party? Marta was dead before he really knew her; but she looked a little like Virginia . . . and talked like her . . . and laughed like her. The diary was the only place where he could ever know her now. And so every night ended with new gloom, matched only by the dreams of morning.

Of course Marta found the West End mines bobbled. She stayed a few months, and left some billboards. It was not safe country. Packs of doglike creatures roamed. At one point she was trapped, had to start a grass fire and play mirror tag with the dogs among the bobbles. Wil read that part several times; it made him want to laugh and cry in the same breath. For Marta, it was just part of staying alive. She moved northwards, into the foothills of the Kampuchean Alps. That was where Yelén found her third cairn.

Marta reached the Peacer bobble two years after she was marooned. She had walked and sailed around the Inland Sea to do it. The last six hundred kilometers had been a climb over the Kampuchean Alps. She was still an optimist, yet her words were sometimes tinged with self-mockery. She had started out to walk halfway around the world, and ended up less than two thousand kilometers north of where she started. Despite her year's layover, the shattered bones in her foot had not healed perfectly. Till she was rescued (her usual phrasing) she would walk with a limp. At the end of a long day's walk she was in some pain.

But she had plans. The Peacer bobble was at the center of a vitrified plain 150 kilometers across. Even now, not much life had returned. Her first walk in, she carried all her food on the travois.

< < The bobble isn't super large, maybe three hundred meters across. But its setting is spectacular, Lelya; I had not remembered the details. It's in a small lake bordered by uniform cliffs. Concentrically around those cliffs are rings of ridges. I climbed to the edge of the cliffs and looked across at the bobble. My reflection looked back and we waved at each other. With its moat and the ringwall, it looks like a jewel in a setting. Equally spaced along the wall are five smaller gems—the bobbles around our lookout equipment. Whoever—whatever—marooned me has locked them up, too. But for how long? Those five were supposed to have a very high flicker rate. I still can't believe anyone could subvert our control systems for a jump of longer than a few decades.

< < Wouldn't it be a joke if I were rescued by the *Peacers!* They thought they were making a fifty-year jump to renewed dominion. What a shock it would be to come out on an empty world, and find exactly one taxpayer left. Amusing, but I'd rather be rescued by you, Lelya. . . .

< < The jewel's setting is cracked in places. There's a waterfall coming into the lake on the south side. The water exits through a break in the north wall. It's very clear; I can see fish in the lake. There are places where the cliff has collapsed. It looks like it could make decent soil. This is probably the most habitable spot in the whole destruction zone. If I have to stop, Lelya, I think this is really the best place it could happen. It's the most likely to be monitored; it's at the center of a glazed flatland that should be easy to mark up. (Do you think our L5 autons would respond to KILROY IS HERE written in letters a kilometer long?)

< < So. This will be my base, forever till I'm rescued. I think I can make it a nice place to live, Lelya. > >

And Marta did. Through the first ten years she made steady improvements. Five times she trekked out of the glazed zone, sometimes for necessities like seed and wood, later to import some friends: she

450

hiked three hundred kilometers north, to a large lake. There were fishermonkeys on that lake. She understood their matriarchal scheme now. It wasn't hard to find displaced trios wandering the shores, looking for something bigger than they that walked on two legs. The fishers loved the ringlake. By year twelve, there were so many that some left every year down the river.

From her cabin high on the ringwall she watched them by the hour:

< < Back and forth in water and bobble there are reflections of the ringwall and my cabin and our bobbled monitors. The fishers love to play with their reflections. Often they swim against its surface. I'll bet they feel the reflected body heat, even through their pelts. I wonder what mythology they have about the kingdom beyond the mirror. . . . Yes, Lelya. Sentiment is one thing, fantasy another. But, you know, my fishers are smarter than chimpanzees. If I'd seen them before we left civilization, I'd have bet they would evolve human intelligence. Sigh. After all our travels, I know better. In the short term, the marine adaptation is more profitable. Another five megayears, they'll be as agile as penguins—and not much brighter. > >

Marta gave names to the friendliest, and the weirdest. There was always a Hewey and a Dewey and a Lewey. Others she named after humans. Wil found himself chuckling. Over the years, there were several Juan Chansons and Jason Mudges—usually the most compulsive chitterers. There was also a succession of Della Lus—all small, pale, shy. And there was even one W. W. Brierson. Wil read that page twice, a trembling smile on his lips. Wil the fishermonkey was black-furred and large, even bigger than a dominant female. He could have run the whole show, but kept mostly to himself and watched everyone else. Every so often his reserve broke and he gave a great screeching display, rushing along the edge of the ringwall and slapping his sides. Like the first Dewey, he was odd man out, and especially friendly to Marta. He spent more time with her than any of them. They all played at imitating her, but he was the most successful. She actually got some useful work out of him, pulling small bundles. His most impressive game was the building of miniature versions of the pyramidal cairn Marta used to store the completed portion of her diary. Marta never said he was her favorite, yet she did seem fond of him. He disappeared on her last big expedition, around year fifteen.

< < I'll never name one of my little friends after you, Lelya. The

fishers live only ten or fifteen years. It's always sad when they go. I don't want to go through that with a fisher named Yelén. > >

As the years passed, Marta concentrated on the diary. This was where the words piled into the millions. She had lots of advice for Yelén. There were some interesting revelations: It had been Phil Genet who persuaded Yelén to raise the Peacer bobble while the NMs were in realtime. It had been Phil Genet who was behind the ash-shoveling incident. Genet consistently argued that the key to success lay in the explicit intimidation of the low-techs. Marta begged Yelén not to take his advice again. < < We will be hated enough, feared enough, even if we act like saints. > >

In the middle decades, her writing was scarcely a diary at all, but a collection of essays and stories, poems and whimsy. She spent at least as much time with her sketches and paintings. There were dozens of paintings of the ringlake and bobble, under every kind of lighting. There were landscapes done from sketches she had made on her trips. There were portraits of many of the fishers, as well as pictures of Marta herself. In one, the artist knelt at the edge of the ringlake, smiling at her own reflection as she painted it.

It came to Wil that though there were periods of depression, and physical pain, and occasional moments of stark terror, most of the time *Marta was having a good time*. She even said so:

< < If I'm rescued, all this becomes a diversion, a few decades on top of the two centuries I have already lived. If I'm not . . . well, I know you'll be back sometime. I want you to know that I missed you, but that there were pleasures. Take all the pictures and poems as my evidence and as my gift. > >

It was not a gift for W. W. Brierson. He tried to read it straight through, but the afternoon came when he couldn't go on. Someday he would read of those happy, middle times. Perhaps someday he could smile and laugh with her. Just now, all he felt was a horrid need to follow Marta Qen Korolev through her last years. Even as he skipped the data set forward, he wondered at himself. Unlike Marta, he *knew* how it all ended, yet he was forcing himself to see it all again through Marta's eyes. Was there some crazy part of him that thought that by reading her words he could take some of the pain from her onto himself?

More likely, this was like his daughter Anne's reaction to *The Worms*

Within. The movie had been in a festival of twentieth-century film that came with the kid's new data set. It turned out that part of the festival was horror movies from the 1990s. The old USA had been at the height of its power and wealth then; for some perverse reason, slash-and-splash had its greatest flowering the same decade. Wil wondered if they would have spent so much time inventing blood and gore if they had known what was waiting for them just around the corner in the twenty-first; or maybe they feared such a future, and the gore was their way of knocking wood. In any case, Anne rushed out of her room after the first fifteen minutes, almost hysterical. They trashed the video, but she couldn't get the story out of her mind. Unknown to Wil and Virginia, she bought a replacement and every night watched a little more—just enough to make her sick again. Afterwards she said she kept watching it—even though it got more and more horrible— because there had to be *something* that would happen that would make up for the wounds she'd already suffered. Of course, there was no such redemption. The ending was even more imaginatively grotesque than she feared. Anne had been depressed and a little irrational for months afterwards.

Wil grimaced. Like daughter like father. And he didn't even have Anne's excuse; he knew how this one ended.

In those last years, Marta's life slowly darkened. She had completed her great construction, the sign that should alert any orbital monitors. It was a clever scheme: She had journeyed out of the glazed zone, to where a few isolated jacarandas grew. She gathered the spiders she found on the display webs and took them into the desolation. By this time she had discovered the relation of those webs to tree and spider reproduction. She set spiders and seeds at ten carefully selected sites along a line from the center of the glazed zone. Each was on a tiny stream; at each she had broken through the glaze and developed a real soil. Over the next thirty years, the spiders and their sprouts did most of the construction. The seedlings spread a small way down the streams, but not as much as ordinary plants. The spiders saw the faraway display webs of their brethren and thousands of seeds were deposited on the path between, each with a complement of arachnid paratroopers.

In the end, she had the vast green-and-silver arrow that did eventually alert an orbiter. But a problem came with that line of trees. They broke the glaze, made a bridge of soil from her base to the outside. The jacs and spiders were awesome defenders of their territory, but not perfect ones—especially when strung thin. Other plants infested the sides of their run. With those plants came herbivores.

< < The little buggers have added a couple of hours' work to each day, Lelya. And some of my favorite fruits I can't grow at all now. > >

Ten or even twenty years into the abandonment, this would have been an inconvenience. At thirty-five years, Marta's health was beginning to fail. Competing with the rabbity thieves was a slowly losing proposition for her.

< < Somewhere in a cairn on the far side of the sea, I said some very foolish things. Didn't I figure an unaided human lived about a century? And then I said something about being conservative and expecting I could last only seventy-five years. What a laugh.

< < My foot has never gotten better, Lelya. I walk with a crutch now, and not very fast. Most of the time, my joints hurt. It's funny what not feeling good does to your attitude and your notion of time. I can scarcely believe there was a day when I expected to walk to Canada. Or that just fifteen years ago I still hiked out of the glazed zone regularly. Lelya, it's a major effort to climb down to the lake now. I haven't done it for weeks. I may not do it again. But I have a rain cistern . . . and the fishers are always happy to visit me up here. Besides, I don't like to see my reflection in the lake anymore. I'm not doing any more self-portraits, Lelya.

< < Is this what it was like for people before decent medical care? The failed dreams, the horizons that shrink always inwards? It must have taken guts to do all they did. > >

Two years later:

< < Today the neighborhood went to hell. I have a pack of near-dogs camped just over the ringwall. They look a lot like the ones at the mines, though these are smaller. In fact, they're kind of cute, like big puppies with pointy ears. I'd like to kill the lot of them. An un-Marta-like thought, granted, but they've driven the fishers away from my cabin. They killed Lewey. I got a couple of the little murderers with my pike. Since then, they've been extremely wary of me. Now I carry a pike and knife when I'm out of doors. > >

Marta spent most of her last year in the cabin. Outside, her garden went to weeds. There were edible roots and vegetables still, but they were scattered around. Getting out to gather them was an expedition as challenging as a hundred-kilometer walk had been before. The near-dogs grew bolder; they circled just outside the diamond tip of her pike, darted occasionally inwards. Marta had several pelts to prove that she was still the faster. But it could not last. She was eating poorly. That made it harder for her to gather food. . . . A downward spiral.

Wil paged the display and found himself looking at ordinary type-script. He felt his stomach drop. Was this the end? An ordinary entry and then . . . nothing? He forced his eyes through the words. It was a commentary from Yelén: Marta had not intended the next page to be seen. Her words had been rubbed out, then overwritten by a later diary entry. "You said you'd walk if you didn't see everything, Brierson. Well, here it is. Damn you." He could almost hear the bitterness in Yelén's words. He looked down the page.

< < *Oh God Yelen help me. If you ever lovd me save me now. I am dying dying. I dont want to die. Oh please please pleas* > >

He paged again, and was looking at Marta's familiar script. If any-thing, the letters were more finely drawn than usual. He imagined her in the dark cabin, patiently rubbing away the words of her despair, then overwriting them, cool and analytical. Wil wiped his face and tried not to breathe. A deep breath would start him sobbing. He read Marta's final entry.

< < Dearest Lelya,

< < I suppose there must be an end to optimism, at least locally. I've been holed up in my cabin for ten days now. There is water in the cistern, but I'm out of food. Damn dogthings; without them, I could have lasted another twenty years. They cut me up pretty bad the last time I was out. For a while, I thought to make a grand stand, give them a last taste of my diamonds. I've changed my mind about that; last week I saw them take on a grazer. Yes, one of those: bigger than I am, with a horn almost as effective as my pike. I couldn't see all of it, just when they were in view from my windows, but. . . . At first it looked like they were playing. They nipped at it, sending it scurrying round and round. But I could see the blood. Finally, it weakened, tripped.

< < I never noticed this when they got smaller animals, but the dogs don't deliberately kill their prey. They just eat them alive, usually from the guts out. That grazer was big; it took a while to die.

< < So. I'm staying inside. "Forever until you rescue me" was how I

used to say it. I guess I don't expect a rescue anymore. With lookabouts scheduled every few decades (at best), the odds are against one happening in the next few days.

< < I figure it's been about forty years since I was marooned. It seems so much longer, longer than all the rest of my life. Nature's kindly way of stretching mortals' meager rations? I remember my fisher friends better than most of my human ones. I can see the lake through one window. If they looked, they could see me up here. They rarely look. I don't think most of them remember me. It's been three years since they were driven away from the cabin. That's almost a fisher generation. The only one I think remembers is my last Juan Chanson. This one's not as loud as my earlier Juans. Mainly, he sits around, taking in the sun. . . . I just looked out the window. He's there now; I do think he remembers. > >

The handwriting changed. Wil wondered how many hours—or days —had passed from one paragraph to the next. The new lines were crossed out, but Yelén's magic made them clear:

< < I just remembered a strange word: taphonomy. Once upon a time, I could be an expert in a field just by remembering its name. Now . . . all I know . . . it's the study of death sites, no? A crumple of bones is all these mortal creatures leave . . . and I know that bones get swept away so fast. Not mine, though. Mine stay indoors. I'll be here a long time, my writing longer. . . . Sorry. > >

She didn't have the energy to erase the words. There was a gap, and her writing became regular, each letter carefully printed.

< < I have the feeling I'm saying things I've written you before, contingencies that now are certainties. I hope you get all my earlier writing. I tried to put all the details there, Lelya. I want you to have something to work for, dear. Our plan can still succeed. When it does, our dreams live.

< < You are for all time my dearest friend, Lelya. > >

Marta did not finish the entry with her usual sign-off. Perhaps she thought to write more later. Further down, there was a pattern of disconnected lines. Through an exercise of imagination, one might see them as the block letters L O V.

That was all.

It didn't matter; Wil wasn't reading anymore. He lay with his face in his arms, sobbing on empty lungs. This was the daytime version of the dream in blue; he could never wake from this.

Seconds passed. The blue changed to rage, and Wil was on his feet. *Someone had done this to Marta.* W. W. Brierson had been shanghaied, separated from his family and his world, thrown into a new one. But Derek Lindemann's crime was a peccadillo, laughable, hardly worth Wil's attention. *Compared to what was done to Marta.* Someone had taken her from her friends, her love, and then squeezed the life from her, year by year, drop by drop.

Someone must die for this. Wil stumbled across the room, searching. In the back of his mind, a rational fragment watched in wonder that his feelings could run so deep, that he could truly run amok. Then even the fragment was swallowed up.

Something hit him. A wall. Wil struck back, felt satisfying pain shooting through his fist. As he pulled his arm from the wall, he noticed motion in the next room. He ran towards the figure, and it towards him. He struck and struck. Glass flew in all directions.

Then he was in sunlight, and on his knees. Wil felt a penetrating coldness in the back of his neck. He sighed and sat down. He was on the street, surrounded by broken glass and what looked like parts of his living-room walls. He looked up. Yelén and Della were standing just beyond the pile of debris. He hadn't seen them in person and together for weeks. It must be something important. "What happened?" Funny. His throat hurt, as though he'd been shouting.

Yelén stepped over a fallen timber and bent to look at him. Behind her, Wil saw two large fliers. At least six autons hung in the air above the women. "That's what we would like to know, Inspector. Were you attacked? Our guards heard screaming and the sounds of a fight."

. . . *and every so often he gave a great screeching display, rushing about and slapping his sides.* Marta had named her fishers well. Wil looked at his bloody hands. The tranq Yelén had used on him was fast-acting stuff. He could think and remember, but emotions were distant, muted things. "I, I was reading the end of Marta's diary. Got carried away."

"Oh." Korolev's pale lips tightened. How could she be so cool? Surely she had gone through this, too. Then Wil remembered the century Yelén had spent alone with the diary and the cairns. Her harshness would be easier to understand in the future.

Della walked closer, her boots crunching on broken glass. Lu's outfit was dead black, like something from a twentieth-century police state. Her arms were folded across her chest. Her dark eyes were calm and distant. No doubt her current personality matched her clothes. "Yes. The diary. It's a depressing document. Perhaps you should choose other leisure-time reading."

The remark should have done something to his blood pressure, but Wil felt nothing.

Yelén was more explicit. "I don't know why you insist on mucking around in Marta's personal life, Brierson. She said everything she knew about the case right at the beginning. The rest is none of your damned business." She glanced at his hands, and a small robot swooped down. Wil felt something cold and soft work between his fingers. Yelén sighed. "Okay. I guess I understand; we are that much alike. And I still need you. . . . Take a couple of days off. Get yourself together." She started back to her flier.

"Uh, Yelén," said Della. "Are we going to leave him here alone?"

"Of course not. I'm wasting three extra autons on him."

"I mean, when the GriefStop wears off, Brierson may be very distressed." Something flickered in her eyes. She looked momentarily puzzled, searching through nine thousand years of memories—perhaps more important, nine thousand years of viewpoints. "When a person is like that, don't they need someone to help them . . . someone to, uh, *hug* them?"

"Hey, don't look at me!"

"Right." Her eyes were calm again. "It was just a thought." The two departed.

Wil watched their fliers disappear over the trees. Around him, broken glass was being vacuumed up, the torn walls removed. Already his hands felt warm and comfortable. He sat in the roadway, at peace. Eventually he would get hungry and go inside.

20

After supper, Wil sat for a long time in the ruins of his living room. He was directly responsible for very little of the destruction: He had punched bloody holes in one wall and demolished a mirror. The guard autons had let that go on for perhaps fifteen seconds before deciding it was a threat to his safety. Then they bobbled him: The walls near the mirror were cut by a clean, curving line. A smooth depression dipped thirty centimeters below the floor, into the foundation. Even the bobbling had not caused the worst damage. That happened when Yelén and Della cut the bobble out of the house. Apparently they wanted their equipment to have a direct view when it burst. He looked at the wall clock. It was the same day as before; they'd kept him on ice just long enough to get him out of the house.

If Wil's sense of humor had been enabled, he might have smiled. All this supported Yelén's claim that the house was not infested by her equipment. The best the protection autons could do was bobble everything and call for help.

Things were different now. From where he sat, Wil saw several robots foaming a temporary wall. Beside his chair sat a medical auton, about as animated as a garbage can. Somewhere it had hands; they'd been a big help with supper.

He watched the reconstruction with interest, even turned on the room lights when night came. This GriefStop was great stuff. Simple drives like hunger weren't affected. He felt as alert and coordinated as

459

usual. He was simply beyond the reach of emotion; yet, strangely, it was easy to imagine how things would affect him without the drug. And that knowledge did make for some weak motivation. For instance, he hoped the Dasguptas would not stop by on their way home. He guessed that explanations would be difficult.

Wil stood and walked to his reading table. The auton glided silently after him. Something smaller floated up from the mantel. He sat down, suddenly guessing that GriefStop had never been a hit on the recreational drug market. There were side effects: Everything moved a little bit slow. Sounds came low-pitched, drawn out. It wasn't enough to panic him (he doubted if anything could do that just now), but reality had a faint edge of waking nightmare. His silent visitors intensified the feeling. . . . Ah well, paranoia was the name of the game.

He turned on his desk lamp, cut the room lights. Somehow the destruction had spared the desk and reading display. The last page of Marta's diary floated in the circle of light. He guessed that rereading that page would be very upsetting to his normal self—so he didn't look at it. Della was right. There ought to be better leisure-time activities. This day would hang his normal self low for a long time to come. He hoped that he wouldn't come back to the diary, to tear at the wounds he'd opened today. Perhaps he should erase it; the inconvenience of coercing another copy from Yelén might be enough to save his normal self.

Wil spoke into the darkness. "House. Delete Marta's diary." The display showed his command and the ideation net associated with "Marta's diary."

"The whole thing?" the house asked.

Wil's hand hovered over the commit. "Unh, no. Wait." Curiosity was a powerful thing with Brierson. He'd just remembered something that could force his normal self to go against all common sense and retrieve another copy. Better check it out now, *then* zap the diary.

When he first received the diary, he'd asked for all references to himself. There had been four. He had seen three: She'd mentioned calling him back from the beach the day of the Peacer rescue. There'd been the fisher she'd named after him. Then, around year thirty-eight, she'd recommended Yelén use his services—even though she'd forgotten his name by then. That was the reference which hurt so much the first time he looked at the document. Wil guessed he could forgive that now; those years would have destroyed the soul of a lesser person, not simply blurred a few memories.

But what was the fourth reference? Wil repeated the context search. Ah. No wonder he had missed it. It appeared about year thirteen, tucked away in one of her essays on the plan. In this one, she wrote on each of the low-techs she remembered, citing strengths and weaknesses, trying to guess how they would react to the plan. In a sense it was a foolish exercise—Marta granted that much more elaborate analysis existed on the Korolev db's—but she hoped her "time of solitude" had given her new insights. Besides (unsaid), she needed to be doing something useful in the years that stretched before her.

< < Wil Brierson. An important one. I never believed the commercial mythology, much less the novels his son wrote. Yet . . . since we've known him in person, I've concluded he may be almost as sharp as they make him out to be. At least in some ways. If you and I can't figure out who did this to me, he might still be able to.

< < Brierson has a lot of respect among the low-techs. That and his general competence would be a real help against Steve Fraley and whoever will run the Peacer show. But what if he opposes our plan? That may seem ridiculous; he was born in a civilized era. Yet I'm not sure of the man. One thing about civilization, it allows the most extreme types to find a niche where they can live to their own and others' benefit. Here, we are temporarily beyond civilization; people we could abide before might now be dangerous. Wil is still disoriented; maybe that accounts for his behavior. But he may have a mean, irrational streak under his friendly exterior. I only have one piece of evidence, something I've been a little ashamed to tell you about:

< < You know I was attracted to the guy. Well, he followed me when I stormed out of Don Robinson's show. Now, I wasn't trying to flirt; I was just so mad at Don's sneakiness, I had to open up to someone— and you were in deep connect. We talked for several minutes before I realized that the pats on my shoulder, the hand at my waist, were not brotherly comfort. It was my fault for letting it get that far, but he wouldn't take no for an answer. The guy is big; he actually started knocking me around. If the rest of the evening hadn't begun my great "adventure," the bruises he left on my chest would have had medical attention. You see, Lelya? Mean to beat me when I refused him. Irrational for doing it with Fred just five meters away. I had to suppress the

auton's reflexes, or Brierson would have been stunned for a week. Finally, I slapped his face as hard as I could, and threatened him with Fred. He backed off then, and seemed genuinely embarrassed. > >

Wil read the paragraph again and again. It hung in the circle of light from his desk lamp . . . and not one letter changed. He wondered how his normal self would react to Marta's words. Would he be enraged? Or simply crushed that she could say such a lie?

He thought for a long time, vaguely aware of the nightmare edge of the darkness around him. Finally he knew. The reaction would not be rage, would not be hurt. When he could feel again, there would be *triumph:*

The case had cracked. For the first time, he knew he would get Marta's murderer.

21

Yelén gave him the promised two days off and even removed the autons from his house. When he walked near a window, he could see something hovering just below the sill. He had no doubt it would come rushing in at the smallest sign of erratic behavior. Wil did his best to give no such sign. He did all his research away from the windows; Yelén might see his return to the diary as a bad method of recuperating.

But now Wil wasn't reading the diary. He was using all the (feeble) automation at his command to *study* it.

When Yelén came around with her list of places to visit and low-techs to talk to, Wil begged off. Forty-eight hours was not enough, he said. He needed to rest, to avoid the case completely.

The tactic bought him a week of uninterrupted quiet—probably enough time to squeeze the last clues from Marta's story; almost enough time to prepare his strategy. The seventh day, Yelén was on the holo again. "No more excuses, Bricrson. I've been talking to Della." *The great human-relations expert?* thought Wil. "We don't think you're doing anything to help yourself. Three times the Dasguptas have tried to get you out of the house; you put them off the same way you do me. We think your 'recuperation' is an exercise in self-pity.

"So"—she smiled coldly—"your vacation is over." A light gleamed at the base of his data set. "I just sent you a record of the party Fraley threw yesterday. I got his speech and most of the related conversation. As usual, I think I'm missing nuances. I want you to—"

Wil resisted the impulse to straighten his slumped shoulders; his plan might as well begin now. "Any more evidence of high-tech interference?"

"No. I would scarcely need your help to detect *that*. But—"

Then the rest scarcely matters. But he didn't say it out loud. Not yet. "Okay, Yelén. Consider me back from psych leave."

"Good."

"But before I go after this Fraley thing, I want to talk to you and Della. Together."

"Jesus Christ, Brierson! I need you, but there are limits." She looked at him. "Okay. It'll be a couple of hours. She's beyond Luna, closing down some of my operations." Yelén's holo flicked off.

It was a long two hours. This meeting was supposed to be a surprise. He wouldn't have forced things if he'd known Lu was not immediately available. Wil watched the clock; now he was stuck.

Just short of 150 minutes later, Yelén was back. "Okay, Brierson, how may we humor you?"

A second holo came to life, showing Della Lu. "Are you back at Town Korolev, Della?" Wil asked.

There was no time lag to her reply. "No. I'm at my home, about two hundred klicks above you. Do you really want me on the ground?"

"Uh, no." *You may be in the best possible position.* "Okay, Della, Yelén. I have a quick question. If the answer is no, then I hope you will quickly make it yes. . . . Are you *both* still providing me with heavy security?"

"Sure." "Yes."

That would have to be good enough. He leaned forward and spoke slowly. "There are some things you should know. Most important: Marta knew who murdered her."

Silence. Yelén's impatience was blown away; she simply stared. But when she spoke, her voice was flat, enraged. "You stupid jerk. If she knew, why didn't she tell us? She had forty years to tell us." On the other holo, Della appeared to be swapped out. *Has she already imagined the consequences?*

"Because, Yelén, all through those forty years she was being watched by the murderer, or his autons. And she knew *that,* too."

Again, silence. This time it was Della who spoke. "How do *you* know this, Wil?" The distant look was gone. She was intent, neither accepting nor rejecting his assertions. He wondered if this were her original peace-cop personality looking out at him.

"I don't think Marta herself guessed the truth during the first ten years. When she did, she spent the rest of her life playing a double game with the diary—leaving clues that would not alert the murderer, yet which could be understood later."

Yelén bent forward, her hands clenched. "What clues?"

"I don't want to say just yet."

"Brierson, I lived with that diary for a hundred years. For a hundred years I read it, analyzed it with programs you can't even imagine. And I lived with Marta for almost two hundred years before that. I knew every secret, every thought." Her voice was shaking; he hadn't seen such lethal fury in her since right after the murder. "You opportunistic slime. You say she left thoughts *you* could follow and *I* could not!"

"Yelén!" Della's interruption froze Korolev in midrage. For a moment, both women were silent, staring.

Yelén's hands went limp; she seemed to shrink in on herself. "Of course. I wasn't thinking."

Della nodded, and glanced at Wil. "Perhaps we should spell this out for you." She smiled. "Though I suspect you're way ahead of us. *If* the murderer had access to realtime while Marta was marooned, then there are consequences, some so radical that they caused us to dismiss the possibility.

"The killer did more than meddle with the length of the group jump; he did not even participate in it. That means the sabotage was not a shallow manipulation of the Korolev system; the killer must have deep penetration of the system."

Wil nodded. *And who could have deeper penetration than the owner of the system?*

"And if that is true, then everything that goes through Yelén's db's —including this conversation—may be known to the enemy. It's conceivable that her own weapons might be turned against us. . . . In your place, I'd be a bit edgy, Wil."

"Even granting Brierson's claims, the rest doesn't necessarily follow.

The killer could have left an unlisted auton in realtime. That could be what Marta noticed." But the fire was gone from Yelén's voice. She didn't look up from the pinkish marble of her desk.

Wil said softly, "You don't really believe that, do you?"

". . . No. In forty years, Marta could have outsmarted one of those, could have left clues that even *I* would recognize." She looked up at him. "Come on, Inspector. Get it over with. 'If the murderer could get into realtime, then why did she let Marta survive there?' That's the next rhetorical question, isn't it? And the obvious answer—'It's just the sort of irrational thing a jealous lover might do.' So. I admit to being a jealous type. And I surely loved Marta. But no matter what either of you believes, I did not maroon her."

She was on the far side of anger. It was not quite the reaction Wil had expected. It really affected Yelén that her two closest colleagues— "friends" was still too strong a word—might think she had killed Marta. Given her general insensitivity to the perceptions of others, he doubted her performance was an act. Finally he said, "I'm not accusing you, Yelén. . . . You're capable of violence, but you have honor. I trust you." That last was a necessary exaggeration. "I would like some trust in return. Believe me when I say that Marta knew, that she left clues that you would not notice. Hell, she probably did it to protect you. The moment you got suspicious, the murderer would also be alerted. Instead, Marta tried to talk to me. I'm totally disconnected from your system, an inconsequential low-tech. I've had a week to think on the problem, to figure how to get this news to you with minimum risk of an ambush."

"Yet, for all the clues, you don't really know who the killer is."

Wil smiled. "That's right, Della. If I did, it would have been the first thing I said."

"You would have been safer to keep quiet, then, till you had her whole message figured out."

He shook his head. "Unfortunately, Marta could never risk putting solid information in her diary. There's nothing in any of the four cairns that will tell us the killer's name."

"So you've told us this just to raise our blood pressure? If she could communicate all you say, she sure as hell would tell us the enemy's name." Yelén was clearly recovering.

"She did, but not in any of the four cairns. She knew those would be 'inspected' before you ever saw them; only the subtlest clues would escape detection. What I've discovered is that there's a *fifth* cairn that no one, not even the murderer, knew about. That's where she wrote the clear truth."

"Even if you're right, that's fifty thousand years ago now. Whatever she left would be completely destroyed."

Wil put on his most sober expression. "I know that, Yelén, and Marta must have known it could be that long, too. I think she took that into account."

"So you know where it is, Wil?"

"Yes. At least to within a few kilometers. I don't want to say exactly where; I assume we have a silent partner in this conversation."

Della shrugged. "It's conceivable the enemy doesn't have direct bugs. He may have access only when certain tasks are executing."

"In any case, I suggest you keep a close watch on the airspace above all the places Marta visited. The murderer may have some guesses of his own now. We don't want to be scooped."

There was silence as Della and Yelén retreated into their systems. Then: "Okay, Brierson. We're set. We have heavy monitoring of the south shore, the pass Marta used through the Alps, and the whole area around Peacer Lake. I've given Della observer status on my system. She'll be running critical subsystems in parallel. If anybody starts playing games there, she should notice.

"Now. The important thing. Della is bringing in fighters from the Lagrange zones. I have a fleet I've been keeping in stasis; its next lookabout is in three hours. All together that should be enough to face down any opposition when we go treasure hunting. All you have to do is lie low for another three hours. Then tell us the cairn's location and we'll—"

Wil held up a hand. "Yes. Get your guns. But I'm going along."

"What? Okay, okay. You can come along."

"And I don't want to leave till tomorrow morning. I need a few more hours with the diary; some final things to check out."

Yelén opened her mouth, but no sound came. Della was more articulate. "Wil. Surely *you* understand the situation. We're bringing everything out to protect you. We'll be burning a normal year's worth of consumables every hour we stay on station around you. We can't do that for long; yet every minute you keep this secret, you stay at the top of someone's hit list—and we lose what little surprise we might have had. You've *got* to hustle."

"There are things I have to figure first. Tomorrow morning. It's the fastest I can make it. I'm sorry, Della."

Yelén muttered an obscenity and cut her connection. Even Della seemed startled by the abruptness of her departure. She looked back at Wil. "She's still cooperating, but she's mad as hell. . . . Okay. So we wait till tomorrow. But believe me, Wil. An active defense is expensive. Yelén and I are willing to spend most of what we have to get the killer, but waiting till tomorrow cuts the protection per unit time. . . . It would help if you could say how long things might drag out beyond that."

He pretended to think on the question. "We'll have the secret diary by tomorrow afternoon. If things don't blow up by then, I doubt they ever will."

"I'll be going, then." She paused. "You know, Wil, once upon a time I was a government cop. I think I was pretty good at power games. So. Advice from an old pro: Don't get in over your head."

Brierson summoned his most confident, professional look. "Everything will work out, Della."

After Della signed off, Wil went into the kitchen. He started to mix himself a drink, realized he had no business drinking just now, and scarfed some cake instead. *Under all this pressure, it's just one bad habit or another,* he told himself. He wandered back into the living room and looked out. In his era, letting a protected witness parade in front of a window would be insanity. It didn't matter much here, with the weapons and countermeasures the high-techs had.

The afternoon was clear, dry. He could hear dry rustling in the trees. Only a short stretch of road was visible. All the greenery didn't leave much to see. The only nice views were from the second floor. Still, he was getting fond of the place. It was a bit like the lower-class digs he and Virginia had started in.

He leaned out the window, looked straight up. The two autons were floating lower than usual. Farther up, almost lost in the haze, was something *big*. He tried to imagine the forces that must be piled up in the first few hundred klicks above him. He knew the firepower Della and Yelén admitted to. It far exceeded the combined might of all the nations in history; it was probably greater than that of any police service up to the mid-twenty-second. All that force was poised for the protection of one house, one man . . . more precisely, the information in one man's head. All things considered, it wasn't something he took much comfort in.

Wil reviewed the scenarios once more; what could happen in the next twenty-four hours? It would all be over by then, most likely. He was barely conscious of pacing into the kitchen, through the pantry, the laundry, the guest room, and back into the living room. He looked out the window, then repeated the traversal in reverse order. It was a habit that had not been popular with Virginia and the kids: When he was really into a case, he would wander all through the house, cogitating. Ninety kilos of semiconscious cop lumbering down halls and through doorways was a definite safety hazard. They had threatened to hang a cowbell around his neck.

Something brought Brierson out of the depths. He looked around the laundry, trying to identify the strangeness. Then he realized: He'd been humming, and there was a silly grin on his face. He was back in his element. This was the biggest, most dangerous case of his life. But it was a *case*. And he finally had a handle on it. For the first time since he had been shanghaied, the doubts and dangers were ones he could deal with professionally. His smile widened. Back in the living room, he grabbed his data set and sat down. Just in case they were listening, he should pretend to do some research.

22

Yelén was back late that evening. "Kim Tioulang is dead."

Wil's head snapped up. *Is this how it begins?* "When? How?"

"Less than ten minutes ago. Three bullets in the head. . . . I'm sending you the details."

"Any evidence who—"

She grimaced, but by now she accepted that what she sent was not immediately part of his memory. "Nothing definite. My security at North Shore has been thin since we switched things around this afternoon. He sneaked out of the Peacer base; not even his own people noticed. It looks like he was trying to board a trans-sea shuttle." The only place that would take him was Town Korolev. "There are no witnesses. In fact, I suspect that no one was on the ground where he was shot. The slugs were dumb exploders, New Mexico five-millimeters." Normally those were pistol-fired, with a max accurate range of thirty meters; who did the killer think he was fooling? "The coincidence is too much to ignore, Brierson. You're right; the enemy must have bugs in my system."

"Yeah." For a second he wasn't listening. He was remembering the North Shore picnic, the withered man that had been Kim Tioulang. He was as tough as anyone Wil had ever met, but his wistfulness about the future had seemed real. The most ancient man in the world . . . and now he was dead. Why? What had he been trying to tell them? He looked up at Yelén. "Since this afternoon, have you noticed anything special with the Peacers? Any evidence of high-tech interference?"

"No. As I said, I can't watch as closely as before. I talked to Phil Genet about it. He hasn't noticed anything with the Peacers, but he says NM radio traffic has changed during the last few hours. I'm looking into that." She paused. For the first time, he saw fear in her face. "These next few hours we could lose it all, Wil. Everything Marta ever hoped for."

"Yes. Or we could nail the enemy cold, and *save* her plan. . . . How are things set for tomorrow?"

His question brought back the normal Yelén. "This delay cost us the advantage of surprise, but it also means we're better prepared. Della has an incredible amount of equipment. I knew her expedition to the Dark Companion made money, but I never imagined she could afford all this. Almost all of it will be in position by tomorrow. She'll land by your place at sunup. It's all your show then."

"You're not coming?"

"No. In fact, I'm out of your inner-security zone. My equipment will handle peripheral issues, but . . . Della and I talked it over. If I—my system—is deeply perverted, the enemy could turn it on you."

"Hmm." He'd been counting on the dual protection; if he'd guessed wrong about one of them, the other would still be there. But if Yelén herself thought she might lose control . . . "Okay. Della seemed in pretty good form this afternoon."

"Yes. I have a theory that under stress the appropriate personality comes to the surface. She's driftiest after she's been by herself for a while. I'm talking to her right now, and she seems okay. With any luck, she'll still be wearing her cop personality tomorrow."

After Yelén signed off, Wil looked at the stuff she was sending over. It grew much faster than he could read it, and there were new developments all the time. Genet was right about the NMs. They were using a new encryption scheme, one that Yelén couldn't break. That in itself was more of an anachronism than polka-dot paint or antigrav volleyballs. Under other circumstances, she would have raided them for it, and diplomacy be damned. . . . Now she was stretched so thin that all she could do was watch.

Tioulang's murder. The high-tech manipulation of Fraley. There was some fundamental aspect of the killer's motivation that Wil didn't understand. If he wanted to destroy the colony, he could have done that long ago. So Wil had concluded that the enemy wanted to rule. Now he wondered. Was the low-techs' survival simply a bargaining chip to the killer?

It was a long night.

Brierson was standing by his window when Della's flier came down. It was still twilight at ground level, but he could see sunlight on the treetops. He grabbed his data set and walked out of the house. His step was brisk, adrenaline-fueled.

"Wait, Wil!" The Dasguptas were on their front porch. He stopped, and they ran down the street toward him. He hoped his guardians weren't trigger-happy.

"Did you know?" Rohan began, and his brother continued. "The Peacer boss was murdered last night. It looks like the NMs did it."

"Where did you hear?" He couldn't imagine Yelén spreading the news.

"The Peacer news service. Is it true, Wil?"

Brierson nodded. "We don't know who did it, though."

"Damn!" Dilip was as upset as Wil had ever seen him. "After all the talk about peaceful competition, I thought the NMs and Peacers had changed their ways. If they start shooting, the rest of us are . . . Look, Wil, back in civilization this couldn't happen. They'd have every police service in Asia down on them. Can—can we count on Yelén to keep these guys out of our way?"

Wil knew that Yelén would die before she'd let the NMs and Peacers fight. But today, dying might not be enough. The Dasguptas saw the tip of a game that extended beyond their knowing—and Wil's. He looked at the brothers, saw unmerited trust in their faces. What could he do? . . . Maybe the truth would help. "We think this is tied up with Marta's murder, Dilip." He jerked a thumb at Della's flier. "That's what I'm checking out now. If there's shooting, I'll bet you see more than low-techs involved. Look. I'll get Yelén to lower her suppressor field; you could bobble up for the next couple of days."

"Our equipment, too."

"Right. In any case, get people spread out and under cover." There was nothing more he could say, and the brothers seemed to know it.

"Okay, Wil," Rohan said quietly. "Luck to us all."

* * *

Della's flier was bigger than usual, and there were five pods strapped around its midsection.

But the crew area didn't have the feel of a combat vehicle. It wasn't the lack of control and display panels. When Wil left civilization, those were vanishing items. Even the older models had provided command helmets that allowed the pilot to see the outside world in terms of what was important to the mission. The newer ones didn't need the helmets; the windows themselves were holo panels on artificial reality. But there were no command helmets in Della's flier, and the windows showed the same version of reality that clear glass would. The floor was carpeted. Unwindowed sections of the wall were decorated with Della's strange watercolors.

As he climbed aboard, Wil gestured at the strap-on pods. "Extra guns?"

"No. Those are defensive. There's a tonne of matter/antimatter in each one."

"Ugh." He sat down and strapped in. Defensive—like a flak jacket made of plastique?

Lu pulled more than two g's getting them off the street; no simple elevator rides today. Half a minute passed, and she cut the drive. Up and up and up they fell, Wil's stomach protesting all the way. They topped out around ten thousand meters, where she resumed one g.

It was a beautiful day. The low sun angle put the forested highlands into jagged relief. He couldn't see much of Town Korolev, but Yelén's castle was a shadowed pattern of gold and green. Northwards, clouds hid the lowlands and the sea. To the south, the mountains rose gray above the timberline to snow-topped peaks. The Indonesian Alps were the Rockies writ large.

Lu's eyes were open but unfocused. "Just want to have some maneuvering room." Then she looked at Wil and smiled. "Where to, boss?"

"Della, did you hear what I told the Dasguptas? Yelén should turn off her suppressors. Maybe a few low-techs will bobble out of this era, but she can't just leave everyone exposed."

"Wil, haven't you been reading your mail?"

"Unh, most of it." All night long it had been coming in, faster than he could keep up. He'd read all the red-tag stuff, until falling asleep an hour before dawn.

"We don't know the reason, but it's clear now the enemy may try to kill lots of low-techs. For the last sixty minutes, Yelén's been trying to remove bobble suppression from Australasia. She can't do it."

"Why not? It's her own equipment!" Wil felt stupid the moment he spoke.

"Yes. You could scarcely ask for better proof that her system is perverted, could you?" Her smile widened.

"If she can't turn them off, can you just blow them up?"

"We may decide to try that. But we don't know exactly how her defenses might respond. Besides, the enemy may have his own suppressor system ready to come on the moment Yelén's drops out."

"So no one can bobble up."

"It's a large-volume, low-intensity field, good enough to suppress any low-tech generators. But my bobblers can still self-enclose; my best still have some range."

For a moment, the purpose of this trip was forgotten. There must be some way to protect low-techs. Evacuate them from the suppression zone? That maneuver might put them in even more danger. Fly in high-power bobblers? He abruptly realized that the high-techs must be giving much deeper thought than he could to the problem. The problem he had precipitated. *Face it.* The only way he could contribute now was by succeeding with his mission: to identify the killer. Della's original question was the one he should be answering. *Where to?* "Are we certified free of eavesdroppers?" Lu nodded. "Okay. We start from Peacer Lake."

The flier boosted across the Inland Sea. But Della was not satisfied with the directions. "You don't know the cairn's coordinates?"

"I know what I'm looking for. We'll follow a search pattern."

"But searches could be done faster from orbit."

"Surely there are some sensors that need low, slow platforms?"

"Yes, but—"

"And surely we'd want to be with such sensors to pick up the find immediately?"

"Ah!" She was smiling again, and did not ask him to point out the equipment he referred to.

They flew in silence for several minutes. Wil tried to see evidence of their escort. There was a flier ahead of them. To the right and left of their path, he saw two more. There was an occasional glint from beyond these, as from objects flying distant formation. It wasn't very impressive—until he wondered how far the formation extended.

"Really, Wil. No one else can listen; I'm not even recording. You can 'fess up."

Brierson looked at her questioningly, and Della continued. "It's obvious you saw something in the diary that—for all our deep analysis, and all Yelén's years with Marta—we did not. She was trying to tell us that the murderer was stalking her, and that the Korolev system had been deeply penetrated. . . . But this story about a fifth cairn"—she raised an eyebrow, her expression mischievous—"is ridiculous."

Wil pretended great interest in the ground. "Why 'ridiculous'?"

"In the first place, it's unlikely the killer lived every second of those forty years in realtime. But if he was so interested that Marta felt his presence, and felt the need to write with hidden meanings—then I think it's reasonable he had sensors watching *all* the time. How could Marta sneak away from her camp, build another cairn, and get back—all without tipping him off?

"In the second place, even if she succeeded in fooling the killer, we're still talking about something that happened *fifty thousand* years ago. Do you have any conception how long that is? All recorded history wasn't much over six thousand years. And most of that's been lost. Only an incredible accident could preserve a written record across such a span."

"Yes, Yelén raised the same objection. But—"

"Right. You told her Marta had taken all that into account. I'll give you this, Wil. When you feel like it, you're one of the most convincing people I've ever seen—and I've seen some experts. . . . By the way, I backed you on this. I think Yelén is convinced; she believes Marta was all but superhuman, anyway. I wouldn't be surprised if the killer does, too.

"My point is, *I'm* on to you," Lu continued. Wil put on an expression of polite surprise. "You saw something in the diary that we didn't. But you don't know much more than what you've said—and you have no clues. Hence this wild-goose chase." She waved at the lands beyond the flier. "You hope you've convinced the killer that you will soon know his identity. You've posted us as targets, to flush him out." It was a prospect she appeared to enjoy.

And her theory was uncomfortably close to the truth. He had tried to create a situation where the enemy would be forced to attack him. What he couldn't understand was the activity around the low-techs. How could hurting *them* hide the killer?

Wil shrugged; he hoped that none of this turmoil showed on his face.

Della watched him for a second, her head cocked to one side. "No response? So *I'm* still on the suspect list. If you die and I survive, then the others will be on to me—and together, they outgun me. You're trickier than I thought; maybe gutsier, too."

The morning passed, slow and tense. Della paid no attention to the view. She was rational enough—and perhaps even brighter than usual. But there was a cockiness in her manner, as if she held reality at a distance, thought it all an immensely interesting game. She was full of theories. It was no surprise that her number one suspect was Juan Chanson. "I know he fired on me. Juan is playing the role of racial protector. He reminds me of the centaur. I think our killer must be like that centaur, Wil. The creature was so trapped by his notion of racial duty that he killed the last survivors. We're seeing the same thing here: murders and preparations for more murders."

Wil's "search pattern" took them slowly outwards from Peacer Lake. Fifty thousand years before, this had been vitrified wasteland. The jacaranda forests had won it back thousands of years since. Though this forest had not existed in Marta's time, it was much like the ones she had traveled. Wil was seeing the heaven side of the world Marta had described. To the northeast, a grayish band stretched along the border of the forest domain. That must be the kudzu web, killing the jungle and preventing invasion. On the jac side, there were occasional silver splotches, web attacks on non-jacs that had sprouted beyond the barrier. The jacarandas themselves were an endless green sea, tinged with a bluish foam of flowers. He knew there were vast webs there, too, but they were *below* the leaf canopy, where the spiders' domesticated caterpillars could take advantage of the leaves without shading them out.

Here and there bright puffs of cloud floated above it all, trailing shadow.

Marta had walked many kilometers before finding a display web. From this altitude, they could see several at once. None was less than thirty meters across. They shimmered in the treetop breezes, their colors shifting between red and electric blue. Somewhere down there was a fossil streambed, the remains of a small river Marta had followed on one of her last expeditions out of Peacer Lake. He remembered what the land looked like then: kilometers of grayness, the water and wind still working to break through the glassy surface. She would have carried whatever food she needed.

Ahead, the forest was splattered with random patches of kudzu. Display webs were scattered everywhere. There was more blue and red and silver than green.

Della supplied an explanation. "Marta's plantings spread outward from her signal line. This is where the new forest meets the old; sort of a jac civil war."

Wil smiled at the metaphor. Apparently the two forests and their spiders were different enough to excite the kudzu reflex. He wondered if the display webs were like animal displays at territory boundaries. The colorful jumble passed slowly below, and they were over normal jacs again.

"We're way beyond Marta's furthest trip in this direction, Wil. You really think anyone's going to believe we're doing a serious search here?"

He pretended to ignore the question. "Follow this line another hundred kilometers, then break and head toward the lake where she got the fishers."

Thirty minutes later they were floating above a patch of brownish green water, more a swamp than a lake. The jacs grew right to the edge; it looked like the kudzu web stretched into the water. Fifty thousand years ago there had been ordinary woodland here.

"What's our defense situation, Della?"

"Cool, cool. Except for the suppressor thing, no enemy action. The NMs and Peacers have buttoned up, but they've stopped shouting accusations. We've discussed the threat with all the high-techs. They've agreed to keep out of the air for the time being, and to isolate their forces. If anyone strikes, we'll know his identity. The bottom line, Wil: I don't think the enemy has been bluffed."

There was no help for it, then. "Exactly which way is north, Della?" Damn this flier: no command helmet, no holos. He felt like the inmate of a rubber room.

Suddenly a red arrow labeled NORTH hovered over the forest. It looked solid, kilometers long; so the windows were holo displays after all. "Okay. Back off eastwards from lake. Come down to a thousand meters." They slid sideways, nearly in free fall. Most of the lake was still visible. "Give me a ring around the original lake site. Mark it off in degrees." He studied the lake and the blue circle that now surrounded it. "I want to get into the forest about ten klicks from the lake on a bearing of thirty degrees from north." They were close enough to the forest canopy that he could see leaves and flowers rushing by. The cover looked deep and dense. "Are you going to have any problem finding a place to get through?"

"No problem at all." Their forward motion ceased. They were just above the treetops. Abruptly, the flier smashed straight down. For an instant, negative g's hung Wil on his harness. Sounds of destruction were sharp around them.

And then they were through. The spaces beneath were lit by the sunlight that followed them through the hole they had punched in the canopy. Beyond that light, all was dark and greenish. Junk was drifting down all around them. Most of it was insubstantial. The underweb carried centuries of twigs and insect remains, flotsam that had not yet percolated to the surface. It was coming down all at once now, swinging back and forth through the light. Some debris—branches, clusters of flowers—was still in the air, supported by fragments of the web. More than anything else, Wil felt as if they had suddenly plunged into deep water. The flier drifted out of the light. His eyes slowly adapted to the dimness.

"We're there, Wil. Now what?"

"How well can the others monitor us down here?"

"It's complicated. Depends on what we do."

"Okay. I think the cairn is southwest of us, near the bearing we took from the lake. After all this time, there won't be any surface evidence, but I'm hoping you can detect the rocks." *And if you can't, I'll have to think of something else.*

"That should be easy." The flier glided around a tree. They were less than a meter up, moving at barely more than a walking pace. They drifted back and forth across the bearing; the sunlight from the entrance hole was lost behind them. Della's flier was five meters tall, and nearly that wide, yet they had no trouble negotiating the search path. He looked out the windows in wonder. Much of the ground was abso-

478

lutely smooth, a gray-green down. That was the top of fifty thousand years' accumulation of spider dung, of leaf and chitin fragments. The abyssal ooze of the jac forest.

The forest floor was as Marta described, but much gloomier. He wondered if she had really thought it beautiful, or said so to disguise a melancholy like he felt here.

"I—I've got something, Wil!" There was real surprise on Della's face. "Strong echoes, about thirty meters ahead." As she spoke, the flier sprinted forward, dodging intermediate trees. "Most of the rocks are scattered, but there is a central cluster. It—it could really be a cairn. My Lord, Wil, how could you know?"

Their flier settled on the forest floor, next to the secret that had waited fifty thousand years for them.

23

The door slid back. Wil stuck his head into the forest air. And jerked it back even more quickly. *Phew:* take mildew and add a flavoring of shit. He took another breath and tried not to gag. Perhaps it was the abrupt transition that made it seem so awful; the flier's air was full of alpine morning.

They stepped onto the forest floor. Gray-green humus lapped around their ankles. He was careful not to kick it up. There was enough junk in the air already.

Della walked a large circle tangent to their landing point. "I've mapped all the rocks. They're not as big as Marta generally used, and not as well shaped. But backtracking their trajectories . . ." She was quiet for second. ". . . I see they were piled in a pyramid at one time. The core is intact, and I think there's something—not rocks or forest dirt—inside. What do you want to do?"

"How long would a careful dig take—say as good as a twenty-first-century archeologist could do?"

"Two or three hours."

Now that they really had something, they had to protect it—and get themselves off ground zero at the same time. "We could bobble the whole thing," he said.

"That would be awkward to haul around if shooting starts. Look, Marta never left anything of importance outside the core. That's less

480

than a meter across in this case. We could bobble that and be out of here in just a few minutes."

Wil nodded agreement, and Della continued with scarcely a pause. "Okay, it's done. Now stand back a couple of meters."

Dozens of reflections of Wil and Della suddenly looked up from the forest floor; the ground between them was covered by close-packed bobbles.

She walked back, around the field of mirrors. "Bobbles are hard to miss against the neutrino sky; if the enemy has decent equipment, he noticed this." Sonic booms came from beyond the treetops. "Don't worry. That's friendly."

The new arrivals slipped through the hole Della had made in the canopy. They consisted of one auton and a cloud of robots. The robots settled on the bobbles, rooting and pushing. The top layer came off easily, revealing more bobbles beneath. These were pushed aside to get at still deeper layers. On a small scale, Lu was using the standard open-pit mining technique. In minutes, they were looking into a dark, slumping hole. The bobbles were scattered on all sides, glowing copies of the forest canopy above.

One by one, the robots picked them up and flew away.

"Which one is . . . ?"

"You can't tell, can you? I hope the enemy is similarly mystified. We've supplied him with seventy red herrings." He noticed that not all the bobbles were flown directly out. One had been transferred to the auton, and one to Della's flier.

Della climbed aboard the flier, Wil close behind. "If our friend doesn't start shooting in the next few minutes, he never will. I'm taking all the bobbles to my home. That's a million kilometers out now. From there we can see in all directions, shoot in all directions; no one can get us there." She smashed straight through the forest's roof, kept rising at multiple g's.

Wil sank deep into the acceleration couch. All he could see was sky. He squinted at the sunlight and gasped, "He may not attack at all. He may still think we're bluffing."

She chuckled. "Don't you wish." The sky tilted, and he saw green horizon. "Twenty thousand meters. I'm going to nuke out."

Free fall. The sky was black, except at the blue horizon. They were at least one hundred kilometers up. It was like a video cut: One instant they had been at aircraft altitudes, the next they were in space. Something bright and sunlike glowed beneath them—the detonation that had boosted them out of the atmosphere. He wondered fleetingly why she hadn't nuked out from ground level. A technical reason? Or sentiment?

The sky jerked again, the horizon acquiring a distinct curve.

"Hm. I have a low-tech on the net, Wil. She wants to talk to you."

Who? "Hold off on the next nuke. Let me talk to her."

Part of one window went flat. He was looking at someone wearing NM fatigues and a display helmet. The space around the figure was crammed with twenty-first-century communications gear.

"Wil!" The speaker cleared the face panel on her helmet. It was Gail Parker. "Thank God! I've been trying to break out for almost an hour. Look. Fraley has gone nuts. We're going to attack the Peacers. He says they'll wipe us if we don't. He says there's no way the high-techs can prevent it. Is that *true*? What's going on?"

Brierson sat in horrified silence. What was the killer's motive, that he would contrive such a war? "Part of it *is* true, Gail. It looks like someone's trying to wipe the entire colony. This war talk must be part of it. Is there anything you can do to—"

"*Me?*" She glanced over her shoulder, then continued in a lower voice. "God damn it, Wil, I'm at the center of our C and C. Sure. I could sabotage our entire defense system. But if the other side really does attack, then I've murdered my own people!"

"None of us will make it otherwise, Gail. I'll try to talk sense to the Peacers. Do . . . do what you can." *What would I do in her place?* His mind shied away from Gail's choices.

Parker nodded. "I—" The picture smeared into an abstract pattern of colors. A screeching noise rose past audibility.

"Signal jammed," said Lu.

"Della? Can you get through to the Peacers?"

Lu shrugged. "It doesn't matter. Why do you think Parker called just then? She thinks she finally broke out of NM security. In fact, the enemy has taken over their system. Letting her through is part of a distraction."

"Distraction?"

"One we can't ignore; he's going to start 'em killing each other. I see ballistic traffic going both ways across the Inland Sea. . . . Someone's blocking my wideband link to Yelén."

A section of window suddenly showed Yelén's office. Korolev was standing. "Both sides are shooting. I've lost several autons. *Both* sides have high-tech backing, Della." Disbelief was mixed with rage and fear. Tears glinted on her face. "You'll have to do without my help for now; I'm going to divert my forces. I can't let my peo— I can't let these people die."

"It's okay, Yelén. But get the others to help you. You can't trust your system alone."

Korolev sat down shakily. "Right. They've agreed to bring their forces up. I'm starting my diversion now." There was a moment of silence. Yelén stared blankly, swapped out. The silence stretched . . . and Yelén's eyes slowly widened. In horror. "Oh, my God, no!" Her image vanished, and he was looking into empty sky.

Wil flinched, the motion floating him against his restraint harness. "More jamming?"

"No. She just stopped transmitting." There was a faint smile on Della's face. "I guessed this might happen. To shift her forces, she had to run control routines that the enemy could not start—but which he had perverted. He's finally shown himself in a big way: Yelén's forces are coming out for us. What she has in far space is moving to block our exit.

"Another minute and we'll know who we've been fighting all this time. Yelén can't take me alone. The killer is going to have to stand up with his own equipment. . . ." Her smile broadened. "You're going to see some real shooting, Wil."

"I can hardly wait." He tucked his data set in the side of his acc chair.

"Oh, don't expect too much; with the naked eye, this won't be very spectacular." And she was humming!

Please God that this insanity does not affect her performance.

The horizon jerked once again. There was no acceleration, no sound. It was like botched special effects from an old-time movie. But now they were better than a thousand kilometers up, the Inland Sea a cloud-dotted puddle. And the Earth was visibly falling away from them; they were moving at dozens of klicks per second.

Surely—even without Yelén—the others could protect the low-techs from a few ballistic missiles? Malicious fate gave him quick answer: Three bright sparks glowed on the southern coast, a third of the way from West End to the Eastern Straits. Wil groaned.

"Those were high air bursts, at Town Korolev," said Della. "If the Dasguptas spread your warning, there may not be too many casualties." There was puzzlement in her voice.

"But where are Chanson and Genet and Blumenthal? Surely—"

"Surely they could prevent this?" Della finished the question. She swapped out a moment. Then: *"Oh . . . wow!"* Her words were almost a sigh, filled with endless wonder and surprise. She was silent a moment more. Then her eyes focused on Wil. "All this time, we were expecting to flush the killer into the open. Right? Well . . . we have a little problem. *All* the high-tech forces have turned on us."

Like a gruesome short story Wil once read: Detective locks self in room with suspects. Detective applies definitive test to suspects. All suspects guilty. . . . Unmarked grave for detective. Happy ending for suspects.

"We are now outgunned, Wil. This is going to be very interesting." The smile was almost gone from her face, replaced by a look of intense concentration. Sudden light and shadow flickered across the cabin. Wil looked up, saw a pattern of point lights glowing, fading in the blackness. "They have a lot of stuff at the Lagrange zones. They're bringing it down on us—while their ground-based stuff comes up. No way we can get to my quarters just now."

And they were back at low altitude, the horizon spread flat around them, the Indonesian Alps drifting by below. His restraint harness stiffened and the flier surged forward at multiple g's, then slammed to the side. Wil's consciousness faded into red dimness. Somewhere he heard Della say, ". . . lose realtime every time I nuke out. Can't afford it now." They were in free fall for almost a second, then more crushing acceleration, then free fall again. Brightness flashed all around them, lighting sea and clouds with extra suns. More acceleration. *Things don't get this exciting when they're going right.*

The horizon jerked, and acceleration reversed. Jerk, jerk. Now each translation of the outside world was accompanied by changed acceleration, the agrav being used in concert with the nukes. Della's words came in broken gasps. "Bastards." Around them the horizon rose, kilometers per second. Acceleration was heavy, spacewards. "They're past my defenders." Jerk. They were lower, hurtling parallel to the vast wall that was the Earth. "They're zeroed on me." Jerk. "Seven direct hits in—" Jerk. Jerk.

Jerk. Free fall again. This last had taken them high over the Pacific. All was blue and ocean clouds below. "We've got about a minute's breather. I regrouped my low forces and nuked into the middle of them. The enemy's breaking through right now." To the west, point suns flashed brighter and brighter. In the sky below, weirdness: five contrails, a dozen. The clouds grew like quick crystal, around threads of fire. Directed energy weapons? "We're the king piece; they're trying to force us out of this era."

Somewhere, Wil found his voice. Even more, it sounded calm. "No way, Della."

"Yeah . . . I didn't come this far to fade." Pause. "Okay. There's another way to protect the king piece. A bit risky, but—"

Wil's chair suddenly came alive. The sides swung inward, bringing his arms across his middle. The footrest moved up, forcing his knees to near chest level. At the same time, the entire assembly rotated sideways, to face a similarly trussed Della Lu. The contraption tightened painfully, squeezing the two of them into a round bundle. And then

24

There was an instant of falling. The acceleration spiked, then stabilized at one g.

The chair relaxed its grip.

The sunlight was gone. The air was hot, dry. *They were no longer in the flier!* The "one-g field" was the Earth's. They were sitting on the ground.

Della was already on her feet, dismantling part of her chair. "Nice sunset, huh?" She nodded toward the horizon.

Sunset or sunrise. He had no sense of direction, but the heat in the air made him guess they were at the end of a day. The sun was squashed and reddish, its light coming sickly across a level plain. He suddenly felt sick himself. Was that disk reddened by its closeness to the horizon, or was the sun *itself* redder? "Della, just—just how long did we jump?"

She looked up from her rummaging. "About forty-five minutes. If we can live another five, we may be okay." She pulled a meter-long pole from the back of her chair, clipped a strap to it, and slung it over her shoulder. He noticed shiny metal where the bobble had cut the chairs away from Della's flier. That bobble had been scarcely more than a meter wide. No wonder he had been cramped. "We need to get out of sight. Help me drag this stuff over there." She pointed at a knoblike hill a hundred meters off.

They were standing in a shallow crater of dirt and freshly cracked rock. Wil took a chair in each hand and pulled; he backed quickly out of the crater, onto grass. Della motioned him to stop. She grabbed one of the chairs and tipped it over. "Drag it on the smooth side. I don't want them to see a trail." She leaned back against the load, dragging it quickly away across the short grass. Wil followed, pulling his with a one-handed grasp.

"When you've got a minute, I'd like to know what we're up to."

"Sure. Soon as we get these under cover." She turned, took the load on her shoulders, and all but trotted toward the stony hill. It took several minutes to reach it; the hill was larger and farther away than he thought. It rose over the grass and scrub like some ominous guardian. Except for the birds that rattled out as they approached, it seemed lifeless.

The ground around it was bare, grooved. The rock bulged over its base, leaving shallow caves along the perimeter. There was a smell of death. He saw bones in the shadows. Della saw them too. She slid her chair in over the bones and waved for Wil to do the same. "I don't like this, but we've got other hunters to worry about first." Once the equipment was hidden, she scrambled up the rock face to a small cave about four meters up. Wil followed, more awkwardly.

He looked around before sitting beside her. The indentation barely qualified as a cave. Nothing would surprise them from behind, though something had used it for dining; there were more well-gnawed bones. The cave was hidden from most of the sky, yet they had a good view of the ground, almost to the base of the rock.

He sat down, impatient for explanations—and suddenly was struck by the silence. All day the tension had grown, reaching a crescendo of violence these last few minutes. Now every sign of that struggle was gone. One hundred meters away, birds flocked around a stunted tree, their cries and flapping wings clear and tiny in the larger silence. Only a sliver of the sun's disk still glowed at the horizon. By that light, the prairie was reddish gold, broken here and there by the dark scrub. The breeze was a slow thing, still warm from the day. It brought perfume and putrescence, and left the sweat dry on his face.

He looked at Della Lu. Dark hair had fallen across her cheek. She didn't seem to notice. "Della?" he said quietly. "Did we lose?"

"Unh?" She looked at him, awareness coming back to her eyes. "Not yet. Maybe not at all if this works. . . . They were concentrating everything on you and me. The only way we could stay in this era and still survive was to disappear. I brought my whole inner guard toward our flier. We exploded almost all our nukes at the same time, and vanished as thousands of meter-sized bobbles. One of those bobbles contained you and me; seventy of them are from the cairn. They're scattered all over now—Earth surface, Earth orbit, solar orbit. Most of the surface ones were timed to burst minutes after impact."

"So we're lost in the turmoil."

Her smile was a ghost of earlier enthusiasm. "Right. They haven't got us yet: I think we brought it off. Given a few hours they could do a thorough search, but I'm not giving them the time. My midguard has come down, and is giving them plenty of other things to worry about.

"We, here, are totally defenseless, Wil. I don't even have a bobbler. The other side could take us out with a five-millimeter pistol—if only they knew where to do the shooting. I had to destroy my inner guard to get away. What's left is outnumbered two to one. Yet . . . yet I think I can win. Fifty seconds out of every minute, I have tight beam comm with my fleet." She patted the meter-long pole that lay on the ground between them. One end consisted of a ten-centimeter sphere. She had laid the pole so that the ball was at the cave's entrance. Wil looked at it more closely, saw iridescence glow and waver. It was some kind of coherent transmitter. Her own forces knew where they were hidden, and needed to keep only one unit in line of sight for Lu to run the battle.

Della's voice was distant, almost indifferent. "Whoever they are, they know how to pervert systems, but not so much about combat. I've fought through centuries of realtime, with bobblers and suppressors, nukes and lasers. I have programs you just couldn't buy in civilization. Even without me, my system fights smarter than the other side's. . . ." A chuckle. "The high-orbit stuff is dead just now. We're playing 'peek and shoot': 'peek' around the shoulder of the Earth, 'shoot' at anything with its head stuck up. Boys and girls running round and round their home, killing each other. . . . I'm winning, Wil, I really am. But we're burning it all. Poor Yelén. So worried that our systems might not last long enough to reestablish civilization. One afternoon we're destroying all we've accumulated."

"What about the low-techs?" Was there anybody left to fight *for?*

"Their little play-war?" She was silent for fifteen seconds, and when she spoke again seemed even further away. "That ended as soon as it had served the enemy's purpose." Perhaps only Town Korolev had been wiped. Della sat against the rear wall of the cave. Now she leaned her head back and closed her eyes.

Wil studied her face. How different she looked from the creature he had seen on the beach. And when she wasn't talking, there were no weird perspectives, no shifting of personalities. Her face was young and innocent, straight black hair still fallen across her cheek. She might have been asleep, occasional dreams twitching her lips and eyelids. Wil reached to brush the hair back from her face—and stopped. The mind in this body was looking far across space, looking down on Earth from all directions, was commanding one side in the largest battle Wil had ever known. Best to let sleeping generals lie.

He crawled along the side of the cave to the entrance. From here he could see the plains and part of the sky, yet was better hidden than Della.

He looked across the land. If there was any way he could help, it was by protecting Della from local varmints. A few of the birds had returned to the rock. They were the only animal life visible; maybe these bone-littered condos were abandoned property. Surely Della had brought handguns and first-aid gear. He eyed the smooth shells of the acceleration chairs and wondered if he should ask her about them. But Della was in deep connect; even during the first attack she had not been concentrating like this. . . . Better to wait till he had a certifiable emergency. For now he would watch and listen.

Twilight slowly faded; a quarter moon slid down the western sky. From the track of the sun's setting, he guessed they were in the Northern Hemisphere, away from the tropics. This must be Calafia or the savanna that faced that island on the west coast of North America. Somehow, being oriented made Wil feel better.

The birds had quieted. There was a buzzing he hoped was insects. It was getting hard to keep his eyes on the ground. With the coming of night, the sky show was impossible to ignore. Aurora stretched from north horizon to south. The pale curtains were as bright as any he had seen, even from Alaska. The battle itself danced slowly beyond those curtains. Some of the lights were close-set sparkles, like a gem visible only when its facets caught some magic light. The lights brightened and dimmed, but the cluster as a whole didn't move: that must be a high-orbit fight, perhaps at a Lagrange zone. For half an hour at a time, that was the only action visible. Then a fragment of the near-Earth battle would come above the horizon—the "peek and shoot" crowd. Those lights cast vivid shadows, each one starting brilliant white, fading to red over five or ten seconds.

Though he had no idea who was winning, Wil thought he could follow some of the action. A near-Earth firefight would start with ten or twenty detonations across a large part of the sky. These were followed by more nukes in a smaller and smaller space, presumably fighting past robots towards a central auton. Even the laser blasts were visible now, threads of light coruscating bright or faint depending on how much junk was in the way. Their paths pointed into the contracting net of detonations. Sometimes the net shrank to nothing, the enemy destroyed or in long-term stasis. Other times, there was a bright flash from the center, or a string of flashes heading outwards. Escape attempts? In any case, the battle would then cease, or shift many degrees across the sky. Aurora flared in moon-bright knots on the deserted battlefield.

Even moving hundreds of kilometers per second, it took time for the fighters to cross the sky, time for the nuke blasts to fade through red to auroral memories. It was like fireworks photographed in slow motion.

The land around them was empty but for moving shadows, silent but for the insect buzz and occasional uneasy squawking. Only once did he hear anything caused by the battle. Three threads of directed energy laced across the sky from some fight over the horizon. The shots were very low, actually in the atmosphere. Even as they faded, contrails grew around them. After a minute, Wil heard faint thunder.

An hour passed, then two. Della had not said a word. To him, anyway. Light chased back and forth within the ball of her communications scepter, interference fringes shifting as she resighted the link.

Something started yowling. Wil's eyes swept the plain. Just now his only light was from the aurora: there was no near-Earth firefight going, and the high-orbit action was a dim flickering at the western horizon. . . . Ah, there they were! Gray shapes, a couple of hundred meters out. They were loud for their size—or hunkered close to the ground. The yowling spread, was traded back and forth. Were they fighting? Admiring the light show?

. . . They were getting closer, easier to see. The creatures were almost man-sized but stayed close to the ground. They advanced in stages—trotting forward a few meters, then dropping to the ground, resuming the serenade. The pack stayed spread out, though there were pairs and trios that ran together. It all rang a very unpleasant chord in Wil's memory. He came to his knees and crawled back to Della.

Even before he reached her, she began mumbling. "Don't look out, Wil. I have them worn down . . . but they've guessed we're on the surface. Last hour they've been trying to emp me out, mainly over Asia." She gave something like a chuckle. "Nothing like picking on the wrong continent. But they're shifting now. If I can't stop 'em, there'll be low-altitude nukes strung across North America. Stay down, don't look out."

The yowling was even closer. When bad luck comes, it comes in bunches. Wil took Della by the shoulders, gently shook her. "Are there weapons in the acc chairs?"

Her eyes came open, dazed and wild. "Can't talk! If they emp me—"

Wil scrambled back to the cave entrance. What was she talking about? Nothing but aurora lit the sky. He looked down. She *must* have weapons stored in those chairs. Climbing down would expose him to the sky for a few seconds, but once there he could hide under the overhang and work on the chairs. The nearest of the dogthings was only eighty meters out.

Wil swung onto the rock face, and— Della screamed, a tearing, full-throated shriek of pain. Wil's universe went blinding white, and a wave of heat swept over his back, burning his hands and neck. He vaulted back into the cave, rolled to the rear wall. The only sound was the sudden keening of the dogs.

There was a second flash, a third, fourth, fifth. . . . He was curled around Della now, shielding both their faces from the cave entrance. Each flash seemed less bright; the terrible, silent footsteps marched away from them. But with each flash, Della spasmed against him, her coughs spraying wetness across his shirt.

Finally darkness returned. His scalp tingled, and Della's hair clung to his face when he leaned away from her. A tiny blue spark leaped from his fingers when he touched the wall. Lu was moaning wordlessly; each breath ended in a choked cough. He turned her on her side, made sure she wasn't swallowing her tongue. Her breathing quieted, and the spasms subsided.

"Can you hear me, Della?"

There was a long silence, filled with the mewling of the animals outside. Then her breathing roughened and she mumbled something. Wil brought his ear close to her face. ". . . fooled 'em. They won't come sniffing around here for a while . . . but I'm cut off now . . . comm link wrecked."

Beyond the cave, the whimpering continued, but now there were sounds of movement, too. "We've got local problems, Della. Did you bring handguns?"

She squeezed his hand. "Acc chairs. Opens off my signal . . . or thumbprint . . . sorry."

He eased her head to the ground and moved back to the entrance. The comm scepter didn't glow anymore; the sphere end was too hot to touch. He thought about the gear Della had in her skull and shuddered. It was a miracle she still lived.

Wil looked out. The ground was well lit: the residue of the nuke attack shone overhead, a line of glowing splotches that stretched to the western horizon. Five of the dogthings lay writhing in the near distance. Most of the others had gathered in a close-packed herd. There was much whimpering, much snuffling of the ground, sniffing of the air. The brightness had burned their eyes out. They drifted toward the rock and hunkered beneath its overhang, waiting for the dark time to pass. Most of them would have a long wait.

Nine dogs paced along the edge of the herd, baying querulously. Wil could imagine their meaning: "C'mon, c'mon. What's the matter with you?" Somehow, these nine had been shaded from the sky; they could still see.

Maybe he could still get the guns. Wil picked up the comm scepter. It felt heavy, solid—if nothing else, a morningstar. He slipped over the edge of the rock and slid to ground level.

But not unnoticed: The howling began even before he reached the ground. Three of the sighted ones loped toward him. Wil backed into the overhang that hid the chairs. Without taking his eyes off the approaching dogthings, he reached down and pulled the nearest chair into the open.

Then they were on him, the lead dog diving at his ankles. Wil swung the scepter, and met empty air as the creature twisted away. The next one came in thigh-high—and caught Wil's backswing in the face. Metal crunched into bone. The creature didn't even yelp, just crashed and lay unmoving. The third one backed off, circled. Wil raised the chair on end. It was as seamless as he remembered. There were no buttons, latches. He slammed it hard against the rock face. The rock chipped; the shell was unscratched. He'd have to get it up to the cave for Della to touch.

The chair massed forty kilos, but there were good fingerholds on the rock face. He could do it—if his friends stayed intimidated. He slid the scepter through the restraint harness and pulled the chair onto his shoulder. He was less than two meters up the wall when they charged.

He really should have known better; these were like the near-dogs Marta had met at the West End mines. They were as big as komondors, big enough they needn't take no for an answer. Jaws raked and grabbed at his boots. He fell on his side. This was how they liked it; Wil felt an instant of sheer terror as one of them dived for his gut. He pulled the chair across his body, and the creature veered off. Wil got the next one across its neck with his scepter.

They backed off as Wil scrambled to his feet. Around the side of the rock, the blind ones growled and shouted. The cheerleaders.

So much for the acc chairs. He'd be lucky now to get himself back to the cave.

There was motion at the corner of his eye: He looked up. Unlike dogs, these creatures could climb! The animal picked its way carefully across the rock face, its skinny limbs splayed out in four directions. It was almost to the cave entrance. *Della!* He stepped back from the rock and threw the comm scepter as hard as he could. The ball end caught the creature on its spine, midway between shoulder and haunch. It screamed and fell, the scepter clattering down behind it. The creature lay on its back, its hindquarters limp, the forelegs sweeping in all direc-tions. As Wil darted forward to grab the scepter, one of its clawed fingers raked his arm.

Wil was vaguely aware of shooting pain, of wet spreading down his sleeve. So the cave was not safe. Even if he could get back there, it would be hard to defend; there were several approaches. He risked another glance upwards. There was another cave still higher in the rock. The approach was bordered by sheer walls. He might be able to defend it.

The sighted ones circled inwards. He pushed the chair under the overhang, then ran to rock face, jumping high. The dogthings were close behind—only this time he had a free hand. He swung the scepter past their noses, then crawled upwards another meter. One of the creatures was climbing parallel with him. Its progress was slow, no more agile than a human's. Was it coming after him—*or trying to get to Della?* Wil pretended to ignore it. He paused again to swipe at those who harried him from below. He could hear the climber's claws on stone. It was sidling toward him, fingerhold to fingerhold. Still Wil ignored it. *I'm an easy mark, I'm an easy mark.*

One of the lower dogs bit into his boot. He bent, crushed its skull with the scepter.

He knew the other was less than a meter away now, coming down from above. Without turning his head, Wil jammed the scepter upwards. It hit something soft. For an instant man stared at dogthing, neither enjoying the experience. Its jaws opened in a hissing growl. Its claws were within striking distance of Wil's face, but the scepter was pushing against its chest, forcing it off the cliff. Brierson tucked his head against his arm and pushed harder. For a moment they were motionless, each clinging to the rock. Wil felt his hold giving way. Then something crashed into the dog from above, and its growl became a shriek. Its claws scraped desperately against stone. Resistance abruptly ceased and it fell past him.

But the others were still coming. As he scrambled higher, he glanced up. *Something* was looking down at him from the cave. The face was strangely splotched, but human. Somehow, Della had beaned the dog. He would have shouted thanks, but he was too busy hustling up the wall.

He hoisted himself over the cave's edge, turned, and took a poke at the dog that was coming up right after him. This one was lucky, or Wil was slowing down: It snapped its head around Wil's thrust and grabbed the shaft of the scepter. Then it pulled, dragging Wil half out of the cave, tearing the scepter from his hands. The creature fell down the cliffside, taking several comrades with it.

Wil sat for a moment, gasping. What an incompetent jerk he was. Marta had lasted four decades, alone, in this sort of wilderness. He and

Della had been on the ground less than four hours. They had made all sorts of stupid mistakes, now losing their only weapon. More dogthings were gathering below. If he and Della lasted another hour, it would be a miracle.

And they wouldn't last ten minutes if they stayed in this cave. Between gasping breaths, he told Della about the cave further up. She was lying on her stomach, her head turned to one side. The dark on her face was blood. Every few seconds, she coughed, sending a dark spray across the stone. Her voice was soft, the words not completely articulated. "I can't climb anywhere, Wil. Had to belly crawl t'get here."

They were coming up the wall again. For a strange instant, Wil considered the prospect of his own demise. Everyone wonders how he'll check out. In a policeman's case there are obvious scenarios. Never in a million years would he have guessed this one—dying with Della Lu, torn to pieces by creatures that in human history did not exist.

The instant passed and he was moving again, doing what he could. "Then I'll carry you." He took her hands. "Can you grab around my neck?"

"Yeah."

"Okay." He turned, guided her arms over his shoulders. He rose to his knees. She held on, her body stretched along his back. He was fleetingly aware of female curves. She had changed more than her hair since that day at the beach.

He wiped one hand on his pants. The nick on his arm was only oozing, but there was enough blood to make him slippery. "Tell me if you start losing your grip." He crawled out of the cave onto an upward-slanting ledge. Della massed more than the acc chair, but she was doing her best to hang on. He had both hands free.

The ledge ended in a narrow chimney heading straight up. Somewhere behind them, a firefight glowed. It brought no anxiety to his mind, only gratitude. The light showed breaks in the rock. He stepped in one on the left side, then one on the right, practically walking up the slot. He could see the entrance to the upper cave, scarcely two meters ahead.

The dogs had made it to the first cave. He could hear them clicking along the ledge. If this was easy for him, it was easy for them. He looked down, saw three of them racing single file up the slot.

"Hold tight!" He scrambled for the top, had his arms hooked over the entrance the same instant the lead dog got his foot. This time, he felt teeth come straight through the plastic. Wil swung his leg away from the wall, the animal a twisting weight on his foot. Its forelegs clawed at his calf.

Then he had the right angle: The boot slipped from his foot. The dog made a frantic effort to crawl up his leg, its claws raking Wil's flesh. Then it was gone, crashing into its comrades below.

Wil pulled himself into the cave and lay Della on her side. His leg was a multiple agony. He pulled back the pants leg. There was a film of blood spreading from the gashes, but no spurting. He could stop the bleeding if given a moment's peace. He pressed down on the deepest wound, at the same time watching for another assault. It probably didn't matter. His fingernails and teeth weren't in a class with the dogs' claws and fifteen-millimeter canines.

. . . *bad luck comes in bunches.* Wil's nose was finally communicating the stench that hung in the cave. The other one had smelled of death, bones crusted with fragments of desiccated flesh; the smell here was of wet putrefaction. Something big and recently dead lay behind them. And something else *still* lived here: Wil heard metallic clicking.

Wil leaned forward and slipped his remaining boot onto his fist. He continued the motion into a quick turn that brought him up and facing into the cave. The distant firefight lit the cave in ambiguous shades of gray. The dead thing had been a near-dog. It lay like some impressionist holo—parts of the torso shrunken, others bloated. Things moved on the body . . . and in it: Enormous beetles studded the corpse, their round shells showing an occasional metallic highlight. These were the source of the clicking.

Wil scrambled across the litter of old bones. Up close, the smell stuffed the cave with invisible cotton, leaving no room for breathable air. It didn't matter. He had to get a close look at those beetles. He took a shallow breath and brought his head close to one of the largest. Its head was stuck into the corpse, the rear exposed. That armored sphere was almost fifteen centimeters across. Its surface was tessellated by a regular pattern of chitin plates.

He sat back, gasped for air. Was it possible? Marta's beetles were in Asia, fifty thousand years ago. Fifty thousand years. That was enough time for them to get across the land bridge . . . also enough time for them to lose their deadly talent.

He was going to find out: The dogs were yowling again. Louder than before. Not loud enough to cover the sound of claws on stone. Wil thrust his hands into the soft, dead flesh and separated the beetle from its meal. Pain stabbed through a finger as it bit him. He moved his grip back to the armored rear and watched the tiny legs wave, the mandibles click.

He heard the dogs coming along the ledge to the chimney.

Still no action from his little friend. Wil tossed the creature from hand to hand, then shook it. A puff of hot gas hissed between his fingers. There was a new smell, acrid and burning.

He took the beetle to the cave entrance and gave it another shake. The hiss got louder, became almost sibilant. The armored shell was almost too hot to touch. He kept the insect excited through another ten seconds. Then he saw a dog at the bottom of the slot. It looked back, then charged up the chimney, three others close behind. Wil gave the beetle one last shake and threw it downwards, into the cliff face just above the lead dog. The explosion was a sharp cracking sound, without a flash. The dog gave a bubbling scream and fell against the others. Only the trailing animal kept its footing—and it retreated from the chimney.

Thank you, Marta! Thank you!

There were two more attacks during the next hour. They were easily beaten back. Wil kept a couple of grenade beetles close to the edge of the cave, at least one near the bursting point. How near the bursting point he didn't know, and in the end he feared the beetles more than the dogs. During the last attack, he blew four dogs off the rock—and got his own ear ripped by a piece of chitinous shrapnel.

After that, they stopped coming. Maybe he had killed all the sighted ones; maybe they had wised up. He could still hear the blind ones, down beneath the overhang. The howling had sounded sinister; now it seemed mournful, frightened.

The space battle had wound down, too. The aurora was as bright as ever, but there were no big firefights. Even isolated flashes were rare. The most spectacular sight was an occasional piece of junk progressing stately across the sky, slowly disintegrating into glowing debris as it fell through the atmosphere.

When the dogs stopped coming, Wil sat beside Della. The emp attack had blown the electronics in her skull. Moving her head caused dizziness and intense pain. Most of the time, she lay silent or softly moaning. Sometimes she was lucid: Though she was totally cut off from her autons, she guessed that her side was winning, that it had slowly ground down the other high-techs. And some of the time she was delirious, or wearing one of her weirder personalities, or both. After a half-hour silence, she coughed into her hand and stared at the new blood splattered on the dried. "I could die now. I could really die." There was wonder in her voice, and fascination. "Nine thousand years I have lived. There aren't many people who could do that." Her eyes focused on Wil. "You couldn't. You're too wrapped up in the people around you. You like them too much."

Wil brushed the hair from her face. When she winced, he moved his hand to her shoulder. "So I'm a pussycat?" he said.

". . . No. A civilized person, who can rise to the occasion. . . . But it takes more than that to live as long as I. You need single-mindedness, the ability to ignore your limitations. Nine thousand years. Even with augmentation, I'm like a flatworm attending the opera. A hundred responses a planarian has? And then what does it do with the rest of the show? When I'm connected, I can remember it all, but where is the original me? . . . I've drifted through everything this mind can be. I've run out of happy endings . . . and sad ones, too." There was a long silence. "I wonder why I'm crying."

"Maybe there's something left to see. What brought you this far?"

"Stubbornness, and . . . I wanted to know . . . what happened. I wanted to see into the Singularity."

He patted her shoulder. "That still may be. Stick around."

She gave a small smile, and her hand fell against him. "Okay. You were always good for me, Mike."

Mike? She *was* delirious.

The lasers and nukes had been gone for hours. The aurora was fading with the morning twilight. Della had not spoken again. The rotting dogthing brought warmth (and by now Wil had no sense of smell whatsoever), but the night was cold, less than ten degrees. Wil had moved her next to the creature and covered her with his jacket and shirt. She no longer coughed or moaned. Her breathing was shallow and rapid. Wil lay beside her, shivering and almost grateful to be covered with dogthing gore, dried blood, and general filth. Behind them, the beetles continued their clicking progress through the corpse.

From the sound of Della's breathing, he doubted she could last many more hours. And after the night, he had a good idea of his own wilderness longevity.

He couldn't really believe that Della's forces had won. If they had, why no rescue? If they hadn't, the enemy might never discover where they were hidden—might never even care. And he would never know who was behind the destruction of the last human settlement.

Twilight brightened towards day. Wil crept to the cave entrance. The aurora was gone, blotted out by the blue of morning. From here he wouldn't see the sunrise, but he knew it hadn't happened yet; there were no shadows. All colors were pastels: the blue in the sky, the pale green of the grassland, the darker green in the trees. For a time nothing moved. Cool, peaceful silence.

On the ground, the dogthings rousted themselves. By twos and threes they walked onto the plain, smelling morning but not able to see it. The sighted ones ran out ahead, then circled back, trying to get the others to hustle. From a safe distance, and in daylight, Wil had to admit they were graceful—even amusing—creatures: Slender and flexible, they could run or belly crawl with equal ease. Their long snouts and narrow eyes gave them a perpetually crafty look. One of the sighted ones glanced up at Will, gave an unconvincing growl. More than anything, they reminded him of the frustrated coyote that had chased a roadrunner bird through two centuries of comic animation.

In the western sky, something glittered, metal in sunlight. Dogthings forgotten, Wil stared up. Nothing but blue now. Fifteen seconds passed. Three black specks hung where he'd seen the light. They didn't move across the sky, but slowly grew. A ripple of sonic booms came across the plain.

The fliers decelerated to a smooth stop a couple of meters above the grass. All three were unmarked, unmanned. Wil considered scrambling to the rear of the cave—but he didn't move. If they looked, they would find. Loser or winner, he was damned if he'd cower.

The three hung for a moment in silent conference. Then the nearest slid, silent and implacable, up the air towards Wil.

25

For whatever it might be worth, Wil's side was the winner. He was released by the medics in less than an hour. His body was whole, but stiff and aching; the medical autons didn't waste their time on finishing touches. There were really serious casualties, and only a part of the medical establishment had survived the fight. The worst cases were simply popped into stasis. Della disappeared into her system, with the autons' assurance that she would be substantially well in forty hours.

Wil tried not to think about the disaster that spread all around them, tried not to think that it was his fault. He had thought the search for the cairn would provoke an attack—but on himself and Della, not on all humanity.

That attack had killed almost half the human race. Wil couldn't bring himself to ask Yelén directly, but he knew anyway: Marta's plan was dead. He had failed in the only way that mattered. And yet he still had a job. He still had a murderer to catch. It was something to work on, a barricade against grief.

Although the price was higher than he had ever wished to pay, the battle had given him the sort of clues he'd hoped. Della's system had retrieved the cairn bobble; its contents would be available in twenty-four hours. And there were other things to look at. It was clear now that the enemy's only power had lain in his perversion of others' systems. But, at every step, they had underestimated that power. After

Marta's murder, they thought it was a shallow penetration, the perversion of a bug in the Korolev system. After Wil found the clue in the diary, they thought the enemy had deeper penetration, but still of Korolev's system alone; they guessed the killer might be able to usurp parts of Yelén's forces. And then came the war between the low-techs. It had been a diversion, covering the enemy's final, most massive assault. That assault had been not on Korolev's system alone, but on Genet's and Chanson's and Blumenthal's and Raines'. Every system except Lu's had been taken over, turned to the business of killing Wil and Della.

But Della Lu was very hard to kill. She had fought the other systems to a standstill, then beaten them down. In the chaos of defeat, the original owners climbed out of system-metaphorical bunkers and reclaimed what was left of their property.

Everyone agreed it couldn't happen again. They might even be right. What remained of their computing systems was pitifully simple, not deep enough or connected enough for games of subtle perversion. Everyone agreed on something else: The enemy's skill with systems had been the equal of the best and biggest police services from the high-techs' era.

So. It was a big clue, though small compared to the price of the learning. Related, and at least as significant: Della Lu had been immune to the takeover. Wil put the two together and reached some obvious conclusions. He worked straight through the next twenty-four hours, studying Della's copy of GreenInc—especially the garbled coverage of the late twenty-second. It was tedious work. At one time, the document had been seriously damaged; the reconstruction could never be complete. Facts and dates were jumbled. Whole sections were missing. He could understand why Della didn't use the later coverage. Wil kept at it. He knew what to look for . . . and in the end he found it.

A half-trashed db would not convince a court, but Wil was satisfied: He knew who killed Marta Korolev. He spent an empty, hate-full afternoon trying to figure how to destroy the murderer. What did it matter now? Now that the human race was dead.

That night, Juan Chanson dropped by Wil's new quarters. The man was subdued; he spoke scarcely faster than a normal person. "I've checked for bugs, my boy, but I want to keep this short." Chanson looked nervously around the tiny room that was Wil's share of the refugee dorm. "I noticed something during the battle. I think it can save us all." They talked for more than an hour. And when Chanson left, it was with the promise they would talk again in the morning.

Wil sat thinking for a long time after the other left. *My God, if what Juan says is true . . .* Juan's story made sense; it tied up all the loose ends. He noticed he was shivering: not just his hands, his whole body. It was a combination of joy and fear.

He had to talk to Della about this. It would take planning, deception, and good luck, but if they played their cards exactly right, the settlement still had a chance!

On the third day, the survivors gathered at Castle Korolev, in the stone amphitheater. It was mostly empty now. The aborted war between New Mexico and the Peace had killed more than one hundred low-techs. Wil looked across the theater. How different this was from the last meeting here. Now the low-techs crowded together, leaving long sweeps of bench completely empty. There were few uniforms, and the insignia had been ripped from most of those. Ungovs, NMs, Peacers sat mixed together, hard to tell apart; they all looked beaten. No one sat on the top benches—where you could look down through the castle's jacarandas at the swath of burn and glaze that had been Town Korolev.

Brierson had seen the list of dead. Still, his eyes searched across the crowd, as if he might somehow see the friends—and the enemy—he had lost. Derek Lindemann was gone. Wil was genuinely sorry about that—not so much for the man, but for losing the chance to prove he could face him without rage. Rohan was dead. Cheerful, decent Rohan. The brothers had taken Wil's warning and hidden beneath their farm. Hours passed. The autons left. Rohan went outside to bring down the last of their equipment. When the bombs fell, he was caught in the open.

Dilip had come to the meeting alone. Now he sat with Gail Parker, talking softly.

"I suppose we can begin." Yelén's voice cut across the murmur of the crowd. Only the amplification gave her voice force; her tone was listless. The burden she had carried since Marta died had finally slipped, and crushed her. "For the low-techs, some explanations. You fought a war three days ago. By now, you know you were maneuvered

503

into fighting. It was a cover for someone to grab our high-tech systems and start the larger fight you've seen in near space. . . . Your war killed or maimed half the human race. Our war destroyed about ninety percent of our equipment." She leaned against the podium, her head down. "It's the end of our plan; we have neither the genetic resources nor the equipment to reestablish civilization.

"I don't know about the other high-techs, but I'm not going to bobble out. I have enough resources to support you all for a few years. If I spread it around, what's left of my medical resources should be enough to provide a twentieth-century level of care for many decades. After that . . . well, our life in the wilderness will be better than Marta's, I guess. If we're lucky, we may last a century; Sánchez did, and he had fewer people."

She paused, and seemed to swallow something painful. "And you have another option. I—I've cut the suppressor field. You are all free to bobble out of this era." Her gaze moved reluctantly across the audience, to where Tammy Robinson sat. She sat alone, her face somber. Yelén had released her from stasis at the first opportunity after the battle. So far, Tammy had done nothing to take advantage of the debacle; her sympathy seemed genuine. On the other hand, she had nothing to lose by magnanimity. The wreckage of the Korolev plan was now hers for the taking.

Yelén continued. "I suppose that we really didn't need a meeting for me to say this. But even though what Marta and I hoped for is dead, I still have one goal before we all fade into the wilderness." She straightened, and the old fire came back to her voice. "I want to get the creature that killed Marta and wrecked the settlement! Except for some wounded low-techs, everyone is here this afternoon. . . . Odds are the killer is, too. W. W. Brierson claims he knows who the killer is . . . *and can prove it.*" She looked up at him, her smile a bitter mocking. "What would you do, ladies and gentlemen, confronted by the most famous cop in all civilization—telling you he had suddenly solved the case you had spent a hundred years thinking on? What would you do if that cop refused to reveal the secret except to a meeting of all concerned? . . . I laughed in his face. But then I thought, what more is there to lose? This *is* W. W. Brierson; in the novels, he solves all his cases with a flashy denouement." She bowed in his direction. "Your last case, Inspector. I wish you luck." She walked from the stage.

Wil was already on his feet, walking slowly down the curve of the amphitheater. Someday he would have to read Billy's novels. Had the boy really ended each by a confrontation with a roomful of suspects? In his real life, this was only the third time he had ever seen such a thing. Normally, you identified the criminal, then arrested him. A denouement with a roomful—in this case, an auditoriumful—of suspects meant that you lacked either the knowledge or the power to accomplish an arrest. Any competent criminal realized this, too; the situation was failure in the making.

And sometimes it was the best you could do. Wil was aware of the crowd's absolute silence, of their eyes following him down the steps. Even the high-techs might be given pause by his reputation. For once, he was going to use the hype for all it was worth.

He stepped onto the stage and put his data set on the podium. He was the only person who could see the two clocks on the display. At this instant they read 00:11:32 and 00:24:52; the seconds ticked implacably downwards. He had about five minutes to set things up, else he would have to string the affair along for another twenty. Best to try for the first deadline—even that would require some stalling.

He looked across his audience, caught Juan's eye. None of this would have been possible without him. "For the moment, forget the disaster this has come to. What do we have? Several isolated murders, the manipulation of the governments, and finally the takeover of the high-techs' control systems. The murder of Marta Korolev and the system takeover are totally beyond the abilities of us low-techs. On the other hand, we know the enemy is not supernaturally powerful: He blew years of careful penetration in order to grab the systems. For all the damage he did, he wasn't able to maintain control—and now his perversions have been recognized and repaired." *We hope.*

"So. The enemy is one of the high-techs. One of these seven people." With a sweep of his hand he pointed at the seven. They were all in the first few rows, but with the exception of Blumenthal—who sat at the edge of the low-techs—they were spread out, each an isolated human being.

Della Lu was dressed in something gray and shapeless. Her head injuries had been repaired, but the temporary substitute for her implants was a bulky interface band. She was into her weirdness act. Her eyes roamed randomly around the theater. Her expression flickered through various emotions, none having reasonable connection with the scene around her. Yet without her firepower, Wil knew, Philippe Genet and Monica Raines could not have been persuaded to attend.

Genet sat three rows in front of Della. For all that his attendance was coerced, he seemed to be enjoying himself. He leaned against the edge of the bench behind him, his hands resting across his middle. The smile on his face held the same amused arrogance Wil had seen at the North Shore picnic.

There was no pleasure in Monica Raines' narrow face. She sat with hands tightly clasped, her mouth turned down at one side. Before the meeting, she'd made it clear that things had merely turned out as she had predicted. The human race had zapped itself once again; she had no interest in attending the wake.

Yelén had retreated to the far end of the front bench, as far from the rest of humanity as one could sit. Her face was pale, the previous emotion gone. She watched him intently. For all her mocking, she believed him . . . and revenge was all she had left now.

Wil let the silence stretch through two beats. "For various reasons, several of these seven might want to destroy the settlement. Tunç Blumenthal and Della Lu may not even be human—Juan has warned us often enough about the exterminators. Monica Raines has made no secret of her hostility towards the human race. Tammy Robinson's family has the announced goal of breaking up the colony."

"Wil!" Tammy was on her feet, her eyes wide. "We would never kill to—" She was interrupted by Della Lu's quiet laughter. She looked over her shoulder and saw the wild look on Lu's face. She looked back at Wil, her lips trembling. "Wil, believe me."

Brierson waited for her to sit before he continued; the counts on his display flat were 00:10:11 and 00:23:31. "Evidently, a good *motive* is of no use in identifying the enemy. So let's look at the enemy's actions. Both the Peacer and NM governments were infiltrated. Can they tell us anything about who we're up against?" Wil looked across the low-techs, Peacers and NMs together. He recognized top staff people from both sides. Several shook their heads. Someone shouted, "Fraley must have known!"

The last President of the Republic sat alone. His uniform still bore insignia, but he was slouched forward, his elbows on his knees and his hands propping up his chin. "Mr. President?" Wil said softly.

Fraley looked up without raising his head. Even his hatred for Wil seemed burnt out. "I just don't know, Brierson. All our talks were over the comm. He used a synthetic voice and never sent video. He was with us almost from the beginning. Back then, he said he wanted to protect us from Korolev, said we were the only hope for stability. We got inside data, a few medical goodies. We didn't even see the machines that made the deliveries. Later on, he showed me that someone *else* was backing the Peacers. . . . From there, he owned our souls. If the Peace had high-tech backing, we'd be dead without our own. More and more, I was just his mouthpiece. In the end, he was all through our system." Now Fraley raised his head. There were dark rings around his eyes. When he spoke again, there was a strange intensity in his voice; if his old enemy could forgive him, perhaps he could himself. "I had no choice, Brierson. I thought if I didn't play ball, whoever was behind the Peace would kill us all."

A woman—Gail Parker—shouted, "So you had no choice, and the rest of us followed orders. And—and like good little troopers, we all cut our own throats!"

Wil raised his hand. "It doesn't matter, Gail. By that time, the enemy had complete control of your system. If you hadn't pushed the buttons, they would have been pushed for you." The short count on his display read 00:08:52. A map of the land around Castle Korolev suddenly flashed on the display, together with the words: "WIL: HE IS ARMED. GUNS AS ON MAP. I STILL SAY TO GO FOR IT. I'M READY ON THE MARK . . . 00:08:51."

Wil cleared the screen with a casual motion and continued talking. "It's too much to expect that the enemy would have given away his name. . . . Yet I'm sure Kim Tioulang had figured it out. There was some *particular* person he was trying to avoid when he talked to me at the North Shore picnic; he was trying to get to Town Korolev when he was murdered.

"And that raises an interesting question. Steve Fraley is a smart guy. What would Kim see that Steve would not? Kim went back a long way. He was one of the three planetary Directors of the Peace Authority. He was privy to every secret of that government. . . ." Wil looked at Yelén. "We've concentrated so much on superscientific plots and villains, we've forgotten the Machiavellis who came before us."

"There's no way our enemy could be a low-tech." Yelén's words were an objection, but there was sudden enthusiasm in her eyes.

Wil leaned across the podium. "Perhaps not now . . . but originally?" He pointed at Lu. "Consider Della. She grew up in the early twenty-first, was a top Peace cop. She also lived through most of the twenty-second. And now she's probably the most powerful high-tech of all."

Della had been mumbling to herself. Now her dark eyes came alive. She laughed, as if he had made a joke. "So true. I was born when people still died of old age. Kim and I fought for the last empire. And we fought dirty. Someone like me would be a tough enemy for the likes of you."

"If it's Della, we're dead," said Yelén. *And revenge is impossible.*

Wil nodded. The count stood at 00:07:43. "Who else fills the requirements? Someone high in the Peacer command structure. Of course, GreenInc shows that none of you high-techs have such a past. So this hypothetical other must have eluded capture during the fall of the Peace, covered his tracks, and lived a new life through the twenty-second. It must have been a disappointing situation for him: the Peace forces straggling back into realtime to be mopped up piecemeal, hope for a new Peace dying."

00:07:10. He wasn't speaking hypothetically anymore. "In the end, our enemy saw there was only one chance for the resurrection of his empire: the Peacer fort that was bobbled in Kampuchea. That was the Authority's best-equipped redoubt. Like the others, it was designed to come back to realtime in about fifty years. But by some grotesque accident, its bobbler had generated an enormously longer stasis. All through the twenty-second it lay a few hundred meters below ground, an unremarkable battle relic. But our enemy had plans for it. Fifty million years: surely no other humans would exist in such a remote era. Here was a golden opportunity to start the Peace over, and with an empty world. So our Peacer accumulated equipment, medical supplies, a zygote bank, and left the civilization he hated."

Genet's lazy smile was broader now, showing teeth. "And who might be so high in the Peace Authority that Tioulang would recognize him?" Juan Chanson seemed to shrink in upon himself.

Wil ignored the byplay. "Kim Tioulang was Peace Director for Asia. There were only two other Directors. The American one was killed when Livermore returned to realtime in 2101. The Director for Eurafrica was—"

"Christian Gerrault," said Yelén. She was on her feet, walking slowly across the floor of the amphitheater, her eyes never leaving Genet. "The fat slug they called the Butcher of Eurafrica. He disappeared. All through the twenty-second his enemies waited around likely bobbles, but he was never found."

Genet looked from Yelén to Wil. "I commend you, Inspector, though if you had taken much longer to discover my identity, I would have had to announce it myself. Except for a few loose ends, my success is now complete. It's important that you understand the situation: Survival is still possible . . . but only on my terms." He glanced at Yelén. "Sit down, woman."

00:05:29. The timing was out of Wil's hands now. He had the terrible feeling this had come too soon.

Gerrault/Genet looked at Yelén, who had stopped her advance but was still standing. "I want you all to understand what I have gone through to achieve this moment. You must not doubt that I will show the disobedient no mercy.

"For fifty years I lived in the pitiful anarchy you call *civilization*. For fifty years I played the game. I lightened my skin. I starved one hundred kilos off my normal body weight. I starved myself of the . . . pleasures . . . that are due a great leader. But I suppose that is what makes me Christian Gerrault, and you sheep. I had goals for which I was willing to sacrifice anything and anyone. My new order might take fifty million years to flower, but there was work to be done all along the way. I heard of the Korolevs and their queer plan to rescue the shanghaied. At first, I thought to destroy them; our plans were so much alike. Then I realized that they could be used. Till near the end, they would be my allies. The important thing was that they lack some critical element of success, something only *I* could supply." He smiled at the still-standing Yelén. "You and Marta had everything planned. You even brought enough med equipment and fertilized human eggs to ensure the colony's survival. . . . Have you ever wondered why those zygotes were nonviable?"

"*You?*"

Gerrault laughed at the horror in Yelén's face. "Of course. Foolish, naive women. I guaranteed your failure even before you left civilization. It was an expensive operation; I had to buy several companies to guarantee your purchase would be trashed. But it was worth it. . . . You see, *my* supply of zygotes and *my* medical equipment still survive. They are the only such in existence now." He came to his feet and turned to face the main part of his audience. His voice boomed across the theater, and Wil wondered that he had not been recognized before. True, his appearance and accent were very different from the historical Gerrault's. He looked more like a North American than an African, and his body was gaunt to the point of emaciation. But when he talked like this, the soul within shone through all disguise. This was the Christian Gerrault of the historical videos. This was the fat, swaggering Director whose megalomania had dominated two continents and dwarfed any rational self-interest.

"Do you understand? It simply does not matter that you outnumber me, and that Della Lu may outgun me. Even before this regrettable little war, the success of the colony was an unlikely thing. Now you've lost much of the medical equipment the other high-techs brought. Without me, there is no chance of a successful settlement. Without me, every one of you low-techs will be dead within a century." He lowered his voice with dramatic effect. "And with me? Success of the colony is certain. Even before the war, the other high-techs could not have supplied the medical and population support that I can. But be warned. I am not a softhearted pansy like Korolev, or Fraley, or Tioulang. I have never tolerated weakness or disloyalty. You will work for me, and you will work very, very hard. But if you do, most of you will survive."

Gerrault's gaze swept the audience. Wil had never seen such horrified fascination on people's faces. An hour ago they were trying to accept the prospect of slow extinction. Now their lives were saved . . . if they would be slaves. One by one, they turned their eyes from the speaker. They were silent, avoiding even each others' eyes. Gerrault nodded. "Good. Afterwards, I want to see Tioulang's staff. He failed me, but some of you were good men once. There may be a place for you in my plans."

He turned to the high-techs. "Your choice is simple: If you bobble out of this era, I want at least one hundred megayears free of your interference. After that, you may die as quickly or as slowly as you wish. If you stay, you give me your equipment, your systems, and your loyalty. If the human race is to survive, it will be on *my* terms." He looked at Yelén. He was smiling again. "I told you once, slut: *Sit down.*"

Yelén's whole body was rigid, her arms half raised. She stared right through Gerrault. For a moment Wil was afraid she might fight. Then something broke and she sat down. She was still loyal to Marta's dream.

"Good. If you can be sensible, perhaps the rest can." He looked up. "You will deliver system control to me now. And then I'll—"

Della laughed and stood up. "I think not, Director. The rest may be domesticated animals, but not me. And I outgun you." Her smile, even her stance, seemed disconnected from the situation. She might have been discussing some parlor game. In its way, her manner was scarier than Gerrault's sadism; it stopped even the Director for a second.

Then he recovered. "I know you; you're the gutless traitor who betrayed the Peace in 2048. You're the sort who bluffs and blusters but is basically spineless. You must also know *me.* I don't bluff about death. If you oppose me, I'll take my zygotes and med equipment, and leave you all to rot; if you pursue and destroy me, I'll make sure the zygotes die too." His voice was flat, determined.

Della shrugged, still smiling. "No need to puff and spit, Christian dear. You don't understand quite what you're up against. You see, I believe every word you say. *But I just don't care.* I'm going to kill you anyway." She walked away from them. "And the first step is to get myself some maneuvering room."

Gerrault's mouth hung open. He looked at the others. "I'll do it, I really will! It will be the end of the human race." It was almost as if he were seeking their moral support. He had been outmonstered.

Yelén shouted, her voice scarcely recognizable, "Please, Della, I *beg!* Come back!"

But Della Lu had disappeared over the crest of the amphitheater. Gerrault stared after her for only a second. Once she got out of the way, suppressor fields and tremendous firepower would be brought to bear on the theater. Everyone here could be killed—and Della had convincingly demonstrated that that wouldn't bother her. Gerrault sprinted for the floor-level exit. "But I'm not bluffing. I'm not!" He stopped for an instant at the door. "If I survive, I'll return with the zygotes. It is your duty to wait for me." Then he was gone, too.

Wil held his breath through the next seconds, praying for anticlimax. Dark shapes shot skywards, leaving thunder behind. But there was no flash of energy beams, no nukes. There was no shifting of sun in sky as might happen if they were bobbled; the combatants had moved their battle away from the amphitheater.

For the moment they lived. The low-techs huddled in clumps; someone was weeping.

Yelén's head was buried in her arms. Juan's eyes were closed, his lower lip caught between his teeth. The other high-techs were caught in less extreme poses . . . but they were all watching action beyond human eyes.

Wil looked at his display flat. It was counting down the last ninety seconds. The western sky flashed incandescent, two closely spaced pulses. Tunç said, "They both nuked out . . . they're over the Indian Ocean now." His voice was distant, only a small part of his attention devoted to reporting the action to those who could not see. "Phil's got his force massed there. He has a local advantage." There was a ripple of brightness, barely perceptible, like lightning beyond mountains. "Firefight. Phil is trying to punch through Della's near-Earth cordon. . . . He made it." There was a scattered and uncertain cheer from the low-techs. "They're outward bound, under heavy nuke drive. Just boosted past three thousand klicks per second. They'll go through the trailing Lagrange zone." Christian Gerrault had some important baggage to pick up on his way out.

And Wil's display read 00:00:00. He looked at Juan Chanson. The man's eyes were still closed, his face a picture of concentration. A second passed. Two. Suddenly he was grinning and giving a thumbs-up sign. Christian's baggage was no longer available for pickup.

For a moment Wil and Juan grinned stupidly at each other. There was no one else to notice. "Five thousand kps. . . . Strange. Phil has stopped boosting. Della will be on top of him in . . . We've got another firefight. She's chewing him up. . . . He's broken off. He's running again, pulling away from her."

Wil spoke across the monologue. "Tell 'em, Juan."

Chanson nodded, still smiling. Suddenly Tunç stopped talking. A second passed. Then he swore and started laughing. The low-techs stared at Blumenthal; all the high-techs were looking at Chanson.

"Are you sure, Juan?" Yelén's voice was unsteady.

"Yes, yes, yes! It worked perfectly. We're rid of both of them now. See. They've shifted to long-term tactics. However their fight ends, it will be thousands of years, dozens of parsecs from here." Brierson had a sudden, terrible vision of Della pursuing Gerrault into the depths forever.

Fraley's voice cut across Chanson's. "What in *hell* are you talking about? Gerrault has the med equipment and the zygotes. If he's gone, they're gone—and we're dead!"

"No! It's all right. We, I—" He was dancing from one foot to the other, frustrated by the slowness of spoken language. "Wil! Explain what we did."

Brierson pulled his imagination back to Earth and looked across the low-techs. "Juan managed to separate the med equipment from Gerrault," he said quietly. "It's sitting up there in the trailing Lagrange zone, waiting to be picked up." He glanced at Chanson. "You've transferred control to Yelén?"

"Yes. I really don't have much space capability left."

Wil felt his shoulders slowly relax; relief was beginning to percolate through him. "I've suspected 'Genet' almost from the beginning; he knew it, and he didn't care. But during our war, all the high-tech systems were taken over to fight Della. Juan—or any of the others—can tell you what it was like. They were not completely cut out of their systems; they had just lost control. In any battle, a lot of information is flowing between nodes. In this one, things were especially chaotic. In places, data security failed; irrelevant information leaked across. Part of what passed through Juan's node was the specs on Gerrault's med system. Juan saw what Gerrault had, where it was, and the exact lookabout timings of the bobbles that protected Gerrault's zygotes and inner defenses."

He paused. "This meeting was a setup. I-I'm sorry about keeping you all in the dark. There were only certain times when an attack could succeed—and then only if Gerrault had moved most of his defenses away from the trailing Lagrange."

"Yes," said Juan, his excitement reduced to manageable proportions, "this meeting was necessary, but it was the riskiest part of the whole affair. If we trumped him while he was still here, Gerrault might have done something foolish, deadly. Somehow we had to trick him into running without shooting at us first. So Wil told the story you heard, and we played our two greatest enemies against each other." He looked up at Brierson. "Thanks for trusting me, my boy. We'll never know exactly what drove the Lu creature. Maybe she really was human; maybe all her years alone just turned her mind into something alien. But I knew she couldn't resist if you told her the right lies about the zygote bank; she'll chase Gerrault to the end of space-time to destroy it."

Now there really was cheering. Some of the cheerers were a bit exhausted, perhaps: their future had been bounced around like a volleyball these last few minutes. But now: "Now we can make it!" Yelén shouted. Peacers, Ungovs, NMs were embracing. Dilip and a crowd of low-techs came down to the podium to shake Wil's hand. Even the high-tech reserve was broken. Juan and Tunç were in the middle of the crowd. Tammy and Yelén stood less than a meter apart, grinning at each other. Only Monica Raines had not left her seat; as usual, her smile was turned down at one corner. But Wil thought it was not so much disappointment at their salvation as envy that everyone else could be so happy.

Wil suddenly realized that he could leave it at this. Perhaps the settlement *was* saved. Certainly, if he went ahead with the rest of his plan, the danger to himself could be greater than everything up to now.

It was a thought, never a real choice. He owed some people too much to back down now.

Wil broke from the crowd and returned to the podium. He turned up the amplification. "Yelén. Everybody." The laughter and shouting diminished. Gail Parker jumped on a bench and cried, "Yay, Wili! Speech! Speech! Wili for President!" This provoked even more laughter; Gail always did have a sharp sense of the ridiculous. Wil raised his hands, and the uproar subsided again. "There are still some things we must settle."

Yelén looked at him, her face relaxed yet puzzled. "Sure, Wil. I think we can put a lot of things right, now. But—"

"That's not what I mean, Yelén. I still haven't done what you hired me for. . . . I still haven't produced Marta's murderer."

The talk and laughter guttered to a stop. The loudest sounds were the birds stealing from the spiders beyond the amphitheater. Where the faces didn't show blank surprise, Wil could see the fear returning. "But, Wil," Juan said finally, "we *got* Gerrault. . . ."

"Yes. We got him. There's no fakery in that, nor in the equipment we rescued. But Christian Gerrault did not kill Marta, and he didn't take over the high-tech computer systems. Did you notice that he never admitted to either? He was as much a victim of the takeover as any. Finding the systems saboteur was one of the 'loose ends' he intended to clear up."

Juan waved his hands, his speech coming faster than ever. "Semantics. He explicitly admitted to taking over the low-techs' military systems."

Wil shook his head. "No, Juan. Only the Peacers'. All the time we thought one high-tech was stirring up both sides, when actually Gerrault was behind the Peace and *you* were manipulating the NMs."

The words were spoken and Wil still lived.

The little man swallowed. "Please, my boy, after everything I've done to help, how can you say this? . . . I know! You think only a systems penetrator could know about Gerrault's med equipment." He looked imploringly at Yelén and Tammy. "Tell him. Things like that happen in battle, especially when penetration—"

"Sure," Yelén said. "It may seem a farfetched explanation to someone from your era, Wil, but leak-across can really happen." Tunç and Tammy were nodding agreement.

"It doesn't matter." There was no doubt in Wil's face or voice. "I knew that Juan was Marta's killer before he ever came to me about Gerrault." *But can I convince the rest of you?*

Chanson's hands balled into fists. He backed into a bench and sat down abruptly. "Do I have to take this?" he cried to Yelén.

Korolev set her hand on his shoulder. "Let the *Inspector* have his say." When she looked at Wil, her face had the angry ambivalence he knew so well. Together, Wil and Juan had just saved the colony. But she had known Chanson through decades of their lives; Wil was the low-tech that her Marta had damned and praised. There was no telling how long her patience would last.

Brierson stepped around the podium. "At first, it seemed that almost any high-tech could have marooned Marta: There were bugs in the Korolev system that made it easy to sabotage a single bobbling sequence. With those bugs repaired, Yelén and the others thought their systems were secure. Our war showed how terribly wrong they were. For twelve hours, the enemy had complete control of all the systems—except Della's. . . .

"This told me several things. In my time, it was no trivial thing to grab an entire system. Unless the system were perverted to begin with, it took expert, tedious effort to insert all the traps that would make a grab possible. Whoever did this needed years of visitor status on the high-techs' systems. The enemy never had a chance at Della; she was gone from the Solar System since just after the Singularity."

He looked across his audience. The low-techs hung on every word. It was harder to tell about the others. Tammy wasn't even looking at him. Wil could only imagine the analysis and conversations that were going on in parallel with his words. "So. An expert, using expert tools, must be behind this. But Yelén's GreenInc shows that none of the high-techs have such a background."

Tunç interrupted, "Which only means the killer rewrote history to protect himself."

"Right. It needn't have been much, just a fact here and there. Over the years, the killer could manage it. Della's db's are the only ones that might contain the truth. I spent a lot of time with them after we were rescued. Unfortunately, her general database for the late twenty-second is badly jumbled—so badly that Della herself didn't use it. But after the battle, I knew what to look for. Eventually I found an opening: Jason Mudge. Mudge was just the religious fanatic we knew, though toward the end of the twenty-second he actually had some disciples. Only one of them had sufficient faith to follow him into stasis. That was Juan Chanson. Juan was a wealthy man, probably Mudge's biggest catch." Wil looked at Chanson. "You gave up a lot to follow a religious dream, Juan. Della's db's show you were head of Penetration and Perversion at USAF, Inc." In Wil's time, USAF had been the largest weapons-maker in North America; it had grown from there. "I don't doubt that when Juan left, he took the latest software his division had invented. We were up against industrial-strength sabotage."

Juan was trembling. He looked up at Yelén. She stared back for a second, then looked at Wil. She wasn't convinced. "Yelén," Wil said, keeping his voice level, "don't you remember? The day Mudge was killed, he claimed Chanson had been a religionist."

Yelén shook her head. That memory was three days gone.

Finally Chanson spoke aloud. "Don't you see how you've deluded yourself, Wil? The evidence is all around you. Why do you think Lu's record of civilization was jumbled? *Because she was never there!* At best those records are secondhand, filled with evidence she would use against me or whoever else was a threat. Wil, please. I may be wrong about the details, but whatever the Lu creature is, she's proved she would sacrifice us all for her schemes. No matter what she's done to you, you must be able to see that."

Monica's laugh was almost a cackle. "What a pretty bind you're in, Brierson. The facts explain either theory perfectly. And Della Lu is chasing off into interstellar space."

Wil pretended to give her comment serious consideration; he needed time to think. Finally he shook his head and continued as calmly as before. "Even if you don't believe me, there are data Juan never thought to alter. Marta's diary, for instance. . . . I know, Yelén, you studied that for a hundred years, and you knew Marta far better than I. But Marta knew she wasn't marooned by simple sabotage. She knew the enemy saw what she left in the cairns, and could destroy any of it. Even worse, if she slipped a message past the enemy, and you understood it, the act of understanding might itself trigger an attack.

"But *I* am a low-tech, outside all this automation. Marta got my attention with the one incident that only she and I could know. Yelén, after the Robinson party . . . I didn't—I *never* tried to take advantage of Marta." He looked into Yelén's face, willing belief there.

When there was no response, he continued. "The last years of her life, Marta played a terrible double game. She told us the story of survival and courage and defeat, and at the same time she left clues she hoped would point me at Juan. They were subtle. She named her fishermonkey friends after people in our settlement. There was *always* a Juan Chanson, a solitary creature that delighted in watching her. Marta's last day alive, she mentioned that he was still out there, watching. She *knew* she was being stalked, and by the real Juan Chanson."

Juan slapped the bench. "God *damn* it, man! You can find any message if the coding scheme is nutty enough."

"Unfortunately, you're right. And if that's all she could do, this might be a stalemate, Juan. But for all her misfortunes, Marta had some good luck, too. One of her fishermonkeys was a freak, bigger and brighter than any fisher we've seen. He followed her around, tried to imitate her cairn-building. It wasn't much, but she had an ally in real-time." He smiled wanly. "She named him W. W. Brierson. He got lots of practice building cairns, always in the same position relative to Peace Lake. In the end, she took him north and left him in a normal forest beyond the glazed zone. I don't know how close you were monitoring, Juan, but you missed what that animal took with him, you missed the cairn he built, where Marta never went."

Juan's eyes darted to Yelén, then back to Wil, but he said nothing.

"You've known about that cairn for four days, ever since I told Yelén. You were willing to show your full power—and kill half the human race —to prevent me from getting it." Wil stepped off the platform and walked slowly toward the little man. "Well, Juan, you didn't succeed. I've seen what Marta had to say when she didn't have to write in parables. Everyone else is free to see it, too. And no matter what conspiracies you blame on Della Lu, I suspect the physical evidence will convince Yelén and her lab autons."

Yelén had backed away from Chanson. Tunç's mouth was compressed into a thin line. *Even without a confession, I may be able to win*, thought Wil.

Juan looked around, then back at Wil. "Please. You're reading this all wrong. I didn't kill Marta. I *want* the settlement to succeed. And I've sacrificed more than any of you to preserve it; if I hadn't, none of us would have survived to fifty megayears. But now that's made me look like the guilty one. I've got to convince you. . . .

"Look. Wil. You're right about Mudge and me; I should never have tried to cover that up. I'm embarrassed I ever believed his chiliastic garbage. But I was young, and my nightmares followed me home from work. I needed to believe in something. I gave up my job, everything, for his promises.

"We came out of stasis in 2295, just before Mudge's numerology said Christ would put on the Big Show. There was nothing but ruins, a civilization destroyed, a race exterminated. Mudge reviewed his mumbo-jumbo and concluded that we had overshot, that Christ had come and gone. The stupid jerk! He just could not accept what we saw around us. Something had visited the Solar System in the mid-twenty-third, but it hadn't been holy. The evidence of alien invasion was everywhere. Mudge had arrived with scarcely more than sackcloth and ashes. I'd brought plenty of equipment. I could do analysis, back up my claims. I had the power to save what humans were still in stasis.

"Yelén, right from then my goal was the same as yours. Even while you high-techs were still in stasis, I was planning for it. The only difference was that I knew about the aliens. But I couldn't convince Mudge of them. In fact, the signs were so subtle, I began to wonder if anyone else would believe me." Chanson came to his feet, his talk speeding up. "Unless we guarded against the invaders, all the goodwill in the world could not resurrect the human race. I *had* to do something. I—I enhanced some of the evidence. I nuked a few ruins. Surely, not even a blind man could ignore that!" He looked at Yelén and Tammy accusingly. "Yet when you returned to realtime, you weren't convinced. You couldn't accept even the clearest evidence. . . . I tried. I tried. Over the next two thousand years I traveled all over the Solar System, discovering the signs of the invasion, emphasizing them so even idiots could not miss them.

"In the end, I had a little success. W. W. Sánchez had the patience to look at the facts, the open-mindedness to believe. We persuaded the rest of you to be a bit more cautious. But the burden of vigilance still rested on me. No one else was willing to put sentries in far solar space. Over the years, I destroyed two alien probes—and still Sánchez was the only one who was convinced." Juan was staring through Wil; he might have been talking to himself. "I really liked Bil Sánchez. I wish he hadn't dropped out; his settlement was just too small to succeed. I visited him there several times. It was a long, idyllic, downhill slide. Bil wanted to do research, but all he had was that punched tape he'd found on Charon. He was obsessed with it; the last time I saw him he even claimed it was a fake." A faintly troubled look passed across Juan's face. "Well, that settlement was too small to survive, anyway."

Yelén's eyes were wide, white showing all around the irises; her whole body had gone rigid. Chanson could not notice, but sudden death was in the air.

Wil stepped into Yelén's line of sight; his voice was a calm echo of Chanson's distant tone. "What about Marta, Juan?"

"Marta?" Juan almost looked at him. "Marta always had an open mind. She granted the possibility of an alien threat. I think Lu's arrival scared her; the creature was so obviously inhuman. Marta talked to Lu, got access to some of her databases. And then—and then"—tears started in his eyes—"she started asking the db about Mudge." *How much had Marta suspected?* At the time, probably nothing; most of the jumbled references to Mudge had no connection with Chanson. It was tragic bad luck she started so close to Juan's secret. "I should never have lied about my past, but now it was too late. Marta could destroy all I had worked for. The colony would be left defenseless. I had to, I had to—"

"Kill her?" Yelén's voice was a shout.

"*No!*" Juan's head snapped up; the reality around him was not to be ignored. "I could never do that. I *liked* Marta! But I had to . . . quarantine her. I watched to see if she would denounce me. She never did—but then I realized I could never be sure what she might say later. I couldn't let her back.

"Please *listen* to me! I made mistakes; I pushed too hard to make you see the truth. But you must *believe*. The invaders are out there, Yelén. They'll destroy everything you and Marta dreamed of if you don't believe m—" Juan's voice became a scream. He fell heavily, lay with arms and legs twitching.

Two quick steps and Wil was kneeling by his side. Wil looked down at the agonized face; he'd had two days to prepare for this moment, to suppress the killing rage he felt every time he saw Chanson. Korolev had had no such time; he could almost feel her eyes boring death through his back. "What did you do to him, Yelén?"

"I shut him down, cut his comm links." She stepped around Wil, to look down at Chanson. "He'll recover." There was a tight smile on her face; in a way, it was scarier than her rage. "I want time to think of just revenge. I want him to understand it when it comes." Her eyes snapped up to the nearest bystanders. "Get him out of my sight." For once there was no debate; her words might as well have been electric prods. Tunç and three low-techs grabbed Chanson, carried him towards the flier that was drifting down the side of the amphitheater. Wil started after them.

"Brierson! I want to talk to you." The words were abrupt, but there was something strange in Yelén's tone. Wil came back down the steps. Yelén led him around the side of the platform—away from the crowd, which was just beginning to come out of shock. "Wil," she said quietly, "I want—I'd like to see what Marta said." *What Marta said when she wasn't writing for Chanson's eyes.*

Wil swallowed; even winning could be hard. He touched her shoulder. "Marta left the fifth cairn, just like I told Chanson. If we'd found it during the first few thousand years. . . . After fifty thousand, all we could see was that there had been a sheaf of reed paper inside. It was powder. We'll never know for sure what she wanted to tell us. . . . I'm sorry, Yelén."

26

t was snowing. From over the hill came shouts, occasional laughter. They were having a snowball fight.

W. W. Brierson crunched down the hillside to the edge of the pines. Strange that with the world so empty he would still want to be alone. Maybe not so strange. Their dormitory was a crowded place. No doubt there were others who'd left the snowballers, who walked beneath the pines and pretended this was a different time.

He found a big rock, clambered up, and dusted off a place to sit. From here he could see alpine glaciers disappearing into the clouds. Wil tapped at his data set and thought. The human race had another chance. Dilip and a lot of other people really seemed to think he was responsible. Well, he'd solved the case. Without a doubt it was the biggest of his career. Even Billy Brierson had not imagined such a great adventure for his father. And the chief bad guy had been punished. Very definitely, Juan had been punished. . . .

Yelén had honored Marta's notions about mercy; she had made that mercy the punishment itself. Juan was executed by a surfeit of life. He was marooned in realtime, without shelter or tools or friends. Yet his was a different torture than Marta's—and perhaps the more terrible. Juan was left with a medical auton. He was free to live *as long as he wished.*

Juan outlived three autons. He lasted ten thousand years. He kept his purpose for nearly two thousand. Wil shook his head as he surveyed the report. If anyone had known that Chanson was into Penetration and Perversion, he would have been an instant suspect—on grounds of personality alone. Wil had known only one such specialist, his company's resident spook. The man was inhumanly patient and devious, but frightened at the same time. He spent so much time in deep connect, the paranoid necessities of defense systems leaked into his perception of the everyday world. Wil could only imagine the madhouse Penetration and Perversion had become by the late twenty-second. Juan made seven attempts to pervert the auton. One involved twelve hundred years of careful observation, timing the failure of various subsystems, maneuvering the auton into a position where he might take control and get transportation to resources in near space.

Yet Chanson never really had a prayer of success. Yelén had hardwired changes to the auton. Juan had none of the software he had stolen from USAF, Inc, and he was without processor support. His glib tongue and two thousand years of effort were not enough to set him free.

As the centuries passed and he had no luck with the auton, Juan spent more and more time trying to talk to Yelén and the other high-techs who occasionally looked into realtime. He kept a journal many times longer than Marta's; he painted endless prose across the rock-lands north of his home territory. None of it looked as interesting as Marta's diary. All Juan could talk of was his great message, the threat he saw in the stars. He went on spouting evidence—though after the first centuries it lost all connection with reality.

After five hundred years, his journal became at first irregular, then a decadely summary, then a dead letter. For three thousand years Juan lived without apparent goal, moving from cave to cave. He wore no clothes, he did no work. The auton protected him from local predators. When he did not hunt or farm, the auton brought him food. If the climate of the Eastern Straits had been less mild he would certainly have died. Yet to Wil it was still a miracle the man survived. Through all that time he had enough determination to keep on living. Della had been right. W. W. Brierson would not have lasted a tenth as long; a few centuries and he would have drifted into suicidal funk.

Juan drifted for three thousand years . . . and then his immortal paranoid soul found a new cause. It wasn't clear exactly what it was. He kept no journal; his conversations with the auton were limited to simple commands and incoherent mumbling. Yelén thought that Juan saw himself as somehow the creator of reality. He moved to the seashore. He built heavy baskets and used them to drag millions of loads of soil inland. The dredged shoreland became a maze of channels. He piled the dirt on a rectangular mound that rose steadily through the centuries. That mound reminded Wil of the earthen pyramids the American Indians had left in Illinois. It had taken hundreds of people working over decades to build those. Juan's was the work of one man over millennia. If the climate had not been exceptionally dry and mild in his era, he could not have kept ahead of simple erosion.

Juan's new vision went beyond monuments. Apparently he thought to create an intelligent race. He persuaded the auton to extend its food gathering, to beach schools of fish in the maze he constructed on the shore. Soon there were thousands of fishermonkeys living beneath his temple/pyramid. Through a perversion of its protection programs, he used the auton as an instrument of force: The best fish went to the monkeys who performed properly. The effect was small, but over centuries the fishers at the East End had a different look. The majority were like the "W. W. Brierson" that had helped Marta. They carried rocks to the base of the pyramid. They sat for hours staring up at it.

The four-thousand-year effort was not enough to bring intelligence to the fishers. Yelén's report showed some tool use. Towards the end, they built a stone skirt around the lower part of the pyramid. But they were never the race of hod carriers that Chanson probably intended. It was Juan who continued to drag endless loads of dirt up to his temple, repairing erosion damage, adding ever-higher towers to the topmost platform. At its greatest, the temple covered a rectangle two hundred meters by one hundred, and the top platform was thirty meters above the plain. Its spires crowded tall and spindly all about, more like termite towers or coral than human architecture. Through those last four thousand years, Juan's daily pattern was unchanged. He worked on his new race. He hauled dirt. Each evening, he walked round and round the intricate stairs of the pyramid, till finally he stood at the top, surveying the temple slaves who gathered on the plain before him.

Wil paged through Yelén's report. She had pictures of Juan during those last centuries. His face was blank of all expression, except at day's end—when he always laughed, three times. His every motion was a

524

patterned thing, a reflex. Juan had become an insect, one whose hive spread through time instead of space.

Juan had found peace. He might have lasted forever if only the world had had the same stability. But the climate of the Eastern Straits entered a period of wet and storminess. The auton was programmed to provide minimum protection. In earlier millennia that would have been enough. But now Juan was inflexible. He would not retreat to the highland caves; he would not even come down from the temple during storms. He forbade the auton to approach it during his nightly services.

Of course, Yelén had pictures of Juan's end. The auton was four klicks from the temple; Juan had long since destroyed all bugs. The wind-driven rain blurred and twisted the auton's view. This was just the latest of a series of storms that were tearing down the pyramid faster than Juan could maintain it. His towers and walls were like a child's sand castle melting in an ocean tide. Juan did not notice. He stood on the slumped platform of his temple and looked out upon the storm. Wil watched the wavery image raise its arms—just as Juan always did at day's end, just before he gave his strange laugh. Lightning struck all around, turning the storm darkness to actinic blue, showing Juan's slaves huddled by the thousands below him. The bolts marched across the fallen temple, striking what was left of the spires . . . striking Juan as he stood, arms still upraised to direct the show.

There was little more to Yelén's report. The fishermonkeys had been given a strong push toward intelligence. It was not enough. Biological evolution has no special tendency toward sapience; it heads blindly for local optima. In the case of the fishers, that was their dominance of the shallow waters. For a few hundred years, the race he'd bred still lived at the Eastern Straits, still brought rocks to line the stub of his pyramid, still watched through the evenings. But that was instinct without reward. In the end, they were as Juan had found them.

Wil cleared the display. He shivered—and not just from the cold. He would never forget Juan's crimes; he would never forget his long dying.

The snow had stopped. There was no more shouting from over the hill. Wil looked in surprise at the sunlight slanting through the trees behind him. He'd spent more than an hour looking at Yelén's report. Only now did he notice the cramps in his legs and the cold seeping up from the rock.

ACROSS REALTIME

Wil tucked the data set under his arm and slipped off the rock. He still had time to enjoy the snow, the pines. It brought echoes of a winter just ten weeks old in his memory, the last days in Michigan before he'd flown to the coast on the Lindemann case. Only these snowfields were almost at the equator, and this world was in the middle of an ice age.

The tropics had cooled. The jacaranda forests had shifted down-slope, to the edge of the Inland Sea. But none of the continental ice sheets had reached further south than latitude forty-five. The snow around the site of Town Korolev was due to the altitude. Yelén figured the glaciers coming off the Indonesian Alps wouldn't get below the four-thousand-meter level. She claimed that, as ice ages go, this one was average.

Wil walked a kilometer through the pines. A week before—as his body counted time—this had been the glazed crater of Town Korolev. So much destruction, and not a sign of it now. He climbed a ridgeline and watched the sunset gleaming red and gold across the white. Something hooted faint against the breeze. Far to the north he could see where the jac forests hugged the sea. It was beautiful, but there were good reasons to leave this era. Some of the best ore fields were under ice now. Why cripple the new civilization when it was weakest? . . . And there was Della. She had lots of valuable equipment. They would give her at least a hundred thousand years to return.

Suddenly Wil felt very bleak. *Hell. I would give her a thousand times a hundred thousand.* But what good would it do? After that night with the dogthings, Wil hoped she had found herself. Without her, he could never have set up the double play against Chanson and Gerrault. A crooked smile came across his face. She had fooled both the killers into defeat. The plan was to force Gerrault to run, to chase him long enough to trick Juan. And it had worked! She had played the old, crazy Della so well. *Too well.* She had never returned. No one knew for sure what had happened; it was even conceivable she had died fighting Gerrault. More likely, some battle reflex had taken over. Even if the mood passed, she might pursue the other for unknown millennia. And if the mood didn't pass . . .

Wil remembered the scarcely human thing she had been when he first saw her. Even with her computer-supported memories and all the other enhancements, that Della seemed very much like what Juan

526

Chanson had become towards the end of his punishment. For all her talk of being tough, Della had nothing on Juan when it came to single-mindedness. How much of her life would she spend on this chase? He was terribly afraid she had volunteered for the same fate that had been forced on Juan.

Wil decided he didn't like the cold at all. He glanced at his data set. It showed the date as 17 March 2100; he still had not reset it. Somewhere in its memory were notes about the stuff Virginia wanted him to bring back from the Coast. How much can happen in ten weeks; one must be flexible in these modern times. He turned away from the sunset and the silence, and headed back for the dormitory. He should be satisfied with this happy ending. The next few years would be tough, but he knew they could make it. Yelén had been friendly towards almost everyone the last few days. In the weeks before, she would never have thought of stopping in the middle of this glacial era just to give them a chance to look around.

The tropical twilight snapped down hard, faded quickly into night. When Wil came over the hill above the dorm, its lighted windows were like something out of a Michigan Christmas. Sometime early tomorrow morning, when they were snug in their beds, Santa Claus Yelén would bobble them up once more. Her sleigh had certainly had a bumpy landing, popping in and out of realtime over the last sixty thousand years. Wil smiled at the crazy image.

Maybe this time they could stop for keeps.

That night was the last time Wil ever had the dream in blue. In most ways it was like the ones before. He was lying down, all breath exhausted from his lungs. *Goodbye, goodbye.* He cried and cried, but no sounds came. She sat beside him, holding his hand. Her face was Virginia's, and also Marta's. She smiled sadly, a smile that could not deny the truth they both knew. . . . *Goodbye, goodbye.* And then the pattern changed. She leaned toward him, snuggled her face against his cheek, just as Virginia used to do. She never spoke, and he couldn't tell if the thought was only his, or somehow comfort from her. *Someone still lives who has not said goodbye, someone who might like you very much.*

Dearest Wil, goodbye.

Brierson woke with a start, gasping for breath. He swung his feet out of bed and sat for a moment. His tiny room was bright with day, but he couldn't see outside; the window was completely fogged over. It was very quiet; normally he could hear plenty of activity through the plastic walls. He got up and stepped out into the hall; not a soul in sight. There was noise from downstairs, though. That's right: There was a big meeting scheduled first thing this morning. The fact that Yelén was willing to meet the low-techs at the dorm was more evidence that she had changed; she had not even demanded his presence. His sleeping late was a half-conscious test of his freedom. For a while he wanted to be a bystander. Managing the last meeting had been a bit . . . traumatic.

Wil padded down the hallway to the second-floor washroom. For once, he had the place all to himself.

What a *weird* dream. Wil looked at his image in the washstand mirror. There was wetness around his eyes, but he was *smiling*. The dream in blue had always been a choking burden, something he must forcibly ignore. But this time it reassured him, even made him happy. He hummed as he washed up, his mind playing with the dream. Virginia had seemed so real. He could still feel her touch on his cheek. He knew now how much hidden anger he had felt at Virginia; he knew, because suddenly the anger was gone. It had cut deep that Virginia had not come after him. He'd told himself that she always intended to, that she was still gathering her resources when the Singularity overtook her. He hadn't believed the excuse; he'd seen what could happen to a personality over a century. But now—for no reason but a dream—he felt differently. Well, what if Della's explanation of the Singularity was correct? What if technology had transcended the intelligible? What if minds had found immortality by growing forever past the human horizon? Why, then, something that had been Virginia might still exist, might want to comfort him.

Wil suddenly realized he was washing his face for the second time. For a moment, he and his mirror image grinned sheepishly at each other, conspirators realizing the insanity of their scheme. If he wasn't careful, he'd be another Jason Mudge, complete with guardian angels and voices from beyond the grave. Still, Della said there was something like religion hiding at the end of her materialism.

A few minutes later he was walking down the side stairs, past the cafeteria. The voices from within were loud but didn't sound angry. He hesitated, then turned away from the door. It might be fantasy, but he wanted to keep the mood of that dream as long as possible. It had been a long time since he'd started the day feeling so good. For the moment he really believed there was "someone who still lives, who might like you very much."

He walked out of the dorm, into daylight.

The building was surrounded by a perfect disk of white—the snow that had been brought through time with their bobble. The sun burned at the snowdrifts, raising a sublimation fog all around him. Wil walked across the slush, through the brilliant mist. He stopped at the edge of the snow and stared at the almost-jacarandas and less identifiable trees that grew all around. It was already a warm day. He stepped back a pace and enjoyed the cool coming off the snow. Except for the shape of some of the hills, the world was the same as before the battle. The glaciers were tamed again, lurked near faraway peaks. Across a ravine and a few hundred meters up a hillside, there was a separate plume of sublimation fog; the golden towers of Castle Korolev gleamed faint within it.

A shadow passed over him. "Wil!" He looked up as Tammy Robinson dropped out of the sky. She brought her platform to a low hover, just as she had when she came to invite the soot pushers to her father's party. She was even dressed in the same perfect white. She stood there a moment, looking down. "I wanted to see you again . . . before I go." She brought the platform all the way to earth, just beyond his toes. Now she was looking up at him. "Thank you, Wil. Gerrault and Chanson would've got us all if it hadn't been for you. Now I think we can all win." Her smile broadened. "Yelén has given me enough equipment to leave this era."

She was almost too perfect to look at. "You've given up on recruiting?"

"Nope. Yelén says I can come back in a hundred years, and any time after. With Gerrault's equipment and the zygotes, you can really succeed. Another century or two, and there'll be more people here than I could ever imagine. They won't feel beaten the way they do now, and a good many will be bored with civilization. There will be dozens, maybe hundreds, who'll come with me. And they'll be people we won't have to support. That's more than Daddy ever hoped for." She paused a second and then said quietly, "I hope you'll come with me, Wil."

"S-some of us have to stay in realtime, or there'll be no civilization for you to raid, Tammy." He tried to smile.

"I know, I know. But a hundred years from now, when I come back . . . what about then?"

What about then? The Robinsons thought all mysteries could be known to those who watched long enough, waited long enough. But a flatworm could watch forever and still not understand the opera. Aloud: "Who knows how I'll feel in a hundred years, Tammy?" He stopped and just stared at her for a second. "But if I don't come with you . . . and if you make it to the end of time . . . I hope you'll remember me to the Creator."

Tammy flinched, then realized he wasn't mocking her. "Okay. If you stay behind, I will." She put her hands on his shoulders and stood on tiptoe to kiss his lips. "See you later, Wil Brierson."

A few seconds later, Tammy was disappearing over the trees. *The one who still lives, the one who has not said goodbye?* He thought not, but he had a hundred years to decide for sure.

Wil walked along the perimeter of the mist, intrigued by the way heat and cool battled at the edge of the snow. He circled the dorm and found himself staring at the entrance. They were still at it in there. He grinned to himself and started back. What the hell.

He was only partway to the entrance when the doors opened. Only one person stepped out. It was Yelén. She surveyed him without surprise. "Hah. I wondered how long you'd stay out here." As she came toward him, he looked for signs of anger in her pale Slavic face. She caught his eye and smiled lopsidedly. "Don't worry. They didn't kick me out. And I'm not leaving in a huff. It's just that all the dickering is a little dull; they've practically got a commodity exchange going in there, splitting up all the stuff that survived our fighting. . . . Do you have a minute, Wil?"

He nodded and followed her out of the chill, back the way he had come. "Have you thought: No matter how well things go, we'll still need police services? People really respect you. That's ninety percent of what made companies like Michigan State Police and Al's Protection Rackets successful."

Brierson shook his head. "It sounds like the game we were playing before. A lot of the ungovs might want to hire me, but without threats

530

from you, I can't imagine the governments tolerating the competition."

"Hey, I'm not looking for a cat's-paw. The fact is, Fraley and Dasgupta are in there right now, colluding on a common offer for your
services."

Wil felt his jaw sag. *Fraley?* After all the years of hatred . . . "Steve
would rather die than disgovern."

"A lot of his people did die," she said quietly. "A lot of the rest
aren't taking orders anymore. Even Fraley has changed a little. Maybe
it's fear, maybe it's guilt. It really shook him to see how easily one high-
tech swindled him and perverted the Republic—even worse, to learn
that Chanson did it just to have a thirty-second diversion available
when he grabbed for our systems."

Yelén laughed. "My advice is to take the job while they still think it's
tough. After a couple of years, there'll be competition; I bet you won't
be able to make a living off your fees."

"Hmm. You think things are going to be that tame?"

"I really do, Wil. The high-tech monsters are dead. The governments may linger on, but in name only. We lost a lot in the war—parts
of our technology may fall to a nineteenth-century level—but with
Gerrault's zygotes and med equipment, we're better off than before.
The problem with the women has disappeared. They can have the kids
they want, but they won't have to be nonstop baby factories. You
should have seen the meeting. There are lots of serious couples now.
Gail and Dilip asked me to *marry* them! 'For old times' sake.' They said
I had been like the captain of a ship to them. What crazy, crazy
people." She shook her head, but her smile was very proud. These
might be the first low-techs to show gratitude for what she and Marta
had done. "I'll tell you how confident I am: I'm not forcing anyone to
stay in this era. If they have a bobbler, they can take off. I don't think
anyone will. It's a bit too obvious that if we can't make it now, we
never will."

"Monica might."

"That's different. But don't be too sure even with her; she's been
lying to herself for a long time. I'm going to ask her to stay." Yelén's
smile was gentle; two weeks ago she would have been scornful. With
Gerrault and Chanson gone, a great weight had been lifted from her

soul, and Wil could see what—beyond competence and loyalty—Marta had loved in her.

Yelén looked at her feet. "There's another reason I ducked out of the meeting early. I wanted to apologize. After I read Marta's diary, I felt like killing you. But I knew I needed you—Marta didn't have to tell me that. And the more I depended on you, the more you saw things I had not . . . the more I hated you.

"Now I know the truth. I'm ashamed. After working with you, I should have seen through Marta's trick myself." Abruptly she stuck out her hand. Brierson grasped it, and they shook. "Thanks, Wil."

The one who still lives, the one who has not said goodbye? No. But a friend for the years to come.

Behind her, a flier descended. "Time for me to get back to the house." She jerked a thumb at Castle Korolev.

"One last thing," she said. "If things are as slow as I think, you might want to diversify. . . . Give Della a hand."

"Della's back? H-how long? I mean—"

"She's been in solar space about a thousand years; we were waiting to find the best time to stop. The chase took one hundred thousand years. I don't know how much lifetime she spent." She didn't seem much concerned about the last issue. "You want to talk to her? I think you could do each other good."

"Where—"

"She was with me, at the meeting. But you don't have to go inside. You've been set up, Wil. Each of us—Tammy, me, Della—wanted to talk to you alone. Say the word, and she'll be out here."

"Okay. Yes!"

Yelén laughed. He was scarcely aware of her walking to the flier. He started back to the dorm. Della had made it. However many years she had lived in the dark, she had not died there. And even if she was the creature from before, even if she was like Juan Chanson at his ending, Wil could still try to help. He couldn't take his eyes off the doorway.

The doors opened. She was wearing a jumpsuit, midnight black, the same color as her short-cut hair. Her face was expressionless as she came down the steps and walked toward him. Then she smiled. "Hi, Wil. I'm back . . . to stay."

The one who still lives, the one who has not said goodbye.

AFTERWORD

The author's afterword: that's where he explains what he was trying to say with the previous hundred thousand words, right? Well, I'll try to avoid that. Basically, I have an apology and a prediction.

The apology is for the unrealistically slow rate of technological growth predicted. Part of that is reasonable, I suppose. A general war, like the one I put in 1997, can be used to postpone progress anywhere from ten years to forever. But what about after the recovery? I show artificial intelligence and intelligence amplification proceeding at what I suspect is a snail's pace. Sorry. I needed civilization to last long enough to hang a plot on it.

And of course it seems very unlikely that the Singularity would be a clean vanishing of the human race. (On the other hand, such a vanishing is the timelike analog of the silence we find all across the sky.)

From now to 2000 (and then 2001), the Jason Mudges will be coming out of the woodwork, their predictions steadily more clamorous. It's an ironic accident of the calendar that all this religious interest in transcendental events should be mixed with the objective evidence that we're falling into a technological singularity. So, the prediction: If we don't have that general war, then it's *you*, not Della and Wil, who will understand the Singularity in the only possible way—by living through it.

San Diego
1983–1985